THE

VIOLATED

THE
VIOLATED

a novel
by VANCE BOURJAILY

THE DIAL PRESS   1958   NEW YORK

© 1958 by Vance Bourjaily
Library of Congress Catalog Card Number: 58-10571

Second Printing: September 1958

Designed by William R. Meinhardt
Printed in the United States of America
By the Haddon Craftsmen, Scranton, Penna.

FOR
Tina

"MERCY:
Remembur, my frende, the tyme of con-
  tynuance!
So help me Gode, yt ys but a chery time."
Mankind

PART ONE

"Remembur, my frende. . . . ."

CHAPTER ONE

1.

LOOK. IN A condemned house in Brooklyn, some children are performing *Hamlet*.

It is a very serious, single performance. There are measures of brilliance in it, and also measures of monotony. The acting is at times self-conscious, but in general these children are absorbed in their roles to the point of abandon. There is an overall intensity in what they are doing which seems to derive from the fourteen year old girl who plays the title role, and who has been the director.

Her name is Sheila Walle.

We are in an audience of about forty people, mostly adult. There is Sheila Walle's mother, Ellen; she is rather drunk. The husband and father, Harrison Walle, sits next to Ellen; he is bored and fretful, though occasionally something happens on the improvised stage that astonishes him into a few moments of attention.

Some sit on orange crates in this long, chilly room; some stand along the walls. Among those standing is Tom Beniger, Sheila Walle's uncle, Ellen's brother, a tall, gentle slump of a man. In spite of a considerable weight of personal worry which he carried in here with him, Tom is transported by the performance.

Also in the room is an odd, hard little man named Eddie Bissle,

3

who is connected with Tom and Ellen. Eddie Bissle's responses to life are of two sorts, the most frequent of which is malediction; the play, however, is presently producing his second kind of response, which is brooding.

Not present tonight, though he promised to be—and generally he keeps his promises—is Guy Cinturon, whom columnists call The Chihuahua Sugarplum, and whose connection with the Walle family and with Tom Beniger is very like Bissle's. Guy is across the River, in Manhattan, attempting a seduction. Eddie is brooding. Tom is transported. Ellen is drunk. We shall see them each like this again. And again.

Now. Look at Tom and Ellen quickly and then back to the girl at center stage. Isn't Sheila's face quite like her uncle's, her coloring precisely like her mother's? There is nothing of the Walle family in her appearance; it's all Beniger. Her grandmother, Tom and Ellen's mother, has said this, and even Sheila's father would concede it.

Yet this maternal grandmother, who, by the way, is among those absent, says the name Beniger with some distaste, and it is not her own name, hasn't been for years. Her name is Mrs. Coombs. Sheila's middle name is Coombs. Why the distaste? Why Coombs? Why the grandmother's absence? Surely, as life used to be lived, grandparents would have been on hand for an occasion like this, sitting in the front row, objects of honor and solicitude? Where are they?

Do not touch Sheila on the shoulder as she flings off-stage, to give her answers to these questions. As life is lived now, they are not her questions; she has never asked them, though they affected quite decisively her mother and her uncle. And even if they were her questions, it would be a crime to interrupt Sheila now, for anything.

But we may answer them for ourselves. The Walle grandparents are dead. Mr. Beniger and Mrs. Coombs are far away.

2.

Mr. Beniger is an irascible old man, rat shrewd, who lives in San Francisco, and has other children, other grandchildren. Tom and Ellen do not know this, and will not; they have not seen their

4

father, nor heard from or of him, since Tom was two and Ellen six. Their mother, after Beniger left for the West, never spoke of him; she does not know where he is, either, and does not care to know.

The fact is that the old man, proprietor of a fair-sized chemical company in San Francisco, is asleep in his big house on Pacific Heights. He plans to get up at three a.m. to go duck hunting, and therefore took enough brandy to put himself to sleep early, after an early dinner. He is unavailable, even to his own consciousness.

Let the old man sleep.

Life baffled him when he was eager, passionate, brilliant and young; life didn't yield until he learned the way of the rat and how to enjoy it.

The young man arrived in Tennepin, Connecticut, forty years ago, in the uniform of a second lieutenant of infantry. He was on weekend leave from Plattsburg, and had come to visit a retired professor who had taught him chemistry at Yale. Came back for other leaves and, on his final one, married the professor's handsome niece, Ruth. Went to France; returned just four months later with a shattered hand that had caught a German grenade, caught the grenade and threw it out of the trench, but not quite quick enough; got back in time to see his daughter Ellen born.

His wife, the professor's niece, was very sympathetic about her husband's wound until the child was born; then she seemed to feel she had a wound of her own, inflicted by the grenade that Charlton Beniger carried, explosively, between his legs. Kept the thing away from herself as best she could after that, for he was Hun enough to try to toss it at her from time to time, especially after a drink or two; and eventually, of course, she didn't throw it out of the trench quick enough and got wounded all over again by her son, Tom. No more grenade throwing after that; armistice. Polish corridor.

Before the Polish corridor—her name was Elaine Potowski— several more public things had happened. Charlton Beniger's hand mended; he thawed out enough, away from his Southern home, to play the organ in the Congregational church Sundays; he'd been raised Episcopal, but in Tennepin nice people went to the Congregational. His organ playing was pretty fair.

One day he made a friend. He was practicing organ, had been for over an hour, when he looked up and saw that an enormous,

5

hairy man, about his own age, was sitting in a front pew in the empty church, listening to him. Charlton knew who it was: Kaiser Coombs, back three weeks, after helping to occupy Germany, and already called Kaiser by everyone because of the doughboy songs he loved to sing.

Charlton smiled, and started playing "Over There" on the organ. The Kaiser raised his pretty tenor voice and sang the words.

"Let's go get a drink," Charlton said, after they'd done another song or two.

"Prohibition's coming," said the Kaiser, assenting.

"What whiskey we don't drink up this month, they'll pour out next," said Charlton.

For a buck, a handshake, and a bottle of pre-war Rye, the Kaiser rented Charlton office space, up on the second floor of the Coombs Fine Printing Company building, largest building in town and housing the closest thing to an industry. In this office, Charlton kept his chemistry books and did his paper work. He already held a patent for a little process in use in the dye industry. The family lived on its royalties, Ruth's inheritance, and the money which Charlton earned through consultation fees.

His consultations took him all over the East, from time to time, even out into the midwest once; it may be a wonder, under the circumstances, that he should have taken his cold bed problem to Elaine Potowski, rather than keep the solution out of town. But Elaine was awfully pretty; she was Kaiser Coombs's secretary. The two men teased her constantly, and often the three would drink a little bootleg whiskey together after work, up in Charlton's office, and sing a few songs. They all liked each other, but the Kaiser, though he was a bachelor, was too shy or something to do anything about liking Elaine, so finally Charlton took on the job. And almost immediately got caught; he had not discovered, yet, that he had a normal human talent for deviousness.

Getting caught happened in the seventh year of his marriage, when his girl, Ellen, was six and his boy, Tom, only two. The professor's niece got everything: her divorce, the house all but paid for. The car, a Durant. The bank account. The patent, with its royalties. Probably would have taken the clothes off his back, too, if she'd figured they'd fit her. Had an understanding he'd never show his face to Tennepin again, never try to see her, never try to see the children. He never did. He felt guilty enough to agree to it all. He left Tennepin, with Elaine Potowski, pregnant, and train fare west. Nothing more. Once he sent a money order back to Tennepin, to buy the kids Christmas presents; it was returned. Another time, he sent an even larger sum, two hundred dollars, demanding it be used to start his children savings accounts, supplying no return address. That was the last sign of life he ever showed them.

Two things brought them to mind, as he worked to build his new family, his new life, in the west: he was aware, being in the industry, that his first little patent process had been superseded, after a few years, by a simpler one, and that the woman back in Tennepin wouldn't be collecting royalties any longer. He was far enough along the way to rathood by then to dismiss the realization with a sour Southern squeak, a sort of "heeul" sound; for he also knew by then, through a much-forwarded letter from his former friend, which was the last word he ever had or wanted out of Tennepin, that the professor's niece had remarried Kaiser Coombs. The last word he ever had or wanted. The world had taught Charlton Beniger quite a lot about itself by then, and he had a pretty fair idea of what it was about Kaiser Coombs; imagine having your children—your boy—brought up by a man like that?

3.

Just now, as we are watching Sheila's *Hamlet,* old Mrs. Coombs is no more available, even to her own consciousness, than is old Mr. Beniger. Mrs. Coombs sits fully clothed, in a comfortable chair, in a nursing home in Arizona, and appears to be awake; but she has been unavailable since some time this morning when, by being a bully and a schemer, she managed to outwit her nurse:

She did not like to be a bully; she sat among photographs of her son Tom, her daughter Ellen, her grandchild, Sheila, and her late husband, Kaiser Coombs, and it was as if they all supported her, a dutiful family council, all smiling. She was right, they said. Bully or not, everything she got from Mr. Coombs' insurance, from her widow's social security checks, went straight to the management of the Sun City Rest Ranch, except for those few dollars a month which she spent on clothes and extras. So, as she said to the nurse:

"You people make a very decent profit on me. I expect a reasonable amount of attention."

"Now Mrs. Coombs," the nurse said. "I'm sorry. I was busy with poor Mrs. Lathrop. She fainted."

"It's the sun that does it to her. You shouldn't let her sit out in the sun."

"Yes, Mrs. Coombs," the nurse said. "What can I do to make you comfortable?"

"I'm perfectly comfortable," Mrs. Coombs said, sitting straight up in her chair. She knew better than to say directly what it was she wanted, even to a nurse like this one who was more or less new. "I'd like some lemonade and I'd like to know if Mrs. Ryder is well enough to visit."

The nurse concealed a sigh but not completely. She picked up the room phone, and made the calls for lemonade and to Mrs. Ryder, saying to herself, Mrs. Coombs supposed, that the customers could perfectly well make these calls themselves. That, of course, was true, but there were other things, not to be spoken of directly, which the customers could not do for themselves; so, as the nurse finished making the second call, she was no longer permitted to be a nurse.

"Ellen," Mrs. Coombs spoke to her sharply. "I don't think you should wear white to school today. It's too early in the year for white."

"I'm not your daughter, Mrs. Coombs," the nurse said.

"I want to see Tom, too, before you leave for school. And you back here in a suitable dress."

"Mrs. Coombs, dear, please, relax . . ."

"Don't talk back to your mother," Mrs. Coombs said, and braced against the arm of her chair. "Honestly Ellen, I don't understand you. I think you do it just to annoy me. . . ."

The nurse sighed, called Mrs. Ryder back, and suggested that the visit be put off.

"Nonsense, nonsense, nonsense. I want to see Tom now, not in a few minutes, I say now. Now."

She was faking. Now the nurse would have to bring a pill; because she was new, she could still be outwitted rather easily—Mrs. Coombs had used a similar strategem the morning before. Some times, of course, her lapses into the past were genuine—and genuinely painful; the girl would learn, all too soon, which were which.

8

The others would tell her; the others called Mrs. Coombs Tricky Dicky.

The pill came. Mrs. Coombs did not like being a schemer any better than she liked being a bully; it wasn't ladylike. But only now, that she actually had the pill, and the nurse was filling a glass with water, could Mrs. Coombs dislike the means she had used.

Smiling, wanting to be nice, she said:

"Did Mrs. Ryder look very closely at you this morning?"

"What do you mean, Mrs. Coombs?"

"I told her to be sure to notice your skin when you went in to her this morning. You have the loveliest smooth skin." It surprised the girl into smiling. "Really, it's a pleasure to look at."

"Thank you," the nurse said.

"What do you use for it? Some terribly expensive cream?"

"Soap and water."

"Soap and water and good health. That's the best beauty formula, isn't it? My first husband was a brilliant chemist . . ." She caught herself; that had nothing to do with what they were talking about. She made an effort: "You wear the uniform so smartly, too. A pretty nurse is better than medicine." Mrs. Coombs could still mix charm with command when she wanted to; those who called her Tricky Dicky did so partly in admiration.

The new nurse was a pleasant girl; as she found things to do around the room, quite obviously keeping an eye on Mrs. Coombs, they chatted. The nurse admired the photographs, and Mrs. Coombs identified them: the Kaiser, a bearish boy in the uniform of the first World War; Tom, grinning just as awkwardly, in the uniform of the second. The Kaiser, with his big face lined by age, in a sports shirt, with a fishing pole, taken in Florida a few months before he died. There was a more recent picture of Tom in a drawer, not on display because Tom's friend Guy was in that picture too, and Mrs. Coombs did not like Guy. She was not particularly fond of her son-in-law, Harrison Walle, either, but Harrison's image was there, in a group which included Ellen, and Sheila as a little girl of four. Standing alone, set apart from the others, was a two year old portrait study of Sheila at twelve; it was a good photograph. The photographer had caught the girl's energy and sensitivity.

"What an interesting face your grand-daughter has," the nurse said. "And doesn't she look like her uncle?"

"Her mother was a prettier girl," Mrs. Coombs said. "I was dark myself."

The nurse left. The pill was beginning to take effect.

Dark, yes. And tall, with a straight back that never ached, and a long neck, a small, proud, fine featured head. Ruth Coombs' hand rose to touch thin white hair, the fingers felt their way across her forehead, counting wrinkles, searching for an eyebrow. She thought she felt, though her fingers no longer had in full their sense of touch, a hair or two over the ridge of bone. A hair or two. Once, slashing across a glowing forehead, crow's wing black. . . . she spoke to Sheila's picture.

"I can't tell you how pretty I was, Sheila," she said. "You wouldn't believe me."

Now the pill was finding its grip; she knew because her back stopped hurting, and her legs seemed to straighten a little.

"I wish you looked as I did, Sheila," she said.

And then: "I wish the Kaiser were here."

And then, after five minutes, when she didn't hurt at all, anywhere, any more, she let herself remember voices that had asked her what she did for her complexion, now that she had the pill she would not slip away again into regret. Not until night, when the pill was wearing off, did she answer the voices:

"Nothing but soap and water. Only soap and water. Good health."

Handsome, straight-backed, happy Ruth.

Happy Ruth Small. Unhappy Ruth Beniger. Ruth Coombs.

Ruth Coombs, 28 years old, uneasy at first in her strange second marriage; nobody knew but themselves how strange. For the Kaiser—everyone in town called him that. Even the children.

The Kaiser, gentle, undemanding, hesitant man, uncontaminated by the curse of brilliance, a bachelor at thirty-two, had never touched a woman before their marriage, and never touched one afterwards, Ruth included.

4.

He would hold her sometimes, quite chastely, fully clothed, for warmth, not lust. To this Ruth was carefully unresponsive at first; male deviousness was something she had learned to fear

10

from Beniger, the disarming caress, the treacherous tenderness, the insistence which wouldn't remain gentle. She and her new husband slept separately.

Ruth had the large double bed, the Kaiser a hard cot which he claimed to prefer. The cot was in the dressing room; every morning, first thing, Ruth stripped the cot and hid away the bedding, disguised the cot as a day bed with slip cover and pillows so that not even the maid would know.

In the sixth week of their marriage, Kaiser Coombs shouted out in his sleep one night, loudly enough to wake her. It was a frightened shout, and it frightened Ruth. She switched on the lamp by her bedside and sat up. A moment later, and in he came, barefoot, wearing pajama pants without a top. He stopped, one step past the doorway, mumbled apologetically, went back to the dressing room.

She called to him, puzzled, still alarmed. The instant he reappeared, she regretted calling.

He came in again, diffidently, wearing his dressing gown; but she had noted, seeing him for the first time with his shirt off, though they had been six weeks married, that he was remarkably hairy; there was even hair on his shoulders.

She pulled the sheets and blankets up to her neck and set her teeth to refuse whatever form he might use: plea, request, demand.

"I'm sorry I . . . made such a noise. Was it very loud?" he asked.

She nodded.

"I'm sorry." He had stopped; he looked at her, pleadingly, from half across the room.

"I hope the children didn't hear," she said, to remind him that there were children—Tom two, Ellen six. She reminded him because he had said that the stewardship of Beniger's children, and the comfort of living in a household, were all the things he wanted from his marriage.

They were both silent for a moment, listening for the crying of a baby or the night questions of a little girl.

Then the Kaiser said, shuffling his feet which must have been getting cold, "I had a dream."

"Do you have them often?"

"Sometimes." He was not attempting to come closer.

"What was it?"

11

"I don't know."

She could tell that he wanted to come closer, perhaps to sit on the bed, most likely to crowd his enormous body into it. Suddenly his size made her tremble.

"Well, we need our sleep," she said, shifting her position. To her shame the tension with which she gripped the protecting sheets and blankets at her throat went out of balance; her right hand, the farther from him, jerked the screen suddenly to one side, exposing her bare shoulders, her nightgown, through which, for it was more or less transparent, he might have seen a breast.

But the Kaiser looked away. "We need our sleep," he said, repeating her words.

"All right. I'll see you in the morning."

He nodded, turned away, started back towards his cot.

Suddenly she said: "Was it something about the war? In France?"

He turned back. She was secure again, behind her shield.

"What?"

"Your dream—was it about the war?"

"Why do you say that?"

"Well, it's what you read. And people talk about. That the men who were over there have bad dreams of battles and guns . . ."

He hesitated a moment. Then he said, slowly: "I don't think it was about battles."

Once or twice a month, in the first years of their marriage, the Kaiser seemed to have those dreams; or others. Sometimes he said he could remember them, though his descriptions were vague; sometimes he couldn't recall them at all. After the first time he didn't come to her room again until, six months later, she said:

"When one of your dreams troubles you, if you want to come in and talk, you may."

"Thank you," he said. "I never know if . . . if I've wakened you or not."

"When you wake me, I'll turn on the light."

She found herself lying awake nights, waiting for it to happen; but when it did again, she was asleep. She did not know how long he had been calling or what he was saying. To her amazement, he was laughing when she was fully enough awake to identify the sound. The laughter stopped, very abruptly, and she turned her light on. It seemed that he might not come in. She waited. When

12

he finally appeared, this second time, he had remembered his dressing gown. Even though he had been laughing, he looked as pale, as frantic, as he had before. He was too large a man to look that way.

"You must have been having a good time," she said.

His mouth opened in surprise.

"I mean . . . I mean in your dream, you were laughing."

"I was?"

"It couldn't have been so bad if you were laughing, could it?"

He shook his head, doubtfully.

"Come sit on the bed," she said, by now as unalarmed about his intention as if he had been little Tom. "Come on." She actually patted the bed beside her.

He dragged towards her. He put a knee on the bed, down near the foot, and let his big body sink over it; he was about as far from her as he could get.

"Do those dreams always frighten you?" She asked.

He did not look at her. He nodded.

"Why?"

He shook his heavy head; it was not clear whether in refusal to answer, or in wonderment. After a while he spoke. "Never mind, Ruth," he said. "It doesn't happen so often now, does it?"

"Not so often." But she wasn't sure this was true.

"I wish I knew how to stop."

"Stop dreaming?"

"Stop disturbing you. We could close the door."

"But I'm not thinking about myself . . . here, lie down." He looked at her in fresh alarm. "Just on top of the blankets, I mean." He nodded. Gratefully, he stretched out alongside her, with the covers between them. He turned his face away. She settled back as well, but left the light on. She turned on her side, towards him, and put out her hand; his face was buried, and he didn't see the hand. For a long minute it hovered over the back of his neck. Finally, stiffly, it touched his shoulder.

It was the first time she had touched him voluntarily, though they had been married over a year.

Whatever it was that troubled the Kaiser, he never came any closer to discussing it than he did that night. Whatever it was, it had no place in a town like Tennepin. Ruth Coombs grew bold about touching him and, as long as the touching was not intimate,

13

as nearly happened one night, it didn't seem to alarm him. On that night, when Ruth's curiosity, impulse—something—got the better of her own fear, her own discretion, she was able to pass off the strayed hand as an accident. This she knew she must do, for his body had gone quite rigid in protest when the hand touched flesh at the waist. They pretended that it hadn't happened. Ruth Small (Beniger) Coombs, and her virgin husband.

There came a time when it was she who held him, for warmth, not lust, and they both liked that; they had, as far as anyone could tell, what they seemed to need from one another; or if they didn't, nobody knew. Nobody ever knew.

If the Kaiser would have liked children of his own, he never said so. If Ruth, as the years went on, found sensuality in herself and would, on some restless evenings, have released him from his vows, she never hinted at it; she wouldn't have known how. She was only thirty when her prettiness began to lose its glow; no one noticed especially. She was busy with her children. She did a good deal of committee work; she undertook so much of the responsibility in that kind of thing that even people who knew better thought of her as five or six years older than she actually was.

5.

Yet there was nothing mysterious, after all, about the Kaiser and his dreams. If Tennepin, which was a little town, from which no New Yorker had yet thought of commuting to the city, seems unsophisticated, looking back, and the Kaiser's young manhood a time of innocence, there were yet names for what was wrong, both popular and scientific. There have always been. And there have always been men like Asa Buxton Coombs who, because he was big physically, with massive arms and shoulders, and furry as a coon, because his nature was kind and his attitude uncomplicated, because he was raised to be a man of character and courtesy, was beyond suspicion in his town and deserved to be.

Asa Coombs—he wasn't called the Kaiser until he returned from the war—had never been afraid of anything before he went overseas as a second lieutenant. He was an accomplished and a highly goodnatured, wrestler and boxer, rural style; he loved work, water, domestic animals, wild ones too; he loved the guns with

14

which he hunted; he didn't mind darkness and he wasn't superstitious. Although he wasn't insensitive, the ordinary terrors of boyhood simply didn't occur to him. He was shy, perhaps, of girls, and almost embarrassingly respectful to older women, but these traits were considered appropriate and boyish. People said: "Asa will get over being girl shy, and then watch out." That was before he went to France. When he got back, they said: "He'll find the right girl," and when he married Ruth Beniger, they said: "If old Charlton hadn't run off with that Polack, Asa might've waited for Ruth Coombs all his life and never said a word."

In France, as an infantry platoon leader, he was still unafraid, except in the healthy way that makes any sane man keep his head down when shells are falling. He was so level-headed, in fact, that he became executive officer on the death of the exec, and acting Company Commander when the CO was wounded, both before his promotion from second lieutenant came through. He was then twenty. He was immensely valued at Battalion Headquarters; at first they spoke of him with pride, as a boy who could do a man's job and then, because there was little boyishness left in his appearance after two months in France, he was simply spoken of as a good man. He was mentioned in dispatches several times. He might have had a personal medal but Headquarters, at the time it was being mentioned, felt that to buck through too many individual medals just then might jeopardize the delicate politicking for a unit citation which, on merit, the entire battalion received.

Asa Coombs loved his men. He loved them virily and sentimentally, as he loved his country, his home town, and the widowed mother who had brought him up. The men's loyalty to him was of the same emotional kind; they followed him because they trusted him, liked him, wanted him to know it, because they knew he cared more for them than for himself, because he was clearly the best man. He was the best man physically, the best with weapons, the best in the other sense, the sense of goodness. If they had been permitted to elect a commanding officer, instead of having had one assigned to them, Asa Coombs would have been unopposed for his office.

There came a particular midnight; the company was in the trenches; the war was straining in both directions. The sky was full of German flares; mortar shells were dropping forward of them, around the barbed wire. About one a.m., small artillery shells began to search in their erratic clusters, now landing in behind them, now blatting away whitely in front. By two, heavier batteries had joined in the barrage, and Allied artillery began to reply; it was a noisy night of unmistakable significance: it meant the Germans would attack, and almost certainly at dawn. Lieutenant Coombs woke in his dugout when it started; he had been asleep for only half an hour.

He checked his watch, scratched himself patiently and thoroughly, digging his fingernails through the heavy cloth of his uniform. Then he left the dugout, and went crouching along the short communicating trench into the lateral one along which his men were spaced out, far too few of them for the distance they were detailed to defend. They were tired, but none of them were sleeping.

Lieutenant Coombs moved slowly along from man to man, smiling at the grumbles, speaking encouragement, asking about equipment and ammunition. When a flare went up he would stop; when it died, he would move on to the next man. It took him half an hour to cover the company position in this way, and when he had finished in one direction, he started back, prowling like an animal which senses fight but has not yet seen its form.

Although the Company had been at less than half strength for weeks, there was only one replacement in the ranks that night, an eighteen year old from Virginia named Mawbrey Danforth. He was slight and fair; he spoke with the soft whine of the hill country, and because he had curly hair, the men called him Molly; although this made him blush, he didn't seem to mind it seriously. He had been with the company two weeks and was something of a pet.

Acting CO Coombs had plans for Molly Danforth. He was going to make him company runner if they ever got up near strength again. This would keep the boy around Company Headquarters, and away from any possible bestiality from the men—for bestiality was not unheard of among the doughboys of the AEF. Why the possibility should have occurred to him in regard to this particular replacement, Asa Coombs didn't stop to think.

It was Molly Danforth's first time under serious fire. The boy was scared. Doing his man's job, working back and forth along his trench as the night went banging on, Asa Coombs found that he was staying longer with Molly than with any of the others,

16

saying soothing things, showing him how to fix his bayonet, putting a reassuring arm around the kid's shoulders. It was the waiting, the boy whispered, that got to him; he had never seen a Hun yet.

"Maybe you'll see some in the morning," Asa Coombs said. The air was never silent, now that counter battery had started; it was full of sighing, rustling, whistling between explosions; he tried to explain to the boy which sounds were which. He was with him when the other end of the Company trench caught a shell.

He was rather confused about what happened next; he had an image of himself trying to get away, down along the trench to where the wounded were, and of the boy clinging to him, sobbing. He remembered pushing Molly away, down into the mud they had been standing in, and he thought the youngster might have soiled himself.

At about four in the morning a reserve company came in to reinforce them; by five, their whole battalion was in the trench. A French battalion, so the newcomers said, had been shifted over by forced march to be in reserve. And almost at the moment of six, the barrage stopped.

They saw the Germans come out of the facing trench, four hundred yards away, and start for them. They fired their rifles; mortars and machine guns from the weapons company joined in. Some Germans fell. The rest lay prone, returning the fire, rising to run forward a step or two before falling again. Word arrived that yet another battalion was now in support behind them, and the men cheered.

Then, something perplexing in the familiar order: the Germans were sliding back towards their trenches again. The men cheered once more, but nervously; there was no reason yet for their adversaries to withdraw.

A runner was looking for the CO of the reserve company; there were orders for it to pull back, immediately, leaving the trenches to Company K alone once more.

"What are they doing, Captain?" one of the squad leaders asked. "What the hell's their idea?"

"Keep your men firing," Asa said. "Let's cover this."

The men from the reserve company were disappearing now, one by one; Company K felt vulnerable, unprotected, as the strange soldiers left their sides, going out behind the dugout, running back somewhere, leaving the trench half empty and the

17

men of Company K curiously lonely. Molly Danforth started to cry, and that was the first time the acting company commander had thought of the boy as an individual in a good many hours; he heard the crying with uncharacteristic irritability, and had to suppress an urge to shout angrily at Molly to be quiet.

As the morning went on, getting silent, getting sunny, and no renewal came of the attack, they began to understand that it had been a feint. The real attack had taken place elsewhere, with the reserves out of position; they felt illogically cheated, and shot their rifles in useless frustration in the direction of an enemy they could not harm, until Asa told them to stop wasting bullets.

In the afternoon came word which could not depress them further because they had anticipated it: the German strategy had succeeded; a hard won salient, six miles up, had been lost back again.

Ten days later, Company K was relieved, bivouacked in a rest area. From there they went back even further to a better bivouack, a better rest area. For once, Acting Company Commander Asa Coombs found himself quartered at some distance from his men, sharing a pyramidal tent with officers from other line companies. He was not completely comfortable with them; for the first few drinks they were fine. Asa was getting quite a taste for cognac himself, and it was always fun getting started. But once the first stage was past, his brother officers would begin to tell appallingly dirty stories—not jokes, but stories of things they said they had actually done; he did not fully believe them, but it made him uncomfortable nevertheless. No amount of trench warfare and cognac could convince Asa that men and women should behave that way, and if they did, it wasn't decent to talk about it. But he did not want to be a child among them; he dissimulated. He even laughed.

One night his tentmates organized an expedition to a farmhouse where there were said to be girls for sale; Asa declined to join them, gently enough. He had no wish to impose his feelings.

After his fellow officers left, he decided to visit the area, a hundred yards away, where the enlisted survivors of his company were quartered in shelter-half pup tents, few enough of them.

There seemed to be no one there. To a man, as far as he could tell, the remnants of his company were out for the evening, very likely headed for some inn or farmhouse of their own discovery. Asa was more disappointed than annoyed; he had brought a bottle of cognac with him. He had thought they might sit around, remi-

18

niscing, singing perhaps—"Oh, We'll Hang Kaiser William from a Sourapple tree," "There's a Long, Long Trail," "My Buddy."

He called several of the men by name, thinking there might be a few sleeping in the little pup tents, but got no answers. Then, just as he was about to leave, he heard the soft hill voice of Molly Danforth.

"Captain, sir?"

He had almost forgotten the boy.

"I'm a lieutenant," he said. "Where are the others?"

"They went off and told me to stand guard," the voice came from one of the pup tents. "They made me stay."

"We're not responsible for posting guards," Asa said.

"Well, I don't mind. They're going to see some old French girls," the boy said. "I just as soon lie here in my tent and look at a paper."

Asa Coombs knelt at the entrance of the shelter to peer in, and found his nose not more than two inches from Molly's, who was peering out. Asa started back.

"You want to see inside, sir? We got it fixed up a little."

"Who's your tent mate?" Asa asked.

"Sergeant Salter."

"I see," Asa said, irritated with himself. He ought to have made this kid Company runner as he'd meant to. Salter was a brute, perfectly capable of that bestiality which was sometimes talked about, which was said to be so prevalent among the British troops, the French, the Belgians, the Negroes; said to go on among the white Yanks from the South, the West, the cities—anywhere but in one's own company.

"I wonder . . ." he began.

At the same time, Molly said: "I got a flashlight, captain. You want to see how we fixed it?"

Asa knelt again and put his head inside the flap of the tent. The soldiers had dug out a little, underneath it, and the two rolls of bedding nested together side by side. There were some French magazine covers, pictures of female entertainers, hanging down along the pole at the far end.

"Sergeant Salter cut us some pine branches for underneath the bedding," Molly said. "Sure is comfortable."

"I . . . I can imagine," said Asa, more stiffly than he meant to.

The boy turned his flashlight out. "Come on. Try one bed and see," he said.

19

Not allowing himself to think why he should comply with so silly an invitation, Asa crawled into the tent and lay down. Instantly, he felt the boy's body against his, unmistakable in its intention. There was a second of involuntary compliance in Asa's own body, so terrible that he roared, as if it hurt, and heaved violently to his feet, picking the pup tent up around his shoulders.

"No," he cried, kicking his way out of the bedding, roaring again. "No," fighting off the entangling shelter halves, the magazine covers which had risen with him.

"But you liked it. I felt you," Molly was shrilling after him as Asa Coombs ran his lumbering run away from there, a frightened man for the first time in his life.

It was a fear that remained with him until, a few years before his death, he found that nothing, not even dreams, could trouble him any longer.

Nuns and priests, saints of many religions, accept celibacy as a condition of their lives. Perhaps it is not so hard for them, for their curious determination is supported by a ritual of magic vows, of approval from their special publics, of belief, they say, that they are meeting a requirement laid down by something supernatural. Perhaps it is not so hard for them as it was for Asa, Kaiser Coombs, who required the same performance of himself secretly, because he was unwilling to think of himself as other than the kind of man that he appeared to be.

His friendship with Charlton Beniger, the tears in his eyes, when, on an evening of Prohibition whiskey drinking, he would sing doughboy songs, the eagerness with which he took Charlton's children into his charge—none of these things seemed connected in the Kaiser's waking mind with sex. Even the bargain which he kept with his wife seemed to him to have been made to spare a delicate woman the pain and risk of further childbirth.

And in the public mind of Tennepin which was, after all, to Kaiser Coombs an entity as powerful as any god to any nun, there was never the least suspicion of deviation on the part of its good and faithful servant. The public mind was right; any god who might be said to disagree is wrong. A man is what he is, not what he dreams; we all have fantasies, in varying degrees of consciousness, in which we seem to act in ways we would not act. These fantasies are not ourselves but the vapors of self, product of the inner heat and secret pressure under which we live.

20

CHAPTER TWO

1.

To HIS STEPDAUGHTER Ellen Beniger, who was twelve in 1930, Kaiser Coombs was a perfect parent with a single, and to her a tragic flaw.

The first item in his perfection was that he was nice. To Ellen, a realist, nice was not a trait of character; it was a description of status. In Tennepin, it described the highest level. Below people who were nice came those who were really very nice. And below them the perfectly nice. Quite a ways below, in the tradesman class, were the wonderful. The lowest class of all included people who were simply the most marvelous.

From this standpoint, Kaiser Coombs was better than her real father, half-remembered, for Charlton Beniger had come from too far away to be classified; as an outsider he merely acquired his wife's status without ever really ceasing to be an outsider. There were other, more homely standpoints, from which the replacement father was an improvement: Ellen could remember Beniger as a man of anguish and temperament, a man who upset her mother; the Kaiser never upset anybody. The Kaiser's strength and calm were always at his stepchildren's disposal, even for standing between them and their mother when she was cross as she often was. The Kaiser's beautiful, light voice always soothed, never scolded. The Kaiser's affection was a steady quantity in a steady life.

The flaw, however, gave all this goodness a kind of unimportance. Sometimes she blamed him for it, more often her mother. They were both at fault but he was easier to forgive, because he was sorry for it and mother wasn't: it was that the Kaiser was a stepfather, not a father, and everybody knew it. And would always know it, no matter what happened. And nobody else had a stepfather, not Margie. Not Connie Green or Connie Marston. Not Bev. Ellen spoke of it to Bev, who was also twelve.

"Sometimes people call me Ellen Coombs, and it makes me so mad."

"Why?"

"Because it's not my name and they know it."

"Do you wish it was?"

"It doesn't matter what I wish." Ellen frowned.

"I'll bet the Kaiser wishes that it was. He just loves you."

"Mother's trying to get me to change it," Ellen said.

"Are you going to?"

Ellen didn't know; the idea had been brought up recently, now that she was about to start high school. The idea bothered her, but why should it? Wouldn't being Ellen Coombs fix everything?

"I wish my father and mother didn't drink all the time," Bev said pensively, filling the companionable silence that had fallen between them. "Even in the morning they do it." It was a shocking lapse in relevance, just when they had been talking about something important. Bev—and Margie, and the two Connies—were all the same; persons like that didn't understand. Their fathers hadn't left them when they were too little to say anything, for old Polish girls; they didn't have stepfathers and divorces. There wasn't one of them you could talk seriously to, about serious things: Connie Green, for instance. Her face would get solemn but you knew she wasn't really listening to you; she was thinking of her first cousins, Dan and Brabber, who were not bright enough to go to school. Connie Marston, the doctor's daughter, would complain because her father was so nervous that he couldn't hold the food he ate without taking stuff to calm himself, and he would keep trying to break himself of this, and it would go all right for a week or so and then it would start again, every meal, excusing himself to go to the bathroom and be sick, even when there was company.

They were a flock, nevertheless, these girls, of pretty birds.

And Ellen was prettiest. She was plump-armed and green-eyed,

22

with light yellow hair, a freckle or two, and the sort of short-barreled body which matures with the least stress, the least embarrassment. Connie Green was the boldest: she knew naughty things. Bev was sweetest. Marge tried to boss them and often they let her. Connie Marston was the fastest runner and knew all the rules of baseball. They had been a flock from the time they could remember—walking together, playing, discovering, shrieking, giggling, advancing, withdrawing—all together from the time they had first marked one another, tiny girls in ruffled dresses, just old enough to be taken by girlish mothers to one another's houses to play on rainy afternoons.

Now they would go to high school together and, after the first strange day, it would be just like junior high, like grammar school, like play school; the important things would not change. It was 1930 and the ways of Tennepin were eternal.

Although she had moments of presence at home when she was very nearly as commanding as her mother, Ellen was a rather passive member of the girl flock. Her being prettiest permitted it; her shame, it seemed to her, required it. And now her mother had said:

"Ellen, it's quite unnecessary for you to go to High School as Ellen Beniger. It will simply confuse all the new people, the new teachers, who won't know who your family is."

"Ruth," the Kaiser said, in a warning voice. They were sitting at the table after supper. Tom had been excused, and Ellen asked to wait. It was a warm spring evening, and Ellen could hear Tom yelling "Bobby" at the eight-year old who lived next door. She found herself wishing she were out there with them. "Ruth, you agreed. . . ."

"Yes," her mother said. "We decided to let you make up your own mind about this, Ellen."

"About . . . changing my name?"

"Yes."

"I didn't know you could. I mean, people could."

"Dear," said the Kaiser anxiously. "If you want to keep your own name, of course you may. We . . . we just thought you might like to be Ellen Coombs, but if you wouldn't. . . ."

Ellen looked at him, loving him. Her mother started to say something, but the Kaiser, who never interrupted, did for once. "When your mother and I were married, we talked about changing your

23

name and Tom's to Coombs. But we thought we should wait until you were old enough to decide for yourself."

If he would ask her now, Ellen thought, and her mother would be quiet, she would say yes. Doris came from the kitchen just then to clear the dishes, so Ellen pretended she was thinking it over; actually, she was listening to Tom and Bobby make what they seemed to think was a very funny joke; it consisted of shouting at one another, "Look out! There's a bumble-bee!" and then yelling with laughter.

"There isn't anything much to discuss about it," her mother said. "I imagine whichever you decide to do, Tom will do also, later on. . . ."

"Oh," said Ellen. "But maybe he wouldn't want to do the same thing later on. That would be worse."

"Of course he would," her mother said. It was true; Tom did whatever he thought people would like.

"Ruth, please," the Kaiser said.

"Couldn't I think it over a little?" Ellen asked.

"Ellen, once you start high school with a name, that will be your name," said her mother.

"But that isn't for three more weeks. Do I have to decide this minute?"

"No, of course not," said the Kaiser.

"What on earth is there to think three weeks about?" Her mother asked. "I should think you'd want to get it over with. After all, it's not as if the name Beniger meant anything here. It's. . . ."

"It's her father's name, Ruth," the Kaiser said.

Then they both stopped talking again and looked at Ellen.

"But I can't just decide, just in a minute . . ." Ellen began.

The Kaiser stood up. "Never mind, Ruth. She doesn't want to."

"But . . ." That was not what Ellen said; it was not what she meant. Of course she would rather be Ellen Coombs; of course, of course. It was just hard to say so when they were both looking at her like that, expecting her to.

"Why not?" The mother snapped, and with that the Kaiser left the room, turning his face away from them quickly.

Her mother seemed quite shaken. "Ellen," she whispered violently. "Call him back. Call him back. Tell him you want your name to be Coombs."

It made Ellen stubborn. The Kaiser shouldn't have left her like

24

that; it wasn't fair; she heard him going slowly upstairs and told herself the Kaiser didn't care about leaving her all by herself with mother getting cross about something.

"Can I go out and play?" Ellen asked. Her mother stared at her and Ellen thought she would probably be sent up to her room; instead her mother bit her lips and nodded.

After that they argued about it whenever the Kaiser was not around. It was an argument Ellen longed to lose, but mother was always trying to trap her or surprise her or overwhelm her, and Ellen would get stubborn again, meaning to lose the argument some other time.

Ellen made a plan, finally; she would do as they wished, but she would not tell them until breakfast, the morning of the day high school started. Then she would bring it up herself, and say it to the Kaiser, not to mother: "I want to be Ellen Coombs."

Tom, Mother, the Kaiser—they were all waiting at the breakfast table that morning when she got down, having taken extra care with dressing. She was eager to get to High School quickly, to walk around with the girls. And as she sat down there, next to her place was a present; the Kaiser never let an important day go by without a present. He smiled at her as she picked it up, and she knew she was meant to open it right away. Pearls?

A wrist watch; a little gold one, with a black band—she had wanted it more, even, than she wanted pearls, which she would now get for her thirteenth birthday in December.

"Put it on," said the Kaiser.

She started to, and then she noticed he had had the back engraved.

E.B.

Ellen Beniger. What could she do but kiss him, and kiss her mother and kiss Tom who shouted, "No, no, no?" She didn't stop to think that the initials could have been changed—well, she did think of it, for a moment, but that would mean the watch would be sent back to the jeweler's and she wouldn't have it to wear today for Bev, and Margie and the two Connies.

2.

The day after his twelfth birthday, Guy Cinturon, having at last found himself potent the night before, sought out a certain nursemaid named Angelica. With him he carried a whip.

This took place in the Mexican state of Chihuahua, in the year 1934. Guy was a handsome, hard-bodied boy who had spent his life riding horses, kicking soccer balls, and beating with his fists such Indian and half-breed boys from the mud village that stood on the Cinturon acreage as seemed to invite it. He had also beaten boys, and once or twice been beaten by them, on or near the Cinturon holdings in the States of Oaxaca, Veracruz, Arizona and Texas, some of which properties were held more directly than others. This small-boy fighting, undertaken with a certain smiling enthusiasm, had been forbidden by father and by elder brothers when he became ten, and had ceased therewith. Guy was dutiful; he did not miss the fighting very much. He was more interested in guns by then, owned several, and was a fine shot for his age. He had been wolf-hunting, even, in the Chihuahua hills, and while they did not get the wolf who had been preying on the Cinturon herds of beef and fighting cattle, Guy had shot a mountain lion out of a tree at close range. There were, of course, men with guns backing him up at the time, but not because young Guy wanted it so; it was rather fear of what Guy's father might do if his youngest boy were injured, which accounted for the semicircle of wolf-hunting herdsmen, all sighting their guns on the same mountain lion at the time the kill was made.

Guy considered using a gun in his reckoning with Angelica. He decided it would be unmanly and unnecessary. A whip should do to offset the difference in their sizes.

Angelica had been Guy's nurse until the age of eight, at which time she was assigned to a younger sister and Guy turned over to a young man from Yale for tutoring. During his years in Angelica's charge, and she had raised him not to tell, Guy had been her toy, and, in a strange way, her love. Angelica had been in her early twenties, then, married, deserted, and a mother. Her own child, a daughter, was cared for by her mother; the husband had gone away

26

to the United States and not returned. Angelica lived in the village, the puebla, and earned the family living at the Cinturon house.

She was a lush, heavy breasted, rather dark woman, and full of self-confidence. She was strong and had handled the fiery little boy with ease; he protested, but he never told that from the time he could remember she had handled him sexually when she bathed him, using her hand, her mouth—sometimes, when she was certain they would be undisturbed, stripping off her own clothes and holding him on top of her, laughing at his struggle to get away. She loved Guy, and he sensed this, not as nurse to boy but with all the feeling of a particular woman for a particular man. She made a fierce public scene when the tutor from Yale arrived, and hated him bitterly, but Guy, to his delight, was not returned to her.

In the four intervening years, Angelica had cared for Guy's little sister; but Guy knew that she was always on the watch for chances and, now and then, she would catch him and work upon the boy some fast, damp, passionate spasm, improvised to fit the circumstances.

"Guyito," she would breathe in her soft, pure village Spanish. "Soon you will be able, like a man, and then you will pursue Angelica and she will run and cry to be let go."

He believed her, as he struggled silently; the image of himself with a weapon which would rout her sustained his hope of self-respect.

Finally, Guy could outrun Angelica. He developed a special talent for avoiding her in close places. She rarely caught him, and when she did he had learned to scratch, kick, box at her, marking her in ways that would be hard to explain; when he was just eleven, the younger sister came upon them one day, struggling, and Angelica was frightened. She stopped stalking Guy; for almost a year there had been no hateful passages of love between them.

Then he was twelve, and the phenomenal thing happened. He was able. His mind turned, before he slept, to the image she had created for him, of herself running, crying to be let go. It was in his mind still when he woke in the morning; it did not leave his mind all day.

In the evening he put on boots and spurs, and took the whip. He left the rooms of the huge, cool, adobe house in the after supper heat, as if he were going to the stable. It was the day off for the Yaleman, and the tutor was pursuing those anthropological researches which had, he said, brought him to Mexico, in company with the man who helped him spend his salary in the pulcheria. The tutor disapproved of families like the Cinturons, who had managed to evade in various ways, many of the land division laws of the Cardenas government; the tutor was a democrat.

Guy slipped out along the rutted road which led from the house to the puebla a mile below. He strode along, scowling, until he reached a certain outbuilding, halfway between. It had once been a watchman's house, but was no longer in any sort of use. It stood at the edge of a gully, deep enough to be shaded now in the setting sun. Guy placed himself between the wall of the building and the edge of the gully and waited. There was a reason for his having chosen this place. Once Angelica had caught him here, and taken him into the little building, onto its damp floor. He remembered it vividly, purposefully; it steadied him to do so.

The maid was putting his sister to bed now; the thought of Angelica putting a child to bed made Guy momentarily wistful; he was annoyed with himself. She would finish. She would come down the road towards the puebla, for Angelica did not sleep every night in the big house, having her own family.

Guy felt the rough wall behind him, thought about the little building and what had happened, and was once more able to wait coldly. His excitement was not sexual; his passion was for revenge, unconnected in his mind with lust. Once, worried, he fixed his mind on a secret thought about himself—it had nothing to do with Angelica—to be sure that the new potency indeed existed. There was enough response to assure him that it did; there was some temptation, even to test the potency still further, to a climax, but he rejected the idea.

After a time, he heard Angelica singing.

He peered around the corner of the building. She was coming along alone in the hot dusk. He gripped the whip.

She walked level with him, unaware, still singing, a smile on her broad face. He let her go past a step, moved swiftly out and cracked the whip sharply across her back; she yelled, and there was no question about his potency now—this was so true that he had to hold back at himself as he swung the whip again. She had run a step or two and the second blow missed. The second blow, actually, had not been planned. He had meant to tumble her into the gully as she cowered. Now, although the plan was no longer

28

practical since she had run the wrong way, he started for her, confused, still meaning to push. She saw who it was, and he raised the whip a third time.

"Into the house, cow," he said. But he had meant to say gully. "I am not a boy today."

Angelica began to smile. *"Guyito,"* she said.

Her smile stopped his arm, poised to deliver a blow.

"Of course, a man. The darling one," she said, stepping towards him.

"No," said Guy. She enfolded him, whip and all, in her big arms, cooing to him: "Yes, the house. The house. Did you think you must whip Angelica?"

"No," said Guy, as she bore him into the building. "No, no . . ." She paid no attention. Laughing, kissing him, fondling him, she enveloped him, as always before, with the hated warmth and dampness. He was silent now, struggling only occasionally, trying to concentrate against the new potency so that it might insult her by deserting him. But Angelica knew too well how to make that part of him respond, and she took him as completely as he had meant to take her, even, finally, rolling him on top of herself, chuckling with passion; he found himself unable to restrain the motion that his hips had to make.

He hated it, all of it, and especially the climax, as if he were giving her, against his will, something of great value.

Later that summer, Guy had his revenge. He avoided Angelica, but that was only part of it.

Angelica's child was a daughter, fifteen, a big-eyed, serious girl and a bright one. It was her mother's dream that Petra would be educated, a teacher for the puebla. Guy, a hard twelve-year old on horseback, studied this girl's movements. He caught her one day, in full daylight, as she was bringing a basket of his sister's mended clothing up to the house from the village. He blocked her way with his horse; Petra was on foot.

He simply commanded the girl, three years older than he and half a head taller, to put the basket down and go into a field where the corn was high. He dismounted calmly and tied his horse. He followed her in among the rows of corn, told her to stop and to lie down. He supposed that she had to obey because of the power of his family over hers. Whatever Petra's motive for complying, Guy did to her as her mother had taught him, that day and many times

29

thereafter until the girl was pregnant. Then there was no longer any question of her becoming a teacher; she was sent three miles away, to work in the fields of a cousin in another puebla. Guy was sent three hundred miles away, to a military school in Texas.

3.

Eddie Bissle's heart broke young, so he threw the damn, cub scout pieces away. It was not clear why the vessel should have shattered so easily; it would not seem to have been a particularly fragile heart. But sometimes heavy ware, designed for rough use, has cracks. Potters can tell you: it's things made of thick, utilitarian clay that are most frequently flawed in firing.

In any case it broke, or so it seemed to Eddie, and that was that. To hell with it.

To Tom Beniger, who came to know and think about them both, there was an inexhaustible series of fascinatingly warped parallels between the origins of Guy Cinturon and those of Eddie Bissle. Both were produced by immigration from the Mediterranean area, intermarried with North American-Anglo stock. Both families were wealthy. Both were agricultural. Both had political power.

But the Cinturones had brought a proud name from Spain in the 1500s, and had owned the boat that brought them, at a royal viceroy's personal request, to Veracruz; Eddie's grandfather discarded whatever his name had been in Malta, and came steerage of course, in the 1890's, at no one's request, to Long Island.

The Cinturones had begun to make North American marriages out of prudence two generations back, taking brides from the wealthy mercantile families of California and Texas, instead of going to Spain for wives—just as the same men began going to Stanford and Princeton instead of to Seville. The North American Eddie's grandfather married was partly Shinnecock Indian, and had very little idea who her family were.

Both boys had the Mediterranean in their appearance, but Guy grew romantically tall, and Eddie stayed short; both had black hair, but Guy's was soft and wavy, and Eddie's coarse—he kept it cropped too short for it to be known whether it might have waved or not. Even their teeth followed the oddly consistent divergence—Guy's small, white, very strong; Eddie's strong too, but

30

yellowish, separated, and thick at the roots. All the conventional animal comparisons were made, at one time or another, about Guy's grace—gazelle, horse, whippet; of Eddie, somebody once said that he was built like a wart. Eddie, when he heard it, considered this description true and just.

The Cinturon family money was vast, somewhere in the many millions; there was no product their farms and plantations didn't raise somewhere in the world, and their holdings spread over five countries. They were involved internationally in trading and manufacturing, in Central American railroads, even in steamboats, for Guy's grandfather had married the heiress of a San Francisco shipping family. Their holdings had been diminished by Mexican revolutions, Texas cotton booms, California fruit men; but they had ability and they had luck. What the productivity of their empire might lose in one area would be gained back in another, through oil being discovered, or a wartime demand that they reopen closed mines.

The Bissle wealth was small beside this, something under a million dollars; its agricultural foundations were not much varied, except as there is variation on outer Long Island between cabbages and potatoes; they had only one manufacturing concern, a profitable little shop which sewed potato bags; and their shipping interests consisted of the ownership of a dozen rather dirty trucks.

As for politics: Cinturon, Cinturon-Avila, Cinturon y Prieto, were names that went back through the Spanish histories of many states, crossing and recrossing international borders; they had been the names of governors, ambassadors, secretaries in national cabinets, generals and archbishops. Eddie's father served his community as head of the trucking corporation which bore his name, and as Democratic committeeman in his district.

About hearts, perhaps the parallels fail; it could be argued either way. In any case, Eddie was twelve when his went, the same age as Guy lying in wait for Angelica, the same age at which Tom Beniger had a six-month illness. The same year: 1934.

Eddie was a silent boy, and his smile was indistinguishable from his scowl.

He was born as the result of a bargain. His father, being pretty well set financially, married for political and social advantage: Mrs. Bissle had a family name so immemorially common on Long Island that it was a local synonym for commonness. Its Colonial bearers had manned the kitchens and the grog shops before the Revolution. If the son of a Maltese immigrant and a part-Indian woman wanted to be Americanized, and wanted to be connected with as many voters in the community as possible, Mrs. Bissle's was the family to marry into. Eddie's father wanted one more thing from his marriage, and that was a son to whom to leave all the money he planned to make.

Eddie's mother, who disliked the idea of having children on the ground that it was strenuous, agreed that she would have them, nevertheless, until the first boy was born; since no girls preceded him, Eddie completed Mrs. Bissle's end of the bargain. She did not avoid her husband's bed after that nor, indeed, beds in general. She liked beds; she was a good scout, on the dumb blonde model; she enjoyed parties and didn't discriminate much between men at a party's conclusion; but she never allowed herself to be so overcome either with drink or passion that she didn't make sure that there was plenty of rubber guarding both portions of engaged flesh, her partner's, husband or not, and her own as well.

To Eddie she paid no attention at all.

As far as Eddie was concerned, his mother stank and his father was a slob. His grandfather was all right, but too dumb to speak English right. His grandfather still worked personally, in the cabbage and potato fields, and still lived in the plain frame house in the midst of them, where his wife had died a bride. Since young Eddie had to be someplace, he supposed, he preferred to be there, at his grandfather's. Some mornings he'd wake up and the stupid stucco house of his parents, on the residential street, with its soft furniture and soft lawn and soft, overnight smells of food and whiskey and his mother, would be too goddamn much. It might be as early as four-thirty or five in the morning, summer or winter, and Eddie would get up angry, put on whatever he'd been wearing the evening before, and walk out to his grandfather's house, four miles away. He would sit patiently until the old guy woke up, and watch him stumbling around, yawning, in his long underwear, boiling coffee, splashing cold water on his face.

The old guy would see Eddie, sooner or later, and say something rough:

"Boy, where coffee pan?" or, "What you sitting? Get wood;" never any question about what his grandson was doing there; Eddie would chuckle. Nothing soft about that old man.

32

He would stay there as long as they left him alone, eating the food his grandfather got from cans, drinking a lot of water, working with a hoe or riding the cultivator, maybe not saying one damn word from morning till night. After a day or two, his father would drive out to get Eddie and take him home, put him back in school, pretending it was all a kind of joke about a little kid running away.

Eddie didn't care what the man wanted to pretend. He had nothing to say to his father. He had nothing to say to anyone, Miss Pig Ears Beal included.

Who was Miss Beal, anyway? Some kind of assistant head mistress of the day school he went to; she was supposed to worry about dopey kids that couldn't get along in their work. So what did she want to worry about Eddie for? He never got anything less than a C in his life. So what, if he only came to school two or three times a week? Why should Pig Ears care as long as he was passing everything, and always had and always would?

It was Eddie's stupid father that put Pig Ears on him, and once she got on him she stuck like a tick—"Eddie dear, Eddie dear, Eddie dear." Come to her office, see her after class, see her at the stucco house drinking tea with his mother, which was pretty funny in a way: his mother with a goddamn tea cup. Pig Ears even tried to nail his grandfather one day; Eddie walked out of the house when he saw her car stop outside. He went to the barn and ran corn through the sheller for about an hour, for the old guy's chickens, till she left. Then his grandfather came out, just as Eddie's arm was about to drop off, and said:

"You don't like go to Sunday School, huh?"

Sunday School? What, was Beal working for the Sunday School, too, now? Eddie shook his head, the old guy nodded, and that was the end of that.

Pig Ears was always giving it to him about extracurricular activities: wouldn't he like to be in the hiking club, or be in a play, or go out for a team? Sure, why not? If Pig Ears wanted to get herself a football team, like the Public High School had, Eddie'd go out for it, but if she thought he was going to play volley-ball with the saps, or run around the track in a pink sweat suit, she was so far off her nut she couldn't reach it with a rake.

It seemed to Eddie that he'd better make up his mind to do something, so he made up his mind to be a football player, team or no team. He decided that in the summer, after he saw a news-

33

reel of some college guys training, knocking hell out of each other. He disregarded the fact that he was a head shorter than other boys his age, and that he had never seen an actual game. He had observed training apparatus in the newsreel, and he stuffed a potato sack with an old mattress and tackled it for hours. He collected twenty old tires and spread them on the ground in a staggered line, and he would run, spread-legged, back and forth, crouching low, foot into one, foot into the next, going harder and harder until he fell. Then, wherever he had fallen, he required himself to do twenty-five push-ups before he was allowed to get up and run again; they had had tires and done push-ups in the newsreel.

One mid-autumn afternoon, just after school had started in again, he was running intently among his tires; there was a ferocious ecstasy in his mind. He had more muscles than a lot of kids three or four years older; he could do a hundred and four push-ups. He had shattered the potato bag with a tackle once. He could throw himself on the ground head first, as hard as he liked, and it didn't hurt. He decided he had earned a football and would buy himself one, not one of those stupid, light, thin things that the fruity kids played touch with—touch!—no, a real, heavy, fat bladder on which to roll, dive, jam his stomach—as he thought of this he was aware of a grunt different from his own boyish grunting; someone was watching. All right, let some slob watch. Eddie would look up and see who it was when he finished running his course in one direction and turned to start back. He did, jumping into the last pair of tires with both feet landing simultaneously; then whirling, switching feet and direction in the same movement.

It was his grandfather, who should have been in the fields overseeing the harvesters.

"What you do boy? Play?" his grandfather asked, slowly and loudly.

Eddie was about to answer when he noticed something else: the automobile of Pig Ears Beal. He raised his glance and by it stood Miss Beal herself, watching then, smiling. Smiling!

"You play little boy game? That's good," roared old Bissle, looking around at Miss Beal for approval. "Good, good, good." He started to laugh.

Eddie held himself still, puzzling it out, holding against the strain of his body to be off among the tires again.

"But you got no one to play with this game," his grandfather

34

said, and there was no puzzle any longer. He wasn't to pity Eddie; not even him; especially not him.

Instead of replying, Eddie began his run, sprinting hard, low, stiff, from tire to tire, forgetting that Beal was watching, coming to the end of his course and keeping on.

He charged his grandfather low and furious. He hit the stout old legs with his shoulder, feeling pain and liking it. He brought his arms together and drove forward. The old man roared and went down like a tree.

They fell together to the ground, the grim twelve-year old, the astonished farmer.

Immediately Eddie felt ashamed. "Yeah I . . . I got somebody to play with. You," he muttered quickly, weakly, hoping it might be taken as an explanation.

But his grandfather was not deceived. He pulled himself away, along the ground.

"You break somebody leg?" he said, without bitterness, sadly. "No good, boy."

Eddie couldn't answer; he couldn't even get up, for Christ's sake, as long as his grandfather was sitting on the ground looking at him like that. Finally the old man did rise, and Eddie did too. His grandfather turned away; he didn't speak again. He limped towards his house without looking back. Just before he got to the porch, he raised his hand and pointed at Miss Beal. Then he went inside, and Eddie went to the car.

That was the big, important deal about how the heart broke, if anybody liked, and if anybody didn't like, what did they want Eddie Bissle to do about it? Pee out of his eyeballs?

He and his grandfather made it up, more or less, by cajolery on the old guy's part, soft-headedness on Eddie's: what the hell, Eddie asked himself, did he expect the dumb farmer to do, kiss him? Pat him on the head and give him a stick of candy, for Christ's sake? Get out the ball and kick it around some, was that it?

Guy, curiously enough, kept the strange parallels going by becoming an apprentice football player too, that fall, learning the game at the Texas military school, excelling effortlessly in the light team competition for younger boys.

Coombs Fine Printing, established in the middle nineteenth century by the Kaiser's grandfather, had once employed fifty men. A local newspaper, which failed in the panic of 1873, had been one of the least of its projects. It had done books and magazines for New York publishers, calendars and timetables for railroad and stage lines, directories and registers for towns and cities all over the state. On the death of the Kaiser's father in 1904, his mother had taken over the management in the name of the heirs— the Kaiser and his sister. The mother was generally admired for this, and said to be a smart woman; it was far from true. Her business judgment was influenced now by a conservative lawyer, now by an expansion-minded foreman, even once, secretly, by an astrologer. No consistent business policy was followed; old contracts lapsed because the lawyer advised against replacing the equipment needed to service them; new contracts of great volume often seemed, when they had been fulfilled, to have been handled at a puzzling loss. The work force became inefficient, and was reduced in anger just at a time when speedy production would have solved a major problem in client relations. The foreman, having been proved wrong on one occasion by the lawyer, was dismissed, and could never be replaced to anyone's satisfaction. Mrs. Coombs, accepting the public valuation of herself as a smart woman, blamed the times; as she grew older she grew more erratic. To the Kaiser and his sister, growing up on the family farm, all this was quite impossible; they believed the legend of their mother's Yankee business sense. When the old lawyer, who had held things together pretty well, passed along, their mother's choice of advisors went from vacillating to irrational.

For the Kaiser, returning to manage the plant in 1919, it was never possible fully to apprehend the total silliness of his mother's business career. While she lived he consulted her daily on management problems, devoting his own judgment and energy to the mechanical aspect of the business for which he had great talent. His men—there were eleven of them when he began to run the place, so it was still large enough to be called a plant—said he was the best pressman in the state. He had a fine touch with machines and a great love for them. Over half the floor space was occupied by unused and antiquated equipment when the Kaiser took over, and each time he sold something off it was like the passing of a friend. Finally, however, at rather too much capital expense, he had his plant modernized and the work force built up to twenty again; his mother had died, he had married. Nothing very ambitious could be undertaken in the way of a contract, but through the twenties there were some periodical and mailing jobs, though not concerned with publications of great influence; there was a good deal of local and regional business printing; and there were some mail-order catalogues, though the four-color covers had to be sub-contracted.

In 1929 the bank was considering making the Kaiser a loan to install new color-printing facilities; in 1930 the bank failed. A man named Murray had been responsible, in part, for the move to expand, a former customer working towards partnership, showing the Kaiser how, by extending more generous credit, business could be increased; the increase had been accomplished temporarily and disastrously, for in 1930 many of the beneficiaries of the liberalized credit defaulted on their bills. Half a year's work had been done which would never be paid for. In 1931, in January, the man named Murray left town leaving his luggage behind at the hotel. Murray had not been a thief, only in over his head like everybody else; there were quite a few small bills owing which the Kaiser quietly paid.

Ruth agreed that he should do this—pay Murray's local bills— though the few hundred dollars was suddenly more than they could afford. The farm on which the Kaiser's sister lived, a maiden, was producing a deficit which the Kaiser had to meet. He began, once more, to reduce his work force, even to sell equipment to meet his obligations; by the end of the year, with five men working for him, his machinery occupying barely twenty per cent of the floor space, the whole upstairs of his building shut off so that it needn't be heated and even his desk moved to a small front room with a separate stove, the Kaiser began to think of himself as a local job printer, and rather a struggling one, no longer as the proprietor of an old solid, national company.

Ruth Coomb's personal income had stopped as well; it had come from two sources—a small inheritance, and the royalties from her first husband's chemical patent. Neither was productive any longer,

37

and in the first years of the depression what remained of the inherited capital went to buy the children's school clothes, buy the car and pay the maid's salary.

After that there wasn't any maid. The children's clothing in 1933 was bought from the savings accounts established some years earlier—about three hundred dollars altogether now—by money order from Beniger. Then, in the fall of 1934, Tom was ill, and the illness lasted until the following spring, and there were no more savings, no more personal banking for Ruth Coombs to do, ever again. With her husband and daughter, she nursed the boy back to health again through a sad winter; when Tom was well, in the spring, having missed a year of school, she found that he had outgrown all the clothes bought for that year without having worn them; Mrs. Coombs went to bed herself where she was to spend most of the next four years. She cried over the unworn clothes.

Tom had gone to bed in October, a thin leggy child with a big head, and got up in the spring a tall, heavy-limbed and reasonably proportioned boy.

It was painful for him, lying in bed and growing so hard. It seemed to him sometimes, during the long days when his sister was at school, the Kaiser at work, his mother downstairs or out of the house, that he could feel growing happen to him, feel his bones reaching, skin stretching, ribs being forced apart by a swelling chest. This was confused, both in mind and in body, with the longing to be active, the yearning for grassy hills, sparkling water, dusty roads, so strong that it could almost make him sob, almost. He didn't sob; Tom knew how to hurt. Hurting was not strange to him.

His own personal ache was born in Tom, a slight, hidden deformity, an out of line arrangement of nerve and bone, in under the left shoulder blade, which produced a constant, low-degree pain, so familiar that he neither noticed nor questioned it. For years, in fact, the condition was not even known to his mother, for the boy didn't mention it, assuming perhaps that human bodies were made that way, that under everyone's left shoulder blade was a dull, congenital ache.

It didn't bother him especially, throbbing away. He could throw hard, being right handed; he could lift, unnoticeably askew, having learned unconsciously to favor the left. The pain never became harsh except when, now and then, he wrenched his shoulder in a

38

certain way. It affected his posture a little; possibly it would have bothered him if he had tried to hit someone with a left-handed punch, but Tom never had much impulse or much need for throwing punches. He was a gentle boy, thoughtful; in spite of his somewhat awesome intelligence, people liked him.

The intelligence was like the pain: something congenital, something too familiar to Tom ever to seem exceptional, even after it had been proved over and over again in school situations that his power to learn was well above the human average. He wanted to know, and it seemed to Tom that everyone must want to know, just as everyone wanted to eat; what he read or heard of knowledge, he attended, understood, remembered, and he didn't realize for a long time that this process, involuntary for him, might be laborious for others. Tom hadn't known the strength of his own mind.

By the time he was able to assess both the defect and the intelligence, it was characteristic of Tom that he should feel a little apologetic about both.

The trouble that winter was respiratory. Asthma, Doctor Marston called it; a hard time breathing. Medicine had begun to wonder if asthma weren't partly psychological, but Doctor Marston of Tennepin, while familiar with these speculations, could see nothing in Tom's personality to indicate maladjustment that severe, nothing in the family situation that might be called causative. The family situation seemed no more, no less, troubled than that of any other family in town that Doctor Marston treated or studied. His own girls, for example, or little Beverly Hill, or the Green kids—or the grocer's or the druggist's children—if you called one of them neurotic, you would have to call them all neurotic, and then you might as well throw your pediatrics books in the river; and your stethoscope and yourself in after them. Doctor Marston used to wonder whether, if he had chosen to practice in some other town than Tennepin, or in some other section of the country, his professional outlook would have been so persistently haunted by ambiguous evidence.

Tom Beniger's asthma, or whatever you wanted to call it, followed an attack of pneumonia from which the boy seemed, at first, to be making a good recovery. But as the doctor made his daily visits to the home, he kept putting off by a day the time when Tom would be allowed up again. The chest didn't sound right; and then the asthma started, and worries about the heart. It was rough to keep a boy like that still, keep him on bed-pans and complete rest, even harder because he was such a nice kid about it; never begged. But he couldn't keep the disappointment off his face when the doctor would finish examining him, listen to the chest, and say:

"Not tomorrow after all, Tommy. Maybe the next day."

The hard growing Tom was doing complicated things. At first no one was alarmed. It was almost amusing that he should have gained eight pounds lying in bed for a month, and still look as thin as ever. In the second month, while Mrs. Coombs kept up an optimistic bustling, assuring the family, in terms of Doctor Marston's current prognosis, that Tom would be up in a week, the Kaiser grew gradually alarmed.

"He'll be so weak," he kept saying, over and over again, brooding about it evenings. "All that new growth, all unexercised."

After a month of thinking about it, the Kaiser called on Doctor Marston.

"I want to rig up some weights and pulleys," he said, "so that Tom can exercise his arms and legs."

"Exercise is what we're trying to avoid," the Doctor said.

"These won't wind him, James. Just work his limbs."

The Doctor thought about it. "All right," he said. "Rig them up. Start him out very slowly. And if his chest starts sounding any the worse for it, or the heart kicks up, you'll take them down."

"All right," the Kaiser said.

The arm exercises were simply pulleys attached to the ceiling, with weights on the floor, and loops in the ends of the ropes over Tom's head which he could reach without sitting up. The leg apparatus was more complicated. It consisted of the chain and pedal set from a bicycle, and a series of reduction gears, built onto the footboard. Again there was a weight on the floor, and a check to keep it from slipping backwards if the pedaler paused with the weight half-way raised. It took about five minutes pedalling to bring it into view, over the footboard, and to the weight the Kaiser attached a small American flag that appeared first, fluttering.

It took ten minutes to set-up the flag raiser, every morning, and another ten to dismantle it for the day; the Kaiser got up half an hour early to do it, and when he got home from work at night, he would hurry first to Tom's room to prepare the thing for its evening use.

40

At first these devices tortured Tom; his body had been unused, had grown away from him. There was a deep physical languor, sleepiness of limb, tiredness of bone, laziness of muscle—a kind of total exhaustion that seemed impossible to overcome. He would try, to please his stepfather, one arm at a time, and it would seem as hopeless as trying to pull open a locked door.

The Kaiser would take the arm, at the wrist and behind the elbow, and start gently to work it up and down. Then he would put Tom's hand in the loop and say:

"Please try."

And Tom would pull weakly at the rope a few times, hearing the weight bump on the floor as he shifted it. Then they would try the other arm, and the legs. But after ten days, it started to take effect. Tom knew it first from the way in which he stopped hating the things, began to look forward to the Kaiser's coming, even to practice a little, secretly, with his arms during the day. It was not long before they began to be able to count the number of times he could raise the arm weights—three in a row with the right, two with the left. Four and three. Six and six. A contest between arms. And by Christmas he could raise the flag—the Kaiser always cheered when it appeared, and saluted—in under five minutes without getting out of breath at all.

These sessions of exercise were the parentheses between which Tom's long days were spent. After the Kaiser left for the shop, always saying something cheerful, trying to pretend that business didn't worry him nearly as much as Tom's being ill, Mrs. Coombs would come with a breakfast tray. The Kaiser had taken care of the bedpans—Mrs. Coombs didn't like to. Over breakfast, Tom and his mother would talk, and his mother would tell him all the worrisome things which the Kaiser had concealed—another man had been let go, another periodical gone out of business without paying its printing bill, the roof had begun to leak on the house and there was no money for repairs. Sometimes, if she didn't sleep too late, Ellen would have her breakfast in Tom's room, too, and then it was jollier, because Ellen talked about school or teased Tom; he liked to have her tease him.

School, as she spoke of it, was a place of infinite romantic intrigue, fresh boys and virtuous girls, though some of the boys were smooth as anything if a girl knew how to make them behave. Tom lived Ellen's dating life with her that winter—she was a junior in

41

High School—jubilant when Henry Armbruster asked her to the Fall Dance, crushed when she couldn't do better than Sorley Green as her date for the first basketball game. Sorley was only Connie Green's brother, and had pimples; and Ellen, whose hair had begun to shine with a special, sixteen-year-old lustre, whose skin glowed with pink, who held herself like a short, proud princess, ought not to have had to do a boy like Sorley the favor of going anywhere with him.

As far as Ellen would let him, Tom lived her academic life, too. He read her school books, all of them, even trigonometry, and tried to get her to explain what he couldn't understand in them. She had sold her second hand sophomore books at the beginning of the year, but sometimes she could borrow one for Tom, and he would read it and try to puzzle out how the preceding information affected what Ellen was now studying. He felt a great frustration because things wouldn't come together, wouldn't fit and relate to one another; the paragraphs for reading, in the back of her beginner's Spanish book, which he taught himself to translate, ought, for example, to relate somehow to the Spaniards he read about in Ellen's history book. There was an encyclopedia downstairs; he would ask his mother to bring him volumes of it, and read more about something. And then, because his mother had gone out somewhere and couldn't bring him another volume, he might start to read the other articles, unrelated except by alphabetical position, in the same volume; it increased his sense of the terrible disorderliness and profusion into which the world's learning had been allowed to fall. He imagined Greece as a place where things were better organized until, one day, something in the encyclopedia led him to suspect that it was ancient Greece that they were speaking of and he shouted, almost angrily, for his mother to bring him the volume which would contradict this awful suspicion. When it was confirmed that two and a half thousand years had passed since Greece commanded knowledge, Tom began to want to learn its former language, which was quite impossible. There were no books available for him to puzzle over, and even the Kaiser, for all his kindness, didn't understand Tom's need of one.

Tom did not read and study all day long. He thought a great deal, and dreamed, dozing; he dreamed himself into every sort of heroic role—winning World Series baseball games with his incredible curves, fighting forest fires, shooting policemen, making ora-

42

tions in the Athenian market place—and, since the growth was affecting his genitals as well as his arms and chest, he would sometimes, not very often, dream of secret things that he might be asked to do by one of the girls who came to the house after school from time to time with Ellen.

It was Connie Marston—he thought of her as Ellen's friend, not as the doctor's daughter—who was most often the object of Tom's fantasies. Bev Hill was prettier, but she was too sweet to imagine doing things with; she was more the kind one might fall in love with and want to marry. Margie was too bossy. Connie Green was all too obviously bored with Tom; when she and Ellen sat in his room, Connie Green would want to talk to Ellen about older boys whom Tom didn't even know. But Connie Marston, who said she was going to be a nurse and then work with her father, liked Tom and sometimes she would sit with him even when Ellen wasn't there. She liked to give him back rubs; she was a tanned, rather lean girl, without much bust, but what she had could be seen, sometimes, when she leaned over him.

Once she put her hand under the covers and into his pajama pants; he liked that, but it brought on an asthma attack which didn't happen when he touched himself. She decided she'd better not do that; another time, after he had hinted every way he could think of, and she had laughed and pretended she didn't know what he meant, until finally she made him come right out and say it, she lifted her skirt, pulled aside her pants and let him look at her. That was even worse for the asthma, so afterwards about all she'd do was tell Tom whatever dirty joke was being told in school just then; they did this secretly, too, because Ellen never heard the jokes. Connie got them from some of the faster girls, who weren't in the high school sorority but whom Connie saw because they were on athletic teams together.

He didn't really see Connie Marston very often. Neither did he see much of Bev Hill, with whom he fell secretly, and of course hopelessly, in love. His sister Ellen kept him informed about Bev.

Now and then his own friends came to visit, scrubbed up terribly clean by their mothers for the occasion. But most of the winter Tom spent alone.

The year turned. The weak sun on the roof, outside his window, seemed a little stronger each noon, lasted a little longer each day. His mother was afraid to open the window, and one day Tom eased himself out of bed to open it himself, and fell to the floor, so dizzy did it make him to be on his feet.

On another day, early in March, the weather was suddenly clear; Tom called downstairs to his mother, who wasn't there; then—it was a rare thing for him to do—he cried because the sky was so very blue. March went slowly. He tried not to be peevish about it, but the Kaiser's exercisers bored him now. His stepfather was reading *Penrod* to him, a chapter a night; Tom had read *Penrod* twice, when he was eight and nine. The Kaiser was a slow reader; he was much more interested in the story than Tom was. And there came an evening in April when the chapter had been especially short and the Kaiser said:

"It was such a short one, shall we have another?"

And Tom burst out, "No, I'm . . . no. Please don't read it any more. Read something else."

The next day the Kaiser called for a second time at Doctor Marston's office.

"I have a funny feeling, James," he said.

"What?"

"About Tom. If that boy doesn't get up this spring, and get outside, he may never get up."

"I can't permit it, Kaiser," Doctor Marston said.

"I have a lot of respect for you as a doctor, James, but you don't live with him. It's killing Tom to be indoors."

"I don't think you understand," the doctor said. "To let him exert himself now would probably do permanent damage to his heart."

Kaiser Coombs looked at the doctor and thought about it. "Probably?"

Doctor Marston said: "I can't give you a figure, odds, but it would be too much of a chance to take."

"People with damaged hearts live on and on," the Kaiser said. "I've known plenty."

"Adults. Men, not boys."

"What are the other risks?"

The doctor hesitated. "We don't know as much about anything as we should," he said. "All I can tell you is that my total judgment recognizes merit in your feeling that Tom should be up this summer, but that as long as he's in my care I can't permit it until there's some improvement."

44

"How long since there's been any improvement?"

"There hasn't been."

"Then maybe if you let him up, there would be."

Doctor Marston shook his head. "We can't risk it."

"James, if I took the boy out of your care, and started to get him out of that bed and into the air, very slowly . . . ."

"Is that what you've been thinking?"

"I've been thinking of nothing else for weeks," the Kaiser said. "Ever since the first warm day, I've been thinking of doing that."

"What would the boy's mother say?"

"She'd be against me, as long as you were," the Kaiser said. "And if anything happened to her son because I'd let him up . . ." he shrugged.

There was a silence between them. Then the doctor said: "You're determined to do this, aren't you, Kaiser?"

Kaiser Coombs nodded. "Yes, James. I've pretty much decided."

"I'm doctor to your whole family," Marston said slowly. "Not just to Tom. You're overworked; strained. You could have a breakdown and I don't suppose you'd have any more cash to see you through than any of the rest of us." The Kaiser shook his head. "Ruth is in bad shape. I don't know what her complaints amount to physiologically, but there's no doubt she feels lousy. If you got Tom up and, and something happened . . . well, it's always seemed to me the bond between you and Ruth put you ahead of a lot of people in town in this damn depression. How's Ellen?"

"She's all right," the Kaiser said.

"Helps you in the shop, doesn't she?"

"Yes. I don't think she likes it very well. It's . . . we were okay, James, until Tom got sick. Everything's been running down since then. It's like the clock stopped."

"All right, Kaiser," Doctor Marston said. "Let's try it your way. A step or two today. And tomorrow. Then I'll check him. If he seems no worse, we'll start letting him go to the bathroom. If that works out, we'll bring him down for meals—and maybe when it's really warm, we'll have him out of the house. Promise me something?"

"Thank you, James. Of course."

"The moment I see the slightest symptom that he's getting worse for this, you'll take my word it's so and put him back to bed."

45

The Kaiser agreed.

It was Ellen who was allowed to speak the news to Tom, while Mr. and Mrs. Coombs stood in the doorway, smiling.

"Doctor Marston changed his mind. Next week, you might even be coming down for meals, Tom!"

"Can I . . . can I go outside?" Tom asked, trembling all of a sudden.

"Next month, Tom," his mother said. "If you get along all right around the house, we'll start taking you out next month."

By summer Tom was running and throwing as hard as any other boy. He was big, suddenly, not really strong, but not weak either; his shoulder seldom bothered him and though there were times when breathing was difficult, he told no one. It generally happened outdoors, and when it did he would lie down somewhere, out of sight, in the grass, and stare hard at the sky. Pollens bothered him; he would get hives. But as he had once learned to ignore discomforts, now he learned to conceal them.

He got brown; his light hair bleached even lighter. Ellen and Bev Hill said he was getting cute, though Connie Marston wasn't much interested now that he was a patient no longer. He cared very little; all winter he had craved to play hard, with boys, and now he could.

The heart seemed to strengthen, if anything, and perhaps the chest healed; Doctor Marston said it seemed fine; first rate.

If there were striking effects from the long winter of illness and recovery, they were characteristics of personality rather than physique: Tom had acquired, through a young boy's loving imitation, and would have for the rest of his life, the Kaiser's hesitant way of speech, the Kaiser's gentle manners, the Kaiser's warm, consoling smile.

46

CHAPTER THREE

1.

WHEN ELLEN WAS a senior in high school, and Tom a freshman, there was a scandal.

It involved a girl in Ellen's class named Dorianne Bates; she was a tall, dark, rather crazy girl whose father was a salesman of novelty goods; her mother was a waitress in the local tavern.

As the story got around, it began on a Tuesday morning with Dorianne sitting in the car of a boy named Dickie Dee, who was two years out of high school, parked down the street from the school building and watching the kids go by. She had stopped a smaller kid, a freshman named Hines, and asked him, with much laughter, to deliver a note to her home room teacher.

According to consensus, the note was in Dorianne's hand-writing with her mother's name signed at the bottom, also in Dorianne's hand-writing, and said: "Please excuse Dorianne Bates from school today. She is drunk."

By the time Hines, the innocent messenger, had been interrogated and someone sent out from the principal's office to where the car was parked, it was gone.

In the afternoon, just before school let out, Dickie Dee was seen by some boys, who reported it to other boys, getting Dorianne's jacket out of her locker.

On Wednesday morning no one at school talked of anything else. Dorianne seemed to have spent the entire night in Dickie Dee's car, parked just off the shoulder of Flying Pond Road. It was said that cars containing several other young men of Dickie's generation had visited the parking place from time to time during the night, and there were two senior boys who could give an eye-witness account. They had driven out, they said, just to see; there were two cars besides Dickie's. Four guys had been sitting outside on the ground with bottles and had given each of the senior boys a drink. An older man, a laborer named Rand, who was apparently buying the liquor, came out of the back of the car, pulling up his pants, they said, and leaving the door open. They had heard Dorianne yell:

"Next man in bring me a drink."

According to the senior boys, both basketball players, they had no intention of joining the activity though invited to by Rand; however, one of them, he said, had looked into the back to see if it was really Dorianne. Dorianne had asked who it was, he had told her, and she had yelled:

"Hey Dickie, I said no school kids. Damn it, no school kids."

The senior boys had been leaving when one of the group of drinkers stood up and said he thought he'd just see how the lady was getting along. Wouldn't do to let her get thirsty. Then he'd gotten in back with one of the bottles and closed the door.

It was pretty much supposed that this had been Dorianne's second night in the car, because of her having written the note Tuesday morning.

At four Wednesday morning, Dorianne's father had driven in from the selling trip which had taken him out of town. He had stopped at the all night diner for coffee, and heard some rumor of his daughter's position. He had been unwilling, however, being tired, to believe that it was anything more than a normal date from which she would be home late, and had gone to his apartment. There he found his wife, the waitress, asleep with her uniform still on; whether there was also evidence of recent male presence differed with whose version of the story you listened to. There was not much variation, however, in reports of what happened next. Dorianne's father had tried to awaken his wife; failing to make any sense out of what she said, he had taken his things out of the apartment and gone back to his car, utterly disgusted. On the way out of town, he had called the local constable, getting him out of bed,

48

and insisted that the officer go out to Flying Pond Road and bring Dorianne home. This the constable finally did at about seven in the morning. The girl, somewhat out of her head, didn't understand, and kept believing that the constable wanted her for the same reason that the other men did; in one version of the story it was said that the constable was himself an occasional visitor to Dorianne's mother, and even that it was he who had been with the mother earlier Wednesday, in her husband's absence.

The mother had recovered by then, and she, Dorianne, and the constable had breakfast together; the girl was frantically hungry, having had nothing to eat since Monday. The constable had left, saying that he would return when Dorianne was capable of making better sense; Dorianne went to sleep. About nine thirty her mother was out, seeing acquaintances who might know where the father had gone; Rand, the laborer, having seen the mother go out, had slipped in to tell Dorianne to keep quiet, and waked her up. She promptly asked for a drink as the price of silence, which Rand gave her reluctantly. While they were talking, and he was trying to calm her down, the phone rang and Dorianne answered. It was the principal's office at school, inquiring about her, and Dorianne, laughing wildly, claimed to be her own mother. She said that if they wanted that bad girl at school, she would send Dorianne to school right away, and that the principal could take down Dorianne's little blue panties if he liked and spank her, but she said, laughing at Rand's face, that the principal must be careful where he spanked Dorianne because she was a little bit sore. This conversation was filled in later by men in town who played pinochle with the principal, and who claimed that he had told them.

Dorianne made Rand drive her to the school building, then staggered out and up the front steps. She went directly to the principal's office. Even the pinochle players had no consistent version of what took place during the interview, though it was known that the principal had been wise enough to have Miss Kershaw, the formidable old science teacher, present during the session. Dorianne left the office sobbing, and went to her home room to get her books and her lunch box, and leave school forever. No one was quite sure whether she had been instructed to make this final call or simply decided to.

The few minutes in the home room were sensational. A senior English class was in progress. Dorianne opened the door, stepped

49

in, and stopped when the teacher spoke her name sharply. Dorianne's hair was a mess; she had no make-up on. Her blouse had several buttons missing, and hung outside her rumpled skirt, unmentionably stained. There was a slip under the blouse, which was transparent, but quite apparently no brassiere. She was wearing bedroom slippers.

The teacher told her to go away, and Dorianne muttered that she was sorry and only wanted to get her books. All the girls in the class, having looked up when she entered, now turned their eyes away; some of the boys continued to stare. Dorianne went unsteadily to her desk, which, her name being Bates, was just in front of Ellen Beniger's.

Dorianne knelt down by the desk; she began crying while she took the books out, and even the boys who had been staring studied the texts in front of them now; the teacher had turned her back and started writing on the blackboard. Dorianne stood up, holding the books; no one would look at her, and she wavered for a moment.

"I'm sorry," she said again to the teacher, Miss Wax, whom she had liked and whose back was still turned. There was no response; her classmates, all of them, pretended hard that they were absorbed in their books. Dorianne slapped Ellen Beniger's desk with her hand and Ellen looked up, startled.

"What do you think yours is for, then?" Dorianne said, shrill and desperate. "You think you're supposed to put grains of sand in it and make pearls . . . ?" And she reeled out of the room.

Dorianne, it was said, slept for two days and, when she woke up, left town on the bus for New York, forty-one miles away. Rand, the laborer, was beaten up by some men from the volunteer Fire Department, led by the constable who took no more official action in the case; Rand, who had a wife and four children, left town too, taking his family elsewhere. Rand had tried to divert the anger to Dickie Dee by saying that Dickie had charged them a dollar apiece for Dorianne, but none of the others involved supported the story so it was not believed. Dickie, who had done most of his dating among girls who were Dorianne's friends, had trouble getting dates for a while, but solved that by making forays to nearby towns; he was smooth enough to have won dancing contests, and soon even local girls were going out with him again—not girls of the class called nice, but they had never dated Dickie anyway. Dorianne's father, the salesman, returned to his wife and, as the winter went on, the episode lost interest.

Except to Ellen Beniger.

It made a peculiar mark on Ellen. Never very aggressive outside the family, she had never seemed particularly vulnerable either. Through her sophomore and junior years, she had been steadily popular as befitted a girl as pretty as she, a member by right of looks and family of the dominant clique of girls at school. But in her senior year, the clique was not very strong; the girl flock had diminished. Bev Hill was gone, sent by her family which maintained a certain prosperity even in 1936, to private school. Margie Hamner had grown very unpopular; she was plain and tried to control school politics, and the boys had discovered it was a great joke to vote against her for such offices as year book editor, in a solid male block. Connie Green, though still at public school, was having a romance with a boy at Yale and was therefore partly withdrawn from school social life. Connie Marston and Ellen were discovering that, while they had always been associated, they didn't really like each other.

This had begun to work against Ellen's self-confidence, comparatively serene in the years before, and to make her quite defenceless to an attack like Dorianne's. Her schoolmates sensed this, and, instead of acknowledging the circumstance of the remark's having been addressed to Ellen accidentally, as they might have a year earlier, they fastened Dorianne's description to her. Boys in the locker room referred to Ellen as "Pearlie," sometimes, and thought of a hundred different related jokes to make about her. Other girls, once jealous of Ellen's secure position, now found that they could make less candid girls' versions of the same jokes about her to one another, without incurring the dislike of anyone important, except Margie Hamner, whom everybody called "Mussolini" these days, anyway.

The jokes, of course, did not reach Ellen directly. They did not reach Tom either, three classes below; the freshman world was a separate one, a reflection of the senior world, not a part of it. And in any case, Ellen would never tell Tom exactly what Dorianne had said to her. So Tom was able to continue to believe that his older sister was the personification of a teen-age romantic image, even if he was the only boy in school who thought so.

Along with the breaking up of the girl flock, a second reason for

Ellen's vulnerability lay in the family's continued financial decline. They were not alone in this, of course, but the print shop was doing very badly and the Kaiser called on people trying to sell encyclopedias evenings in pursuit of the small, occasional commissions which might enable them to have butter on the table for a week instead of margarine, a roast instead of macaroni. Mrs. Coombs was still generally in bed. Ellen did the cooking now, and, with the Kaiser's help, the rest of the housework. Tom tried to help too.

At the shop itself there was only one employee left, a linotype operator. Two of the three remaining linotypes were turned off, their pots empty, but could not be sold because of the mortgage. In the afternoons, after school, Tom often went in to feed the hand press if there were a small business form or stationery order; except on Fridays, Ellen went home to clean the house.

On Fridays Ellen, Tom and the Kaiser all worked together on the only job which kept the shop in business—the printing and mailing of a small religious weekly edited in New York. It was done at Coombs Fine Printing because the rates were lower than city rates. It was called *Faith First;* the copy reached Tennepin Wednesday afternoon. By Friday, after school, the magazine would be printed and stapled, ready for Tom to stamp addresses onto long rolls of gummed tape from standing type in a proof press. He would hand the tapes to Ellen who cut off the individual addresses and pasted them onto the magazines. The compositor would be sitting at his linotype, making corrections, additions, deletions— many deletions—for the mailing list. The Kaiser would be cleaning his press, sorting type, and stacking the magazines in cartons to take to the post office as Ellen finished.

Tom and the Kaiser would sing. That was the way Ellen always thought about the winter of 1936, which became 1937 without her having had a New Year's Eve date—as a time of pasting labels in a grimy print shop, while a boy's tremulo and a man's tenor sang foolishly, a linotype clicked and hummed, and she brooded about her mother's desertion of responsibility, her friends' desertion of affection, and a wild-haired girl who had made Ellen's innocence a thing of public ridicule.

She was so preoccupied with herself that she didn't notice an odd thing that began to happen under the grey March sky. Connie Green had to point it out to her:

52

"He must really think you're something."

"Who?"

"Dickie Dee."

"Dickie Dee?" Ellen was astonished.

"Are you blind? He's always looking at you when we go down the street. He comes up to the window of the radio store and looks." Dickie was a clerk.

"Maybe it's you," Ellen suggested.

"No. He knows me. But he asked Sorley to introduce him to you at the winter dance."

"What's he need to be introduced for?" Ellen asked. "I'll bet he didn't wait for someone to introduce him to Dorianne."

"That wasn't so much Dickie's fault," said Connie, making an observation which had become conventional. "They say he didn't tell everything he knew, cause he didn't want to make it worse for her."

"How could it have been any worse?" Ellen asked. Then, "Anyway, what's he want to look at me for?"

"You can't blame a man for looking."

"Why didn't Sorley introduce him when he asked?"

"Would you have wanted him to?"

"No."

"Well, that's why he didn't."

The next day, when they walked by the radio store, Ellen looked to see whether what Connie had said was true. It seemed to be. Dickie Dee even had the nerve to smile.

2.

After midterms in Guy's second year at the military school in Texas, his father was asked to withdraw him. Guy was accused of paying no attention whatsoever to the students who outranked him in the cadet system, of breaking regulations whenever he chose, of spitting on the floor, once, in the required course in Texas history, when Sam Houston's name was mentioned. He was also accused of mocking teachers by affecting to speak with an absolutely repulsive Mexican-American accent, of fighting, and, as a final act of insolence, of turning in blank blue books at the recently held examinations. This behavior was particularly intolerable because

53

Guy had done very well in his first year at the school, made A's and B's, played excellently on all teams for which he was eligible and been promoted to corporal.

His campaign of provocation had begun just after the close of football season, and he had influenced another boy to behave just as badly. When asked the cause of his behavior, Guy had replied that he didn't like to have his mail censored; the school authorities took the position that they didn't censor mail, merely checked spelling, grammar and punctuation. No exception could be made for one boy, they said, or the whole system would break down.

Guy, whose English, while not perfect, was quite beautifully spoken, had grinned and replied: "I theenk thees very bad action, meestaire, to poor Mexican greaser boy," and the campaign began. Behind it was nothing more than a particular note he had wanted to send to a girl in town without its being read.

Because of the season, Guy's father and mother were in Mexico City, and Guy went to them there.

"What did they try to do?" His father asked.

"Nothing. The teachers were pigs. The boys were stupid."

"Your mother is unhappy."

"I am sorry. I will apologize to her."

"I did not like to hear you had been fighting."

"Everybody does there. One has to."

"What is this about spitting when they said Sam Houston?"

"A joke. I was joking that I was very Mexican. Very patriotic."

His father said: "It doesn't seem funny."

"No. Not here. There in Texas it seemed funny."

"And about not speaking English well, this was more of the same joke? This your mother is unhappy about."

"I will apologize."

"Guy, it will be more difficult now for you to transfer to another school, in North America."

"They must know this happened?"

His father thought a moment. "No. I think you will go to Chihuahua, and have a tutor. He can say you studied with him up to now."

"I would like to stay here."

"No. In Chihuahua, with a tutor."

"Yes, father. A North American?"

"Yes."

"Will you find one who has played football, please? I would like him to train me."

It was not a difficult request to fulfill. There were many college graduates who had played excellent football looking for jobs that year. The choice was narrowed very quickly to a man who had been a fullback in the Southern Conference, and one who had played varsity end in the Big Ten. Guy chose the end; he wanted to learn to catch passes.

But football, for Guy, was only an enthusiasm—not an obsession as it had become for Eddie Bissle.

3.

"Do you think he's cute?" Connie Green asked.

"Dickie?"

"Yes."

"I don't know."

"He's got bedroom eyes."

That was one way of putting it. Dickie Dee's eyes were large and brown, and protruded. His nose was short and turned up at the tip. His face was round, his skin dark and smooth, his beard and eyebrows heavy. His lips were a little thick, but he could manage to look wistful; once Ellen had heard a girl call him pig-faced and been amused. She no longer thought it amusing; she preferred what Connie said about his eyes.

Dickie had still not spoken to her, but his admiration was constantly evident.

Then one day in April, when the sky was half-clear and a pulse of warm wind was running through the long-chilled air, Ellen saw his car on the street as she and Connie walked home from school. She was careful not to look at it again; and ten minutes later, when she had left Connie at her corner and started down her own block, Ellen was unsurprised to have the car come cruising quietly by with Dickie alone in it. If it had passed on by, she might have been alarmed; but it stopped.

"Hi, Ellen Beniger," he said. "Let me drive you home."

"I only live three houses down from here," Ellen said.

"I know. That's much too far to walk." He smiled and opened the door on the side towards her. "Come on. Get in."

55

Her brother Tom would be at the print shop; her mother in bed. No one would see if Ellen got into Dickie's car for a minute, just to see what he was really like.

She affected a careless shrug and got in; she started slightly when he reached behind her to close the door.

"I meant to catch up with you sooner," he said ambiguously.

"Mine is the yellow house."

"I know." He let the car roll forward very slowly. "It may take hours to get there. I'm a careful driver."

"I like to go fast," Ellen said, daringly.

"You allowed to go out week nights?"

"Once in a while, if I want to bad enough."

"How bad is that?"

"Enough to kick and scream."

"You must like someone awfully well to kick and scream for him."

She had no reply for that, and she gave him a soft glance and lowered eyes instead. It had not occurred to her that you might kick and scream to see a particular boy; when you fussed to go out, it was for the event, not the person who was taking you to it.

"Do you ever sneak out?" He asked.

"Sometimes," said Ellen, who never had. "My stepfather's very strict." She knew instantly, though Dickie was careful not to smile, that she had made an error; Dickie would know the Kaiser and know that she was lying. He continued to roll his car slowly along at that absurd pace, and she tried to repair her position. "Very strict with me, anyway."

"I'd be strict, too, if I had to take care of a girl like you," Dickie murmured.

"How would you keep me from sneaking out?" Ellen asked, finding the conversation delightful.

He frowned as if he were really considering the problem. "I'd take all your clothes away and wrap you up in cotton," he said. "And I'd put you in a pretty white box and tie it with silver ribbons." He had a low, insinuating voice. She laughed.

They had rolled past her house, and Ellen said: "Take me for a ride."

"No." He touched the brake lightly with his foot, and shifted gently into reverse. "No, Ellen, but I'll take you to the movies tonight, if you want to kick and scream for it."

He stopped in front of the house, and they debated. Finally she agreed to go to the movies with him on Friday.

Once there had been a Friday when they finished the *Faith First* mailing as early as four-thirty. But this week everything went wrong. Tom spilled a galley. The linotype jammed, which meant the Kaiser was busy for half an hour, getting it straightened out; that delayed everything. Harry, the compositor, was cross, and spoke sharply to Tom who was being too exuberant.

Ellen began to panic; it took half an hour in the bath to get the ink off, after a Friday's work. She was never certain that a tight kerchief would really keep the ink out of her hair. Dickie was not asking her out because she was blonde and cute and fascinating, but only because she was down to his level, now, Dorianne's level. Ellen thought of Bev Hill, off at the school they had always thought they would attend together, and could have cried. It was almost six o'clock. Harry, the compositor, had left at five-thirty; the Kaiser couldn't afford to pay him overtime and was now sitting at the linotype keyboard himself. It was even getting dark, and they were only two-thirds done.

"Ellen," the Kaiser looked over at them and smiled. "Ellen, you and Tom go on home and get your supper. I'll finish up."

"Oh, Kaiser," Ellen said. "We can't. You'd be hours."

"Won't they be mad," Tom argued, "if we're late with their mailing again?"

"We're already late," the Kaiser said. "Yes, they'll be mad." He got up and came over to them. "Now you kids go along."

"No," Tom shouted, ducking past their stepfather and seizing the next galley. "Come on, Bismark." It was Ellen's family nickname. "Who's hungry? Let's rally round the flag."

The Kaiser smiled again, and caught the galley out of Tom's hands. "You're hungry, boy," he said haltingly. "And I imagine your sister has a date. Here." He reached into his pocket and took out a nickel and two dimes. "You walk her home now, Tom, and then you go to the movies." He looked at the change in his hand again; the movies were thirty cents. "Can you . . . can you let him have a nickel, Ellen?" he asked.

"Yes," said Ellen. "Sure I can."

They went out into the cool evening, leaving the Coombs Fine Printing building as the street lights came on.

"Let's run," Tom said.

She grabbed his arm. "You walk along slowly with me," she said. Being tired physically always excited Tom too much. "And walk outside. Boys walk outside—I've told you that."

He shifted and walked gravely along between her and the street. He crooked his elbow towards her. "Hey, do you really hold someone's arm when you walk with him?" he asked.

"Sometimes." She took the arm.

"That's sappy."

"Not if it's slippery or something like that."

"Oh. Who's your date tonight? Sorley?"

"No." She must be careful to say it unemphatically. "Dickie Dee."

"What?" Tom stopped and looked at her.

"Well, I want to see the movie," Ellen said. "And he's the only one that asked me."

"Couldn't you go with Connie, or Margie?"

"Just because I'm going to the show with him doesn't mean I like him."

They started walking along again, but Tom was almost a step away from her, too far for her to take his arm again. After half a block in silence, he said:

"Does Mom know?"

"Well, I don't know whether I mentioned it or not . . . anyway, I don't guess she knows him."

"How come you know him?"

Ellen decided to stop answering, and they walked the rest of the way without speaking. As they went into the house, she said:

"Here's your nickel."

"I don't want it," Tom said, and ran upstairs to his room.

When she had had her bath and was dressing, Tom brought her some soup and a sandwich. He was always doing things like that without being asked. That was what made it hard to have him feel reproachful.

He put the food down without saying anything; she opened her purse and took out fifteen cents, all the money she had, and offered it to him.

"Please?" she said. "You can have Cokes afterwards."

"All right." He took it, smiled, cleared his throat, looked down at the carpetless floor, and then up at her finally. "You aren't going

58

to be ready, are you? Want me to go talk to him while he waits? I mean . . . Mom doesn't feel like getting up."

"What did you say to her?"

"Nothing. Just if she wanted to get up or not. I took her supper."

"Tommy, he's really nice."

"You really don't like him?"

"I don't think so. I just. . . ." But instead of completing the sentence, she gave her gawkish brother a big hug, even though she was wearing only a housecoat and still had a towel wrapped around her hair.

Ellen did not see Tom at the movies. Ellen did not care. "That's a very serious kid brother you've got," Dickie had said, smiling, as he helped her into the car. "He knows more about radios than I do." That was the last Ellen thought of Tom, or of her family, or of anything else that wasn't right at hand.

Being with Dickie Dee was so different. You didn't find yourself wondering whether he'd remember to come around and open the car door for you to get out; you knew he would, and he did. You knew he wouldn't make a clumsy joke about the amount of money he had to spend for two tickets to the show, and he didn't. She had been a little apprehensive, even though Margie and Connie both knew, about the effect of her coming in with Dickie to a theatre full of kids who knew her, and he managed it in such a way that they entered just after the lights went out. The seats he chose were what she would have chosen; and while he couldn't be given credit for the excellence and good humor of the movie—it was Fred Astaire and Ginger Rogers in *Follow the Fleet*—Ellen was sure that she enjoyed it more because she'd seen it with Dickie.

By the time the lights came on again, she was pleased with the idea of being seen with Dickie, and she smiled at friends as they went out, heading not for the Spa, where the kids would be having milkshakes, but for Sullivan's out on the highway. The kids only went to Sullivan's after dances, when there were enough of them to take the place over from the older crowd that used it regularly.

"We won't stay long," Dickie said, escorting her into Sullivan's, and since all his decisions had been right for her so far, she didn't question this one. He had been lightly complimenting her appearance as they drove out—the pink of the sweater she had chosen was such a good color for her, he said, and how could anybody's hair shine so, it wasn't fair to other girls; she was happily certain,

59

as they found a table at Sullivan's, that people were looking at her because she was pretty, not because she was with Dickie Dee.

Sullivan's had a juke box and a dance floor. It also had a bar. Ellen half-expected Dickie to suggest that she have a drink—it was said that he had taught Dorianne to drink; she had a refusal ready, and knew it was going to sound nervous.

"Coke or ginger ale?" Dickie said. "Do you like the hamburgers here?" Everything he did and said was reassuring.

While the waiter, who called him Dickie, went to get their order, they danced.

She had never danced with anyone half so good. He was so perfectly rhythmical, so gently persuasive in his leading . . . nor did he seem to expect her to talk while they danced . . . instead, he murmured things that needed no replies: "You're as easy on the feet as you are on the eyes . . . I love the way your hair smells . . . I hope you'll let me really know you, Ellen . . . the sweetest kid . . . the smoothest skin. . . ." Yet it wasn't like a boy using a line, trying to make you believe him; rather the murmuring was part of the way he danced, part of the way he understood you and made you feel warm and safe and highly prized. . . .

They ate their hamburgers, drank their cokes, and danced again. As the record was finishing, he held her tightly for a moment, dipped very deeply and smoothly, and then, taking her hands, let her drift out to arm's length; he smiled apologetically, as if he were going to say something quite unhappy, shook his head slowly, gazing at her. Then he said:

"What I'd like to do is dance with you all night long, but this is our first date, and I mustn't keep you out too late . . ." He had her off the floor and into her coat before she realized that really, she could just have well stayed and danced for another half hour or so.

He drove directly to Lee's Road, the familiar place to park, and she was glad of its familiarity; once again he had decided rightly, for there were a dozen equally untravelled but less conventional by-ways he might have chosen.

He switched on the radio, waited until she put out her cigarette, and then kissed her. And that, she decided, was just what she had wanted him to do; a rule like not letting a boy kiss you on the first date had no connection with Dickie. Instead of trying immediately to kiss her again, he relaxed, with his arm around her, and led her to talk; and suddenly she found herself talking in a great rush, saying everything that was on her mind as she hadn't been able to, even to Connie Green. It was so clear that Dickie would understand; when she paused he would squeeze her, brush his lips against her hair, murmur something encouraging, and she would begin to talk again.

When she was talked out, he began to kiss her again, more firmly now, kissing the way he danced: he did the leading, but only as he sensed that she was willing and able to follow. They stayed ten, fifteen minutes; then, as she found herself getting rather excited, the lights of another car showed at the end of the road, and Dickie slid under the wheel and started his automobile. She wondered if they were going home; she didn't feel quite ready; she decided not to ask. They were not.

He didn't drive very far—back onto the highway from Lee's Road, up a couple of hundred yards, and then into a dirt road that she had never noticed. He drove in only a little way, and she was relieved; any further, and she would have had to ask where they were going, which would be the same as asking what he intended. Stopping as they did, she found herself still fluttering from the last kiss, eager for the next.

"I want to see a lot of you, sweet Ellen," he said, taking her into his arms again, and she believed it. Intermixed with the kissing now were the beginning caresses of the upper part of her body, a stage in necking at which she had always made Sorley Green—and Henry Armbruster, last year's beau—take her home. But it had been partly because she knew that not even Henry had known exactly what he was doing, and there was no question but what Dickie did. Suddenly, she found herself thinking about Dorianne again, but differently than she ever had before; she found herself hoping that it was all true, what they supposed had happened to Dorianne, that Dickie had really been the first seducer, and, instead of blaming him now, Ellen found that she merely wanted to feel sure, from what he said, from what he was doing, that Dickie liked her better. She wanted to ask him but not yet, not tonight, because she didn't know whether she was going to be brought now to the final mystery or only necked more thoroughly than ever before. She knew that she had made a mistake with herself, in not having decided much earlier how far she meant to go; if she had made such a decision, she could relax, she could enjoy what happened up to the predetermined point and then ask him to stop; not having decided, she had no intention of her own and must rely on his.

His hand was under her sweater now, on her breast, and she thought dizzily that she would let him touch flesh there, just for a moment. The moment ended with a shocking crash against the side of the car.

"My God," said Dickie, jumping away. Ellen was paralyzed. There was another crash. She grabbed at his shoulder.

"What is it?" She gasped. "Oh, Dickie."

"Somebody throwing stones," he said, as a third rattled off the side of the car. "Get down." Ellen went half prone along the seat, and Dickie started his motor as the fourth stone hit. Then he hesitated, muttered, "It's on that side," opened the door and ducked out of the car with the motor still running.

"Cut it out for Christ's sake," he yelled.

There was a heavy noise of somebody beginning to run through the underbrush, and the stoning stopped. Ellen was still too scared to sit up.

She heard Dickie yelling again. "All right, damn it. Stop. I see you."

There was silence for a minute. Ellen sat up, biting her lip, got her brassiere rebuckled and her sweater pulled straight. Then she heard Dickie's voice, coming back.

"All right, stupid. Come on. Come on, damn it. Let's see what you've done to my car. Let's just see."

Ellen turned off the ignition and let herself out on Dickie's side, meaning just to peer around from the side and see who it was without being seen.

By the glow of the tail-light, she saw that it was Tom. He was being marched up to the car, his arm twisted behind him in a hammer lock by a furious Dickie.

"If I have to have this car painted," he was saying, "it'll cost your stepfather, kid. I mean it." Then, as Ellen stepped into sight. "Do you always bring him along?" He shoved Tom towards her, letting go the grip.

"Oh, Tom," Ellen said. Her brother's face was scratched, his pant leg torn, and he wheezed for air. He must have been waiting in the chilly night at Lee's Road, seen them come there, followed the lights on foot when they left. She said the next thing that came into her head.

"It's your fault for stopping here," to Dickie. And the next: "I could kill you, Tom Beniger."

Tom looked pale and guilty; he was trembling.

"Go ahead and kill him," Dickie said. "Good idea." He was lighting matches, looking over the side of his car.

"Is that all you care about, your car?" Ellen said, bitterly. Then she noticed that Tom's trembling had turned into actual shaking; it was cold. He had only a light jacket on. How long had he waited on Lee's Road? And suppose they hadn't come there at all?

"Tom you, fool," she said, opening her arms to him. "Oh Tom, you're cold." She mothered him around the car to where she could reach her coat which was draped over the back seat. She wrapped it around Tom's shoulders, and left him for a moment.

"Dickie," she said in a low voice, going around the car to him, "will you take us home? Tom's shivering with cold, and he's not very strong. . . ."

"Oh, fine," said Dickie. "He tries to ruin my car and I'm supposed to drive him home. . . ."

Tom had followed, and spoke for the first time. "I wouldn't ride in his old car," Tom said.

"All right," said Dickie. "All right. The car's okay. How about getting out of here, kid, and letting us alone and we'll forget about the scratches?"

"No," said Ellen.

"I'm staying right here," Tom said.

"Come on, Ellen," said Dickie. "Let's take a drive."

"You'll have to run over me," said Tom. "I'll lie down in the road. I will."

"Dickie, take us home," said Ellen, insistently.

"You heard the kid. He doesn't want to ride home. I'll take *you* home."

"Tom," Ellen said. "Tom, get in the car."

Tom hesitated.

"Get in the car."

Tom got in.

Disgusted, Dickie drove them to their house. He stopped. Ellen looked into his eyes, regretting. He returned the look impassively, and she thought that she loved his eyes, even when they were angry. Then she turned her face away, and let herself out. Tom came blundering out of the back; he had stopped shivering.

63

The minute they were out, the doors closed, Dickie let out the clutch, gunned his motor, and roared off, letting his engine say the last word for him.

"Ellen," Tom said, in a squeaky voice. "Ellen, I'm sorry."

She didn't answer until they were indoors. She walked into the living room, thinking, and turned the lights on and off just for something to do with her hands; it was plain that Dickie Dee would not ask for another date. There was only one thing that could be salvaged now, and that was Tom's comfort so she said, and she would never know how sincerely she meant it: "It's all right, Tom. Honestly, it's a good thing you came along when you did."

4.

Eddie Bissle's grandfather died the summer Eddie was fourteen, and as far as Eddie could see nobody was sorry except himself. Eddie's father promptly sold off about five damn good growing acres, and Eddie heard a man say at the house one evening:

"It's a good thing the old man didn't wait till winter to die. We could never have held the government boys off that long."

The acreage was to be split by a federal highway construction project, financed under WPA; the land was sold to a group of builders.

The grandfather died in his fields. He was riding a tractor, and apparently fell off the seat. How long he lay, baking in the sun, and whether he was dead when he fell were unanswered questions. He was nearly eighty.

Eddie found him. Eddie had been over at the ocean surf swimming, that day, and in the evening he considered going to his grandfather's house but he was pooped. He worked on a model airplane he was building instead, a lousy model airplane with a big deal gasoline engine, and he didn't get out until the next morning, by which time the old guy had been dead a long while. When he saw the body, lying in a freshly plowed field, Eddie knew at once what state it was in. He looked at it; then he went over to the stalled tractor and turned off the ignition.

There were a couple of buzzards, way up in the air. Eddie sat and watched them for a while, on the tractor seat, without realizing what the buzzards wanted. Then, realizing, he got furious. He got

64

down off the tractor and tried to lift his grandfather's body; it was pretty heavy for him. He thought of dragging it to the house, but the house was three fields away. He squatted by it for a long time, watching the buzzards and cursing them in every way he knew.

For a long time he couldn't think what to do; he didn't know much about buzzards, and he was afraid that if he left, to go to the house and phone, they would come flying right down and start to peck at his grandfather's body. Finally he found himself staring at the tractor, and it occurred to him that he was being very very stupid, even for Eddie Stupid Bissle. There was a spike-tooth harrow hitched behind the tractor, and its top was flat. He could put the body on that, and pull it behind the tractor to the house.

He started to haul the body over; then he paused, and thought how much stupider he was even than he had been before, because all he had to do was start the tractor and drive it over.

He had to crank the thing for a long time before it started; then he had to practice driving it a little, because his grandfather had never let him do it by himself. It had a hand throttle, and if he sat right on the edge of the seat and stretched his body as far as it would go, he could get the clutch about halfway in with his foot. He stalled the thing a couple of times working this procedure out, and each time he had to crank again. But it wasn't so hard now that the engine was warmed up. Finally he drove it alongside the body, took it out of gear, and let it idle while he moved his grandfather's corpse onto the top of the harrow. He didn't figure on doing any gear shifting once he got going; low would be fast enough.

He started to move the machine and its burden along, watching behind; he couldn't help noticing how smooth the path was that he was leaving. Probably if the old dead guy could say what he'd like to say, he'd say, "Finish field, boy. Go on. Finish." He'd probably say that.

Maybe he'd be proud of the way Eddie was driving the tractor, too.

It took about half an hour in the hard sun to get in. Eddie had gotten quite a lot of sun at the beach the day before, and it was making him feel sick, but there was no breakfast in him to lose; the body was jouncing now, because they were on a part of the field that hadn't been harrowed before, but Eddie was afraid to

65

slow the machine down because it might stall again. So of course they hit a bump, and the body rolled off.

Eddie stopped the tractor, and got his cargo back on. This time he fastened it to the harrow top with belts, the old man's and his own. He was able to drive on in, then, very slowly. There was some music in his head as they went along that way, and he thought maybe it was a funeral march. This was like a funeral, like riding his grandfather's body in a kind of hearse.

He drove the tractor right into the barn, and then closed the big doors so the damn buzzards couldn't fly into it; he didn't know whether they would or not. There were probably rats in the barn, but Eddie would hurry back and guard against them. When he got to the phone, he didn't call his father. He called the police.

"My grandfather's killed," he said.

Later, some smart Sherlock Holmes cop wanted to know why he said that, instead of *my grandfather's dead*. They were sitting in the living room at Eddie's house, and this Sherlock Holmes cop was asking questions with a notebook, just about as peachy as a cobbler. Eddie knew the answer to the question, too, but he wasn't going to tell Sherlock the Peachy Cobbler Cop. Let Sherlock detective that one for himself if he was so god damn smart.

Eddie had said his grandfather was killed because he was a little crazy by the time he got to the telephone, and he was thinking of the buzzards as having killed his grandfather so they could eat him. He had even taken a rifle out of the house to shoot up in the air at them, only the buzzards were gone by then. In fact, Eddie was wandering around with this stupid rifle when the cops came.

"Why did you think you needed a rifle, son?" said Sherlock the Cop.

"I was going to shoot some buzzards," Eddie said.

"That's what you told Sergeant Imbrie, but the sergeant said there weren't any buzzards when he arrived."

Eddie shrugged.

"You loved your grandfather, didn't you?"

Eddie looked at his father. If his father was such a god damn big politician, why didn't he make Sherlock shut up?

His father answered: "Yes. Eddie was always with the old man."

"You understand why I'm asking you about this, son," Sherlock said. "By the time you rode that body in all that way, and it fell

66

off, and you put it on with the belts, it was pretty marked up. It's hard for us to tell what condition your grandfather was in when you found him."

"He was all right," Eddie said.

"What do you mean? He wasn't dead?"

"I mean he wasn't marked up."

"How did the body look?"

"Just like you'd look if you fell off a tractor dead," Eddie said.

"You say you were swimming yesterday?"

"Yeah."

"What beach?"

"Watermill."

"That's about eighteen miles. How did you get there?"

"Bike."

"It was pretty cold wasn't it?"

"I like it cold."

"Nobody else swimming?"

"No."

"Your father told us you were at your grandfather's yesterday."

"That's what he thought."

"Don't you tell him when you're going someplace eighteen miles away?"

"No."

"That's right," Eddie's father said. "He's always going off."

"Take your lunch?"

"No."

"Where did you eat?"

"On the beach."

"I thought you didn't take your lunch?"

"I didn't. I bought a loaf of bread and some other junk at a grocery store."

"You must have had some left over."

"Yeah."

"What did you do with it?"

"Threw it on the beach, I guess. I don't know. Not on the sand. I hate guys who throw crap on the sand."

"You're a pretty tough kid, aren't you Eddie?"

Eddie looked up surprised.

"Take it easy, Carmichael," his father said. Sherlock looked at his father.

67

"All right," he said. Then back to Eddie, more of his peachy cobbler questions. "How come you went swimming alone?"

"I always do."

"Why?"

"I like to."

"The kid's a loner," Eddie's father said. "He doesn't like other kids. We never see him."

"Sure," said Sherlock. "Eddie, are you sure you weren't at your grandfather's farm yesterday? Now wait, before you answer. Let me tell you how it looks."

"What do you think, I killed him?'" Eddie suddenly yelled, standing up. "You dirty son of bitch. You dirty. . . ." His father caught him as he was going for Sherlock with his fingernails.

Sherlock was on his feet now, too. "I said wait, didn't I? Will you let me finish, you crazy brat?"

Eddie subsided. Then he wrenched himself loose from his father's weak grip and went over and sat across the room.

"Look, Eddie," Sherlock said. "I don't say you killed your grandfather. But maybe you were out there when he fell off, maybe you did something that helped him fall off, I heard at your school about how you had a scuffle with the old man once. . . ."

Eddie didn't look at him. He didn't bother answering.

"I didn't say that happened," Sherlock went on. "I just say it could have happened. But probably it didn't. You know why? Because of that rifle, Eddie. I'll tell you what else could have happened, shall I?"

"Carmichael, for Christ's sake . . ." his father started. Then seeing that Eddie wasn't going to answer he stopped.

"Why do you want me stop, Mr. Bissle?" Sherlock said.

"Because he's a kid. Thirteen years old. That's why."

"I'm about through. Is it all right with you if I go ahead, Eddie?"

Eddie didn't say yes; he sure as hell didn't say no. He was tired of looking at Peachy Cobbler and his big red Sherlocky face, and he wasn't going to have anything more to say at all.

"All right. Now listen to this Eddie. Your grandfather was holding onto some land that a lot of people in this community thought he ought to let go, for the public good. . . ."

"Carmichael!" said Eddie's father, but Sherlock went on.

"People were mad about this. They were saying that your

68

grandfather was preventing federal money from coming in that would make jobs for people in town who needed them. Did you know that?"

Eddie didn't answer. He looked at his father, and his father was furious.

"So maybe you were there yesterday, and saw something," Sherlock said. "And maybe after you got the body in, you were getting down that rifle to do something about it. Listen to me Eddie. If that's what happened, I'll do something about it. The police will do more about it than you possibly could." He stopped, and now Eddie had to look at him again.

So Sherlock had to have an answer? Okay.

"Bullshit," Eddie said.

In later years he used to think that Carmichael had been a pretty straight cop, risking a lot on a hunch. He must have known that he couldn't accuse Eddie's father that way and stay a cop long if he were wrong. And he had to be wrong; Eddie'd been swimming, all right, and he knew his father too well ever to share Carmichael's suspicion. Eddie's father might be crooked, but Eddie knew he was a gutless slob, and would never have pushed anybody off a tractor seat, no matter how much he wanted to.

Eddie refused to go to his grandfather's funeral. He knew that he was considered odd enough so that people who might be gossiping along the lines of Carmichael's theory would notice his absence and talk about it; he had to put up with quite a lot of begging and ordering and pleading and threatening from his old man about it, too. Even his mother had one of her rare little talks with him, probably at the old man's request. Eddie thought of a lot of things he would have liked to tell his mother at the time, but he didn't say any of them. He just said no.

He had his own idea about his grandfather's funeral. He waited until it had been over for a couple of days, and practically forgotten, and then one evening he went out to the cemetery and took the model airplane he'd spent the winter building. It was a beautiful piece of work; it was designed to have the tiny gasoline engine in it, and to fly at the end of a control wire. He'd saved about a zillion allowances to buy the motor, and on the evening he came back from swimming and failed to go on out to his grandfather's as planned, he'd been installing the motor and tuning the thing up. Worked at it till his mother screamed for him to stop the noise.

When he arrived at the grave, he knelt by it, and got the airplane motor going. He hoped it would fly. He emptied a can of lighter fluid over the plane, lit it, gave it a toss. The propeller took hold and up it went, climbing in circles over his grandfather's grave; one minute it was a model plane, the next, a ball of flame. Eddie stood dry-eyed at what he supposed must be something like attention, and watched it hesitate in the air; then one of the burning wings fell off, the plane came flaming down, and Eddie turned and left the cemetery. Why he conceived and carried out this plan was obscure to him; his grandfather was no soldier or anything; Eddie just got the idea and did it.

5.

That same summer, Coombs Fine Printing Co., Inc., closed its doors. The religious weekly had found a non-union shop whose rates were even lower; a radical weekly, which followed, and which, equally avid for a bargain, nevertheless needed a union label, lasted only a month or two before it lost its subsidy. The Kaiser sold the building and equipment, for only a little more than the amount of the mortgage.

"We've come out fairly well, Ruth," he said to his wife one July evening, when the last of the transactions had been completed.

"How well is that?" She was propped up in bed. She had been making an effort, recently, to get herself up and been partially successful.

"We don't owe anything. We have about four hundred dollars in cash. I . . . the fellow who got the *Faith First* job from us wanted the model K Lino; that was a break. This house is clear, and they won't foreclose the farm before Lucia dies even if I'm late with payments—they've promised that."

Lucia was the Kaiser's maiden sister.

"You're not thinking of mortgaging the house?"

"No. No, I've got a job."

"A job?"

"The paper in East Bixton. They're doing quite well."

"How can they be, Kaiser?"

70

"It's a county seat. They get all the legal ads, the bankruptcy sales—and the merchants can't afford to stop advertising."

"What will you do?"

"Be a printer, just as I've always been."

"It's twenty miles."

"Only nineteen. There's an early bus. The workers in the Bixton soap factory use it. You and Ellen will have to fix me a lunch."

"What about your insurance?" She asked.

He hesitated. "It's . . . all paid up," he said. Then, as she continued to look at him, "I've inquired about borrowing against it, Ruth. It can be done."

"And you want to?"

"Ellen ought to go to college. Tom will be all right, I'm sure. His high school grades have gotten him the scholarship to Roper. I'm sure his . . . Roper grades will get him just as good a one to college. Anyhow, a boy can work."

"Is this one of the things you've made up your mind about, Kaiser, that I can't budge?"

He shook his head. "No, I . . . I want to do it for Ellen. And to get Tom his clothes. But . . . the insurance is yours, really, Ruth. In intention you know. So I'll respect whatever you wish."

It was not an easy thing for Ruth Coombs, who had been secure in all her younger years, whom financial difficulties, when they came, had made physically ill. But she nodded her head, after a while, and said he was to make the loan.

"I haven't done as well as I meant to for my children," she said.

He patted her hand. "They'll be fine," he said. "Ellen is a very pretty girl, and everyone likes Tom."

CHAPTER FOUR

1.

TWO WEEKS AFTER he had entered Roper Preparatory School as a sophomore, Tom was sitting in his room one evening, doing Latin with secret joy, when a proctor appeared at the door.

"Beniger."

"Yes, sir." Tom rose. You were supposed to stand when a proctor was in your room.

"Put on your coat and tie. You're wanted."

"Oh, boy," Chowderhead Grant said. He was the boy Tom had been assigned to room with. "Now you're going to get it. You ever been to the Head's office before?"

"No," Tom said, putting a necktie on, wishing his shirt were cleaner.

"You'll be maimed and crippled," Chowderhead said.

"Shut up, Grant," said the proctor.

"Do you know what it's about?" Tom asked.

The proctor, whose name was Rogers, looked at Tom severely. "I imagine they found out," he said.

"About what?"

"About you putting the turds in the toaster."

Chowderhead shouted with laughter.

"Shut up, Grant," said the proctor. And to Tom, in a bored voice: "Aren't you ready yet?"

Tom got his jacket on, and followed the older boy down the hall. They went down two flights of stairs silently, and out across the yard to the main building.

You stand up until the Head tells you to sit," Rogers instructed him. "And when he does, sit straight in the chair. Don't slop around."

"All right," Tom said. "Thank you."

They went into the main building. Tom couldn't imagine what he might have done. He had been very quiet, very inconspicuous, as a new boy ought. He had been thrown in the pond once for crossing proctor's grass without permission, but he hadn't known; and plenty of new boys had been thrown in practically every day. He wondered if he had done something really awful without knowing it, and he remembered what they had said to him when he protested that he hadn't known about the proctor's grass:

"Ignorance of the law is worse than no excuse, because if you're ignorant you're dumb, and if you're dumb you're an animal. Are you an animal, Beniger?"

"No, sir," Tom had said.

"Then you must be a fish," and they threw him into the pond. If you said yes, you were an animal they said you were an herbivorous bastard, and made you get down on your hands and knees and eat grass.

The proctor knocked on the door of the Headmaster's study.

"Here's Beniger, sir."

"Ask him to come in."

With the Head was Mr. Fairless, who taught French and Latin. The proctor closed the door behind Tom, and remained outside.

"Sit down, Beniger," the Head said.

Tom sat.

The two men looked at him for a moment then the Head said: "According to your high school record, you have not previously studied French?"

"No, sir," Tom said.

"Yet Mr. Fairless says you appear to have the ability to do work in that language on the same level as boys who have studied the subject for two years."

"Well, sir, I had Spanish," Tom said.

"Perhaps you will explain the connection to us, Beniger?"

"Well, sir." Tom knew he was squirming. He made himself sit

still. "We have a French dictionary at home, because my stepfather was in France during the war. And he. . . ."

"Go on."

"Well, my mother thought the high school should teach French instead of Spanish. And my stepfather said a lot of the words were the same, so I started looking them up when we'd come to them in Spanish. To see if they were the same, that is." He felt as if he were confessing to some kind of cheating.

"And were they?" the Head asked, drily.

"Oh, yes, sir, quite a bit," Tom informed him.

"For example?"

"Well, like . . . well, knight. It's cabellero in Spanish, and chevalier in French and . . . well, it's like cavalier in English, isn't it?"

"Why do you suppose that should be?" the Head asked.

Tom thought a minute. "The . . . the Norman conquest?"

Mr. Fairless beamed.

"We thought perhaps there might have been an error in your high school transcript," the Head said. Then he nodded at Mr. Fairless.

"Tom, we'd like to test your Spanish if you don't mind," Mr. Fairless said. He held up a piece of paper on which appeared some typing. "This is a passage of Spanish. Would you read it aloud to us, and then translate at sight?"

"I'll try, sir," Tom said, rising and taking the leaf. He glanced at it and saw with relief that it was very easy. All in the present tense. He began to read it aloud; the Head interrupted and told him he might sit down. Tom did and began again.

Mr. Fairless followed a duplicate as Tom read, giving him encouraging looks when he stumbled; when he had finished the sight translation, Mr. Fairless was smiling happily.

"Very good, Tom," he said. Then to the Head: "As I told you sir, I have only a reference knowledge and I'm not at all sure that his accent is intelligible. But the translation was very accurate."

"I see. Well. Thank you, Beniger," he said. He paused, and then went on: "We have a Mexican boy transferring to Roper. You're to be his roommate."

"A Mexican boy, sir?"

"If you have some objection, I'm quite prepared to consider it."

"Oh, no sir," Tom said. It was like a daydream; he was to speak

74

a language with someone who spoke it natively—they were counting on him for it. In the next moment he thought of the hard two weeks he had just been through, of being a new boy, of how much Chowderhead Grant had helped him, explaining rules, warning about the personalities of older boys and masters; but the instant of dismay at the thought of being deprived of Chowderhead's guidance was immediately replaced by pride that he would be able to serve the same function for the little Mexican kid.

The Head was speaking again: "This is not to go any farther," he said. "The boy has had some trouble at another school. We would not have relaxed our admission rules, ordinarily, but one cannot refuse, ummm, Government interest. Which there is in this case, Beniger. You are not to speak of this."

"Oh no, sir," said Tom.

"I thought it best that you understand. We haven't even been able to determine how much of the trouble is due to language difficulty. But we hope that Cinturon will adjust to Roper."

"I don't think I know enough Spanish really to talk to him," Tom said.

"No, we don't imagine that you do. But perhaps enough to help him through the first days. And if you don't get along, we may be able to make some change after Christmas vacation." His tone changed. "Thank you, Beniger."

Tom understood that he was to rise. "Thank you, sir."

The proctor was still outside when Tom left the study.

"What'd he want?"

"A new boy is coming," Tom said. "A Mexican. They're making me his roommate."

"Oh." The proctor said. "We had a Turk here once. Find your way back all right?"

2.

Eddie Bissle did not go to Roper Prep. He considered it, and chose Mount Pennell Academy instead. He made his choice on the basis of comparing football scores as published in the rival catalogues of these and two other schools; Mount Pennell had beaten them all. He was able, from a local boy who went to yet another Massachusetts school, to learn that Mount Pennell's success was consistent. In fact, the local boy insisted that Mount Pennell recruited its team as colleges did. That sounded all right to Eddie; that sounded like what he was looking for—a tough coach.

Coach Ericson was tough; his favorite joke was that his name ought to be Bitchison. At least once a season he would knock a boy down with his fist; this boy would be one of his best and biggest players, and the occasion for the slugging was always the star's lapse of attention during practice. The star would be lounging, talking to someone about girls, or about classwork, or school personalities, perhaps dangling his helmet picturesquely against a padded hip; Ericson would overhear, turn red, stride up to the boy, and tell him to drop the helmet and put up his hands. When the hands were about halfway up, the coach, whose reflexes were excellent, would hit him in the stomach, close, put a foot behind the boy's ankle, hit him in the chest, and then crowd him down backwards over the tripping foot.

"What is this, football practice or girl practice?" he'd roar. Then, turning to the others on the field: "Anybody else want to practice girls?"

Eddie's first year, the victim of this was an enormous redheaded fullback named Brad. After Ericson had drawn everyone in around him, extending the abuse to all the members of the squad, he suddenly seemed to recollect himself.

"Oh, Jesus and Mary," he said, kneeling by his fullback. "I haven't hurt you Brad?" He helped his star up. "You're all right boy? Here, walk a step or two."

"I'm okay," Brad muttered, more embarrassed than hurt. Ericson, an arm around him, was visibly fighting for emotional control.

"Brad," he said, "do you want to turn in your uniform?" Then turning from Brad who hadn't had time to mutter a negative, Ericson roared at the squad. "Anybody here want to turn in his uniform? Anybody want to leave me in the lurch right now? Now listen, boys, we're overmatched Saturday. Who wouldn't be wrought up? Overmatched, against a team that's really got the cannons. You saw them last year when we whipped them, 36 to nothing. And I'll tell you something. That hurt. That hurt them. You can understand that. And they went out and they scouted up a team of giants; a team of nineteen- and twenty-year olds. You know what they'll be doing in the dressing room, while you boys are putting on your equipment, getting yourselves set for that game? They'll be shaving, shaving just before the game, trying to conceal those beards by powdering their faces. Take a deep breath when you face them in the line, you linesmen, you'll smell powder! Talcum powder! And you'll know what it means. Now I never coached dirty football, never once in my life. You men have played for me and you know it. Is there anybody here who doesn't know it?" A pause. No answer. Intense attention. "And I never will. I'd rather leave this game we all love than ever see the day I felt I had to coach dirty football to meet an unscrupulous opponent. But I'm not going to send you in there unprepared, either . . ." And he didn't.

He had other methods. He would take the boys who were Catholic, like himself, to church with him to pray for victory, instructing the others to pray for that goal in their own ways. He would read, generally just before the Roper game, a tattered letter he had once received from the mother of a former player who had gotten a football scholarship to a major college, a letter full of semi-literate praise of *everything you, Coach, have did for my big boy* . . . "Did I see somebody smile? Did some fine gentleman here smile at that frail old mother's grammar? If so, I don't care who he is. He can leave this room and not come back. . . ."

Eddie adored him.

On Eddie's first day out for football, looking tinier than he really was, in a uniform too large, Ericson had actually picked him up, held him up for the others to see.

"Look, I asked them for football players. What did they send me? A monkey." He turned Eddie around in the air to face him. "What can you do, monkey?" he asked.

"I can block and tackle," Eddie said, meaning it as a statement of limitations; he had played sandlot football every afternoon of the previous fall, and he knew he could do those things.

"Block and tackle?" Ericson roared. "Not throw fancy incomplete passes? Not kick useless dropkicks?" He set Eddie down, and slapped his bottom. "All right. You can come to practice. Don't get in anybody's way."

As they worked on the dummies, on calisthenics, on drilling in the fundamentals, in the opening days, Eddie was able to show that he had not been boasting. He was already too muscle bound, at fourteen, to be especially fast, but he had enormous pushing power in his legs, he was tireless, and nothing hurt him. Ericson made him

77

running guard, on the fourth team, and by the middle of the season Eddie had won the same position on third string, replacing a soft fat kid with an infant face who outweighed him by twenty pounds. As a third stringer, Eddie made the trips to the games away, though he wasn't used in them. At first the others called him Monkey, and tried to make a pet of him as the coach had. This lasted a few weeks until some of the older boys had felt the impact of Eddie's shoulder, tried to run out of the clasp of his short, heavy arms in scrimmages. As Eddie learned his position, even players the size of Brad knew you couldn't run over him carelessly. They stopped calling him Monkey; they didn't call him Eddie, either; they called him Bissle.

When Eddie won the promotion to third string, Garoway, who was co-captain, remarked to the coach: "It's too bad Bissle isn't faster. At his weight he ought to be a back."

"Don't kid yourself," Ericson said. "He won't get into a game this year, but next fall he'll be ten pounds heavier and he'll be my starting guard. And the year after he may not weigh an ounce more, but he'll be All State."

3.

"Dear Bismarck:"

Ellen got letters from Tom twice a week, and tried to reply at least to every other one. Tom's letters were often long, and always conscientiously newsy; she didn't always read them through on the day of arrival.

"Dear Bismarck:"

She kept meaning to find a way of suggesting that she'd like him to stop using Bismarck, a family nickname which had once been supposed to designate her function in the Kaiser's court; she kept delaying asking Tom to drop the nickname. She had a sense that their family was beginning to work loose, and she didn't want to communicate this sense to Tom. She thought of him as not being old enough to feel it for himself.

Dear Bismarck:
I moved in with my new roommate yesterday. His name is Guy Cinturon, and he is very handsome although I don't

78

know if you'd think so. I started off wrong because the first thing I did was try to say hello to him in Spanish, because I thought he didn't know much English; anyway, I thought he was going to be a little kid and he's almost as tall as I am and I'm the tallest in my class. So I said hello in Spanish, and he laughed at me and said something very fast back, and I said "Como?" which means "what?" And he said "I bet I speak damn more English than you do Spanish;" that's the only mistake he's made. I guess whoever taught him English didn't teach him to swear. Anyway, he's a football player, and I guess he's about the only one in our class who's good enough so that he'll get into any games; at least Chowderhead says he will, because Guy was at practice today, and Chowderhead said Guy was a very fast runner and was catching passes better than anyone else.

I don't know what kind of trouble Guy got into at his last school, but I think it was something about girls. I don't want to ask him, but about the first thing he said to me, after what I told you, was he asked me if I was his roommate, and I said I was, and he said, "Too bad for you." So I said, "Why?" and he smiled (he has a very bright big smile, but it isn't very friendly, just big) and said because he was going to get in trouble. Then today Chowderhead said that after football practice this proctor Lew Archibald who's sort of the head of the school was being very friendly to Guy, and the others were too. So anyway Archibald was being nice and asking Guy where he was from, and where he'd been, and Guy told them the other school he was at, and Lew said: "How could they let you go if you can catch passes like that?" and Guy said that wasn't the only thing he could catch, he could catch girls. Well, I guess the others didn't like to hear a sophomore talking like that, or maybe they didn't like the idea of him being a Mexican and the girls being American; anyway, Chowderhead said that the seniors froze right up, and Archibald (the proctor) walked away without answering.

Anyway, the feeling all around school now is that Guy is very fresh, and they're mad because he's a foreigner and if they picked on him he'd think it was because of that, not be-

79

cause of being fresh. He got thrown in the pond yesterday, and he tried to fight with them when they did it, which you aren't supposed to do.

I guess nobody likes him very much, and I don't guess I do either. He said I was the school grind, because I said I wanted to study tonight and he wanted to play his radio; it isn't allowed during study hour, but he's doing it anyway, and I finished my work, so now I'm writing this in a composition book (that's why the lined paper). Anyway, I wish he'd speak Spanish with me, instead of just saying things like, "They always put me in with the school grind." I'm not really; I mean the other guys like me all right.

Please write me about Bev and the other girls from Tennepin. I had a letter from mother and she said that all the news she has about you is what I pass on when I write home and have been reading one of your letters. I'm awfully glad you're so busy.

Love,
Tom

P.S. I was right about Guy's trouble. Just after I finished the letter, and I said the radio wouldn't bother me, even if it was still study period, he smiled that smile I told you about, and turned the radio off and asked me how often we could go to town, and what were the girls like. So I said I didn't know, but we could go once a week, and I decided to ask whether it was a girl or something at the other school. And he said it was a girl they called Morbid Mildred, and he got caught with her by her father, and her father called up the school. I guess he meant they were necking. I said I didn't think he should say anything to the guys here about it, because I don't think they like the idea of seeing girls except seniors (it isn't like Tennepin High), so he said, "Who are you worried about? Me or you, Mr. Beniger?" So I said what did he mean, and he said did I think if he got in trouble I would too, because of being his roommate, and I said of course not, but he didn't believe me, because he said: "Tell them what you want . . . tell them you don't like me. I don't care. They'll
80

leave you alone and I'll worry about Mr. Cinturon." I didn't know what to say, so I asked if he wouldn't let me try to speak Spanish to him sometime, and he just smiled and turned the radio back on. I even had the Kaiser send my High School Spanish book. Ha, ha on me. T.

What a break for poor Tom, Ellen thought; he had said that he liked his first roommate, Chowderhead, so much. Chowderhead had sounded like a nice kid; Tom wasn't a grind. She found herself feeling quite angry with the Cinturon boy; Tom must be really quite upset to have written so much about it, and Ellen suddenly thought very fondly of her brother, that this was what he would do; he wouldn't, if he were unhappy about his new roommate, go and talk to Chowderhead about it. He might write about it to Ellen, but if he hadn't been able to do that, he'd never have said a word to anyone.

Ellen wished she were as wise.

Two days after Ellen arrived at college, Bev Hill, one of her very best friends in Tennepin, had come to Ellen's room. Ellen had hoped to room with Bev, but they hadn't seen each other in time to plan it. Bev, having been away in school Ellen's senior year in Tennepin, had spent the whole summer at her family's beach place in Rhode Island, and gone to college straight from there. When they finally met, in a line to register for courses, Ellen had asked Bev whether her plans were made and Bev said yes, she was going to be with another girl from her school, in Carter Hall—not even the same dormitory. Ellen, of course, didn't say what she'd been hoping; there had still, up to that moment, been some hope of switching, if both had been assigned roommates. Then, when Ellen heard that Bev and the girl from her school had a corner room on the ground floor, she was relieved that nothing could be done; ground floor rooms were more expensive, and corner rooms most of all.

Bev had been sweet enough to come see Ellen the very next day. Ellen's assigned roommate, a heavy, rather good-natured scholarship girl from upstate, was out; Bev came in and admired everything, which was sweet just to begin with.

"What's your roommate like?" Bev asked. "Someone you knew before?"

"No," Ellen said. "But she's terribly nice."

81

"You're as lucky as you are pretty," Bev said, which was the kind of thing Bev was always saying. And that was what made Ellen kind of go off her head and start raving to Bev about herself, how much fun she'd had senior year at high school; how she'd been queen for the homecoming game, and, in the spring, had her picture on the front page of the East Bixton paper in cap and gown as "Miss Girl Graduate, 1937" ("Of course they used your picture," Bev said, "if you photograph half as nice as you look. . . .") And Ellen had gone on and on, about how smart Tom turned out to be ("But your whole family is"), and, omitting Dickie Dee, the boys ("Sorley Green was crazy about you from the time he could talk"). Until finally:

"Honestly, Ellen, I've got to tear myself away. I know you're going to be the maddest success here at this place, and I'll just be watching and envying."

Two weeks later, Sorley Green, who was a freshman at Brown, asked Ellen up for a football game, and asked her to find a date for his roommate. Ellen went to Bev.

"Ellen, how darling of you to think of me but all of us can't just go out and dazzle boys who are complete strangers." Ellen took her roommate, Ronnie, and was a little ashamed of her. Later she learned that Bev and her school friends—there were four of them—had been to Yale that same weekend; it was then that Ellen realized how very much too much she had talked on Bev's first visit.

Not that Bev wasn't always sweet; but she and her school group were being rushed for Elm Club—sororities weren't allowed on campus; instead there were clubs named for trees. The rushing took all Bev's free time and for two weeks Ellen saw her friend only in the two classes they had in common. Just before club rushing closed, Ellen herself was invited to join Maple, which, she knew by then, was the least of all the clubs—the one that won scholarship prizes, and had activities girls. Marge Hamner, from Tennepin, knew girls in Maple and had written to them about Ellen. There was still a chance that she might get a last minute bid from Elm, or, failing that, Silver Birch at least. Ronnie, Ellen's roommate, who knew she wouldn't make a club herself, held out hope for Ellen; Ronnie's sister had been to Hazlit Woman's College, too.

"They always try to get the prettiest girls so they'll have somebody to run in the festival elections," Ronnie said.

Bev felt the same way: "I can't understand why all the clubs aren't after you," Bev said. "Oh, they're so stuffy over at Elm, I mean it's more a quiet group for stick in the muds like me. But Silver Birch and Live Oak—but you know what Ellen?"

"What?"

"I think you'd be right to join Maple. They're so active in everything, I mean all the prominent girls, they just practically run the school. I'd be so flattered if they wanted me. . . ."

It was Bev's way of telling Ellen that she didn't have a chance for Elm.

Ellen was not an ungracious girl, only a disappointed one. She thanked the rushing committee of Maple sincerely and accepted membership. She acknowledged to herself that she was not going to be great friends with Bev Hill, after all, and looked for others. She found Ronnie, her roommate, rather trying, but she concealed her impatience; she made friends with a girl named Hannah Ryan, from upstate New York.

Hannah was a clown; Hannah had a brother at Yale; Hannah was tall and thin and wild; Hannah confessed, with great secrecy, that she had not been a virgin since her fifteenth year. She made this confession, if you stopped to think about it, on rather short acquaintance, so it was best not to stop and think about it.

"I'm a sexy witch," Hannah said. "I guess I was born wanting to, and I did as soon as I was old enough." This, it turned out in a second stage of the confession, was not quite accurate; Hannah's first man had been a riding instructor, who didn't sound very scrupulous to Ellen. She liked Hannah. They could be gay together. They spent a weekend at Yale, with Hannah's brother and a friend, and Ellen and the brother were in love for a week; it ended the next weekend, at the Ryan's home, a big place on the Hudson River, when Hannah and her date spent most of Saturday out of sight and the brother got drunk and tried to insist that Ellen yield to him. On Sunday the brother was abashed, not much fun until he'd had a few beers; then he was discourteous and that was less fun. Hannah and her date seemed tired of one another; Hannah and Ellen left the boys and went riding, which was wonderful. When they got back Ellen felt too fine to let the weekend be spoiled by disgruntled boys, so she put some energy into cheering things

83

up and it ended quite pleasantly; but she and Charlie Ryan weren't in love anymore, and she didn't suppose he'd ask her back to Yale.

Dear Tommy:

Your new roommate doesn't sound very pleasant, and I'm sure I wouldn't think him handsome. Maybe you can get back with Chowderhead next year.

I've been awfully busy. We have these clubs here and I'm in one called Maple (they're all named after trees). Bev Hill is as sweet as ever; she's in a club called Elm, and I was sorry that she and I couldn't be in the same club, but actually I'm making a lot of new friends and she is, too.

I went to stay at Hannah's (I told you about her); you should see the place! There were some Yale boys, too—one is Hannah's brother. We rode horseback, which I wasn't very good at, but Hannah said I looked wonderful in her riding clothes, and you know how I love flattery. She's a little taller than I am, but the clothes didn't fit too badly, except the boots. Anyway, I'd like to take riding here if it weren't so expensive, but it costs about a million dollars an hour. Bev says the horses here are very good, and that I would be a natural rider, but I'm not so sure.

Well, I've got a million things to do, including write home as you so sweetly remind me. Mother says (she probably did to you, too) that the Kaiser is getting along better and better at the paper, so everything is wonderful for everybody, except poor you with the new roommate, but just ignore him if he won't be nice.

I'm sending a dollar for you to buy five milkshakes with all at once if you want to.

Love,

("O well," Ellen thought, as she signed it.)

Bismarck

the boy sitting next to him, as Brad came limping off on the Coach's arm.

"Oh, yes sir," the substitute said. "It bothers him all the time, but he just tapes it and plays. He's got guts."

The man in the grey overcoat nodded, and lit a cigarette, his face perfectly composed, thinking, Eddie figured, that he had just saved himself four or five hundred bucks.

There was no scoring in the last quarter. With Brad out, Mount Pennell played conservative football, a pleasure to watch, punishing the line, kicking out of bounds to minimize any runback heroes, containing Roper's frantic attempts to pass or run wide with crushing efficiency.

The only thing that looked like trouble came two minutes before the game ended, when Roper's Number 16 outran a pass defender and was clear, downfield. But the pass was long, or misjudged, or something.

5.

Tom knew that every sophomore there, wild as he might be for the team to score again, was glad that the pass to Guy was incomplete. For Guy's successes had been of the most galling kind to his classmates; he was the only one of the fourteen and fifteen year olds who had played with any regularity, and he had no modesty about it. His attitude was a perfect reflection of the way he played: interceptions, long runs, impossible catches, showboat stuff—but the solid playing was done by the other ten men. For Guy would fail to gain on ordinary plays; he needed an open situation to make use of his flamboyant running ability. He was an undependable blocker, and poor defensively, often missing tackles. No one had called him yellow to his face, but several boys had used the word to Tom.

Tom would neither agree nor disagree; the whole situation continued to trouble him. He kept trying to be nice to Guy, because he felt the Headmaster had asked him to; this the Proctors seemed to approve. Lew Archibald, who was Chief Proctor, had even taken Tom aside one day to say so.

"Look, Beniger. Nobody's going to hold your roommate against you. We know why the Head put you in with him."

"You do?" Tom was surprised; he hadn't said anything.

87

"Sure. It's what they always do when they let an odd ball into school. They put him with a scholarship kid who can't kick."

Tom hadn't realized they knew he was a scholarship boy, either.

Chowderhead was pounding Tom's shoulder: "He dropped it, Tom. He should have had it, shouldn't he?"

"I don't think so," Tom said, and a minute later the game was over. The team huddled to cheer Mount Pennell, the spectators scrambled over the field, running to get warm; Tom watched Guy, looking suddenly frail as he walked off the field by himself, still wearing his helmet.

Chowderhead came tearing back past Tom.

"Come on," he shouted. "We're going to make cocoa in the room."

Tom shook his head; he had decided to go to the Field House and wait for Guy. He didn't much want to, but he felt he should.

It was getting colder; as he went into the center room of the Field House, off which the dressing rooms opened, Tom told himself that it was going to snow.

A number of boys were waiting for members of the team to come out of the dressing room, and Tom stood with them; as a player appeared, his friends would close around him, crying, "Good game, good game," and walk him away.

Guy was neither first nor last. He came out walking gracefully as ever, a little over-dressed, wearing a suit and tie when the others had on sweaters or jackets; he was not smiling.

There was not precisely a silence when he appeared, for no amount of jealousy could make him the sole goat of a badly played game; it was rather that there was no shouting, no one to move towards Guy except Tom.

"Nice game, Guy," Tom said, more loudly than he meant to.

Guy stopped and looked at him. There was still no smile. "I stank, Mr. Beniger," he said, and walked past Tom out of the Field House. Tom did not see him again that day.

It was customary, on the Friday night after the Roper game, for the seniors on the football team who had just played their last game for the school to break a number of rules: they went off bounds at night, they went to town without permission, and once there they drank beer. This custom was abetted by the faculty, who stayed in their rooms, and by the non-football-playing proctors who pretended to be scowling and alert but could always

88

manage not to catch the privileged ones escaping. The chases and alarms, in fact, were part of the fun. The player would leave his room, hide in the yard, seize a moment to run off across the field towards the road to town, while a proctor and some younger boys ran after him, laughing and shouting, "Stop," but unable, of course, to recognize him. That year there was a grand coup as well; Lew Archibald and his roommate hid in the back of the headmaster's station wagon, and let the Head himself transport them to town.

The school was still laughing about this on Monday when a shocking rumor started. The rumor was that Guy Cinturon, a sophomore, had been seen in town by one of the seniors, sitting in the restaurant which was too expensive unless one's parents were visiting and paying the check, having dinner with a girl.

Monday after supper, Tom was called to Archibald's room, where the proctors were gathered. Archibald said:

"This isn't going to get to the masters. They might take away the Senior Football Sneak forever, just because one stupid kid doesn't know how to behave. You see that, Tom?"

"Yes," Tom said. It was the first time Archibald or any other proctor had called him by his first name.

"We saw you at the Field House Saturday waiting for Cinturon after the game. That was the right thing to do. You've done a lot of right things for him, or tried to, and we know the Head appreciates it. But you don't have to take any more of Cinturon's crap, Tom; you've probably taken too much already."

Tom didn't know what to say so he kept quiet.

"You have to sleep in the room with him, but there's no reason why you can't move your clothes and books back into Grant's room, and do everything there but sleep. Grant likes the idea."

"What are you going to do to . . . Cinturon?" Tom asked.

"Don't worry about it," Archibald said.

Tom walked away down the hall; the suggestion that he move back in with Chowderhead for everything but sleeping pleased him, except that it wasn't a suggestion really. It was a command.

Guy was at his desk studying. Tom spoke to his back in a very quiet voice.

"The Proctors are awfully mad about Friday night."

Guy looked up.

"They want to know when I came in?"

"No. I guess they know all they want to know."

89

"What they going to do? Give me the silent treatment?"

"That's what it sounds like," Tom said.

"I had it before." Guy turned back to his desk.

Tom stood in front of his own desk, looking at the books, considering whether to pack the things he must move or carry them to Grant's room in several trips. He supposed Chowderhead would help if asked.

"You going to talk to me, Tom?"

Tom was startled; Guy's tone was that of a request for information, but a plea was quite implicit. Tom was dismayed; if Guy did not want to be disliked, after all, how could Tom dislike him?

"You want me to talk to you?" he asked, but this was pushing it too hard.

"Do what you like," Guy said. Perhaps because of the slight foreignness of intonation, it sounded not like a pat phrase but like advice on conduct. Tom stood, looking at his books, thinking about it. How could one do what he liked? How could one know what it was? Guy did what he liked, apparently, and if it meant disregarding rules, flouting the system, Guy knew the consequences and shrugged at them. The problem was clear in Tom's mind only for a moment; perceiving it, he retreated from it.

"I . . . I've got to get this history paper done," he said; he didn't move his books that night; he thought he might do it in the morning.

During the night the snow finally came. In the morning the proctors caught Guy on the way to breakfast, removed his pants, and packed snow into his underwear shorts. They said he must learn to keep cool. Tom did not see this, having left for breakfast early, but when he got back he found Guy in the room, still trembling with outrage.

"Jesus Christ, Tom, it hurts," Guy said. "Like being kicked there. Dirty guys."

They walked to class together silently. Tom wondered which would be noticed—the walking together or the silence.

At eleven they were back in the room when the bell rang for milk break.

"You want to go over to the dining hall, get some milk?" Guy asked.

"I've still got to finish the history paper," Tom said. He hadn't been able to concentrate very well the night before.

90

"I got to go over," Guy said, frowning. "I didn't get any breakfast." He dawdled a moment in the room, watching Tom set up his work. Then Guy took off his suit coat and his necktie; he pulled his belt in tight, put on a light sweater and a pair of pigskin gloves.

"I'll see you," he said, and went out.

Tom waved and, an instant later, felt violent shame. He got up and went to the window of their room. He saw Guy go out of the building and saw Guy stopped by Chowderhead Grant and three other sophomores. Archibald and another proctor were nearby, watching but apparently taking no part.

Suddenly Tom heard himself sob. He ran out of the room in his shirtsleeves, down the two flights of stairs, and out into the cold air. He heard Archibald say:

"He's your problem now, Grant. He's in your class. We're through with him."

"Let's get his pants again, guys," Chowderhead cried. Guy stood lightly, his fists clenched in the light gloves. Chowderhead saw Tom. "Let's get his pants, Tom," Chowderhead said, and started to charge Guy.

Tom stepped past his roommate; he meant only to get between the two, take Chowderhead's rush, and argue; but his feet hit snow, and he found himself pitching into Chowderhead shoulder first, clutching for support. It was more effective than a blow. They went down together, out of snow, onto a bare spot, and there was pain in Tom's imperfect shoulder from the shock. He got to his feet, meaning to help Chowderhead up, and saw that the other three had closed towards Guy and were hurling their fists at him inexpertly, just out of reach of Guy's returning jabs. They were too heavily dressed, and, instantly, Tom realized why Guy had been so careful in choosing his sweater, and along with the clarity of mind which permitted this thought came the observation that one of the three sophomores was about to duck in from the left. Tom forgot about helping Chowderhead up, leapt on the boy's back and bore him down to the ground. He was angry and it was a strange sensation, he had known it so seldom. As he pushed the boy's face into the snow, he saw that Guy had tackled another one and was kicking at the third.

Guy was also screaming something in Spanish, Tom noticed, just as Chowderhead's arm went around Tom's throat in a choke hold,

91

and the boy underneath caught Tom on the ear with a wild fist. Tom rolled away, his head ringing, and managed to dump Chowderhead. He kept seeing peripheral things: now it was the proctors, watching impassively. Now it was Guy catching at a finger, breaking a choke hold himself.

Tom crawled, gasping, towards the boy who had hit him on the ear and slapped at his mouth, open handed. Tom rolled on his back, and kicked at Chowderhead. A moment later he was on his feet, somehow, and diving towards Rails, who was hammering Guy's back. Tom caught Rails with a fist in the side of the neck, and, at the same moment, someone crashed into Tom's back, knocking him prone.

Tom got to his knees and pounded at the face and chest of Rails, who was kneeling beside him, screaming. Rails didn't hit back. Tom jumped up and found his own shoulder against Guy's for an instant. Chowderhead was coming in, and he and Tom stood close, plowing fists into one another. Then Guy jumped back, sending Tom sidewise, and Chowderhead's fist, traveling in a short arc, caught Tom a solid blow on the nose. It seemed to him that he was blinded for a moment, and he realized that his arms were thrashing at Chowderhead as if of their own accord, smashing at the head, while Tom's feet kicked out at someone who was on the ground, interfering with his movement.

A boy had grabbed Guy's arms from behind and Rails was hitting Guy's face hysterically with one hand. Tom crashed into the boy holding the arms, uncertain who it was, and they all went down, Guy springing away and up, instantly. Chowderhead landed on Tom's back, then, and Tom felt a hand against the back of his head, pushing his face into dirty snow. Bloody snow. He yelled, mostly with the frustration of not being able to get up and fight, though his arms were so weary they wouldn't push when he tried to shove himself up. He started to roll desperately, and felt Chowderhead leave him, much too easily, so that he rolled completely over and back onto his stomach again. Then he felt a hand pulling at his shoulder and he heard Archibald's voice say:

"All right, you little saps. Break it up."

Both proctors had moved in, and the six sophomores were being pushed and pried apart. As Tom let himself be lifted and set back, he saw that Mr. Fairless, the French and Latin master had come up, prompting the proctors' action; Tom realized the extent of his

92

exhaustion. He had come out in shirtsleeves, and he might as well have been naked as the chilly wind dried his sweat; but the comparative lightness of their clothing, he thought, was what had enabled him and Guy to fight so long. Even so, another minute would have finished them.

He stood shoulder to shoulder with his roommate, heaving for air, scowling at the other group. There was a lot of blood around on the snow, quite a pool of it at his own feet—gradually Tom decided it must be his own nose bleeding, and began to snuffle back with what breath he could summon. The blood was over all of them. Tom glanced sidewise at Guy; his roommate's face was beaten raw, but Guy was smiling, or trying to. Tom looked at their adversaries again, to find out what there was to smile at; one of Chowderhead's eyes was nearly closed already; another boy was spitting fragments of tooth and gum; Rails held one hand in the other and whimpered. It turned out later that Guy had broken a finger, prying off the choke hold.

"All right, you little dopes," Archibald said. "Go get cleaned up." Then to Mr. Fairless, "It's like wading into a dogfight, sir. You have to watch that you don't get bitten." Fairless nodded, and turned away; this was the proctor's province.

Guy touched Tom's arm. *"Compadre,"* he said.

But Tom was so filled with a growing sense of self-approval, for having been in a fight and fought it, that he paid as little attention to the fact that Guy had said a word in Spanish to him as he did to Lew Archibald's remark, as they turned away:

"What happened, Beniger? You find out he was rich?"

6.

"I tried to apologize to Grant," Tom said. "He wouldn't let me."

"But I don't understand," said Ellen quite puzzled. "I thought you didn't like the Cinturon boy?"

"Cinturon," said Tom, correcting her pronunciation. It was an evening of Thanksgiving vacation; they were both home.

"A boy's finger was broken, and your nose?" Ellen said; she had finally got Tom alone to ask about the injury. "I think it's terrible."

"Captain Hook," said Tom, grinning, pointing to the bump where his nose had mended.

Their mother came in. "We're going to bed," she said. "Do you want to sit up and talk?"

"Yes, please," Tom said. "If Ellen wants to."

Ellen smiled. "Go on, Mom," she said. "We'll bring you both breakfast in the morning."

"You'll do no such thing," her mother said. "Tom needs to sleep late. And it wouldn't hurt you either, Miss."

They said goodnight. The Kaiser had already gone up to bed; his work at the East Bixton print shop, where he was foreman now, exhausted him these days. He made more money, but his sister was ill and the hospital bills were high.

"I was sorry about the fight afterwards," Tom said, when their mother had left. "I mean not at first; at first I thought I'd done something great. Then, when I heard about Rails' finger, I just about cried. He can't play basketball until after Christmas, and he's supposed to be pretty good. . . ."

"But I still don't understand why you did it," Ellen said.

"Oh. It wasn't me that broke his finger, it was Guy."

"I don't mean that. I mean why you had the fight."

"I had to," Tom said. He frowned at her. "I don't understand this: it seems like I do things because I have to, and Guy does things because he likes to."

He paused. He seemed to be waiting for her to explain this to him, but it wasn't Ellen's kind of conversation. Sometimes, when Tom wanted to be serious, she found her brother boring. She said: "Well, school kids don't stay mad about things like that, do they?"

"Oh, I don't know."

"Didn't you shake hands and all that?"

"Well, I don't guess Rails could shake hands with a broken finger."

"But Chowderhead?"

"I told you. I tried to apologize and he wouldn't let me."

"What did he say?"

"He didn't say anything."

"You mean he just turned away?"

"Yes. He sort of just, oh, got up and walked away."

"What about the other two?"

"I didn't try to apologize to them."

"Why not?"

94

"Well, I . . . I thought the same thing would happen. Anyway, I wasn't too sorry, except about Rails' finger."

"But why would the same thing happen, Tom? You mean any of those four boys would just walk away?"

"I don't know what they'd do," Tom said. "Yes, I guess they'd have to."

"Tom, what do you mean, 'they'd have to'?"

"They aren't allowed to talk to us," Tom said. "Nobody at school is."

"What?"

"We're getting the silent treatment." Suddenly he grinned. "We don't care. We're driving them crazy."

"Tom, what. . . ?"

"Guy's teaching me Spanish," Tom said. "We never speak English any more except in class. Boy, you should see the guys who sit at the table with us in dining hall, when we jabber away and they don't know what we're saying."

Ellen looked at him amazed. The grin seemed perfectly sincere.

"*Cabeza de Sancocho tiene una espinilla féuco en la frente hoy,*" Tom said. "That means Chowderhead has a repulsive pimple on his forehead today. I just about died when Guy said it." Tom laughed at the recollection. "*Sancocho* really means stew more than chowder," he said.

"Tom, how long is this, this silent treatment going on?"

"I don't know. Till they decide to stop. You know something? Guy wanted me to go down to Mexico with him. Instead of back to school after vacation. He said we could spend the winter in Chihuahua, and his father would get a tutor for us, and we could just stay there, if we wanted, until we were ready to go to college. And travel around—I nearly did, too."

"Tom!"

"Well, I didn't really nearly go, but it sounded wonderful. And at first Guy said he was going to do it anyway, so I had to come. Then, when I said I couldn't, he said . . . well, he said then he'd stay at school and not let himself get thrown out, because he wouldn't leave me alone with those guys."

"I should think that's the least he could do," Ellen said.

"We're *compadres,*" Tom said. "That's a special kind of friend."

"But what kind of a boy is he? I thought . . . I'm confused about him, Tom. You didn't write about any of this."

"I didn't want you telling Mom."

95

"But the last letters that you mentioned Guy in, you didn't even like him."

"I didn't know him then. At first I thought it was going to be awful, being on silent treatment, but really I've never had so much fun. Guy's been so many places, and he's done everything, and he's very funny about it. . . ."

"In Spanish," Ellen said.

"No kidding, Bismarck, you'd like him."

"Tommy," Ellen said. "I'd sort of like you to stop calling me Bismarck."

"Okay," Tom said. There was a pause. Then he said: "Honestly Ellen, about the fight. You don't know what they were trying to do to Guy—what the proctors already did to him."

"What?"

"I can't tell you."

"Something nasty?"

He nodded.

Ellen was shocked. "You mean they . . . ?" She had a vivid image of something completely unnatural; apparently it communicated itself to Tom, for he spoke quickly.

"Well, not . . . well what they did was took his pants off and rubbed snow around, well, all around down here."

"Oh."

"He was very frightened. He thought it might hurt him there permanently. So he couldn't . . . you know. Could it hurt him that way, Ellen?"

"How awful," Ellen said. "I don't know, Tom. You could ask the Kaiser."

"Well it didn't, anyway."

"How do you know?"

"He told me."

"How does he know?"

Tom was blushing.

"How, Tom?"

"He . . . knows this girl in town," Tom said, hunching his shoulders in shame. "He . . . sneaked in to see her."

"This boy is fifteen?" Ellen said.

"Almost sixteen."

"He's quite a boy."

"I thought it would shock you," Tom said.

96

She shook her head. "I know girls that do it, one that was younger than that when she started."

"So was Guy."

"He was?"

"He was twelve. Or . . . well, he told me about this nurse that used to take care of him when he was little. She wanted him to, and he'd try to kick her. He laughs now because he used to fight with her about it. Anyway, he said when he was twelve, he . . . listen, Ellen. Maybe I shouldn't tell you this."

"Go ahead, Tom. It's all right."

"But I mean you'll probably meet him sometime."

"It's fascinating, Tom."

"It is?"

"Oh Tom, girls are interested in sex too, you know. Not just boys."

"We never talked about it before."

"You were a little bit young."

"I used to talk about it to Connie Marston."

"Connie Marston?"

"Yes. When I was sick."

"I'll be darned," Ellen said. "So that's what you two were doing."

"We didn't do anything."

"Too bad you didn't wait a couple of years," Ellen said.

"You mean she does now?"

"Tell me the rest, about Guy and his nurse."

"Well, when he was twelve, he waited for her one time with a whip."

"A whip!"

"Yes. He was going to make her do it, because then he was bigger he said . . . big enough." Tom turned shy again.

"I see," Ellen said, smiling encouragement at Tom and trying to picture this boy, Guy Cinturon. But heavens! "A whip?"

"Yes. He hit her with it, too. But then she was stronger than he was, and she took the whip away. . . ."

"What did she do to him?"

"Well they . . . you know."

"After he hit her, she still did?"

"Yes. Guy said she mocked him. He laughed about it when he told me."

"What else has the young man done in this field?" Ellen asked.

"He has a book," Tom said. "A loose leaf book, and he has a page for every girl that he meets and tries to . . . well, tries to do it with. And he writes everything about her, and how far they went, and if they went all the way, he pastes a gold star on the page. You know, like you get for perfect Sunday school attendance?"

"Well, how many stars does your friend have?" Ellen asked.

"Seven."

"Wow."

"He doesn't count when . . . well, sometimes in Mexico he paid girls."

"Oh, I see. They're called prostitutes, Tom."

"I know."

"They're not girls, really. Women."

"Guy says they're girls in Mexico."

"He hasn't tried to take you to one of those women, Tom?"

"Oh, no. Guy says he's never going to pay any more."

"Nice of him."

"For one thing, he can't put it in his book if he pays. He has pictures of some of the girls, and a lot of details. . . ."

"I think that's awful about the book, Tom."

"You do?"

"Well, imagine being one of those girls, and thinking of your name and picture and everything about you in a book like that, and other boys could see."

"Oh, he doesn't show it to anybody."

"Not to you?"

"No. Just a picture of one of the girls once. He says . . . well, it's like a diary. I mean, it has dates that things happened."

"Oh. That's different, if it's like a diary," Ellen said.

"Ellen?"

"Yes."

"You really know girls at college who . . . who do it?"

"Sure."

"Do they like to?"

"I know one girl that probably likes it as well as your friend Guy," Ellen said.

"What about Connie Marston?"

"I'm sorry I said anything about that."

"Why?"

98

"It was just a rumor, anyway. And you shouldn't repeat things about sex, Tom; especially, boys should never repeat them to other boys. It can ruin a girl."

"Is that what happened to Connie? I thought she was going to be a nurse."

"Well, she used to say that. But then she decided to be a doctor. She was taking pre-med in Boston."

"What happened?"

"She . . . she had an affair with some man who was married, and the man talked, and Connie got sent home."

"Is she here now?"

"Why? Do you want to see her?"

Tom blushed again.

"She's in New York, anyway. Some people say the man from Boston is down there too, or he comes down there."

"Have you seen her?"

"No."

"Would you want to?"

"I don't know. She's an old friend of mine."

"How's Bev?" Tom asked.

"She's fine."

"Are you still . . . do you see a lot of her at college?"

"Oh, sure. Bev's the most wonderful girl."

"I'm glad you're having a good time, Ellen."

"I am. Marvelous."

"Getting in the club was fine."

"Well, now, Tommy. Most girls do. But the rushing was exciting."

"I'll bet you're the prettiest in your class, aren't you?"

"Why Tom Beniger, what makes you say a thing?" She teased him with a smile; he was a cute brother.

"You are. I'll bet you are. If they have an election, I'll bet you win it."

"How much?"

"A billion dollars."

"What's pretty about me?"

"Your hair. Your eyes. The way you smile."

"Not my figure?"

"I don't . . . sure."

"Stop blushing, silly. Haven't we talked about enough things tonight so you don't have to blush like an old silly?"

"You never did it, did you Ellen?" The question burst out of Tom with scared fervor.

She checked herself on the point of a light answer. "No," she said, tenderly. "No, funny little brother. I never did it and I won't till I'm married." She smiled. "But I'll bet you will."

And he blushed again. He was silent for a minute, and Ellen was considering what other turn to give this delightfully candid conversation, when Tom said:

"Do you think the Kaiser looks all right, Ell?"

"About the same."

"I thought he looked tired."

"I guess he does."

"What did his sister die of, Ellen?"

"Aunt Lucia? I don't know."

"Maybe that's why he looks tired."

"Maybe," Ellen said.

They talked on and on. They actually didn't get to bed until two A.M.

CHAPTER FIVE

1.

BY THE FALL of Guy and Tom's senior year at Roper, they were both proctors. This was not altogether a reflection of popularity: it was customary that the high man academically and the football captain, which they were respectively, be elected. But their old adversary, Chowderhead, was Chief Proctor, and while all three now thought back on the fight and the punishment with the nostalgic affection of participants for a legend, they never became friends; it was because Guy thought liking Grant would be a waste of time, though he knew this made it hard for Tom, who wanted to like everybody.

There had been many triumphs: Tom's gift for classic languages had persuaded the school to restore Greek to the curriculum. Tom had made a speech, recommending conscientious objection, in the school forum that was talked of for weeks; he was not a good speaker, Guy thought, but he had a sincerity that overcame the shy diction, the hesitation to assert. He was so persuasive, for example, that there was hardly a boy at school who did not, in emulation of Tom, profess to worship President Roosevelt—even Guy, to whom American politics seemed a bore, let Tom convince him that Roosevelt was the world's best hope for prosperity and justice.

Among Guy's accomplishments were new school records in the two-twenty low hurdles and the hundred yard dash. He had taken Tom to Mexico for spring vacation, junior year, flown down and back by private plane. He had got his general average up to B which, lacking a photographic memory like Tom's, seemed high enough for anyone. And there were sixteen gold stars in the pages of Guy's book.

Tom was pretty funny about the gold stars. "Did she go to Sunday school?" he'd ask, about a new girl. "Yes, she's quite devoted," or, "It was her first time," or, sometimes, "No," and Tom would say: "Little atheist."

They could look back on the winter of 1937 and laugh; they could also admit to one another that it had been rough. They were on silence for a long time; it lasted until Guy got tired of it.

He had by then observed all the other boys in school quite carefully, and decided which few he might like, since, for Tom's sake, he was going to stay in this place. "We're lucky, Tom," he explained. "When we get ready to talk, we only need to talk to the ones we want to."

He selected the proctor named Rogers as the man through whom to crack the ban. There were several reasons: Rogers was Lew Archibald's rival for school power. Rogers had taken no part in the snow-stuffing episode. Rogers represented sophistication in the school mind as definitely as Archibald represented sincerity, the cult of athletics, being clean cut.

Rogers drank. He was feared for a sharp tongue. He was lazy and sardonic. Tom seemed alarmed at the idea of Guy's risking Rogers' ironies; Guy laughed it off. He thought they might like Rogers; he thought he could handle Rogers; and what had they to lose?

Rogers roomed alone. Guy went up to see him one evening in February. Mid-term averages had been posted that day, and Tom led the school. Guy felt it was time for a move.

Rogers' door was open, so Guy knocked and stood in the doorway. Rogers looked up, tilted back in his desk chair, and hooked his thumbs into his pockets. Guy smiled.

"Well, for Christ's sake," said Rogers. He had a nasal voice which he accentuated in self-mockery.

"May I come in?" Guy asked.

"I doubt if I see you," Rogers said. "I'm sure I haven't spoken to you, Señor."

"Pretty childish, isn't it?" Guy said, still smiling.

"Childish things are good for children."

"Listen, I want to thank you. I've been wanting to."

"What in hell for?"

"You were the only proctor that didn't try to make me a snow jock strap that day."

"Maybe I was just tired."

"Thanks for being tired. You know something? There was sand in that god damn snow." Guy laughed. "Boy, it was like being worked on with a file."

Rogers laughed. Then he stopped. "All right, Cinturon. You've got me talking. What do you want?"

"Will you give Archibald a message for me?"

"What are you going to do? Appeal to his great big sense of fair play?"

"No, I decided I'd like to knock his ass off," Guy said, "if he'll fight with me."

"Now what the hell is this?" Rogers asked. "Code of honor? I can see the headlines: 'Prep School Duelers Die at Dawn'."

"No, I'd just like to fight him," Guy said. "With gloves, if he wants, in the gym. Or anywhere."

"Figure he's the author of all your goddamn woes?"

Guy shook his head. "No, I fixed it for myself along those lines," he said, grinning. He felt pretty certain of Rogers now. "I just think it would be a shame to let an Archibald get away without socking him in the head a couple of time, for being dreary."

Rogers laughed. "Get out, Cinturon," he said, "before I start to appreciate you too much."

Guy reported his success to Tom.

"What do we do next?" Tom asked.

"Wait for him," Guy said. "He'll come."

And the next night he did, opening the door of their room without knocking, and looking in at them.

"You guys finding each other pretty entertaining?" Rogers asked.

"Circus every night," Guy said quickly.

"Where do you keep the señoritas? In the closet?"

"Nothing there but gin." It was a gibe at Rogers' drinking. Guy didn't figure on being cravenly friendly.

"Going to ask me in?"

"Please." Guy stood. Tom had already risen.

Rogers stepped in and closed the door. "What's your friend doing?" he asked Guy. "Putting me on silence?"

"No tengo palabras," Tom said, in an undertone.

"Poor fellow has forgotten English," Guy said fast. "It's been so long."

Rogers laughed. He sat down and chatted with them for ten minutes.

The next day Rogers greeted them outdoors from Proctors' Grass. Tom and Guy returned the greeting happily, and saw Lew Archibald go up to Rogers and say something in an angry whisper. Rogers' reply was quite audible:

"Archibald, were you born childish or did you have to study?"

"Listen Rogers. . . ."

"I'll bet you're going to major in childishness at Harvard," Rogers went on in his tired nasal, and, as Archibald spluttered, "Well listen, Lew baby, it isn't every boy who can do that." Rogers' influence over the school was growing, Archibald's waning; Guy had his family's instinct for politics.

He never got to fight Archibald, which was rather a disappointment; he'd supposed he'd be beaten, but thought it would be a pleasure to hit the chief proctor a few licks. By spring, about a third of the school approved of Guy, and he and Tom could pick their friends. It split the student body disastrously from the standpoint of general morale, but Guy didn't care much, except that he couldn't manage to soothe Tom's sense of guilt for being one cause of the general peevishness of tone which settled over school life as the year finished. They had enemies, particularly in their own class, and Guy learned that Tom would never get used to that and accept it comfortably as something natural.

Junior year a couple of their enemies didn't return. Guy trained hard for football season, and had a brilliant year; the team was reasonably successful. They made the trip to Mexico. Senior year Guy had gained a few pounds and was faster than ever. The team was the best in seven years.

They heard about the hot Roper team at Mount Pennell. They heard about it till it was dripping down their pants legs, Eddie felt. Roper, Roper, Roper. Spell it out the cruddy way. Football would be a good game if it weren't for all the cruddy talking that went with it.

Yet he maintained his affection for Ericson; he had to. The Coach might be a little bit stupid, but he was tough; his speeches got results. Eddie varied between thinking Ericson knew what an ass he was, and thinking that he didn't; thinking that Ericson played it that way perfectly, and thinking that he was all bull and a yard wide. Eddie also varied between caring and not caring. On the whole he cared—whether it was a matter of being tickled by Ericson's cunning, or of just forgiving the coach's stupidness because the toughness outweighed it. Eddie had to care about him. Because if he didn't, who in hell else was there in Eddie's cruddy little corner of the world?

So Eddie went along, trying to be the Coach's boy, for most of the season. But he had a hard time with his affection, and it got worse after the all-conference selections were announced, Monday before the Roper game. They had been in the morning paper, a small enough story on the sports page but the news of the day in Massachusetts' prep schools.

Ericson gathered the squad around him before practice. He stared at them.

"Every year," he said "just as we face our biggest game, the sports writers from Boston upset my squad with this all-conference twaddle. I have generally been fortunate enough to have a player or two selected; in fact, I may say that this is the only year I can recall when only one of my players has been selected. One. Why? Because they will not wait until we have completed our schedule; they will not watch my team fighting its hardest against its most formidable opponent. And boys who would surely have been selected have been passed over."

He lowered his voice. "But let me tell you something. I had a sportswriter come up to me, after a Roper game one year, come right up to me and shake my hand, with tears in his eyes, and say:

105

'I was wrong. If I could have seen X, and Y, and Z play the way they have today, the all-conference voting would have been different.' Yes. I could name that writer to you, you read him every morning, but I'm not going to. No. I'm going to let him name himself. Because if you play the game you can play on Saturday, that sportswriter won't be apologizing to me. No. He'll be coming to the dressing room after the game *to apologize to every one of you!*

"Men, I have never before, in all my coaching career at Mount Pennell, had only one man picked for an all-conference team, and I am here to tell you that we are going to show those sports writers how wrong they are. And as for that one man, if he thinks he can lie on his back, dreaming dreams of glory this week, he can turn in his uniform."

And as for that one man, who was Eddie, he didn't mind the speech so far, though his whole body ached to be running and crashing in scrimmage, not standing around getting cold while the coach spouted. What offended Eddie was what came next:

"Not that the one man is undeserving of the honor. I do not say that; I would fight anyone who said that, old as I am. Because that one man has played his heart out for me. I'd take that one man over all the others the sports writers have seen fit to choose. If Jack Smalley, who coaches the Roper team, were to come up to me tomorrow, and say, 'Eric, I'll trade you my three all-conference players for your one,' I'd say, 'Jack, who do you think you're talking to?' I'd say, 'Jack, you've got your Mexican jumping bean in at half, and my team with Bissle's going to cook him in chili sauce.' I'd say, 'Jack, You've got a blocking back called Grant, and my team with Bissle's going to make him wish that he'd stayed home on his rich father's fancy estate'. I'd say, 'Jack, you've got your center, Kelley, and my team with Bissle's going to work him over so hard he won't know what he's trying to pass between his legs—the football or his own aching head.' But Jack Smalley isn't going to make me that offer, because he wasn't born yesterday either; he knows I'm right!" He paused. Then he said in a soft, soupy voice: "Eddie boy. Come here."

Eddie supposed he had to go to the coach. He did.

"Can this team win, Eddie?"

"Sure." Sure, Coach, just make that trade you were talking about and we'll win by fifty points.

"Say it louder, Eddie."

"Sure. We can win." We can stop Cinturon if Grant breaks a leg. We can stop them in the line if Kelley breaks an arm. He had played against Kelley and Cinturon the year before; he had heard about Grant.

"Louder!"

Eddie looked at the coach amazed. What did the man think he was, a goddamn juke box? Put a nickel in me, Ericson, and I'll play *Begin the Beguine*. He wasn't going to stand there all afternoon hollering "Sure!" at the top of his voice; if his teammates had found him the inspirational type, Eddie figured, they'd have elected him captain. So he moved away a step, tried to goose a little enthusiasm into his voice, and said:

"How about some practice, Coach?"

Ericson blinked. Then he picked it up. "All right," he yelled back. "That's my kind of talk. How about some practice?" But Eddie noticed, as he ran that afternoon, that Ericson kept looking at him.

Eddie figured he knew what came next. In spite of his being just about tall enough to climb on the can without help, he was supposed to be the hardest guy in school. Very hard school. So that, along with the all-conference selection, which Eddie figured he damn well deserved unless Roper had a better guard, which he doubted, would make him pigeon for Ericson's annual target practice, just as big Brad had been two years before. Just as Underwood, who was now playing for the Princeton freshmen, had been last year.

Eddie hated the whole prospect. Not only did he hate the idea of Ericson slugging him, he hated the idea of Ericson enshrining him, after he went on, as one of those inspiration cases—like Bert Wampole, who left a Roper game in agony never to play again, or the boy whose mother wrote an ungrammatical letter, or Brad himself who, as the coach liked to put it, "would play better football on one leg than most boys on two, dragging a bad knee behind him as he ran because he knew what it meant to love this game." What would Eddie be? Boy, he could hear it: "Came out here the size of a monkey and what did he say? 'I can block and tackle.' And he could. And the week of the Roper game, what'd he say? Been selected all-conference and what'd he say? 'Let's get some practice, Coach!'" Eddie could hear it, just as clearly as he could see himself getting slugged for nothing.

The trigger for the annual slug was always inattention; Brad had been talking about girls, Underwood about grades; Eddie decided he would watch his step.

Every day as practice started he'd remind himself: think football every minute, stupid, if you don't want to go tumbling over with Ericson's fist in your gut. He might as well have saved himself the damn worry. Ericson was bound to get him; it was something the coach needed to get himself ready—Eddie could see that. Ericson just had to biff some kid the week before the Roper game; Eddie could almost feel sorry for the man, having to depend on being convinced by his own song and dance the way Ericson did.

When it came Eddie wasn't talking about girls or grades. As a matter of fact, he wasn't even talking. They said around school that sometimes Bissle didn't say three words a week and when he did two of them were *crud,* and that was true enough. So what he was doing at the time Ericson turned red and started for him was rinsing his mouth with water.

They'd been running plays for over an hour, and the fact was that when they ran plays, it wasn't the backfield that did most of the running, it was Eddie. He was so goddamn deft at the plays where the guard pulls out of the line to become an extra blocking back that Ericson had built a whole offense around Eddie executing this maneuver; so one back might run on one play, and a different one on the next, but Eddie ran on every play. When Ericson told them to rest five minutes, Eddie wasn't tried; but he was dry. He headed for the water bucket. He waited until Garabona was finished drinking, and took the dipper. He saw Ericson coming.

"What is this?" The coach was yelling. "Football practice or gossiping around the water bucket? What?" His fist was already cocked, his foot sneaking around to trip Eddie from behind.

Still holding the dipper. Eddie jumped backwards. As he did, he felt a lot of pity for Ericson. The man had slowed down a step or two since the year he tagged Brad. Eddie almost wished he had the guts to hold still for this, but. . . .

God damn it.

Thrown off in his timing by Eddie's anticipating him, Ericson put out a hand, reaching for Eddie's shoulder. Eddie pushed it off and jumped away another step.

"Bissle!" The coach roared.

Eddie couldn't help it. He jerked his hand forward as if he were

108

going to throw the dipper of water in Ericson's face; it stopped the man.

"Keep your hands to yourself, Coach," he said. Then he poured the water on the ground.

"You're excused from practice, Bissle," the coach yelled. Eddie tossed the dipper in the bucket and walked off the field.

The next day he went out at the normal time, changed his clothes with the other guys, and went out on the field. Ericson neither looked at him nor spoke to him. When calisthenics and dummy drill were over, Ericson named two line-ups for scrimmage, without Eddie in either one. Eddie watched for a moment; then he went over with the third and fourth stringers, appointed himself guard on the fourth, and scrimmaged with them. Had a pretty good time knocking the kids around, showing the apprentice guards what to do, under the baffled supervision of the young English teacher who was Ericson's assistant.

In the evening Garabona came to see him. Garabona was right end, pretty good; Captain.

"The Coach wants you to apologize, Eddie," he said.

"Yeah?" Eddie put it mildly.

"That's what he said. I mean, then it'll be all over; you'll be back with the team."

"Swell."

"Will you do it?"

"Sure."

"You will?"

"Yeah."

"That's wonderful."

"Now go ask him what I'm supposed to apologize for."

"Oh, come on, Eddie."

"Gee, I'm sorry I wouldn't let you slug me, Coach. Think that will do it?"

"He didn't mean anything personal, Eddie. You know how he is."

"I'm sorry, Coach. Try it again and I'll hold still. Okay?"

"Don't be that way, Eddie."

"Crud."

"Please, Eddie. It's important."

"I've been Bissle to you for a long time, Garabona."

"Jesus, Eddie. Jesus." He got up, but did not start out of the room.

Eddie looked up at him. Garabona was a tall guy.

"Who's this Eddie you're talking to?"

"Bissle. Come on, Bissle. Be a good guy. Do it for the team. Doesn't that mean something to you?"

"Sure. Ten other guys that play football."

"You're always saying that you're not going to pay to go to college. They're going to pay you."

"Yeah?"

"I've heard you say it."

"I talk too much."

"Don't you care about a football scholarship?"

"I got a rich father, with a fancy estate."

"You always said you wouldn't take any money from your father to go to college."

"Nice of you to worry about it."

"Damn it, Bissle, every guy on the team's counting on you to square things with the Coach."

"I'll be there."

"What do you mean?"

"I'll be there in my uniform every day, until he tells me to turn it in."

"Come on."

"I'll get on the bus to go to Roper unless he tells me not to. And I'll play if he tells me to play. He's the Coach."

"You won't apologize?"

"Sure. Go find out what for."

That was the way it went. Eddie went to practice; when the Coach didn't call his name for scrimmage or drill, he walked over and worked with the scrubs. When it came time to get ready for the trip, he packed his gym bag, threw his uniform in a duffle, and turned them over to the manager. Then he got on the bus and sat by himself, not in the front and not all the way in back.

In the past there'd always been a speech on the bus. Today there wasn't. Eddie had a magazine. Eddie read it.

Just after they'd turned into the town where Roper was, Garabona came and sat by him.

"Eddie?"

Eddie closed the magazine and looked at the captain.

110

"Will you do it, Eddie? You can just say 'I'm sorry.' You don't have to say what for. Listen, the Coach knows he's wrong, Eddie. Look, we were at his house for supper last night. All the seniors except you. And Mrs. Ericson told us, she said: 'Eric's terribly broken up about this boy Bissle.' Now listen, Eddie."

"I was listening," Eddie said.

"'Eric's terribly broken up over this boy Bissle. Eric says the boy is more or less in the right. Eric says Bissle is the greatest football player of his size he's ever coached.' And you know what she says? She says the Coach just about cries when he talks about you. What do you think about that?"

"Why," Eddie thought about that a moment. "Maybe he cries because he's going to lose a ball game that he was going to lose anyway."

"No, Eddie." Garabona could be a little bit stupid. "It's because he's afraid you'll go away hating him."

"I don't hate anybody," Eddie said.

"But that's why it's so important to him for you to apologize. So that he knows you don't hate him. He told his wife that the most important thing wasn't the score of a football game, but for a coach to have the respect of his players. So if you won't apologize, he just can't use you; because the kids on the team who'll be back next year, they wouldn't respect him."

Eddie thought Garabona was beginning to sound quite a lot like Ericson, and decided to stop talking about it. He opened his magazine.

"Excuse me," he said. "Were you finished?"

Garabona looked stricken. Garabona wasn't a bad guy.

"I just want to finish this article before we get there," Eddie said, politely. He didn't figure on telling Garabona what it meant to him to play in this game, where there'd be some scouts watching, so that he might have a chance to get picked up by an important football college, to play for a big time coach; and maybe, if he could only start growing again, put on some weight, and play like hell for four years, it was almost conceivable that he'd get to do what he wanted to do with his life which was play pro ball. Or if he didn't get that heavy, at least know the game well enough to be a coach himself.

Maybe stuff like that hung on this game. Maybe it didn't. But it figured that there'd be people there watching Roper's two backs

111

and their center who hadn't seen a Mount Pennell game because the team was poor. Being all-conference was nothing Ericson couldn't spoil if he told a scout that Eddie was a problem child; and why wouldn't Ericson do it, if Eddie didn't truckle up an apology? Otherwise, he supposed he'd have to truckle one up for his father. For living. Truckle you, Eddie Bissle. Truckle you, x, y, z. Z for apologize.

Garabona was still there, looking at him.

"He reads me in the starting line-up, I start the game," Eddie said, patiently. "He doesn't, I sit on the bench. He tells me to get off his bench, I stand on the sidelines. He tells me to go take off his football suit, I go take off his football suit. He's the coach, not me."

Ericson did not read Eddie's name in the starting line-up. Ericson paused in the dressing room, holding the slip of paper which contained the line-up in his hand, and asked if anybody had anything to say before they started talking about today's game. Eddie glanced around to see if anybody had anything to say; no one seemed to.

They moved out, trotting, tumbled around on the field. When the referees called Garabona and Cinturon to midfield, Eddie trotted over to the bench. He drew a substitute's blanket from the manager, the first he'd used all season; he'd been in sixty minutes of every other game. He found himself a place on the bench, not next to the coach in the middle, not all the way out at the end. He watched the kickoff.

Roper received. Some guy caught the kick, and threw a lateral to Cinturon who cut across the field and went up the sidelines and scored. Just like that. 6-0.

They'd known the play was coming for weeks; Roper used it once a game. They'd practiced against it for Christ's sake.

Missed the conversion.

Mount Pennell took Roper's kick and got up to the forty. They ran three half-assed plays, Eddie's plays, and made about two yards altogether. Average of two-thirds of a yard per play. Very good. They kicked, Garabona dropping back from end to do the kicking. Not badly; kept it away from the Mexican, anyway.

Roper started right back in, tearing hell out of them in the classic pattern—a gain through the line, a gain through the line, pull in the defense and sprint like hell around end for the first

112

down. Then Grant threw a long pass to Cinturon, and it was 12-0. They lined up to kick the extra point, but it was a fake. The center went to Grant who threw a hard flat pass to nowhere, and Cinturon's head and arms appeared, rising out of a crowd of defending players as if they'd tossed him into the air to meet the ball, a big grin on his face, to take the pass. 13-0.

Mount Pennell received again. Their rooters had been yelling, "Get that ball," for about ten minutes, but the only way they could get it was let Roper score and then take a kickoff. It took them three plays after the runback to come up with something ingenious. It had no number. It consisted of missing every block in the line so that the whole opposition line could get in with the Mount Pennell backfield. By the time Snider, who had the ball, and was supposed to throw a lateral pass, had finished faking his end run, every eligible ball carrier had at least two Roper men with him, and Snider had three. There was absolutely no question of throwing the lateral at this point, so of course Snider threw it. The Roper tackle in whose arms it landed looked rather surprised. Probably never carried before in his life. Ran clumsily along for quite some distance, without anyone bothering him, and then tripped about ten yards short of the touchdown and fell flat. And instead of Roper's supporters groaning when their man fell, they laughed; that's how confident they were.

The laughter seemed to make Mount Pennell's team mad. They lined up on the ten and held. Garabona shifted himself in, from pass defense to line-backing, and he was a good ballplayer. The best Roper could do was move the ball out, away from the sidelines, until, at fourth down, they were nicely centered on the goal posts. At that point they came out of the huddle smiling, having apparently decided to do something practically unheard of in the conference, which was try a field goal. They made it; in fact, Kelley made it, Kelley the center who did their kicking off but didn't ordinarily kick even for extra points, made the field goal. Grant went up and centered to him. Roper seemed to think it was fun, giving their center a chance to score that way. 16-0.

The quarter ended. The teams changed goals. Eddie was dying.

He had never in his life wanted anything so much as to be in there spoiling some of Roper's fun. He figured he could at least keep Kelley out of the backfield. He had watched Grant carefully, and seen more than one play where he'd have spilled the blocking

113

back right into Cinturon's feet. There were six or eight plays which his quarterback hadn't called yet which would gain ground, the way Roper was working defensively; but if they were called without Eddie, they wouldn't work. The two teams weren't that uneven, not sixteen points a quarter; what would that make? Sixty four to nothing? While Eddie was making this calculation, Roper recovered a fumble and started to move again.

"Hey, Bissle."

No, it wasn't the coach's voice. It was that of the kid next to him. "Watch your elbow, will you Bissle? Every time they center the ball you damn near knock me off the bench."

"Sorry," Eddie said. He honestly hadn't realized he was doing that, going with his body on every play that way. He would have said he was just sitting still watching. What an idiot. Roper would pass next play, and their passer was getting the ball off very slow. A guard who could get past Kelley could have that passer for a fat loss. Fat. The pass was good to Cinturon, who jumped for it. Garabona, back on pass defense again, was with him and pulled him down before he could start running. Same play, Eddie told himself; same play coming, different receiver if they've got one. Then when we're opened up for passes, they'll run off tackle, Grant will get Garabona and they'll score. He was hanging on to one hand with the other to keep his idiot elbows still; he was also damn near pulling his fingers off. His teeth hurt from so much biting against one another. If he could get in, he would stop the next pass, hurry the passer if he didn't nail him; he could spill Grant on the off tackle play that followed; he was breathing as loudly as if he'd already done it; it seemed to take all the strength he had to hold himself still.

A figure moved in front of him, blocking his view, and Eddie leaned around to watch so as not to miss the play, not to miss an instant of the torture of seeing it succeed. The figure shifted as he did, moving in front of him again, and Eddie nearly screamed as he jerked himself back, trying to see the field.

"Eddie?"

The figure was the coach. On the field Garabona called time out.

Eddie looked at Ericson, at the stern beefy face staring down at him; Eddie felt love. He was small, hunched in a blanket, looking up at all the strength in the world. Now let the man slug him. Let him slap Eddie's face, back and forth, grab Eddie off the bench

114

by his jersey front and shake him, throw Eddie on the ground, and curse him for the stubborn, sullen little bastard that he was; and then, then let him kick Eddie's ass into that ballgame.

"Eddie boy. . . ?"

Oh no.

Ericson leaned towards him, the big face pleading.

Not like that, coach.

Not like that.

"You say you're sorry, Eddie?" The coach said wildly, loudly, to the silent figure. "Well, that's all right, then. Thanks, Eddie. My fault, too. Now get in there, boy, and play."

Eddie rose slowly, unbelievingly. He hadn't said a word. He let the blanket fall off his shoulders and took a step towards the field. He couldn't look at the coach any longer. He took another step and felt Ericson grab his arm.

"Say it again, Eddie," Ericson pleaded. "Again, so the squad can hear."

"All right," Eddie spat, wrenching his arm loose. He had to be on that field. "Then I'm sorry." And he ran out, crying with anger.

He broke up the pass play just as he'd planned, just as if the Roper team had been kind enough to call it for him. He broke it up, going under Kelley and hitting the passer while he was still loafing back, driving with a passion that had more fury in it than a boy can use. Roper understood the uselessness of this fury, and started the off-tackle play that Eddie had expected next. But Eddie didn't stop it. They'd added a very ordinary little hand-off to it, and just as Eddie realized he was about to clobber a man who no longer had the ball, the man turned out to be Grant, and the man dropping behind Eddie was Kelley, and they mousetrapped Eddie and damn near broke his legs. Cinturon outran Garabona and scored on the play. 23-0.

Grant was more or less sitting on Eddie when the ball went across the line, a cozy way, there on the ground like that, to watch a touchdown.

Eddie blocked the kick for extra point; he swindled Kelley nicely on the play, cool now, dumped the center and went in. He took the ball in his face off the kicker's foot, and that was the caress he'd been needing. After that the afternoon settled into a satisfying contest; Kelley was the best linesman Eddie had ever faced, and they worked fiercely on one another, both of them en-

115

joying it. When Eddie was defending, Kelley was his to rush; when Mount Pennell had the ball, and Kelley became line-backer, there were a number of plays on which he became Eddie's man to block if he could. This was football, Eddie found himself thinking; why let coaches spoil it for him?

He got to tangle with Grant from time to time, too, and Grant was a good ballplayer. Eddie never once got his hands on Cinturon; the Roper quarterback just didn't run Cinturon to Eddie's side of the line. Eddie could understand that; Cinturon was supposed to be a little bit brittle.

In the third period there was a score on each side, making it 37-7, and in the fourth, playing against a bunch of Roper substitutes, Mount Pennell scored again, moving the ball through the line behind Eddie in four and five yard clips. A 37-14 ballgame.

Coach Ericson said it was the worst loss a team of his had ever taken; he also said he was proud of the way they fought, and that the linesmen had reported smelling talcum powder on the Roper team's faces. He didn't say any of these things to Eddie, however, because Eddie and Ericson never spoke to one another again. Perhaps they were equally ashamed.

3.

Lover Man Haynes was an Oklahoma towhead with a sly, tired face. When he was sixteen he married a California woman of thirty-five, and when he was sixteen and a half he married a second, very much like her. Both women seemed rather stout in the newspaper photographs, and both had incomes, one from alimony, the other from a real estate business left by a deceased first husband. When the bigamy was discovered to the newspapers by Lover Man's mother, from whose wretched home the boy had run away, and who was about the same age as the two wives, both women promptly refused to prosecute; neither wanted to give Lover Man up. The realtor's widow told reporters, in a widely published interview: "I'll stand by Lover Man. He is more of a man at sixteen than my husband was as a man." The meaning of this quotation shone through its phraseology to millions of newspaper readers—readers who were indignant, or envious, or who simply found the whole thing a good, harsh joke.

116

The second woman, whose divorce was still interlocutory, so that the marriage to Lover Man had to be set aside, wanted him just as badly. She had, she announced, to enforce her claim, bought him a car, a second-hand Chevie coupe for a hundred and forty dollars. Lover Man didn't know how to drive it, but he liked to sit in it and play the radio.

The newspapers published many photographs of Lover Man, along with interviews of all the principals and reports on his fan mail, which was considerable; it was equally distributed between men who wanted to beat him up and women who offered to wait for him should he happen to go to jail. Just when it appeared that he would not go to jail and the newspapers were ready to forget him, a woman in Oregon, who had been too mortified to say anything up to that point, confessed to her minister that she was a third Mrs. Haynes.

THIRD MRS. LOVER MAN, said the papers enthusiastically, and revived the photographs. The Oregon lady, guided by the preacher whose picture began to appear as well, said that she felt it her duty to prosecute. She said that only she really loved Lover Man, that he should be punished for his own sake, and that she would be waiting for him. She was somewhat more attractive than the others and only thirty-one, but she had children who absorbed much of her income. The reporters hinted that otherwise she would have won Haynes' heart, but they were probably seeing his situation through their own eyes; Lover Man himself never expressed any preference. He only asked to be allowed to keep the car.

"Dear Lover Man Haynes:"

It was Ellen's favorite joke in the spring of her junior year at college, to write Lover Man Haynes fan letters and send them to Tom. Tom was the same age; he looked a little the way Lover Man did in the newspaper pictures—both blond, both rather given to squinting when photographed, though Tom was considerably more robust.

Ellen's roommate, a girl named Alice Hewitt, collaborated on the notes sometimes. Ellen was between men; she and Alice had asked Tom up to college for the Maple Club dance, the informal Easter dance, and they planned to introduce him to some of the younger girls as Lover Man Haynes. It would embarrass Tom tremendously, and he was very cute when he got embarrassed.

117

Dear Lover Man Haynes:
Here is the latest photograph of you from the New Haven
paper. We think you are as divine as ever in it. A whole
house full of glorious young womanhood is waiting here to
squeeze and squash you, so don't let them put you in jail.

Your devoted,

Mystery Fans

P.S. The one eighteen is the best train Saturday and we will
meet it unless we hear differently.

4.

"Tom," Guy said cautiously. "Your sister is not fooled about
you?"

"No," Tom said. He had given Guy the picture to look at; Guy
was pretty fascinated with Lover Man lore, but his appreciation of
Ellen's teasing was quite cautious. "She isn't fooled. Hell, I've got
virgin written on my forehead. That's the point of the joke."

"You go to see her next weekend?"

"Yes."

"Tom, I think we should turn this joke around."

"Be pretty quick turning," Tom said, casually.

It was Tuesday. On Wednesday they had town permission, and
had planned to see the current movie. Wednesday morning Guy
said he wanted to make a phone call; this was at milk break. He
came back looking serious.

"Have a graham cracker," Tom said. "They've opened a really
loathsome box of graham crackers."

"No thanks." Guy poured himself some milk. They stood by
themselves near the head table in the dining hall, where eleven
o'clock milk and crackers were spread.

"But you've got to taste one of these to know how bad the
graham cracker can be."

"Tom."

"What?"

"Today, both of the Browning girls will be home in the afternoon. I talked to Ruby; she is playing hookey."

"Oh."

118

"She says to come and see them. Both of us."

"Oh . . . well."

"Ruby wants to meet you. She's been asking for weeks."

"She's the younger one?"

"Yes. Very cute. She has your picture I gave her."

"Yeah, I know but . . . she's awfully young isn't she?" Tom put the bitten graham cracker down; it didn't seem to taste so hilarious any more.

Guy shrugged. "I don't know. Fifteen. Sixteen. God knows how many boys she has had. She loves it. She wants to meet you."

"Yeah. Well. What do you know?" Tom made himself grin.

"We'll go, huh?"

"All right." Tom put the milk down, beside the graham cracker. He wished he hadn't already drunk some of it. "All right. What do you have to do? Call them back?"

"No. No *compadre*." Guy drank off his own milk, slapped the glass down, hit Tom lightly on the arm and went into a fighter's crouch. He spoke in Spanish. "I told her we'd come." Feinted with his left. "Told them, Tomaso, that we'd be there. Miss Ruby is excited." Crossed with his right, stopped it just at Tom's chin, and held the knuckles there until Tom smiled back.

Between then and three o'clock, when the school station wagon left, Guy gave Tom much advice:

"Don't neck with her. That changes the subject," and, "You know what she told me? Said she might be only Jeanette's little sister, but she wasn't going to miss anything Jeanette was getting out of life."

"She'll hate you if you don't. She expects it. I told her."

"Yes, I'll give you some; with her you must use them."

"If you don't tell her it's the first time, how can she know?"

Tom couldn't eat any lunch. Tom couldn't pay attention in class. He gave a wrong answer to a Latin vocabulary question which so astonished Mr. Fairless, the teacher, that he checked the word in a book before telling Tom he was wrong. By the time Tom sat in the station wagon, Guy humming confidently beside him in the rear seat where only proctors might sit, Tom had sweat through a shirt for the second time.

Jeanette and Ruby Browning were Numbers 13 and 16 in Guy's book. He had known Jeanette for some time; he had told Tom of catching Ruby twice when her older sister was out. He also said, chattering along in Spanish as they rode to town, that he had been planning an encounter for Tom with one or the other Browning sister for some time, delaying only because he couldn't be sure which was more suitable.

"Since Jeanette is jealous, clearly it must be Ruby."

"Ruby is not jealous?" Tom asked in Spanish.

"Ruby does not care."

As they left the other students, who were headed for the movies, and turned up the hill, Guy gave Tom his final instructions: "Don't try to keep thinking what you're supposed to do next. Relax. Be natural. Don't let her think she can get away with anything less, but as far as details go, leave it to Ruby."

To get to the apartment where the Browning sisters lived, you went through a tailor shop. The tailor was no connection of the family; he rented from Mrs. Browning who had been left with the old building by her husband, once the operator of a newspaper and magazine shop, where the tailor now worked. The tailor was a Lithuanian who spoke little English; he stared at the boys but said nothing as they came into his shop.

"Is this the only entrance?" Tom asked.

"No. There's one to the kitchen from the alley. But if someone sees us coming in this way, we're having clothes made."

It was a warm day in March, and the little shop was overheated. Guy asked the old tailor how a sports jacket he had ordered was coming along; the Lithuanian shook his head.

"Fitting him next week."

Guy nodded. He joined Tom again and they moved on towards the rear. Tom felt weak and out of control below the waist, numb and stifled above. The last time he had felt this way was in Guadalajara, on their trip to Mexico the year before, when Guy had wanted to take him to a brothel; they had some beer then, and he had thought that was the trouble. It had given him a reason for refusing the brothel; now he could only follow.

Guy pushed aside a curtain; there was a door behind it. They went into a short corridor. The air was colder but very stale. Guy opened the next door and called out:

"Hello."

A voice said: "Guy. Hey, Jeanette, it's Guy. They're here." And Tom was standing in a living room, staring at Ruby Browning.

She was a wary-looking girl, short, rather full in face, shoulders

120

and chest, tapering considerably to a small waist and narrow hips. Her hair was dark, her face quite pretty in a firm-jawed way, her skin smooth and dusky. She was wearing a skirt and sweater. Guy glanced at her; Tom supposed he winked.

"You two kids get acquainted," Guy said. "I've got business inside." And, giving Tom a covert push towards Ruby, Guy went into the next room where, presumably, Jeanette was waiting.

Ruby, who had not gotten up, smiled at Tom. He had no idea what to say or what to do, but, because Guy had pushed him, he continued moving towards her until he was too close to do anything but lean down and kiss her. She lifted her face for this readily enough. Buzzing so with his own awkwardness that he made no record of the sensation of her mouth on his—though the girls he had kissed before were few enough—Tom sat down beside her, clutched at her convulsively, and kissed her again. This time she put her arms around his neck and kissed back, a sensation of which he couldn't help being aware because it had never happened before and was surprising. He felt no real desire, only a superficial acknowledgement that she was desirable.

They held the kiss until she broke away and said,

"Wow! Come up for air."

Tom had no control over the expression on his face, but it felt like a smile.

"My mother said a cute thing this morning," Ruby said. "She's so cute. She works for the telephone company, and Jeanette was trying to get into the bathroom but Mom was there first. So she said: 'Sorry, Miss. The line is busy.' Isn't that cute?"

A laugh achieved itself out of Tom's dry throat and, to prevent her hearing how forced it was, Tom kissed her ear which moved towards his mouth and became the closest thing to him. Guy had once said something about kissing ears; Ruby squealed quietly and hugged him till he took his mouth away.

"You're fast," she said. "Aren't you? Wow!" He didn't know how to answer that. She pushed his hands away and stood up. "Don't you want some wine, Tom?" she asked. "Guy brought us a bottle." Tom shot to his own feet beside her; he supposed he had spoiled everything and the supposition brought him great relief. He nodded, and started to say thanks, but she went on:

"Jeanette doesn't like it, but I do. Just a minute, Tom." She looked at him and added. "You're nice, Tom. Standing up like

121

that for me. I like boys who do things like that." She started out of the room, and paused. "Most boys aren't very polite, are they? Guy gave me your picture." He started to say that he knew, but she was already moving again, this time towards a door, not the one Guy had used. "I'll be right back."

Tom looked around the room in which they had been sitting. In addition to the sofa there were two overstuffed chairs which matched it; they were all covered with something faded, and the seats were lumpy. There was a small worn rug, wrinkled on the floor. One of the table lamps made some pretense of elegance, with an elaborate gold-fringed shade; it looked like the kind of shade you might win at a shooting gallery. There were two calendars on the wall, and a photograph of a young sailor.

He stepped towards the door by which Ruby had left the room, and saw her in the kitchen. She had already poured wine into two jelly glasses; beside them on the table was some store cake and half a package of hot dogs, remaining probably from her lunch. Ruby had her hand up under the back of her sweater and he supposed he must have disarranged her brassiere somehow, and that she was fixing it. Tom stepped away from the door and looked at one of the calendars. It had a drawing of a girl in a sort of cowboy suit but with very short, tight pants and a bolero jacket fastened over the points of bulging and otherwise naked breasts.

Ruby came in. "Caught you," she said, and then laughed. "I didn't mean anything. Here." She handed Tom one of the glasses of wine. He took it, thinking that two minutes before he couldn't have kept it down. Now that nothing was going to happen, he drank it to kill his extraordinary thirst.

"Hey, you like that, don't you?" Ruby said, sipping at hers; it seemed to Tom that her face no longer looked wary; now it was a greedy face, but in a childlike and not unattractive way. "Me too. Do you like her? On the calendar, I mean? Jeanette looks something like that. That's why we put it up." She went back and sat on the sofa, just where she had been before. "You'd have seen Jeanette, only she's drum majorette at school, and when she comes home from practice she likes to take a shower and not get dressed. . . ." She caught herself. "Ooooh, what I said."

Tom laughed, somewhat more easily this time, and thought of Guy and the girl who looked something like the calendar drawing, together in the other room. His head must have turned to the door because Ruby said, dropping her voice:

122

"You can't peek. She leaves a key in the keyhole."

Just then a new girl's voice spoke from behind the very door she was speaking of.

"Don't you kids drink any of my wine," it said.

Ruby gasped and gulped hers down. Tom moved to take the glass from her and she cried: "Don't come in," and clutched his hand. Tom knelt and shoved both glasses under the sofa.

"Don't do anything we wouldn't do," the other girl's voice said, and there were steps shuffling away from the door. Ruby was whispering and Tom leaned close to hear.

"It isn't her wine. Guy brought it to both of us." She was grasping Tom's shoulder and he sat beside her once more. She moved around to be kissed and Tom thought, rather calmly, oh, maybe it is going to happen, after all. A moment later, not certain how his hand had managed to make such a trip, he thought with an equally surprising calm, oh, she wasn't fixing her brassiere in the kitchen, she was taking it off. Some rather purposeful twisting was going on, and it seemed to place his hands conveniently without any particular directing of them on his part. Every half minute she would stop kissing, hold one of his hands with hers, and say: "Gosh, you're even fresher than Guy," or, "you've got Roman hands," and finally it seemed as if he were pushing her down though he hadn't tried to. They clung together and he dug at his clothing and found, as he did, that he was thinking of the movie they hadn't seen. *Snow White and the Seven Dwarfs;* now he wouldn't get a chance to see it because today was Wednesday and they would change the bill tomorrow.

"Don't look at me, Tom. It isn't nice," Ruby said. She too was getting her clothes off, much more efficiently than he. He sat up and finished removing his. When he turned back she had put a sofa cushion on top of her midsection, and she kept it there until they were lying together again; then she reached around his back to drop it on the floor. I'm in for it, Tom thought, losing whatever touch of excitement he had felt when the cushion dropped, in the blind delay of putting a condom on.

He began to copulate with her and it felt all right, but somehow remote; he wondered how long he would have to keep doing it. He pretended to be excited because she was, but he really found himself disinterested and wondered why; he felt that he could keep this up indefinitely but doubted that he would have an orgasm; she was calling him "Lover," now, and he thought of Lover Man

123

Haynes and of how they were turning Ellen's silly joke. It was distasteful to think of Ellen, so he kept moving in what seemed to be the inevitable way, and tried to review what had happened, how he had gotten into such an odd position. Guy was right; Ruby had done it all. She had put him through all the steps that might have occurred in a normal seduction with an experienced boy, he thought, and put herself through all the responses; she had used him like a dummy, almost—and he had been a dummy, Tom thought suddenly. An exact dummy. Because he hadn't said a word since he entered this room, now that he thought about it; not one. Several times he'd been about to say something and been prevented. Golly.

He'd better open his mouth. He'd better make some sound in this room besides forced breathing and fake laughter—golly, you could rig a dummy up to laugh.

"Ruby," he said, experimentally. He thought his voice might come out strangely, after all the silence, but it was like the rest of him, perplexingly unaffected by what was going on.

She misunderstood. "Wait, oh, just a second lover. A second." Then, "Now," and she relaxed under him, pushed his face away from her cheek and looked up.

"You're some man," she said. Tom guessed she must mean for him to start moving again so he did.

"Hey," she said, holding stiff for a moment; then she began to move again against him. It went pretty much the same way; he remained capable but unresponsive, trying to puzzle out how long he must keep this up in order for her to be convinced of his competence. She relaxed once more, going through quite a lot of thrashing before she did. By the time they repeated it all again, and she relaxed for the third time, his back was getting very tired; the bad shoulder throbbed as it hadn't for over a year; still, for all the effort, he felt no real participation, no tension and, of course, no release. She said:

"Oh golly, Tom let's rest. Are you all right?"

He knew what she meant but he dissimulated. "Sure."

"You're so terrific. You mind resting?"

The words were welcome. He rolled away quickly and got her sofa cushion for her. He found that he was curious to look at her, and he did for a moment, holding the cushion away. She snatched it.

124

"Don't be naughty," she said. She adjusted the cushion. She sighed. "I never knew a boy like you. So terrific. Not even Guy." Tom guessed that was meant to be flattering. "You think we better get dressed?"

Tom nodded, stood up, and pulled on his underwear shorts. She got up, turning away too. Suddenly, as they stood back to back, dressing, two or three feet from one another, he felt very tender towards her. He wished he could say something to her that would be wise and helpful, but it was quite impossible. He wasn't wise.

He turned to look, buttoning his shirt, and she had put on her skirt and top but was still barefoot; her pretty dark hair was a mess, and as she glanced around, meeting his eyes, the mouth, with its lipstick gone, looked childish and swollen. And sorry.

"Tom," she asked, unexpectedly wistful. "Did you like me all right?"

He nodded, slowly, sat down on the sofa and held out his hand. She came over and sat down, and he put his arm around her. He stroked her arm and felt about ninety years old and as if, in spite of the way it had happened, he had taken advantage of innocence.

"You're a lovely girl, Ruby," he said.

"Oh, I love you too." She said it with such gratitude, such intensity, such earnestness, that he could not bring himself to correct her about what he had said himself.

"Listen, Tom, I'll . . . I mean, I'll save it for you. Really. I don't date this way with boys at school. I don't . . . do you believe that?"

"Yes," Tom said, as if it mattered whether he believed it or not, as if anything mattered but whether he cared. He wondered if he did. He tightened his arm around her, seeing the room again, thinking how dreary school must be for her if she preferred to play hookey, to stay in this drab place alone, morning after morning, with hot dogs and store cake for comfort.

"You and Guy are different," she was saying. "I mean you've been around so much, and you know what it's about . . . but I won't even with Guy any more; honestly."

She paused, waiting for him to accept the offer.

"All right, Ruby," he said, troubled. "All right."

Guy waited until they were outside again, out past the tailor shop, before he said: "All right, mister? All right?"

"Oh, yeah, sure," Tom said. "Wonderful." He had half forgotten

125

the first purpose of the afternoon in his wonder at a girl's having said she loved him.

"She's a crazy little thing, isn't she? The sister's different."

"Crazy?"

Guy shrugged it off. "I mean the way she likes it so much. Hey you know when you went to the john, I asked her. How she liked you. She didn't want Jeanette to hear, so she came over and whispered: 'I didn't know a boy could be that good.'"

"I didn't do anything," Tom said. "Not really."

"You must be a genius for this, too. You must be."

Tom shook his head. He was too tired to explain.

Tom lay awake that night a long time after their lights were off, thinking of Ruby. He thought of the different ways her face looked: wary, greedy, childish, wistful. The next afternoon he broke bounds, leaving school through a patch of woods and walking half a mile to the road, then on in to town because there were no rides, to see her again. Breaking bounds was something he had never done before, though Guy had a hundred times. Guy had work to make up but he offered good-humoredly to go along. Tom refused.

"Once you start in," Guy said, sending him off, "you're like a grass fire. Watch out, girls." Tom didn't mind his friend's incomprehension; he began to understand that there were things in the world for Guy which were not for Tom. What took him to town that day was a compulsion as strong as sex but much different: it was pity. He was going to tell Ruby Browning before it was too late that he wasn't honestly in love with her.

Yet when he saw her, he couldn't be sure that it was so. Her sister was not at home, though she might come in any time; they went into the bedroom, as tawdry as the rest of the place, and sat together on the bed holding hands. Tom no longer felt ninety years old. He felt nine; he felt confused.

Ruby said that Jeanette had poured out the rest of the wine to punish them for drinking it without permission, and Tom said that was all right. Ruby was visibly restless because he didn't make any move to do more than hold hands, and Tom began to see that the renunciation he had planned, which was to have impressed her with the beauty of its self-sacrifice, would have no such effect. Renunciation would be as selfish as anything else; she didn't want to be renounced. Yet what else could he do for Ruby, without being

126

a fraud? Again he had that sense of needing wisdom and of lacking it.

"Gee, you were such a whirlwind yesterday," Ruby said. She pulled his cheek to her and started to kiss it quite violently. Crazy? Tom asked himself. Who was crazy and what did crazy mean? He thought that probably he had better do it again with her, and that would reassure her. He felt an even greater disinclination than he had the day before but he managed to repeat his performance except that this time it was not so easy to stay erect. He found himself bringing to mind an image of Connie Marston, and pretended that he was lying in bed sick, with Connie showing herself to him, and that helped. But there was still no climax, no release of tension, for there was no tension.

It was all wrong. He thought, as Ruby finished and he got away, that she must have sensed it.

To his dismay she said that he was even better than the day before.

"Ruby," he said, sitting up, naked and miserable. "This is all wrong."

"What is?"

"I was a virgin till yesterday," Tom said. "In a way, I still am."

"What?"

"I am."

"I don't get you," Ruby said. She sat up herself, so disturbed by what he was saying that she forgot to cover herself. As she did the sight of her moving naked broke his resistance to the whole thing, like a chain snapping, and he seized her and bore her backwards, murmuring hoarse and urgent things, reaching his long-delayed conclusion in a moment's passionate crowding.

Now he felt triumph. Now he loved her.

"Tom," she complained, struggling out from under his weight. "You didn't use a . . . thing."

"But that was more like it, wasn't it?" He cried. "Wasn't that better. I mean at last. . . ."

"No." She shook her head, drawing farther away from him. "You shouldn't be like that. I couldn't even move and you hurt my arm."

They dressed in silence after that, and then, just as he was about to say goodbye and go out, thinking that the thing had solved itself, she said: "Tom do you still love me?"

"Oh, God," he said, not as a curse but in confusion.

"I love you anyway, only you scared me then."

"I'm sorry."

"You won't be like that any more? Because you loved me yesterday and you weren't like that."

She said this with perfect certainty.

Tom thought: but we don't know what we're doing. We're like four year olds playing with a loaded shotgun. We're like those religious people who think they can handle rattlesnakes.

"Yes, I did love you yesterday," he said, trying at last to be honest. "But it wasn't when we were . . . doing it. It was afterwards. Because you were sad."

It was too late for honesty. "I'll be scared, Tom, till I have my monthly. You know? So we'll know it's all right? Tom, you have to call me up every day when you can't come and see me, or I'll be so scared."

"I can't," Tom said. "I have to go and see my sister this weekend."

Ruby started to cry. Ruby tried to stop herself. Tom loved her worse than ever. He said he would come tomorrow, he would call her from Hazlitt Saturday night, he would call from school when he got back on Sunday.

When Ellen and Alice Hewitt, her roommate, greeted him as Lover Man Haynes that weekend, Tom knew that they supposed they understood his flushing at it; actually he hadn't stopped to think that the joke would be sure to come up. He tried to act as if it were just a funny kind of teasing to him. He hoped they would get tired of it, but when he was dressed, and arrived at the club, and asked Ellen if he could use the phone, she said:

"Tommy! A girl."

He couldn't even deny it.

"I knew you were Lover Man. Oh, Alice, he's calling one of those women in California."

"He has us," Alice said. "But we aren't enough." They laughed him into the phone booth, where he closed the door. Class after class of Maple Club girls had written numbers on its walls, and drawn hearts around them, and erased them, and written others; he stared at the numbers. He saw Alice and Ellen watching him, making swoon faces at him.

Ruby was demure on the phone; she said she was fine and that she missed him.

Tom had a weird time at the dance. The younger girls weren't interested in him of course, but he was kid enough so that girls in Ellen's class could make him the evening's pet; ordinarily he would have played up to this and enjoyed it. It was a younger brother role that he had played easily for years, even the embarrassments were easy. Or had been.

It wasn't a large dance, just an informal one with a small local orchestra, a cozy, friendly sort of party; but every time he started to forget himself a little in enjoyment, some girl would swoop down crying, "Lover Man Haynes." There was a big girl in red called Willa who was especially shrill about it. At intermission, she wanted to clear the floor and introduce him as Haynes. She and several others tried to pull him into the center; it was beginning to rattle him. He hung onto a column and wouldn't be pulled.

Then he was afraid Ellen would think he was being a lousy sport about the joke, and decided to try to keep taking it. They were dancing again; he was with someone called Valerie who wanted to know what his secret was, Mr. Lover, should she try to guess? Ellen came up and cut in, and led him out onto the porch.

"Something the matter, Tommy?" she asked, as they stood in the quiet.

He yearned to tell her. "No," he said.

"Come on. What's wrong?"

He couldn't tell her. Not Ellen. She was too beautiful, this sister, too immaculate; he looked at her shining blonde hair and knew she could never be touched by anything like this.

"There's nothing wrong, Bismarck," he said. He felt very lonely; there was no one he could tell, not even Guy.

The big girl in red opened the door on them. "Lover Man," she said. "Lover Man Haynes."

Ellen said: "I think that's enough of that one, Willa," but before she finished the sentence Alice, Ellen's roommate, pushed past Willa and said:

"There he is. You can't keep him to yourself, Ellen," and ran to Tom. After her came other girls, crying "Lover Man," laughing and pushing. There weren't enough men at their dance. They were trying to pull Tom back to the dance floor, and he looked at Ellen, feeling almost frightened by them, Ellen nodded permission.

129

"I'm sorry," Tom said edging off. "I've got to go. I'm . . . I've got to go now. Good night everybody." He had a room at a professor's house.

"No!" cried Willa; she caught his arm.

"Back to his wife?" a girl said.

"His wives you mean."

"Don't leave us, Lover Man."

"Oh, sigh. Oh sigh."

"Kiss us all goodnight."

"Yes. Kiss us."

They surrounded him.

Tom ran.

The last thing he saw was that a girl in blue had followed onto the lawn, and laughing voices were calling, "Lover Man. Come back. Lover Man. Come back."

When he called Ruby Sunday night, back at school, she was very excited at the thought of seeing him again next afternoon, so he didn't tell her that he couldn't get town permission; he broke bounds again. And again on Tuesday. He no longer questioned whether he was in love with her. He had to be. On Wednesday he went in with the station wagon, with Guy, but Guy was not seeing Jeanette; he asked Tom to tell Jeanette that he was restricted to school. He had a new girl. Tom didn't much like the thought of lying to Ruby's sister the first time he met her, but Jeanette wasn't there, any more than she had been Monday or Tuesday. They skipped Thursday, but Tom spent so much of it thinking of Ruby that on Friday he broke bounds again. There was sex every day, her way, not his, though he was fully potent now.

There was a pay phone on which the boys were allowed to make out-going calls—incoming ones were received in the Head's office and the boy called to an extension by the duty proctor. Tom phoned Ruby every morning, during milk break. She hadn't gone to school all week.

The phone calls were beginning to be noticed; several boys were aware of how consistently Tom was breaking bounds. The school began to talk about it. Younger boys told each other Tom was planning to get married, and looked at him curiously.

Chowderhead, who was Chief Proctor, came to Tom's room Saturday morning and asked if it were true that Tom was seeing a lot of a girl in town.

130

"Yes."

"What's she like?"

"I don't know. A girl."

"You in love with her or something?"

"I guess so, Chowderhead."

"Be careful, will you Tom? You're going to get caught, breaking bounds. Fairless was looking for you yesterday."

"I'll be careful," Tom said.

He made the same promise to Guy; he broke it on Monday, because Ruby didn't answer when he called in the morning and he couldn't bear not having word from her.

"There're other girls, Tommy," Guy said that evening. "You've got all your life."

"But she has to see me, or she gets scared and lonely," Tom said, and confessed to Guy that Ruby was afraid she might miss her period.

"It won't help her if you get caught breaking bounds."

"Oh, Guy, when did you ever worry about getting caught?"

"For me, never. For you, all the time." He smiled at Tom affectionately. "Through you I am paying for the sin of not worrying."

5.

Ellen, between men, was not unhappy. She had a gift for small gaieties, and she liked other girls. There were always little jokes, ceremonies, endearments, developing from day to day at college, a mild, pleasant flow of mild excitements between girls into which concern for a man could seem intrusive and upsetting.

On the weekend of Tom's visit she was just over, by two weeks, having been quite seriously in love with a wild and very attractive boy from Tufts, who drank too much and drove cars too fast—a spoiled, explosively charming boy with curly hair. Tad and Ellen had been a celebrated couple through the winter. Other girls told one another how they met: that Tad had come for Christmas Formal as the date of a rich Silver Birch girl, seen Ellen at the dance; stopped dancing with his date, crossed the floor, cut in on Ellen without an introduction, danced with no one else, shaken his head when anyone tried to cut, and the Silver Birch girl had burst into tears as the evening went on, and had to be taken home by friends because Tad would not leave Ellen.

131

This romantic anecdote was true enough, except that when Ellen's supporters told it they said that Ellen had been cool to him that evening, which wasn't so. A Silver Birch version which had Tad too drunk to know what he was doing and Ellen leading him on was not accurate either. Tad had done the leading; Ellen, however, had not been cool. Excited, she had played his enthusiasm back to him in a way she knew was shameless; they had adored each other instantly. Or rather, Ellen came to think after it was over, each had adored the image of himself, herself, as half of the beautiful couple they would make.

They did. People—except of course at Silver Birch, and to some extent at Elm—responded to the sight of Tad and Ellen as an incarnation, a movie-made-flesh, a magazine cover come to life: Tad curly and shining, Ellen flushed and always laughing as he pulled her after him, always moving fast, fast to the next place, the next game, the next thrill.

Silver Birch said that Ellen slept with Tad, had spent a weekend with him, unchaperoned, in Boston; the first statement was false, the second true. They were in too great a hurry, almost, for kissing, let alone bed; they hadn't seen a bed at all the weekend in Boston, slept for an hour in an armchair someplace fully clothed, too busy having fun; there was something unworldly, newborn, in their joy together, and simply to see them dancing, running, driving, was to know all there was to know about them. A fast kiss, a hard squeeze, public or private, and off they'd race. . . .

"Honestly, Ellen, I knew you'd be famous," Bev Hill said. "I just wish I had your courage." Courage? There was no time, for once, to stop and think what Bev could mean, not with Tad on the phone, or about to drive up, about to . . . do you know what he did? He was taking flying lessons, part of a college program, had someone fly him over Hazlitt one day in a little red plane, circle Maple Club three times, and Tad jumped out, arriving in the middle of the campus to call on Ellen by parachute.

Would she not sleep with such a jumper, such a flyer, if he wanted her to? Ellen supposed so, Ellen promised herself she would, but he never suggested it.

She wasn't sure why they should have had a quarrel; only one. Something slightly critical she said, to something slightly irritating he did, some small exchange of crustiness that spoiled the perfect ease with which they had gone along—or perhaps it was only she

132

who had gone along, resisting nothing, finding nothing to resist, delighted to do whatever he liked, to cry yes to whatever he said. There was only that one slight quarrel, but one was more than perfection could stand. Should she have known that?—anyway, it was over in March. Bad things always happened to Ellen in March.

After a day or two of numbness, she found herself in Alice Hewitt's hands; Alice, her sophomore friend and junior roommate, took on the task of interesting Ellen in life again with characteristic energy. Alice's was the drive that kept the Lover Boy Haynes joke going once Ellen had thought it might be fun to send the first fan note to Tom. Alice's was the capacity for making plans that got Tom up for the weekend. In fact, Alice's was the six dollars loaned to send Tom his train fare.

Alice was a new kind of friend for Ellen, a girl with serious ideas, convictions, political opinions, an earnest student of history and sociology, dreaming of democracy in Spain, death to Quisling, and a master's degree. It made her very much a Maple Club sort of girl except for one thing, which was her bust. She had very large, out-thrust breasts and she dressed to emphasize them, which interested men very much. Alice, of course, didn't mind interesting men, yet a bust like that seemed inappropriate for her, as if a mistake had been made and Alice were wearing the breasts of some more frivolous girl, who really needed them.

The rehabilitation of Ellen, after Tad had gone, required, of course, other measures besides having a kid brother up for a dance; the only cure for man trouble is more man trouble. So Alice began taking Ellen to Yale.

This was a rather odd thing. Yale was where Elm Club girls did their dating, and Silver Birch to some extent; but Alice Hewitt, Maple Club and proud of it, went to Yale for every function, and through her Ellen learned that only in the eyes of Elm Club colonizers did all the natives of New Haven look alike. There were men at Yale who were untidy poets, long haired drama students, bearded painters; there were even Democrats and radicals. It was to parties with men like these that Alice went and took Ellen that spring, and though these men talked of writers and revolutions, and were impatient at not being in the war, they seemed to find Ellen's hair and Alice's bust as bewitching as did any other kind of man, except perhaps for those few strange ones of whom Alice whispered that they didn't like girls at all.

Ellen was easily popular with Alice's friends. The men did not despise her naiveté, far from it: they instructed it. And from her standpoint, it was lovely to be going to Yale at last. She didn't let it spoil things when Bev Hill, inquiring who Ellen was seeing in New Haven, had never heard of any of the men ("They must be the interesting ones at Yale, not the old, dull silly things I see.") Bev was half-engaged to the captain of the Yale crew, president of a senior society.

It was at one of the political parties, with men on both sides of her crying that international morality required a U.S. declaration of war against the fascists, that Ellen first met Harrison Walle. He was a quiet-looking man, sucking on a pipe, a little more formally dressed than the others, and he was listening to the arguments with attention.

"There should have been an expeditionary force in Ethiopia," one was saying. "There should have been an AEF in China."

The other was arguing, retrospectively, for a League of Nations with teeth and Ellen was, she hoped, looking intelligent, and trying to suppress a silly image of a league of toothless nations which had come into her mind.

The quiet man moved away from their group after a moment, and Ellen watched his back; he was wearing a tweed suit, the only suit in the room. Most of the men were in shirt sleeves.

"Who's he?" one of the boys asked; the other didn't know. A little later, off to her right, she heard their host at the party challenging the man in tweed to state an opinion on Lindbergh's position about American involvement in the European war. The man in tweed said he admired Lindbergh, and thought the liberal press was crucifying the man unfairly.

There was a great storm of rebuttal, which seemed to leave the quiet man unshaken; he stated his case much more politely than his opponents, Ellen noticed. He was for neutrality. Alice was one of those arguing at him and Ellen suddenly thought that Alice was being shrill, even a little coarse. She wondered what the stranger was doing with this group. She left the ones she was sitting with, after the argument subsided, and joined some others. She kept seeing the stranger in tweed in the crowded room, and once or twice their eyes met.

Someone told her, though she didn't ask, that the man's name was Harrison Walle. Someone else said that he came from Michi-

134

gan and thought like a midwesterner. Someone else said he was a first year graduate student of economics and had made a senior society as an undergraduate, and that he sometimes sought out their group to hear opinions other than his own—Walle and the host knew one another from some advanced economics course in which they had been the only students enrolled the year before.

So Harrison Walle was out of place here, Ellen, thought, and began to wonder if she were out of place herself; before the evening ended they had managed to wonder this confidentially to one another.

He phoned her at Hazlitt the next day; within a short time, and rather to Alice Hewitt's discomfort, Ellen and Harrison were seeing one another steadily. It was a staid, even humorless, romance, but there was peace in it, or so it seemed to Ellen.

6.

Mr. Fairless was correcting papers. He was, curiously enough, correcting one of Beniger's Latin papers when the phone call came. He was thinking with a certain testiness, for his pride was involved in this boy's work, that he must find some way of speaking to Beniger about the carelessness of his papers. They were accurate enough, but sloppy, words crossed out instead of erased, handwriting hasty; Newt Parker had been digging into Mr. Fairless quite nastily about Beniger's lapse in attentiveness to his classwork; Newt Parker had had boys twice in his science courses, in former years, who led the school academically, who got spectacular scholarships to college. And while Mr. Fairless had had a good modern language student from time to time, he had never had, never hoped to have, a boy in classics who would challenge the records of Newt Parker's famous Morcombe, in physics, or little Bimstein in biology.

So, when the phone rang, Mr. Fairless had just written on a sheet of scrap paper, and was considering transferring to Beniger's Latin composition, the sentence: "I am entering a mark of 50 in my grade book, which is an average between 100 for the correctness of this composition and 0 for its neatness." The only thing preventing him from using the formula was that he didn't actually want to put a fifty in the grade book for Beniger.

135

And the phone rang.

Mr. Fairless was at the Head's desk, because he was Duty Master that morning.

"Hello."

"Is this the Roper School?" It sounded like one of the other master's daughters.

"Yes it is." He said it in the pleasant, slightly teasing voice one uses to children on the telephone. He was still thinking more of Newt Parker than anything else. Newton Parker, Newton Berwell Parker. Once Mr. Fairless had grown a mustache, spending weeks and weeks on it, and Newton Berwell Parker got smart and grew one, too, and the Head made a very embarrassing joke about the mustaches in faculty meeting, all but telling them to shave them off, and Mr. Fairless did shave his off, only New Ton Ber Well Par Ker laughed and kept his and still wore it today and it was bushy and horrid, not light and unobtrusive as Mr. Fairless' mustache had been.

"Could I talk to Tom Beniger?"

"I beg your pardon?"

"Could I talk to Tom Beniger?"

He remembered that Beniger had a sister; perhaps the boy's family was in town.

"I'm sorry. The boys aren't allowed to have phone calls during the day," Mr. Fairless said. "But if you leave your number he can call you at eleven."

"He knows my number."

"Does he?"

"Oh yes, he usually calls me at eleven, but couldn't you get him now? It's awfully important."

"Who is this calling?" Mr. Fairless asked.

There was a short silence. Then the child repeated in a breaking voice, "Couldn't you get him please? Please?"

"No, the boys can't have calls except in the evenings; anyway, I imagine he's in class. But if you'll tell me who it is, he can call you at eleven."

"Are you . . . are you a teacher?"

"Yes. This is Mr. Fairless."

"Oh . . . oh, golly. Oh, golly," the girl said.

"Tom is a student of mine, and I'm very fond of him," Mr. Fairless said. "Won't you tell me what this important matter is?"

136

"Oh. . . . Oh, goodbye."

"Wait a minute. Perhaps I can help you. Wait." Mr. Fairless said. She obeyed. "Do you know Tom very well?"

"Oh, yes," she said.

"Are you his, uh, girl friend?"

"Please, Mister, couldn't you just get him? Just this once? I mean if you like him and everything."

"But if I were to get him, who would I say was calling?"

"Ruh . . . Ruby."

Ruh . . . Ruby? That certainly wasn't Beniger's sister. Beniger's sister was Ull . . . Ellen. Or perhaps Ulleanor. No, there were no Ruh . . . Ruby's in the Beniger family. "Ruby who?" asked Mr. Fairless.

"He knows."

"And what shall I tell him it's about?"

"He knows. Honestly, he'd want to come and talk to me. I know he would."

"You say he calls you every day?"

"Yes."

"And what is it that can't wait until eleven o'clock today?"

There was a silence. Then she said, tearfully:

"Will you get him now?"

"I told you, I can't Ruby. Tom's in class."

"But you said you'd help."

"You haven't told me what it's about."

Ruh . . . Ruby hung up.

Mr. Fairless couldn't move for a moment; he was more or less transfixed with agitation. It ran through his mind that a policeman would signal the operator and command her to trace the call, and his hand actually moved towards the tines in the phone cradle to put this wild, cinematic impulse into operation. Embarrassment about what the operator would think, how curtly she might refuse, stopped the hand, and Mr. Fairless hung up. Then he seized his marking pencil and scrawled "O," on Beniger's Latin composition. He clenched his fists and rubbed his temples with the knuckles. Then he looked at the Duty list, and saw that Cinturon was Duty Proctor from nine to ten, which meant now. He rang the Proctor's buzzer furiously, and Cinturon came in.

"Yes, sir?"

Mr. Fairless detested the boy. He was about to confront him

137

with Ruby's name, and demand information which he was certain Cinturon would have, but checked himself; if he did he would get nothing but supercilious lies. So he controlled the urge to accuse and said, as casually as he could:

"A phone message for Beniger. He has a sister, doesn't he?"

"Yes, sir."

"I suppose it's she." He wrote, *Please Call Ruby* on a piece of paper, folded it, gave it to Cinturon to deliver, and pretended to be absorbed in his corrections.

". . . but you mustn't try to call me at school . . ." Beniger was saying, as Mr. Fairless walked past the phone booth, an open book in his hands, at eleven.

". . . I don't dare this afternoon . . ." Beniger was saying as Mr. Fairless walked back again. And then: "Oh, Ruby. Yes, darling. I'm sorry. Yes, I will."

Darling? Dar Ling Ruh Ru By.

Classes were out at three; Beniger had history until then. At two forty-five Mr. Fairless stationed himself in the woods, sweating. At three ten, Beniger practically ran into Mr. Fairless' pudgy arms.

7.

After the first couple of days, Tom took it pretty well, but Guy had lots of trouble with him those first couple of days. It wasn't the list of restrictions themselves, though the Head had invented some new ones for Tom—it was the purpose of them which made Tom so rebellious; the purpose, of course, was to make it impossible for Tom to see or speak to Ruby. To that end, he was not only restricted to school bounds, but assigned to work details and remedial study hall in all his free time. Guy added another restriction of his own: since he was the courier, he thought he had better do a little censoring of correspondence. Tom had tried to defy the Head, said he would leave school and go away somewhere with Ruby, and the Head apparently made the same three points Guy made: Ellen, the Kaiser, Tom's mother.

Tom yielded part way: he said, after calculating, that he would finish the school year but, that if Ruby were pregnant, he would marry her as soon as school was out. He wanted Guy to assure

138

Ruby of this. Guy said he would, provided Tom promised not to put the offer in writing; hence the censorship of messages. Guy felt that he had got his friend into this, and Guy was determined to get his friend out.

Ruby's call had been to say that she was certain, now, that her period would not occur. It was Guy who phoned her, after Tom was caught, to say his roommate couldn't come in now and that she would hear from Guy. Then he devoted the next two days to calming Tom.

Once Tom admitted that the restrictions, the work, the special study halls, could be made to hold him, since every other proctor was made personally responsible for his presence at school, he devised his formula of delay until June. Then he became quite passive; he said he rather enjoyed the work details, mowing grass, rolling tennis courts. Remedial study hall was tough, since he had nothing to study, and since younger boys would come and stare at him as he sat in the library with the school dullards; the little ones would whisper to one another that Tom was, was almost, was not really, married. Tom said he mostly just sat there, without even thinking, waiting for news to come about Ruby's condition.

The news came as far as Guy: in a Wednesday afternoon conference with Ruby and Jeanette, Guy was convinced that the girl was over a week past due; whether it was pregnancy or nerves, of course, he didn't know. Nerves, most likely. Ruby cried and wanted to know when she could see Tom.

Guy returned to school and told Tom that everything was fine; he said that Ruby had begun to menstruate, and had had a date with a sailor. Guy watched Tom carefully while he invented the sailor, and decided that his friend's reaction was only partly jealousy; there seemed to be a measure of relief in it. Guy felt enormously relieved himself.

Tom wrote a seven page letter to Ruby, not mentioning the supposed sailor, so full of turgid philosophizing that Guy felt certain the girl would not read it through; it seemed safe to deliver.

Jeanette was being a tremendous bitch about the matter. Ruby by herself would have been no problem to handle, but the older sister was protective, vindictive, and ambitious. She envisaged a marriage of her sister to Tom; she imagined herself living with them, in some glamorous place, continuing to protect her sister and making great things of new opportunities. She did not believe

139

it when Guy said Tom's family was poor, and that Tom could not hope to go to college if he married Ruby. Jeanette offered an alternative: Guy didn't know how she arrived at such a figure, but Jeanette figured the wrong could be righted by the payment, to herself as trustee, of two thousand dollars. She said she would then take Ruby to New York and arrange for an operation.

Guy haggled with Jeanette, while Ruby sat by, staring at them, for three afternoons running. At the end of the third afternoon, Jeanette said:

"All right. Tonight I'm going to tell Mom."

"No," Ruby said. "Oh, no."

"Yes," said Guy. "That is a very good idea. Tell your mother I will come here to see her tomorrow in the afternoon. Tell her I am ready to talk to her about a reasonable sum of money."

"She won't listen to you," Jeanette said. "You can be damn sure of that."

Guy smiled, and nodded, and said that they would see. Jeanette stared at him with so much hate that he was afraid she might try calling on the school authorities, so he stayed another ten minutes, smiling and cajoling until he had her softened up enough to kiss him goodbye. Then he left the apartment and called the phone company, where Mrs. Browning worked.

He told Mrs. Browning that he was a boy from Roper, who knew Jeanette and Ruby, and that he would like to meet her for a few minutes as she came off from work. He got a cab, drove to the phone company's offices, and waited. He knew her when she came out because she had a face so much like Ruby's; she was a worn, older version, but not unpresentable. He said he'd like to buy her some coffee or a drink, and she hesitated before she said all right, coffee.

He had them driven to the Hotel, where he took her into the coffee shop.

"Of course," he said, "I'm not old enough to have a drink in the bar, but I'd be very happy for you to have one if you would like. I have an aunt in New York who looks very much like you, and I have taken her many times to bars in New York. It's fun."

"Well, all right," Mrs. Browning said. "I think that might be kind of cute." They went to the bar.

She ordered whiskey, and while she was drinking it, Guy began to talk about her daughters. Then he told her a little about Tom.

140

Then he told her what the situation was. Mrs. Browning was astonished, and hurt with the girls; she was also angry at Tom, but she showed no sign of wanting to be angry with Guy. He ordered another whiskey for her, and told her that Tom was a very sweet boy but a little bit stupid. He said that Tom had a half-witted sister, poor little thing, and asked Mrs. Browning if she considered those conditions hereditary.

She said she'd heard of such things.

Guy didn't labor the point. He went on to say that Tom's family was desperately poor, that his stepfather had been to prison and was an alcoholic, and that Tom's mother was an invalid; poor Tom was only barely managing to stay in school. Then he left the subject, and began to talk about Jeanette.

Or rather, he let Mrs. Browning talk about Jeanette. It seemed, as Guy had gathered long ago, that the mother did not get along well with her older daughter. Guy let her say that it was Jeanette's fault if Ruby had gone wrong, that Ruby had always wanted to do everything Jeanette did, and been so influenced by her sister that Mrs. Browning sometimes felt those girls didn't want a mother.

Guy bought Mrs. Browning a third whiskey, and held her hand while she talked. She said he was a sweet, sweet boy. She said he was a very handsome boy, too, and that she could have understood it better if it was a boy like him that Ruby had got in trouble with. Guy squeezed the hand and assured Mrs. Browning that he was going to see that everybody got out of trouble, that he himself was not rich but could get a little money; he suggested that if Mrs. Browning could get the afternoon off tomorrow, he would meet with her, and Jeanette, and Ruby, and they could settle the whole thing. Then he sent Mrs. Browning home in the cab.

That evening Guy was summoned to the Head's office and told that the faculty were not satisfied that he had been totally innocent in the difficulties that Beniger was having, and that they had decided to restrict him for two weeks.

Guy accepted the restrictions politely. Then he went to Mr. Fairless' room. Mr. Fairless was not in. He went to his own room, and told Tom, who was musing and rather distant, that the sailor had returned to his ship and that Ruby's and Jeanette's mother was planning to take her daughters for a trip some place.

In the morning Guy finally found Mr. Fairless, and asked to speak with him.

141

"The Head put me on bounds," Guy said.

"Well," said Mr. Fairless. "What an injustice, Cinturon."

"For two weeks."

"Well, Cinturon, I hope you'll spend them in meditation," Mr. Fairless said. "You can meditate on—on crime and punishment."

"Yes sir."

"You must ask yourself constantly, whether, uh, you are successfully resisting the design of the experience, to correct your deficiencies, or whether you are still nursing the pure flame of revolt in your lawless and romantic heart."

"Yes, sir," Guy said, hoping that Mr. Fairless was now through being funny. "I have a chance to get Beniger out of the mess he's in."

"Oh? You arouse my curiosity. Just what kind of a mess is he in?"

"Just the kind you think, Mr. Fairless," Guy said. "It's going to cost either money or marriage to get him out. I've got the money."

"I see. Does Beniger know this?"

"No," Guy said. "I told him she was all right. I'll even tell you it was my fault in the first place. Tom never was with a girl before."

"I see. And you, uh, didn't instruct him in the, uh, precautions?"

"Yes," Guy said. "He had bad luck. Anyway, he's over her. Or getting over her. But if he knew I was lying to him, he'd leave school and marry her."

"Under age, aren't they?" Mr. Fairless asked drily.

"Not in Maryland."

"I see." Mr. Fairless began to look a little agitated.

"I've got the money," Guy said. "I've seen the girl's mother. I'm supposed to straighten it all out with her this afternoon."

"I see," said Mr. Fairless. "Why are you telling me, Cinturon?"

"Because I've got to go to town this afternoon, and the Head restricted me."

"I see."

"I'm going to go," Guy said. "Through the woods. I'm going to stay late, and I'll get caught. That's all right. I just don't want to be stopped from going."

Mr. Fairless pondered. "I won't stop you," he said finally. "But when you get back, I'll see that you get all the same restrictions Beniger is on."

"All right," Guy said.

142

"It's you who deserves them. Not Tom."

"All right. Will you cash a check for me?"

"A check?"

"Yes."

"For how much?"

"A hundred dollars in tens."

"No one carries that much money in this country, Cinturon. I'd have to go to town to cash it."

"Yes sir. Will you?"

"Can you actually pay these people off for a hundred dollars?"

Guy hesitated a moment. Then he nodded. There was no point in telling Fairless any more than that.

"All right," Mr. Fairless said. "I'll get you the money."

At eleven, Guy called his cousin, Jose, who worked for an export bank in New York. At one, he called Jose again, and Jose had made the arrangements. At three Guy headed for the woods, with ten ten dollar bills in his pocket and his fawn colored flannel suit on.

Arriving in town he bought a suitcase, a nightgown, and a few toilet articles. He packed these and went to the hotel.

"I'm at Roper. I want a room for my mother."

"All right," said the clerk. "What's your name, son?"

"Browning," Guy said. "I'll pay for it now. I don't know what time she's coming yet. Would you put the bag in her room?"

"She sent that ahead?"

"The chauffeur left it off," Guy said. "He has to take the car over to New Hampshire with my father. I . . ." he lowered his eyes. "You see, my Mom drinks, and then—she and Dad have these quarrels. . . ."

"That's all right," the clerk said. "Don't take it so hard, kid. Parents are like that."

Then Guy went to the Brownings. He was pleased to see that Mrs. Browning was quite dressed up; so was Ruby. Jeanette was defiantly wearing an old pair of slacks and a boy's shirt.

"I'll bet you think you're smart, getting to Mom first," Jeanette said.

"No," said Guy. "I just had an impulse after I left. I've been dying to meet your mother."

"Did Tom send a note?" Ruby wanted to know.

"No," said Guy. "Not today. They're giving him special tests today, all day."

"Oh," said Ruby. "I hate tests."

"I hate tests," Jeanette mimicked. "What are we going to do? Talk about homework?"

"It sounds to me like you've been doing quite enough homework, young lady," Mrs. Browning said.

"Oh for heaven's sake, Mom," Jeanette said. "Don't let this Mexican brat start soft-soaping you again. Honestly."

"I think I can talk about what's best for Ruby without your help," Mrs. Browning said.

"What's there to talk about? The only question is when we get the money, and I mean how much I told you, too."

Ruby started to cry. "I don't want any money," she said. "I just want to see Tom."

Guy said: "Ruby, wouldn't you like to take a trip to New York? And go to the big stores, and buy clothes? And go to Broadway?"

She stopped crying and looked at him tearfully; then she remembered to shake her head.

"Now he's working on Ruby with the Mexican soap cake," Jeanette said. "You give us the money, Guy; we'll decide what to do with it."

"Will you?" Guy asked. "Do you know a doctor, a clean good one, who won't injure Ruby's health? Do you?"

"I guess I can find a doctor," Jeanette said.

"I don't want to go to a doctor," Ruby said.

"I suppose you don't want to go to New York either?" her sister said.

"Will you girls be quiet?" Mrs. Browning said. "Honestly Guy, the bickering that goes on around here, I can't hear myself think."

"I think you and I could settle it, Mrs. Browning," Guy said, respectfully.

"Oh no you don't," said Jeanette.

Her mother got angry. "You think I wouldn't know what's best for my daughter? Who got her into this kind of trouble? Not me. I'm not the one who brings boys here in the afternoon, and lies around drinking wine."

"Where do you think I got the wine?" Jeanette shrieked.

Guy rose quietly: "Shall we go someplace and talk, Mrs. Browning?"

144

"Yes."

He took her back to the hotel bar, and he bought her quite a lot of whiskey. Then she said she was feeling groggy, and he suggested going up to the room. Once there, she sat on the bed. Guy gave the elevator man a ten dollar bill and asked him to get some sandwiches and a bottle of bourbon. When the man came back, Guy gave him another ten. He fed Mrs. Browning, and wrote out for her, carefully, full instructions on the trip to New York: what date to go, what hotel the reservation was at, the time of the doctor's appointment Jose had made for Ruby.

"You'll need some cash to spend," Guy said. He put fifty dollars and the schedule in Mrs. Browning's purse. Then he put in two checks, for twenty-five dollars each, one made out to Jeanette and the other to Ruby. He made out a third, for fifty, to Mrs. Browning.

"You can cash these at the hotel desk when you get there," Guy said.

He closed the purse, and asked if they would need anything else. Mrs. Browning said no, it all sounded fine. He gave her a drink.

Then he seduced her.

Then he promised sincerely that the girls wouldn't find out, and insincerely that he would see her and they would have another party when she got back from New York.

Then he went back to school, surrendered himself to the custody of Mr. Fairless, went to his room, told Tom that Mrs. Browning was taking the girls to Atlantic City for a few days, and pasted the 17th gold star into his notebook.

145

CHAPTER SIX

1.

TOM BENIGER AND Guy Cinturon were graduated from Roper Prep and were accepted at Washburn College in the spring of 1940, the same spring Tom's sister Ellen finished her junior year at Hazlitt Woman's. Tom's choice of Washburn was a plain matter of money. With some helpful pressure by Mr. Fairless and his Headmaster—the Head was a Washburn graduate—Tom received a prize scholarship specifically endowed by a nineteenth century will to provide a classics scholar with tuition and maintenance. Guy decided on Washburn because Tom was going there; his father would have preferred Princeton but Washburn was one of half a dozen smaller schools to which there was no objection. Eddie chose it too, but not before the summer was mostly gone.

2.

The Kaiser said: "I'm terribly pleased about the scholarship, Tom. Since my sister Lucia died there isn't a great deal to keep your mother and me in Tennepin; with Ellen finishing and you so well set, we'll be able to do as Dr. Marston advises."

"Move south?"

146

"Yes. The winters are very hard on your mother here."

"But leave Tennepin. . . ."

The Kaiser nodded.

"How will you be able to, Kaiser?"

"I've been able to pay off the mortgage on the farm," the Kaiser said. "It's finally clear. The house has always been. I've listed them both for sale."

"But you always planned to move to the farm," Tom said.

His stepfather smiled. "I know. And I wanted to leave it to you, and the house to Ellen. Well, it hasn't worked out that way."

"No," Tom said.

"You haven't noticed," the Kaiser was musing. "You've been away. Tennepin's changing, Tom. It's turning into a commuting town. There are eight busses to New York now every morning."

"Are there?" Tom didn't think he cared.

"The farm. It won't be a farm after I sell it. It will be cut up, I suppose, into five and ten acre plots, and they'll build homes there . . . this house, I can't believe the money I've been offered for it."

"Where will you go, Florida?"

"Yes."

"What will you do there?"

"I suppose I should do some kind of defense work," the Kaiser said.

"But what would you like to do?"

The Kaiser smiled. "I'd like to buy a little orange grove," he said. "I'd like to see fruit grow. That would help defense, too, wouldn't it? And fish a little, early mornings. And I could have a handpress and a type case in one of the outbuildings, and print things sometimes just to amuse myself. Stationery for you and Ellen at college, things like that."

"Please do it, Kaiser," Tom said. Then, after a moment: "How funny. To tell people in college that I come from Florida instead of Tennepin."

"No," the Kaiser smiled again. "You'll always be from Tennepin. We both will."

"Only there won't be any Tennepin," Tom said.

Ellen, who was working away from home, giving dancing lessons at a resort that summer, came in the middle of each week for her days off. She seemed to mind the idea of their parents moving more than Tom did.

"How funny," she almost repeated to Tom what he had said to their stepfather. "Not to say that I'm from Tennepin. Not to be coming here for vacations and . . . I don't know. Not to think of living here, and having my children go to school and take English from Miss Wax."

"Did you really think you'd live here?"

"I don't know. I suppose not."

"Even if Mom and the Kaiser were staying, wouldn't you have to marry someone in town if you were going to live here?"

It made her smile. "I haven't any candidates," she said.

"I'm sure Sorley Green would be glad to help out."

Ellen laughed now. "I wonder where I will live?"

"Michigan," he teased. "I hear it's very nice there." Harrison Walle was from Michigan.

"Never," said Ellen. "Never, never, never." Then: "I do feel funny about the Kaiser and Mother leaving Tennepin."

"Me too," Tom said.

That was early in the summer.

Late in the summer, after Connie Marston's suicide, it was clear that Ellen felt differently. Ellen didn't seem to care if she never saw or heard of Tennepin again.

3.

Connie Marston came home in August to marry and to die. She had met in New York a very suitable young man, a fellow, oddly enough, from East Bixton, the town slightly larger than Tennepin and twenty miles farther from New York, where the Kaiser had worked for the past half dozen years.

With the announcement that there would be a summer wedding of such local importance, all the tired stories about Connie and a married man from Boston, which had been repeated in town for three years, stopped by unspoken consent. It was to be a kind of social event that rarely took place any longer, and further gossip would have marred it.

Ellen and Bev Hill would be bridesmaids. Even Marge Hamner, who had some curious connection with union politics down in

148

Pennsylvania, would be back and in organdy. Connie Green, who had been married two years already, would be matron of honor. Sorley Green, through whom the bride and groom had met, would be an usher. It was the sort of thing the girl flock had planned with one another when they were eight and nine, and only gradually stopped expecting.

The ceremony was everything that had ever been hoped for: the ugly old Congregational Church, transfigured by flowers to an awkward beauty. The reception in the Marston's garden, a pageant of green grass and light dresses. The groom, handsome and serious as a groom could be. Mrs. Marston, grand and tearful; the Doctor looking as if he didn't quite believe it; Kaiser Coombs and Ruth, Uncle Ben Green with Big Connie, the Jepsons, Liddie Hamner, old Steppie Miller, all turned out and dressed up, along with many others who rarely appeared these days—as if something were being reborn through as simple a public event as the Marston girl's getting married.

Connie herself looked surprisingly fresh, considering reports from people like Sorley, who had seen her in the past year and described her as haggard. Connie told Ellen and Bev that she had been asleep all summer.

"I've been doing nothing else since April. Just sleeping. About every two days the phone would ring, and I'd wake up for an hour or so." But this could hardly be so, since she'd met the East Bixton boy in June and had time to announce an engagement and plan a wedding. The older people were especially pleased because the couple were going to live in East Bixton, where the groom would inherit the Water and Gas Company.

"That's where he wants to live," Connie said. "I know I'll love it." There was no particular enthusiasm in her voice, and no particular lack of it either.

Once, just an hour before the ceremony, she clutched at Ellen and looked very carefully at her face.

"So pretty," she said, very seriously. "Why did we stop being friends, Ellen? I don't remember, do you?"

Ellen started to answer, but Connie went on: "It doesn't matter. Oh, God, so many things I can't remember. Bev?" She turned to her other old friend.

"Yes?"

"What's your little sister's name?"

149

"Betsy," Bev said. "You remember. You used to fix her bicycle for her; honestly, she still adores you. She's so excited about the wedding. . . ."

"I thought so," Connie said. "A red bike."

"Blue," Bev said.

"I wonder where I fixed a red bike?" Connie asked. "Or did I dream it?"

Ellen glanced at Bev. The man in Boston, it was said, had had Connie at his house from time to time, supposedly doing secretarial work when his wife and children were away. Could there have been a red bike? If Connie made any such connection, it didn't show on her face. Nothing much showed on her face; nothing at all. Yet the remark about bicycles was the closest thing to a hint of explanation about the whole affair that anybody ever had.

For two days after the wedding, everyone who had been there talked of it; it was a topic, for once, that excluded the nice advertising man who had bought the Dix place, and the families who had built homes along the creek and along Lee's Road, which used to be lovers' lane. On the third day they began to talk of something else: the East Bixton boy had come driving frantically into town to see Dr. Marston, Connie's father, and taken the doctor back with him to wherever they were honeymooning. No further information developed, however, and the talk quieted; Connie and her husband took up residence in East Bixton, and everyone got cards with the new address.

When, on the first day of September, the news came of Connie's having killed herself with sleeping pills, the callous said it must have been her second try.

Ellen heard it from Sorley, who had been at the newlyweds' home for dinner the night before, and whom the groom had called first, after Dr. Marston and the police. It was Ellen whom Sorley called first. He said that Connie had been in New York, early in the week, to finish moving out of the apartment she had lived in there. Among the things Connie brought back was a cowhide overnight bag; this, it was discovered on the morning of September first, as the bride lay dead, contained enough sleeping pills of different sorts to stock a hospital, along with prescriptions from a dozen different doctors for more. Connie must have been working at the collection for months.

Sorley called Ellen at eleven; it was disproportionately shocking to her, considering the distance that had grown between herself and

150

Connie and at first she refused to believe it. When Sorley finally convinced her, Ellen hung up the phone before he was quite through talking. She sat with all the knuckles of her left hand crammed into her mouth to keep from crying. Then she got up and walked out of the house, over to Bev Hill's, three blocks away. The sun was very bright.

When she got to the Hills', Mrs. Hill and Betsy were packing. They were going back to their Rhode Island place for the last two weeks before school would start again; they were giving a big party up there, Bev had said. The mother and sister were rather cool to Ellen, and said that Beverly was taking a nap. Ellen didn't want to tell them what she'd heard, but Mrs. Hill said:

"You've come to talk about poor Constance Marston, I suppose?"

"Bev's heard about it?"

"Oh yes. So perhaps you won't feel we ought to disturb her." Mrs. Hill gave Betsy an armload of folded dresses, and Betsy carried them to a trunk in the next room, ignoring Ellen. Then Mrs. Hill excused herself and went out of the room; Ellen was about to leave when she heard Bev's voice, coming down the stairs in the room to which Betsy had gone.

She heard Bev cry out, in that sweet, throbbing voice that was so much a part of Ellen's life: "Betsy, darling. I've just finished the invitations—oh, honestly, you mustn't pack my things for me. You'll spoil me."

Ellen left the house as quietly as she could, swallowing tears since there wasn't anyone to cry them with.

4.

Guy's father sent him off to college with a car; so did Eddie's. Guy, thoughtful about such things, for he had learned at Roper, garaged the car in Boston and didn't actually have it at school until they had been there for a month. Eddie arrived driving his, a green convertible.

It was ridiculous that he had it at all. His father had offered him a job that summer, offered to pay him sixty dollars a week. Eddie said thanks, he wanted to do some swimming; he wasn't surrendering any of his independence.

Every day he went to a beach, riding the same bike he had

151

ridden at thirteen which, disgustingly enough, was still the right size. He went to lonely beaches and swam hard in the surf. He turned the color of cocoa. He stayed, most nights, in his grandfather's house which was still standing in the potato fields.

One evening when Eddie was home, his father got up nerve to say: "You're going to college, Eddie?"

"Yeah."

"Which college?"

"I'm accepted at three," Eddie said. "Two of them want me to play ball. The third, they don't have football scholarships. I guess it's out."

"Which is that?"

"Washburn."

"Oh." Mr. Bissle thought a moment. "Basil McHugh went to Washburn." Basil McHugh was a gentleman politician, not a very big shot.

"I know," Eddie said.

"Do you want to go there?"

"I told you. No football scholarships. It's the Ivy League, only smaller and older."

"I'll send you there."

"No thanks."

"How about the money your grandfather left in trust, Eddie? I could let you have some of that to go to college."

"You could?"

"What about that? Wouldn't you rather be paying your way, instead of having to play football, whether you feel like it or not?"

"I feel like it," Eddie said, but slowly, because the idea took hold.

Look, Eddie never said his father was dumb, or didn't understand people; he only said his father was a slob. Listen, a guy doesn't have to be so stupid he knocks down a good idea, just because he doesn't respect the source. "Maybe you're right," he said.

His father looked surprised.

"Eddie," he asked. "You ever do any drinking?"

"No," said Eddie. "I'm always training."

"You want to have a drink with me, talk about college? I never went; I'd have given anything I had to go, but your grandad thought it was nonsense."

"I'll bet he did."

"He used a dirtier word than nonsense."

"I'll bet he did." Then: "Sure. Give me a drink."

His father got him drunk. His father got him silly, staggering drunk, and they spent the whole damn evening crying together, and Eddie more or less remembered telling good old Dad that he didn't hate him, and just to show Dad what a nice guy he, Eddie, was, why he, Eddie, would accept good old Dad's offer of a car, and let old Dad pay his college bills, and even take seventy-five a month to spend. . . . How can you be any nicer to your father than that?

He woke up about six the next morning, stumbled out and onto the bike, and spent the day fighting undertow at a beach where they had red warnings up; there were waves like charging elephants, and Eddie slammed into them and under them, and chopped his way back to the beach when they tried to pull him back with them on the way out, until finally he was so beat he lay on the beach with his teeth chattering—and damned if the green convertible wasn't there when he got back to the house, parked right in front with the keys in it. Brand new.

It made Eddie shake his head in wonder at himself, but he found he was very pleased to be going to Washburn where Bantie Gans was celebrated for turning out winning small college football teams with strictly amateur material, and where nobody would give a damn if a football player wanted to spend some of his time with a history book. All right.

On the wave of these big deal decisions, Eddie decided there was another matter that needed to be taken care of and that was getting laid; he'd never so much as had a date in his life, but he didn't figure on arriving at Washburn and having every guy there be a master of the pastime but himself. So he went cruising in his green convertible one evening after supper, and he happened to cruise by Myra Andahl's house.

And he happened to know about Myra: she'd gone steady all through high school with Billy Galway, who was the local football hero, and who had once played on the same sandlot team as Eddie. Billy wasn't exactly a friend, but he and Eddie were close enough so that Billy told Eddie once that going steady, for him and Myra, wasn't just a matter of good night kisses.

Okay, Billy was away. Billy had a good life-guard job, supervising tail at Jones Beach. Billy could have driven home to Myra

153

every night if he'd wanted, but Billy didn't want. Clear enough. Eddie stopped at Myra's house.

She was sitting on the porch. Eddie got out and crossed the lawn.

Eddie said: "How do you like my new car?"

Myra said: "Oh, Eddie, it's beautiful."

Eddie said: "Take a ride?"

Myra said: "I'll bet you've been riding every girl in town."

Eddie said: "Come on. You want to or not?"

Myra called in to her mother that she'd be back in a little while, and walked down off the porch. She was half a head taller than Eddie, had reddish hair and kind of a pouty face, a little bit dished in. Eddie was no great judge of figures, but hers seemed all right, about like any other girl's. She was wearing a brown corduroy jumper and a white shirt.

They crossed the lawn and got into the car. He drove her out of town. She talked along at him—he didn't bother answering very much. When they got to where the road was quiet, he pulled off on the shoulder and she objected.

"Listen, Myra. I never had a date in my life," Eddie said. "I wouldn't know what move to make."

"Really, Eddie?"

"Yeah, really."

"Why'd you want me to come riding?"

"I talked to Billy about you a couple of times," Eddie said, not realizing until he saw her face that he was saying something brutal.

It took her a few minutes to compose herself, and then she asked to be taken home.

"Wait till you hear what I've got to say," Eddie said.

"You've said enough."

"All right. You're mad. Let's wait till you stop being mad and then I'll tell you."

She sat silently for a while, and then asked him for a cigarette.

"I'm sorry, I don't smoke," Eddie said.

After another minute she asked: "What were you going to say, Eddie?"

"I'll give you twenty bucks," Eddie said.

"What for?"

"I told you. I never went out on a date. That's what for."

154

"You mean. . . . Eddie Bissle, do you think people do that every time they go out on a date?"

He was embarrassed. He had thought so, more or less, the way guys talked.

"Oh, Eddie," she said, and laughed. "You really don't know anything, do you?"

"All right, I don't. But I'll still give you twenty bucks."

"Eddie! I couldn't. Girls don't take money like that."

"Some do."

"Not nice girls."

"Thirty bucks?"

"Eddie, you're going to get me mad again in a minute. What do you suppose Billy would do if he heard you talking to me that way?"

"To tell you the truth," Eddie said, a little bit sarcastically. "I hadn't planned to send Billy a telegram about it. Had you?"

"Well no. Of course not. . . ."

"Nobody will know," Eddie said. "Maybe this is a bigger deal than I thought. I'll put the price up." He got his money out of his pocket and counted it. "I've got fifty-four dollars," he said. "You can have the fifty. I need four for gas."

"Fifty dollars?"

He nodded.

"Eddie, you must want to awfully bad."

"I guess so."

"Did you want to for a long time, and you were scared of Billy, or what?"

"What do you mean?"

"I mean was it always me you . . . wanted to do it with? You like me?"

"Sure. I like you all right," Eddie said.

"You always have?"

"Tell you the truth, I just got the idea when I saw you sitting on the porch tonight with nothing else to do," Eddie said.

That little piece of telling her the truth cost another two minutes of silence; like Memorial Day or something.

"You like me now?" she asked finally.

"I said I did."

"You aren't being very nice," she said. "Don't you understand, if I do things with Billy, it's because I love him. He's my guy."

155

"Sure," said Eddie.

"I'm not wild."

"No."

"I mean there are probably lots of girls who'd be glad to take twenty dollars and nobody the wiser."

"Sure. Only I said fifty." Eddie remembered a phrase he'd heard in the locker room. "Why give it away when it's worth good money?"

"I've heard girls that say that," Myra said. "Maybe you should see one of them."

"You want the fifty bucks, Myra?" Eddie asked.

She didn't answer, so he put the bills in her hand, started the car and drove through the fields to his grandfather's old house.

"I've been staying out here," he said. Again she didn't reply, so he got out, went around and opened the door on her side. She got out without a word and went straight into the house, still holding the money. He followed her into the living room, and snapped on a light.

He pointed to the cot he used, and asked if that was okay. She put the dough away, took off the jumper, the blouse, and a slip, with her jaw tight; she started on underwear and Eddie didn't watch her jaw. She lay down on the cot, coldly, and when he joined her she turned her face away but he didn't know whether he was supposed to kiss her anyway. She was plenty tight lipped about the whole thing, but Eddie didn't mind. He enjoyed himself on top of her; he had been more or less set for a disappointment, and it turned out to be a pretty solid little medium sized deal.

The only other thing that Myra said was as he let her off at home: "You might have been a little nice about it."

He supposed he'd forgotten to say thanks, so he said it. She slammed the door. It made Eddie decide, as he drove off, to test her indignation by trying to buy her at least once more, and by the end of the summer he had her price down to ten bucks, and she had to let him try whatever he wanted. By that time he understood enough about this particular little medium-sized deal so that he wished she'd slapped the hell out of him the first evening for even suggesting such a thing; he didn't know why, he just wished she had.

5.

Freshman year?

Well, Eddie was considered just about the grubbiest kid who ever arrived at Washburn. They didn't like his looks, they didn't like his car, they didn't like his talk and they didn't like his attitude. Ninety-eight per cent of the school was unaware that he played freshman football and ninety-nine per cent didn't care. They shaved his head the second day on campus, not that it changed his appearance much; he always wore it about one eighth of an inch long anyway. Nobody asked him to join a fraternity, and his roommate moved out at the end of the first week; that suited Eddie all right—except for his first year at prep school he'd always managed to room alone.

Let the college forget about Bissle except for the guys who played freshman ball with him, and the teachers who got uncomfortable at the way he scowled back at them when they were lecturing, listening hard to every idiot word they said. There was also a certain sophomore named Fellwen, who didn't forget Eddie, because he was damn careful to stay out of Eddie's way.

Fellwen came from more or less the same part of Long Island except that his town was fashionable. Right at the height of the hate-Bissle campaign, which started and was over in the first two weeks, after which forgetting set in, Fellwen bought himself two minutes of attention by telling some guys that everyone in his part of the Island had heard Eddie's father—Old Man Bissle, he said, had started as a small time bootlegger. This got back to Eddie; Eddie looked up Fellwen's room number in the office, and went up to the sophomore dormitory one evening. He walked in to Fellwen's room without knocking, and, seeing a key in the door, locked it behind him. Eddie said Fellwen was wrong, that Old Man Bissle never had the guts to be a bootlegger. Eddie then told Fellwen to keep his mouth off Eddie and Eddie's family; Eddie then beat Fellwen till he couldn't scream any more. Fellwen was six feet tall and weighed about a hundred and seventy; Eddie was five feet five, and weighed one forty five; Fellwen was quite badly coordinated, so it was more of a beating than a fight in spite of the difference in sizes. There were a lot of sophomores in the hall,

157

banging to get in, and when Eddie came out some ran to take care of Fellwen who was lying on the floor, and the others took turns hammering Eddie. The word around the college was that Fellwen had a weak heart and was generally defenceless; most of the freshmen believed this and Eddie was pretty well ostracized, except by Cinturon and Beniger who had the room next door.

Cinturon and Beniger seemed to say and do just about as they pleased; but Guy said it was less bother if you made people like it. They were both pledged to Omicron, which was the best house at Washburn; when they held the class organization meeting, Guy could easily have been elected president if he'd wanted. He declined the nomination, so they elected Tom class secretary instead.

Guy was polite, a little remote, pleasant when he had to be; Tom was kind and funny, but not really cordial, and people were cautious about approaching him because of Guy. The two were admired, and allowed to go their own way—our own snobbish way, Tom said gently, and any minute they'll see through us; maybe being nice to Eddie was a kind of counterbalance. It was Tom who was nice; Guy seemed to have a certain respect for Eddie as a ballplayer, a disinclination to let his attitude be dictated by that of the rest of their class—beyond that, Eddie's skin was tough enough so that when Guy was snotty Eddie didn't scare off. Tom was never snotty; Tom would talk to Eddie even when Guy was obviously impatient about it; Tom Beniger was the first guy who ever insisted on liking Eddie Bissle, and Eddie knew exactly how it started.

It was at the end of the first week; Eddie's hair had just been shaved; he hadn't beaten up Fellwen yet, and his roommate had only just announced that he was moving out. Eddie couldn't help being grateful that Guy was willing to walk back from the first freshman football practice with him. They got to the door of Guy's room, and Eddie waved and walked on towards his own. When he got there, he saw the roommate sulking at his desk, and Eddie still felt too good from practice to share four walls with young rancid ass. So he turned away and went back towards Guy's door which was open.

Guy was saying to Tom: ". . . quite a squad. Manstan who was that fullback at Royal; five yards a try. We never did stop him. Little Bissle was all-conference guard at Mount Pennell. There's a big tackle from New York who was supposed to be one of the

158

best linemen in secondary school history; Notre Dame was after him, but his father went here. And this kid Parker, from New Hampshire; if I'd had a passer like that in school, we'd never have lost a game."

"Aaah, we're all aces," said Eddie, from the doorway, more harshly than he meant to. Guy looked at him politely, and stopped talking; Tom Beniger smiled. "Did you ever think how many aces there are?" Eddie asked. "Ten thousand prep schools, and everyone had a big ace last year. Ten thousand aces. And the high schools; think of all the aces in the high schools. How the hell can any college freshman team ever beat another one with all us aces around?"

Guy was stony, and Eddie saw, without being able to stop himself, that every word he said made the stone a little harder. But Beniger, Beniger was smiling.

Beniger said, in that nice, hesitant voice: "Come in, Eddie. Guy, here's a bald little gnome come to see us."

Eddie didn't go in, but his panic left him. For some reason he continued speaking to Guy: "Look at Beniger. Big ace in studies. Listen, every one of those schools had a big study ace, too. And a . . . I don't know. A kid who could draw pictures like nobody's business. A kid who could write compositions like his teacher never saw before. And a pitcher and a catcher and a half-miler." Why was he talking so much? Who was he talking to? If it wasn't too late already, he could still shut up and maybe have two guys left in the place who'd at least walk to class with him. He didn't shut up. "Look at all us aces, coming into the colleges," he said. "Take football right here. Forty of us who were hot in prep school, but only eleven can play first string, and only one or two of those is going to look like a star when the season's over. And when the four years are over, maybe one of this year's squad will be a big star and maybe he won't—and the same way with the half-milers and the kid who could draw the pictures. That's all I was thinking." He ended abruptly, awkwardly; he felt deeply embarrassed but, as he turned to go, he heard Beniger say:

"We're going to eat downtown, Eddie, in half an hour. Would you like to come?"

A few days later, after the thing with Fellwen, Eddie figured he had to lose Beniger now, particularly with the big rumor going around about Fellwen's weak heart. Beniger was kind of a pacifist.

159

But Tom came to Eddie's room where he was nursing a couple of bloated fists just before lunch, hoping the swelling would come down by football practice time.

"Want to try putting some cold water on those?" Tom asked. "Come on. Let's go to the washroom, and stick them in a bowl. I'll get you some ice from the Union."

"Listen, you know what they're saying?" Eddie asked him. "They're saying the guy I beat up was an invalid."

"Invalids ought to have more sense, shouldn't they?" Tom said kindly. "They ought to wear signs saying, 'Careful, weak heart.' " Then: "I don't know Fellwen, but Guy says he looks healthy enough." As they were going down the hall to soak the hands, Tom said:

"Guy and I had a fight once in school, for a lot sillier reason, and did a lot more damage."

"You?" Eddie was amazed. "Had a fight?"

Tom laughed. "Careful of me, E. Bissle," he said. "I'm a dangerous man."

As the semester went on, Eddie decided, and even said it to Tom, that Guy might have the potential for All-American if he were at a larger school; as the semester went on, he never said it to anyone, but Eddie decided he just about worshipped Tom Beniger. It was the biggest switch of Eddie's life, because there wasn't a tough wrinkle in Tom's nature. Everything the idiot did and said was gentle. Eddie watched for weeks to find the dishonesty, the selfishness, the piss and corruption, and there just wasn't any. Eddie gave in; he supposed people figured he was just sucking around the two most admired guys in their class, making use of the lucky opportunity of living next door. Eddie couldn't be concerned what people figured. It made him happy to know there was a human being in the world like Tom; and Guy's careless civility was close enough to tolerance so that Eddie could feel that he had two friends.

They didn't take him on their weekend trips to women's colleges; they didn't try to interest Omicron in pledging Eddie, or anything like that. But they would walk on campus with him, ask him along for hot dogs and shakes at the Union late at night, take him to the movies when they went, make Moultrie, who sometimes came down to their room for bridge, accept Eddie as a fourth.

160

These things were enough. Eddie had found his own way of keeping occupied on weekends.

He was writing a paper that was going to toss the smart asses in the Washburn history faculty right onto their hairy ears; all it did was prove that Andrew Johnson was the closest thing to a great man who ever held the presidency of the United States, that's all. Eddie was working on that paper like he'd once worked to learn football, saying nothing about it to anybody, not even Tom and Guy. He spent every weekend in the library, reading and making notes. He was going to turn it in at midyears', when there was a fifteen page paper due in American history—only Eddie's was going to be forty pages, or fifty.

The one thing he yearned to do was talk about the Andrew Johnson paper to Tom, but he didn't dare. Tom was so damn smart. Tom might not think it was any good. Anyway, Tom wasn't in the course.

But finally, a week before the thing was due, Eddie had to show it to him; Eddie was about to take his paper down town, get some broad to type it, and he had to know that it wasn't just absolutely ridiculous before it got put in so permanent a form. So he went into Tom and Guy's room one night and said:

"Tom. Would you read something for me?"

"Sure," Tom said. "What is it?"

"Something I wrote," Eddie told him. "For American History. I want to know if it's all right."

Guy, who was in the course with Eddie, said: "Sure it's all right, Eddie. Thaxter's going to give you a good mark because he's terrified of you."

Tom smiled.

Guy pantomimed a cringe, and said: "Thaxter looks like this every time Eddie walks into the room."

"Would you mind, Tom?" Eddie said.

"I'll be glad to read it. I don't know anything about the subject."

"Have you got time?"

"This evening?"

"Oh no, Eddie," Guy said. "Tomorrow's when Tom has two Greek classes the same day."

"I've got time," Tom said.

Eddie took the pages out of their folder.

161

"My God," Guy said. "It's a book."

Tom smiled, and held out his hand for the manuscript. "You must have done a lot of work on it," he said.

"Yeah," Eddie said. "Well, it's a term paper."

"Give me an hour," Tom said, looking into the manuscript. "I'll go through it right away."

Eddie checked his watch and left the room. When it was one hour to the minute, he made himself wait five minutes more. Then he went back into Tom's room and sat down. Guy had gone out. Tom was on the last few pages. Eddie watched him finish reading. Tom was smiling as he put it down.

"Aaah," Eddie said. "That's the way a hangman smiles."

"Eddie," Tom said. "This is kind of amazing."

"Come on. Good or bad?"

Tom pointed a finger at him and the smile widened. "Listen, you Eddie Bissle," he said. "Stop trying to scare me. I'm not a miserable little history teacher."

"All right," Eddie said, unable to keep himself from returning Tom's smile. That was something about Tom; you talked to him and you stopped feeling so tense about things.

Now Tom stopped smiling and began to speak very earnestly. "Let me tell you why I wasn't quite finished when you came in," he said. "I stopped in the middle because I didn't know anything about Andrew Johnson, so I read through the chapter about him in Guy's textbook."

"That crud," Eddie said.

"I think you'll get an A on your paper."

"You do?"

"But not the kind of an A you want."

"How many kinds are there?"

"Look, they'll give you A because you've done so much work. Because you're a freshman and you've tried to be original. They've got to encourage you for that. But you try to turn Johnson into Robin Hood, Eddie. Take the land from the rich white, give it to the poor white. I don't think they'll take it seriously, Eddie. They'll only give you A for encouragement, and maybe . . . well, laugh about it."

He shook his head. "What do I do then?"

"Well, you could work on this some more. Cut out all the opinion and the slanting, and see what was left."

"I wouldn't know how to start," Eddie said.

"I could help you, but you'd hate me for it."

"What else?"

"Well, you're going to major in history, aren't you?"

Eddie nodded.

"If it's just a question of strategy," Tom said, beginning to smile again, "it's easy. You write your paper on something else, don't let them know you've made any special study of Johnson. Then when you take the exam, you find the essay topic this material can be included under, and wham, you let them have it. Impromptu. And the guy who reads the blue book has to assume that you'd have known just as much about any other topic you'd chosen . . . but maybe you do."

"No," Eddie said. "No, I'm a big Johnson specialist."

"It'll rock them harder, coming that way," Tom said. "A guy reading exam papers is always grateful for an unexpected answer."

"Is that the way you write exams?"

"Well . . . no," Tom said. "But I've got this trick memory. Anyway, I'm a queer. I like to study stuff." He blushed, and then grinned again at Eddie. "Anyway, I don't just do it to be able to beat history teachers around the ears."

"Stop reading me," Eddie said. "I'm no book."

"No, you're a gnome," Tom said. "I'm sorry your hair grew back. Hey, you know what you ought to do?"

"What?"

"Save that paper. And all your notes and everything. Then when you're a senior, and really know the enemy, you can write it into a real big club and beat them good with it."

Eddie laughed.

He took part of Tom's advice. He didn't turn the paper in. But he didn't save it either. It wouldn't have been like Eddie to save that kind of thing, not with all the wastebaskets there are in the world.

6.

Senior year for Ellen was a year of excursions, with Harrison Walle waiting for her at the end of every trip. There were Warren, from Wesleyan; Edgar and Stan from Amherst; Dab, who

163

came to see her twice, all the way from Virginia, who could drink more than any man she'd ever encountered before. Between each one and his successor was Harrison. If the trip had been rough—the one with Dab was very rough—she was glad to see Harrison; if it had been a mild cruise, as it was with Edgar and Stan who were Amherst roommates, so that neither wanted to leave her alone with the other and the big thing was the laughter, the sight of Harrison could be pretty dreary.

He never chided, though he sometimes let her see that he was hurt; he firmly considered Ellen his girl, but he never spoke of marriage—except for one evening when he said that he couldn't consider being married (to anyone), because it was fairly obvious that Roosevelt was going to get us into this war (one way or another), and Harrison would (he presumed) have to go, and it would not be correct (would it?) to be married before such hazards were faced. Afterwards, afterwards; meanwhile he was finishing his second year of graduate work in economics, and had decided to join the Navy.

Estimable decision; Ellen was perfectly willing to concede this, but somehow it didn't interest her much. And that was odd, because she had learned, just recently, and with a considerable catch in her throat, that Tad, her golden boy of last year, was already in the RCAF and might be off to join the Battle of Britain any time. She had neither seen or heard directly from Tad since their one quarrel, but the news of his enlistment seemed somehow to carry more emotion in it for her than did Harrison's projected naval service.

She was too fair to feel that the trouble with Harrison was really Harrison; it was herself, Ellen felt, herself. Hers was the gift of response; with merry people, she was merry, even, perhaps, made them merrier; with drab people she was drab, pulled them down. She was like an uncertain tennis player who plays a fast game against a fast opponent, a faltering game against a poor one. She tried to explain this to Alice Hewitt, who was her roommate again senior year.

"Silliness," said intelligent and forceful Alice, who had almost always found Ellen perfectly intelligent and forceful.

Then Tad showed up for home leave, the final one before going abroad, lean and beautiful in his flyer's clothes. It was in March, of course.

It was the time of the same annual Maple Club dance to which Tom had come as Lover Man Haynes the year before. Tad? He arrived uninvited, in uniform, and Harrison was already there as Ellen's guest; Tad danced and danced with Ellen, and Alice tried to talk to Harrison and keep him away, just for a little. If only Harrison had gotten mad, and driven back to Yale or something, but of course he didn't. If only Ellen had had the courage to say yes, yes, when Tad tried to sweep her away. Instead she said,

"Oh, I can't. I can't." And Tad was as sulky, hurt, mad, as Harrison.

Tad left Ellen and started dancing with a little freshman girl called Sonny, a delicious little brunette all the way from California; Tad took Sonny off.

Ellen left Harrison sitting with Alice, and went to their room. Ellen had been chairman of the Dance Committee, and had charge of buying a little brandy to spike the punch with; there was half a bottle of brandy left. She poured it out, into her toothbrush glass, and started to sip it. She took off her dress and stockings and garter-belt, and drank some more.

By the time Alice came up, two hours later, Ellen was lying on the bed, wearing nothing but a strapless brassiere, and the brandy was nearly gone, and Ellen didn't care at all that Harrison had left, or that Tad was downstairs, had brought Sonny back, was asking for Ellen. All Ellen cared about was that there was a sip of brandy left, and she drank it off quickly, not because she felt she needed it but because otherwise Alice might try to claim it.

After that, Harrison called up a lot and finally, promising herself that when college was over, this would be too, she started seeing Harrison again but much more casually than she had before. She wouldn't neck with him any more.

Harrison came to her graduation in Navy uniform; he looked quite well in it, and it was sweet of him to wear it. He'd gotten a direct commission in the Supply Corps and would start his training right away.

Tom came too. The Kaiser and Mother were in Florida, which was too long a trip; they were living in St. Augustine, in an apartment, near the beach house of a woman with whom Mother had corresponded for years. The Kaiser had some sort of job in a plant that made airplane parts, and said that he was required to stay in it, now, until we had the allies fully armed.

Harrison and Tom seemed to get along pretty well.

Harrison stayed for the Graduation Ball; Tom had his summer job—at a camp this year—to get to. As they danced Harrison asked Ellen what her plans were; he knew perfectly well, of course, that Ellen and Alice were planning to take an apartment in New York and find jobs. Ellen didn't understand why Harrison was making her repeat all this until he told her his surprise: the Navy wanted him to have six months to a year of special training in accountancy and auditing, and for this Harrison was going to be in New York, too.

CHAPTER SEVEN

1.

YOUTH LONGS FOR catastrophe as it longs for love.

By September, 1941, for Tom and Guy, even for Eddie, their participation in a war seemed inevitable, one of the guarantees of adolescence, certain to follow, like work, marriage, full growth, gradual decline, and death. But just as these fulfillments were inevitable, so they were remote; none would come tomorrow. The seat of longing is a chair in a waiting room.

Concerning war, if the question had always been when, never if, seldom why, the answer was always, sometime. Like the other certainties in the waiting room, war was nothing much to think or speak about.

Coming back for their sophomore year at Washburn, Eddie, Guy and Tom thought and spoke of football, girls and one another.

2.

"Williamstown, Mass., Sept. 26—The most deadly marauder since Pancho Villa, El Pistolero Cinturon led his Washburn bandits on raid after raid into Williams' territory this afternoon, plundering 26 points on 4 touchdowns and 2 conversions. . . ."

". . . the Mexican Mailtrain turned out to have a special delivery bomb for hapless Tufts, yesterday. . . ."

"Brunswick, Me., Oct. 8—Perhaps if they had stopped to think, Bowdoin would have elected to defend the North goal here today; before the first quarter ended and the teams switched, the amazing Conquistadors from Washburn had demonstrated twice that nothing could keep them from going South of the Border."

"WASHBURN CLICKS LIKE
CASTANETS AS RHUMBA MASTER
TEACHES WESLEYAN DANCING
IN A HURRY"

At first it was only undergraduate sports writers, on college weeklies, who responded so energetically to Guy's amazing first season of varsity football, for Washburn was not an important college athletically. But by the final games, metropolitan dailies in New England were, on occasion, covering Guy as well. He had always had color on the field, but that season his color developed as remarkably as his ability. It was a kind of color worth regional attention, and with it went luck, for there was a press association stringer in town, a Washburn alumnus, who appointed himself Guy's publicity man and saw to it that attention was called.

Of what did the color consist? It was a question for Tom to ponder with a good deal of interest. First, there was the physical accident of the smile; unlike most smiles, Guy's had range. You could see it from the stands. It showed in coarse screen news photos. And Guy was always smiling.

He smiled when he scored, when he fumbled, when he jumped for a pass, when he caught it, when he missed it—a wild smile, communicating exhilaration. If there were a pile-up of tacklers at the end of a play, the sort that makes spectators catch their breaths, expecting injury, and Guy were at the bottom, he was smiling when the pile cleared off—smiling, miraculously intact, springing up excitedly to flip the ball with special smiles—for the umpire as if he were grateful to the man for supervising play so well, for the tacklers as if he were fond of his opponents for providing the thrill of opposition. Because of the smile, no one ever had to ask which one was Cinturon, what his number was—but the

168

smile was only half of it, in Tom's analysis. Even without it, Guy was a spectacle; people who didn't follow the game came to watch Washburn play that fall, just for the sight of Guy running with a football. He was graceful, elusive, a performer of tremendous speed and verve—yet there was something in his running that created empathy, a touch, almost, of fear; it was as if the man were moving desperately to avoid violation, running for self-preservation, skittering past menacing tacklers, flying away, to escape from personal devastation at their hands. It was the contrast of this quality of movement with the astonishing smile which made Guy's playing so forceful a projection of personality, Tom thought, hence colorful, hence the thing you would remember from a game even if someone else had done the scoring. But Guy did the scoring, too; he was called the best scat back in New England, a stylish ball handler, a dexterous faker; could go up in the air for a pass like a picture in the Sunday supplement, and even did a workmanlike job of punting though he never got over a tendency to hurry his kicks.

But in spite of the way he caught the public imagination, sportswriters knew, his coach and teammates knew, eventually even Tom knew, that there were flaws in the perfect player. The important flaw was defensive, and after midseason it became—not obvious, but apparent enough to those who were looking for it.

What happened to expose it? The fullback who had played safety went to the infirmary with mononucleosis, leaving Guy the only man with the speed for the job. And there were, it developed, certain kinds of tackling from which Guy—slightly, involuntarily, just enough to lose advantage—cringed. He could overtake most runners from the side, even the rear, and bring them down neatly. He could, and did more often that he ought to have as a defensive maneuver, knock a runner sprawling with a beautifully timed block. But when it was Guy and the runner head on, or at any angle less than oblique, Guy could not keep himself from guarding his face. The situation was infrequent; a whole game might be played without its happening. But when it did occur, the runner, unless he were too slow-thinking to exploit it, scored.

This was not a glaring thing, and nothing much was said about it, either in the papers—except by one columnist who earned his paycheck by belittling—or in campus gossip. Members of the team never spoke of it; Eddie, for example, gave Tom no answer

169

when Tom, innocent at first, inquired why a certain touchdown had been scored in the Wesleyan game.

Banty Gans, the coach, tried other, slower men at safety the next weekend against Amhurst, returning Guy to pass defense at which he was superb. But there came a situation in which Guy's speed would have enabled him to make the oblique tackle and save a score; and another in which the runner got away, down the sidelines, and could have been knocked out of bounds. In the final quarter, and in subsequent games, Guy was playing safety again.

Guy's other flaw was brittleness. He had no bones broken but he never played without an ankle taped, or a knee, or, perhaps, wrapping on his ribs; this meant saving him to some extent, as the season went on, though he was always eager to be in and the crowds were always calling for him. He continued to score, to smile, to draw a following; he was mentioned for small college All-American though he was only a sophomore; yet the season ended for him—and for Tom, who felt so strongly what Guy felt—with a sense of anti-climax.

As Guy played less and less, so Eddie played more and more. It gave Tom two players to watch—Guy and his reverse.

Eddie had finally made a hundred and fifty pounds, but that was still a ridiculous weight for a guard in college football. It took a while for Bantie Gans to convince himself that Eddie could do, on guts and drive, all the things his freshman coach had claimed for him. But Eddie proved it. His strength was amazing, and the way he used it, Bantie once said, was worth thirty pounds of weight. Eddie never ran out of hustle; his skill in pullout plays was not particularly important in Bantie's style of offense, though occasionally such a play would be used for surprise and when it was, Eddie made it effective. It was, however, in contrast to Guy, as a defensive player that Eddie was most valuable. He was a little block of buried cement in the line, immovable unless you picked him up and carried him away, never willing to concede himself out of a play, always trying to wriggle under a blocker, bull towards a runner, meet the flying knees of any size ballcarrier with head, shoulder, face—it didn't matter to Eddie. He was savage; you could bruise his cheek bones, bang his nose, kick his jaw; he kept coming in. He didn't feel the blows sustained in the joy of the blows inflicted; when he caught a man, Eddie never tackled easy. It was always grab, strain, slam.

Eddie played quite a lot, but he was never mentioned for small college All-American, or anything of that sort; he wasn't even noticed especially.

"Maybe," Tom wrote to Ellen, "Eddie's a great football player for his size, but that still leaves him miles from being a great player, because in football size is the first element of greatness. It's too bad." Tom mentioned Eddie fairly often when he wrote to Ellen; Tom rather minimized Guy. He knew precisely why he did this, and knew how silly it was; sooner or later, Guy and Ellen would meet, and Tom was jealous of the idea. Call it boyish, but to think of his sister being and remaining virtuous was important to Tom; and Guy's reputation as an enemy of chastity was really quite formidable. Even before their freshman year had finished, Guy's string of conquests was spoken of beyond their own campus; college girls warned one another about Guy; Tom was perfectly aware that these warnings helped his friend's campaigning quite a bit. There were more than thirty stars, now, in the notebook.

So Tom wrote a good deal about funny, peevish little muscleman Bissle, as if Eddie were just as close a friend as Guy, and just as fascinating an individual. He did this, somewhat abashed at himself, thinking it juvenile, but without power to stop himself, and he mailed the letters to Ellen's new address in New York. She had moved from her first apartment, with Alice Hewitt, to someplace uptown.

3.

"I want to break training with champagne," Guy said, declining a glass of scotch that Moultrie, a fraternity brother, was trying to put into his hand. Moultrie looked as if he suspected arrogance. "Really," Guy said. "The Stuff's in the bar, getting cold." He turned away, looking for Tom.

The game had been over not quite an hour. The faternity living room was full of chattering boys and sleek girls; Guy looked at the girls and wanted them all in a general, not very pressing sort of way. He was tired, and his right leg ached. His own date for the weekend had come down with mumps on Thursday, and sent a frantically disappointed wire; Guy had not bothered calling in a replacement. It would have meant urging some girl to break a date, since this particular weekend, when most New England colleges played their final fooball games, was not one on which any very desirable girl was likely to be free. He had thought of several who would break dates to come to Washburn for him, and rejected them all—some because he was through with them, though they might not quite know it yet; one because it wasn't time for this kind of date in her course of preparation; two more because they would too readily break dates for Guy, thus reversing carefully constructed orders of obligation.

Now, seeing the girls, he regretted having come to the fraternity house at all; he had meant only to have some drinks with the boys and look things over, perhaps establishing a potential or two for later in the year if he met something nice. But he wasn't at all sure, now that he saw girls, that he would be able to restrain himself to that extent, and he didn't really like playing the wolf; too easy to initiate, too uncertain thereafter. And for another thing, to do it—though he felt no urge to be considerate of the brothers in Omicron, most of whom he disliked—would be to offend someone; and offended people are a nuisance.

He was still wondering whether or not to stay when he recognized the Mariatt girl by the back of her honey blonde head; she was very much in the category of those who were not certain yet whether Guy was finished with them. She was with Pratt, the same boy she'd been with when Guy met her, early in the year; Guy thought, without vanity, that she'd probably accepted Pratt's invitation hoping to see Guy; he walked quickly away, into the library, and almost collided with Judy Held, from Baltimore, whom he had seduced last spring and not seen since. She was coming out of the library with an empty glass. She oughtn't to have been at Washburn at all. She dated at Harvard.

Judy Held frowned at him, but her mouth opened at the same time to expel breath; and her lips trembled a little.

"Hello, Judy," Guy said. "Excuse me." He stepped aside, smiling, to let her pass, and heard her breathe his name but pretended he hadn't. Then she said it again, so he had to turn around.

"Oh, Guy."

"Are you going to be here tonight?" Guy asked. She nodded. "Good, we'll dance together," he said lightly, and this time got away. And there, sitting on the arm of a leather chair, laughing so hard she didn't see him yet, was a girl named Helen Face, a young girl from town; her father owned the weaving mill; she was the

172

one he had considered calling when he heard about the mumps, whom he was not quite ready to take up seriously yet.

It was no evening for Guy at the Omicron house. It was not rare for him to find himself in accidental contact with a girl he didn't want to see, but suddenly the room was full of them. He found Tom, talking to Moultrie, and called him aside.

"Do you want to stay here for supper?"

Tom shrugged. "I don't care. No date." Tom's date was quarantined with Guy's. "I suppose we could help wait on table."

"I've got to get out," Guy said. "Why don't you get the champagne when it's cold and bring it over to the room? And then we'll go down town and get a steak?"

"All right," Tom said. "We can come back later if we feel like it."

There were no further girls for Guy to duck on the way out, but there was a recent alumnus who wanted to discuss a pass interception Guy had made—fifty-two yards and a score, called back because Bissle got over-enthusiastic and clipped someone; Guy smiled his way out of that one, and made the door; there, clustered around it, blocking his way, was the group of Omicron brothers who drank at games, without dates, and came back to the house drunk, and wanted to discuss football strategy.

As he made his way through their questions, and finally gained the porch, Guy had a vision of his life as a football game, in which he was forever evading tacklers—the Mariatt girl, Judy Held, Helen Face—what kind of a name was Face?—the recent alumnus, the strategists; only he had forgotten something. He had forgotten to find out where the goal was. This vision had the sharp confusion of a dream, and he supposed that he was tired from the game; he needed the champagne. He thought, with longing, that soon he would be drinking it with Tom.

As he walked across the campus in the chilly dusk, people called out to him and he smiled automatically and waved back; a drunk encountered him near the chapel doors, where it was dark under the elms, and the drunk said:

"Sophomore flash. Hey, sophomore flash. . . ."

Guy went past him quickly. He knew that he could reassure himself by turning around, going back to the Omicron house, and getting Judy Held whose lips had trembled when she said his name, whom he had meant to see again last spring; or better, he

173

could phone the house, have her called, tell her to meet him—he stopped himself from plotting it out. What he needed was to lie on his back, and drink champagne out of the bottle, and talk quietly with Tom.

He thought about Tom, the only friend he had ever made or needed to make. What an accident in his life it had been; what a fortunate one.

The only friend; there were two or three others Guy liked, several he tolerated; most acquaintances he despised or didn't bother to judge. He took a certain pride in thinking that, though the categories were quite distinct to him, no individual could tell, from Guy's behavior towards him, in which he had been placed. Guy was precisely the same to everyone, polite, charming when he cared to be, never friendly enough to invite intimacy; if anything, he was a little more polite, a little more often charming, to those he disliked. If they had been Mexican, they would have understood perfectly that this was a way of expressing hostility; but no American, not even Tom, could really understand that.

Guy hesitated at the door of the dormitory, feeling very Mexican, very alien; he could beat them at their game, take away their women, outspend them which was all they really respected, have the best of them for his friends. But to beat them made him less one of them than it would have to fail. Winners are lonelier than losers; there are fewer of them.

In Mexico it was different, not because he felt any more resemblance to the people, but because he had the family there. Brothers, cousins, father, uncles. That was the difference; and he thought, looking up the brick wall of the dormitory, at one or two meaningless lights showing among the dark windows above him, that Tom was like family to him. Well, then; his fidelity to Tom had been engaged by accident, but once engaged, there had never again been, could never again have been, any question of it, any more than there could be a question of fidelity to a brother.

Boy, Guy thought, oh boy, I need champagne. And he willed himself to stop thinking; the trouble with this was that it brought Judy Held back into his mind.

He realized, late and guilty, that she was very sweet.

The dormitory seemed utterly empty. If he had seen lights from outside, they must have been left on carelessly, by celebrants in too great a hurry to get to the parties; it was so quiet. He had never

174

heard it this way. It was meant to be a place of shouting, showers running, phonographs and radios playing—now, in the dusk, with only the hall lights burning, it was empty and sad.

If I die, Guy thought quietly, I will go to Hell. He didn't believe in Hell, but he went to church now and then in case he was wrong. I'm a Mexican, Guy thought, a superstitious Mexican.

Even though it made him feel guilty, Judy Held was pleasanter to hold in mind than God's vengeance, and as he climbed the stairs to the third story, where the rooms were, Guy urged Judy back into his head. He had promised to dance with her, and he remembered how he had danced with her in the vanished spring, when the issue of their interest in one another was still excitingly in doubt, and how, as the tune finished, she had closed against him for a sweet moment, sweetly, without words, resolving the doubt. A solitary radio could be heard now, left on somewhere on the fourth floor, playing quietly to itself, accentuating the sadness of the building and Guy's nostalgia for that lost moment when Judy pledged herself. Oh yes, sweet. So sweet. A face bright as a new leaf and as easily bruised, and he came to the head of the stairs in this curious, hallucinating mood, and saw a face looking down into his. The dark, ugly face of Eddie Bissle.

"Guy," Eddie said. "I wondered who in hell could be coming up. The place is empty."

Guy nodded; he couldn't speak.

Eddie was walking along down the hall, a step ahead of him. "How come you're not stretched out in a villa, with a bunch of tomatoes dripping warm oil on it?" he asked.

The meaning of the words was very slow in coming to Guy; he found himself translating them into Spanish, something he hadn't done in years: Tomatoes, *jitomates,* oil, *aceite* . . . they were at the open door of Eddie's room and Eddie paused, staring at Guy's face in the light shining through from a desk lamp.

"For Christ's sake," Eddie said. "What's the matter, Guy? I thought you were going to fall back down the stairs. Who'd you think I was?"

Guy stared back: "I thought you were . . . the devil," he said.

"What?" Eddie looked away. "Crud," he said.

It took the sound of the familiar word to restore fully Guy's assurance that Eddie was merely himself.

"Come on in," Eddie said. "You want a drink of gin?"

175

Guy followed Eddie into his room. He had seldom been inside it. Eddie was admitted to the small category of those Guy liked only because of Tom; it happened more often than Tom could possibly have realized that Guy accommodated to one of Tom's attitudes or sympathies—it was part of the pattern of fidelity, not even strictly necessary for, since Guy was the more positive, his own attitudes could have prevailed. But Tom was his friend, and Guy accommodated, and without resentment.

Yet even while consenting to Tom's fondness for Eddie, Guy knew it was softness on Tom's part. They had not extended friendship to Eddie; he had merely claimed it. Because he and Guy were football men, because he had arranged, once again, to have a room near theirs, because he had no use for anyone else at college, Eddie had chosen Guy and Tom as friends. Snubs had never deflected him from this; if he minded being omitted from their excursions, he never said so. He was not as unpopular this year, was accepted as an odd character, a crank, even thought amusing— but he only responded to Tom and Guy. He insisted on putting his car, his allowance, himself—none of them especially wanted—at their disposal, as if he were one of them. It wasn't in Tom to resist so open a plea to be liked; it wasn't in Guy to refuse to share a feeling with Tom.

"You're part Indian, aren't you?" he muttered, finally, to Eddie.

"Did I tell you that?"

"Yes. Or Tom. I guess I saw it in your face for a minute, there on the stairs. I'm sorry I said you were the devil."

Eddie seemed perplexed. "I don't get you tonight, Guy," he said. "You crapping me or what?"

Guy thought: he doesn't know what I'm saying. I don't know what he's saying. He shook his head,

"Indians scare you?" Eddie asked. "You've got a lot down in Mexico, haven't you?"

"It's an Indian country."

"You mean like boogies in the South?"

"No," Guy said. "No, it's their country. We never took it away from them and exterminated them, the way you did here."

"Yeah?"

"But they never got us out, either. They didn't really try. Maybe they should have."

"Why?"

"I thought you studied history?"

176

Eddie shrugged. "This is a different angle."

"What happened was a mixture, a new race. Indian-Spanish. A bad, hysterical race. And *they* threw the Spanish out. I was wrong. It's not an Indian country. It belongs to the mixture."

"Hell, we're all mixtures," Eddie said. "Except you, I guess. You're pure Spanish, aren't you?"

"No. American mother, American grandmother," Guy said. "Less than half. All European, though. I guess Tom could say that too."

"If it's anything to say. I don't see much in this race crap, do you?" Eddie smiled, if you called the thing a smile. "Pure crud is just as bad as mixed crud, isn't it?"

We are talking, Guy thought with surprise; Bissle and I. He looked at Eddie carefully, and around his room. Eddie was sitting now, back at the desk from which he must have gotten up when he heard Guy on the stairs. There was a single lamp on, the desk lamp. There was a book on the desk, but it was closed; Eddie had not been reading. There was a bottle of gin, but it had not been opened.

"What were you doing?" Guy asked.

"Nothing," Eddie said. "Thinking about having a drink of this goddamn gin." He lifted the bottle. "I've had it a year now. You'd think I might open it."

"You don't drink much?" If Tom were here, Guy thought, Tom would urge Eddie to open the bottle, knowing Eddie wanted someone to accept a drink from it; Tom wouldn't even consider that it might spoil his taste for champagne.

Eddie shrugged. "I can't see the point of it," he said. "I like to get drunk sometimes, but I can't see the point of just drinking." He pondered. "Sometimes, I go get drunk in a bar."

"Is that what you're going to do tonight?"

"I hadn't decided," Eddie said. "I don't figure to go out and get drunk just because it's supposed to be the night for it. Like all the other football jerks. Breaking training. Big deal. You know the last time I got drunk?"

"When?"

"Friday night before the Amherst game. I drove down to Lowell, and got stinking and then slept it off in the car. A cop woke me about four A.M. and I drove back. Got here at five."

"Why?" Guy asked. "If Bantie had found out, you'd have been off the squad."

177

"Yeah. That was the deal," Eddie said. "Six years now I've been letting them smother me in crap about training rules. So I just thought I'd see how much it hurt to break them all. Christ, I ate fat food, I couldn't find a whore house so I pulled my pod in the men's room, and after I got back here I read till morning so I wouldn't have any sleep. And what happened Saturday?"

"You played sixty minutes, didn't you?"

"Yeah. And felt perfect. I admit, I went to bed right after the game and slept eighteen hours. Look, you don't want to hang around with me."

"I beg your pardon?"

"Thanks a hell of a lot for dropping in," Eddie said. "But you're probably on your way someplace. I don't want to hold you up. I uh, got reading to do." He struck the closed book a smart blow with his open hand.

Guy rose. He understood perfectly. Eddie didn't want him to leave, he only meant to anticipate Guy's leaving. The thing to do was respect the intention, wasn't it? But Tom wouldn't; Tom would say to himself that Bissle wasn't any happier about the idea of spending the evening alone in an empty dormitory, with a book and an unopened gin bottle while the college celebrated, than any other undergraduate would be. Probably, if it were Tom, it would be a contest to see whether Tom could invite Eddie to join them before Eddie invited himself. As Guy thought this, he heard Tom coming upstairs.

He might as well forestall the contest, Guy thought. It would save awkwardness. "Here's Tom," he said. "Come break training with us."

"Yeah?" Eddie said, too readily. "Shall I bring the gin, or what?"

"We have champagne," Guy said. "Try a little of that."

"Thanks, Guy." Eddie rose, obviously very pleased. "I've never had champagne. Hey Guy."

"Yes?"

"I'm sorry about clipping that crumb halfback, on your interception. He turned on me."

"That's all right," Guy said, surprised yet again. Why should mistakes be mentioned when a game was over?

They drank the champagne, two big bottles of it. They began, later, working their way through Eddie's gin bottle. They forgot to eat, almost, until it seemed silly to go all the way down town,

178

so they accepted Eddie's offer to bring up hamburgers from the Union, just before it closed. Now and then they would hear somebody in the dormitory, coming in to get a jacket or a bottle or something, but mostly they continued to have the building to themselves.

The strange mood of guilt and vision which had seized Guy early in the evening left completely. He had never felt that way before and hoped he never would again. It became very cozy, drinking there with Tom and Eddie, eating the hamburgers, listening to Tom and Eddie argue about girls.

Eddie said there were two methods: a little crude strength at the right moment, or a little cold cash. It didn't sound as if Eddie spoke from very wide experience, and Tom's countering was based, Guy knew perfectly well, on just about no experience at all. Tom hadn't had a girl since funny little Ruby, at Prep school; Tom didn't really seem to want a girl. He went along with Guy on weekends constantly, and Tom would keep his date at the tavern or the dance or whatever it was while Guy went off. Tom might or might not kiss a little with his date; he seemed just as content if the evenings came to nothing more than talk and laughter. He said he was mostly interested in having a pleasant time; it perplexed Guy. He wondered if the business with Ruby had scared Tom off. Well, it was funny to listen to Tom and Eddie arguing, and Guy sat and listened, sipping his gin from a water glass, concealing a smile.

Eddie kept saying, "Let's hear from the expert," but Guy declined to testify. He thought he must feel something like a professional gambler, listening to beginners talk about cards; there was no point in joining the discussion, because the difference was a matter of attitude. Sex to them was an amusement and a mystery. Sex to Guy was, by this time, his occupation.

For Guy, there could be none of the generalizing about girls that Tom and Eddie were doing. Each girl was a separate study. Some liked strength, some gifts, some attention, some neglect; most responded to an appearance of sympathetic understanding and almost all, at some point, to physical urgency. But these responses were only the beginning, the salesman making a prospect talk to him; closing the sale was something different, a higher order of skill. One must be able to feel very accurately what the individual wanted—if it was ruthlessness, as Eddie seemed to think, very well, but the ruthlessness must be subtly applied, a re-

179

fusal to accept refusal, not an exercise of force. And that was only one of many ways of closing; there were girls with whom the only way, finally, was to keep all pressure off, give them plenty of time, let them bring themselves in.

Guy did not consider himself irresistible; he was not that stupid. He knew, moreover, that there were many things outside himself that contributed to his successes: his being a foreigner, a Latin; his being wealthy; the accident of his appearance; the newspaper stuff; his reputation as a dangerous man. But he also considered that, with or without these things going for him, he had a better than even chance with any woman to begin with and that, though a mistake might lose him the advantage at some point, the percentage of chance was reduced in his favor in direct proportion to the amount of time and care he chose to spend. Leaving Tom and Eddie to their foolish debate—Tom's position was that you could only do what the girl had already decided to permit, which was a piece of the truth about the same size as Eddie's piece—Guy slipped away, into the bedroom. He stayed there half an hour, looking through his notebook; there were thirty-seven gold stars in it now, against nineteen pages without stars, to prove him right. He counted them to make sure; he had counted them day before yesterday. He entered the totals and the date, something that he did periodically, on a separate leaf. The Mariatt girl's was the most recent page; it had been a long time getting its star, and he had no photograph for it; difficult girl. For a while.

He found himself turning back to Judy Held's page; he felt quite drunk. Not difficult at all. There was a snapshot of Judy looking uncertainly demure. Pretty. Pretty thing. Though it was nothing as complex as the early evening mood, Guy found himself crying a little over the picture, an actual tear or two. He abandoned the intention he had been nursing all evening of calling her away from the fraternity house. He felt better about it. He closed the book, put it away in its locked metal box, and went back to Tom and Eddie.

Now Eddie was saying extravagantly bitter things about the British, for some reason, and even worse things about the Irish. Tom seemed quite amused with these crotchets, and the more he laughed at Eddie, the more Eddie caricatured his own malevolence. Guy laughed at it, too. He poured himself some more of the gin. Eddie jumped to his feet, went jigging slowly around the

180

room like an old man, and said, in an abominable attempt at brogue:

"I'm half British and half Irish and all crud, lads, and I'll kick the man with a good word to say for either nation."

"What about Afghanistan?" Tom asked.

"You say anything kindly toward Afghanistan, I'll beat your head bloody with a gin bottle," Eddie growled. "Yes, I will."

It was all right with Guy if Tom wanted to be friends with this irascible little *mestizo;* but it was Tom who could be out of the mood for concourse with Eddie, not Guy.

It was Tom who, a night or two later, turned off the light in their study when they heard Bissle out in the hall, so that it would appear that Tom and Guy weren't in.

"I'm sorry," Tom said, when Eddie had gone away from the door. "I just couldn't take it tonight, I guess."

And it was Tom who said, "No, Guy. We can't take Eddie to Radcliffe," when there were three girls available there one weekend early in December. They took Moultrie, instead; Guy supposed Tom had worried that Eddie might use the occasion to try to prove his theories about girls.

4.

Once Eddie Bissle wrote a poem. He had this friend, Tom Beniger, who was a tall idiot, who was raving about T. S. Eliot. So Beniger and Eddie's other friend, Guy Cinturon, went away one early winter weekend, just after Thanksgiving, tail-chasing to some woman's college, and Eddie read the whole book of poems by T. S. Eliot. Read it, reread it, took it to the library and looked up some of the stupid references, until he figured he had it sawed up into boards.

When Beniger and Cinturon got back from delighting their dongs at Miss Duckworth's, or wherever it was, the volume of Eliot was back on Beniger's desk, with Eddie's poem written in the flyleaf (but in pencil, and lightly, so that Tom could erase it in case he really cared about the damn book):

POEM
I sit and cry:
"The world is full of broken glass."

I should have stood to cry.
Oh, my bleeding ass.

E. M. Bissle

He heard Tom and Guy coming back in the afternoon, and he waited for a few minutes. Then Tom came into his room, grinning, and said:

"I think you're a minor poet, Eddie, but a strong one."

They talked for a while, and when Tom left, Eddie turned on his radio; there was no pro football game being broadcast, but sometimes he liked the Sunday afternoon music. He was too late to hear the title and composer of what they were playing, but whatever it was, it put him to sleep.

When he woke up, he thought for a minute that it was intermission and some crumb was laying out the cultural situation, the way they did, and he felt a slight annoyance because he usually managed to be up and out of the room before the crumb could get started.

Only this wasn't the cultural crumb; it was a different voice, a news bulletin voice, and it was the first report of the attack on Pearl Harbor.

Eddie always wondered what had wakened him; was it just that the music stopped, or was the news bulletin crumb's a voice he had to wake up for, because he had been waiting for it all his life?

He jumped up; he ran out into the hall, meaning to go to Tom. He found the hall full of jerks running back and forth to tell each other the news they were all hearing. He stopped in his doorway and watched the faces go by—serious, excited, full of importance —and he thought: what a pukey thing to go running around about. What a puke I am to be going to Tom.

He stepped back into his room, and closed the door.

The news bulletin crumb was still running off about all the ships that were sinking, and Eddie sat by the radio for a while and tried to listen to it all and understand what the hell had happened. Finally, he stood up and looked around for his gin bottle. It was in the closet and there was about half an inch of liquor left in the bottom. The crumb on the radio was beginning to repeat.

Eddie took off the cap and walked back to the desk. Tom caught him pouring the gin over the radio, saying to the news bulletin crumb:

"Here. You need this more than I do."

182

CHAPTER EIGHT

1.

Two weeks after Pearl Harbor, Tom arrived in New York to spend Christmas vacation with Ellen in her third apartment. The first had been with Alice, the second uptown; this one was in Greenwich Village, a large one-room place which Ellen shared with a girl named Harriet Newton. Harriet was going home for the holidays.

Tom arrived the night before Harriet left, and there was a memorable evening of laughter and prurience, concerning the fact that they must all three sleep in the same room, Tom on sofa cushions on the floor; the prurience got rather high-pitched when they began taking turns in the bathroom, to prepare for bed. They had done a good deal of whiskey drinking.

Tom could not be sure whether Harriet, a handsome girl with a lavish bust, intended that he have various intimate glimpses of her during the preparations or not; he could not even be sure what she intended when Harriet came out of the bathroom struggling with a transparent nightgown and a handtowel, crying that Tom must shut his eyes, she had forgotten her hairbrush. Ellen said, laughing:

"If he wants to look, let him. Tom's seen girls before."

Tom looked as much as he dared; by the time he woke next

morning, Harriet was gone. And there were Tom and Ellen in New York together, all grown up, owlish eighteen, svelte twenty-two.

It was Saturday morning, and Tom and Ellen sat a long time over breakfast, finishing a coffee cake that had been supposed to last until Sunday, talking about the fall. Ellen was quite frankly fascinated to hear about Guy; Tom spoke of him cautiously.

"Isn't he in New York?"

"Yes. I don't know how much I'll see him. He's going to a lot of debutante parties and stuff like that."

"Maybe I'll get to meet him," Ellen said. "After all I've heard— what a shame he's so young. What about Eddie? Is he going to be around thrilling debutantes, too?"

"No, he lives out on Long Island," Tom said. "As a matter of fact, Eddie said he was going to go duck hunting every morning if the Coast Guard doesn't have too much barbed wire around the marshes."

"Maybe he'll come to town."

"Maybe," Tom said.

"We could have a party—for you and Guy and Eddie. I'd love to give it. It sounds as if Guy could find you girls."

"Sure," Tom said. "Well, listen, I know a couple of girls myself. Matter of fact. . . ."

"Matter of fact what?"

"I might just get myself a date tonight. What are you going to do?"

"I promised to see Harrison," Ellen said. "Want me to break it?"

"No. Why don't we all go out together?" Tom said.

They saw a lot of Harrison that vacation. Tom found him awfully dull, though he dutifully tried to like him; and, as a matter of fact, Harrison in Navy uniform wasn't altogether useless; he looked very well. Headwaiters and bartenders responded to the young officer, and Harrison had a certain Yale-bred assurance with such people, which made going out in New York very smooth.

Tom and Guy talked on the phone two or three times a week; they went to a couple of hockey games together, met in bars afternoons when Ellen was at work, double dated several times. Tom, grimly foolish about it, kept managing to put off a meeting between Guy and Ellen, but by the day before Christmas it no longer seemed possible. An uncle of Guy's was giving a Christmas

184

Eve party at the Plaza, and Tom and Ellen were both invited. It was to be a dressy, diplomatic set version of some sort of traditional Mexican celebration, and Ellen was quite excited. Tom grew resigned. He began to regret now, that he hadn't let the meeting take place earlier, in some less splendid setting, for now Ellen's first glimpse of Tom's friend would be of Guy in tails, assisting his uncle as a host. Well, it was going to be a dazzler.

Then, at the last moment, came a wire from the Kaiser; he and their mother were flying to New York, arriving that day.

"BECAUSE OF WAR," the telegram said, "MAY NOT HAVE FAMILY TOGETHER AGAIN. . . ."

Ellen, who received it at her office, phoned Tom and read it to him. Then she said:

"Tommy, I hate to disappoint you but, well, I don't guess we ought to plan on going to Guy's party, should we?"

Tom felt lousy about it; he knew the disappointment was more Ellen's than his. So he said:

"Ellen, we'll dress for the party, and then we'll settle Mom and the Kaiser and have Christmas Eve with them. And then we'll go to the party late, after they've gone to bed."

"You don't think Mom's feelings will be hurt?"

"I'll fix it with her," Tom said. "I'm sure I can."

Then, after all, when they got to the Plaza at one, Guy wasn't there. It was a sumptuous party—neither Tom nor Ellen had ever seen anything quite like it; Guy's uncle was very cordial, and there were a lot of young Latin American officers who flirted with Ellen, Guy, the uncle explained, had waited for them until midnight, but now must be off, representing the family at a series of similar parties which would go on until everyone met at church, early Christmas morning. He suggested sending them around with Guy's cousin Jose, to look in at the other parties and find Guy; Tom was for it, but Ellen sighed and said they'd better not. The Kaiser wanted very particularly to see her first thing in the morning, she said, for a private talk. The folks had a plane reservation to go back, Christmas afternoon, for the Kaiser was now frozen in his defense job which he took very seriously.

"There has been a great deal of absenteeism, and I don't like to participate in it," he had said. "Any more than a soldier should leave his post." He was a section foreman now, and had an example to set.

Going home in a cab, Tom said:

"I think the Kaiser is working too hard. He's fifty now. He shouldn't be working overtime every night."

"No," Ellen said. "He looks tired. But Mom looks better than she has in years."

The cab turned into Bleecker street, where her apartment was.

"What a heavenly party," Ellen said. "Tom, thank you so much for taking me."

"How many phone numbers did you have to give out?" Tom asked. "You should have it printed on a card."

"They can look in the phone book," Ellen said. "I do hope that pretty Brazilian boy knows about phone books."

"The Brazilian?" Tom said, as the cab stopped. "Listen, those guys study the New York telephone book in grade school."

"I'm so tired of just seeing Harrison and Harrison's friends," Ellen said. He helped her out and paid the cab.

"Yes, I imagine Harrison gets a little heavy."

She looked at him.

"Heavy?"

"Oh, I like him all right, Ell. But he's awfully . . . I don't know. Proper. Isn't he?"

She gave him a curious look, and then nodded. "Yes, he's proper. Come on. Let's not stand out on a cold street talking about Harrison Walle at three in the morning."

In the week between Christmas and New Year's the vacation, which had been fine, got altogether marvelous. Having found that they more or less agreed about Harrison, it became easier for Tom to see the man so constantly with his sister; he wasn't anyone Ellen was serious about. Good. The Brazilian called, and gave Ellen a great two day whirl before he had to return to Washington, putting her into a wonderful mood. She forgot about wanting to meet Guy. And then there came an enchanted late afternoon moment which, it seemed to Tom, contributed to the vacation the note of poignancy, of things about to be lost, which underscored all the gaiety and made it real.

He had a date, with a dark-eyed girl he sometimes saw at Radcliffe, Angie Berkhead. They were to meet Ellen and Harrison in a bar on Sixth Avenue, and go on to a cocktail party.

They walked into the bar a few minutes late, and saw Ellen and Harrison and some of Harrison's friends, all standing at the other end. The men were all, like Harrison, graduate students in Naval

186

uniforms; Ellen was wearing winter white, and she was laughing. Everyone in the bar was aware of the handsome group; these accounting officers looked, the war being only three weeks old, no less military, no less profoundly endangered, than any others. And some would have sea duty, of course. Ellen was looking up at one of them, not Harrison, a tall thin boy Tom didn't know, who wore the uniform with particular style; just as she finished laughing at whatever it was he said, the juke box began to play "Anchors Aweigh," in a pretty, dance band version, and the bar grew quiet. Everyone looked respectfully at the Navy men and at Ellen, and the group, which had been laughing a moment before, grew quiet too, and serious. A crooning voice was singing words about a last night on shore and suddenly Ellen pressed her shiny blonde head against the blue of the tall boy's uniform, and Tom thought that he saw tears in Ellen's eyes. Angie caught his arm, and held him still, so perhaps she saw them too. If tears were there, they were gone in an instant for Ellen pulled her head away and smiled at Harrison and his friends, a smile of almost unbearable radiance. That was the moment, so it seemed to Tom, that would always characterize the vacation for him, the thing he would remember when he too was in uniform and needed something to recall.

Better and better. Harriet Newton was coming back. A man had phoned her from New York, insisted that she be on hand for New Year's Eve. When she arrived, Tom offered to move over to Guy's hotel room but, to his concealed delight, Harriet wouldn't hear of it; all three had shared the apartment before she said. They would again, she said, and pinched Tom's cheek.

What could she mean? What could she intend? This was an older girl, a year older than Ellen even, a girl who knew what she was doing. She kept Tom in an almost continuous state of excitement through the following days, always around in some stage of undress. Tom tried to hide the excitement both so that Ellen wouldn't know, and because he imagined that the less interest he showed, the more careless Harriet would be about her clothing. This seemed to be so. It became quite commonplace for Tom to see her in her slip; she stopped leaving the room when she pulled on stockings.

On New Year's Eve itself he let himself into the apartment about eleven; he had left one party and was on his way to another.

187

Both Ellen and Harriet must have left, he assumed—Ellen with Harrison, Harriet with the man who had called her back.

All the lights were on but it didn't seem to mean anything. Clothes were strewn all over the room. The place looked empty but happy; Tom was so sure that he was alone in the apartment that he actually picked up one of Harriet's undergarments and held it against his cheek for a moment. Then he started into the bathroom. It was bright, full of steam, and Harriet stood naked in the middle of it, drying herself after a bath. Tom was so startled that he forgot himself for a long moment, and stared; Harriet was so startled, apparently, that, for the same long moment, she neither shrieked nor moved the towel to cover herself. Then she did both as Tom backed away, profoundly embarrassed, closing the door. He was almost too choked to call through it that he was sorry; she didn't answer. He supposed she must be furious. But just a second later she came out, holding a large terry cloth robe around her, brown-haired, vigorous and damp.

"You little fiend," she said to Tom and then, before he could apologize again, she smiled, took his face in her moist hands, pulled him against the folds of the robe, and kissed him deeply, filling his mouth with her tongue, her face and arms radiating the warmth and wetness of the shower. Then she stepped back, observed him, and said, matter-of-factly,

"Hurry, will you Tommy? I'm late and I need the whole place to myself just this once."

Baffled, Tom got quickly on to his next party which was one Angie Berkhead's family was giving, and where there were gay young girls, unfathomable enough, but not with the total mysteriousness of over twenty.

Tom was the first one home. He fell into bed at five. At six, Harrison and Ellen came in, quite drunk, and sat on one of the beds. Tom talked to them for a minute or two, and then pretended to go to sleep and watched suspiciously through slitted eyes; promptly and decorously, Harrison went to sleep with his clothes on, and Ellen got ready to nap on Harriet's bed. Tom woke again, briefly, when Harriet came in at eight; they didn't know he was awake. They moved the sodden Harrison onto cushions on the floor, in much the same sort of arrangement Tom had for sleeping; Harriet seemed displeased with her evening, but Tom was too sleepy to apprehend why. Something the man had done or wanted to do,

188

something irregular. . . . Tom tried to stay awake to use the slit-eyed treatment on Harriet undressing, but the slits kept closing. When he woke again it was noon, and Ellen and Harrison had gone out.

Harriet made no reference to what had passed between them the evening before and, in fact, went rather ostentatiously to the bathroom to take off the robe she had on over her slip, and change to a dress. It was, in some ways, a relief to Tom; the degree of erotic fantasy he had reached over Harriet had begun to fill his mind almost to the exclusion of sense.

The next morning, Ellen and Harriet began to work again at their jobs. Harriet taught in a nursery school; Ellen was assistant to a man who did promotional work for a number of charities.

In the evening, Ellen had a headache which she ascribed to arguing with Harrison for two solid days. Tom was going to a movie with Guy; on impulse, he asked Harriet to join them. He was curious to see whether Guy and he really seemed as young to a woman this age as he supposed they did. She refused. When he got back, shortly before midnight, Ellen was sitting up in bed in her pajamas, sleepily drunk and rather contented. Harriet was brushing her marvelous long brown hair.

Tom made himself a drink, and gradually, the whole ambiguous thing began again: Harriet bared her legs. Harriet took off her dress without quite leaving the room. Harriet walked past a lamp which shone through her slip. Ellen went to sleep, sitting up in bed.

Tom followed Harriet clumsily into the corridor off which kitchen and bathroom opened, where she let him press her against the wall and kiss her. They did this silently because of Ellen. It lasted for some time until Harriet pushed him away and went into the bathroom. Tom, grotesquely excited, drank some straight whiskey out of the bottle, set it down, and paced around the room; the wait was interminable. The thought that anything further was impossible because of Ellen kept buzzing at him, and he kept slapping it away.

Harriet's coming out, when she did, took him by surprise; she was wearing only a nightgown this time; that should have been a good omen, but she eluded him and slipped into her bed. He followed recklessly and she, holding the blankets tightly around her neck, gave him the merest peck of a kiss and said:

"You'd better get ready for bed."

189

And another, when he insisted, and said:

"I have to work tomorrow. Go on."

Tom turned away, went to the wall switch and turned out the light. He went into the bathroom, pulled off his clothes, leaving them piled on the floor, and put on a pair of pajama pants. Then he banged back into the room, painfully charged with excitement, so much so that he was no longer a social creature but an animal, possessed; he went directly to Harriet's bed, where she was pretending to be asleep. He didn't pause. He got into the bed and instantly her excitement seemed to be as painful as his for they both gulped air harshly and she received him with some indistinguishable sort of cry. For two or three blind minutes he was unaware of time, place, of Ellen sleeping—he was unaware of Harriet except as femaleness. And within five minutes, Tom was back on his pile of cushions as if nothing at all had happened, though it took him more than an hour to go to sleep.

The next morning, he woke very pleased with himself though it took a moment to remember why he should be. Ellen and Harriet were both gone. He jumped up, and called Guy; they had breakfast together in a restaurant, and Tom knew he was being an infant about it but he couldn't resist telling Guy the whole thing in close detail. Guy listened carefully and philosophized about girls that age; he saw significance in the man who had brought Harriet back for New Year's. He seemed to know what he was talking about, and Tom began to think: no, it was not ridiculous to prevent Guy and Ellen's meeting. Ellen was a girl that age, and the prettiest one there was, too.

When they had finished with Harriet, they planned when and where to meet the next day to take the train back to college.

All in all it seemed to Tom that he had finally had a satisfactory sex experience, where nobody had to fall in love, and get their feelings hurt and it was just fun and felt good. Fine.

That evening a subdued Harriet muttered that she was going to be an overnight sitter for one of her nursery school charges, put some things into a small suitcase, added in overexplanation that she supposed Tom and Ellen would want to talk on Tom's final evening, and disappeared. Tom, his own suit-cases half-packed around the apartment, was not too sorry; the euphoria of the morning was somewhat dampened by the way she avoided his eyes.

He and Ellen had supper and, afterwards, inevitably, she opened

the last and most confident of his boy's illusions—that his sister was wise and pure—had been, steady and warm.

Now he had to see this sister as she really was, and his pain was as much a protest at the destruction of a beautiful false certainty as it was the pain of jealousy and the pain—he could not escape this either—of fellow feeling, her personal pain of which he now assumed a share.

Here now was Ellen plain, no blesser of heroes with a brave and tragic smile, but only a very pretty girl, without quite enough money to have ever dressed really well, or quite enough family to have ever been really sure; with a small, endearing gift for gaiety; with a good mind that would never be used; with a hunger she couldn't acknowledge for a fulfillment she couldn't name; with an obscure sense of hurt, more wistful than resentful, at finding herself in a world that does not yield nameless things, that may not even have them.

After a while she was crying because, she said, she had messed things up so; by walking out on the arrangement with Harrison, because its very staidness bored her, she had thought to offend him; instead he had upgraded her from the good scout with whom to share a proper bachelor's bed to the one woman he must desperately and forever love. It was such a mess; and most of the other men she knew in New York were Harrison's friends, to whom she was Harrison's girl.

Once he had settled down to listen, Tom was able to decide that, even if there had been someone there to feel sorry for him, he would hardly deserve it; that his sense of loss represented the loss only of a tissue of silliness, illusion, unnatural jealousy—an oversensitiveness on his own behalf. So he swallowed his bereavement, and gave himself over to comforting Ellen, and they sat up most of the night, occupied with it.

That was the vacation, except for an odd thing: when he got back to college and unpacked, he found that Harriet had put into his suitcase, under the socks, half of a greeting card—the rear half which read, in print, "and a Happy New Year." Under it she had written: "With you, back to college, goes a piece of my heart. H."

He wrote to her immediately, but got no reply. And since she moved away from the apartment not long afterwards and Tom never saw her again, he never quite knew what she meant.

193

Tom needn't have worried about Guy and Ellen's meeting. He learned that later in the winter; 1942.

College life was beginning to come apart. Nearly everyone was in some sort of program now, Army, Navy or Air. A number had left school; others planned to, or fell below in their grades at mid-years and were drafted right out of the dorms. A faculty committee had been appointed to devise an accelerated program, which would keep them all in school through the summers.

In this time of rumor and change, Ellen wrote that she was taking two weeks' leave of absence from her job; she had to get out of New York and away from Harrison with whom she had broken for good; she was going skiing, all by herself, but she would stop off Saturday, on the way to the ski slopes, in the Massachusetts town where Washburn College is. She wanted to see Tom; she wanted to meet his friends. Please.

He could sense from the letter that it was important to Ellen to find him secure, and he was glad he hadn't written to her about the changes that were going on at Washburn. He and Guy cancelled plans for a trip to Mount Holyoke, and got local dates instead.

"She wants to take us all to dinner," he said. "Then I guess she'll go on up to the hills on the nine-eleven."

"She doesn't really want us," Guy said, sadly. "In the world of twenty-two year old girls, we are only large babies who have lost their cuteness."

"What's she want me for," said Eddie. "She got a grudge against herself?"

But they both agreed; they were both pleased.

Tom met the train in Eddie's car; Guy's was being repaired. He took Ellen to the most familiar of the local beer joints; she enjoyed it. It was reminiscent for her of her own undergraduate times, though she had never dated at Washburn. As they drank the beers, Tom learned that she did not plan to go on; she had intended all along to spend the night. They drove over to the Rolmer Hotel, the old, barny hotel by the railroad station where everyone had to stay, and took a room for her. Tom said that he and Guy would break their dates—he would, anyway—but Ellen wouldn't have it.

"We'll eat," she said. "Here." She gave Tom a twenty. "You pay the check for me, will you? And then I'm going straight to bed after dinner. I have to get a morning train at 7:15, and I'll be out skiing by noon."

Late in the afternoon they drove up to the sophomore dormitory to get Guy and Eddie. She was worried about their liking her, which made Tom laugh; she looked very New York in the short fur coat, with a hat which didn't hide much of her air, and a style of making up her face beyond the skill—or, perhaps, outside the custom—of the college girls whom they regularly saw. No, Guy and Eddie would like her; and she would like Guy. He was a little concerned about what she'd think of Eddie. Back in the silly time, when he had been so worried about Ellen's being swept away by Guy, he'd overdone the build-up on poor Eddie.

They stopped the car, got out, and waved at the windows. A girl couldn't go into the dormitory, not even a sister. Guy and Eddie waved back and left the window. Other acquaintances came to other windows to look out at Ellen and make ridiculous gestures, hands covering eyes, pretended faints—she was really something to look at.

There was only one slight irritation, and yet Tom had to sympathize with it; it was the way, when his friends came out, that Eddie was careful to stay on the side of the car visible to the gesturers in the windows. He was letting the boys know that he, Eddie Bissle, was with his friends Tom and Guy and a blonde from New York who might have been a model but was, in fact, his friend Tom's sister.

Built into one end of what was still an enormous bar-room at the Rolmer Hotel, an almost amateurish attempt to adapt to changing customs, was a dark little room with four booths, two tables, a juke box, and a sign over the door which read "Cocktail Nook." There they sat and had two rounds of drinks. Guy was very talkative; suddenly Tom thought that Guy was being too talkative. And then realized that this was deliberate. Ellen was getting from Guy the facile friendly charm, the pleasantness, the treatment Guy had for a girl's mother or a lady chaperone, not the direct, slow pulsing, but infinitely stronger magnetism that a girl faced when Guy was seriously in pursuit.

195

Tom thought: how stupid I have been. Guy would never make a pass at Ellen. She's my sister. He felt as if he owed everybody at the table an apology, but the time was passing too pleasantly to dwell on that.

They played a tango on the juke box with the third round of drinks, and Guy danced it with Ellen; he was a considerable expert at it, and she had taught dancing.

"Fine to watch," Eddie said.

As the record ended a waiter came in to protest that they had no dancing license. Eddie bluntly offered the man a dollar bill to go and see if the roof wasn't leaking upstairs, and to everyone's surprise the man finished serving their fourth round of drinks, accepted the bill, and went away. They played the record again, and Ellen asked Eddie if he wouldn't like to dance, too.

"No," said Eddie. "We got no license for amateurs. I like watching you and Guy." So the two danced the same tango over again, with flourishes; then they all finished their drinks and went in to dinner.

Tom and Eddie stuffed themselves. Guy quoted what he claimed was a motto translated from his family's coat of arms: *Eat moderately and go to a good barber.* Tom put it back into Latin for them. Actually, Guy never ate much before a date, and he was seeing Helen Face that night, the girl whose father owned the weaving mill. Tom's date was a professor's daughter, home from college for the weekend. Ellen wanted to hear all about both girls and Tom said they would bring them to Ellen's room at midnight for a loving cup. Ellen said that would be a very good way to get hit with a ski pole, and they all laughed immoderately.

Ellen didn't actually have much to say or much to eat either; instead she drank through dinner, smoked, and laughed flatteringly at everything everyone said.

They were debating brandy when Guy noticed that it was past time to go for their dates; they were shamelessly requisitioning Eddie's car, because of Guy's being in the garage for repairs. Eddie said he would walk back up to the dorm, assuming he could ever move again. Ellen said he was to stay while she had her brandy, and Tom and Guy left.

Tom was delighted with the way the long-delayed meeting had gone. As he and Guy got into the car, he even permitted himself

196

a moment's illogical indignation because Guy hadn't been a little more overwhelmed, a little less guarded. But then Guy started talking about how perfectly wonderful Ellen was, and Tom's indignation was over with.

3.

Ellen said: "You don't have as much to say as those fast talkers, do you?"

"It's because I'm an ugly customer type," said Eddie, whose most frequent object of misanthropy, especially when he had been drinking, was himself.

Tom's sister seemed to take it for wit; she laughed.

Eddie was surprised. Immediately calculating, he said: "You mean Tom hasn't told you? When it's ugly day, they fly me from the flagpole."

"You aren't ugly," Ellen said.

"No, I'm Bissle," Eddie replied. It was a standard joke form of the day.

"To tell you the truth," Ellen said. "I think Tom's been keeping both of you away from me."

"Guy Cinturon is my best friend, and a yellow bastard," Eddie said. "Tom Beniger is my best friend and soft in the head. I already told you my secret."

"Why do you say Guy's yellow?" Ellen asked. "He's the one the girls swoon over, isn't he?"

"It depends," Eddie said, "on the girls. There are some stupid girls who swoon on ugly day. Of course, it's just possible those girls were born unconscious."

For some reason this delighted her. Eddie was amazed. Didn't this girl believe her eyes?

"Listen," he said. "If I die from overeating, it's your fault. You admit that?"

"Are you really uncomfortable?" Ellen asked. "I'm sorry."

"So you think I could lie down in your room a little while?" Eddie asked. He had nothing to lose; he took no risk.

"All right," said Ellen, apparently not displeased. "I'm sure it will be all right. They probably don't know which one my brother is, anyway."

197

On the way upstairs, Eddie kept counselling himself to go slow. The idea of making a pass at Tom's sister was extremely stimulating, as much for the prospect of symbolic retaliation at Tom—he did not ask himself why Tom deserved this—as for her own very evident desirability. It did not seem to Eddie that he would be particularly successful, but he intended, when dinner had worn off a little, to force himself to make the pass. He thought he could probably kiss her, if only because she so plainly wanted to be nice to Tom's friends. Hey, Tom, Eddie thought, as they got to the door; your big, pretty sister's going to get kissed in about two minutes. Actually, it was more like half an hour before he nerved himself to make the move.

Ellen, sitting and watching him with a drink in her hand as he lay on the bed with coat, tie and shoes off, was rather fuzzy from all the liquor. She kicked her own shoes off. She became aware of Eddie's curious, overdeveloped little body—the knotty muscles in his wrists and fingers, the heavy forearms, the corded neck; he had seemed a funny little fellow to her, and, taking her cue from Tom, endearing. Now she saw him as a male, as well; his face was rather attractive in a knobby way, a bit coarse but as strong as the rest of him. She made the judgment automatically, without real interest in him.

Eddie, trying to keep his face inexpressive, was remembering, for encouragement, that when he had taken the key out of her hand to open the door, and touched her for a moment, she hadn't drawn her hand away.

All right, Ellen thought, half forgetting about the silent Eddie; I have come away from Harrison Walle now. There had been no one else in her life, really, for almost two years; what she knew of lovemaking was all in Harrison's sedate terms. She thought she might find a man at the ski place—a tall instructor with a winter tan, a go-to-hell downhill champion—someone exciting. That was all she would ask of him; that he be exciting. It had not occurred to her that she might find one of Tom's young friends exciting, and did not now, though she had had a natural curiosity about Guy. But Guy seemed bland to her; she told herself, as an interior joke, that she could not actually be sure, on the basis of what she had seen of them, that this powerful little man lying so nonchalantly on her bed, more or less ignoring her, was not the one with the reputation for irresistibility. The thought amused her; the joke was on silly Tom.

Eddie, of course, was not ignoring her at all. Eddie was intensely aware of her and straining at his indecision. "Hey you know?" He said suddenly, sitting up. "You're shorter than I am. How many girls can say that?"

"You're not especially short," Ellen said, and gave him a smile. And sipped a little at the drink, which tasted good.

"I'm a dwarf." Eddie made himself bounce to his feet, in front of her chair. "Quasi Goddamn Modo. Put your drink down and stand up."

Ellen obeyed, for no particular reason. "You're not a dwarf," she said, standing in front of him, and touched him on the chest.

"Look at that." Eddie stepped close to her, as if he meant to measure. Then he put his arms violently around her and, in his agitation, twisted at her so vigorously, trying to bend her into a kissing position that they toppled sidewise onto the bed. There was a scuffle then, during which he did finally succeed in kissing her.

Ellen at length managed to push him away. "Lord, are you always so rough?" she asked, holding him off, for she had mistaken accident for intention. She supposed that his purpose, far from being fulfilled, was barely initiated. "Are you always so rough?" She had never felt anything like the pressure of this boy's grip, the hardness of his arms and shoulders.

There was something permissive about the way she said it, a failure of indignation; so, experimentally, still watching his step, Eddie got rough. He was ready to quit the moment she seemed genuinely frightened or angry, but the fighting she did seemed to be for no more than the pleasure of resistance, for she didn't cry out.

There came a point where Eddie ceased to watch his step, and Ellen ceased to resist.

"Lord," she gasped, and relaxed under him, making for herself, as reservation, a notation to the effect that she was really quite drunk. What followed excited her, as nothing ever had before. There was real brutality in Eddie, and real response to it in Ellen. But it left her sober.

Eddie felt fine.

She watched him swaggering around the room, picking up his clothing; she counted with more wonder than displeasure, the places where she hurt or would hurt.

"You won't tell Tom?" she asked.

"Depends," said Eddie. "Depends on how nice you are to me."
She looked at him and smiled weakly, but not insincerely. A
curious placidity came over her. "I'll be nice," she said, and he
dropped the clothes he had been gathering and came to her again.

She skied for eight days. There were a couple of men there,
but, preposterously enough, she was less interested than they were.
She kept thinking, off and on, of ridiculous Eddie Bissle, and by
the evening of the eighth day he didn't seem ridiculous at all to
her. She called him up. He said that Guy and Tom were leaving
Friday night for a long weekend at Pembroke, so she waited
around on the ninth day and on the tenth was back in her room
at the Rolmer Hotel. And Eddie with her. Friday night and Saturday night. She was supposed to see him Sunday morning, too, but
she woke early, scared and bruised and hung over; she packed and
got an early train back to New York.

Sunday she drank. She went to sleep about four in the afternoon, and woke up just in time for work, on Monday morning.

4.

"Hello."
"Hello. Harrison?"
"Yes. Hi."
"This is Ellen."
"I know. How was skiing?"
"Fine. How'd you know I'd gone skiing?"
"I called Harriet."
"Oh. Well, it was fine."
"No broken bones?"
A pause. "No."
"Did you see Tom?"
"Yes."
"How is he?"
"Fine. Harrison?"
"Yes?"
"May I ask you something?"
"Of course."
"Do you . . . do you still want me to marry you?"
200

"What?"

"I said, 'Do you. . . .' "

"I'm sorry. Yes, I heard what you said. I mean, I was just surprised at your saying it."

"Oh. Well, do you?"

"Well, yes. Yes, darling."

"All right."

"Well, listen Ellen. Listen. I can't get away now. Or maybe I can. Can you?"

"No. I'm at the office."

"But . . . well, darling. It's sweet of you to call and tell me. Did you make up your mind while you were skiing?"

"No. Yes. Yes, I guess so Harrison."

"Ellen, this is wonderful."

"I'm not exactly the same as I was last fall, Harrison. Do you care?"

"Do you mean what I think you mean?"

"Yes."

"Please don't . . . talk about it, Ellen. Of course I care. But . . . well, it's been a rough time for both of us, hasn't it?"

"I'm sorry if I've made it rough for you."

"Oh, darling, that's all right now."

"Do you want to marry me right away?"

"Well, I . . . I don't see how we can. I mean shouldn't we wait until I have leave, and you can meet my parents?"

"No. I don't want to wait now. Please."

"Oh."

"Couldn't we . . . just get a license and get married?"

"You don't want a wedding?"

"No."

"Or an engagement ring?"

"No."

"Ellen, wouldn't it be better to see each other, later on today, and settle it?"

"No. No, Harrison. If you really want it settled, it's got to be now. I mean it. It's got to be."

"Over the telephone?"

"Please. If you really want me to."

"I do, Ellen. Let's see . . . Thursday. I only have one class

201

Thursday, in the morning. If we get blood tests done today, and I apply for the license, we can do it Thursday."

"All right. Yes, Harrison. Let's."

"Can you arrange for your blood test?"

"Yes."

"Ellen, I love you."

"Thursday. All right. I'll get the day off."

"I love you, darling."

"Harrison, thank you for wanting to marry me. You really do, don't you?"

"Yes. Really."

"Thank you, Harrison."

"What about tonight?"

"What? Tonight?"

"Could we . . . well, Phil and Fred are still in with me. I mean. . . ."

"Yes. I'll get Harriet to stay away. She has a cousin. She wants to move anyway, so you can come here."

"Shall we live there?"

"Yes, if you want to."

"I want to. Ellen, listen to me. *I love you.*"

A pause. "Yes."

"I love you."

"IloveyouHarrisongoodbye."

Sound of hanging up.

"Wait. Wait. . . ."

He had to call back to ask her where to meet that evening.

5.

"Hello."

"Hello. Is Ellen there?"

"No. She's not in. Who's calling?"

"I'm just a . . . a friend of her brother's."

"My name is Harrison Walle. Ellen and I are being married tomorrow."

Eddie hung up. Guy was waiting for him, out in the station by the Incoming Trains Bulletin Board. He walked over there.

"No date for me. Damn girl's getting married," Eddie said.

202

"Good. Then I'll get you a girl and we'll celebrate together. Who was she?"

"Just a tomato I laid a couple of times," Eddie said. He would never tell anyone about Ellen; not anyone.

Guy got him a date that night, and they roared around New York together. Eddie's date didn't like him; Eddie didn't care. The date Guy got him the next night liked Eddie even less, and Eddie cared less; Guy seemed to think it was funny. That was okay too; splendid. Wonderful. Eddie felt very close to Guy. The third night, they were still drunk from the first, more or less, and Guy turned up a really crude dish for Eddie who liked Eddie fine. Excellent.

They had left college together suddenly; just got the midweek itch and left, like you might cut a class. Left poor old Tom to keep the books from blowing away. Came to New York for a good, splendid, okay, excellent bat. Guy was heading for the Air Corps. Eddie wanted Infantry.

After that third night Eddie was out of money, so he went out to Long Island, saw his father, avoided his mother, put the car in a garage, went over to Brook Street and enlisted. He guessed Guy would make it in the Air Corps all right; old Tom wanted to be a pilot, too, but Eddie had some doubts about that; being a pilot was only one of several ideas Tom had stewed about.

The most surprising thing Eddie did during his infantry training was to get married. It didn't happen during Basic, every minute of which was damn good; it happened at Officer Candidates' School, at Fort Benning, where they were busy making Eddie a lieutenant in ninety days. That was good duty, too. When the army meant lying around waiting, Eddie hated it; when the army was rough, Eddie loved it. Every other guy was either hard or trying to be hard, and Eddie averaged a couple of fights a month in basic; got his ass whipped some, too. In O.C.S. they weren't supposed to scrap with one another, but the training was even stricter; if you put out the way you were supposed to, whether they were watching or not, you didn't have a hell of a lot of fight left in you evenings. And then, by God, some sergeant was apt to turn you out about two A.M. in your bare feet for fire drill, or extra rifle inspection; those sergeants were cuter than hell, the things they thought of to do to you.

The guys with him in O.C.S. had Eddie pegged; they handed out some pretty sharp kidding; after a fire drill or something, one of them was apt to say:

"Hey, sarge. Bissle wants another one."

"Bissle, they've got the floodlights on in the obstacle course, and we're going to get to go run it, right now."

"Isn't that grand?"

"Look at him smile."

"He's purring like a kitty cat."

"Crud," Eddie would say, and the kidders would look at each other, in mock amazement:

"Did the man say crud?"

"My, my. I believe he did."

"Hey sarge. Bissle said crud."

Eddie was able to take this kind of thing pretty good naturedly; the hard physical life, with its sense of sharp purpose, kept him in a good mood most of the time. He had little urge to issue personal challenges among his fellow-candidates for posts as infantry platoon leaders; the way they told it there were going to be some mighty dee-funct asses out of this group, and shortly, and maybe Eddie's, too.

Julia was a Georgia girl who came to Officer Candidate dances. It was said that she was absolutely faithful to a new candidate every ninety days, and the cadre—the men permanently assigned to the base—considered her rather affected in view of this. Unjust: Julia was a lady. On the other hand, it was perfectly true that they kept sending her men away.

Eddie just plain fell in love with her. It happened over a goodnight kiss, which he had to stand on tiptoes to deliver, and she was nice enough to scrunch down to receive it. Probably the feeling for Julia was an overflow of the general sense of well-being that so marked Eddie in that period. They were married, after a chaste but tender courtship, in the Post Chapel the day after graduation.

Julia said she had always known she'd be married in the Post Chapel.

She was almost a head taller than Eddie, dark, with a quiet look and a flighty nature; pretty enough. Wore the wedding gown her mother and grandmother had worn; Eddie bought a dress uniform for the occasion, and rented swords for the members of his training squad, all of them fellow 2nd Lieutenants now. The swords were to make an arch with.

He was as gentle with Julia as he had been rough with Ellen. While Eddie had never seriously considered marrying Ellen—the sheer inappropriateness of such a match made it bewildering to think about—her marriage had quite a lot to do with his own; for one thing, he had decided to enlist with the thought that Ellen might want to make herself available near wherever he was training. He had wanted the affair to go on, and had wanted to move it as far away from Tom as possible. Well, it was probably a hell of a lot better for her to be marrying this Walle bird; Eddie could see that. But he had been pretty wild for Ellen, and the failure of his plan left him, for the first time in his life, with a strong sense of needing a woman; hence, perhaps, a reason why falling in love with Julia should have led to marrying Julia. But it may have been simpler than that; there were an awful lot of swords rented every time a class graduated at Benning, and you waited for the Post Chapel the way you waited in a chow line.

Julia insisted—can you tie this?—that Eddie was an old sweet thing. She seemed kind of embarrassed by his stature. She said she'd never thought of him as a short little man until she saw him with his clothes off. After that she took to kissing him quite a lot on the top of his head, can you tie it? Can you? Jesus, what a girl.

She enjoyed the trip north, where they went for Eddie's pre-embarkation leave. She was delighted to find that Eddie's family were as prosperous as he'd said they were; hell, they were more so. Eddie's old man was really making money, now, with the war on; Eddie, happy to be an Infantry officer, happy to have a pretty Southern bride on his arm, didn't want to know any of the lousy details of how his father was making it. There was nothing anyone could do, short of shooting, to stop it.

Eddie's father didn't take much to Julia, but Eddie's mother, of all things, cuddled right up with the girl. What a pair. Eddie probably said more polite words to his mother in those ten days than he had in all his previous life.

The Air Corps had snatched Guy out west someplace, but Tom hitchhiked down to see Eddie and Julia during the one weekend of Eddie's leave, and the younger Bissles offered to drive Tom back to college; or Eddie did. It turned out Julia didn't really want to go along. Well. The trip would have been hard for her, so they compromised by just driving Tom down to New York and putting him on the train Sunday. Julia was fascinated with New York.

Tom hadn't had much to say during the visit, except for a couple of hours he and Eddie spent out in the grandfather's house when Julia was at the beauty parlor getting ready for New York; in those two hours they talked about the war a lot. Probably Tom's silence at other times was caused by a kind of discomfort about seeing Eddie in uniform; or married; or meeting his cruddy father; something like that.

Anyway, it was time, very quickly, for Eddie to go ree-place some dee-funct in North Africa, and Julia went on back to Georgia. That was September; the preceding time had been, without question, the best six months Eddie ever spent.

Word reached him overseas, just before Christmas, via a letter from Tom who was still at college, that Ellen Beniger Walle had given birth to a girl and named her Sheila. This letter was brought up by a mail orderly who had to lug it because his jeep hit a mine; luckily, it was an anti-personnel mine. It tore hell out of the tires, but didn't hurt the mail sacks. Or the orderly. At the time Eddie accepted the sacks and distributed the letters to his platoon, they were not under fire, but they had been and were apt to be again, any minute. There was a particular fucking 88 that the Germans kept finding new emplacements for, that the stupid planes couldn't hit. In fact, the stupid planes couldn't hit much of anything except maybe a few Allied troops from time to time. Anyway this 88— they called it Grandma—was always after Eddie's platoon with air bursts; that meant digging fox holes instead of slit trenches and damn well staying in them. They were lucky Grandma wasn't on them when the mail came, because the jerks came rising out of their holes as if it were maneuvers and they'd been told to take ten. They were a pretty lucky platoon; they hadn't had a casualty yet except for guys who'd been stupid enough to try native food or native girls, none of this since Eddie got assigned to them.

Eddie was eating a K-ration while he read Tom's letter. He absorbed the news of Sheila Walle's birth, and half forgot it.

The next day two British tanks went by them, and found Grandma and blew her all to hell, though she got herself a tank in the scramble. Eddie's company, which had been pretty well pinned to the same little hillside for four days, moved half a mile on to a new little hillside, and Eddie's guys bitched about having to dig again in spite of being half a mile closer to Wadi Guitar, which was what they called the regimental objective. While they were digging, the platoon ran out of luck. They got strafed and dive bombed by two planes, one pass each, and within ten seconds they had fourteen casualties, four of them dead. While they were trying to figure out which were dead and which wounded, one of the planes came back for a second pass and got three more guys, just like that. You felt helpless as hell. After that it was ten minutes before Eddie could get enough guys out of their half-dug holes to help put field dressings on the wounded ones; the medic had gotten hit on the second pass, making five dead altogether. Then there was a pretty horrible hour while company Hq tried to get them some ambulances; but after a long, quiet, jittery wait in the hot sun, during which a sixth man died, two stretcher-bearing jeeps drove up and started hauling. They could only handle six at a time—two lying down and one sitting in each jeep, so they made two trips. There was still a guy left over, one of the squad leaders with a big piece of hand shot off, but he was full of morphine, and another squad leader, who was his buddy, sat next to him in the shade, keeping the wounded man's eyes away from the hand. For a long while it looked like the jeeps had forgotten to come back for the odd man, and Eddie was on the walkie-talkie, asking for company transport, when the medics finally did show up. They got the wounded man in, and his buddy the other squad leader, fellow named Rackerman, thought he ought to go along. At first Eddie thought this was just a misapprehension, and tried to assure Rackerman that no further nursing service was needed from him. It gradually developed that Rackerman was out of his head with fear, and wouldn't get out of the jeep for anything; Eddie pulled him out, and tried to argue. About the time Eddie became convinced that he might as well send Rackerman back to the Aid Station, too, and be rid of him—Rackerman was crying by then and having to be restrained physically from getting back into the jeep—the driver suddenly yelled: "Hey, I'm not hauling that crazy son of a bitch," and took off.

Then there was word on the walkie-talkie to be ready to move out, and a few minutes later along came a tank to be followed, this one American. It was called "Sweet Lorraine." Eddie had to kick Rackerman's ass over the hill personally, not because the sergeant was any use by then but because they couldn't very well just leave him to bake his addled head in the sun. Good thing nothing went pop as they moved on after the tank; if there had, Eddie figured, the twenty-one men he had left would have gone in twenty-one different directions.

In the evening they were digging again. Rackerman was under guard, and a detail had to dig a foxhole for him and put him in it. If fear really has a smell, Eddie was thinking, we must be stinking up the desert for miles around. A tistard. A tastard. A green and yellow bastard. Twenty-one tistards, twenty-one tastards; make it twenty-two. Don't neglect our peerless leader.

Eddie finally managed to get Company to take Rackerman off his hands. They told him the platoon was to start following "Sweet Lorraine" again at o-one-four-five, taking point duty for a company advance, and were willing to concede that Rackerman's services might not be helpful in this; so they sent a couple of quaking cooks and the mess sergeant up, with side-arms, who marched Rackerman away in the dusk. Eddie had forgotten the man before he was out of sight.

At o-one-four-five, instead of "Sweet Lorraine" coming up, the C.O. arrived to see what their position was like. Something, some ordnance mess, was holding back the tanks; Eddie was to be ready to go, on five minutes' notice. Meanwhile they were to stay right where they were, in a dry little draw that Eddie didn't like the looks of at all. He dispersed his twenty one survivors on the sides of the draw, and, in spite of the fact that they didn't expect to be there long, there was no bitching about digging. They spent a quiet, uncomfortable morning. About eleven, they were allowed to move out of the draw to a somewhat less inviting position, and the stupid Germans, who could have had the whole platoon with one shell earlier, starting dropping mortar shells around in the sparsely covered, hillocky terrain where shells now fell fairly harmlessly. There was nothing much to return fire at, so they dug again; Eddie didn't have to tell them to. You stay yellow longer than you do green.

About half the guys had thrown away their packs the day before, on the first move after the strafing, and, with the packs, their K-rations. Eddie and the platoon sergeant had a couple of extra each, but it still wasn't enough to go around. Eddie got onto the walkie-talkie for permission to send a detail back to Company supply for more rations, and heard that battalion supply had misplaced the truck that carried them. The first sergeant said he'd do what he could and let Eddie know. So, when they saw the crazy mail orderly crawling up with another sack, they figured it was food coming and cheered—but quietly, because they didn't want to get the Germans on the mortars, two or three bumps over, too excited. It wasn't food at all, for Christ's sake; it was written permission for Eddie to send a detail back for the food—and some more goddamn mail. Eddie was for throwing the mail sack away at that point, or sending it back unopened. He couldn't imagine that any of the guys would want to take time to read letters, but the platoon sergeant said they would; sentimental jerks. It was goddamn funny to see them crawling on their bellies over to Eddie's fox hole when he'd call their names, to get letters from their broads or their mamas. Eddie's letter that day was from Julia's father; it said, in rather elegant Southern attorney's language, that Julia was in love with a Polish refugee colonel, observing now at Fort Benning; a nobleman. A Count. My, my. And a way had been found to annul Eddie's and Julia's marriage, so that she could have this Count; it meant a little less than nothing to Eddie and he would have dropped the letter into the bottom of the fox hole instead of sticking it in his back pocket, if they hadn't been short of toilet paper.

When he had occasion to get it out again, it was the next morning, and they still hadn't changed position. Instead, the situation had changed. Regimental artillery had been sending shells over their heads all night long, and there didn't seem to be any more German mortar teams dug in two bumps away. Eddie had his guys fire rifle grenades over, to make sure, and even got a few rounds of light mortar fire from their own weapons platoon; nothing stirring. Very shortly afterwards, Eddie found both Tom's letter and the one from Julia's father in the back pocket, and re-read both of them as he squatted behind a big rock. Things were pretty busy overhead, but the activity was all American planes, coming and going. He disposed of the letters. In the afternoon, along came good old "Sweet Lorraine" with another tank called "Jean T.N.T.," and Eddie had to get his boys up to follow them; this was the same assignment they'd missed, thirty hours before, on point for the company advance. They made four or five miles; "Jean T.N.T." wasn't much of a tank; it kept getting overheated or something and having to rest, but it was comfortable to follow —the tanks exploded the A.P. mines, the castrators. It meant that the guys wanted to stay right in the track marks, even when they knew they were not in a mine field, but nevertheless, it was better than going by yourself. On the next day they started out the same way; then "Jean T.N.T." broke down completely and became a target; they were still in that bumpy, hillocky country, and it seemed very much as if there was fire coming at "Jean T.N.T." from three sides. The crew opened the turret and tried to come out, and Eddie, on his belly watching, couldn't be sure what kind of fire got them but they sure got got. "Sweet Lorraine" spun around and came chugging back, probably looking for some cover to fire from, started to turn in to a promising little indentation, and had her tracks blown off by about the biggest mine explosion Eddie'd ever seen; there must have been six or eight mines all wired together. The Germans weren't so stupid. That crew got out all right; the C.O. sent second platoon up to hold ground with Eddie's remnant, and they found themselves in their first real fire fight. The Germans didn't seem to have tanks, but they had some artilley, 88's again, come up behind them, and the mortars were murderous; Eddie couldn't keep track of his casualties, and no one paid a hell of a lot of attention to his attempts to direct fire. They were really getting creamed, until planes came along and bailed them out; the planes were getting better. So were Eddie's boys, what were left of them.

There was fairly constant skirmishing from there on into Wadi Guitar; Eddie had one squad left, and an extra rifleman; his platoon sergeant became first sergeant, the first having been sent back with some violent disease—no one knew quite what, though it sounded like dysentery. It made Eddie a sort of glorified squad leader, not that he minded. At the same time he was getting the piss scared out of him, he was learning combat; you either learned it fast, or you never did. He got smart enough to improvise a sweet little piece of tactics with his one squad, the day before they entered Wadi Guitar. The tactics involved a bothersome machine gun, and cost no loss at all. Eddie used three B.A.R.'s firing from different places to confuse them, having the guns fire at separate intervals so that it seemed like one B.A.R. team mov-

There is a man here who was a flyer of sail planes; that is
called soaring and he says it is like the sensation I had imagined. Also an instructor says that in a fast fighter there is
more thrill. In the multi-engines where I am going, it be-
comes very mechanical, they say, and you must work a great
deal with instruments; I suppose this might become interesting. Of course, even now there are things like night landings
without lights, and flying in very close formation which are
exciting; all I meant to say was it was a different kind of excitement. There is chow call; I am always hungry.

I must get this finished now and mail it. I have had overnight leave—someone with a pass didn't want to go and gave
it to me. Texas is very strange to most of the men who are
training with me, and very familiar to me. Once, before
I went to Roper or even to New England, I went to a military school near here, and I feel sometimes as if I am still
there, and nothing has changed. It is because even now they
treat us like children; everything you try to join in this world,
it seems, has an initiation period, like an endless series of
adolescent fraternities. It was that in preflight, now in flight,
next I suppose in multi-engine and even, perhaps, when one
is assigned. They think of it as psychology, but it is really
an attempt to manufacture superstition, to make one feel
that something is better than it actually is. It's like the tribes
in anthropology books, no better.

I think I am telling you all this because I now believe that
you should stay at college as long as you can, until you are
actually torn away. It is so very petty and depressing, but of
course one hopes it will be less so when training is over. In
a multi-engined plane, I will be able to bomb against Germany.

Guy.

Guy must be depressed, Tom thought, to have spent so much
time on writing to him. Tom wrote regularly to Guy and Eddie
both, college news, even family news, but with the feeling that
they couldn't possibly be interested. What could Eddie care in
Africa—that was where the APO number probably was—or even

Guy in Texas, if Tom had been down to New York for a weekend to see Ellen, home from the hospital and proudly nursing her baby; or if the Kaiser's little plant had been awarded a flag with an E on it for production excellence; or that Moultrie, in the Marines, might be on his way to the Pacific?

Tom could imagine the vehemence with which Eddie would say crud. Is it the boys who are cheered up by letters from home? Tom wondered. Or merely the people who write the letters?

The campus was a strange place; even faculty, those ancient, unimperiled creakers around academic corners, were disappearing into the services. There had already been college chapel services for there former undergraduates—one shot down flying with the Canadians, one dead in the American Field Service with the British in Egypt, another flyer in a training accident in Florida. There was a bulletin board, gradually filling with the names of those who joined up, and the color of the lettering would be changed, from white to red, when a death was reported.

Of the students who remained, almost half were in uniform or signed to some program which permitted them to stay in college pending a call from a particular service branch. The uniformed ones were marched to classes now by actual army sergeants and navy petty officers, detached to this strange station.

Even those who, like Tom, were not in uniform, were required each day to do an hour of calisthentics and swimming, and the strokes which the swimming coach taught in the college pool were ones designed for swimming a long time after a boat was sunk; and, in case any of them should have to go under a sheet of blazing oil on the surface of the water, they were taught the value of swimming underwater, rising for air with a great thrashing motion that might break up the flames for a moment.

Yet the letter writing, the uniforms, the hour of militant exercise and swimming, did very little to relieve the general pallor of college life; for who were left besides Tom? The halt and the blind, people with limps or heavy glasses, a monstrous fat boy known as Man Mountain Varnesky, little Dave Grey with his hearing aid. And the striplings, freshmen too young to be drafted, manning the college teams now. . . .

At night Tom was an Air Raid Warden, charged with patrolling the campus at certain hours. This was chiefly to enforce the dim out, for Washburn was close enough to the sea to be part of the

214

program for reducing shore lights so that there would be no glow against which passing allied ships might be silhouetted for submarines.

It was during the lonely walks in the dark, helmeted, looking for lights in windows, that Tom thought about the war, far away, inapprehensible. After a half an hour or so he would begin to be able to think quite consecutively; it was as if he could speak without the usual interruptions such as an audience makes, to himself as listener:

"I can imagine Guy, in flight training, but that is because I have seen planes in the air, and flyers.

"But how can I imagine Eddie in command of men, deploying them into positions where they will shoot back and forth with a real enemy?

"And am I, after all I have said about it, going to enlist for pilot's training?

"For there is a great mass of things I have felt and have not said.

"Who would I have said them to?

"Guy? He would be sympathetic only because it was I speaking; it would bother him.

"The Kaiser? He would be hurt, and conceal it, and speak awkwardly of patriotism; it would bother them.

"I do not want to bomb civilians.

"Not German ones, much less French ones who might be living near a target.

"I don't want to bomb anybody, really, not even a man firing an anti-aircraft gun, trying to shoot me down.

"The soldiers are all drafted, on both sides; there are no volunteers for this kind of war, and very few professionals.

"I don't want to kill people at all, not even the professionals.

"I don't want people to try to kill me.

"But all these don't wants are little personal quantities on one side of an equation.

"On the other side is the feeling that one has to stop the Nazis.

"And if I think they have to be stopped, I can't ask others to stop them for me on the ground that a different area of conscience tells me it is wrong to kill and injure people.

"So if I should be among those stopping Nazis, I should be among those doing the most damage and I suppose that's a flyer and especially, if Guy is right about where my size would put me, one who flies a bomber and kills civilians.

"Even after Pearl Harbor I thought I would wait until the time came and then, as quietly as I could, bothering as few people about it as I could, I would be a conscientious objector.

"And go to prison.

"Because limited service doesn't make any sense, and if one is willing to do any part of it, one should be willing to do the worst part, the killing.

"I don't have a deep political feeling about fascism or anything else if I look into myself honestly, not a feeling deep enough to justify killing to suppress the idea.

"It's not the idea I feel must be stopped, then, but any idea which develops to the point where people use it to justify slavery or murder.

"The democracy of the French Revolution was murderous, communism in Russia is murderous, Catholicism in the time of Cortes was murderous, racism in the south is murderous, and when they were or are murderous they should be or should have been suppressed.

"I suppose.

"Which is to say that people who hold any idea to the point of murdering and enslaving should be or should have been . . . what? Killed?

"Is war a kind of mass capital punishment for murderers?

"That is one of its effects, and since these idea-murderers insist on their right to continue murdering, then we have to adopt capital punishment as the only means to contain them.

"And therefore we should be fighting to establish a supernational system that could go in anywhere, including the American South and the Russian salt mines and the Spanish police stations and the places in Africa where a big tribe enslaves and murders a little tribe, a system that would have all the armies and weapons and be absolute boss of the world.

"To put down people holding any idea, any belief, any theory political or religious, strongly enough to kill for it.

"Then the war would be about something.

"But it isn't. It concerns only the capital punishment of one particularly poisonous group of idea-murderers, and that is what is on the other side of my equation.

216

"What is the good of inspecting one's own confusion?

"And suppose I were able to say those things not to Guy or the Kaiser, but to Eddie, crawling along beside him wherever he is crawling.

"Eddie would say crud.

"Eddie would say, Grab that rifle Tom and shoot that bastard over there before he shoots you. . . ."

Or whatever people say in whatever situation Eddie is in.

So?

It was, of course, not the weight on either side of his equation that finally determined Tom's course. It was much simpler, more emotional. It was the sense of everybody going somewhere Tom wasn't going. Of something unimaginable happening Tom wasn't seeing. It was sheer youthfulness, which insisted that he had to test himself, his courage, against that of the men who had fought in the last generation's war, and written its books and developed its attitudes. And it was, least worthy of all, a general sense of staleness about what he had been doing all his life.

As, for example, one day in Greek class with Bunky Layman, a teacher for whom Tom had always had great feeling, a man, in fact, whose career and personality Tom had once thought his own ought to resemble.

That particular day, Tom was the only student attending. Of the two others in the course one had left for the Navy, and the other was cutting. They had been reading the *Crito,* the story of the death of Socrates; Bunky was talking about the ship which figures in it.

"Try to imagine that ship, Tom. For thirty days each year, it summed up religion and law, because no Athenian could be put to death until it returned from consulting the oracle at Delos, and all of Socrates' friends, like Crito, had been waiting without hope for its . . . its inexorable return. So in comes Crito to the prison and says, 'I have bad news.' You see?"

Tom nodded.

Bunky nodded too. He had a heavy head of white hair and a mustache. "Then try the sentence again with that in mind," he said.

Tom translated: *"Socrates:* Oh, then I suppose the ship is in from Delos, and the arrival of my death."

"No. The ship's arrival. Not the death's arrival."

217

"Oh," Tom said. "Yes, I see. '. . . the ship, whose arrival . . .' "

"Yes," Bunky said. "You know, I think I've dreamed about that ship. I'm sure poor Crito did. It hadn't really arrived, you see. But travellers from it had been put ashore at Sunium, a day's sail away, and had arrived in Athens already, and been seen by Crito. . . ." It is more real to Bunky, Tom thought, the imprisonment and death of Socrates two thousand years ago, than is the current war to me, which has already bloodied half the world.

"Plato," Bunky was going on. "An extraordinary writer as well as philosopher, a great narrative poet. His characterization of Socrates has such economy and such reality. Just from the few exchanges with which some of the dialogues start, we know the old man—his flirtation with Alcibiades, his troubles with his wife. We know that the last thing that came into his mind as the poison took effect was a small debt, of a cock, that he owed. That was Socrates. Remember what he says in the *Apology?* 'I am a man like any other, a being of flesh and blood, nor rock or oak.' There are times when the dialogues are like a novel, and you can pull your truck around back and put the laundry in the service entrance."

He stopped speaking. Tom looked at him.

"Excuse me?" Tom said.

Bunky chuckled. "I said, 'You can pull your truck around back and put the laundry in the service entrance.' "

Tom had to laugh. "Was I being that inattentive?" he asked.

"Not a very Socratic question," Bunky said. "Why don't you go on, Tom?"

"Go on?"

"To war. That ship that let the passengers off at Sunium will still be on its way to Athens when the war is over. You'll be back to think about what happened after it arrived, I'll be here to talk about it with you. Or if we aren't, there'll be another student and another teacher. . . ."

He should have been moved, Tom thought, leaving class. It was a powerful thing Bunky had said, about the persistence of culture, the immortality of art and knowledge. It was the way Tom wanted to be able to feel about these things in the world; Bunky Layman's values ought to be Tom's values. But, to be honest, they were not. He began to plan a trip to Florida to say goodbye to his parents, a weekend in New York to say good bye to Ellen and to settle the Air Corps enlistment in his mind.

218

2.

Eddie was trying to decide how to puke. There was no longer any question but that he would. They had been bumping around in the landing craft, or whatever in hell it was, for over two hours. He couldn't see out of the damn thing. He couldn't see anything except some guy's pack which was sticking into his face, smelling of mold and tobacco. He was hot and overloaded with equipment, and he had lost all sense of where shore was; there seemed to be fairly steady firing in both directions, and the sky was full of planes. He knew they were preparing to go ashore at Salerno, Italy; the orders had said they would go directly in, as soon as they were aboard the landing craft. Whatever the fuckup that was caus- ing the delay, Eddie was not grateful for it; he'd rather be any- where, including dead on the beach, than feel like this. The image of himself lying calm and dead on the beach, with a little cool salt water lapping over him from time to time was soothing. . . .

Not soothing enough. He decided the only place was his helmet. If he puked on the floor, it would start general puking, and they would all be wading around in it. He slipped off his helmet, took the liner out, put the liner back on his head, and let go into the steel part. Then Bing, who was his new platoon sergeant and about nine feet tall, said:

"Gimme, Sir. I can reach up and dump it for you."

Eddie gave Bing the helmet and his canteen. Bing dumped the helmet and rinsed it, and returned the things to Eddie.

"Thanks," Eddie said.

About fifteen minutes later, as Eddie was beginning to think the helmet would have to come off again, the engine noise increased and they seemed to be going in a straight line for a change. "Okay," Eddie yelled, not feeling wretched any longer. "Get those goddamn cartridge belts fastened."

There was ten minutes of grim, bumpy riding, during which a lot of chow hit the deck and Eddie was glad he'd gotten rid of his early. Then there was a scrape and a bump, and the ramp started to go down. Eddie hurled himself forward, through his men, and was first one off, landing in water up to his ass. Shore was exactly one million yards away. The Navy bastard could have done bet- ter, Eddie thought, starting to wade bent forward, fast as he could go. There was no sense trying to fire now. The thing to do was get to shallow water fast, and hope the planes and Naval artillery would cover them. He looked back and most of the platoon was with him. He saw that two men, he couldn't identify them, were still in the landing craft; a third was just coming off the ramp in a hurry, and the Navy bastard was already starting to hoist his ramp to get out of there. Maybe the Navy bastard was drawing fire; there was some splashing around there. One of the stragglers was coming off the lifting ramp, jumping into the water, and it was Bing; he must have been kicking the other tails off the boat. Damn good sergeant. One guy would get a ride back and a court martial, and Eddie might or might not ever know who it was because there were others spread out, struggling in towards shore, who were getting it right in the water and this wasn't any time to stop and read their dog tags.

There was a fine sight forward; two Navy planes, skimming the beach, dropping fire bombs. Very good. Better than hauling the flame thrower Eddie's company hadn't been able to get.

He made the beach as the fires were going out and, for a moment, it looked as if there wasn't going to be any small arms fire, nothing more than the German artillery which was still whamming stuff out into the water. Eddie dropped prone anyway and started looking, and so did the others as they came up by him, spreading out in a line. Then Eddie got up in a crouch and ran about ten steps inland, and dropped again. Another man came up and another, and finally the whole platoon. Still no trouble. Eddie jumped up and tried ten more, and just as he fell, he heard the machine gun start. Then he and everybody with him were pinned to the beach without cover, and all they could do was hope that Navy planes or Navy shells would come along and give them a chance.

There was a piece of seawall fifty yards farther up, and the barbed wire covering it had been well enough beat up by the shelling so that they could get next to it. Once there, they'd be out of the trajectory of the machine gun, not just under it. Eddie wondered why there weren't German troops right behind the sea wall; he thought there must have been. It was a good position, and if the defenders were there they'd have every man in Eddie's platoon by now; the fire bombs must have finished the Germans. That was probably it. And why not mortars, now that the machine gun had

220

them lying still? As if in answer to the question, a mortar shell burst up the beach. Then a lot of others in the same empty area. Good. No observation then, except by the machine gun crew which couldn't leave its weapon to straighten the mortar boys out. Very good. Eddie started forward on his belly. It was going to be a nice fifty yard crawl, and plenty of sand down the neck.

Then the Navy shells came in again, and a couple of big blasts went off over where Eddie had the machine gun located, so he took a chance that concussion would have rocked the gunners for a moment, got up, and ran like hell for the sea wall. Bing arrived beside him. As soon as they had their breath Eddie said:

"Come on," and took the long chance, vaulting the wall. Bing came over with him, and they were safe. There were the German infantry, burned crisp and smelly by the fire bombs, about twelve of them. Bing landed right on one, and cursed, and Eddie had to laugh at him.

Now they were cozy, able to work up close along the wall right up to the pill box. There were three other guys with them, now, and they could pump rounds at the horizontal slit the gun stuck out of; the pill box was a concrete bubble, commanding a lot of beach. The gun wasn't firing for some reason, and the rest of Eddie's platoon was making it over the wall as Eddie and Bing, with the other three covering, worked along right up to the box. There they crouched; Eddie pulled the pin out of a grenade, let it fly off, counted two and stuffed the thing in the slit. They heard it drop. There were no shouts inside, no response, and, after a moment, the explosion. Then he and Bing went around back with bayonets ready and went inside. As far as they could tell, there had only been a single man on this gun after all, not a crew, and he was probably dead from the Navy shell before Eddie and Bing got there. Guys who got killed got killed two or three times, two or three different ways, Eddie was thinking, as he moved toward the gun itself; Eddie unloaded the gun, while Bing unscrewed it from its base. Then they toppled it crashing onto the floor. Then they put another grenade on the floor, under the open breach, with the weight of the gun holding it in position, pulled the pin and ran outside again. When the second grenade had gone off, they checked to see that the gun was really useless. A counter-attack could lose them this side of the sea wall, and they didn't want to have the same gun to take all over again.

Paralleling the sea wall was the road Eddie remembered from the map. They were supposed to cross it and dig in. And for once the orders made sense; there was good cover across the road.

He looked at it longingly. On the other side, they could rest; until Germans tried to come back, anyway. If they did. Naval artillery was raising very commendable hell a few hundred yards farther along. Maybe no counterattack. Just go across the road.

"No tank to follow today," he muttered, not quite sure why he had thought of it. Then he sensed something that made him drop; it wasn't until after he was down that he put any name to it:

"Short round coming," but he hadn't finished thinking it when the big Navy shell hit, right across their road, right where they were going. It made a tremendous noise; it rocked the ground they were lying on; fragments from it took Pauling's head off, right at the neck, and left one of the replacements gut-wounded. But Eddie wasn't mad at the short round; because it detonated every mine in the area, and made it possible to move in.

"Let's go," he said, and sprinted across the road. While they dug, he sent a guy to find the beachmaster and report their position; they wouldn't be able to use any further help from Navy shells. He made sure the medic took care of the wounded replacement, poor screaming bastard, and settled his platoon down. By night, when it started to get cold as hell, they had a good position, and there were lots of troops on the beach, moving right through Eddie's platoon and going into Italy.

3.

Ellen hadn't wanted to go to the movies, but Harrison insisted. There she was, unwilling to have her hand held in the dark beside him, while the newsreel showed the Salerno landings, a series of blurred, long-range, meaningless pictures, a confusion of boats, smoke puffs, airplanes, while canned sound made gunfire noises, moderately well-synchronized. It ended. Then there was something about Roosevelt; he was puffing on his long cigarette holder and saying that everyone should have some of the new issue war bonds; Ellen clapped for Roosevelt, not because she had voted for him herself—she had forgotten to vote in 1940—but because her brother Tom loved the man so. Harrison didn't clap. After Roose-

222

velt, an admiral was interviewed on the deck of a carrier in the Pacific. No action.

Then white letters appeared on the screen and said,

GRADUATION DAY

A line of men in flying suits and parachutes were standing at attention, their hands being shaken by an officer. The announcer said that this was the first class trained in the new something or other bombers, and the camera closed up on one representative graduate, a very handsome man. . . .

"It's Guy!" Ellen said.

"Who?"

"Never mind," Ellen said. "I'll tell you later."

The formation broke, and the camera picked up Guy again— they didn't give him any name—jumping into one of a line of vehicles which went whirling over a runway to a formation of huge airplanes. The camera closed up on Guy again, ordering his crew into the plane, hesitating a moment, looking keenly up at the heavy nose. It was a fairly corny shot, and he had quite obviously been directed in it;

"Another of America's new pilots takes to the air," the announcer said, as Guy ran up into the plane, and the film next showed planes taking off, etc.

"How funny," Ellen whispered. "Guy's a Mexican."

"Who is he?"

"Guy Cinturon, Tom's roommate."

"Oh yes. You sure it was him?"

"Yes."

There was even a funny little item about it in one of the columns next day:

GOOD NEIGHBOR BOO BOO. . . . handsome U.S. Flyboy in World News Cam's pilot graduation sequence, playing the nabes the other day and getting femme sighs (MGM please note), was really a handsome Mexican flyboy, Guy Cinturon, son of a family that owns plenty cactus, plenty sage brush, and just an eensy teensy bit of magnesium. . . .

Ellen cut it out for Harrison to see when he came home from class.

"Sounds like an interesting kid," Harrison said. "I'd like to meet him."

223

Ellen saved the clipping for Tom. He was in Florida now, seeing mother and the Kaiser. He would be staying with Ellen while he took his Air Corps physical, next week.

Tom said, smiling, "Guy's always getting into the papers," when he saw the item.

"Does he arrange it?" Harrison wanted to know.

"Not consciously," Tom said. "But he's always getting mentioned. Even in prep school, where the paper was two mimeographed pages twice a month, there was always something about Guy—nasty, half the time. Hey, how about let's all have another drink?"

"Not you," Ellen said. "You're going to bed."

The first day of Tom's physical was tomorrow, and Ellen had great anxiety about it. She was more pleased when he passed it—when they didn't discover the shoulder misalignment or question the asthma history—than she was with Harrison's being promoted to Lieutenant j.g. But she was proud of Harrison, too, of course; proud of everybody, even Sheila who was now, at three months, trying to raise herself in the crib.

They saw Tom off to pre-flight in a real party mood, the first Ellen had felt since the war began. She wanted to boast to people when they heard that Tom had been top man in his class at pre-flight.

Then, three weeks after the beginning of flight training, Tom wrote to say that he had washed out. He simply didn't have the coordination, and there were questions, after the pressure chamber tests, about his stamina. He might yet be sent to navigator's school; it depended on how bad the pressure chamber test results really were.

Whether it was the tests, or a mix-up, or just that the program was full, Tom didn't go to Navigators' School. He didn't go to school at all. He was sent, as a private first class, to be a driver in an Air Corps ordnance unit. He would have been terrifically disappointed, he wrote, except that the unit had been brought up to strength so hurriedly for a particular reason; it was to be flown overseas, most likely to England, immediately.

CHAPTER TEN

1.

YANK TROOPS WHISTLED wherever Lala Herald walked. Their officers didn't whistle; they called up on the phone. Why not? She had a lovely complexion, nice hair, and was friendly to them at the dances and things one went to; she was nineteen. Her father was a colonial civil servant, retired; customs—Lala had been born in Hongkong. She and the boys were all sent back to England to stay and go to school; then her father came back, in '38, and they'd begun staying with him and a housekeeper. Mother was dead; had been for ever so long. Daddy was Home Guard now; fierce old thing. Mustache. They had a pretty cottage, nothing grand; other pretty cottages stood along the same road, all in sight of one another.

Most of the Yank troops in their town were airmen; there was a drome not far away. Lala saw it frequently at night, at the officers' club, and sometimes, while they were dancing, she would hear the planes take off. Rather thrilling.

Just now there was a particular airman—Lala was partial to airmen; it's what her brothers were, one dead, one still flying. The particular airman—flyer, rather, was a very young captain called Chuck Little. About twenty five, and rather like a movie American: tumbly hair, vigorous, a good deal of enthusiasm; a wisecracker,

225

spendthrift; full of public assurance and private boyishness when it came to girls. What a dancer—he taught Lala the shag and the Lindy. He came from Maryland, which was one of the states south of New York, and went to a college (University?) called Princeton. Had gone. Graduated, he said. He was very popular and was practically a legendary flyer. Quite. If he got dangerously drunk every Saturday night, Lala understood that it was the effect of tension, responsibility. After all, a Captain; she wasn't sure just what the rank meant in terms of command, but the brother who was still living didn't have his captaincy yet and he had a great deal of responsibility.

One Saturday night at the regular Officers' Club dance, Chuck's colleagues decided he was too drunk to drive Lala home. The decison was based on the fact that Chuck was fast asleep. On the other hand, he would wake up from time to time and offer to tear the place apart if some one of the colleagues attempted to do the chore; and the girl had to be got home. A compromise was effected; they phoned the motor pool. They told the sergeant on duty to send a jeep and a driver; the sergeant came himself and reported his name as Beniger. He was very tall and rather pale and had lower class posture.

They made a joke of briefing him: "You will go directly to your objective, release your bomb, and report here."

"Report here?" The sergeant seemed confused.

"We're going to time you," one of the Lieutenants said.

"Both hands on the wheel, you noncommissioned wolf," said another, whom Lala knew as Curtis.

"I think that's a little insulting to me, Curt," Lala said, and then wanted to bite her tongue off as the sergeant looked soberly her way; what she said had not sounded as she had meant it to.

She sat in the front seat of the jeep with him as he drove carefully away, and the young flyers, crowding out onto the front steps of their club, shouted lost messages into the summer air. She wondered whether she should apologize to the sergeant in some way, and couldn't, but supposed she could overcome her tactlessness by being friendly.

"Is it a terrific thrill to be a driver for someone like Captain Little?" She asked.

"Yes," he said.

226

Then she remembered that they had sent to the motor pool for this man—"Oh, but your captains don't have drivers, do they?"

"No."

"Perhaps you don't even know Captain Little?"

"No, I don't."

"But he must have a great reputation."

The sergeant didn't answer.

"Doesn't he?"

"Yes. He's supposed to be a fine pilot."

"You don't like him?"

"I don't know him."

"But whatever you know of him, sergeant? Do you like that?" She thought she might be in love with Chuck, and she wanted to hear how devoted his men were to him.

Sergeant Beniger looked at her, shook his head, and looked back at the road. "I'm sorry. I just don't know Captain Little," he said.

It made her angry. "I suppose you're going to tell me that in civilian life, he'll be a taxi driver and you'll be a millionaire?"

"I'm sure I won't be a millionaire," the sergeant said. "I don't know what he'll be. A pilot for the airlines?"

"Sergeant," Lala said with icy sweetness, "have you ever heard of Princeton College?"

It was light enough so that she could see what seemed to be a momentary smile, but he replied gravely enough: "Yes. I have."

"And do graduates of Princeton College often become airline pilots?"

"I don't know that much about airlines pilots," he said. "It just seemed like a logical job for a man who likes flying." After a moment he added: "But perhaps if Captain Little went to Princeton, he'll go into business." He looked at her again, and said, with what was apparently intended to be kindness: "From what I've seen of him, I imagine he'll be very successful."

She would not be treated like a child; besides she had him trapped. "Oh, you *have* seen something of him?"

"Oh, yes."

"Then why do you keep saying you don't know him?"

Didn't want to answer, did he? "Why, sergeant?"

"Well . . . it seemed fairer than saying I disliked him," the sergeant said. "Is this your house?"

227

It occurred to Lala that this might be one of the religious Americans. Most were some variation of the girl-whistling, boyish, movie kind, but a few were serious, teetotalling and religious. A girl she knew had been stuck for hours sitting beside one at a dance; it seems the man didn't approve of dancing, and perhaps it had struck this Sergeant Beniger badly to see Captain Little enjoying himself.

He had got out of the jeep and was coming round to her side. "I can manage," she said, hopping out. "Thank you, Sergeant."

Gloves. In her eagerness to get away from that grim, religious, teetotalling American she had forgotten her gloves. Two evenings later he called round at the house to return them, and asked to see her. She was quite cross; she had worked long hours at her job that day, a job with the ration board.

It seemed very cheeky of him to ask to see her; she was tired of spoiled American enlisted men who got more pay than British officers, the best food, medical care, clothing, and who complained constantly.

"What is it, Sergeant?" she asked, staying on the stairs down which her father had called her.

He put the gloves on the ballustrade, and said hesitantly: "I wanted to apologize for saying I . . . I disliked Captain Little. Since it seemed to matter to you. . . ."

"Yes, well. It's very kind of you to take an interest, but it's really no concern of yours, is it?"

"I suppose it was envy speaking," he went on. "I tried very hard to become a pilot. In any case, I'm sorry."

"Thank you," she said. "It's quite all right." She half turned to go back up and resume lying down.

"Would you . . . would you like to know something about him?" Sergeant Beniger asked.

"What do you mean?"

"Well when . . . well, you told me that he'd gone to Princeton. And there's a man I . . . I know, who went to Princeton too. About the same time. I play bridge with him sometimes."

"Yes, Sergeant?" she said impatiently, wondering if he would ever get out what he was trying to tell her.

"Captain Little's a fine fellow according to this man I know. Very popular in college, very active in things. Comes from quite a prosperous family; they have something to do with marketing shellfish."

228

"Shellfish?"

"Crabs and oysters and so on. The Chesapeake Bay is a great center of that."

"Sergeant, did you call me downstairs to tell me about crabs and oysters?" Lala asked.

He smiled. "It does sound silly now," he admitted. "I . . . it just seemed the other night that you wanted to know about him, so I thought I'd find out for you. By way of apology. The men who fly with him expect him to have another promotion soon, by the way. He's quite religious and that makes him stand well with his commanding officer, who's very high church. . . ."

"Are you, Sergeant?"

"What?"

"Quite religious?"

"No. I'm afraid not."

"I can't make you out."

"I'm sorry."

"Did you really come here to tell me about the shellfish? Or did you, well, hope you might see something of me, or what?"

"It really was the shellfish," he said, smiling quite broadly now. "And . . . I knew I'd been unfair. My Princeton man says you and Captain Little are quite serious, and I thought you'd like to know that as Americans rate young men, he's the best kind."

"Then you like him now?"

The man actually grinned. "I still don't know him," he said.

"What makes you so special?" she asked exasperated, coming down several steps towards him. "You're saying that you approve of him for me, of all cheeky things, but he won't do for you."

Sergeant Beniger laughed.

"And don't laugh at me!"

"I'm sorry. It is a funny situation, though, isn't it? Yes, I approve of Captain Little, for you, and it's terribly cheeky of me. You know, he's something like the man my sister married only much lighter hearted, and I certainly approve of lighter hearts. For you and me both."

"Oh, goodbye Sergeant," Lala said, more puzzled than annoyed now. Perhaps he was an eccentric, an artist, a misfit.

"Goodbye," he said, and turned to go. She watched him stoop out and close the door quietly. He's very young, she thought, unexpectedly; younger than Chuck. Then she thought: he did mean to be kind.

In the late fall of 1943, Guy, having been first assigned as an instructor in multi-engine school, and having requested transfer to combat regularly each week, was reassigned to the Ferry Command, and in 1944 he started flying back and forth across the Atlantic, arriving in New York for a day or two off about twice a month. He spent several of these brief New York leaves at the apartment Harrison and Ellen Walle had taken in Brooklyn Heights.

Brooklyn Heights is the somewhat chic, middle class section, just across the river from Wall Street; for people employed in the financial district, Brooklyn Heights offers a faster subway ride to work than most residential parts of Manhattan, as well as general quiet and a view of water. The location was not very convenient for Harrison at the time, since he was still going daily up to Columbia, but he thought they would live in Brooklyn Heights after the war and, he explained to Guy, the New York apartment shortage would almost certainly grow worse, not better, when the war was over.

Not only were apartments short; hotel space was too. Guy, who could never be certain when he might be in town, had a problem: he didn't want to bother trying to argue his way into hotels. On the other hand, if he were going to be at a fixed place—a fixed phone number—that, too, could be a nuisance. He did not relish his new assignment, and continued making regular transfer applications, but he felt that as long as the situation existed, the problem of a place to stay in New York might as well be solved pleasantly. So he had three places.

One was with his uncle at the Plaza, another an apartment whose rent he shared with four other Ferry Command pilots, the third was with Harrison and Ellen. In many ways he preferred the third.

Staying with his uncle was best, of course, if he planned to see a girl and she were social—but this involved giving time to family matters and was, in addition, no place he could take the girl when it came to that point.

The apartment with the flyers he used if he were dating a showgirl; it was the sort of place they expected, and did not suggest that he might have the kind of money worth a girl's trying to attach permanently. The drawback here was the necessary intimacy with the other flyers who shared the place, something with which Guy could put up well enough but for which he had no real relish. In addition, the others tended to rely on Guy to find dates for them when their leaves coincided with his, and he found himself having to be more widely acquainted in showgirl circles than he quite meant to be.

Ellen's and Harrison's was the place for comfort and quiet. He never took a girl there or gave one its phone number. There were times now when Guy simply felt tired of sex, times when he preferred to muse and read, to sleep, wake up by himself, perhaps slip off to the St. George Hotel pool for a long, slow swim. At these times, he was very contented to be at the Walles', sleeping on a cot in a screened off corner of the living room, bringing them scarce food and liquor items, cigarette brands, flown back from foreign post exchanges, helping with the dish-washing, even minding the infant Sheila while Ellen went shopping.

"Guy, you're so domestic," Ellen would say. "What will happen when all those women discover the secret?"

He wasn't really domestic, of course. He had no greater feeling for the Walles' kind of family life than he had for being apartment buddies with the flyers. But it was the price of inaccessibility, of quiet, of staying in New York incognito, of meditation. It was not an unpleasant price.

And he was fond of Ellen. She was often depressed in the year after Sheila's birth, and Guy felt that cheering her up was a service he could render Tom. He tolerated Harrison as being one of Tom's relatives; there was no difficulty in talking to the man. Harrison was endlessly curious about the Cinturon holdings and operations, so there was almost always a topic of conversation to move to. When they ran out of that, usually because they got to a point where Guy's knowledge no longer matched the depth of Harrison's interest, they could talk about the job Harrison was to have after the war. He would be in economic trend analysis for an enormous midwest insurance firm, and there were always reports to be made to Guy on the latest maneuvers between Harrison and this firm in reaching their somewhat secretive rapprochement.

Then in March it fell apart.

"It would be March," Ellen said, when Guy called next day, to say how much he regretted it all.

Guy had slept, twice, at the flyers' apartment, with a tall, brunette nightclub dancer who called herself Sue Z. Robling. She was quite an exciting girl physically, which was pretty much the only way Guy knew her, and on March 2, returning from a flight to Casablanca, he felt he'd like to see Sue Z. and phoned.

The phone was answered by a male voice, Sergeant Someone it said; seemed odd. Sue Z.'s taste ran pretty much to officers.

"May I speak to Sue?" Guy asked. "This is Guy Cinturon."

"Spell it please," Sergeant Someone said.

Guy laughed at this rather heavy example of GI humor, and obligingly went along, spelling out his name. "Your phone number and address?" The man was pretending to be a secretary or something.

"She has them," Guy said.

"What did you want with Miss Robling?" the Sergeant asked.

"Why, I think I'd rather tell her than you," Guy said, good-naturedly.

"Don't you read the papers, mister?" the Sergeant asked.

"What are you talking about. By the way, it's lieutenant, not mister."

"The morning papers."

"No. I just got in from Casablanca."

"You a friend of hers?"

"Yes. But I don't see why all the questions," Guy said. "Has something happened to her?"

"Yeah. Something did."

"But you . . . you said you were Sergeant . . . ?"

"Detective Sergeant Berger, New York Police. Miss Robling got herself strangled last night."

There wasn't much war news for the headlines. The death of the beautiful, brunette dancer dominated the tabloids for three days.

There was no great mystery about it. The strangler was a married garment manufacturer, who had been paying Sue Z.'s bills; Guy had heard about him from the girl. The manufacturer gave himself up, and talked to any reporter who would listen about the motive.

232

The motive, unfortunately, was Guy.

HANDSOME FLYER FERRIED SUE Z.'S HEART AWAY, said one headline.

Guy, who was constantly troubled with the notion that his life was predetermined, had a feeling that those words had been set in type at his birth, and that the papers had been waiting for the time to come to use them, as they set in type both possible results of an election.

WHEN HE FLEW IN, GARMENT KING HAD NO LOVE TO KEEP HIM WARM.

It was a thin story. The garment man's career showed no interesting irregularities. Sue Z.'s was the showgirl's usual past, of aspiration and pathos.

Guy was all they really had to work on.

He was not Joe Flyboy as Sue Z. thought in her trusting heart. He had a million dollars for every bobby pin on her dressing table. . . .

It was an old song in a wartime uniform: she was in love with the honorable Lieutenant Soandso. When he saw his society friends, Sue Z. waited. . . .

In their clipping files, the tabloid people found all kinds of things: records of deb parties Guy had gone to, football games he'd played, deals in which his family was involved; they could assemble almost endless material from the social, sports and finance pages of years past, and transfer them to page three, right hand column. Pictures too. What the reporters couldn't use, the columnists could.

At that, it would have been forgotten, was already being forgotten on the morning Guy got orders for his next flight, if another showgirl, one Guy hadn't seen since leaving college, hadn't given an interview about the torch she would always carry for the Flying Caballero. This was not page three material except that somebody—a publicity man perhaps—had arranged for the new girl to be photographed meeting Sue Z.'s mother at Grand Central Station. Perhaps it was the same publicity man who called up Guy and tried to sell his services, and whom Guy, getting rather rattled by now, told to go to hell. Whatever the mechanism, Sue Z.

233

was dead, the manufacturer was in jail and forgotten, and a public figure had been born: the Chihuahua Sugarplum, Guy Cinturon.

An inconvenient thing to be.

A public figure is permitted no easy subterfuges. His family could no longer choose to disregard what they had known all along: that Guy didn't spend every leave with his uncle. There could hardly be a girl left around Broadway, or Fifty-second street, who still thought of Guy as a nice young pilot from someplace, drawing flight pay. There could hardly be a mother left in society, for society mothers are the most diligent of tabloid readers, who did not realize that there was a greater danger in a daughter's being out with Guy than the risk of incurring flattering gossip. Thank God for orders; thank God for the speed of airplanes; thank God for the Walle apartment to come inconspicuously back to. And goodbye, pretty, long-legged Sue Z. Should I not have believed you when you said of your garment king, as we lay laughing and naked in the narrow bed, that you could handle him? I'm afraid it didn't seem to matter to me at the time whether I believed you or not. . . .

When he returned to the city, ten days later, Guy bought all the papers and was pleased to find himself unmentioned in any of them, first time through. Then he began to check the columnists, and found he'd been too hasty. There were items in two. One was simple enough:

. . . Candy Kobitt alone by the telephone these days, waiting for the call from G.C., involved in the Sue Z. Robling tragedy and out now flying for Uncle Sam. Candy, the 'I Can't Help It' Girl of the Chez Mamo show, can't help it. . . .

Guy did not know Candy Kobitt.
The other item was nasty:

Air Force high brass are laying aside matters of global strategy to debate the transfer of Guy Cinturon to another theatre. Seems he's doing more damage to home front femmes than he is to the enemy; but family pressure may keep the Chihuahua Sugarplum right here, where the field is open and the only ack-ack is from cigarette smokers at the Stork Club.

Guy phoned his uncle. There had been quite a lot of that sort of thing, his uncle said. Lawyers had been consulted and nothing could be done that wouldn't make things worse; Guy's best course was to stay out of sight; Guy agreed. Grateful that such a sanctuary existed for him, he went to the Walles'.

He spent a pleasant, unrecognized afternoon pushing Sheila's perambulator for a long walk beside Ellen in the winter sunshine. People looked at them, and must have taken them for a young Air Force couple, to judge by the smiles. The appearance enabled them to buy a beautiful steak from under the counter at a butcher store.

Ellen had the steak ready to broil, Guy had the martinis all mixed, when Harrison got home. Harrison, Guy thought, was a man with pictures in his mind, movie stills, shot of how Americans lived from the pages of magazines; Harrison tried to fret the visual aspects of his own life into conformity with such images and this ought to have done it for once: the pretty blonde wife, Harrison himself in Navy uniform, the young friend from the Air Corps, the dry drink—even the baby was quiet for once, asleep early.

"Hi," Guy said, putting the drink into Harrison's hand.

"Guy." Harrison stared at him rather strangely; something must be wrong with the image after all.

"Just got in this morning," Guy said. "I tried to call you at school."

"Oh."

Guy smiled. "I didn't want to leave my name. I'm afraid the reasons are obvious." Harrison nodded, and looked to his wife.

Ellen, who had been waiting for her kiss, received it now. "Darling," she said, "Guy's made it up to us for the imposition again. Steak this time."

And wouldn't that supply the missing element for Harrison's picture story? The rich steak? No, apparently not.

"Yes," he said, abstractedly. "Oh, yes."

"Well, let's all have another drink first," Ellen said.

Harrison was rather quiet during drinks and dinner. Usually he had quite a bit to say; not tonight.

After dinner he sat with Guy in the living room, while Ellen washed the dishes; dinner dishes she liked to do alone, Guy knew, because she could have a quiet highball along with them. Harrison didn't like to drink after dinner.

"Anything new on where you're likely to be shipped?" Guy asked. The man almost always had a fresh rumor to report.

Harrison shook his head. "The, uh . . . main topic of conversation around the school these days is you," he said.

"Me?"

"Just after that girl was killed," Harrison said doggedly. "When they had your picture in the paper. The one of you kicking the football?"

"Oh yes." NOW KICKS HEARTS AROUND, had been the caption.

"Well, I . . . I got damned angry about it. And I told some of the men in training with me that it was unfair. I said I knew you and that you stayed with us sometimes."

"I see. Thanks."

"I didn't realize you had . . . several other places to stay, Guy."

"Neither did my family," Guy said. "I hope it didn't hurt your feelings, finding that out."

"No." Harrison shook his head. "Guy, I've been taking a terrible riding about this. It might . . . it might even affect my Naval career."

"How, Harrison?" Americans and their tiresome kidding; it was like constant street fighting with the hands tied behind the backs.

"Ellen's an awfully pretty girl, Guy. The Navy doesn't like the kind of publicity there'd be if some photographer were, oh, to see you out walking with her and snap a picture. Something like that."

"Well," Guy said. "I'll be careful. By the time I come in again, they'll have forgotten me."

"No," Harrison shook his head. "They aren't forgetting about you. It's . . . well, take the men I train with. They're probably a pretty representative group, but more educated. And even they . . . well, it's amazing how strongly they feel about you, Guy."

"About me?"

"They resent you. You're . . . you've become the kind of celebrity they resent. It's a good thing you're in uniform or it would be much worse. Anyway, they never let me alone about it: 'Ellen down there with the Sugarplum today?' They say things like that. 'What's he got, Harrison, or aren't you the one to ask?' "

"What are you saying, darling?" Ellen had come into the room.

"What I told you, Ellen. About the boys at school riding me about Guy's coming here."

"Oh. I . . . I wish you hadn't told Guy."

236

"Do you?"

"I just thought he had enough worries," Ellen said. "Guy comes here to be quiet, and relax."

"But they don't stop, Ellen. They keep after it."

"Why?"

"You know why."

"Oh, Harrison."

"Look," Guy said, sympathetically. "I'm awfully sorry you've been embarrassed about this Harrison. I won't come any more, of course."

"Guy!" Ellen protested.

"In fact, I can go up to my uncle's tonight. He'll be quite tickled to see me and be able to bawl me out."

"But your bed's all made," Ellen said. "Sheila will be so disappointed in the morning."

"Ellen, a five month old child does not feel disappointment," Harrison said.

"I'd forgotten you were such an authority on children's feelings," Ellen said.

Guy rose. "If Sheila likes me, it's because I look like her teddy bear," he said with a smile.

"Don't go," said Ellen. "Guy, don't go."

"Well, I don't want to rush," Guy said. "But my uncle goes to bed rather early."

"At least have a drink with us first, and we'll talk about it," Ellen said.

"Ellen, he wants to go," said Harrison, quite impatiently.

"Now you're an authority on him, too."

"Ellen, this is an awkward situation, and you aren't helping it," Harrison said.

"I didn't cause it, either."

"And why should you feel I did?"

"Well it wasn't Guy and me who went bragging to the boys that they knew someone in the papers," Ellen said.

"Ellen!"

"And it isn't Guy or me who's sitting there in a petty jealous sulk because a friend of my kid brother's comes to see me now and then."

"I am not jealous," Harrison said. "I told you that the other day."

"Again and again," Ellen said.

"I like Guy just as much as you do, and I'm sure he understands that."

"Then why don't you spit in somebody's face up at Columbia instead of spitting in Guy's?"

"Ellen. . . ."

"If you insist on being jealous, I'm damn well going to give you cause one of these days," Ellen said.

"You already have," Harrison shouted back at her, and there was a silence in the room.

"Thank you so much, Harrison," Ellen said, rather quietly. "For mentioning it to Guy."

"Oh." Harrison began to flop now, like a fish on a hot dock. "Guy, I . . . I didn't mean anything that's . . . that's taken, uh, place since our marriage . . . of course. I . . . I'm sorry Ellen. You're quite right. It was most. . . ."

"Go on," Ellen said to Guy, quite deflated herself. "Please go on if you like. This isn't exactly fun for you."

"Never mind," Guy said, to both of them. "When people get mixed up in tabloid murders, I'm afraid it causes a lot of discomfort. I'm sorry you've had to share it with me." He turned to go.

"Guy," Ellen crossed to him and took his hands. "Sheila *will* be disappointed. And so will I."

Guy smiled, squeezing the hands, and dropped them.

"What was she like? The girl, Sue Z.?"

"I don't really know," Guy said sadly. "I only saw her twice." He crossed to Harrison. "Good night, Harrison," he said, offering a hand to shake.

Harrison jumped up and accepted the handclasp. Guy rather sympathized with him. If Guy'd had a wife, he wouldn't have liked it so much to have something called a Chihuahua Sugarplum on casual visiting terms.

He had the luck to find a cab, and rode across the bridge. He had the driver try several hotels until he found a midtown room; he registered, using the name Peter Rice. Then he went to a movie, but left shortly after it started, because a very young girl who seemed to have recognized him in the lobby sat down a few seats away and kept staring. He remembered his uncle's saying that the newsreel pictures of himself had been reshown, very widely, in connection with the murder reporting, but this silent teen-ager who was now following him out of the theatre, was the

238

first stranger to have shown recognition. He decided he'd better speak to her so, as she came up, he said:

"You'll miss the picture."

She said: "I don't care."

"But I do," Guy said. "I want you to see it."

"Will you give me your autograph?"

"I'm not anybody famous," Guy said. He took out a pen, wrote Peter Rice on a piece of paper, and handed it to her. "Here, though. If you want it."

"Oh." She read the name. "Oh, I thought you were . . . that Mexican."

"Do I talk like a Mexican?" Guy asked.

"No."

"Go see the movie."

He walked out of the lobby, onto the street. As he went along, he began to get annoyed. It was all very well to be discreet, but he would, after all, be flying away again tomorrow. He could not let this miserable business exclude him forever from the places he liked, the things he liked to do. Perhaps, if they insisted on his being a celebrity, the place to hide was not in hiding places, but among real celebrities, in places where he would be inconspicuous because of low rank and brief establishment. With this in mind, he bought evening papers and went into a restaurant which was a meeting place for theatre people. Shows had just let out and it should be filled with the legitimately famous.

The headwaiter knew Guy, of course; had, long before all this started. Had had good tips from Guy for years; why should he bother noting Guy's presence for the columnists when there were movie people in his restaurant, stars of current shows? There was William Roster, a king once more in movieland, now that the younger matinee idols, who had replaced him, were off to war; Roster, with his group of young girls, his court of heavy looking men, his wavy grey hair and deep tan—that would be tonight's item. He would be the one for whom the columnists would invent quips worth repeating, and allege that they had been made in this restaurant. Not Guy.

Guy asked for a single table, sat at it, ordered a chicken sandwich and a beer and started to read his papers. He was just finishing the first, finding with pleasure that there was nothing at all about him in it, when he felt a hand on his shoulder.

He looked up. It was William Roster, the star, very drunk.

239

"You're Guy, huh?"

"Hello, Mr. Roster," Guy said. "Yes."

"Well, up yours, Guy," Roster said, weaving.

"Okay, Mr. Roster," Guy said, turning away and sitting again. He certainly wasn't going to get into a fuss with a middle-aged drunk.

"Hey, come on. Be pals," Roster said, grabbing Guy's shoulder again and trying to turn him back. Guy sat absolutely still. "All right, all right," Roster said. He let go the shoulder and Guy thought he had moved away. Guy reached into his pocket and found some bills to leave for his order which hadn't come yet. He had been wrong to come to this particular playpen. Suddenly his hat was snatched off.

"Hey, Guy," Roster said. 'What are you doing with a U.S. hat on?" Guy stood up and turned towards him. Roster, smiling loosely, ducked away, waving the hat. "Look at that. U.S. hat."

Guy walked away without it, leaving the man to hold it and yell obscenities after him, at which people in the restaurant laughed as if they were funny.

BILL ROSTER DECLARES WAR ON MEXICO.

FIGHT IN NIGHTCLUB.

CINTURON DOES THE HAT DANCE IN IMPROMPTU FLOOR SHOW.

Yep. Fight in nightclub. Picture of Roster with a black eye, grinning; picture of Roster holding steak on eye, grinning, saying, "Cost me a meat stamp, too"; interview with Roster, saying, "It was worth it. I came all the way across the country to hang one on that Chihuahua jerk. No kidding. That was the whole reason for the trip." Lieutenant Cinturon could not be reached for comment.

Lieutenant Cinturon supposed the black eye was genuine and envied whatever nameless private figure, in the course of Roster's night, had been privileged to throw the punch. Apparently they needed their diversion, the readers of war news, and Guy wondered how long he was going to have to be it.

240

The next time Lala saw the pale young sergeant, it was business. He had come into the ration board to arrange about papers for some civilian employees of his unit who were going off American rations onto a different system. Chuck Little, the Princeton man was gone by then and there was somebody new, another captain, a serious dramatic man. Lala suspected that this captain was lying to her about not having a wife, and, except that she disliked the idea of his lying—whether he had a wife was his own business, and he needn't have brought it up—he might have been her first real lover. Chuck had always got too drunk; it had made Lala wonder if he really wanted to. Men made such a surprisingly complicated fuss of the matter, Americans did at least; those of her countrymen whom she saw—but there were never any of them around now—hadn't ever brought the matter up. It was all rather mystifying, and not a bit like novels.

Novels, yes. Perhaps the sergeant. . . .

"May I ask," she said, when they had finished their business, "are you an artist, sergeant? Or a writer of some kind?"

"No. I came to this straight out of college. I hadn't become . . . well, much of anything."

"What did you think you might like to become?"

"Oh, some . . . some sort of scholar I guess. I don't seem to know any longer."

"But a scholar in what field?" she asked.

"I used to think. . . ." He smiled anxiously at her, as if he doubted that what he was saying could really be interesting. "Classics. That I'd like to teach classic languages," he said.

Oh. A schoolmaster. At last he was approaching classification. "Why, 'used to'?"

"Well," he smiled again. "When I thought that, I hadn't done much of anything else. And I . . . I still haven't but I know it now." His hesitancy was not especially charming; it was something better. It was nice. She could see into him amazingly, and what she saw was a real reluctance to talk about himself fighting with an unwillingness not to answer her questions as honestly as he could. "Do you think classics are very . . . relevant?" There,

241

you see. He was trying, awkwardly, to find out whether she really cared to talk to him.

She smiled. Now she understood why he had come to her that day about Captain Chuck Little and the shellfish. It was just as he had said, nothing more than a desire to correct an injustice—a small thing most men would have forgotten. For her to admit this spoke better for his character than it did for her power to fascinate. Because she was nineteen and couldn't abide anything less than total possession of every man in the world, she said, "And now you've come to take me to tea after work?" She accompanied this with the least of her ravishing glances, and of course the poor sergeant stammered and said might he. Poor sergeant.

She was quite right. He was nice. Perhaps the thing that made her like him most was that he didn't seem to have any idea how very nice he was.

Nothing much came after the tea, until her second brother was killed. And then Lala, whose upper lip was stiff by birth, who would have found it harder to cry than most men, thought it might be all right to see someone nice for a while. There was no difficulty about bringing herself to his attention; she simply phoned him up and asked him to take her to tea again.

Thereafter, it was he who did the phoning; because he was so nice, she made it easy as she could for him, always saying yes right away. The one time she was a little bit bitchy and wanted to put him off for a Saturday night, waiting to see whether she might feel more like accepting an invitation she knew would come for the officer's dance, he was so eagerly decent about it that she felt simply awful. In fact, she had to accept the dancing invitation then to relieve him, and had a rather horrid time; the man who'd asked her was the kind, apparently, they called a wolf, and kept fighting so hard against what he supposed would be resistance that it became resistance. Lala didn't mean to be overwhelmed any more than she meant to be lied to.

Then came the air raid. It was absurd that she should have been frightened in it; she had been in far larger ones, in some of the really tremendous ones in London in fact, and this was no more than a dozen planes, trying to do something about the American aerodrome which wasn't even in town. One of the reasons she was afraid was that they couldn't get to a shelter; another was that the

242

planes came in rather low. But perhaps the real reason was that, since her brother Bert's death, she'd been in rather a flap.

They had been to the cinema and were sitting in the parlor. She'd made Sergeant Beniger a sandwich for which the poor man was very grateful, and was watching him eat it when the sirens began. He switched off the lights, and she supposed at first that it meant he would come after her in the dark; she hadn't started being frightened yet.

Instead he said, in the dark: "I'm not going to let it spoil the sandwich."

"Have you been in one before?" she asked.

"No. Is there a shelter we're supposed to go to?"

"Not this far out. We can go to the cellar if you like."

"No. Do you supposed I could watch at the window?"

"We're supposed to stay away from windows."

"Oh, yes." She heard him sit down again in his chair.

That was when they heard the first plane going right over the roof, the sound coming up so suddenly and loud that it sounded as if it would have to crash into the house. When it was past, she found herself in his arms, but he hadn't moved; she had. He had only risen to meet her.

"Sorry," she said; he was holding her very gently.

"Don't go away," he said, stroking her shoulder. "Unless . . . shall I take you to the cellar?"

"No. It isn't like me. . . ."

Another plane came over the same way, and again she went against him; this time a bomb went off not far away, and the concussion rocked them. She began to sob drily, and he tightened his arms around her a little.

"It's all right," he said. "Be afraid if you like. I'm going to take you to the cellar now."

"No." For some reason she was even more frightened of the cellar.

"All right." He stopped trying to lead her, and put his arms around her again. "Just stand still then. Here with me. Everything's all right, Lala. . . ." he was speaking to her as if to a little girl, and she nestled against him. When a third plane went low over them, she found that her fear was over.

"Let's do go to the window," she said sniffling. "The barrage is awfully pretty."

243

Sheltering her still with an arm, he let her lead him to the window, honoring her bravado, and together they crouched down and watched the lights, the bursts, the tracers in the sky. There were no more planes. The all clear sounded. For the first time she was aware of how large a man he was.

"Don't turn on the lights, Tom," she said.

"All right."

But he was releasing her.

"No." She wanted him to kiss her. When he didn't, simply continued holding her, she said: "Please kiss me."

He did, very nicely. Tenderly . . . or was it only kind? She would have to have another to find out.

When she had it, she stepped away for a moment; her eyes were accustomed enough to the dark now so that she could see him a little.

"Tom," she said. "I'm a virgin, you know."

"No," he said. "I didn't know." She wondered if he were smiling.

"Would you?" This seemed correct to her. To pick a man who was gentle and uninsistent, yet obviously—why obviously? well, he just was—experienced, and simply ask him. Yes, why not?

He hesitated. Then he said: "Shall we talk about it?"

She shook her head in the dark. "Please not. I'd hate that. If you don't like me well enough or something, then I'm sorry. . . ."

"Oh, Lala," he said, touching her arm. "Of course I like you . . . more than well enough."

"Come along," she said before he could say anything more. It absolutely must be matter-of-fact. She had promised herself that. "Let's go to a bedroom, shouldn't we?"

As they went upstairs she chattered along, trying to deny her excitement, explaining that she had always meant simply to pick a man and be matter-of-fact, and that she should have hated him if he'd refused on the one hand or been soppy about it on the other; Americans were so prone to soppiness, weren't they? Not the least hard-boiled, really. . . .

But she rather liked what he said when they were on the bed together:

"Lala, this may sound soppy to you but I . . . feel a certain reverence at your having chosen me."

And then afterwards it was she who was soppy, telling him she loved him, feeling it, too, completely; asking him to light a match so that she could look at his face.

244

Was it the match-light, or did he really seem bewildered, almost pained at her saying she loved him?

Was it his characteristic uncertainty about exactly what to say, or did some real spasm of anguish pass through him before he could reply,

"I love you too."?

4.

What day do you remember when they are all the same?

If you are only a piece of tired dirt, dirt-colored, why should one monotonously violent episode be any different from another? If you are so weary you have forgotten how to sleep, how can you remember. . . .

. . . a German sitting next to Eddie on a hillside, about a step below and to the left, so that Eddie could keep the carbine on the back of the guy's head. A lieutenant, a big joe. Because he was blond it took Eddie a long time, sitting in the sun, to figure out who this joe reminded him of; because the man he reminded Eddie of was someone he used to know in college called Guy Cinturon, who, Eddie was pretty sure, was dark. That was a long time ago, but anyway, if you could keep your stupid dirt-colored mind on it for a minute, persuade yourself that it was worth keeping a mind on, this joe had the same way, or Cinturon had the same way, of making you like him just by smiling. Something like that. Bastard spoke fair English, too, and they'd been chatting off and on, liking each other, one old pro to another, about weapons and crud like that, for about twenty minutes, while Eddie decided what to do with him.

On the forward slope of the hill over the ridge and a little east, was a draw which both sides patrolled every night, each making sure that the other wasn't trying to sneak through it. Patrolling was for information, not casualties; so Eddie, who had a company now, let the Germans have until midnight to take their look; he sent his own boys out towards dawn. Whoever his opposite number was had seemed to respect the hours pretty well up to now. But Eddie's morning patrol had found this blond joe and brought him in; found him lying between two corpses; what got them? Artillery probably. Anyway, the joe was lying between the two corpses, pretending to be a third. Cute. Cute little grease gun under his belly. Apparently, finding himself alone and caught, he'd figured to let Eddie's patrol go past, raise up and let them have it.

Bing, in charge of the patrol, said he'd been suspicious, but Eddie figured it was more like greedy. Not much question but what if Lugers hadn't been bringing a hundred bucks in the rear area, the German lieutenant would have got himself four GI's. Eddie's boys were over the souvenir crap for themselves, too many boobie traps. But they hated to miss anything worth a hundred bucks to someone else, boobie traps or not. Couldn't blame them in a way. It gave them something to fight along for: money. They were smart enough to know the risks and how to handle most of them, not that it wasn't skin off Eddie's ass; he never got over hating to lose a man, though he could no longer remember the names of all the one's he'd lost. Hell, sometimes you'd get a replacement and lose him before you've even heard his name.

Anyway, the guys carried ropes when they went patrolling in Italy in the summer of 1944, and they kept the ropes hidden from Eddie, stuffed into their fatigue pants, wound around their waists. If they came to something they wanted to have a look at, they tied the rope around it, went off, lay down behind something, and gave a pull. Sometimes the German engineers would mine whatever was the most likely thing to lie down behind, but Eddie's boys were wise to that; they were born neutralizers. There wasn't a man in the company who'd hesitate to go through a piece of ground with his bayonet and come up with a mine and disarm it.

When Eddie'd sent Bing out with his patrol he'd said sarcastically:

"Got your rope?"

Bing said: "Rope, Eddie? Come on, Eddie."

Eddie said: "Rope, Bing. Take off, Bing."

Bing said he never been so surprised in his life as he was when they heaved on the rope, and the big blond German lieutenant they thought was dead let out a yell and tried to grab for the grease gun they were pulling him away from. They hadn't even thought about tying the rope on easy—just dropped a loop over the boot and apparently blond joe hadn't been aware. It was a cute war.

Only now what was Eddie going to do with this prisoner he didn't want?

246

Intelligence always claimed they wanted prisoners, but what for? They knew the name, hair color and favorite ice cream flavor of every son of a bitching German across on the next ridge by now; and the Germans had the whole picture, looking back towards Eddie, too. Didn't do anyone a damn bit of good.

When the heavy thinkers decided it was time for Eddie to be on that next ridge, they would start by sending attack bombers to which the Germans no longer had enough ordnance to reply effectively; then they would get up enough artillery to shoot twenty rounds for every one the Germans had to shoot back; then Eddie and his boys would steam across. Jerry Stein would take his company on the right, and whoever had replaced Herb Rascoe would go across on the left, and they'd each be a few men short when they settled down on the new ridge and counted up—one or two dead, half a dozen wounded, no worse than that. And the Germans would settle on the next ridge behind their present position, casualties about the same, and fire the screemie-meemie mortars which were the chief thing they had now and which were damn good. The Germans would know that they were only there until the heavy thinkers decided it was time to move them back again, and they would pass the time thinking up mine and booby trap angles for Eddie's scavengers to figure out.

"Where'd you learn English?" Eddie asked his prisoner. He didn't really want to shoot the bastard in the head, but he supposed he had to. This was what everybody claimed happened to prisoners but, as far as Eddie knew, nobody ever really saw. Ever had seen. Watch this; watch this.

"School."

"What kind of school?

"Army school. I was by parachute into England going."

"Oh yeah? Why didn't you?"

"I don't know. I think we could done it. Who knows those things why they decide them?"

"Same way all over," Eddie said. If he fired, the round would go in right where the guy's skull showed pink in the sun, under his hair cut. "You must have been out of the line recently."

"Excuse me?"

"That's a fresh hair cut. Where'd you get it?"

"Trieste. You have a good time in Trieste when you get there."

Then Eddie saw the scars, almost invisible the way they followed

247

the folds of the guy's neck, and knew he must have been in the hospital in Trieste; well, Eddie had a couple of legs full of scars himself, some with the metal still in.

"When do you think we'll get there, to Trieste?"

"Who knows? After time. They keep taking supplies away from us, put them in France."

"Yeah."

"Maybe today, tomorrow, they would take me away to put in France, if not for your cowboys with the rope."

"Yeah," Eddie said. "I'll bet France is all right."

"When I was in France, that was best. I learn to drink wine."

"Hope you left some for us," Eddie said.

"Plenty there. Next year."

Next year. What a stupid conversation. Maybe the guy was trying to flatter Eddie, save his ass. But he didn't seem like that kind of guy. And he seemed pretty confident that he'd be marching back to P.O.W. Camp soon; he'd asked a lot of questions about the camps.

"Hey," Eddie said. "What do you think of Hitler?"

The German shrugged. "What do you think of Roosevelt?"

"I don't like him."

"He is a Jew?"

"No."

"I did not think so."

"Is Hitler crazy?"

"No different from everybody."

That disposed of international politics.

"Want another smoke?" Eddie asked.

The German took a cigarette out of the pack that Eddie tossed in front of him.

"On our side, 400 lira for your cigarettes one package."

"They get across to you, huh?"

"Yes."

"What's 400 lira worth on your side?"

They couldn't figure out equivalents; that took care of international finance. Eddie knew he'd have to decide what to do pretty soon now. About lunch time, the Germans were apt to throw a few mortar shells over; just a habit. And the prisoner had no helmet.

Okay German, Eddie thought, you're a good enough joe. And I'd send you back to that fairy major in Intelligence if I could spare the guys to take you. Maybe he'd like you; Jesus, they say one German prisoner came out of the interrogation tent wearing the bastard's wristwatch. But look, German, I got nobody to send you back with, and I don't guess I'm the type you get watches off; anyway, buddy, we got no tent even if I were, so now I'm going to shoot you, German, while you look up towards the top of the hill and wish you were over it, getting your orders to France, bang.

Eddie tightened his finger on the trigger; nothing happened.

For Christ's sake, he'd forgotten to take the safety off. Think about it. The most automatic thing in the entire range of human action sequences was to flick off the safety on the carbine he carried before pressing the trigger; as automatic as opening your mouth when you bring a glass to it. It requires absolutely no conscious thought; well try it, for Christ's sake. Get yourself a glass, and lift it up there to your little pink lips, and keep them closed—that's the kind of feeling. The whole conscious thought in Eddie's head was: I'm going to shoot you now, German . . . bang. So having made that decision, his cruddy unconscious decides to veto against him, just like that. Safety on, no shot fired, yellow belly Bissle.

"So Trieste is okay?" Yellow Belly muttered.

"Excuse me?"

"Bing!" Eddie yelled.

Bing came over.

"You brought me this cruddy bastard," Eddie said. "You gotta take him off my hands."

"What do you mean, Skipper?" Bing asked.

"I mean take two men and march his ass back to Battalion, for Intelligence," Eddie said. "Probably Major Henbill will give you a big wet kiss when he sees what you've brought him."

"Okay, Eddie," Bing said. "We're not supposed to lose him along the way, huh?"

"No," Eddie roared. He wasn't going to ask Bing to do something he was too yellow to do himself.

Bing unslung his M-1 and took over. "All right, Lieutenant," he said to the German. Bing had a nice manner, even like this, with a prisoner. "On your feet, now."

The prisoner got up. Eddie watched Bing organizing his detail, starting down the hill, Smalley the goldbrick in front, Bing and the guy they called Cheerio in back. Eddie was still wondering at himself, at his failure of nerve or whatever the hell it was, and just as he was forgiving himself on nice, humanitarian grounds, his big German did the inevitable thing—reached forward, grabbed the M-1 out of goldbrick Smalley's lazy hands, whirled and caught Bing a tremendous butt stroke and ran; you could hear Bing's skull crack, all the way up the hill. By the time Cheerio started firing his rifle, the German was halfway back up and angling off, running like a good halfback, and Eddie sent a couple of carbine rounds off the hip without any goddamn effect whatever. Then he stopped because he was firing into the area where his own guys were dispersed, and someone started the B.A.R. on Eddie's German but wild as hell. Eddie ran up the hill to cut the man off, stopping and dropping to one knee just before he reached the ridge line. Somebody's wild shot clipped the German in the shoulder and he went down, twisting, trying to get the M-1 working. Eddie aimed one and plunked it into the German's back, but it wasn't enough; the guy was over a hundred yards away. The German got up and staggered towards the top with the whole damn company firing at him, like a bear hunt. God knows how many rounds were in him by the time he showed over the ridge line and his own side started shooting at him, too. Boy it was wild as hell for a minute; nothing was holding him up except that the force of bullets going into him from both sides wouldn't let him fall until a leg actually came off. Then, as Eddie kept yelling to cease the goddamn firing, and it gradually did stop, this goddamn Cheerio, who was a big buddy of Bing's, went up on his belly, crazy as a blinded cat, and started pulling the meat back, looking for something to stick a trench knife in. Very cute war.

All the cuteness and fun brought a nice steady little afternoon shower of screemie meemies onto their area; the mortar men on the other side must have figured the German was part of an outfit trying for an unsupported daytime attack, as if such a thing were ever used any longer. Eddie wished he could get them on the radio to explain that it was just one of their boys, trying to get back and see if his orders had come for France.

So Bing was dead, the German was dead, and Eddie couldn't have the cooks bring up hot chow that evening because of the mortar shells coming in; they all had to stay in their holes to eat so they wouldn't get hurt. And that's the kind of Infantry officer Yellow Belly Bissle was and when, sometime later in the campaign,

250

they told him he was going to get a Silver Star for a lucky company strength night patrol he'd led, which got some fire going in an underground ammo dump, Eddie thought about his yellow belly subconscious and the safety on the carbine and wondered how many other Silver Stars they were handing out to pukes like him.

5.

" 'All Counties and Hundreds, Trething and Wapontakes,' " Tom said softly, " 'shall be at the ancient rent. . . .' "

He stood with Lala on a hilltop in the soft British summer of 1945, looking out over other hills, with slow sheep on them, seeing the reflection of the sun off a lake yet farther on, seeing occasional outcroppings of stone, Druid grey, and a boy kicking dust. Nothing would bother this land now. The war would be over in a few weeks, a month, like all the other wars, and there they would be forever as he saw them now, the Counties and the Hundreds, the Trethings and the Wapontakes. . . .

"What on earth?" Lala said.

. . . at the ancient rent now and forever.

He pointed a finger at her: " 'Trials upon Writ of Novel Disseisin, of Mort d'Ancestre and Darrien Presentment, shall not be taken but in their proper manner,' " he said sternly.

"I'm not King John," she said. "And I think it's more of your bloody American cheek to trap me on Magna Carta." She put her arms around him and her face against his chest.

"I feel as if I'd been born here," he said, tightening his own arm across his shoulders.

"Do you?" She looked up. "Where were you born?"

"A town called Tennepin, in Connecticut."

"Anything like this?"

"No," he said. "Not really. Sometimes the air felt like this."

"How d'you happen to be able to quote Magna Carta, anyway?"

"Read it one day in your father's library," Tom said. "Things like that stay in my mind. Whole pages."

"Is it any use to have a mind like that?" she asked.

"It must be," Tom said, smiling. He pointed out over the gentle hills. "Do you think that might be a Wapontake over there?"

She laughed. "How would you like it if you took me to Philadelphia and I stood under the Liberty Bell, saying your Declaration of Independence. With gestures?"

"I'd think it was beautiful," Tom said. "If it was you."

"And I think you're a big soppy goof," Lala said, kissing him. "I can't think why I should be in love with you."

"But you are."

"Oh yes. And I'm going to marry you and there's no chance at all of your wiggling out of it."

"Don't have a wiggle left in me," Tom said.

"Shall we live in that place you said? Tennepin?"

"No. I don't think so."

"Where then? New York?"

"First we'll go back to where I was in college," Tom said. "So that I can finish. I think you'll like that."

He was rather confused about their future; they would be married, he would finish college. Perhaps he'd do graduate work; he couldn't decide. Perhaps he'd get a job, but he had no idea what sort of job. First, though, he would marry Lala; that was the one thing so far that was altogether clear.

"What about Tennepin, Tom? You don't care for it?"

"Oh, yes," he said. "But, well it's disappearing, in a way. Being absorbed by the creeping city. It's sort of a disinheritance, isn't it? To have your hometown vanish." She seemed interested, and he went on, lightly enough: "They're levelling the hills and covering the places where they used to be with little houses and new streets. I don't know. It used to be a comfort to think that there was a place where one could always go and not be an outsider." He tightened his arm around her. "But it's better to have a person to whom one isn't an outsider, isn't it?"

"Much," she said.

He was very fond of her. It seemed to him that he was in love with her, but if this were so, then love—love was a quieter, less stirring thing than he had thought. Nice, warm, fine in every way; but, it seemed to him, with none of the tears and sighs and suffering it was said to have. Or was it him? Tom wondered, sometimes, about his own capacity to feel; there was always something in him, near the core, that resisted being stirred. A month or two before, Roosevelt had died. There was a corporal with whom Tom worked, a leathery, salacious boy from the Boston slums. When the news came, they were both in the mess hall; the mess sergeant had come in, telling the news quietly, and Tom had been shocked and sorrowful, had felt as he might at the news of a friend lost, or a parent. Had risen quietly, to go out and think about this by himself and just then noticed the Boston corporal, sobbing unselfconsciously, his head down in his arms on the table. Perhaps I don't feel fully, Tom thought, and it made him frown unhappily and hug Lala all the tighter.

6.

There was a war on. Germany was falling, Europe smelled peace, but there was a war on in the Pacific. Guy went to it.

Family pressure had been used in behalf of Guy's service career at last. It was used, at his insistence, to get him transferred out of the Ferry Command and into heavy bombers, one of which he flew, with great skill, for the final months of the war with Japan. Though he took his plane through anti-aircraft fire from time to time—quite a lot of it over Okinawa—he rarely saw an enemy fighter plane and his gunners never got a shot at one. So he had little sense of really having been involved in combat.

Guy found an odd situation on joining the Squadron. Navarro, flight engineer of the crew whose pilot Guy replaced, happened to be Mexican—Mexican-American. The crew, like all the rest of the Air Force, had read about Guy in the papers at the time Sue Z. Robling was killed; Guy had been, briefly, a topic of general overseas Air Force debate, a temporary symbol of the universal sense of complaint. He had been succeeded, of course, by other symbols —except in the particular crew he took over. Here, because of Navarro, who was plump and warm and excitably witty—a general favorite—the topic had been kept alive with Navarro in defense. They were all incredulous that Guy himself, Navarro's hero, should arrive to take over.

Fortunately Guy was an exceptionally good flyer; that overcame any initial difficulties—they had confidence in him and soon enough they liked him. It was a happy crew; when, in fact, they got themselves a new plane, they insisted that it be called The Chihuahua Sugarplum and Guy had to give in. His feeling about the nickname and the notoriety was still distaste; but he had begun to wonder, since leaving New York, whether, if his celebrity per-

253

sisted, the attention it brought couldn't be made useful. If he could not avoid it, he must learn to cultivate it so that it would grow properly; if a man must have a press, better a good press than a bad. So when Navarro came up to Guy grinning one day, with a correspondent, proud that he had persuaded the man that Guy should be interviewed about the christening of the new plane, Guy was happy enough to sit down and answer the man's questions. Yes, he was happier now; yes, he had been applying for transfers to combat command long before the trouble started; no, he had no grudges against anybody, only the Japs.

There was a singer, a rather nice man named Horace Winters, who was navigator on one of the other planes in the squadron. And a gunner, a former competitor in beautiful body contests. There came a visit from a U.S.O. troop which produced some photographs of Winters and Guy and the beautiful body man with a well-known movie actress. Consequently, in the few dispatches that accompanied these pictures, their squadron was called "The Glamor Squadron," and the rest of the boys liked that fine.

When Guy was discharged, early in 1946, he was still a public figure, a minor one of course, but there were photographers to record his discharge. He got two movie offers, and one to play professional football, which made him smile; he was also a U.S. citizen now, if he wanted to be. He consulted his father about this, and his father thought it might not be a bad idea from the overall family viewpoint. Guy could live wherever he liked in the States— New York, he thought; have the proprietorship of a good deal of Texas and California property in his name, which would be a legal convenience. If, when he married, Guy wished to return to Mexico, that could be arranged, too.

He decided, arriving back in New York in civilian clothes, to take a hotel apartment, and found one on the East side, in the thirties. He was in a nice position, coming back, because the break of almost a year would enable him to resume only those connections he chose to maintain; all the others could be ignored.

Except the Walles. He would have preferred to ignore the Walles. But Tom would be back soon, and Tom's young British wife would be arriving. They would stay at the Walles', most likely, for a while at least, and so it was Guy's duty to assure himself a welcome in Brooklyn Heights. He did it by phoning in the evening, asking for Harrison, and inviting them out to dinner; Harrison hesitated for a moment, and then accepted with apparent pleasure.

7.

So the war was over, both wars, all the wars, and who got killed? Not Guy, not Tom, not Eddie—not even the Kaiser, though he had worked himself pretty close to death.

Edward M. Bissle, senior, that's who got killed, Eddie's father. Eddie never wanted to figure out all the details; he didn't even hear about it until he got home—thought his old man was alive and everything; what he learned was all he wanted to know.

Apparently, it had started even before the war; his old man, sensing that gas and tire rationing was coming, had bought up and added to his small trucking company a fleet of several hundred truck carcasses, assembling them from junk yards for sixty or seventy dollars each. None of them would run, but each was entitled to four good new tires every six months, and gallons and gallons of gasoline as long as Bissle senior's man stayed on the ration board. This was the beginning of an operation which got pretty big, got involved with meat and sugar and counterfeit ration stamps, needed more and more protection, not just from the politicians, whom Bissle could count on, but from the real, professional gangsters, too. It was too close to New York City maybe; anyway, they wouldn't let Bissle have it all, that way, and when he started grabbing war construction priorities, which meant the proprietorship of scarce industrial materials, and which was as big as black market business could get, they must have decided it was too much. Materials of that kind were controlled by the same men who controlled unions; they were tough men. Not like Bissle senior, who was only crooked.

They had him shot, using a cuckoo discharged Marine who got Bissle through his car window at a red light. The Marine was cut down by cops. The car which was supposed to wait for him drove away, leaving him, even before the cops appeared. That's the way the boys who got Eddie's old man played.

Eddie's father had been trying to get out from under, or so Eddie

255

was told. Because Bissle senior was involved in transferring funds around in a somewhat precarious way in the effort to get out, most of the funds disappeared; the man who told Eddie this, his father's lawyer, said there was no way of knowing how much loss was involved. The rest of the money had been squandered on the Ten Acre Flag project.

Eddie had a hard time imagining his old man really playing with gangsters—it must have just grown away from him, and Bissle senior hadn't known how to stop. But Eddie could sure see his old man pissing away dough on the Ten Acre Flag.

The basis of this was the supposition that travel from Europe to the United States would be more and more by plane as the postwar age opened, and that the planes would come in over Long Island. So instead of passing the Statue of Liberty, these planes would be going over nothing at all to tell the passengers where they were and what it was all about.

Some politician had suggested to Eddie's father that what was needed was a ten acre U.S. flag, on outer Long Island, something visible from the air, and Eddie's father went for it hard. He had bought the land for it, at ten grand an acre, having to pay that kind of price because the plot had to be rectangular; he had hired soil chemists to develop the dye that would be plowed deep, deep into the ground, packed with dyed stones or perhaps concrete for absolute permanence, in a pattern of stars and stripes. He had had to hire publicity people, and a man to go to the airlines, and the Federal commissions, and the State for tax forgiveness; and get in a New York legal firm to set the thing up as a foundation, the Ten Acre Flag Foundation, to which, the day before he was killed, he had made over the acreage. Thus, the lawyer said, something Eddie's father had planned to start off with fifty thousand dollars—a public subscription was to have raised the rest, and repaid part of the land purchase—had actually cost the estate close to a quarter of a millon.

There was enough left, the lawyer suggested, for Eddie's mother, who had moved to Florida, to live out her life if she didn't live too high. What remained for Eddie was his grandfather's house and land; the trust fund, his father had got into—there wasn't much more than enough left in it to buy seeds and equipment for a crop. But the lawyer didn't think Eddie ought to use it that way; the lawyer suggested that Eddie could sell the farm, and have some capital that way, and maybe not bring the name Bissle back to that part of the world. . . .

Eddie thanked him and said he thought he'd worry about getting a crop in. He was still wearing his uniform with two rows of ribbons, a discharge medallion and a combat infantry pin.

"Edward," the lawyer said, as Eddie got up.

"Yeah?"

"You wouldn't . . . you aren't thinking of trying to do anything about it are you?"

"Anything about what?"

"Those . . . the men who had your father killed. You aren't planning to try to do anything about them?"

"Grow up," Eddie said. "My old man screwed with that kind of thing all his life; I never offered to underwrite him."

It made the lawyer uncomfortable. "Edward, your father wasn't a dishonest man. That is he . . . he wasn't like the men who, who, got angry at him. He was a business man. . . ."

"He was a crook without guts," Eddie said. "I knew that from the time I was ten. And when he got old and scared he tried to wave a ten acre flag."

"Edward, about the Foundation. . . ."

"Yeah, I know. You're treasurer. And you're going to sell off the land so that you can vote yourself payment of legal fees. I understood that first time around."

"Edward. . . ."

"Don't bother," Eddie said. "I don't want the goddamn money. I just hope a few more of you guys shoot one another, squabbling over what's left."

The lawyer—maybe he wasn't such a bad guy; but he probably was. He'd been in with the old man over the years. Anyway, he reminded Eddie of the Colonel who had sat on the screening board when Eddie was discharged, day before yesterday.

Eddie had figured, going in before that Board, that his life was cinched now. He had three almost uninterrupted years of combat infantry experience, the last eighteen months of it handling a company; he had a Silver Star and two Purple Hearts, and a very deep desire to stay in the Army. The Regular Army.

And what did the Colonel say, in a voice just like the lawyer's?

"I suggest that you not transfer to the Regular Army, Captain.

257

As long as you stay an active reservist, you will hold your present temporary rank, and very likely be promoted to Major."

"But when the reserves get inactive?"

"Why . . . there's no immediate possibility of that."

"I like the sound of Regular Army," Eddie said. "That's a career, not an emergency job."

Then they explained it to him. His permanent rank might be staff sergeant in the regulars, maybe platoon sergeant; he would have to work back up to a commission from that, and, though there were several ways to do it, the best would be to apply to West Point and start his college training over. But then, when he was permanently commissioned, he would, of course, be overage in grade, and promotions would be much slower now that the emergency was over; much slower.

Eddie had stood there, at ease, feeling lousier and lousier. He'd counted on being in the army. He'd thought they'd need people like him, with all the guys crying to get out.

"Okay," he said.

"You wish to remain in the service in your present rank and status, Captain?"

"No," Eddie said. "I don't wish to be done any favors, thanks."

They tried to argue with him a little more, but Eddie was getting tired of standing there; his legs still had some metal in them, just tiny pieces, but they hurt after a while. He said thanks again and turned to go without saluting. The Colonel called him on it.

"Are we to infer that the oversight was deliberate, Captain?" He asked.

"No," Eddie said.

"You do intend to salute this board?"

"Doesn't matter to me one way or the other," Eddie said, throwing them a salute and turning and going out without bothering to notice whether it was returned.

Then he'd gone up to Long Island to find the house closed; nobody'd bothered to write him a letter about what happened to his father, and the first he knew about it was from a cop who didn't know him and wanted to know who was trying to get into the empty house. Shame in a way that Eddie hadn't been notified; if he had, the Regular Army might have had itself a damn good staff sergeant.

258

Tom and Lala met and hugged in the Walles' kitchen.

"Are they too much for you?" Tom asked.

"Oh, no. They're all quite sweet. But your sister isn't going to like me."

"She's a little bit drunk," Tom said.

"Your stepfather is a dear. Why on earth do you call him Kaiser?"

"I don't think anybody remembers," Tom said.

"And we'll have to go to Florida to meet your mother?"

"Yes. In the spring, I guess."

"Couldn't we go one day this week?"

"Florida's over a thousand miles away," Tom said.

"Oh." She laughed. "Think you're pretty big, don't you?"

They had another hug on that, and he asked her what she thought of Eddie.

"He looks quite lost, poor soul," Lala said.

"Yes. I guess he is. His father was killed while Eddie was overseas; Eddie didn't know anything about it till he got home and found the house empty."

"Poor man," Lala said. "How terrible."

Guy was out there, too, in the living room, with the girl he had just become engaged to, the heiress of a celebrated fortune. Eddie, Guy and his girl, the Kaiser, Harrison, Ellen, and a Navy couple— a man Harrison had known at Pearl Harbor and his wife. Tom had been sent to the kitchen to make drinks.

"What about Guy?" He asked Lala.

"You'd spoken of him so much I ought to have been disappointed," Lala said. "But I wasn't. He looks very much the great lover."

"Wait till you see him stepping up the voltage sometime, with some hapless creature," Tom said. "It's really quite a sight."

"I think he's stepped it down for me," Lala said. "I have a very distinct feeling of a man holding back."

Tom laughed. "Guy has to be careful," he said, "That reputation's a terrific liability."

"Yes. I can imagine."

"He once told me that he'd developed a special sort of approach to make to ladies with whom he wished to fail but who'd be hurt if they didn't think he'd tried."

"Oh, Tom!" Lala said. "Do you believe that?"

"I don't know. Yes, I think I do."

"How does he work it, then?"

"He said the secret of failure was verbalizing at the wrong moment," Tom said.

"So that's where you learned," Lala teased, gave him a kiss, and carried off some of the drinks he'd fixed to the party in the living room. It left Tom smiling but uneasy. He believed Lala loved him; he thought that he loved her. They were having a wonderfully friendly, wonderfully affectionate time together. But he did not think he was a very satisfactory husband physically; perhaps his sexual vitality had always been low, Tom thought. Whatever it was, even from the beginning there had been a physical insincerity in his relations with his wife which, it seemed to him, she must sense. Nothing fooled Lala for long; he found himself hoping that they would begin to have children soon, which would mean long periods of affectionate companionship without physical commitment.

He finished fixing the tray of drinks, and went back into the room. How odd, no, how nice, that Ellen should have found both Guy and Eddie for them, to welcome Lala; how unchanged they all were to look at after three years—Guy a little heavier, but it made him more virile than ever; Eddie a touch more wrinkled, even with a few grey, bristly hairs on one temple though he was what now? 23 or 24; Ellen still looking like a plump teen-ager at 28. He himself, Tom thought, sloppier looking most likely, in spite of all the drills and inspections. But these things were not transfigurations, nothing more than the changes that would have taken place if they had all stayed on at college; he began taking the drinks around. Another day or two, he was thinking, and we will start to forget the war, we will think of it less and less often, as one thinks a little less each day of a girl one still loves and has lost.

Harrison and the Navy couple had got up and were going upstairs. The Walles had taken another apartment, a much larger one, in this same building, and were preparing to move to it. Harrison said he was taking his Navy friends up to see the place which was being painted and having some cabinets built in; Tom had been up already. He gave them their drinks to carry along.

260

Lala was talking to the Kaiser. Ellen was talking with Guy and his fiancée. Tom distributed the drinks and sat down beside Eddie.

"Eddie," he said. "It's awful good to see you." Eddie in a grey tweed suit, as bristly as his hair.

"You said that twice before," Eddie told him. "You're losing your marbles."

"Last two times you agreed."

"I don't know how to talk anymore, Tom. I used to be more of a talker, didn't I?"

"Speeches every night," Tom said.

"Hey, that's a nice wife you got."

"Thanks Eddie."

They sat quiet for a moment. Then Tom said: "Eddie?"

"Yeah?"

"What happened to Julia?"

"Julia."

"None of us knew anything had happened. Fact, I expected to see her walk in with you tonight."

"Julia." Eddie looked at his glass. "I haven't even thought of her in so long." Suddenly he swore a loud oath. "Jesus cruddy Christ, Tom."

"What's the matter?" Tom was a little alarmed.

Eddie hit his leg violently with the glass. "You know what I did? Down at the goddamn place they discharged us. Now listen to this, I just remembered it. Look, the first night in. Guys sitting around the beds, talking about their wives they're going to see. Some guy asks me if I'm married. I say no. He says I ought to try it. I say maybe I will some time. Listen to that. Just as if I never had been. I didn't even think of Julia."

"Maybe it's just as well," Tom said.

"Yeah." The explosiveness left Eddie as suddenly as it had come. Maybe he was a little changed at that; he was musing now. "You saw her, didn't you?"

"Why yes. Of course," Tom said.

"That's right. You came down to the island and saw her."

"It was only three years ago."

"I don't know what you thought of Julia. But she was wonderful, Tom. A wonderful girl. Smart and pretty and loving. . . . I was the crud in that deal. I let her down, Tom. I was bad to her."

What was he talking about, Tom wondered? Must have got into something overseas.

261

"Hey did you see Sheila?" Eddie asked. "Ellen's baby?"

"Sure," Tom said.

"I haven't seen her yet. Is she beautiful?"

Lala and the Kaiser sat down with them. A moment later Tom saw Ellen starting to wander; it was an odd thing she did when she reached a certain point in drinking. She walked away, sometimes in the middle of a conversation, and would begin to drift around a room; but towards nothing. Tom got up and went to her. He had seen her only twice since his discharge, because he had spent most of the time in Canada, waiting for Lala's boat to come.

"Is this where you stayed when Harrison was in Honolulu?"

"What?"

He repeated the question; he could see in her face and eyes that she was focusing herself on it.

"No. It was a smaller place. Two blocks over. Where Guy used to visit."

"How long have you had this?"

She could make perfectly good sense once she got focused. "Six weeks. Harrison paid the superintendent a hundred dollars."

"And in two more weeks you move upstairs?"

"Yes. Going to be our home for always. For another hundred dollars. Harrison paid the man another hundred dollars. You know, Harrison's prob'ly the best superintendent briber in New York City today? A very talented boy. . . ."

"Ellen." Tom put his arm around her waist and smiled down at her.

"Thank you."

"Was it a pretty lonely year for you, while he was away?"

"Yes."

"Poor Ellen."

"No. Had Sheila for company."

"No friends?"

"Nope. Loyal wife. You know what, Tom?"

"What?"

"Never mind. Sure, I had a friend. Another loyal wife. Lived downstairs at the other place. Janet. We used to see each other every day."

"Oh," Tom said. "Has she left there, too?"

Ellen shook her head. "Nope. Still there. She's got a little one-room hole of a place. Husband's back too, I guess."

262

"You don't see her any longer?"

"Never mind." She brooded for a moment. Then she said: "All right, I'll tell you. I'm so ashamed, Tom; don't tell anybody. I was going to invite her over here tonight. But it . . . it seems her husband was a coxswain. Harrison didn't want to have them. Stupid of me, wasn't it? Not to ask her what her husband's rank was the night she sat up, all night long with us, when Sheila and I both had the virus."

"Oh, Ellen."

"What I'm ashamed of, Tom, I guess I could have insisted. I mean, Harrison wasn't all that awful about it. But I . . . it was night before last. I got drunk instead."

Unchanged? Ellen had changed a little, too, then, just as Eddie had; a little. A little loss of fibre. Out of himself too? Out of Guy?

He and Guy spoke in Spanish, pleased to be doing so again, standing in a corner.

"I like your girl, Guyito. She's even prettier than her pictures in the paper."

"But we're not being married, Tomás."

"No? Why not?"

"Sometimes to be engaged is a mutual convenience," Guy said, grinning. "She said she hadn't been engaged to anybody in a coon's age."

The English idiom, translated literally into Spanish, was funny, and Tom laughed.

"Tom? Guy?" Eddie came over to join them. "Are you snotty bastards talking Spanish again?"

"*Si*," Tom said, ruffling Eddie's short, absurd hair. "*Mira al precioso.*" Speaking Spanish at Eddie was an old game; Eddie liked it, too. It gave him something to rail at. But presently he had something serious to say. His father had left a cottage not far from what was now Eddie's farm, his grandfather's old place. Maybe Tom and Lala would like to stay there for a while? The beach in winter was pretty, in a grisly way, to walk on, if you were stupid enough to like that kind of thing.

Tom said they were quite stupid enough, but they would be going up to Washburn next week for the February semester. The GI Bill. Quite a deal.

"Neither of you thinking of coming back, too?"

Neither Guy nor Eddie was. Eddie said he had to get a crop

263

in, he had a living to make, for the first time in his life. No loving arms of college or army to protect him any longer. . . . Guy's plans were less specific, but equally clear to him. He would live the life in New York he'd always meant to live, looking after some family matters from time to time, nothing very arduous.

And Tom?

He still meant to be a cruddy professor?

A college president? Or publish very elegant translations from Greek and Latin?

No, a pukey college president, so one of these days he could give Eddie an honorary degree in Cabbage Cultivation.

"I don't know," Tom said. "It depends a lot on how Lala likes it. How I like it, too, I guess." As they talked Tom thought: another change: Guy puts me off a little now; I'm fonder of Eddie.

Harrison and the Navy people were back. When Ellen saw them, Tom noticed—he had been keeping an eye on his sister—she stopped wandering. She came directly over to their group.

"Eddie Bissle," she said.

"Yes. Hello again, Ellen."

"Eddie Bissle. You come see our new apartment upstairs now."

"Should I?"

"Yes."

"All right. Shall I get myself a drink?"

"Yes."

While Eddie went to the kitchen, Ellen said to Guy: "I don't dare take you upstairs. Harrison would bust a seam." Then she laughed a strange laugh, as if she'd made a joke.

She stopped laughing, and put a hand on Tom's shoulder, pulling him down towards her. "Tom," she said. "I wasn't lonely when Harrison was away."

"No," Tom said. "You told me, Bismarck. About your friend. . . ."

"I'm lonely since he got back," Ellen said. Then Eddie came back from the kitchen, and Ellen gave her brother a push, before she guided the short man out of the room.

Tom went over to the Kaiser and Lala.

"I was telling Captain Bissle," the Kaiser said. "A strange coincidence. We met his mother in Florida."

"Eddie's mother?"

"Yes. She's living in St. Augustine, too. Your mother met her

264

at a Red Cross function I think. And recognized the name immediately of course."

"That is strange," Tom said.

"A very pleasant woman," the Kaiser nodded. "Captain Bissle comes from a fine family, Tom. Has he told you about the ten acre flag his father was planning, just before his death?"

"No," Tom said.

"A wonderful project," said the Kaiser. "As I said to Captain Bissle, if there's any hope of saving it, I'd feel privileged to contribute fifty dollars myself. As a sort of memorial, you know. . . ."

9.

It had been, the Kaiser told himself, the happiest evening of his life. Lieutenant Cinturon and his girl, who were quite famous, both of them, had left, and Captain Bissle with them; what fine friends Tom had. But that was only the personal part of it. How reassuring to see them, from a public standpoint, just coming home from their war this way, young and strong and more earnest, the Kaiser judged, than his own, irresponsible generation. Oh, the world would be better off in the hands of young men like these; he would tell Tom and Ellen's mother that, yes, he would tell Ruth, and she would be reassured. She had read entirely too many newspaper words about the maladjusted veteran. Look at these boys. . . .

"The war hasn't really affected them, has it Tom?" He said.

He and Tom were standing in the doorway of Sheila's room, Tom's new wife beside them; they had been looking in at the sleeping child, and now the light was off again.

"Excuse me?" Tom said.

"The war hasn't made oh, a generation of misfits out of your bunch, has it?"

"No." Tom smiled at him. Tom had the nicest smile. "No, I've been thinking about it Kaiser. The war may have speeded up our . . . development a little; but I don't think it's changed the various ways we were headed."

Exactly what the Kaiser meant. "Yes," he said, approvingly, "You've all matured. I was thinking of how we came back after my war. I'm afraid we were a good deal more headstrong, dissi-

265

pated. Oh, I mean it was just youth and high spirits . . . capable hands, Tom. I'm glad to think things will be in capable hands."

"Oh? Oh, yes . . ." Tom said, doubtfully. Tom's modesty was one of his nicest qualities.

"I'm going to start picking up," the young British girl said. The Kaiser'd half forgotten she was standing there.

"Nice girl, Tom," he said softly as she left. "The English are a very conservative people, aren't they? But she'll steady you."

Tom was smiling again. "Yes," he said.

"Funny, I never liked the English when I was young."

"You knew some?"

"In the first war. We called them limeys. Our men used to get into fights with them. . . ."

"How funny, to think of you being prejudiced against anyone," Tom said.

"We were all very prejudiced in my time. Only we didn't think it a sin. Ellen's all right, isn't she Tom?"

"Oh, yes." Tom said. Ellen was sleeping on the sofa, Harrison having gone to bed when his Navy friends left.

"Just celebrating her brother's return. And marriage. Do her good."

"Yes."

"You've made fine marriages, Tom. Both of you. Ellen's husband, now, he got her off to a bad start, of course. But he did the decent thing, and I must say I like the man."

"Yes."

"A man's no worse for a bit of hell in him. Perhaps you other fellows should have been more like him, had a little more fun before you settled down to run the world for us."

Tom looked away. Then he said: "You'll be running it for yourselves a long while yet."

The Kaiser cleared his throat and didn't answer.

He was in the hospital twice a week now, for deep radiation therapy, but he was still feeling pretty well. He didn't like to use a word like cancer and, as a matter of fact, if that was what he had— well, it was, of course—there was still no reason to speak to Tom about it yet, or anybody else.

"It's been a happy evening, Tom," the Kaiser said, finally, and very quietly because of the sleeping baby. "I'm glad to see you and Ellen off to such fine starts. Married to such fine people. I'm glad to see. . . ." He gestured towards Sheila. "The little girl." She was three now; she had called him grandfather. He felt like her grandfather; he had never really quite felt like Tom and Ellen's father, though he'd done his best for them, such as it was, but he really did feel like Sheila's grandfather.

Pity he couldn't do more for her, but Ruth would need the use of everything he could leave.

Suddenly the Kaiser felt sadness, the kind that follows happy evenings. He wouldn't be here to see how it all came out.

"Tom," he said, taking his stepson's arm. "Tom, you're all so young."

"Yes, sir."

"I seem to be . . . Tom, I haven't lived as good a life as I might. But I've . . . I've lived as good a life as I knew how, and it hasn't been a bad one."

"No," Tom said, and his arm came around the Kaiser's shoulders, a gentle arm, a young arm, a great comfort to a large, tired man who had tried his best.

PART TWO

". . . the tyme of contynuance! . . ."

CHAPTER ONE

1.

Sheila Walle and Amy Cuzenus found the house one day, walking home from school. It was a narrow brownstone, five stories high, standing on a quiet street, not a short cut but with a candy store on the homeward corner.

The street was just outside their neighborhood, Brooklyn Heights, and would be inside it when the old houses were torn down and a new, modern apartment building put up in their place. There were five of these old houses, all alike, with dark little side entrance ways between them, each entrance way now blocked by a padlocked iron gate.

They had walked by them many times without paying any special attention, but on this particular winter day Amy tapped Sheila's arm and pointed out that one of the padlocks was broken.

"I wonder who did that?" Sheila said.

"Tough kids."

They went to look between the bars of the gate; it swung away from the weight of their hands. Amy looked at Sheila.

They went through the gateway together.

The passage between the houses was narrow and filled with rubbish. Halfway along the wall was a side door which ought to have been boarded up; the boards had been torn away and left scattered on the ground.

271

"Wait," said Amy. She ran back and closed the gate. Sheila waited fearfully. She was a slim, fair girl with short, careless yellow hair and a keen face, dimly freckled. She was fourteen. She was almost a head shorter than Amy, who was four months older, swarthy with a big mouth, a low forehead and, already, something close enough in warmth to a woman's smile to bother the older boys at school.

Amy came back from closing the gate; Sheila caught at her.

"Maybe they're still in there," Sheila whispered. They listened but there was nothing inside the house to hear. Amy gave a push at the door. To Sheila's secret relief, it didn't move.

"Try the handle," Sheila said. Amy did, and pushed. The door moved slightly. Suppressing dismay, Sheila threw her weight with Amy's against the door and together they opened it and went in. They were in a kitchen, but all its fixtures had been removed, even the sink; the side door had been a delivery entrance.

"Should we close it?" Sheila asked.

"What do you think?" Amy was not used to being in command.

"I guess we'd better."

They closed the door and started through the ground floor holding hands. The kitchen, long and narrow, went along one side of the house, a parallel corridor along the other; both opened into a dining room at the rear. The girls crossed the dining room and peered through cracks between the boards which covered French windows at the very back of the building, Sheila's eyes at a crack six inches lower than Amy's.

They found themselves looking across thirty feet of paved back yard, filled like the entrance way with rubbish, to the blank rear of a brick warehouse. As Sheila stared, Amy moved away from her side.

"Where are you going?"

"Upstairs."

This time they moved through the corridor instead of the kitchen. It was dark and smelled wet. At the end it forked into a stairwell at the left, a foyer giving onto the front door at the right. Sheila went into the foyer and tried the front door. It was nailed tight and immovable. Amy waited. Sheila turned to her.

"Let's go upstairs."

"That's what I said."

A truck went rushing by outside, and both girls stood motionless until it passed.

"Wouldn't it be awful if those kids were up there? The ones that broke in?" Sheila said, certain they weren't. Step by step the girls made their way up the dark flight. It was altogether cold and still in the house, and a sense of four flights of empty and unmoving air, enclosed and chilly, looming above them, made them watch their feet as they went up. Halfway there and Amy was clutching Sheila's waist as hard as Sheila Amy's. The steps turned right; three more and they were at the top. They looked ahead and gasped.

The whole second floor was all one room. A certain amount of winter sunlight reached in, finding its way between the window boards. To eyes conditioned on the dark stairs, it seemed striped with brightness. The room was empty, except for a blue plush armchair, tipped away towards the rear in the middle distance. A row of small plaster columns, running from floor to ceiling, stood out a few feet from, and paralleled each of the windowless side walls. The effect was of tremendous length.

Sheila expelled her breath and, seizing Amy's wrist, led her all the way to the rear of the room. There they turned and faced one another.

" 'Now Mother, what's the matter?' " Sheila cried defiantly.

" 'Hamlet, thou hast thy father much offended,' " replied Amy, projecting dignity.

" 'Mother, thou hast my father much offended,' " said Sheila, bitingly, turning away; she whirled back to face Amy's reply, and they played the scene; they had been doing it all winter long, ever since the drama teacher had said it was a great scene. For the first time now they were able to raise their voices to full cry—scolding back and forth, the queen reduced to fear that Hamlet means to murder her, the stabbing of Polonius—

" 'Dead for a ducat, dead' " cried Sheila and ran to kick viciously at the blue plush armchair. She discovered it was Polonius, and addressed the cushionless seat:

" 'Thou wretched, rash, intruding fool, farewell!
I took thee for thy better. . . .' "

And back at the queen mother, battering at her imperiousness with accusations, until Amy begged, " 'No more, sweet Hamlet.' "

They had a marvelous time, skipping casually past the indicated entrance of the ghost in the pleasure of shouting at one another, rollicking through the movements which had formerly been confined, in school corridors, to half steps and small gestures; at the end of the scene they fell into one another's arms, laughing at the pleasure and freedom of it.

"Tomorrow, after school, let's make Theodore come," Amy said.

Theodore was Amy's twelve year old brother, drafted as Polonius for this particular scene one October afternoon, last year, and stabbed by Sheila behind many an improvised arras as the winter had gone on. He was a reluctant player but competent. His real enthusiasm was for train pictures and information, and he delivered lines with much the same self-satisfaction one heard in his voice when he corrected some fellow-hobbyist on the horsepower of the new Diesels used to pull freight cars over Donner Pass. It was the carefully expressionless voice of a triumphant statistician.

"We'll get Theodore tomorrow," Sheila agreed. "And somebody to be the ghost."

"Who?"

"I don't know."

"Not Roy," Amy said. Roy Nevins was, of course, exactly who Sheila had in mind—a tiny, big-headed mite, just eight years old, who had been a surprisingly deep-voiced shepherd in the school Christmas play; Sheila, rightfully, had been Mary, Amy an angel with an alto solo. Ever since, Roy Nevins had had a violent crush on Sheila of which both girls took advantage, sending him on errands, using him like a puppy from time to time when there arose the impulse to have something to pet.

"Why not Roy?" Sheila said. "The ghost only has one speech in this scene, about two lines."

"Six," said Amy.

"He doesn't have to memorize. We'll let him read them."

"Oh, all right," said Amy, who had apparently been hoping for something a little more interesting in the way of a boy. "Get Roy. Do you think we'll be able to get in again tomorrow?"

2.

The following morning in Manhattan, Sheila's Uncle, Tom Beniger, woke up late, determined to tell someone about a personal development which had been occupying his mind for almost a week.

After eleven years of childless marriage, Tom was to become

274

a father; Lala had gone to England the previous fall to visit home, and, as he heated water for coffee, Tom read once again the deeply surprising letter she had written him:

> Darling: I am ready to burst and I mean that for wit. You won't believe it, just as I didn't, but I am going to have a child. Now don't start counting months, which is what Daddy says a man would do instantly (did you?), because of course I've known this was possible for some time. But thought, of course, that it would be another of my miscarriages which is why I haven't said anything before now. . . .

Yes, reticence was understandable. Four times in their eleven years Lala had been pregnant and miscarried. The first time, in graduate school, they had told friends and family; made plans. Tom had left graduate school to take an instructorship in Alabama, anticipating a need for the money, and thereafter they had spent a strange year in the South, working out the contract there was no longer any real reason to have signed. The second and third times, they had consulted only one another; the fourth, Lala didn't even tell Tom until miscarriage was inevitable.

> Anyway, I missed my November period and didn't pay any attention; I'm always missing the damn things, you know. When I missed again in December and started having backaches and things, I went to a doctor who said aspirin and rest and keep warm, so I went to another doctor a week later, who did some sort of test with a frog (doesn't that seem obscene? What do you suppose they *do* to the poor frog?), and said I was pregnant. Well, said I, then of course I shall miscarry. Nonsense, said the doctor, who is younger than I am, take these pills dear child, and aspirin and rest and keep warm. In January I was all set for the annual sorry event; I went to bed and bled quite a lot (Daddy was horrified; he knew nothing about these things, and I had to have quite a little nature talk with him), and assumed that was it. But when I felt strong enough to go see the doctor again he said I still had it (he didn't even have to sacrifice another frog). So then I said I would send you a cablegram, a long happy one, and he said no, wait one more month to be sure. So now the doctor is sure and I'm sure; I'm getting quite fat and

275

glossy, like a mare, and the baby is due in mid-June and the Doctor and I and Daddy and the woman who comes in to clean all feel that you should come over for the delivery; I'm not allowed to fly back or really do much of anything. Anyway, the doctor's reasons are probably psychological—he won't exactly tell me—and Daddy feels it's your duty, and the cleaner woman says it's women who bear the burden and men who have the pleasure, and I just want you to. Can we manage, Tommy? Just for a few weeks, and then, if you can't stay over and travel around Europe a little (wouldn't that be wonderful? Any chance?), why then we'll all come home together. All *three*. Oh, Tommy, imagine!

He had cabled Lala, cleaned out their bank account to send an extra check, started to make plans for the trip in June; but he had not told anyone, and now he wanted to.

He mixed the soluble coffee and drank it slowly, not noticing its flatness as he usually did, not renewing for once his regular morning resolution to stop at a hardware store and replace the glass stem of the percolator which had broken over a month before. He was considering whether to call his mother in Arizona and tell her.

He finished the coffee; then he stripped and folded the bedding from the sofa on which he'd spent the night. Although he was much too long for this sofa, and there was another room in the apartment, a bedroom, he often went to sleep out here these nights with Lala away; he would be reading, get cold, get himself a comforter; would prepare for bed and, instead of going to it, return to the sofa and comforter and the companionship of the colored evening light of Greenwich village and voices from the bars, rising five stories to come in through the front windows.

Now, as he dressed, he decided tentatively that he would make the phone call though there were Arizona calls on the bills, going back three months now, which he was trying to get paid. These were his mother's rambling, collect calls to him, undertaken on an old woman's erratic impulse, never having any real purpose. Or their purpose was real enough, but indirect—the calls were to assure herself that affection for her still existed in the world. This was why Tom could never tell the inquiring operator that he would not accept the charges, even though he knew that his mother had nothing in particular to say and would only spend the time, the money, fussing away about irrelevancies. Her husband had died eight years before; she was self-enrolled at the Rest Ranch; she would not call Tom's sister Ellen in Brooklyn, whose household could more easily have absorbed the expense, for while with Tom, Mrs. Coombs fussed one-sidedly, with Ellen there was still enough life left in their relationship to produce quite genuine quarrels.

He placed the call and eventually his mother was on the line. At first she did not understand who was calling. She mistook the name Beniger for the word banker, though it had once been her own name, and told the operator firmly that she knew no bankers. But she was not hard of hearing, and so Tom knew, even before they began to talk, that this was not one of his mother's lucid mornings.

She was pleased that he had called; he listened, biting his lip, as she told him about a Mrs. Kelcy who had taken the most expensive cottage on the grounds, who was wearing furs right out in the sunshine. "Of course she's old, Tom, seventy-one," said Mrs. Coombs, who was sixty-six. "But it was already quite hot, and there she was in a mink cape, having orange juice in the patio. . . ."

Tom talked gently to his mother. He had first heard about the unladylike Mrs. Kelcy and her preposterous mink cape two years before, though his mother was speaking now as if the episode had just occurred. It was no morning to tell Mrs. Coombs about the expected birth of a child, not if his mother didn't recall that she and Mrs. Kelcy had become friends, and remained friends until three months ago when, in spite of her furs, the older lady died.

When he hung up, Tom decided he would do three hours' work at the library; then he would go out to Brooklyn Heights, if his sister were home, and, in spite of the fact that she and Lala didn't get along, discuss the news with Ellen.

3.

Five blocks from the abandoned house was the apartment building in which the Walles occupied seven large, expensive rooms. Here, that afternoon, Ellen Beniger Walle, Sheila's mother, wondered what she would do with the rest of the day. Her cleaning

277

woman had come in the morning, so there was no housework. The things for dinner had been delivered, the laundry called for. There was a bundle of clean laundry, still wrapped in brown paper, lying on her bed, which Ellen might have unpacked; but it wasn't enough of a job to be worth starting at. In the state of mild, habitual apprehension in which she passed so many of the daylight hours of her life, it did not occur to Ellen that she might go out somewhere. She seldom left her apartment, and almost never alone.

Her hand was resting on the cabinet of a large, color television set, but she had no inclination to turn it on. An elaborate phonograph system and over a hundred records were across the room, and above them were three long shelves of books. She left the room.

There was something they needed from the drug store; in a moment she would remember what it was and call up for it. As she paused, trying to recollect, hand hovering over the telephone, it rang. She snatched her hand away, startled; she told herself to calm down, it would be her husband, Harrison. It rang again. Or it would be a school friend of Sheila's to be told that the girl wasn't home yet.

When the phone rang for the third time, Ellen picked it up and said hello.

"Hi, Ellen. It's Tom."

"Tommy. Tom." She was delighted. She hadn't heard from Tom for a week. "Tom, hold on just a moment, will you?"

She put the phone down on the table and ran to the kitchen. Not bothering about ice, she poured some whiskey into a glass and hastily ran tap water into it. Apprehension gone, she trotted back to the telephone without sipping. She sat, resting her elbow for comfort on the table, and picked up the instrument.

"All set, Tom," she said, smiling at her glass.

"What was wrong?"

"Left some water running in the kitchen."

"Oh. Well, how are you?"

"Fine. Just fine." She held the receiver away from her lips, and took a swallow of the drink. It was warm; she must, in her haste, have turned on the hot water faucet instead of the cold. It was quite repulsive. She drank it off quickly, trying not to taste, as Tom talked. It seemed he wanted to see her about something, rather not say on the phone, would like to come over. She agreed warmly; she was grateful to Tom for calling. If you were talking to someone on the telephone, it didn't count as drinking alone.

278

While she waited for Tom to arrive, Ellen had a second drink, this one more slowly, with ice in it, and took some pains with her appearance. What would he want to talk about? A new job. It would be funny, if it weren't so hard on him, the way Tom changed jobs every year. Of course he should be working on a campus some place, but the little English bag wasn't happy on campuses; at least, that was Ellen's opinion. It didn't make sense to believe Tom's reason, that he found the academic life withdrawn and meaningless. What had he done instead? A year of newspaper reporting in the midwest, which he gave up because he said he lacked cynicism to work for an organization which propagandized for ideas so dissimilar to Tom's own. Turned down, after probationary training, in the State Department because they asked him how he felt on certain issues and Tom told them honestly. Worked for token pay for the World Federalists, for almost a year, until he and Lala'd gone through their savings from the newspaper year. Tried a teaching job again. Found he'd let his G.I. Bill run out, so that he couldn't finish taking his Ph.D. courses, and didn't want Lala living on graduate assistant standards by then, anyway.

But of course, none of these was the worst, the craziest, the most horrifying and, well, touching. The job that was all those things was the one Tom tried to get in 1950. Ellen could still remember Tom and Lala coming in to a little dinner she was having to give for some of Harrison's business friends; they had called Ellen away from the table, and Lala had said:

"Ellen, Tom's enlisted."

"Enlisted? For what?"

"In the army," Tom said. "To go to Korea. I . . . I thought I had a little experience, and. . . ."

Ellen had been appalled. She couldn't believe it at first. Then when Tom got into one of his characteristic explanations about the meaning of the war, the new concept of nations acting together in the manner of policemen, she could believe it all too well. And Lala sitting there, smiling placidly, refusing a drink, not unduly proud of Tom but apparently perfectly satisfied to let him do as he liked. The thing that made it touching was that Tom was turned down, finally, in his physical; the thing that made it craziest was that a few months later, when MacArthur started chasing the North Koreans back over that parallel, whatever it was, Tom turned as bitter against the war as he'd been thrilled at first. No telling about Tom.

279

Now finally he was in, of all things, television work, because a friend had been asked to submit some plans to a network for an educational series. Worked very hard on that, full of enthusiasm, only the network decided not to do the series. So Tom had got his present job, also in television, and Ellen smiled, as she mixed a third drink, quite certain that today she would be hearing about some new plan.

She carried the fresh drink back to the dressing table and glanced at herself in the mirror. She liked to look well for Tom, and thought that now she did. At thirty-eight, Ellen still had her figure; the plumpness had hardened, not spread out. Perhaps alcohol had seen to that, for Ellen never had an appetite. The only puffiness she could find, unless, of course, she stripped, was around her eyes—make-up which filled the tiny wrinkles minimized that, just as a squirt of lacquer from a spray can disguised the tonelessness of Ellen's hair.

Her brother, she thought, no longer looked younger than she; he had the same light coloring and greenish eyes, but unless he got often into the sunshine, his skin tone was pallid. His hair was quite thin. At this time of year—she thought back to the last time she had seen him—he looked like all New Yorkers in the winter: unhealthy, bloodless, peculiar, one of a race of invalids.

The bell rang, and she left the drink on her dressing table, pushing it behind a tall can of talcum powder. She trotted happily to the front door, opened it, and there was Tom.

"Hi, Ellen."

"Tommy." How convenient to be enough shorter than he so that she could squeeze her arms around him and press her cheek against his diaphragm, thus preventing him from stooping to kiss her and smelling the whiskey.

"You can't be that glad to see me," he said.

"But it's been weeks, and you're my Lover Man Haynes."

4.

Tom knew, from her calling him Lover Man Haynes, that Ellen had begun her day's drinking. There was an area of the past that it pleased Ellen to inhabit when she drank, not with any sense that it was real, but with a recollection so fond that it almost seemed to yearn for delusion. Had she really been so happy then,

Tom wondered? And could there—here was another thing to wonder—could there be any connection between their mother's suffering frequently from dislocated time sense, and Ellen's alcoholic impulse backwards? This thought, casual as it occurred to him, became shocking as it grew to a realization and shook his mind with a kind of fright.

"I wonder what ever happened to Lover Man?" Tom said, seizing the only words available between them.

"You're him." Ellen had her arm around his waist now, as they walked into the living room, and the cheek was pressed against his side. "You always were and you always will be."

"World without end," Tom said.

"Poor Lover Man," said Ellen, breaking away. "I think they finally put him in jail. Remember the picture of him I sent you from college? From the New Haven paper? He looked just like you."

"He was a mean, weary-looking boy," Tom said.

"But proud. Which wife said Lover Man was more of a man at sixteen than her husband as a full-grown man?"

"That was number one," Tom remembered, sitting on the sofa. "The other one bought him a car. A second hand Chevie coupe. He didn't know how to drive it but he liked to sit in it and play the radio."

"How long have you remembered that? More than twenty years," Ellen said, admiringly.

"Only nineteen," Tom said. He had done the memory trick for her almost in spite of himself because it was something he could do that she enjoyed. In a moment, if they kept this up, he would be able to quote headlines. "It was 1938."

"How about a drink?" Ellen said it brightly, as if it had just occurred to her, and rose.

"No thanks," Tom said. "Go ahead if you want one."

"Nice of you to give me permission," Ellen said. "Maybe I feel it's too early in the day." Her tone was pure sassiness; sometimes, these days, Ellen insisted on responding to a challenge when none had been issued.

"Do you?" Tom said it as mildly as he could.

"I may and I may not."

"Never mind, Bismarck," Tom said.

"Meaning what?"

"I imagine you've already had a drink or two."

"Oh, do you?" A kind of clipped brightness was coming into her voice as if, having defeated Tom in a pleasant skirmish, she was now going to toy with him while deciding whether to put him to rout or let him go.

"Let's not fuss about it," Tom said.

She ignored this. "As a matter of fact, I've had hundreds of drinks today."

"Hope you enjoyed them."

"Hundreds." She was still standing, ready to skip off to the kitchen.

He only looked at her.

"I had one bottle before breakfast and two afterwards. I'd have had three," the brightness was beginning to get giddy, "but I had to stop and lay the laundry man."

"Okay," Tom said. "Bring me one, too, and stop treating me as if I were Harrison."

Now she giggled. "I wouldn't dare say that about the laundry man to Harrison."

"Sure you would," said Tom.

She started out to the kitchen, paused, and said: "How'd you know, Tommy? That I'd had a drink?"

"No special signs, Bismarck," Tom said. "I just knew."

5.

Amy put older sister pressure on Theodore. Sheila needed no pressure to enlist Roy; the little boy was solemnly excited from the moment he heard the word "play," and by the time they were all together in the empty living room, even the stolid Theodore was exhilarated to the point of strutting around, shouting his lines as they prepared.

"I don't need the book, Sheila," Roy said. "I already learned what you showed me. In study hall." He was a red-headed mushroom of a child, as wide from ear to ear as he was from hip to hip. Sheila hugged him.

Then she let him recite the Ghost's six-line speech in the scene they were about to do; he had memorized perfectly, but without comprehension.

"Roysie," she said. "This Ghost: he's Hamlet's father. My

282

father." Theodore laughed, and Sheila gave him a squelch look. "He was murdered. He's come to see Hamlet before, to tell Hamlet that his mother—that's Amy—helped with the murder." Roy nodded. "Well, in this scene, Hamlet's up in his mother's room. His mother thinks she's going to bawl Hamlet out for sulking around and stuff, but really it's Hamlet that's going to bawl her out—because of what the Ghost told him."

"Bawl her out?" Amy said. "It's all Hamlet can do to keep from killing her."

"That's right," Sheila said. "She's done a terrible thing, and her son knows it, and this is where he tells her what a wicked woman she is."

"Then what's the Ghost do?" asked Theodore.

"He's come to make sure that Hamlet doesn't feel any pity for his mother," Sheila said. "He reminds Hamlet that the idea is to get revenge."

Roy nodded again.

"What am I doing?" Theodore asked. "How come I get killed, anyway?"

"Because you're listening in, you rat," Amy said.

"I think it's a plot," said Sheila, who wasn't quite sure. "You were supposed to get Hamlet up here to his mother's room, and listen in. Hamlet hears you moving, and kills you. Anyway, it doesn't matter. I want to read Roy's speech to him." She read the Ghost speech aloud; Roy said it after her, mimicking her points of pause and emphasis. The second time through, he had most of her inflections as well. By the third, it was so pat his voice had begun to sound like Sheila's.

"Roy, you're a regular phonograph," Amy cried. "Come on Sheila. Let's go. Let's go."

"I'm ready," said Theodore and struck an important pose, for it is Polonius' scene to open, with advice to the Queen on what she is to say to this sulking son Hamlet—Hamlet who is already in league with ghosts and madness, whose plan of revenge is already working out.

The scene went wonderfully. They had a splendid time. At the end of it, Sheila actually dragged Theodore, a corpse red with laughter, for several feet, then stopped and yelled,

"Listen to the clapping."

Roy danced out to the front, impersonating an audience of thousands, clapping and shouting "Hooray."

"We ought to do it," Amy said. "The whole play. And have people come."

"Oh, easy," said Sheila, with great sarcasm, and the boys laughed with her at Amy, crying, "Oh, easy. Easy."

6.

As she mixed their drinks in the kitchen, Ellen thought how much she loved Tom; from this it followed that she could forgive herself for having been piqued at him. She giggled again, thinking of what she had said about the laundry man, whom, as a matter of fact, she had never seen—he dealt with the cleaning woman. Then she remembered that Tom had said on the phone that he had something he wanted to talk to her about, the new job or something, and, contrite, she hurried back and handed him his glass.

"Here," she said. "What did you want to tell me?"

"Nothing we need to start on now," Tom said. "What's Sheila up to these days?"

"Oh, come on," Ellen said. "You came all the way out to tell me something."

"Sometime when we're both feeling highly serious," Tom said, and sipped his drink. "Ooooh, Bismarck. You really made one."

"Poor Lover Man. I'm sorry."

"It's all right. Feels good once you're used to it." He smiled and sipped again.

"No, I mean sorry about not being highly serious."

"It doesn't matter," Tom said. "When's the girl get home from school?"

"What time is it?"

"Ten after three."

"Depends on whether they're having rhythmics today," Ellen said. "She tells me every morning, and it goes out of my mind the minute she leaves the house."

The phone rang. She left Tom and went to answer it.

It was Eddie Bissle, calling from the country, saying he would be in town tomorrow. He asked Ellen if she could meet him in

284

the afternoon, at the hotel they had used, two or three times a year, ever since Eddie had got out of the army. It annoyed her, being asked so calmly, just when she'd been having a nice time talking to Tom. She decided to refuse. She said she was having dinner guests tomorrow and asked Eddie to join them. Eddie asked if Tom would be there, and Ellen said yes, though she hadn't yet asked Tom, and Eddie said all right, he'd come. He also said that he'd be staying in town a week, and so perhaps they could get together; Ellen didn't answer. Then Eddie asked, in the special tone he had for the question, how Sheila was.

This made Ellen furious. She had denied God knew how many times over the years the possibility Eddie insisted on, that Sheila was his child. She had told him that it was physically impossible, and Eddie would reply, chuckling, "Sure. You've got to say that Ellen. Stick to it, baby." And the fact was, damn it, that it wasn't physically impossible at all. It was something no one would ever know for certain.

They said goodbye, and Ellen went back to report to Tom. She had punished Eddie, just a little, by not saying Tom was there. Now she told Tom he would have to come to dinner, and Tom said he couldn't, and reminded Ellen that the television show he worked for had a planning meeting every Thursday evening. That meant Tom's news wasn't a new job, after all.

And it also meant that Ellen was trapped. She'd promised Eddie Tom, and couldn't deliver him, and Eddie'd be very uncomfortable here with Tom not present, and when he got Ellen to the hotel—but Ellen wasn't going to the hotel with Eddie any more. It was too hard on her. She quaked pleasantly, nevertheless, thinking about it.

That was how she happened to call Guy's apartment, just after Tom left, leaving the message that she'd like Guy for dinner Thursday; Eddie would be placated if Guy could come.

7.

When Tom left Ellen's, he too, had decided to call Guy. He had thought several times of Guy's as the natural ear for his news, and hesitated; over the years, Tom had felt less and less close to Guy. Lala had nothing to do with this; she was no censor of friendship, got on quite well with whomever Tom liked. But of Guy, Tom sometimes almost disapproved. Dissembled, of course, and Guy seemed as fond of Tom as ever, but might it not be a little dishonest, under the circumstances, to make Guy the first recipient? If it were going to be an old friend, he'd almost rather it were Eddie. Not really. He could hardly expect Eddie to produce much in the way of congratulation for the event.

So it was going to be Guy, and Tom had a sense of relief at making the decision, a feeling that whatever lack of closeness had grown up was in his own mind and the result of a finickiness on his part which was not generous. He went into a drugstore and found a pay station. The first time he dialed Guy's number, however, the line was busy.

He drank a cup of coffee at the counter, then went over and dialed again. I shall stop being so particular, Tom thought; stop making secret conditions for my listener. After all, Ellen was not so drunk that she wouldn't have been interested; Mother might, if she had heard the news, have become quite lucid, and suppose she hadn't? Would I have lost anything in particular? I shall say hello to Guy, and simply tell him this unremarkable but pleasant piece of news, and he'll say something sympathetic and joyful, and this thing I am building up in my mind about it will go away. . . .

He finished dialing and listened to the phone ring twice on the other end. Then there was the click of receiver removed and connection made.

A mechanical reproduction of Guy's voice, said: "Hello, this is Guy Cinturon's phone. This is a recording. I'm sorry not to be in. Will you say please, who is calling and what the message is? This machine will record it. . . ."

Tom could think of nothing that he wanted to tell a machine, so he hung up.

8.

By the time Sheila got home she was persuaded, although she recalled perfectly laughing at Amy for suggesting it, that a full performance of *Hamlet* in the old house had somehow been her own idea. Sheila was ruthlessly double-minded. She could, with perfect clarity and only an occasional sense of conflict, hold any opinion and its opposite. As, on letting herself noisily into the

286

apartment, searching for her mother, and seeing Ellen at length, stretched out dozing in her bedroom, Sheila could mutter to herself:

"Drunk again," but in tones of teenage worldly joking, and both mean it and not mean it. She knew perfectly well that her mother was drunk and in a reverie, and she knew perfectly well that her mother couldn't do anything as sloppy and awful as be drunk.

Dismissing it, and deciding not to call her mother out of it—she might be cross—Sheila went to her own room. She had a choice of her mother's being cross now, at being got up, or cross later because Sheila hadn't called out. Sheila automatically chose later. There was something she wanted to do.

The apartment was laid out on two sides of a central hallway. Three bedrooms opened off one side, the living room opened off the other and, at the far end, the kitchen. Between living room and kitchen were two more rooms; the first, connected to the living room by an arch, had the phonograph, television and books in it. The next was a small dining alcove, its arch opening on the kitchen. All the way back, behind the kitchen, remote from anything else, were a maid's room and bath. These Sheila had insisted on having, not long before, leaving the third of the large bedrooms off the central corridor to be used for guests and for storage.

The other two bedrooms connected; one had been furnished by her father as a study and he slept in it sometimes. The other was the room in which Sheila had left her mother undisturbed.

Now the girl went serenely through the kitchen, stopping at the refrigerator, drinking what was left of a small bottle of grapejuice, and on to her private little place where she shut the door. In a moment she was out again, and into the room where the bookshelves were. She looked through the books and found, just as she had thought, that *Hamlet* was included in a paper-bound volume of four Shakespeare tragedies. It was a practical omen of great importance; since Hamlet was one of the plays in the thirty-five cent book, every actor could have his own copy.

The other book she needed was already in her own room, an old volume called *Worldwide Manual for Direction of the Play.* She sat at her small desk with the two volumes closed in front of her. She knew perfectly well that they would never produce *Hamlet,* and she was entirely certain that they would.

She had put off the pleasure she had been tasting for over an

287

hour now, ever since leaving Amy and the boys, long enough. Now she would have it. She opened the paper bound volume and found the play. She turned to the cast list. She took her pen and painstakingly printed, "Sheila Walle," after the name "Hamlet"; then she printed "Amy Cuzenus" after "Gertrude, Queen of Denmark," and "Theodore Cuzenus" after "Polonius." She did not immediately write in little Roy as Ghost. There were lots of bigger kids at the Haddix Town School, and Roy would be whatever they told him to be.

The ink ran through the paper and blotted. She hauled her portable typewriter onto the desk and copied the cast. She typed in the three names. Then she took the sheet out of the typewriter and began to write in the names of other schoolmates after most of the other parts. She was very judicious about this, constantly crossing out and substituting. Some of her first choices she had to reject because the ideal person was too far ahead in school, wonderful but unapproachable.

They must be secret about it, not risk asking anyone who might refuse and tell. With two exceptions, Amy and one other, she chose only kids younger than herself; she had to be able to control them.

After an hour of absolute absorption, she had the cast list completely filled in except for Horatio, ready to retype and show to Amy in the morning. Of course some of those she had selected might be unwilling; some might even be inappropriate and have to be changed to other parts. Sheila could not be absolutely certain. She had never read the play.

9.

At a quarter to five, Tom found himself walking past the building in which Steven Even productions, the television packaging concern for which he worked, had its offices.

He had persuaded himself to be amused with the dilemma of where to tell his news. To whom did modern city people unburden themselves? Their doctors? It took ten days to get an appointment with the man Tom and Lala went to. There were various other people he liked, of course, but after Guy and Ellen, Eddie and his mother, the degree of intimacy seemed too slight; a piece

288

of family news would be an imposition. Now seeing the vast network building on which, but on a different floor from the network of course, Steven Even was located, Tom thought sardonically:

"A man should be able to talk to his employer."

He grinned. Then, because he had begun to feel that he would like to talk to almost anyone about almost anything, and because there might be one of several people he liked up at the office just now, preparing to leave for a five o'clock drink—the writer on the program, or the director, for example—he went into the building and rode the elevator to the ninth floor.

In the reception room several actors were waiting; Tom asked the receptionist first for Paul Wuss, the writer on his show, and was told that Paul hadn't come in that day; Tom asked for Charlie Hinkle, the director.

"I'm sorry, Mr. Beniger," the receptionist said. "Mr. Hinkle won't be with us any longer."

To his surprise Tom felt a mild anger. Their director on *Golden Words,* a vocabulary quiz show for which Tom was a consultant, had been extremely likable and none too competent. Charlie's friends had been assuring one another all winter that *Golden Words* was just the slot for Charlie—not a director's show, after all; what d'you do? Go from a shot of the contestant to a shot of the emcee, and maybe pan the audience now and then. Anyone in the control room could do it; so you had to rehearse the contestants a little bit, old Charlie could handle them, they loved him.

Unreasonable Tom, to be irritated at the word that Charlie's shortcomings had been dealt with as they deserved. He was about to turn away from the receptionist when a heavy voice hit him in the back.

"Tom. How are you Tom?"

Tom turned around. "Hi, Steve," he said.

The man who called himself Steven Even was six inches shorter than Tom but he was still the larger man. Immensely broad in face, neck and shoulders, he always stood off far enough so that he did not have to raise his head to look into Tom's eyes. If anything, Steve would push his chin deeper into his chest and let the intense blue eyes swivel up, independently. No one knew what this man had started as, for he had manufactured himself, he said, physically as well as personally—made his breadth by lifting barbells; subcontracted the replacing of his natural teeth and hair, whatever they had been, to the most artful recappers among theatrical dentists and barbers; made his voice in a studio; manufactured his name which, as he said, "you never forget—it irritates itself into your memory the first time you hear it."

"What's on your mind, Tom?" Steve boomed. "You don't know how literally I ask that question: what's on your mind?" He dropped his voice like an orator hitting decrescendo. "Listen, Tom. We've got to sit around and let it flow sometime. I'll let you put me off now, and I'll let you put me off next time, but I won't let you put me off forever." The man's persuasiveness was immense; although it was precisely opposite to the truth of the causal situation between them, Tom found himself almost persuaded that Steve had been waiting patiently to see him for weeks.

"I'm free right now, Steve," Tom said.

The blue eyes stared into him. Steven nodded. "I envy you your freedom," he said, after a moment, and went on with as much conviction as if what he were saying was urgently pertinent. "Freedom, it's a quality of mind. You have it. I knew it when I first saw you, Tom. You emanate it. Maybe freedom's won by shooting guns at tyrants; when the tyrants are dead, then the burden's on men like you. I realize that about you, Tom. Maybe I don't always show it, but I do. Look, I'm embarrassing myself." He turned away; his eye fell on one of the people Tom had taken for an actor—a slim young man, conservatively overdressed, large-eyed. "You know Ned Kildeer, Tom." Steve made the statement gruffly as if it were impossible that Tom should not know Kildeer. "Our new director." He stepped away now, paused in front of Kildeer. "Ned, how can I say how good it was of you to come in?"

Kildeer rose. "Didn't you want to see me, Steve?" he asked. Tom's mind immediately, hatefully, began to classify: homosexual, sensitive, fretful, possibly overbearing when he's in authority. He had heard of Kildeer as a director of dramatic shows with a reputation for artiness. And this was what they were to have now, in place of old agreeable Charlie Hinkle. Tom sighed, privately, and turned to leave.

As he started out of the office, he could hear Steve booming at the new director: "No, I didn't send for you Ned. The meeting's

290

tomorrow. Some fool here crossed the wires. But I wish I *had* sent for you, and I wish we were sitting down together now— Ned, there are things about this business nobody knows but you because you haven't expressed them yet, things we need to know if we're ever going to conquer our fatal talent for bastardizing. You're a torchbearer, Ned, a torchbearer, they know that on every floor of this building. . . ."

The door closed behind Tom and he was in the corridor. He walked slowly towards the bank of elevator doors, regretting Charlie Hinkle yet again. Just as he reached the elevators, the new director came out of the office and then over to wait by Tom. They stood side by side, watching the elevator dials, a long wait at this time of evening, in the embarrassment of people who haven't quite met, know they must, and have no reason to suppose that they will like one another.

Each knew, Tom thought, that the other was searching for the right kind of thing to say to ease the awkwardness; Kildeer achieved it first:

"My name's Kildeer," he said, shakily poised.

"I know," Tom said. "Oh, I'm sorry. Tom Beniger. You weren't told, were you?"

"No," Kildeer said. His diction was very precise. "Not that it mattered."

Just then an elevator should have stopped, for the situation was satisfactorily neutralized. Instead one went past, too full, apparently, at going home time, to stop for passengers, no matter how constrained. Tom smiled.

Ned Kildeer returned the smile. It was good to see the stiffness leave his face. Suddenly the man seemed innocent and friendly.

"My . . . my wife's going to have a child," Tom heard himself say. "It's . . . our first in eleven years."

"Really?"

"She's in England," Tom went on, amazed at what he was doing. "And . . . I don't know whether I'll be able to get there."

"Oh, I hope so," Kildeer said, and apparently would have gone on, but just then a car stopped and people of whom Tom had been unaware shouldered them into the car and packed them into separated body spaces among the other descending travelers of the day's end.

The operator cried, "That's all. That's all," and closed the door in the face of a running man. No one spoke until they reached the bottom, when there were exasperated mutters of excuse me, the door slid open, and, alive once more, they pushe don anothr out. For an instant Tom caught Nd Kildeer's big eyes; then they went sweeping past him, looking. The eyes found another man, a little younger than Kildeer, similarly dressed, waiting; the eyes returned to Tom once more, trying to express something, and then the slim director hurried across the lobby to join the one who was waiting.

10.

When Ellen woke in was dark. Her tongue was thick and bitter, and the arm she had been lying across had gone numb, something that always frightened her. She sat up, flopping the arm around, working sensation painfully back into it. She looked around vaguely for something, what? A clock. It was not very dark and the clock said six forty-five. Six forty-five?

Why was the place so quiet? Wasn't Harrison home? Sheila? Fighting an urge to lie back down, drift off again, she struggled up and over to her dressing table, turning on a light. She held her hair back and looked at her face, sagging back at her from the mirror. The large can of talcum powder had a meaning and she moved it; behind it was the drink she had hidden when Tom arrived. She started at it, not wanting it. She wanted to hear something, some sound that would tell her she was alive and surrounded by life, but no sound came. She slipped towards the corridor, hesitating, listening.

"Harrison?" She called so quietly that he could not have heard her if he been five steps away. She went into the unlighted corridor, trembling a little, and called again, trying to make her voice louder; it came out even more softly. She could barely hear it herself.

"Harrison? Sheila?" said her voice, whispering.

She peered into the living room; it was unlighted.

Then a strange, loud, aggressive voice said:

"Now Mother, what's the matter?"

Ellen jumped around and it was Sheila coming towards her in the dark corridor; only Sheila.

"Oh, Sheila," she said. "Where's your father? Isn't he home?"

292

Sheila stopped, tossed her head, and said in the same hateful voice as before: " 'Mother, thou hast my father much offended.' "

"Sheila, what are you saying?"

Sheila turned on the light. "Hi, Mom," she said. "It's Wednesday."

"It is? Oh." On Wednesdays Harrison ate dinner at his desk in the office, because it was weekly report day; the whole trend analysis staff worked late, writing the report and having it mimeographed.

"Where'll we go?" Sheila asked.

Sometimes on Wednesdays Sheila and Ellen had supper out, and saw a movie. "Don't you have homework?"

"Finished it. Didn't you hear me typing?"

Ellen shook her head. "Do you want to go out?"

"I don't care. Will you let me cook supper?"

"All right," Ellen said. "Sure." Cleaning up the mess Sheila would make would be no worse ordeal than going out, the way she felt. She thought of the pans to scrape, the dishes and glasses and mixing bowls and measuring cups, for Sheila always tried ambitious things, which seldom turned out well; the thought of all those things to clean was not discouraging. It was rather comforting. Hot dishwater and bright suds and something to do with her hands, something to keep her on her feet; yes.

"All right," Sheila said. "There's something I want to try. You have to stay out of the kitchen—a secret."

Ellen nodded and her daughter turned to go skipping down the corridor. "Sheila?"

Sheila stopped and looked back, twinkling. "Yes, Mom?"

"Did you say something, a minute ago, about my offending your father?"

Sheila said, "Oh, that. It was . . . it was a play. I was just saying something from a play."

"What play?"

"Just, ah . . . one we're reading in Enlgish. Wait till you see what I'm going to cook tonight."

"I thought you were reading *Ivanhoe,*" Ellen said.

"Oh. Well, we're reading this play too," Sheila said glibly, and dashed away to the kitchen.

CHAPTER TWO

1.

EDWARD M. BISSLE, JR., a farmer, was dressing to go to New York, but he was not thinking about it. He was thinking about Puerto Ricans.

He didn't know the first scabby thing about Puerto Ricans. But since when did the human, excuse the profanity, mind, prefer knowledge to prejudice? When? All right. Then any objection to Eddie thinking that Puerto Ricans were sneaky and yellow? Foreigners were. His own damn grandfather, who went to bed in his underwear in this house every night for fifty years was a foreigner, therefore sneaky and yellow. Eddie's father, half-foreigner, half-sneaky, half-yellow. That made Eddie one quarter of each, but wait:

It's going to get kind of exquisite. No foreigner ever thought of being as sneaky and yellow as a genuine native American, which was to say an Indian, and what was Eddie's grandmother? What? Try to squirm your human—excuse the profanity—mind out of that one: two quarters. And as for the flabby little race of British sharecroppers and waitresses who had produced Eddie's mother as one of their soo-preme achievments . . . all right. Any Puerto Rican who wanted to try matching Eddie in the sneakiness and yellowness departments would have to get pretty low and pretty lemony.

He pulled the belt of his tweed pants in until it squeezed. He was always interested in seeing whether he could pull it so tight it would hurt; he couldn't. He liked to test one set of muscles against another. Arms against stomach; arms lost. Stupid arms. Stomach bulged back at them, like a lead popover.

Dressed now, except for his jacket—Eddie wouldn't own an overcoat—and with almost half an hour left before train time, he paced up and down in his bedroom, continuing his consideration of the Puerto Rican question.

Puerto Ricans. The harvesting and marketing Co-operative of which Eddie was a member—his damn grandfather had founded the miserable thing, so Eddie wouldn't pull out, much as some might have liked it—was proposing to bring Puerto Rican labor in for the harvest, eight months hence. Planning a harvest already for crops which hadn't even been planted was absolutely typical of the Co-operative; Eddie, pacing, decided he didn't care what breed of bum came in to cut his cabbages, pick up his potatoes after the plow, as long as they stayed off his property after work. All right. So he decided he would not have to be back on Monday for the meeting, to fight getting Puerto Ricans; he smiled at the thought of how relieved the softheads who ran the Co-op were going to be when he failed to appear and make the expected speech damning the idea. Not that Eddie could command many votes or wanted to; as a matter of fact, he despised the hicks who voted with him on such issues, perhaps more than he did the ones who followed the leadership. But his speeches, always brief, always scurrilous, caused turbulence in the meetings, and the officers didn't like that. Too bad about them. They were perfectly entitled to get their egos fed by conspiring to be elected officers so that they could sit on the goddamn platform at the meetings. But Eddie, too, had an ego, he figured, charming little thing, just as warped and empty as any of theirs, and his happened to feed on making nasty, stupid little speeches now and then.

And here was a little syllogismee to ram up your gismee if you didn't think Eddie knew what he was saying about Puerto Rismees: What was a Puerto Rican? A Mexican living on an Island. And what was Eddie's second best friend? A Mexican. And what were this Mexican friend's characteristics? Sneakiness. Yellowness. Q.E. Dismee.

Eddie was just a touch more race-prejudiced than most; Eddie was prejudiced against the human race.

Get your jacket on, you dark-skinned, knobby-knockered,

mustache-wearing little crud (all men are cruds; all cruds are sneaky; I am a man. Signed, Edward M. Bismee); get out the door, that's right, kick it open; admire yourself pretty heartily for that, do you? Get in the car; get on the train; get to New York, they're having a world's crud fair.

2.

"If you weren't so tall and beautiful," Sheila said, "it wouldn't matter."

"Oh stop," said Amy.

"No really. Suppose some squeak like Freddie Jones were the king? Nobody'd ever believe you went for him the way Queen Gertrude does." The night before, after supper, Sheila had read almost half of *Hamlet,* and an outline of the rest. She knew the Queen was pretty gone on King Claudius. "Look."

They were once again in the long, deserted living room; it was even colder today. They kept their coats on. Sheila found the place in the book to prove her point; the lines thrilled her, as she read them, more for their candor than their poetry. It was the Ghost, the murdered King, speaking of what his brother Claudius had accomplished:

" 'Oh, wicked wit and gifts that have the power.
    So to seduce!—won to his lust
    The will of my most seeming-virtuous queen.' "

Sheila held the book against her breast. "Now, does that sound like you and Freddie Jones?"

"Well, thank you if you think it sounds like me and Ben Chaffin," Amy said. "Won't you ask Mac?"

"Will you?"

"I can't," Amy said.

"Will you if I do it with you? Mac's never looked at me." The much-admired Mac, who was almost seventeen, had recently taken to teasing Amy when they met in the corridor.

"I just couldn't," Amy said.

"Then it's got to be Ben Chaffin."

"But he's stupid."

"Well, thank you if you think that's why he likes me," Sheila said. Ben Chaffin had no skill at teasing in corridors; though he

296

was sixteen, he was awkward, a blurter, and both girls felt quite superior to him. "I can *get* Ben," Sheila said. "And I can make him come to rehearsals and learn his lines, too. Do you think both of us put together could do that with Mac?"

Amy lowered her eyes. "Give me time," she said, but it was a way of conceding the point, because she added: "All right. But if you get Ben, that means you have to get Fats, too." Fats Gunderson was a fresh fourteen year old, a class behind them; Fats was Ben's cousin and since the boys Ben's age hadn't much use for him, the two cousins were generally together.

"We've got a perfect part for Fats," Sheila said. "He'd be much better than who I have because he's such a show off."

"Which part?"

"Lair-tus. That's Polonius' son, Ophelia's brother. The one Hamlet fights with in the end."

"How'd you say his name?"

"All right. You say it." Sheila showed Amy the name.

"Lay-er-tees."

"You sure?"

"Yes."

"Okay." Sheila wrote herself a note in the book. Nothing had been said about her directing the play. Nothing needed to be said. It was implicit.

"What about Horatio?" Amy asked. "Hamlet's friend?"

"I've got to think some more."

"Well, who will we have? To see the play, I mean?" Amy asked.

"Oh, I don't know. Parents, I guess. Other kids."

"Teachers?"

"I guess so." It didn't matter much to Sheila yet. She was quite convinced now that they would do the play, and had been since English class that morning. During English, she had folded the typed cast list she'd prepared, addressed it to Amy, and had it passed as a note. It came back with question marks after some names, O.K.'s after others, and a big "No!" after Ben Chaffin's. And at the bottom: "Let's not tell any of them until we talk." This practical warning somehow moved the project, in the realms of Sheila's mind, out of the kingdom of fantasy, into the republic of possibility.

Tom Beniger sat immobile in a straight chair, squinting out the front window of his apartment, waiting for his camera to stop buzzing and click. He had decided, since there was film in the camera and there was a self-timing apparatus, that he could save trouble and time and expense by taking his own photograph for the passport application.

He was very conscious of expense. He had been calculating finances, worrying about the trip to England. There were thirty-two dollars in the checking account. He would earn, in the fifteen weeks between now and early June, $2250, his *Golden Words* fee of $150 a week. If he lived on $30 a week, that was $450. And three rent payments, of $125 each was $375. Deducting these costs from the $2250, left $1425. But there were three hundred dollars in bills, some to department stores carried over from last fall, for clothes he had urged Lala to buy for her trip. To pay the bills would leave $1125. And utilities, at $25 a month times three, left $1050. Comfortable enough, except for the big trauma of any man's fiscal year, which was income tax. Tom had earned, from his work in television, from some translations he had done from Spanish, from providing the notes for an anthology of Greek literature, nearly $8800. What might have happened to it he had no idea; nor had Lala. In the first year of their marriage their income had been less than fifteen hundred dollars, from the GI Bill mostly, and they had managed to live, and had none left. Each year the income had gone up a little, and each year they had none left. Only in one year, when Lala worked too, had they managed to save anything—seven or eight hundred—and that had gone the following year into living. Now, at $8800, they were still managing to live, and still had nothing—no appliances, no furniture, no car, no memorable dissipations—only a little travel and some books and worn luggage and just enough clothing. When a dress or suit wore out it was always a crisis; but why? Isn't $8800 a lot? Well, Lala's going abroad, of course, and the money he'd loaned his friend Brestman who was trying to work up an educational TV series, never mind . . . no sense counting. There would be $1050 left, after paying up everything, and the tax would be $650

298

more, if he could take off Brestman's thousand as a bad debt. And that would leave him four hundred dollars for passage to England and back—Lala had her return ticket. The baby. Would they have to pay passage for the baby? And a stay in England; Tom would have to find some more money, a few hundred dollars more. And be very careful with what he had. And then it might be possible.

Click.

He had had his eyes closed, figuring, when the camera went. Umph. Photography of the self. He had been busy saving all this time, trouble and the fifty cent expense of ordinary passport photos, for over an hour. In principle it had seemed a simple enough thing, though Tom was no very dedicated photographer; gauge the light, set the lens and shutter, put the camera on something solid, focus, sit down in front of it. . . .

But to begin with, it had taken a quarter of an hour to find the exposure meter, which should have been with the camera. He had located the thing, at length, in Lala's drawer in the dresser; it was in a box with some costume jewelry she had left behind; then it took Tom several minutes more to get over being touched at this—the meter had always seemed an object of great value to funny Lala, though it was actually worth far less than the camera; so she put the meter in the dresser drawer to keep it out of his awkward path. Dear, funny Lala.

Next he had discovered that the sun, which had been coming in splendidly through one window to begin with, was now shifted past it; it would be several minutes before it started coming in the other. He began to fuss with books, trying to make a pedestal on the window sill that would hold the camera at the proper height. This arranged, he realized that it would not, after all, be the back of the chair he was photographing but an object—his head—at an undetermined height. So, more ingenious in imagination than with his hands, he had tried to twist up an arrangement of wire coat hangers onto the back of the chair in such a way that he could sit, tie a handkerchief to the top hanger at the height of his nose, and then get up, leaving the thing there to focus on. The improvisation was a mechanical failure. The hanger would not stay firm. He then realized that if he simply moved the chair back, he would increase the area to be photographed sufficiently so that his head would

299

have to be included—and that an enlargement of the head, discarding the rest, could be made from the negative.

Feeling decidedly harassed, he had made the new arrangement and, between the time of setting the self-timer and the click of the camera, had gotten off onto his financial figuring which was climaxed by the realization that having enlargements made would increase the cost of passport photos after all, and it was this that had made him close his eyes at the moment of click.

He leapt up to take the picture over. He had no particular vanity of appearance to be gratified by the result, but supposed one ought not to look asleep.

The whole thing made him so impatient that he forgot to advance the film, so the second shot combined with the first as a double exposure.

It was time to leave now for Guy's hotel, for Tom had reached Guy that morning and arranged to go over. But he would not be defeated by the camera; he quieted himself with a silent moment of self-ridicule, and, achieving the second wind of patience, adjusted the film and checked the setting. He kicked a hassock into place in front of the chair, which would bring his head, now, to the height of the chair top, enabling him to focus closer and avoid enlargements. He rechecked the light and adjusted the lens. With unexpected ease, he made the picture and removed the roll of film.

Unfortunately, he then withdrew his attention, so it was likely that the drug store wouldn't actually get the film for many days—perhaps not until Tom remembered to change suits and the cleaner found the roll of film in his jacket pocket. He set out for the hotel in the East thirties where Guy now lived, in two rather luxurious rooms, with a kitchenette and a terrace. It was a comfortable, noiseless sort of place, new rather than modern, with heavily carpeted corridors and efficient, invisible service. From this address, Guy still represented family business interests in the international financial community of New York, a sort of ambassador to it as had been an uncle before him, the one who had lived at the Plaza when Tom and Guy were in college. There were other brothers and cousins who had succeeded other uncles and fathers in similar functions in Rio, in Paris, in Los Angeles and Mexico City. His father's generation, Guy said, stayed pretty much on the ranches these days.

"Tom, come in, come." Guy hugged him ceremoniously, the Mexican greeting. "Let me tell you a coincidence," Guy went on,

300

stepping back and smiling, the teeth as white as ever, the head fleshed out, and as handsome now, in an adult way, as it had once been in a boyish way. "Yesterday afternoon, Ellen called up. Twice—first to leave a message. Then, just as I was about to call her back, the phone rang, it was Ellen."

"Really?" Tom said.

"But she never calls," said Guy. "I haven't heard from Ellen in three months."

"What did she want?" Tom asked.

"Forgive me, Tom for saying so—I think she was feeling sad and nostalgic for impossible days. . . ."

"A little tight, you mean," Tom said, and smiled. "I know. I was there earlier."

"She told me. And that Eddie was coming for dinner tonight. Do you know, I think I'll go?"

"To Ellen's for dinner, on a day's notice?"

"Well, after dinner. I always like to see your sister. And I have something to speak of with Eddie."

"I haven't heard from Eddie yet," Tom said. "I imagine I will when he arrives. Why after dinner? Ellen cooks pretty well."

"Wonderfully," Guy said. "But I have a date. One who will expect to linger in an expensive restaurant, waving to people she knows and eating some . . . some one of those conspicuous desserts they turn the lights down for and light a fire. But then—a drive by car over Brooklyn Bridge, why not? And some civilized conversation; I think it will be all right."

"What do you have to tell Eddie?" Tom asked.

"The strangest deal . . . have you any money, Tom? To invest?"

"I won't laugh hollowly," Tom said.

"It concerns a painter, a moron, named Ernest Goswith. You haven't heard of him?" Tom shook his head. "No, you wouldn't have . . . but hell, you don't want to hear about it if you can't come in."

"No, I'm curious," Tom said. "What's so extraordinary?"

"I think you must see the pictures first, Tommy. Then I will tell you. What have you on your mind? Something special?"

Tom understood from this that the deal, whatever it was, must still be confidential to non-investors. He didn't mind being turned aside by Guy's tact for he understood that it was automatic, a product of personality rather than of calculation.

"A very special thing to me," Tom said, and paused a moment.

Then he looked at his friend: Lala's going to have a baby."

Guy whooped, lifted Tom bodily out of his chair, set him on his feet, crying, "Yes, yes, Tom. You will be Papa." Then he shook him, grinning, embraced him, and knocked him back in the chair again, crying that Papa was to wait.

Guy ran to his kitchenette, and Tom, grinning happily, didn't need to be told what for. There were always a dozen splits of champagne cold in the refrigerator—it provided the right touch at times, Guy said, late at night, just before reaching the critical point with a girl; worked pretty well in the morning, too.

Now he came back, laughing and twisting at the wire on a bottle, with new shouts as Tom laughed back, popping the cork across the room, seizing Tom's head under his arm and tilting back to pour the foaming stuff into a willing mouth.

Guy let go, poured the rest of the champagne from the small bottle into his own mouth until it was emptied, and then flung the thing across the room.

"Now Tomás," he said, in Spanish. "What shall we call this boy? Hey? Xavier? Heriberto? Galdenzio?"

Tom said: "Perhaps it will be a girl, *compadre.*"

Guy said exuberantly that he would go with Tom to England, they would stay with a cousin in London, then out to the country. And Tom replied that he was not certain he would go, because of. . . . Before he could advance a reason, Guy was offering to lend him money, any amount, though Tom owed his friend already something over a thousand dollars on which he insisted on paying interest. The debt went back to a trip he and Lala'd made abroad, and only a few small payments had been made through the years—payments that were always acknowledged with a gift, or by Guy's sweeping him and Lala out to dinner and a night-club, for Guy insisted that no money was due. Tom suddenly thought: this was part of it, this embarrassment about money, part of the reason for not having come to Guy instantly with the news. But there was more to the reason, more even than Tom's occasional disapproval of Guy, withdrawal from Guy. For, though he had not thought of it the day before, there was sometimes withdrawal on Guy's part, too, or if not withdrawal, impatience.

Guy now, relaxed, sitting on the floor, jumping up to get another of the little splits of champagne over Tom's protests, barefoot, strong, outgoing, happy and a little wild, was wonderful. But such moods were rarer now than formerly; Guy's temper grew shorter every year, though there was, of course, no sign of this as he talked excitedly with Tom about the birth and future of Heriberto Xavier Galdenzio Beniger.

The subject was exhausted, the second split of champagne emptied; Guy said he had the little bottles only because you could arrange to finish one at whatever moment seemed to require such a pause; Guy said therefore they had not really had a drink yet and he would open another. Tom said no, he had the *Golden Words* meeting to go to at six and Guy yielded; Guy drank very sparingly, in any case.

"Who's the date tonight?" Tom asked, quite relaxed now that he had spoken fully of his fatherhood. "Who's gets the romantic ride over Brooklyn Bridge?"

"A foolish, deformed girl," Guy said, naming an actress who had just then been receiving an extensive publicity buildup. "Tom, she is nice enough of her kind, but what has done this to her breasts? Is it some exercises, or drugs? So big they are silly. Undressed, Tom, Dorothy is a well-proportioned young woman— shoulders, hips, legs, all in scale, even a small waist—but these great weights hang from her chest. She must hold them up with her hands, until she can lie down. . . ."

"How long have you been seeing her?" Tom asked.

"Three weeks. But it is getting to the difficult time, now. The first fun over, and I must decide whether there is to be more fun or not . . . I don't know. She has a nice, simple little unbalanced mind, and is rather a moralist at heart—the kind who makes sentimental exceptions for practical reasons, you know? It can be tiring."

"What's her number?" Tom asked. "You're still numbering?"

"Yes. Miss Dorothy is 205. And the score in the other column, 43."

"You aren't getting turned down much these days."

"You don't like the scoring," Guy said. "The notebooks. But I will tell you something, Tom. I am getting like an old ballplayer, who is more interested in his lifetime averages than in the day's game. Sex is . . . I confess to you; nobody else. I am less interested in sex than in statistics. My rate, very high just after the war, for two years. Then down, one a month sometimes, ignoring the chances for more casual seductions because I wanted to know the woman—I get tired of their personalities, as tired as of their bodies, Tom." Guy looked almost sad. "Sometimes I would like

303

to stop. But you know what? I have this score. I have ten more good years left, I think, till I am forty five, and by then, I would like. . . ." He looked at Tom with an apologetic smile. Tom nodded. "I would like to have made 350 scores in my left hand column, and to be under 50 on the right."

"That's about fifteen a year," Tom said. "And only one refusal."

"Yes. And I make it hard for myself; I don't know why. Not to take whatever I can get, for an easy score; no. Only a girl that I really desire. . . ."

"Suppose you stop desiring them?"

Guy nodded rather soberly. "That is the danger of course. Sometimes it happens to me. I go a month, two months, and meet nobody to excite me. And drag along with the girl I am having an affair with, not desiring her either, making her angry, reseducing her, just for the game. . . ."

"Guyito," Tom said. "It exhausts me just to think about it."

"350—you think that is a stupid ambition?"

"I don't know," Tom said. "Either all ambitions are stupid, and that no more so than the others—or anything a man can set himself to make his life interesting is worthwhile. I don't know. Artists, scientists, leaders—we honor their ambitions; but we honor the ballplayer, too, who wants to make 200 hits. He doesn't seem stupid to us. Only limited—and doing what he can with his best ability."

"And seducing women is my best ability?" Guy said.

"It isn't one society values much," Tom said. "But . . . well, a lot of men would; and some women. And it's not like committing 350 murders, after all."

"No," Guy said. "Only a little like that."

"I think you would have been a great ascetic, Guyito." Tom said lightly, but Guy nodded in rather serious agreement.

Tom got up to leave. "Don't worry about it, Guy," he said. "Either you'll renounce your score or you'll achieve it. I don't think you'll fail."

Guy smiled. "One must have something . . ." he said. "And you think it would be all right with Ellen to bring this girl?"

"I think Ellen would love to have someone like Dorothy Conn drop in," Tom said. "What hostess wouldn't?"

"And Sheila, too. An actress. Sheila will like that?"

304

"She may not be Sheila's kind of actress . . ." Tom began, but Guy, who was grinning again, brushed it aside.

"Good. I will call Ellen now to confirm. And Tom, after your meeting, come out. Maybe you will arrive no later than I do. And Eddie will be there. . . ."

"It might be good," Tom said. "Depends on how much we leave of one another at the meeting."

4.

"Mother. Hey, mother." A door slammed.

Sheila was home.

Ellen was once again in her bedroom, lying down, but this afternoon she had not been drinking; she had been a little frightened yesterday at the way she'd gone into numbness, into forgetting. About three today, being jittery, she had taken some aspirin and come in to lie down.

"Mother." The girl came down the hallway and opened the bedroom door. "You all right?"

Ellen was sitting up now. "Sheila, when are you going to learn to knock on doors?" She asked.

"Well, you were just napping, weren't you?"

"That's not the point," Ellen said. "You insist on your privacy often enough. Don't you think your parents are entitled to some, too?"

"Oh, all right. I'm sorry," Sheila said. "Hey mother. . . ."

"And don't say 'Hey,'" Ellen said. "Guess who we're going to see tonight?"

"I already know," Sheila said.

"How can you? He only called twenty minutes ago to say he'd be coming."

"Who only called twenty minutes ago?"

"Guy. He. . . ."

"Guy's coming," Sheila shouted. "Mister Gorgeous."

"Sheila hush. He's coming after dinner, and he's bringing Dorothy Conn."

"Who?"

"Dorothy Conn. You know, the actress."

"Oh, the one with the big booz," Sheila said.

"Sheila! And the Helds are coming. Do you remember them?"

"Yes," Sheila said. "They have that pretty drippy boy. Drippy Peter."

"Sheila. I wish you'd listen to me," Ellen said. "For just a minute. I was talking to Tessie Held today; Peter's quite grown up now. We were saying perhaps you and he could go to the movies or something. . . ."

"Mother," said Sheila. "He's only fourteen."

"And how old are you?"

Sheila ignored the question. "What are we having them for?" she demanded. "Business reasons?"

"They're very nice people," Ellen said. "Your father wants us to know them better."

"Business reasons," Sheila repeated.

"So the Helds and Guy and Miss Conn. . . ."

"And Eddie Bissle," Sheila said. "Listen, I'm going to eat early and study, is that all right? I'll fix it myself. And you call me when Guy comes?"

"All right. But you have to come say hello to everybody, as they arrive. . . how did you know Eddie was coming?"

"Because I just let him in, Mother," Sheila said impatiently, starting for the door. "He's waiting for you in the living room."

Ellen jumped up, ran across the room in her stocking feet, and seized Sheila's arm.

"Why didn't you tell me?"

"Is it so important?" Sheila asked. "I tried to."

"What time is it, anyway?"

"After five."

"Sheila, Sheila honey. Would you . . . I mean, could you do me a little favor? If you'd . . . well, read or study or something in the television room? I mean while I'm talking to Eddie, until somebody else gets here?"

"Why, what do you think he'll do?" Sheila asked.

"Oh, nothing, just . . . will you do it?"

"All right," Sheila said. "As long as I don't have to talk to him." And started down the hall to put her books away.

"Why are you home late again today, dear?" Ellen called after her.

Getting no answer, she went back into the bedroom and slipped into her shoes. Then she went into the living room and greeted

306

Eddie. He seemed if anything shorter and more gnarled each time she saw him. She disliked the bristly little mustache he wore; and the single temple which had started to grey during the war and was now a patch of white made her feel old. His clothes, as always, asserted that he was just in for a stay from the country, and saw no particular reason to dress up for it; his face changed least of all, from one encounter to the next—bumpy, scowling, tight at the jaws, and the skin lined and weathered. His appearance always affected Ellen ambivalently and she could not help looking closely every time she saw him; now she was glad Sheila had moved ostentatiously into the adjoining room, and was noisily preparing to play some records. It would spare Ellen the proprietary kiss, the hard pinch at whatever part of her his hand happened to fall on, with which it had become Eddie's habit to greet her through the years. It was a demeaning practice, and intended to be, and often enough Ellen had offered herself to this symbolic statement of their relationship dutifully, finding it a foretaste of pleasure; today, the prospect made her shudder. The years have taken over for you, lover, she thought; they punish me enough. It was time they were done with one another, and before the evening was over, she would tell him so.

"Hello, Eddie."

"Hello, Mouse," Eddie said, using an endearment she disliked; and got up. "How's it going?"

"I'm way behind with dressing," Ellen said, staying in the corridor doorway; she did not want to be too obviously depending on Sheila's being present through the arch. "I'm going to get you a drink and then run and get dressed. What would you like?"

Eddie looked at her and smiled, rather a pleased smile, as if he liked her trying to impose distance. "I can mix my own," he said, and walked towards her. When he reached the doorway, out of Sheila's angle of sight, he crowded Ellen briefly against the edge of it. He raised his knee between her legs, hooked his ankle behind hers, to trap her, pinched the flesh over her ribs through the blouse she wore, and waited, holding on, smiling at her, his face eight inches away. She bit her lips together in refusal; he tightened the pinch. When it became too painful she released her lips, put her face forward and kissed him. It was over in a dozen heartbeats, and he let her go and strutted back to where he'd been sitting.

"On second thought, you can get the drink, Mousie," he said, affably. "Scotch and water, please. Not much water you know?"

Furious with herself, Ellen fled down the corridor and into the kitchen. She mixed Eddie's drink automatically, and as she did her daughter came up behind her, through the dining alcove.

"Mother," Sheila said, mischievously. "Mousie!"

"Here." Ellen turned on the girl. "Take it to him." She thrust the glass into Sheila's hand, took another she'd fixed for herself, and ran back to her bedroom.

5.

Sheila watched her mother go. Then, thoughtfully she tasted the drink. She wondered if Eddie had said something, whispered it perhaps. There was nothing Sheila could think of that he might have done to rout her mother in the few seconds they were out of Sheila's sight. She decided that her mother was just in a peculiar mood, and carried the drink through.

"Hey, Sheila, thanks," Eddie said. "Sit down and talk to me."

"I can't." Lies came effortlessly to Sheila. "I have to play some records for music homework before the people come."

"I'm people," Eddie said, sipping the drink and gazing at her. "You're a sweetheart. This is wonderful."

"Excuse me," Sheila said, and started back to the television room.

"That's all right," Eddie got up and moved after her. She tried to feel a sense of menace about it, and couldn't. If she could have thought Mr. Bissle sinister, she would have liked him better. "You go right ahead," he said. "I'll listen, too. Go ahead."

Sheila went to the machine which she had already turned on, and put on the second of the LP's she had gotten out. She was having a Beethoven period, and she played the Third Symphony constantly. But if he watched, she couldn't pretend to conduct it.

"Don't you want to sit down and listen?" She suggested.

"Okay. Sure," said Eddie. "Thanks." But instead of going back into the living room, as she had meant him to, he moved over and sat in a chair next to where she stood, continuing to look fondly at her over the rim of his glass.

It puzzled her. He was always like this with her and he was

308

supposed to be such a cross patch. She supposed that she was just terribly likeable. The only thing that interested her about Eddie Bissle was the idea that she alone, of all human beings, had charm for him—infrequent fantasy material, but valid enough for an occasional daydream.

Now she put the record on top of the other, and tripped the switch. The bottom one dropped onto the turntable, and the music began. Since she couldn't very well conduct, she acted entranced.

"You like that music, sweetheart?" Eddie asked, when the first movement ended, and before the funeral march began.

"I love Beethoven," Sheila said, more primly than she intended.

"Beethoven," said Eddie.

When the record finished, Sheila left the room, explaining hurriedly that she had to write her essay on the first two movements, and she wanted to run and do it while they were fresh in her mind. The rest would go on playing if he wanted to listen.

6.

Eddie waited until she was gone and looked at his watch. It was a quarter past five. He got up, took out a pen and a scrap of paper from his pocket, and started going rapidly through the record folders. Whenever he came to something by Beethoven, he would jot the name; there were eleven different things, but the guy wrote more than that. Sure he did.

Still alone, Eddie walked out into the hall, opened the telephone directory, and called a department store where he had a charge account; he asked for the record department. It was twenty of six; just in time.

"Listen," he said, when he had a clerk. "I want to order some records. Now will you listen to me?"

"Yes, sir," the clerk said.

Eddie gave his name and address. "Now," he said. "I'm going to read you the names of some Beethoven records. You got that? And I don't want any of the ones I'm going to read you. These are the ones she's got. I want to order ones she hasn't got. Do you understand me?"

"Beethoven records not on your list, sir?"

309

"Yeah. Yeah. You got it?"

The clerk claimed to have it, and Eddie was happily ordering seventy dollars worth of Beethoven records, and stick in some other things, same kind of stuff by different guys if you follow me, when Ellen came into the hall and asked what he was doing; there was an empty glass in her hand.

"Listen," Eddie said into the phone. "I want you to hold on a minute, understand? I'm not finished but I have to talk to someone, and I'll be with you in a minute. So hold on."

The clerk promised to obey.

"Just ordering a couple of records," Eddie told Ellen. "From you to Sheila. There'll be a card in it, 'Love, Mother'. Okay?"

"Oh, Eddie," Ellen wailed, and he grinned at her and finished his ordering. When he hung up he put a hand out and held her arm, not giving her a pinch this time because they'd already said hello, and asked her when would be a good time for her to come to the hotel and she said tomorrow morning, Eddie, tomorrow morning.

CHAPTER THREE

1.

HAVING LEFT EDDIE BISSLE, Sheila went to her room and finished reading the play. She thought it was quite good. There were places in it she didn't understand too well, but the *World Wide Manual for Direction of the Play* had a special chapter on Shakespeare, and it said that directors always cut things out, and that would be a help. What she liked best was the part where Hamlet has killed Polonius and is dragging the body around and hiding it like a real maniac, and won't tell anybody where he's put it; awful, wild-eyed Hamlet, and teases them. Murders the old man and then drags him around different places, and teases them when they want to know where the body is. When Hamlet starts in being a bad boy, there couldn't be anybody worse—more aggravating, unreasonable and awful to everyone. Except to his best friend, Horatio.

Horatio was still the big problem. If only Amy could be Horatio and the Queen, too. Suddenly Sheila had an idea; and sometimes an idea is exactly half of what you need, and the other half is luck. She opened her door slightly so that she would know when the Helds arrived; they had to bring the luck.

They were a zippy little couple; Mr. Held worked on Wall Street, like her father. And they had this drippy son, Peter. Drippy and stuck up. So stuck up he must have done some acting. You didn't, except for Amy, get kids you liked a whole lot for a thing like this; kids you liked were too sensible. They wasted time being nice. They were nice enough so that other people wanted them to do other things. You got drips, stuck up drips or any other kind. Come on, Helds.

Sheila started reading the play again at Act Two. Act One was easy, and they could do the whole thing—the soldiers on watch, the first appearance of the ghost—but she must get to know the rest of the play and find out what to cut before she could start teaching the kids; already she half-knew her own part and learning it perfectly did not present itself to Sheila as a major problem.

2.

Ellen had gone to finish dressing. Eddie sat in the living room, pretty pleased with himself, content now to wait and see what happened next.

What happened was that Harrison Walle came home, Harrison with his wavy chestnut hair which was always a surprise. People thought of Harrison, when he was out of their sight, as being less good looking than he actually was. He was well built, had attractive features and that fine head of hair. He was also, on the other hand, one of those who do not wear glasses very well; the bridge of his nose was too shallow for his glasses to set in comfortably against the face, so there was a look of forward thrust about them, as if they had just been jarred loose. He wore excellent clothes, and always had color in his face; he was three years older than Ellen, but didn't look it.

Harrison had developed. Eddie could remember a time when even Tom, who was kind about everybody, used to groan at the mention of Harrison, and with reason. This was no longer especially true; Harrison was not the bore he had been as a younger man. It was as if he had had to complete his education, his serious training for life, get job and family established, before he could take time to discover in himself a personality. Now he had become an agreeable man, not overconservative, good at his job— he was Chief of Section; he earned a good deal, drank a good deal, went back to Yale every other year for Harvard games, maintained just that minimum of self-dissatisfaction which invites tolerance without taxing sympathy.

312

"Eddie," he said. "Good to see you. How's the cabbage crop?"

"It's all right," Eddie said.

"Got a drink? Good. I'll get myself one and join you."

Harrison went out; Eddie could hear his voice raised in greeting to Ellen as Harrison went by her room; Ellen seemed to be saying that she would be right out. In a moment, Harrison was back.

"Tom coming out tonight?" he asked.

"Don't think so," Eddie said. For all the fury with which Eddie constantly addressed himself, his drawing room manners were not profane; the fury became more and more self-contained the longer he sat with strangers. "Guy's coming, I believe."

"I heard that. And bringing this girl, Dorothy Conn. Be pretty interesting to have a look at her."

"Sure," said Eddie.

"I imagine you saw the famous picture of her? With the Afghan hound?"

"No," Eddie said.

"Oh," said Harrison, good naturedly. "Of course. The recluse. But you have seen a picture of the girl?"

"Can't miss her, can you?" Eddie said.

He and Harrison chatted; they enjoyed patronizing one another.

3.

Ellen looked in to make sure they were all right and that the Helds had not arrived. She saw that their glasses were empty, and suggested that Harrison might fix Eddie a drink. She went along with him to the kitchen. Harrison asked what they were going to eat, and Ellen said roast beef, she had a beautiful roast.

She waited until Harrison left the kitchen; then, quickly, she got the roast out of the refrigerator and began to get it ready for the oven, something she ought to have done an hour ago. It was a big roast and would take over two hours; she knew she was forgetting something, but couldn't think what. She heard the bell and remembered, simultaneously, what it was she had forgotten; the bell meant the Helds, and what she had forgotten was preheating the oven. Quickly she shoved the roast into the unlit oven so that no one would see it, looked wildly for something to wipe

313

her hands on, couldn't locate a dish towel; she hitched her skirt up and wiped her hands on the stocking-tops on either side, shook herself out and went to the living room to greet her guests. Harrison passed her, on his way in to get them drinks.

The Helds lived in the same block; Ezra Held and Harrison often walked to the subway together, mornings, but the two families did not know each other well. Ezra was a chirpy, cheery little man, who bounced around on the balls of his feet, and began to banter with Ellen about how they lived too close to one another to ever get together; Tessie was pretty and coquettish, and more direct than her husband.

Harrison came back with drinks and said:

"Quiet please, Helds. I'm going to drop a name and when I drop a name I want it heard."

Ezra Held came to attention, Tessie parted her lips and sat forward, and Harrison said that Dorothy Conn was going to be dropping in after dinner.

"Honestly, Harrison, do you know her?" Tessie asked. She made her eyes big and touched Harrison on the knee as she spoke; her husband twinkled.

"No," Harrison said. "A friend of ours is bringing her out. Fellow called Guy Cinturon."

"Oh, but he's a name, too . . ." Tessie began, but Ezra's crow of laughter cut her off.

"A double delayed name drop," Ezra said. "Perfectly done, Harrison. Perfect. Never saw a better example."

"But he's the one who always takes out the beautiful women," Tessie persisted seriously, not getting it. "You know what they call him. . . ."

" 'Celebrated *bon vivant,* man about town and raconteur,' is the phrase isn't it?" Ezra said. "When will they say that about us, Harrison?"

"You're half a century behind," Harrison said.

"The Walles have the most fascinating friends," Tessie said, and turned to Eddie. "What do you do Mr. Biddle?"

"Bissle," Eddie said.

"Call him Eddie," Harrison said. "If he bites you, we've got serum in the bathroom."

Laughter.

"But what does he do?" Tessie pleaded.

314

"I'm a farmer," Eddie said, unemphatically.

Sheila came in, and the Helds cried greeting.

"Hello," Sheila said. "Mom, there's a great big piece of raw meat in the oven. Is it supposed to be turned on?"

"It's not quite time," Ellen said, furious. "I'll take care of it in a minute."

Sheila turned to Tessie Held. "How's Peter?" she asked.

"I'm afraid he's just about the handsomest thing on the block," Tessie said. "A friend of ours wants Peter to model for boys' clothes ads."

"Is he going to do it?"

"I suppose he'll find time."

"He'd better," said Ezra. "For twenty-five an hour."

"But Pete's so busy," Tessie told Sheila. "Singing lessons and fencing lessons. . . ."

"Fencing?" Sheila asked.

"Yes. He used to do it just at school, but now he goes to New York every week, to a . . . *salle d'armes.*"

"Would you let your 14-year old son go to a *salle d'armes?*" said Harrison to Eddie, mock severe. "Oh, tut tut, tut. Every week?"

"Maybe I ought to talk to Peter," Sheila said, still to Tessie, ignoring her father.

"Why don't you call him up?" Tessie asked.

"Oh, Tessie," said Ellen. "Why doesn't he call Sheila up?"

"That's right," Ezra said. "Just because you called me night and day, Tess, doesn't mean that's what all girls have to do."

"I got you, didn't I?" Tessie said.

"I don't mind calling him," Sheila said. "Is your number in the book?"

4.

Naturally they teased her about it, a thing she would not ordinarily have stood for a minute. Now she endured it patiently until the Helds told her their number, and Mr. Held asked if he might keep a finger on her pulse while she was talking, just as a precaution. Sheila gave him a blank stare while the others laughed, except Eddie Bissle who looked mad about something. Then

315

Sheila went out into the hall and dialed the number. Behind her the adult voices rose in an extravagance of babble and laughter.

"Pretty drunk out tonight," Sheila said darkly, as the phone began to ring at the other end.

Peter answered.

"Hello."

"Hello, Peter. This is Sheila Walle."

"Oh. Hello. Are my parents there?"

"Yes, they're all drinking cocktails," Sheila said. "What are you doing?"

"Mom left some supper for me. I just ate it."

"Do you like the theatre, Peter?" Sheila asked.

"Yes. Sometimes I get excused from school," Peter went to a boys' school, she remembered, "and go to a matinee. Only I really don't, well, generally take anybody because I like to go alone so I can concentrate. You see, I'm planning to be an actor."

And that was just what Sheila thought.

"Are you?" Sheila said. "Oh, how wonderful. Have you been in any plays?"

She listened carefully to his voice as he described having been in *The Bluebird* when he was younger, and in some French plays at his school. He said he loved to act, he really felt he'd rather do it than eat. His pronunciation was artificial, almost affected. That would be all right.

"Some kids I know are going to put on *Hamlet*," Sheila said. "Don't tell anyone. We're going to rehearse secretly, and not tell anyone until it's ready."

"Really?" Peter sounded interested.

"Of course, if you've just done French plays, I guess Shakespeare would be pretty hard for you."

"Oh, no," Peter said. "I've done Shakespeare before. We had scenes from *The Tempest* and *Midsummer Night's Dream* at school last spring. I was Puck."

"That's the toughest part all right," Sheila said, wondering which play Puck was in. "You must be terribly good."

"Who's going to be Hamlet in your play?" Peter ventured.

"Oh. I am," said Sheila.

There was a pause. "Really? A girl?"

"I'm going to get my uncle to see it," Sheila said. "He's in television. And I'm going to get him to bring some directors and people like that. And Guy Cinturon is a friend of my family's, and he'll bring some producers. And that actress, Dorothy Conn, she's a friend of ours, she's coming, too. And my dramatic teacher at school; she's a professional."

"So's mine," Peter said. "He goes out and acts in summer theatres every year." But the drip was obviously impressed.

"Do you want to be Horatio?" She asked.

"Which one is he?"

"He's Hamlet's best friend," Sheila said. "It's one of the longest parts in the play. He makes all those wonderful speeches, like 'Good night, Sweet Prince.' And you could direct the fencing scenes. I hear you're a terrific fencer."

"Yes, I could do that," said Peter. "Yes, I'd like to, Sheila." Apparently the idea pleased him so much that he forgot to ask who was going to be directing the whole play. He agreed to meet Sheila the next afternoon at the candy store, and offered to bring his foils. Sheila said they weren't ready for that yet, but to bring a book if he had one, and they hung up.

She went back to her room without going through the living room again. Her mother was in the kitchen, finally starting the oven for her roast. Eddie Bissle was there too, opening a bottle. So apparently Mom wasn't avoiding Mr. Bissle any more.

5.

Golden Words was a quiz show in the medium money bracket, based on vocabulary questions. Tom did the research. He and the writer on the show found the words and classified them. Tom also sat with the director during the performance as a judge. After a contestant had defined a word, he could double his prize of five hundred dollars by spelling it. He could double the thousand by using the word correctly in a sentence. Finally, the contestant could make it four thousand and win the right to try another word if he correctly gave the first word's origin. Each of these steps had to be judged by Tom, who signalled right or wrong by buzzer; each doubling involved risking the contestant's previous winnings, but once one had a new word he kept all winnings from the previous one.

Tom's winnings of a hundred and fifty dollars a week were paid

317

him for two afternoons of work, an evening, and one full day which, since it included the performance, lasted about sixteen hours.

In spite of its unoriginal formula, the show had been reasonably successful for a season and a half; as it entered the final half of its second season, there was some talk of the sponsor's dropping it at the end of the year, and the Steven Even office was searching for ways of improving the rating which indicated audience interest.

Tom's evening work, in addition to the performance, was done on Thursday. Each Thursday, at six, there was a meeting at which the next week's show was planned.

Today Tom was early. In the reception room, where he had meant to sit and read trade papers for half an hour, Steven Even was leaning over the couch, talking to a middle-aged man. The fact that Steve was so engaged indicated two things about the listener: that he was somehow useful, and that he was nevertheless being brushed off. If you couldn't be ignored, but he had no particular business with you, Steve came out of his office when you called and met you in the reception room. It took less time.

Tom hung up his coat, told the receptionist that he had merely come early for the meeting, not to see anybody, picked up a magazine and sat as far away from Steve and his visitor as possible. He tried not to listen, but Steve's voice was too big to ignore.

"We're not getting any action on it, no action at all," he was saying. "Every morning I pick up the phone and call Jo Anne, you know? I'm very polite: 'Jo Anne, you stupid cow, when are you going to get off your tricycles over there?' Some morning she's going to get tired of me being polite, and she's going to say let's go, and you know who'll be the first to know? You. You know that's straight. You know how I feel about you. . . ." Steve now had talked the caller onto his feet, and was propelling him by sheer voice power to the front door. "You're the, what shall I say? —indispensable ingredient? Is that too much like cooking? Lonny, will you permit me that metaphor?" There was the sound of genuine entreaty in the question. Lonny, whoever he might be, cleared his throat, which Steve seemed to take as permission for the metaphor. "The indispensable ingredient for this confection, then . . . listen, do I have to tell you that? Everybody knows that. Everybody in this office knows it; they're sick of hearing me say

318

it . . . so long, Lonny. We know where to get you. . . ." And the door closed.

Steven Even started back across his reception room, big, manicured hands swinging easily at his side, wearing the expression of a man who knows the danger of wearing expressions. He had on a fawn-colored gabardine suit, the jacket riding easily over the great width of his shoulders. His clothes were beautiful, but he looked the same in any of his suits, regardless of cut or color. Some things about him were known: he had been an actor once, had gone to Hollywood and failed. Went to get a new agent one morning, so said the story Tom had heard, and sold himself so effectively that he wound up with a desk at the agent's office. Succeeded well enough as a Hollywood agent, but within the limits put on bright young men in large firms; realized it would take years to achieve the degree of connectedness in the film industry which could bring real money, real influence. And so came East in the time when television was still a flickering wonder-toy. He learned production—more than learned it; Steven Even was one of the men who had invented television production. He had been on his own as an independent producer, a show packager, for seven prosperous years.

Much of this went through Tom's mind as he looked, past the magazine, at Steve's back, going out of the reception room. He didn't think Steve had noticed him, but just as the producer reached the door, he said in a low, peremptory growl, without looking back:

"Come in, Tom."

Tom got up to follow, caught up with Steve at the door of his office and said:

"I'm not really here to see anyone before the meeting. . . ."

"Come in," Steve said. "I never get a chance to talk to you."

They went into the office. It was a big room, without a desk; Steve worked at a heavy table around which were six or seven comfortable chairs. Except for telephone and intercom, there were no machines in the room and no papers. Such things were for secretaries to bring in and out as needed. There were, at the moment, legal pads and lead pencils on the table, but these were for the meeting. On one wall were two Dufy water colors, originals, and opposite them a large blackboard on which was chalked information about the situations of the two shows which Steven

319

Even productions currently had on the networks. One was *Golden Words*. The other was a drama series about a girl newspaper reporter called *Carole of the Comet*. It was practically the last of the half hour, non-comedy shows being done live; it had, however, recently been moved from fairly good evening time, by a new sponsor, to the afternoon. Information about rehearsals, scripts in preparation for *Carole* and so on, covered half the blackboard; the other half had the schedules, the current contestants' names of *Golden Words*.

Tom took his eyes from the blackboard—why should they always travel there rather than across to the Dufy's?—and saw that Steve had sat and was waiting for him to sit, too. He did.

Steve looked at him. Tom smiled.

Steve did not return the smile. He looked very serious. He said: "Well, Tom, what can I do for you?"

Tom was slightly flustered; had he been misunderstood? "I'm sorry. I mean, I didn't come in about anything. Just . . . just here for the meeting."

"No. No." Steve shook his big head. "I know you're not here to see me. Why should you be?" He looked steadily at Tom who could think of no reply. "What can I do for you? What can this, how shall I say, improvisation center of dirt and aspiration that I find myself commanding do for you? What can television do for you—let me tell you that I ask because I have some idea of what you can do for us. We need your help, Tom, but do you need ours?"

Tom had heard Steve talk too often to be astonished; yet the sincerity was so well done, it was hard to disbelieve. Each time you saw Steve, you thought, this time, this time we are really getting through, establishing something; we have been waiting to work together and now the waiting is over. Each time you left Steve you wondered what it was you thought had been established. Well, Tom thought, I can tell him I need money. . . .

But Steve had composed his next paragraph of conversation and now began to deliver it: "Shall we consider you? Will you permit me to be that embarrassing, just as a concession to the need of an uncreative man to order his thoughts? Tom, you're a man of cultivation. Range. How many people like you do you think we have in this industry? I'll tell you something that will surprise you: hundreds. They're attracted to this stumbling medium for its potential as the most extraordinary living influence on people man has ever devised, or ever will. They join it and they let themselves be misused by it, and often enough they leave it. But why? Why are they misused? Because guys like me don't know how to use the man of cultivation and range. And why don't we? The burden's on you, Tom. Because you won't instruct us in how to use you. You have a further responsibility than simply putting yourselves at our disposal. . . ."

Tom finally got himself in balance, disbelief and credulity both put aside, to enjoy the performance. When Steve started to pitch, it was like brilliant old-fashioned oratory, reduced to the volume and intimacy of person to person conversation. You had to remember two things to enjoy it: that it was not insincere, for Steve was interested in his ideas. And that it didn't necessarily relate to anything at all. When it did relate to something, it could be magnificently convincing.

"What about program ideas?" Steve was saying. "Do you have them? Structure . . . do you understand structure? Would you want to write a script, say, see what it's like to wrestle with content? Do you think you might derive some, some sense of the program as a unit, from doing that?"

"Why. . . ." Could Steve be offering something specific?

"I suppose you could use the eight hundred bucks, but that's beside the point. Or is eight hundred bucks ever beside the point? I know you're not a writer, Tom. I'm not sure that matters. Sometimes a writer's beside the point." He stopped, as if waiting for Tom to say yes or no.

"I must have lost you, Steve," Tom said. "Do you have an actual script in mind you want me to try?"

"Yes," said Steve. "Carole. *Carole of the Comet*. Did you ever see it? Don't. You have the intelligence to derive the formula from reading one script; hell, half a one. Why don't you write one? Be scared to? I'll take this chance you can do it: I'll pay you half, even if we don't use it . . . and then you'll have an idea what the elements are, even in a bad show. Do you think I don't know Carole's bad? They didn't swing us out of evening prime time just because they hate me, which they do. But we've still got that afternoon audience to win, Tom, and we need a fresh element in the scripts. Believe it or not, there's good-bad, as well as bad-bad. We need new good-bad. You want to take a pile home with you, fool with it, see what you come up with? Say no if you don't want to, Tom, don't give me a reason, just say no."

A buzzer sounded. Steve flicked the intercom button.

"Mr. Cassidy is here for the meeting," said a soft, secretarial voice.

Steve flicked the button over and spoke into the box. "Put a pair of handcuffs on Cassidy and send him in," he said. "The bastard always puts the left-over cigarettes in his pockets." Steve stared moodily at the full cigarette boxes, in leather, standing open on the table. "You don't have to answer today," he said to Tom. "Think it over."

Tom was trying to think what Steve's offer really meant; probably a reduced production budget now that the show was daytime, and the regular writers wouldn't take the cut, didn't need to, could work elsewhere.

"I'd like to try it, Steve," Tom said, almost doubting, after the way Steve's voice filled the room, that his own was carrying across the table.

Steve turned on his intercom again. "Somebody get a pile of Carole scripts, and put them in an envelope for Tom Beniger," he said. Then: "Hello Cassidy, you crook."

Cassidy, a thin man with a high voice who worked for the advertising agency which stood between sponsor and producer, said: "What do you mean crook? Steve, you say I'm a crook?"

"Me?" Steve shook his head. "No, I didn't say that. You may be the only man I know I wouldn't say that to, you know it, Cassidy? I'm a crook. Men are crooks. Those loyal little girls who sit at typewriters in the outer office, worshipping you and me in their innocence, are crooks. But Cassidy, you're, how shall I say it? One of the pure in heart. I can count all the pure in heart I've ever known on the fingers of one dishonest hand, and you're the only one I've ever dealt with in television. I mean it. You know Tom Beniger?"

Every week, at the meeting, Steve introduced Tom and Cassidy to one another as if they'd never met.

"How're you, Tom?" Cassidy said. "Steve, you're a great man."

"No, I'm not," Steve said. "But I know why you say it. It's because you're a kinetic personality, Cassidy. People with tongues a foot thick are eloquent in your presence. I never find myself with you without feeling I'm a bigger, smarter, rangier man than

322

I thought I was. Cassidy, if I were rich, I'd implore you—not that you'd consider it—to join me so that this firm could have the benefit of being directed by the man I become when I'm around you."

"Steve," said Cassidy, "humility is the finest coat that greatness owns. . . ." They addressed these things to one another with such a scrupulous absence of irony that its absence became ironic.

Someone else opened the door. It was Phoebe Andrews, representing the sponsor. With her was Gus Forhan, who emceed *Golden Words.* Just after them came Paul Wuss, the writer on the show, and after him Ned Kildeer. Tom was slightly embarrassed to see him.

"Ned Kildeer." Steve pointed at him. "Ned Kildeer. Stand still a minute. These are your colleagues. This is Ned Kildeer, our new director."

"How do you do?" Kildeer said. Three others, minor functionaries, not important enough to have the privilege of arriving early, came in; it was just six.

"You all know why we hired Ned," Steve said. Everyone took seats. "Shall I be tiresome and recapitulate? May I indulge my vice of garrulity to that extent? You all know Ned's contribution to the evolution of the dramatic show. Without him, they'd still be shooting them with one camera. Ned is one of the most resourceful users of the camera in the field. He is convinced that he can make our show more exciting, visually, and I believe that if we give him scope, he has the eye, the imagination, the intensity to do it. You've seen the show, Ned?"

"Oh, yes," said Ned. His public look, the look of frightened poise, was back. "And many of the kinescopes."

"And been in the studio?"

"Yes. Last week."

"Do you want to tell us anything, yet?"

"No. Not yet," Kildeer said.

"All right," Steve said. "Now you've all seen the ratings for last week's show. Were they bad? Considering that there was a big color show on the other network. . . . Does someone want to take that position?"

They looked back at him, nine people around the table. Cassidy and Phoebe Andrews were his antagonists, of course, and probably had prepared something together. But they didn't look at one another; whatever it was, the time had not come for it. Nobody spoke.

Steve, apparently, was not going to let them pick their own moment.

"How did you feel about last week's show, Cassidy?" He asked.

"I'd say . . . it was a very characteristic episode of a very high grade quiz," Cassidy said, not yielding.

"How did the sponsor feel, Phoebe?"

Phoebe went for the bait. "The show dragged," she said.

"Perhaps Steve would agree that it's in the nature of our present formula that we have an . . . occasional slow moment, Phoebe?" Cassidy said.

Argument developed along these lines. Agency had long felt that the contestants ought frequently to be celebrities; sponsor had been persuaded, up to now, that the solution was to find more colorful, unknown contestants. It looked as if sponsor might be going to agency's point of view; Steve, who had held for the status quo, moved to hold sponsor against agency. The addition of celebrities would give more control to the agency, since there would be less interviewing and searching among the unknown, a producer's function.

"More colorful people. Yes. Fresh people, yes." Steve said. "I'm perfectly willing to step up the interviewing, and will tomorrow if you say the word." More interviewing, on the same budget, would mean that increased work hours would have to be charged against Steve's general overhead. "We now process six hundred letters a week, and interview thirty people to find four. Want us to step it up, we'll interview a hundred to find four. We'll devise new methods of getting leads—the classified sections; have a casting director monitor the other quizzes, talk to more people. But I'm against having celebrities on the show and I'll tell you why. It destroys one of the most interesting points to be made about the quiz show, destroys it, yet it's a point that's never been made and maybe we ought to start trying to make it." He was going now into a high degree of pitch. "Now look: read the columns, the editorial pages, listen in on meetings of civic groups—what do you hear? They all despise the quiz show. But what are they for? Educational television. Why don't those people stop and think? What gives them education on television? What dramatizes facts, learning, scholarship? The quiz show. Not only that, not only dramatizes education, but drives home a crazy, wonderful

324

American moral—something no college ever dared to claim—that learning pays big money? Our educational value, our public service value, is just as big as our entertainment value—and the quiz show is the closest thing to a guaranteed half hour of unfailing entertainment the American viewer has."

It carried, for the moment anyway. The educational TV pitch interested Phoebe Andrews, and would be repeated to management at the sponsor's offices. She wondered if the idea should be offered to the public through direct incorporation in the commercials. Cassidy, representing agency, was much against yielding any selling time to institutional build up of the program itself, and Steve mediated by suggesting indirect incorporation in the emcee's chatter and by planting remarks for the contestants to make, unrehearsed.

This was not paradox. It was easy to plant an unrehearsed remark. By the time a contestant, having been selected, was prepared, through an afternoon of further interviews on his opinions, by Gus Forhan and the staff, his opinions could be made to resemble almost anything; even wording would be suggested to him in such a way that he thought the phrase he had been admired for was of his own coinage, and would repeat it on the air. Paul Wuss, the writer, was directed to work this out with Gus, and the meeting got to its specific business, which was planning questions for the coming program.

"What have you got, Tom?" Steve asked.

"Well, for categories . . . history always seems to go pretty well. I thought maybe Byzantine history."

"Sounds fancy," Phoebe Andrews said.

"Could be one of the ones nobody ever chooses," Paul Wuss remarked.

"Let's hear the words," said Cassidy. "What are they, Tom?"

"The easy word would be Caesaropapism," Tom said, and there was a laugh.

"That's the *easy* one?" The assistant director said.

"Well it's easy because all you have to do is think about it to figure out the meaning," Tom said.

"Sure," said Steve. "What other words in the category?"

"Wait," said Phoebe. "I'm dumb. I want to hear what it means."

"Well, it describes the situation in which the emperor makes himself head of the church," Tom explained.

"Oh. Caesar and pope," said Paul Wuss.

Phoebe frowned. "What other words on this Byzantine history?"

"Ecumenical," Tom said. "And Iconodule."

"I'll bet they're both religious," Phoebe said. "Doesn't ecumenical mean something like Catholic?"

"Well, it means universal," said Tom. "Just as Catholic does. But it isn't as specifically religious in connotation. You're right about iconodule."

"Is it the opposite of iconoclast?" Paul Wuss guessed.

"Yes. It's the hard word," Tom said. The words in a category were graded according to difficulty. "The Iconodules were more or less the winning sect, the Iconoclasts the losers until the Reformation."

"We can't use it," Phoebe said. "Catholic reaction."

"But they're just interesting words," Tom said. "I mean we're not recommending Caesaropapism, or endorsing the Iconoclasts, any more than we were recommending parricide in the crime category. . . ."

"Phoebe's right," Cassidy said. "We got mail on the crime category."

"What's next, Tom?" Steve asked.

Tom had prepared the Byzantine history category pretty much with the idea that it would give them something to turn down. Now he would offer one they'd be sure to like. "Category is Superstitions," Tom said. "I'll give you the hard word first. Traikaidephobia."

Once again they laughed.

"I love it," said Phoebe. "What is it?"

"Fear of the number thirteen," Tom said. Everybody loved it, and they accepted that category with its words, and the next set he had done as well. The next one he had was another of the ones he'd included for probable rejection; setting these up was something he had learned he had to do, because if it was given nothing to criticize, the meeting would feel useless and begin to throw out perfectly sound categories, but he hadn't read this next one. It had the word "homunculus" in it, and he'd anticipated someone saying they didn't dare, a contestant might guess it meant a fairy; it was, of course, Ned Kildeer's presence that led to Tom's omission. They spent something over an hour considering Tom's words, and then more time on some Paul Wuss had found.

326

At one point Phoebe interrupted. She had a word she wished they'd find a category for and two other words to surround it. It was antimony. She loved it because an overeager contestant would probably confuse it with alimony and miss; and if he didn't, and knew it at all, he would probably call it a metal.

"It looks like metal," Phoebe said, triumphantly. "It's used in metallurgy. But it's really crystal."

Phoebe was always for trick words. She took the contest aspect personally—it was Phoebe, in behalf of the sponsor's purse, against the contestant. Tom, who didn't mind supplying words of honest difficulty, disliked trying to deceive. He suggested that alimony had unpleasant connotations, should the error be made, and Phoebe withdrew the word.

The meeting went on to production matters, and Tom and Paul Wuss withdrew and went to another office where Tom turned over his notes, and they spent a little time drafting questions. This completed Tom's evening of work. Tomorrow he would confer with Gus Forhan, the emcee, about pronunciation; he would also recheck the etymology on the words which had just been approved, and on those Paul had brought in, and make certain, through consulting British dictionaries, that there were or were not permissible alternate spellings. Then he would be ready for the rehearsal and the show the following Monday.

When Tom and Wuss were finished, the writer went back to consult about chatter requirements, and Tom was free to go. He felt pretty tired; he started, with his head down, through the reception room, now dim, unaware that anyone was there.

"Tom, er Tom."

He stopped. Ned Kildeer was rising from one of the couches.

"Hi," Tom said.

"I thought you might like to get some coffee, or a drink."

"Let's do," Tom said.

"Do they always take so long over this?" Kildeer asked. "I didn't eat first."

"Neither did I," Tom said. "I never have any appetite before hand. I hate to say it but it was a short one tonight." He remembered that this slight man with the big, fast, slightly frightened eyes, hadn't spoken once since being introduced at the beginning of the meeting, three hours earlier. "I can't believe meetings are a very efficient way to work."

"No." They had walked into the corridor together, and now

327

Ned Kildeer smiled. "You gave them that Byzantine history thing just to chew up, didn't you?"

"Yes," said Tom, feeling less and less constraint with Ned. "So much of what goes on there is a formality. They know I give them the first category to chew on; if I didn't, I'd fail them somehow. It's like the flattery game that Steve and Cassidy play with one another. . . ."

"Cassidy's quite good at it, isn't he?" Ned said.

"Almost a match for Steve," Tom said. "Sometimes he even stops him."

They stopped at the elevators and rang. "I'm sorry I ran off yesterday," Ned said. The elevator came and they got into it. It was just nine o'clock, and the building, like the night time operator, seemed out of uniform. "I was interested in what you said—about your wife's being pregnant."

"Thanks," Tom said. "I understood that you had to go. I saw someone waiting. . . ."

"My friend," said Ned; there was a wisp of bitterness in his voice.

Then, as the car stopped and they walked away from it, Ned said, as abruptly confidential as Tom himself had been the evening before:

"I'm in love with an absolutely impossible boy."

Across the street were a bar and a cafeteria. Tom had half decided to have a drink and go on over to Ellen's. Now he changed his mind and decided to eat with Ned.

6.

Shortly after nine o'clock, Ezra Held took Ellen aside and said drunkenly that Tessie was pretty plastered, could they get her just a little something to eat?

"Just a marshmallow, or a little sandwich, or something," Ezra said, whispering confidentially into Ellen's ear in the television room, almost falling on her, ogling and smiling and shifting around, like a man about to initiate a cuddle.

"All right," said Ellen. "All right." It was her impression now that she had spent the entire day in the kitchen cooking, that it was still mid-cocktail time, and that there was no possible solution

328

to the mystery of where all the salted nuts, the crackers, the cheese spread and potato chips she had put out earlier might have gone. She wanted to sit with her guests.

But Ezra, leaping and whinnying like a lascivious pony, crying, "here we go . . . here we go . . . quietly, quietly . . ." pushed her towards the kitchen. "Don't look for us back. Here we go. Oh, boy," Ezra cried over his shoulder to the others, and Ellen, pretty plastered herself, was not so much so that she didn't realize that the more show he made of it, the less apt he was to make a pass at her in the kitchen—nothing she particularly wanted to have happen; but it did seem a sort of stupid performance if all the man wanted was a marshmallow for little Tessie Marshmallow. . . .

A burst of frantic seven o'clock effort had got the meal on. Everything was cooking along now. She went to the bread-box.

"Always keep the marshmallows in here," she said, taking out a slice of bread and putting it in the toaster. "Toast it for her."

Ezra crowed with laughter and danced around "Ellen-y Walleyes," he cried. "You are the cutest little hostess. Here." He stopped by the row of bottles on the kitchen counter. "I'm going to fix you a little drink for that. Yes I am." He put too much whiskey into a glass with ice, cocked his head towards it, said it looked just about right, almost right, splashed in a little more, cried "There!" snatched the glass up as if Ellen had tried to grab for it, crying: "No. No. Water first, Must have water." Then he carried the glass gingerly over to the sink, muttering at it, picked up a teaspoon, filled the spoon, drop by drop with water from the faucet, and solemnly transferred the water from spoon to glass.

"There," he said. "Now."

Ellen laughed, and the toast popped up. She spread it with butter and peanut butter, and offered it to Ezra for his wife.

"No, no, you give it to her. She'll get mad at me if I try to give it to her. Go ahead," Ezra ducked and smiled. "Cutest little hostess." He preceded her and opened the swinging doors ceremoniously between dining alcove and television room. Ellen came along, bringing the toast, leaving the drink he'd made her behind; she wanted a drink but not that drink. My God, not that one. . . .

In the living room Ellen found that Tessie, through flirting with

329

Harrison, had induced him to take his glasses off. That was okay with Ellen, and she gave Tessie the toast with a casual smile so that she could drift way and not interrupt them.

"What's this for?" Tessie giggled.

"Better eat it honey," Ezra said anxiously, bouncing up as Ellen stepped aside. "Dinner won't be for a few more minutes."

"What is it? Something to eat?" Harrison asked, groping around, pretending that being without his glasses made him helpless. The blind man's hand landed on Tessie's bottom for a moment and everybody laughed at Harrison's expression, even Eddie.

"Get that guy a sign and some pencils," Eddie said. "He's in trouble."

"Eat the toast, honey. Oh, eat it," Ezra sang, but Tessie swung to Eddie.

"Trouble?" she asked, holding the toast in front of her face like a fan and peering around it at him. "What do you call trouble, Mr. Farmer?" And she sat down on Eddie's lap; Eddie received her impassively, but Ellen didn't like it. Ezra began trying to persuade Tessie to take just a tiny bite of toast. Finally she put tooth marks into the peanut butter and then held it up for all of them to see that she had drawn Ezra's picture. Then she jumped up to help Harrison look for his glasses, putting the toast aside. A moment later Ellen saw Eddie pick up the toast quietly and finish it.

"Eddie, dear. I'm sorry," Ellen said, sitting by him. "You hungry?"

"Always hungry," Eddie said, shifting away slightly. Sometimes, to be just a little bit mean to him, Ellen would be just a little bit affectionate in public.

"We'll eat in a few minutes," Ellen said. "Awful sorry, Eddie."

"Don't break up about it," Eddie said, and got up. "Get you a drink?"

7.

"My dear," Guy said. "If you prefer, we can do many other things."

"No," said Dorothy. "I like to do what you like to do. Let's see your friends."

330

"All right," said Guy. "That's very nice."

He was being attentive to her, but he was very bored. He had almost hoped she'd say she'd rather not go out to Brooklyn, so that he could provoke a quarrel. The famous bosom rose and fell across the table from him, half-bared, tightly held in, and it was probable that most men in the restaurant must have recognized it, might well be yearning to seize the top of the dress, pull down and expose it, bury their faces in it, nibble, caress; and, Guy thought wearily, why doesn't one? If he so yearns, let him do it; he will have his dream, and what will the heroism of seizing it cost? Being hit by me, being thrown out of this place; a night in jail, a hundred dollar fine, perhaps a story in the papers, perhaps not. It would be a story that the restaurant, Dorothy's press agent, his own, for that matter—for Guy had a press agent, now, not to seek space for Guy but to keep the mentions pleasant—none of these functionaries would want the story used. Maybe the dreamer would get away with it completely, Guy would miss the punch, the restaurant would put the dreamer out gently, Dorothy would run to the ladies' room to sew—that was the minimum cost, and the maximum was not much greater. Guy looked around the room, wishing he could see such a hero, and smile encouragement. Several pairs of eyes which had been directed at Dorothy turned back to their plates.

All right, cowards, said Guy, I will show you what I think of your dream; I will let the ash on this cigarette get very long, and I will reach across the table and drop off the ash into the bosom, let it disappear in cleavage, smiling, and she will only look embarrassed and try to pass it off. How will you like that, dreamers, heroes? He would not do it, of course; nor would he lead expeditions, command revolutionaries, fight duels, swim the Hellespont for love. No; he would only take Dorothy Conn to visit the Walles in Brooklyn, and tomorrow he would do some other inadventurous thing, and on the next day, some other.

"Guy," Dorothy said. "When you look at me that way, I just melt."

He raised his glance to the china blue eyes, floating above the bosom and almost as famous; "Yes, Dorothy," he said.

Behind her he saw a producer they both knew coming towards their table. He dislikes me, Guy thought; he will never take Dorothy out because he has a wife he is terrified of. But he wants

331

to be seen talking to us. And Dorothy will not mind being seen talking to him. And I cannot mind, I am not entitled to. I have made this for myself and will not break its rules.

"Robin," Dorothy said to the producer, who was offering her a flower he had picked out of the vase on the next table over. "Oh, you crazy thing, they'll sue you." She had a slightly addled personality that she slipped into with other theatre people, slipped into it quite unconsciously and out again the moment she and Guy were alone. "Oh, I love it." She leaned past Robin, and spoke around him to the people from whose table the flower had been taken. "You don't mind do you? If I have your flower? It's so beautiful."

The people said no, of course not, Miss Conn, and Robin stood there chatting with them for a moment. Robin asked them to come along with him to a party Guy and Dorothy had already declined, and they declined again. Robin left. Guy said:

"My dear, if you would like to go on with Robin to Henry's party, I will go out to my friends for a little and come later to Henry's to pick you up." If she accepted, he would not pick her up; he would let her find someone at Henry's party, and that would provoke the quarrel, and it might be interesting to try to make it up, tomorrow.

"No," Dorothy said. "I'd rather be with you."

She was relentlessly inoffensive. She was inexorably sweet. He called the waiter and asked for his check, ordered his car brought around to the front. He made himself a promise that he would be nice to Dorothy tonight.

He asked if she would like a liqueur, and she said no, she didn't want to be high when she met Guy's friends.

8.

At nine forty five the roast was done, and Ezra Held, who had conceived the idea that his hostess was suffering terribly from embarrassment because the dinner was late, urged Ellen to forget about the potatoes.

"They won't know, ever know, they were going to have any . . . any p'tatoes. . . ." He snickered at his inability to say the word.

332

"Tater totters, Mizz Hostess . . ." he said, and seized Ellen around the waist and danced a few steps with her.

"No, they'll get done onna topuva stove," Ellen said, laughing and pushing herself away. "Look, I'm going to set this bell, little timer bell, when it rings, all done. . . ."

She went back into the living room; Ezra waited for a second and slyly turned the flame higher under the potatoes. Then he set the timer bell to go off in ten minutes instead of fifteen. When he went through the television room, Ellen and Harrison were having a low-voiced quarrel about something, and Ezra pretended not to see them. In the living room, Eddie the farmer was going around picking up and draining glasses which had liquor left in them and Tess was trotting around after him, admiring him. That seemed like a pretty good game, so Ezra tried to see how many glasses he could find to finish, too, and then Tess admired both of them. Ezra heard the bell go off in the kitchen and charged back into the television room, right up to the Walles whose quarrel seemed to have died down a little—Ellen was turned away from Harrison and he was holding her arm; Ezra charged merrily right up to her and pushed her along with his shoulder towards the kitchen saying,

"Bell, Ellen. Tater bell."

"Just a minute," Ellen said. "Drink. I got to get my drink," and went towards the living room with Harrison following.

"No drinks," Tessie cried. "Eddie finished them all," and Eddie said:

"I finished them. All of them."

Ezra felt a momentary hurt because his wife and Eddie weren't acknowledging that Ezra had helped with the joke; then Harrison went to the kitchen and brought bottles and the ice bucket back and they made some new drinks, and about ten minutes later Ezra remembered the bell again. . . .

He went to Ellen and said:

"Remember. P'tatoes are done?"

"Oh, God," Ellen said. "Come on. They're probably burned."

They ran to the kitchen, and there was Sheila, the Walles' girl. She had taken the potatoes off and was cooking some frozen string beans. The kitchen clock said 10:40.

"I thought I'd better help finish," Sheila said, and Ellen hugged her daughter. Then Ellen said as soon as she made gravy they'd be

333

ready, and Ezra fussed around with them, helping carry things to the table. The meat was kind of cold but he didn't suppose anyone would notice; he broke off a little piece of crisp fat from the outside and ate it and it was delicious.

Sheila, who was in boy's pajamas with a shirt button missing, little bubbies kind of peeking around the corner, and looking very cute that way, came in, and he broke off another piece of fat and said, "Shhhh!" and gave it to her. Then he went chuckling into the living room, and called the others. This time Tess was sitting on Harrison's lap, and Eddie the farmer was telling them that the theory of economic cycles was a great big syllogistic cyle of slop, Q.E.D., and Harrison was applauding with his arms coming up under Tess's arms and the hands clapping together right in front of Tess's bubbies—maybe touching them a little. Ezra persuaded them to come eat, and Eddie the farmer, who must be carrying a tremendous load of liquor by now, started saying something about Guy Cinturon, whom he'd known at college apparently, but Ezra lost the sense of it.

When they were all sitting down and Harrison was doing an awful job of carving, without his glasses, which he said he was never going to wear again, Tess got a little bit shirty with Ellen and said Ezra couldn't eat rare meat, it didn't agree with him. Ezra said "Shhh!Shhh!Shhh!," he'd been planning to ask for the outside slice anyway, but Ellen put some slices back in the oven for him, and they all lay around in their chairs waiting with their drinks, and Ezra kept telling Ellen that he didn't remember, just didn't remember, when he'd ever had such a marvelous time. Finally they were served. Tess held up a slice of beef in front of her face as if it were a fan, and peered around it, giggling, first at Harrison, then at Eddie the farmer. Harrison was eating very fast, cramming food into his mouth, and Eddie was going after it more steadily but just as woozily. Ellen had pushed her plate away untouched and was drowsing. Suddenly there wasn't much conversation or life, and Ezra said to himself that it was after eleven, he had to go turn on the television set because the Price Company's now process tile was being introduced tonight, and his firm, an investment bank, had a big piece of Price Company, and Ezra meant to see how this new product was introduced in the commercial which would follow the eleven o'clock news.

334

So he wandered away from the table, feeling that he'd had his dinner, and went looking for the TV.

Then a bell rang out in the hall, and Ezra went out and picked up the telephone and said:

"Walles' Amusement Park. Good evening," but there was only the hum of the dial tone for answer. Maybe the door.

He hung up, went to the door. Better luck. A beautiful woman with a stole around her shoulders, quite familiar looking. Man, tall man, behind her.

"Walles' Amusement Park," Ezra said, throwing the door wide, knowing he ought to remember who they were. "Get your tickets. Checking on the right. . . ."

"Mr. Held?" The man said. "I'm Guy Cinturon."

Ezra shook hands, trying to pull himself together, and was presented to Dorothy Conn.

A low bow was the only way to atone for not having known who she was, Ezra felt, so he began to execute the bow and fell down on the floor.

9.

Guy would have helped the man up and left immediately, before anyone else had seen them, but just then Sheila came running down the hall in boy's pajamas and threw herself into his arms.

"Guy," she squealed, clinging to him. "Oh, please come in. Hello, Miss Conn. I'm Sheila."

"You're the girl who's going to be an actress," Dorothy said, and smiled very nicely. Held finally had himself picked up and was bustling away, presumably to tell the rest.

"Oh, I don't know," Sheila said. "Come in. Come on. Everybody's drunk and awful."

Ellen and Eddie had appeared in the living room doorway. Guy could see that Ellen was in her dreamy, wandering state; Eddie pushed past her and punched Guy on the arm. At least, Guy thought, Eddie would still be fairly sober, but evidently not, for when Guy presented him to Dorothy, Eddie just stared and said:

"Jesus."

Sheila was hanging onto Guy's arm, and he thought: she's the

335

only thing worth coming over here to see; he thought the same thing all over again when they entered the living room. There was Harrison looking foolish without his glasses and wearing quite a bit of lipstick, probably Mrs. Held's. And Mrs. Held, Tessie, was worst of all, pushing Sheila aside and putting her arms around Guy, ignoring Dorothy, saying that now she could tell people she'd embraced Guy Cinturon.

Sheila was looking at him sympathetically, a little roguishly, and Guy nodded; the girl was doing him good. Without that look, he would have stiffened altogether and perhaps made excuses and left. He smiled at Sheila; yes, they were funny and disgusting. Yes, he would stay and watch them with her. Tessie intervened again; she said she was going to sit on Guy's lap. Guy remained standing. Harrison, perhaps because his glasses were missing, was ignoring Dorothy, keeping after Tessie. Eddie had sat down across the room and continued to stare at Dorothy, and shake his head.

Dorothy said to Ellen: "What a beautiful place you have," and Ellen smiled at her rather vaguely.

"The lady speaks to you, mother," Sheila said, in an odd, harsh voice thrusting herself back on Guy's attention; her voice has changed, Guy thought, it sounds like a boy's. "Will you not answer her?"

"What?" Ellen asked.

"Sheila," said Harrison reprovingly.

"Father, I obey you," Sheila said, and bowed her head to him, crossing her feet and posing.

"What's got into you?"

"Sheila." Eddie got up. "Hey, Sheila. . . ."

"Nothing, nothing," Sheila cried, flinging her arms out. "This company goes to my head. It's too much beauty." She walked, overgracefully, across to where Guy was standing, sank down and sat on the floor at his feet, resting her head against his knee. "You see, I'm quiet now. Go on, go on. . . ."

There was a chair behind Guy. He sat, putting a hand on the girl's head. "Up kind of late tonight, Sheila," he said. She jerked her head away from under his hand, throwing her hair back, and fixed her eyes brightly on his face.

"Oh, much too late. Much, much too late," she said, in that same deep voice. He noticed that a pajama button was missing from her shirt, smiled, and reached out his hand to touch her

336

shoulder. Eddie was staring at them; so, for that matter, was Dorothy Conn. Before Guy's hand reached her, Sheila bounded to her feet and backed away.

"Don't you want to ask Miss Conn about the stage, sweetheart?" Eddie asked, sounding somewhat sober now.

"Yes," Ellen said. "I'm sure Miss Conn. . . ." Her voice trailed off, and she looked at Dorothy. Dorothy smiled encouragingly at Sheila.

"Oh, yes, Miss Conn," said Sheila. "Please. Please tell me all about the stage," and the girl smiled brilliantly and ran from the room.

"What a strange little girl you have," Dorothy said to Ellen, in the silence.

She's not so strange," Eddie said.

Harrison, it seemed, hadn't lost his glasses after all. He was taking them out of his pocket now, releasing Tessie Held's waist, putting the glasses on.

"She can't stand excitement . . . very well," Ellen said, uncertainly.

"Shall I go speak to her?" Harrison now offered.

Eddie, who had taken a step or two towards the rear of the apartment, turned back and sat down.

"No," Ellen said. "She'll . . . she'll calm down. It must be seeing Guy . . . and Miss Conn. . . ."

"I can understand that," Ezra Held said, leering at Dorothy. Dorothy looked automatically for Tessie when this happened, and smiled. But Tessie was already circling Guy again, and Harrison had put the glasses back in his pocket and was circling Tessie, and Ellen was looking vague again and circling the room. Ezra, who had poured liquor, left a glass off with Guy, and was jouncing in now to deliver the other glass to Dorothy.

Guy, trying to get the image of Sheila out of his mind, got up and sat by Eddie.

"How'd you come out last year, Eddie?" He asked. He hadn't seen Eddie since fall.

"Good," Eddie said. "I had a hell of a crop, and prices stayed up."

"You'll be a rich man yet," Guy said.

"I'm making it back," Eddie said. "My old lady kicked off last month and she hadn't spent it all up, for a wonder. Hey . . . I tell you about going down to Florida?"

"No," Guy said.

In January. About six weeks before she died. My old lady was a big lush, you know, and crazy about the boys right up to the time she went."

"It always amazes me that you can speak of your mother so," Guy said, but he felt no offense—merely, as he had said, a certain amazement.

"You didn't know my mother," Eddie said. "Listen, I'm being kind." Guy smiled. "Anyway, there was always some boy; when I went down I'd had a letter from this lawyer asked me to sign a release he's got drawn up in favor of one of ma's gigolos, so he can get some dough out of the will when she dies. And I also get a letter from Ma, first time she ever wrote me a letter in her life. 'Dear Eddie: Don't sign anything.' The lawyer and the gigolo had her terrified, and she had some other punk by then she wanted to give her dough to . . . well, I went to Florida. . . ."

Tessie Held screeched, and came flouncing in from the television room, where she and Harrison had gone to watch a late movie with the lights off. Harrison followed, putting on his glasses again. Nobody paid much attention, and Tessie sat down by Ezra. Harrison came to join Guy and Eddie. Ellen was still wandering.

"Anyway, I went to Florida," Eddie said. "And knocked some heads together. Cleaned them all out—Christ, the lawyer and the gigolo were both living with my old lady when I get there. The other punk's hanging around the corner, trembling. I hired her a bodyguard."

"You didn't?" Guy said.

"Sure," said Eddie. "I didn't want to stay and keep doing the job myself. I got this private detective for twenty bucks a day, and he did a great job. So anyway, I'm about eight grand richer. . . ."

"That's all that was left?" Guy asked.

"Well," Eddie squirmed a little. "Well, this punk that was nice to her, the one she wanted to leave some to. I sent him a check, after all. I mean, he kind of earned it."

"How much?"

"Five grand," Eddie said.

Tessie came and stood in front of Harrison. "Let's watch some more of the picture," she said. "And have a drink."

338

"You won't get scared again?" Harrison asked, a little too broadly.

"Ezra and Dorothy want to see it, too," said Tessie and took Harrison away.

Eddie called to Ellen to come and sit with them; she did. But heaven knew what Ellen was thinking of or hearing. She seemed comfortable at being with them, and quite occupied with whatever it was that was in her mind. Once she said,

"It's a nice party, isn't it? I wish Tom had come."

Otherwise Guy felt free to talk to Eddie as if she hadn't been there; Eddie seemed sober enough now, Guy thought, or maybe it was only that he, Guy, was a little looser. He was on his third drink.

"Eddie," he said. "You at all interested in painting?"

Eddie said sure.

"There's a crazy deal cooking that might appeal to you," Guy said.

"Investment?"

"Yes."

"Everything you ever gave me was good," Eddie said. "Christ those Mexican export loans made me more dough in a year than cabbage does in five."

"This is wild," Guy said. "Really wild." And he told Eddie about Ernest Goswith: Goswith was an idiot, Guy said, maybe an idiot savant. Not that bad, really, but an awful guy. The one thing he could do was paint. Goswith was two kinds of painter: he was a very bad contemporary painter, with a studio full of unsold work, derivate of each successive fad of modern art for the last twenty years. He was fiercely proud of these, and considered himself a master. Meanwhile, however, Goswith had had to make a living. Loathing the society that rejected his serious painting, he had done so by supplying pornographic drawings and paintings to collectors of this kind of material. Now, Guy explained, there was some overlap. Wealthy collectors of serious painting also buy in the pornographic market for their private rooms, and over the years, a collector of taste, or a critic, would see Goswith's work in this vein, and Goswith had begun to achieve an underground reputation as, perhaps, a great painter—but only for his pornography. "You must see it," Guy said. "Much of it is ordinary, of course, but often he will express in one of the paintings some amazing perceptions about sex—the transience of the pleasure, the reduction of the copulating human to a sad, bewildered animal. It is almost a religious feeling. . . ."

"Go on," Eddie said.

"Some people I know, art critics, museum people, collectors, have bought up some of the best of these," Guy said. "We are going to have shows."

"You're kidding," Eddie said.

"No. We will have shows, first in Mexico City, then Paris, then, if it works, New York. A . . . a leading museum has acquired one of Goswith's paintings and will hang it. Critics, several of them, are prepared to testify that Goswith's work is not pornography but great art. . . ."

"You mean you're going to court?" Eddie said.

"Yes."

"You can't win, can you?"

"Not in this country," Guy said. "But those who own paintings for sale while the courts are deciding. . . ."

"Jesus," Eddie said. "What a scheme. The price will go up like crazy, won't it?"

"Yes," said Guy. "The collectors who haven't dared buy Goswith as pornography will have to have him as fine art. We want it spread out. We must not leave any in Goswith's hands or he will sell too soon and ruin the market. Can you take four paintings?"

"What will it cost?"

"Thirty-two hundred dollars. Eight hundred each."

"I don't know," Eddie said.

"Oh, you'll see them first, of course."

"Can I bring Tom to look at them?" Eddie asked. "When it comes to looking at paintings I got two left eyes."

"Sure," Guy said. "I started to tell him the other day . . . but I'm not sure Tom will approve of all the details."

"No." Eddie said. "He won't. But he'll tell me if the paintings are any good."

"All right," Guy said, and Eddie wanted to know how Guy'd gotten onto it, which was a somewhat involved story, starting with Guy's brother in Mexico City.

While they were still talking about it, the others came back

340

from the television room, Tessie saying that Richard Barthelmess was the most exciting man the movies ever had; even Dorothy got involved in the discussion. The party was getting its second start.

10.

". . . this German was sitting right on the hillside with me," Eddie was saying. He was quite convinced that the only reason Dorothy Conn could have had for singling him out to talk to was that she was a wary girl and he was nobody's husband. But he was too cruddy drunk, by now, to care. "So I was holding a carbine on him, trying to decide whether to shoot him in the head."

"Eddie, you didn't?" Dorothy said.

"No, and I've been cursing my yellow-bellied self ever since," Eddie said. "I put him under guard to go back, like a good boy."

"Thank heavens." Tessie was listening, too.

"So he clubbed one guard to death, took off up the hill, and wound up with three hundred rounds of assorted ammunition in him from both sides. There wasn't enough left of him to lift with a fork. I could have had him with one round, and saved my man. . . ."

"Oooh," Tessie said. "Doesn't anybody know a nicer story than that?"

"Get Guy to tell you a story," Eddie said. "He's the one with the stories."

Guy smiled and shook his head.

Ezra Held, who was very drunk, seemed, for some reason, to have decided to resent Guy for his wife's behavior, rather than Harrison who was the one making time with the damn woman. Held said he understood Guy was a celebrated sportsman, *bon vivant,* man about town and *raconteur,* and he thought, by God, Guy oughtta do a li'l' raconting. Tessie sat on the floor, very much as Sheila had earlier, and put her face against Guy's knee; Guy got up and changed seats.

Christ, Eddie thought, what ever got into Sheila? Then he forgot her again as Dorothy Conn started to put the pressure on Guy to tell one of his stories, chiming in with the others and swinging her boobs across Guy's face.

Eddie chuckled, and told Guy to let them have it.

"All right," Guy hit the arm of his chair. "The cat story?"

"Yes," Eddie shouted. "Give them the cat story." He could see that Guyboy the Flyboy had his back hairs bristling at the way the women were crowding him, and he expected a good performance. The cat story was a long yarn about a recently divorced man who had an affair with his cat; the cat was unfaithful; deeply hurt, the man had the cat and kittens destroyed. Subsequently the man had remarried, as Guy reported sadly: ". . . the woman was pretty, a good housekeeper, cheerful, exciting in bed, and he tried to love her, but, as he told me—it wasn't the same thing."

"It wasn't the same thing," Eddie shouted. He loved the line, for some reason, and the story always upset women. Now the women there all reacted against it, Tessie being offended, Ellen saying it was awful. Dorothy looked very hurt.

Ezra rallied to Tessie. Harrison said thickly that the story was ver'ver' interesting. Dorothy got up tensely and got her stole.

Guy was smiling when they left; Dorothy wasn't. She wasn't speaking, either. Eddie hoped he hadn't got his friend in too much trouble with the dame; it had seemed like a funny idea to get Guy to tell the cat story, because that was the kind of mood Guy was in—but since when was Eddie Bissle a pander to Guy's moods?

Maybe it was that actress whore. Jesus, you watched those deep, white things of hers swinging back and forth in the light long enough and you got hypnotized, soft in the cruddy head.

The party was breaking up. It was two o'clock. Ezra, grinning now as if he'd personally run Guy out, was saying they all had to come over for a night cap with the Helds. Harrison wanted to go; Ellen was half-asleep on the sofa. Eddie said he would finish the drink he had and go along back to his hotel. Harrison urged him to curl up in the guest room; Eddie said thanks and declined. Ezra Held shooed Harrison and his wife out of the apartment, twinkly as ever, though Tessie and Harrison were so wrapped in one another's arms as they walked out that it amounted to an ambulatory embrace.

It was Eddie's uninformed opinion that Ezra would watch and twinkle, over at his house while any amount of necking went on, like a benign referee, attentive to the play, watching for fouls; and Harrison would walk back up the street about four A.M. with his nuts aching. That was Eddie's somewhat weary opinion.

342

Now he sat with his shoes off in a large chair, finishing the drink very slowly, thinking how drunk he was, and studying Ellen, who was fast asleep. He felt no lust for her now; he was drunk and he would see her tomorrow. He felt no sentiment at all, and wondered how that could be, how his only feelings for Ellen could be ever re-current lust, followed by indifference.

He got up, soundless in his stocking feet, and walked over next to the sofa so that he could look more closely at her. There ought to have been some tenderness; Eddie felt its lack. Felt a kind of sad and low-keyed anguish at its lack. What tenderness he could summon was reserved to other things, a group of symbols in a gov-ernment box in his bureau drawer: the box, leather-hinged and satin lined, had his Silver Star in it, and Sheila's baby picture Ellen had sent to Italy in the war, and an identification bracelet given to him by the faithless Julia; he thought of Julia with maud-lin reverence, now as if, instead of betraying him, she had died tragically.

He stared at Ellen, wondering why she couldn't be a part of this group of feelings, and moved even closer, thinking that to touch her lightly, on the shoulder, while she slept, would be like a tend-erness.

"What do you think you're doing, Mr. Bissle?"

Eddie spun.

Sheila stood in the archway that led to the television and music room. The girl's voice was cold and angry.

"I don't like you looking at my mother like that."

"I . . . ."

"Where's my father, anyway?"

Eddie struggled for words.

"Did he go over to the Helds?"

Eddie nodded, pointing vehemently towards the door.

Sheila came into the room and sat down. "Listen, can't you see my mother's asleep?"

"Sheila!" Eddie finally choked a word out.

"I'm going to sit right here."

"I . . . I wasn't going to touch her," Eddie said. How could there be such loathing in the girl's voice? How could there? He would, he would . . . fall on his knees to her. He would do any-thing. "Sheila, I wouldn't hurt your mother, sweetheart."

"I'm going to sit here anyway," Sheila said. "I wish you wouldn't call me sweetheart."

"Sheila, I. . . . Oh, Jesus," Eddie said. "Oh, Jesus, good Jesus."

The girl looked at him. "There are your shoes over there if you're looking for them. Why is my mother scared of you?" she asked. And then, as Eddie could neither move nor reply: "You have awfully small feet."

"You have small feet too," Eddie shouted. "You do." I'm so drunk, he thought, staggering a step in the deflation of having said something so stupid; I'm so drunk, or I wouldn't have told that actress whore about the German. When did I ever tell . . . then he caught himself, and thought, with desperate craftiness: I'm so drunk, I could just about, just about . . . Oh, Sheila, honey. You mustn't hate me.

"Don't . . ." he said. "No, don't. . . ."

"Don't what?" Sheila asked, more coldly than ever. "I'm not going to leave you with her."

Then must he tell the girl? Yes, now. Because he could not bear to have her hating him. He would tell her, and she would have to love him, and he was drunk enough . . . a girl had to love her father. Yes.

He took a faltering step towards her. She seemed to look at him more softly, pitying the old drunken, stupid farmer; yes. That would make it easy. Yes. He would tell her, gradually, craftily, hints first, letting her guess it finally for herself . . . and then he would hold her, stupefied with strength and tenderness. He ached to hold her, he was glad. Glad he was drunk enough at last.

"Sheila," he said. "Sweetheart, I . . . I want to tell you . . . I want to tell you goodnight." He picked up his shoes and went slowly away from her, down the corridor.

He figured he could put on the cruddy little leather boats in the hall, and float away, like a turd down the Hudson.

CHAPTER FOUR

1.

LALA BENIGER WROTE to Tom:

Darling:
Here it is March, terribly cold, and I don't mind a bit. The doctor says I have twice as much blood flowing around my bloated body as usual, and it certainly keeps one warm. Are Eskimos terribly prolific?

Her father came into the dining room where she was sitting, writing at the big refectory table.

"Eleven," he said. "What about a glass of port?"

She laughed at him. "The doctor wouldn't like it any better today than he would yesterday," she said.

He turned to go. He was a stout old man, whose mustache had been white so long it was turning yellow, who had never been comfortable with her.

"Sit down, Daddy," she said. "And have your port. I'll have coffee in a moment."

He poured himself a tiny little glass of port; it was like candy to him.

He sat. "Writing to Tom?"

"Yes. Any news for him?"

"Haven't seen the boy in seven years," he said. Tom had come with her to England last time.

Her father looked sad. Perhaps he was thinking of Lala's brothers, both killed flying of course; or perhaps he was thinking that he never had understood Lala's marrying a sergeant. An American—well, if she liked. But a sergeant. Lala could think along with her father on any given topic: a sergeant. Indispensable fellows, of course. Backbone of the army. . . .

Mr. Herald would never understand, really, that Tom could have been a sergeant yet not a professional ranker; he was puzzled that the boy had not chosen to stay with the colors after the war. Stood to reason the fellow wouldn't have made a go of it, trying to become a professor, a journalist. Class was more than a system to old Mr. Herald. It was one of the things you couldn't change in human nature, and wouldn't want to. Solidly fixed by birth, education, career, and in retirement, just in the middle or a hair above, he felt as much comfort, as little resentment that there should be strata above him as he did security in knowing there were strata below him.

Lala quite understood. When she was in England, she felt no great resentment herself; she only yearned for the fluidity of America. And when she was in America, she yearned, a little, for the definition, the knowing where one was and how people would behave, that she felt in England.

"How are you and Buster getting along with the boat?" Lala asked. His father and a crony, a younger man of fifty-odd, were building a boat.

"Oh, does Tom care for sailing?" Her father asked, his mind apparently still on what message he could have for a mysterious, non-commissioned, American son-in-law who now had something to do with a word game on television.

"Oh, yes," Lala said.

"You have a boat, then?"

"No," Lala said. "We don't live near sailing. Sometimes we go out, in the summers, with Tom's friend Cinturon. He charters quite big boats, and we help sail."

"But surely, New York harbor. . . ." How Lala wished Daddy could see America just once, form some images of her life there to replace the confusion that worried him so. "The baby," he said. "Does he still kick sometimes?"

"More and more."

346

"I remember your mother when she was carrying Bert," he said. "Used to say he would have big feet. . . ." He laughed, a wet-eyed, old man's laugh. "I had a nice family, Lala." He sipped at his port. "You must have a nice family." It was not one of the things he would realize, that, in view of Lala's history and since she was thirty-one now, other children were unlikely. Lala said, "Oh yes. I must."

She was thinking, by then, that the remark about the Eskimos was rather too corny, even for her, and that she would start the letter over when her father left the room.

2.

Guy woke too early and couldn't go back to sleep. He was dissatisfied with himself.

At first he thought the dissatisfaction must relate to Dorothy, and he thought back through the car ride, home from the party. He had not felt the liquor particularly; she'd had very little. Dorothy had said nothing until they were going over the bridge, when she asked rather tearfully why he told that awful story. He had chosen not to answer. The silence grew longer and longer. It came time to begin the wiles, the strategems: counteraccusation, coldness, hints of secret cause for anger, to drive her coldly to his apartment, say it was time to have these matters out—the ritual of reseduction. As the silence continued, the moment to initiate this pattern grew more urgent; went. "I think I'll take you home," Guy had said, quietly, and she nodded. They had stopped for a traffic light. He had looked at her; the famous china blue eyes stared back with tears in them; she was really a nice girl, but he had thought of nothing more he could say to her. . . .

Well, he must send Dorothy flowers.

Ellen then. Was the story as offensive as all that? No—he must have told it in a way intended to give offense.

Well, he must send Ellen flowers, too.

Send flowers, send flowers . . . he recognized these imperatives, and the recollections that led to them, as smoke, thrown up in his mind to conceal whatever it was he was truly uneasy about, and waited for the image of real guilt to show through. When it did, it was Sheila in her pajamas and he groaned aloud. He sat up in bed, holding his head in his hands, and groaned again.

Must he acknowledge to himself that this posturing fourteen year-old, who hardly looked like a girl yet, much less a woman, had stirred him more than any woman had in several years? Such a thing had never happened before. The immature had never engaged Guy, even in imagination, except, of course, for Angelica's daughter, the girl whose mother he had tried to threaten with a whip so foolishly—but though that girl had been only fifteen, Guy himself had been only twelve.

He saw Sheila, had seen her, how often? Once or twice a year since babyhood. Had always had an avuncular fondness for her. But last night? He tried to puzzle it out. She had been artificial, that was part of it; given herself a kind of false dimension. And looked at him with a kind of knowingness that must have been false, too. Yet if he saw her again, would she not still have this false, disturbing dimension? And the knowingness? The whole thing was unthinkable. He swung his legs out of bed, his feet onto the carpeting.

He would not, of course, see Sheila herself until this whole ridiculous thing became forgettable. And there should be no trouble at all achieving this. There were, fortunately, in the world, many thin, slight, short, boyish young women, who continued to look and behave as Sheila now did, right into their twenties, even into their thirties. Almost instantly such a young woman came to mind. He would find her, take her to bed, and that would be the end of it. Good.

What was her name?

He had met her at a theatrical party, looking out of place, looking like too far West in Greenwich Village; she had, much as Sheila might in the circumstances, been rather defiant of the sleeker and more successful people who were at the party; she had taken Guy for an actor, and started to scold him when he said he was not studying with anyone. She had been embarrassed when she learned who he was, and made it worse by trying to apologize. She was extremely serious about acting, and felt openly superior to, and at the same time the victim of, the prosperous people with whom she found herself, most of whom were musical comedy players and people on the business side of theatre.

Her name?

It was too early to call the man who had given the party, an agent named Harry Johnson. Guy would have to wait. He put on a pair of shorts, went out on the terrace, and did exercises in the

348

winter sunlight. He came inside and worked on a punching bag on his bedroom wall. When he had worked up a good sweat, he took a shower and got dressed for the day. A breakfast tray arrived every morning at ten, unless countermanded or ordered early, and he was annoyed that he hadn't thought to order it early. He looked in his refrigerator, and there was nothing but that fool champagne. He supposed that with his marvelous new field of interest, it should be Coca-Cola; he should put in some jump ropes and jacks.

Breakfast finally came. He made himself eat slowly. Then, still exerting discipline on himself, he read through the financial section of the *Times* before permitting himself to call the agent. He called the man's office, left his name, and settled down to wait for Harry Johnson to call him back. If he had known this girl's name, and wanted only her address, he would have had the hotel secretary make the call for him, and avoided a certain unpleasantness. It was not embarrassment, for he was deeply indifferent to what a man like Harry Johnson might think of him; rather it was a distaste for exposing himself to familiarities. Perhaps he should simply send Dorothy the flowers, and avoid the whole thing.

He called the florist. He ordered flowers for Ellen; not for Dorothy. A few moments later the phone rang, and it was Harry Johnson returning his call.

". . . a thin girl, very badly dressed, with small, hazel eyes."

"Sounds like anybody."

"There was no one else like her at your party," Guy said.

"Another clue, Doctor," Harry said.

"She tried to find out if anyone would play the guitar. She wanted to sing folk songs. . . ."

"Oh my God," said Harry. "You can't mean little Karen Lord?"

"Yes," said Guy. "That was the name. Thank you."

"She's a real cuckoo, Guy. They call her Lordie Lord."

"Thank you."

"My God. You wouldn't go for that?"

"Thank you, Harry," said Guy, and hung up. It was all he could take from Harry. Now: if Karen Lord were not in the phone book, he would certainly not call Harry Johnson back. He would send flowers to Dorothy, instead. Big pink, waxy camellias for the white vase on her mantle.

But there was a Karen Lord, at a Greenwich Village address, in the phone book.

He dialed the number. It was noon already.

In the middle of the first ring, a girl's voice answered.

"Lordie Lord and Reuben-Shteuben," she said.

"This is Guy Cinturon calling," he said. "Is that Karen Lord?"

"That's what mother calls me," the girl replied.

Guy gritted his teeth. This was going to have to be gotten over quickly.

"I wonder if you'd have dinner with me some night soon," he said. "In fact, the sooner, the better."

Through the telephone he could hear a man's voice rumbling.

"Wait a minute," she said to Guy. And then, turning apparently to the man, "I don't know." Back to Guy. "Who did you say was calling?"

"Guy Cinturon."

"Guy Cinturon!"

The man's voice said, quite audibly, "Oh, for Christ's sake."

"Well this is Princess Margaret Rose, Guy dear," said Lordie Lord. "Let's go change the bloody guard at Buckingham Place, what?"

"Perhaps you don't remember meeting me?" Guy said.

The man's voice said: "Who's the joker? Freddie?"

Lordie Lord's voice said: "I dunno."

"Karen," Guy said. "I've been to a great deal of trouble to find out your name. From Harry Johnson. The last man in the world I enjoy calling up in the morning. . . ."

"Harry would be tough before breakfast," Lordie said. "Is this really Guy Cinturon?"

"Yes. Is it so unbelievable?"

"I feel silly," the girl said. "I told all my friends about meeting you, when was it? Months ago. And they sometimes tease about it . . . well, if it really is you, what's someone like you calling someone like me for?"

"Because I want to take you to dinner," Guy said. "Very much. I . . . I would have called long ago, but I didn't know your name . . . and I wasn't free."

"Would you let not being free bother you?" she asked. "Hey, that's interesting."

The man's voice now came close and said: "Let me talk to him. I'll find out who it is. . . ."

The girl said: "No. It's really Guy Cinturon," and there was, apparently, a scuffle for the phone. "It really is. Stop, Reuben."

Reuben yelled: "What would *he* want?"

"Oh, go sit down," said Lordie Lord, and then, into the phone: "I'm sorry. I'm having trouble with the dog." And she burst out laughing at her own joke.

Why don't I hang up? Guy wondered. He said: "Are you finally convinced? That it's I? And that I want very much to see you?"

"Oh. Yes, I guess so."

"Then can't we set a date? For dinner?"

"Well, I'd love to have dinner with you, Mr. Cinturon—Señor, I'll bet I should say. I mean, I'm very flattered. I really am. But I don't think the boy I live with would like it."

There was a rough guffaw from elsewhere in the room.

"Would it be better," Guy asked rapidly, "if I called you back later?"

"Why. . . ."

"I'll suggest a time, if I may. You have only to say yes or no . . . two this afternoon?"

"No."

"Three?"

"Oh, all right," she said. "Listen you don't have to."

"But I will."

"Hey," she said. "I'm . . . I'm sorry I'm not free."

"Goodbye until three o'clock," Guy said.

"Oh. All right. Goodbye, Señor."

No. He could not possibly call back at three o'clock, Guy decided, hanging up. She had as much as said she would not meet him. She was, also, quite obviously impossible. He would order the pink camellias for Dorothy. But he put off calling the florist. And, in a moment, the phone rang.

For an excited instant, he thought it might be Karen Lord calling back. She could have slipped out somewhere, to a phone booth—but it was only the desk downstairs, saying that Eddie Bissle was on his way up; a moment later, Eddie knocked.

"Hung," said Eddie. "Hung like a crooked picture. You?"

"I didn't have so much to drink," Guy said.

"Do we get Tom and go see this Goswith?" Eddie asked. "You've got me all watered up about it."

"I can't today, after all," Guy said. "Things have come up. You'll still be in town Monday?"

"Yeah," Eddie said. "Okay."

"I thought you were planning to be, for a week?"

"Yeah. I was. Then just now, I was thinking I'd like to get back. . . ." Eddie trailed off. He seemed tired and nervous, now that Guy looked at him.

"Anything the matter?"

"New York gives me the jitters."

"That's all?"

"Guy. Look, all the dames you've had. Did you ever know any that wanted you to beat them? Rough them up?"

"Oh, yes," Guy said.

"You wanted to?"

"Yes," said Guy. "If that was really what they craved. You met such a woman, Eddie?"

"I've known her for years," Eddie said, frowning.

"You beat her?"

"Not exactly. I mean, not like a French whipping novel. But I hurt her, just being rough. And, she seems to like it."

"This pleases and excites you both, there is nothing wrong," Guy said.

"That's what I used to think," Eddie said. "I'll tell you something, Guy—or is this too much of a goddamn bore?"

"No," Guy said.

"I've had damn few women. Most of them I've paid for. Like— oh, the babe that comes out to the farmhouse to clean. I tumble her once or twice a week, fast, no sweat, five bucks a throw. Okay with her, okay for me. No harm done."

"I see," Guy said.

"But this other babe, the one who . . . you know. The one I get rough with. That's all sweat, all excitement. When I was young I figured the way you said—if we both liked it, why not? I guess I'm getting soft, Guy. I still couldn't tell you why, but it makes me feel lousy now; I don't mean I don't get tremendously excited with her, Christ I do. But I feel lousy afterwards; I didn't used to. And I don't know how to tell her that I think we should stop—or whether I can."

"This lady you . . . you see in New York."

"Just spent the morning with her," Eddie said. "Jesus, if you can give me any help with this Guy—I meant to tell her, when she came, just to, well, have coffee with me, and talk it over, and chalk

352

it up to youth and be finished. I couldn't. I got too excited. And I don't think she would have taken no. . . ."

"Maybe you should have a new woman, Eddie," Guy said. "Not a maid you pay."

"Sure," Eddie said. "Easy as that. I haven't made a girl without paying for—" he broke off, and finished the sentence differently than he seemed to have intended—"a long time."

"But I think I'm right," Guy said. "A different woman, whom you could work to please in a different way . . . why not?"

"Got any candidates?" Eddie said, bitterly. "Some babe with a good eye for crud?"

"Yes," said Guy. "What would you say to Dorothy Conn?"

"What?" The suggestion actually shook Eddie. "Me?"

"She'll go out with you," Guy said.

"What for?"

"She liked you."

"Crap me easy," Eddie said. "Jesus, Guy."

"If I write her a note, and tell her you are going to phone, I think she'll go out with you tomorrow night. She had a date with me."

"You're done with her?" Eddie was incredulous.

"We . . . said goodbye."

"Jesus, was it my fault?" Eddie asked. "Getting you to tell that goddamn cat story?"

"No, no," Guy laughed. "I was looking for a way to break with Dorothy. I should thank you."

"What could you tell her that would make her go out with me?" Eddie asked.

"Just . . . you are nice. You have some money. You are lonely."

"Money?" Eddie asked. "You mean there's a price on that?"

"Oh no," said Guy. "There is no purchase. Not even of presents. No, just that she must feel comfortably that you can afford to take her to certain places without it bothering you."

"What places?"

Guy named them.

"Maybe I ought to try it," Eddie said. "What do I do? Just call up and say, 'This is Eddie'?"

"Late this afternoon," Guy said. "After she has my message."

"Oh, to hell with it," Eddie said. "What a goddamn waste of time that would be. . . ."

"Maybe," Guy said. "But I will tell you what you need to know."

"Nice simple language," Eddie said. "She got a button you push or something?"

"Every beautiful creature has a . . . button to push, if only men knew it. The beautiful are the easiest." He smiled. This was a role he liked; the philosopher of sex. After the ambiguous conversation with Lordie Lord, it was gratifying to play it. "You see, one who is beautiful is full of self-love. But: as much love as we have for anybody, there is an equal amount of hate. So the beautiful creature, poor thing, is full of self-hate, too. All you must do is wait for, or perhaps create, the moment when her hate overcomes her love; when she hates herself, she is helpless. Her button is exposed. If you are what is at hand, you are what she needs, because only by having someone make love to her can she persuade herself to love herself again. . . ."

"It sounds so easy," Eddie said. "All you have to be is be a goddamn genius psychologist of women. . . ."

"Do you want to call her? Shall I write the number?"

"Sure," Eddie said, grinning now. "What the hell. Not, to be honest with you, that I expect to work it; but I always wanted to have the kind of date you piss away a couple of hundred bucks on in an evening. It's one of the few stupid things I've never done."

When Eddie had left, Guy spent half an hour, writing and rewriting the message for Dorothy. Then, at last, he felt he had it right; he phoned the florist, gave the name and address, and dictated his composition:

> The flowers are to apologize. I am going away now for a little, because I have forgotten how to be kind. I think you may hear from my old friend, Eddie Bissle, whom you met last night. He is a strange, shy man who owns many acres of Long Island. If you have not forgotten, too, perhaps you will be kind to Eddie.

When the florist had it down, he asked what kind of flowers, and Guy said pink camellias.

Then there was nothing for Guy to do until three o'clock.

354

3.

All right. Eddie would try the actress. Eddie would try anything. The morning with Ellen . . . the miserable morning. Acting like bad children together all their lives. Trying to remake a past that never was. That was the trouble, but he couldn't have explained it to Guy; it might have given the whole goddamn thing away. The way they drank together; the things they talked about; take us to the Rolmer Hotel, twice a year. Make us nineteen again, and twenty-two.

Eddie had never meant the thing to start again, after the war; never even thought about it. Ellen had, she'd said, all the time, during the months of the war she'd spent alone. All the time. But that was the physical stuff Ellen thought about then, the stuff they could both like. Now she thought about something else, about . . . about not dying . . . and the physical stuff, it had to be the same as ever. A kind of ritual. Eddie would have happily let up on her a little, hell, he wasn't a kid from the country any longer, proving his manhood on a New York woman; but there could be no change to easier-going patterns. No. To be less brutal would be the real brutality, now, would be to tell Ellen's body with his own that both communicants were aging . . . it couldn't be very good, for Ellen, renewing, every five or six months, such a lie . . . he didn't propose to start worrying at this point how good it was for Eddie . . . mostly, he wanted to give the thing up because of Sheila last night; he did not want to put the girl in the awful jeopardy, ever again, of finding out.

Crud, crud, crud.

What about that, Big Crud?

Rather than sit around picking his nose, for he had expected to spend the afternoon with Guy and Tom, looking at the paintings, Eddie decided to buy himself a lousy trap, for throwing clay pigeons.

It was one of the reasons for coming into town.

And was there some big, logical, syllogismicruddy preventive. A hole of a sacred cause why he shouldn't roll his revolting little self over to Abercrombie's and buy it?

None. So he did.

And now he could spend the whole spring blowing lead pellets through the air, missing clay birds, at eleven cents a throw for shells and that Puerto Rican Bum up in the sky knew how much for birds.

Eddie could call Big Crud any name he wanted. Eddie had something on Him. Anybody had something on Big Crud who wanted to stop and think. If He was everybody's papadeardaddy, then, when he went after his little daughter Mary, why wasn't it incest?

Maybe someday Eddie'd go too far. Maybe Big Crud would get tired of Eddie's pushing him. Maybe this minute, while Eddie stood at Abercrombie's, waiting for his cruddy change. And that would be all right. Sure. If Big Crud didn't care for Eddie calling Him a Lousy, Incestuous Puerto Rican Bum, why then He was more than welcome to insert Eddie into His Personal Hand Trap, and whirl Eddie into space, and blow hell out of Eddie.

There were times now, had been ever since his mother died, when Eddie felt he'd be glad enough to make the trip.

All right.

4.

Tom was actually hoarse from so much talking. He and Ned Kildeer had sat up until after two, going from the cafeteria finally to the bar next door, each plunging from one confidence to the next. . . .

Tom was writing Lala about it:

> . . . it was a dizzy kind of thing. Ned lives a guarded life, forbidden, apparently, to talk anything but elegant trivialities with this monstrous man he loves. And I don't seem to have talked to anybody since you left, except to Guy about the baby. . . .

It had taken this extraordinary flow of words with Ned to instruct Tom in the answer to a question he had often asked himself: Even with a tolerant wife, who accepted his friends, new or old, why did he not come upon the new ones very frequently; and why did he rarely get as close to them as to the old? And the answer seemed to Tom to be that wives and husband do for one another

356

after marriage one of the great unrealized services for which one depended upon friends before: absorb, be mildly interested in, the great flow of semi-conscious and unfocussed conversation of which so much of human life consists.

We do not talk about particular things any more often than we think about particular things; yet we think and talk continuously, erratically, unconnectedly . . . And a wife or husband, like the friends who preceded them, fills the function of unfocussed listener, not one who cares deeply at all times what we say—that would be unbearable—but one who doesn't mind listening, since he or she will have a turn.

That is why, Tom thought, people who live alone must have someone to phone every day, about nothing in particular, or learn to talk to themselves, or to some god.

That is why a married man who wonders why being married has affected his capacity for making friends, makes a new one every time he is separated from his wife for any length of time. . . .

. . . he told me a great deal about himself: I told him as much about myself, I suppose. Ned grew up in a tough section of the city, was always frail, and hence necessarily acquired a protector. His first was a boy who became a prize fighter, and was subsequently killed in the ring. Ned's pattern, he says, is to enter relationships with men who frighten him in some way—he was terrified of the fighter, who used to come to see Ned even after Ned had broken away from his background and begun the long climb to the intellectual estate. He thinks, and it is curious to hear it put this way, of slum people neither in the stereotype of poor but honest, nor in the other of poor and vicious. He thinks of them as enormously corrupt, almost in the sense of decadent, with a specifically homosexual connotation. I, at least, have tended to think of homosexuality primarily as a product of upper bourgeois, urban life, with a few recruits from the Navy. Ned associates his vice—that's his word by the way, not mine—with poverty; country poverty, especially Southern, he says, produces homosexuals "in absolute droves, Tom, they're arriving every day by the busload and ten at home for every one that gets here." The democracy of decadence. Ned says he is a characteristic example of the metamorphosis: from the rugged background he became (these are all his terms) the young provincial in the world of the arts, his youth overbalancing his gaucherie; acquired elegance by imitation, became an arriviste, finally and genuinely—and this, he says, saved him—found enough creativity in himself to learn to value seriousness (how he hates television); and then made what he bitterly refers to as a marriage.

I suppose that it is his hopeless feeling about the marriage which accounts for Ned's lack of chauvinism about the homosexual. Ned's man is named Hubert; he has managed to obsess Ned with himself sexually and, except for Ned's creative life such as it is, which Hubert doesn't care about, poor Ned is Hubert's creature. Hubert is a great prig, it seems, and wishes Ned to be exquisite at all times.

I asked, perhaps naively, about being cured, by psychiatric treatment, and Ned says he doesn't deny the possibility. But he feels that he has already replaced his fundamental personality structure completely, in undergoing the metamorphosis he speaks of; he has become, in his own mind, a third kind of human being in the world. "Suppose I could be made heterosexual," he said. "Where would I find a set of heterosexual characteristics, a heterosexual outlook? There's nothing of that sort buried in me I want to go back to. How would I know what to become?"

And now I must admit that I don't know how much of it he meant, and how much he said experimentally, just to voice some ideas that had run through his mind and found no previous outlet. A great deal of what I said was in that category, I admit.

Which was to say, odd though the choice might seem, Tom had made a friend.

Well, [Tom had to finish] the important thing is that Ned is coming today to get me started on a television script that Steve is letting me try to write. So now I must stop thinking about you and start thinking about *Carole of the Comet*.

He put the letter aside, neither finished nor unfinished; he no longer wrote separate letters to Lala—wrote one letter, continuing it from day to day, mailing off its installments every day or two. More of the random flow of conversation, he supposed, made less effortless by being put on paper; like keeping a journal.

He began to read the scripts Steve had given him. The formula was not hard to grasp. Carole goes out on an assignment, meets somebody who is in newsworthy trouble, solves the problem, reports back in and breaks a date with her young man in order to write her exclusive story.

There was a sameness about the scripts, as reading matter, a calculated lack of distinction in the dialogue, that made them dreary reading, rather like trying to read the continuity of a poorly done comic strip without having the pictures to look at.

It encouraged Tom, in a way; he thought he could not only do it, he might almost be able to do it better.

He was to begin by thinking of some people with problems for Carole to solve, jot notes, and then consult with Paul Wuss, who, in addition to writing *Golden Words,* was editor for the *Carole* series.

Early in the afternoon he called Paul and said: "Look, I'm such an innocent at this, you're going to have to be pretty patient with me."

"Okay," Paul said.

"I was thinking Carole might go out to do a kind of color story about an organ grinder," Tom said, mentioning the one of his notions which appealed to him most. "And she finds the old man is going to lose his license. . . ."

"Hold it, Tom," Paul said. "That's a marvelous horrible example; it's got at least ten things wrong with it before you say another word."

"Oh," said Tom. "Well, it's a good place to start, then, I guess. Can you tell me the ten?"

"First," said Paul. "This is a live show, not film. An organ grinder works on the streets, outdoors; avoid outdoor sets. Second, he's got a monkey; avoid animals. Third, you'd want to show him with children; avoid children. That one's not absolute, of course, but we don't like using child actors. Fourth, an old organ grinder is a comic Italian; avoid comic foreigners. Avoid old people, too. Fifth, Carole always goes out on big stories; a color job isn't important enough for her. Shall I go on?"

"I'm fascinated to see if there are really ten," Tom said.

"Sixth, loss of a license isn't a sufficiently dramatic problem. Seventh, we might have trouble about music permits. Eighth, there's no violence implicit in the situation. Ninth, there's no danger to Carole herself. Tenth, we did it last week."

Tom laughed. "I love number ten," he said. "What did happen to Carole last week?"

"She uncovered a scandal in the police department," Paul said. "Only it turned out the cop had been framed by gamblers; avoid dishonest cops. What else have you got?"

"I'm afraid most of the things I have are rather gentle," Tom said.

"Avoid gentleness," Paul sighed.

"I did have one . . ." Tom began, tentatively. "Well, the situation works up to a point where Carole is alone with an escaped killer."

"That doesn't sound too bad," Paul said. "Killing take place in the script?"

"Well . . . no."

"That's good. We try to keep the murders down to one a month. What happens?"

"I guess . . . she gets a tip where this guy is hiding," Tom said. "She doesn't tell anyone because she wants to interview him exclusively."

"That's our Carole," Paul said. "Stupidest broad that ever drew breath."

"So she finds him, maybe runs down a series of clues or something. And then, when they're alone, she realizes that if this man is caught he will go to the chair, whether he shoots Carole or not. So he has nothing to lose by shooting her to prevent her revealing the hideout. . . ."

"How does she get out?"

"Tricks him, I guess," Tom said. "I haven't thought just how."

"You're okay for the last ten minutes," Paul said. "What happens before that?"

"Well, as I said . . . she gets the tip, runs down clues, goes out on the story. . . ."

"She gets the wrong tip first," Paul suggested. "Somebody tries to hold her back. There's time pressure. The tip's only good for an hour. Editor tries to take her off story; she defies him, etcetera."

360

"But. . . ."

"Look, Tom. This is a half hour show. A half hour show needs twice as much plot as an hour show. Seriously."

"I wonder why?"

"I don't know. Yes I do. In an hour show you can try to develop character, color, wit. Theoretically. If you happen to strike a producer tolerant enough to stand for such long-hair crap. In a half hour show, all you have time for is story. Why don't you outline that killer thing, Tom?"

Paul explained how the outline was to be done, told Tom he would get a hundred dollars when it was approved, as the first installment on total pay, and they hung up. Half an hour later, Ned arrived.

Tom asked how Hubert had taken Ned's being out so late.

"Furious?" Ned said. "Furious simply isn't the word. He made me cook breakfast this morning, Tom, and then serve it, while he sat at the table without saying a word. Then he took a fried egg, very slowly poached in butter, really, which is the way he likes them; he picked it up very carefully with his fork and knife, off the plate, balancing it so the yoke wouldn't break, and put it down in the middle of the table. Then he lifted the other one and did the same thing. And then the bacon, and the toast, until his whole breakfast was arranged in the middle of the table, just as it had been on the plate. Then he stood up and leaned over and cut it all up with his knife, and poured coffee over it, and said: 'That's how my stomach would look now, if I'd eaten it. Would you like your stomach to look that way?' Then . . . I was speechless . . . he stood up, patted his mouth with his napkin, threw the napkin into the mess he'd made and walked out of the apartment."

"He was home when you got in last night then?" Tom asked. Ned had left Tom saying he hoped Hubert might still be out with some friends from the ballet.

"Yes. He was waiting." Ned took off his jacket, sat down, and accepted a cup of coffee. "But not where I could see him of course. Oh no. He let me come into a totally dark apartment, turn the lights on, look to see if he was in bed yet . . . I was certain the place was empty. He didn't make a sound. I was so relieved— then, when I went to the closet to get my pajamas, after fifteen or twenty minutes, thinking I was alone, I suddenly felt hands grab

361

me by the throat. He'd been standing absolutely still in that closet, all the time, to do that to me—I actually screamed, Tom."

"Of course you did," Tom said.

"Oh, God, how could I have been surprised?" Ned asked. "Hubert . . . never misses a chance at Grand Guignol."

"I suppose if you'd said you were out talking with a woman, it would have been all right?" Tom said, and smiled.

"Not with him," Ned said. "Not if I'd said I spent the evening in church. In Hubert's mind, one can be vile anywhere, with anybody or anything, and he loves to accuse me of it . . ." He mimicked Hubert's voice: " ' You were in a cafeteria, dear? And did you both use the self-service?' I used to think it was funny when he said things like that to other people, when we were first . . . courting."

"Have you thought of leaving him?" Tom asked.

"I couldn't," said Ned. "And he wouldn't permit it. Though I suppose someday he'll move in someone else. I'll know it when I get home, and try my key and the lock's been changed."

"What will you do?"

"Tell everyone I don't care and kill myself," Ned said, quite unaffectedly. "Well, let's talk about your script."

Tom told him about Carole and the escaped killer, and they had a rather entertaining time giving the gunman some of Hubert's characteristics in the outline. Ned had an idea for how Carole turns the tables on her captor: he directs her to make him a pot of coffee while he keeps her covered with his gun.

"They can close up on the percolator for time passing," Ned said. "Or perhaps use one of those glass things, and shoot the moment when the brew passes into the water below and the color darkens—make a nice shot. Then Carole pours out a cup of the stuff, carries it over to Hubert and throws it in his face . . . no, I guess that's too painful. She could scald his gun hand with it, though."

"He drops the gun, she scoops it up and covers him?"

"And calls the police," Ned said, grinning. "Who give Hubert a hideous beating with their nasty little pale blue truncheons."

5.

Tessie Held was making her party call by phone.

". . . but I don't remember," she wailed. "There I was with Guy Cinturon, and Ezra says I was pert. And Guy told . . . some story about a cat? Do you remember that?"

"Oh, yes," Ellen said.

"Why do I do it? Why, why, why?"

"Don't worry about it," Ellen said. "You were no worse than any of the rest of us."

"Have you just got up, Ellen?"

"Me? No, oh no."

"When?"

"Quite early," Ellen said. "I . . . I had to go to Manhattan." She shifted the phone to her right hand, so that she could pick up the drink with her left. Tessie was tiresome, but Ellen didn't want to discourage her. It would be nice to have someone to call, or who would call, afternoons; she took a long swallow. The drinks with Eddie in the morning hadn't affected her enough; this, now that she was home, was better.

"Manhattan? What for, Ellen?"

"Shopping."

"What strength. Dorothy Conn was very nice, wasn't she?"

"Very."

"My maid is so thrilled with me she's scrubbing the kitchen."

"Mine didn't come today," Ellen said. She had a hard afternoon's work ahead of her, and she would have to do it; she would have to be able to say she'd done it in the morning, before crossing the . . . the river. . . .

"Ellen, do you really think Peter and Sheila are somewhere together, this afternoon?"

"They might be."

"But without telling us?"

"More fun that way. Tessie, will you hold on a minute? I think I left the water running in the kitchen."

"Shall I hold on or hang up?"

"No, hold on," Ellen said. "Please hold on."

Little Roy Nevins was close to tears.

"Why can't I be the ghost?" he asked, crouching in the space between two banks of lockers that lined the school coat room, peering up at Sheila, his green eyes brimming, his red hair untidy.

"Who said you couldn't? Amy?"

Roy nodded.

"Amy doesn't know everything," Sheila said.

"I already learned it. All of it."

"The whole part?" Sheila was astonished.

"Yes, and my mother listened to me last night, and watched in the book, and she said I didn't make one mistake, not one."

"Roysie." Sheila finally got him to come out from between the lockers. She pressed his cheek against her stomach and patted him. "How did you know we were going to do it?" She made her voice as soothing as she could.

"I just knew you would," Roy said. "I was going to surprise you. . . ."

"Did you tell your mother?"

She felt the head shake against her stomach; funny feeling.

"Good boy," she said.

"I just said it was for school." He looked up from against the stomach. "Can I be the ghost?"

"I won't promise," Sheila said carefully. "If you're the best one for it, you can be the ghost. I don't care what Amy says."

"I'll be the best. I learned it already."

Sheila patted him again. She was considering how they could overcome his stature in costuming—is a ghost any special size?—and how effective, his weird, gravelly voice, neither a girl's nor a boy's yet, might be. "Maybe you will be best at that," she said. "You be there this afternoon."

Ben Chaffin blushed and said he couldn't possibly.

"Yes you can, Ben," Sheila said caressingly. "You can do anything. And if you have trouble with the words or anything, you and I can stay there, anytime you want to, after the others go, in that old house. . . ."

"What about Fats? Can he be in it?" Fats was the younger cousin with whom big Ben went around.

"Do you think he'd want to?" Sheila asked.

"If he will I will. Let's find him."

They found Fats Gunderson in the play yard, demonstrating the hammerlock; the smaller boy, who was both pupil and subject, was not enjoying the lesson much.

Ben and Sheila waited respectfully until the demonstration was over and the small boy dismissed.

"With girls in it?" cried Fats, when they told him.

"Oh, me and Amy and Margaret Jones and Deedie Freed . . ." Sheila said, casually.

"Did Margaret say she would?"

"Oh, yes," said Sheila. "She's got a very important part."

"Ophelia?" Fats asked. He was always surprising and annoying people by knowing things they didn't expect him to know.

Sheila shook her head.

"Who's going to be Ophelia?"

Sheila hesitated, then decided to risk telling them now since they'd find out in a few hours anyway. "Rosemary," she said. "Because she's so pretty."

Both boys were silent. Then Fats said: "You can't even hear Rosemary when she says something in class. How are people going to hear her in a play?"

"I'll worry about that," Sheila said.

"Thank you, Miss Sheila M. Walle," Fats said, in the tones of a radio announcer. "You sure Margaret said she would?"

"Yes," Sheila said. "I saw her first thing."

"We'll be there," Fats cried, and, feinting with his left, hit his big slow cousin, Ben, a sharp right with the knuckle points on the arm muscle, and then began to grapple with the older, clumsier boy.

"Is Fats . . . and Ben, and all those . . . really going to be in it?" Margaret Jones asked. "They said they would?"

"Yes," Sheila said. "I saw Fats first thing."

"Who am I going to be?"

"You and I and Deedie Freed are going to have boys' parts," Sheila said, putting her arm through Margaret's and walking with her along the hall familiarly, as if they habitually walked so. "Amy and Rosemary have to be the girls."

"I should think Amy would have wanted to be one of the boys, too," said Margaret, happily.

"Well, she gets a long part this way," Sheila said. "You know how Amy is."

Consulting after lunch, Amy and Sheila found that they had approached them all successfully except for Rosemary Bernstein.

Rosemary would be sitting silently by herself somewhere. She always was. It was not because she was disliked; no one felt that strongly about Rosemary. It was rather that there was something strange in her quietness, and it made her schoolmates uneasy. Her eyes were wide and remote; nothing engaged her mind or her glance for more than a moment. Other thirteen year olds might feel strongly about things; Rosemary, so far as could be told, didn't feel. Yet this is not to say that she seemed invulnerable; quite the contrary, her expression said that she expected hurts, and had she asked for recognition, the hurts would surely have been extended. But children who permit themselves to be ignored are generally ignored; and so, in spite of her unearthly prettiness—her skin, as pale and white as the hair and eyes were dark, her personal radiance of delicacy and softness—Rosemary sat by herself, and nobody even knew whether she minded, though Sheila had sometimes wondered.

Yet if Rosemary was surprised to have Sheila and Amy come up to her in the school library, where she was neither reading nor not reading the open book in front of her, she did not show it. Amy whispered to her that she was to come out into the hall, and Rosemary, who always obeyed everyone, even younger children, came out.

"We want you to be in a play," Sheila began, and paused to introduce her first argument. "The thing. . . ."

But already, in the pause, Rosemary had said softly: "All right."

"But the . . . well, the play is *Hamlet,* and you're going to be Ophelia."

Rosemary nodded.

"All right?"

The question seemed to surprise her, but again she nodded, a tiny, slow movement of the head, like a plant barely touched by light wind.

"Have you ever read the play? Did you see the movie?"

"No."

"It's by Shakespeare."

"All right."

"Ophelia's this girl who's in love with Hamlet, he's me, and she goes crazy."

"All right."

Honestly. As Amy said later, if they'd told her that Ophelia had to enter naked and be burned alive at the stake, Rosemary would have said, "All right."

A plan was made and carried out to complete the enlistment of Peter Held, who was from another school, who had agreed to meet Sheila at the candy store, whom they had to have to play Horatio.

Instead of Sheila, it was Amy who was waiting.

He was just too easy for Amy to recognize—curly, blond, rosy, slim, wearing pants that were a little tight across the buttocks, a sleeveless cashmere, carrying his overcoat, exhibiting posture much too good for fourteen.

"You couldn't be anyone but Peter Held," Amy said, going to the door of the shop to meet him.

"How flattering to be recognized," he said, in a voice that made you want to kick him.

"I'm Amy Cuzenus. I'm going to be Queen Gertrude."

"I see."

"Sheila wanted so much to come herself. But we thought there'd better be someone over there the kids would listen to."

"Do they listen to Sheila?"

"Oh yes," said Amy. "You know, she's a genius." Amy felt embarrassed using the word but Sheila had insisted it was the only one which would work.

"Really?" said Peter.

"Oh, yes. People from Broadway are very interested in her. But then . . . well, Sheila says they are in you, too, Peter."

"Yes," said Peter. "Yes. That's true."

"She says you can act in French as well as English. Can you really?"

"Well, I have done some French roles," Peter said.

367

"Shall we go over?" Amy asked. The drip hadn't even offered to buy her a Coke; well, fourteen. What could you expect? They started out. "She's right about your looks," Amy said. "And she says you're just as gifted as you are handsome." Peter smiled, and held the door for her.

"Horatio is a fine part," Peter said. Then, carefully: "I admire Sheila's courage in playing Hamlet. I shouldn't care to try it until I'm older."

Amy stopped, caught his arm, and looked with what she hoped was an adoring look directly into his face: "Sheila was talking about that. She says you'd be marvelous, but you haven't time to learn such a long part this spring." Peter nodded. Now he was ready for it. "She hopes—but please don't tell the other kids—that if we're a little bit successful this spring, maybe next year she could direct you in it, in a really big production."

"I have ten books," said Sheila. "How many have their own?"

Peter Held and Roy Nevins held up their hands.

"Then we need three more," Sheila said. "For now, George and Basil can take one home and use it together. And Margaret and Freddie Jones. And Amy and Theodore, you let Lucy look at yours until I get the rest." There were three Cuzenus children in the cast: Amy, of course, and Theodore, the train fancier, who played Polonius. The third Cuzenus was Lucy who, though eleven, was no taller than eight year old Roy Nevins; she was not exactly a dwarf, but she would never achieve normal height, and there was already a certain exaggeration of feature in Lucy, an inappropriate breadth and dimension of lips, nose and face bones, which made her face a caricature of her handsome older sister's. Lucy was, however, quite smart; she was to be the Player Queen opposite Roy, who, whether he made it or not as Ghost, would definitely be the Player King.

"When I get my allowance next week," Sheila went on, "I'll get the other three books and everybody will have one. Then I'm going to pay myself back later out of the ticket money."

"Oh boy, we going to charge for tickets?" Fats asked.

Sheila looked at him, and then went on without answering. "I've crossed out all the things in the play we're not going to have, in all the books. The way I've fixed it, it won't be too long. And Monday we're going to read it all out loud together, but today Amy and I and Theodore and Roy are going to do a scene so you can see what it's like. But first I'll tell you about who everybody is in the story, so you'll know what you're supposed to be like."

She paused and looked at them. She held up her hand, pointed a finger dramatically at Freddie Jones, and began in a low voice. "It starts with Francisco. He's a soldier, guarding the castle at night. He's Freddie. . . ." She went on, building up considerable intensity, choosing to skip certain events, as she described their parts; deliberately, she over-emphasized the importance of some of the smaller parts, so no one could feel slighted. She had read the play three times now, and talked, in a guarded way, about some of the hard passages with Miss Flexe, her drama coach at school. She had read articles about the play in books.

As she spoke excitedly, shrilling and gesticulating, about Hamlet's madness, grateful for their fascination with the idea of making parents think you're crazy, she was also, with the other part of her mind, looking them over very coolly. Funny bunch; kids and creeps. Except for Amy, and probably Peter, they wouldn't act at all, except as she could force them to. Some would be adequate if they simply learned their lines and were themselves; as much as she could, she had taken this into account in the casting: Theodore Cuzenus, the collector of train information, was stodgy and so was Polonius; Fats was fresh, a show-off, and so was Laertes; the Lafferty twins, only a year away from Ireland and with the voices and manners of English schoolboys, need add nothing to the parts of Rosencrantz and Guildenstern. It had occurred to Sheila that to cast in this way was to ridicule her fellows; this bothered her considerably and, at the same time, didn't trouble her at all.

As for the others in the cast, they would be as much as she could make them be, even Amy to some extent, Roy completely; only Peter Held was mysterious in this regard, she might be able to direct him, she might not.

When she had done with the characters, she said: "Now look. What you've got to understand is, this play isn't just a lot of talking. It's got plenty of excitement in it—fights and duels and murders and plots and a ghost and people going crazy. Hamlet's a boy who's supposed to be king someday. . . ."

Fats snickered. "How old?" He said, under his breath.

"You want to say something, say it out loud," said Sheila.

369

"If Hamlet's a boy, how come they always have old men act him?" Fats demanded.

"The same reason they have fat ladies in operas," Sheila said. "They have to pretend the fat ladies are pretty young girls, because they think the fat ladies are the only ones who sing well enough. Well, they think Hamlet's such a hard part, they have to have one of these old men, forty years old, act him. No wonder everybody's mixed up about the play. . . ."

"Who is?" Fats asked scornfully. "You are."

"If you'd read all the junk I've read about this play, you'd know what I mean."

"All right, what?"

The opposition was good for Sheila's tongue. "I'll tell you," she said. "If you'll just kindly shut up. There's a lot of junk about Hamlet. They say he can't make up his mind, he sees all the sides of all the questions; stuff like that. He can't make up his mind to *do* anything. Well, what kind of man would that be? He'd be a drip, wouldn't he? Well, Hamlet's no drip. He's very smart, but he's just a kid." She saw that Fats was about to say "How old?" so she cut it off. "Sixteen. Or seventeen. Hamlet's away at school; he hears that his father's dead and he has to come home for the funeral. He gets there and finds that his Uncle Claudius, his father's brother, is King. And married to Hamlet's mother already. Then the Ghost comes, Hamlet's father, and Hamlet finds out that Claudius is a murderer. And his own mother, too, she helped do the murder. The ghost wants Hamlet to get revenge. Well, look. If Hamlet was a grown up, what would he do? He'd get angry, and go right up and stick a sword in his uncle and maybe his mother, too. Or if he knew he couldn't, he'd get out of there and raise an army and fight them. But Hamlet's just a kid. His mother and his uncle aren't even scared of him. He's just home from school, and suddenly here's this ghost wanting him to act like a grownup and start killing people. Everybody wants Hamlet to do something different. His mother wants him to stay at the castle. His stepfather tries to send him to England. The ghost wants him to kill people. There's this girl Ophelia's father, he wants Hamlet to leave his daughter alone. And all the time they're trying to get him to do these different things, they're also trying to plot against him and spy on him and find out if he knows anything." She had Fats pretty well shut up now, and as long as Fats was attentive, the others were

370

too. "What do you do when a bunch of adults are pulling you around, trying to get you to do different things, trick you, trap you, be on their side against someone else? You get confused. You don't know what to do. So Hamlet pretends he's gone crazy!" The heads were nodding at her. "He's got this one friend, Horatio. . . ."

She had them now. She went on, outlining the plans that the boy Hamlet tries to make: first to persuade them he's crazy, so as to give himself time to find out. The adults try to catch him, to prove that he's either love struck or isn't really crazy at all. First they try to do this with spies named Rosencrantz and Guildenstern. Then they have the girl, Ophelia, meet him, while the adults hide and eavesdrop. Hamlet outsmarts the spies, and is too worried about his own business to pay any attention to Ophelia. His own plan is to have a play acted by some actors, which will be about the same kind of murder that his mother and uncle did. Then they'll show how guilty they are; Hamlet's plan works. But meanwhile they are trying to trap him into talking to his mother, again with someone listening in. Hamlet knows, now, that he's got to kill his uncle, and on the way up to his mother's room he has a chance. But he's still a kid, he can't kill a grown man, so he thinks of some fancy reason why he can't just do it yet. . . ."

"Yellow," Fats said.

"Sure he's yellow," Sheila said. "Wouldn't you be if there was an uncle you hated and you were supposed to be the one to kill him? Anyway, he goes to his mother's bedroom and now he really starts being a man because he tells her he knows how wicked she is, and makes her beg him not to kill her, makes her confess and say she's sorry. And he hears old Polonius moving around, and sticks his sword through a curtain and kills him. Runs the sword right through him. Now it's too late for him to get King Claudius easily. They know what Hamlet knows and they know he isn't really crazy. The king tries to have him killed by the spies, sending them all on a trip to England, but Hamlet figures that one out and kills the spies. He's getting to be a real killer now. He comes sneaking around. . . ."

"Meanwhile, back at the ranch," Fats said.

"All right. Do *you* know what happens while Hamlet's away?"

"Sure, Ophelia goes nuts because her father got killed. That's when I come back."

"That's right," Sheila said. "Laertes. Ophelia's brother. He's a bully and a show off. He comes back and they all tell him that

371

Hamlet killed his father, and that Hamlet's to blame for poor Ophelia being crazy, too. So Laertes wants to kill Hamlet, now. . . ."

"Yeah," Fats cried.

"The King fixes up a duel," Sheila said, clinging to her perception. "Between Hamlet, who's just a kid, and this big bully who's going to college, Laertes. It's supposed to be a play duel, for fun, but just to make sure, the King gives Laertes a poison sword. And he's got a cup of poison, too, for Hamlet to drink if Laertes doesn't get him. But his plan goes wrong: the Queen is watching the duel, and she drinks the poison cup, by mistake. While she's dying Laertes finally manages to stick Hamlet with the poison sword, but Hamlet gets the sword and gets Laertes, the same way. They're both dying horribly, and so's the Queen, and Laertes tells him the truth: it was a trick the King thought up, to murder Hamlet. The King starts to run away. Hamlet yells for everyone to lock the doors; then he catches the king, and jumps on him and stabs him about twenty times . . . blood, blood, blood, all over the stage. . . ."

They loved it. All of them. While she still had them this way, she beckoned to Amy, Theodore and Roy.

"Now this is the scene," she said. "Remember? Where the old man is hiding, and Hamlet's been called in to see his mother?"

She disposed them: "The Queen's in bed."

But Sheila had miscalculated. The kids were restless. "In bed?" Amy asked.

"When I come in?" said Theodore.

Instantly Sheila changed tactics. "Take five minutes off, everybody," she said. "While we get the scene ready."

"Blood, blood, blood, all over the stage!" cried Fats and leapt on his cousin Ben, pumelling.

"Can we go out and get Cokes, Sheila?" Deedie Freed wanted to know.

"Not yet," Sheila said. "We'll be done in twenty minutes. Then, after we read it Monday, most of you won't have to come very often. Just me. I'll be here every day."

She glanced around; almost all the kids were milling and shouting around the room now, except for Peter, who leaned gracefully against a column, watching her, and Rosemary Bernstein who sat

372

very still, looking at nothing, on one of the orange crates they had brought in the day before.

"Hey, you keep calling me the old man," Theodore said, plucking at Sheila's arm. "How old am I supposed to be?"

"Well you have a boy at college. Laertes," Sheila said. "I told you that."

"Oh yeah. I forgot," Theodore said.

"You can't remember anything that doesn't have wheels and say chug," said Amy. Several others quieted down, and came to hear the quarrel. Peter Held was still watching them.

Sheila darted between Amy and Theodore and seized Amy's arm. "You're in bed, in your nightgown," she said loudly. That got everybody's attention again; there was even a laugh, from Fats.

"Don't worry about whether the old man would see you that way," Sheila said still loud enough to keep them all quiet. "We'll just have him stick his head in the door and go right off to hide, you see? Because I'll tell you the way Hamlet has to feel. You know how it is when your mother's in bed, and she sends for you? How mad it makes you to see her lying there, all comfortable." They were listening now. "Trying to scold you about something while she scratches herself under the covers? And the way mothers smell when they're in bed? That's what Hamlet comes in to."

"All right," said Amy, and pulled an orange crate into position to represent the bed.

"All right, we're ready," Sheila cried, and the rest remained quiet, watching.

"Now you just put your head in from the left," Sheila told Theodore. "The Queen's in bed. You see her, and you say your speech."

Theodore complied, telling the queen that Hamlet was on his way and advising a good scolding.

Sheila moved to the right, behind the pillars, and gave them Hamlet's offstage cry: " 'Mother, Mother, Mother.' " She visualized herself looking for her own mother in a large house, with many rooms, a little hesitant, guilty because she had just had her sword out, ready to kill her uncle, and held back only because the man was praying . . . she let herself feel the guilt very strongly, and knew from the way it affected her that she could play the scene with enough conviction.

Then, once again, she and Amy were off and quarreling in their

373

favorite scene, to the mixed delight and discomfort of the younger children who saw, in Sheila's stage defeat of Amy, a fantasy of successful rebellion against parents.

After it was over, and the others were all going, promising to be there Monday for the reading of the whole play, Sheila said to Amy: "They didn't laugh at Roysie being the Ghost."

"Have it your way," said Amy. "You always do."

But Sheila wouldn't let the stage quarrel carry over, not this time, especially not with Peter Held coming up, so she gave Amy a hug and told her she was beautiful. Then Peter arrived and began to congratulate them both with such fluent and effusive flattery that suddenly both girls began to adore him, accepting everything he had to say as hungrily, as uncritically as Peter had accepted the calculated flattery Amy had delivered two hours earlier to him.

7.

"Lordie Lord, Reuben Shteuben not home."

"Oh, please," Guy said into the phone.

"I had to answer the way I always do, Señor. It might have been Reuben calling."

"We can talk now?"

"Oh, sure."

"There isn't really too much I can say on the phone that I wouldn't rather tell you personally, Karen."

"Isn't it too bad," she said, without any particular coquettishness, "that I can't see you?"

"Karen, look. . . !"

"You can call me Lordie, if you want. Hey listen, maybe if you called again, in a couple more months. . . ."

"You think you might be leaving, er, Reuben."

"No. I mean, I don't feel that way now. But I know me. I'll get tired of it, sooner or later. Or maybe he will. Or if one of us doesn't, maybe we'll get married and then we'll both get tired. Wouldn't *that* be a mess?"

"Karen. . . ." Guy began.

"Lordie." She sounded quite firm.

"Lordie, I don't propose to carry you away on a charger, or anything. I'd just like. . . ."

374

"Oh, you don't? Oh, dear."

"I'd just like you to have dinner with me."

"I'd like that, too, but as I explained, I can't."

"Do you never have an evening to yourself?"

"Oh sure. Half the time. That Reuben is great on drinking it up with the boys. Girls, too, for all I know. I doubt that he'll come back tonight, as a matter of fact."

"And what do you do on such evenings?"

"Chew my nails, and think up mean things to say to him in the morning. Oh, sometimes I go out, too."

"When you do, is it . . . well, with other girls? Or. . . ."

"Listen, I have a lot of friends," Lordie said. "Not like you. I don't mean men. Just . . . oh, kids like Reuben and me, who like to sit around and talk theatre, you know? Sure, I go out like that. Or to see an old movie or something. But you don't mean just go out friendly, do you?"

"I'll promise to keep it that way as long as you want me to," Guy said.

"But I might not want you to," said Lordie Lord. "That's the trouble. . . ." When she did flirt, Guy thought, she was even worse than when she didn't. "I wasn't really very straight with you, Señor, letting you call back," she said. "I guess I just wanted to hear you ask me again. I'm sorry."

"Glad to be of service," Guy said. "Oh, Lordie, this is silly. Do come out. You will, won't you? Tonight?"

"But . . . why?"

"Just to have some supper, some place pleasant. So we can each have another look at the other. Then we'll both know whether I really ought to call again, in a couple of months."

"Would that satisfy you?" she asked. "All right. I don't mean about supper tonight. I mean, we're giving a party next week. You could come to that."

"You mean with Reuben Shteuben and all the kids who like old movies?" Guy asked.

"Well, it wouldn't be much for you, I guess," Lordie admitted. "I mean, sitting on the floor and drinking red wine . . . hey, I know."

"What?"

"Why don't you come, but don't use your real name?"

"What?"

"You can come and be Ossie Parker. That's a boy they all know

I knew, but he's been in Hollywood for years, and none of them know him. See, I used to live with him."

"Have you lived with a great many different men?" Guy asked.

"I don't know. What's a great many?" He didn't answer and she went on. "Do you want to be Ossie Parker? Look, you don't have to stay at the party. I mean, just come in and we'll look at each other, like you said."

Guy sighed. "Where and when?" He asked.

"Wednesday next week. Any time after ten. You don't have to bring a bottle of wine. Oh. Hey, maybe being you, you'd better?"

"What does that mean?" Guy asked.

"The stuff we serve is pretty awful."

"Oh," said Guy. Then he made up his mind. "Wednesday, you said?"

"Yes. Will you come? I promise not to tell anybody."

"Lordie," Guy said. "How disappointing. I'm afraid I must be out of town on Wednesday." But she would agree to no other arrangement, and they hung up.

He paced the floor for a few minutes, trying to think what to do. He decided he would go down and at least look at the outside of the place where she lived; it might suggest something to him. He decided not to take his car, phoned the desk and asked that a cab be called. Guy disliked cabs, but his own car was cream-colored, a new Jaguar coupe; too distinctive.

Once in the taxi, he gave the driver the address, and instructed him to drive slowly past the building when they arrived.

"Drive *past* it?" The man asked.

Guy felt no need to justify or explain himself to a cab driver, any more than he had felt a need to explain himself to Harry Johnson, the agent.

They went coasting by the building, an unremarkable small apartment house, well west on a numbered street in the Village. Guy then had the man go around the block again; the second time past, he watched the opposite side of the street.

"What are you? Detective or jealous husband?" the cab driver asked.

Guy didn't bother to answer. He saw a second-hand bookstore almost at the other end of the block from the apartment building, and decided he would go in there. He rode to the corner, paid his fare and dismissed the man, neither under- nor overtipping.

"Brother!" said the cab driver, and moved off. Guy paid no attention.

In the bookstore, but going to the door from time to time to look around, Guy found a second hand Oxford dictionary in a number of volumes and in good condition. He bargained for it, bought it, and ordered it sent to Tom. He imagined with some pleasure the trips this would save his friend to the library. He was wondering, at the same time, whether he was idiot enough to go and ring the girl's bell, since he was fairly certain she was home alone.

Then he saw someone going past, on the street, who might be she—a short, slight, jaunty girl in jeans and a heavy, navy-blue sweater, carrying a bag of groceries; Guy ran out of the shop. It was not she. At least he didn't think so; he couldn't exactly remember what Lordie Lord looked like. He went back into the shop to be sure the man had Tom's address correctly.

Now that the transaction was finished, he supposed he was going to cross the street, walk down the block, enter Karen Lord's building and ring her bell, though it violated the first two principles of approach: Learn all you can about your quarry. Never move without a plan. If only he knew her, he could judge easily enough whether she would respond to the persistence of his having come in spite of her refusals. If she were one of several sorts of girl, such a move would be precisely correct. If she were one of several others, to importune could be disastrous. He went down the street, to her building.

A printed card on bell 3A said, "Karen Lord"; scrawled under the line of print, in pencil, was the added name, "Reuben Andros." To his profound irritation, Guy felt an instant jealousy, not so much of Reuben Andros as of the unknown names on other cards which had preceded his, the other names, unknown, uncounted, scrawled, written, stamped, in pencil, in ink, under the printed line, "Karen Lord." It was almost enough to prevent his ringing the bell, after all; almost. Not quite.

The responding ring, which released the front door lock, came immediately. Trusting girl, Guy thought; opens to anyone.

He climbed two flights of dark stairs and knocked on the door of 3A.

Karen Lord's voice said, "Coming." A moment later the door opened, and she looked into his face. It was the same girl, in jeans

377

and heavy, navy-blue sweater, the one with the grocery bag, whom Guy had decided could not be she on the street.

"My God," she said. "It's the Señor. Hey, you shouldn't have come."

"But I did," said Guy.

"Well, now we're looking at each other. Just what you said. Hey, I like what I see. I hope you do too. I mean, I'd still like you to call me in a couple of months. You know? Like we were saying, to see if I'm free?"

She really was very little like Sheila, after all; the body, yes, flat, hipless, uninteresting, tubular, like a young girl's. But the face was different, older of course; it was appealing enough, but without the keenness of Sheila's; a forthright little face. Lordie Lord; the hazel eyes were nice, but small, as he'd remembered. The clothes did considerably worse than nothing for her; she'd be cute in a dress and stockings, though, not chic, but cute like a little girl dressed up . . . and in boy's pajamas? . . . "I'd like to," Guy said. "I'd like to call you, and I will."

"Okay." She was swinging the door slightly, now closing it a little, now opening.

"I'd like to talk to you," Guy said. "I'd like to come in, if I may."

"Oh no. Not in this messy place," said Lordy Lord.

"Then come along out for a while. We'll have a drink and talk. Or just walk along." He smiled. "Do come. Come on."

"I can't. I really can't." There was no yielding in her voice, though she seemed not unwilling to argue the point, standing in her doorway, keeping him out, for as long as he cared to go on. He disliked the way in which he was continuing to find her engaging—she had some warmth, he supposed, in spite of the awful mixture of candor and silliness in the things she said. He could not, even yet, guess what to do with his dignity to impress her—whether to preserve it by leaving or squander it by continuing to argue. "But listen, I wish you'd come to the party and be Ossie Parker. That would be howls."

"I can't, Lordie," he said. "That's why I came now. But I *will* see you—and thanks for sharing the look with me." He smiled; she returned it. He turned and left, hoping he had managed to save some shred of the situation at the end.

But in the cab going uptown, he regretted that he hadn't been

378

more forceful about going into her place, more impetuous—no, that was ridiculous. If anything, he should have left her uncertain as to whether she would hear from him—no, not that, either; he had no intention of keeping this matter open for "a couple of months." It had to be got over with, or—no. There was a better way to fix up as miserable a start as he had made on this, and that was to cross off the whole, unalluring enterprise.

This Guy did, quite literally, when he got back to his place; he opened the current volume of his journal, turned to its most recent page, and drew a light line through the name *Karen (Lordie) Lord,* her address and phone, a notation of how he had met her.

Fracaso, he wrote, at the bottom of the page. Failure.

Then he thought: but there is something that I want about her, and she has certainly not said no to me, only wait. And he thought: already it is she I want, no longer poor Sheila; I must be grateful to Lordie Lord for this. And so, under the word *fracaso,* he wrote *a ver,* which meant that he would see.

8.

The letter with the line about the Eskimos was still unfinished. Lala had given in to her father's longing for conversation. They had had lunch. She had taken a long nap. When she came down they had tea and her father suggested a walk.

"If you won't be impatient with me for going too slowly," Lala said.

After half a mile through the lanes, Lala decided to turn back and let her father go on alone. Her route back was more direct, going along a street with motor traffic, leading past the place where a chapel had stood, all the time she was in school, and in which she and Tom had planned to be married.

They were married elsewhere, after all because the very last of the buzz bombs that came into town towards the end of the war, looking blindly for the American air base, had hit near the chapel and caved it in. Now there was neither chapel there nor ruin; odd. She and Tom had looked at the ruin together on their trip here seven years before. She rather missed it, missed both— the chapel of her girlhood, the pretty ruin it had made. Clean ground now. What would they build on it next?

CHAPTER FIVE

1.

"I'm going to Peter Held's house, all right?" Sheila said.

It was Sunday, but Harrison was working today. About twice a month Harrison went to his office on Sunday.

Ellen said: "Sheila, I was thinking about something. . . ."

"What, Mom?"

"I was thinking . . . you and I might go to church."

"Church?"

"Yes. It's Sunday."

"What church? The one we went to Christmas?"

"No. That's in Manhattan. I thought maybe we ought to get sort of acquainted in, in our own church. Here in Brooklyn Heights." For years, how many now?, she had been passing a Congregational Church, the kind she'd gone to every Sunday with the Kaiser and her mother when she was little, on a corner not two blocks away. For years she'd been thinking, intending, to start going to it, get to know the minister, and take Sheila. But Harrison, Harrison was irreligious, as bad as Tom, and cheerful about it. Sheila had gone to Sunday School a little, when she was younger. Ellen had never quite wanted to start the church-going by herself.

"Oh," Sheila said.

"Would it interest you?"

380

"Well, I guess so," Sheila said. "Only I made this date with Peter this morning. He's going to start teaching me to fence."

"I thought . . ." Ellen trailed off. She couldn't really say to Sheila that she had been startled by the girl's erratic behavior to Guy and Miss Conn the other night, that Harrison and even Eddie had spoken about it. Neither had quite accused Ellen of neglect— that didn't mean she couldn't accuse herself of it.

"Can't you just go get acquainted yourself today, Mom?" Sheila said. "And maybe I'll go some other time. I mean, I have this date. . . ."

Go to church by herself? All at once Ellen could feel them, all the Sunday mornings sitting between the Kaiser and her mother, not even allowed to be next to Tom; the tremendous accumulation of tedium seemed still to be inside her head, solidified and heavy. "Sheila," she said, but more weary than stern. "Date indeed. At your age."

"Well, appointment then," Sheila said. "Daddy says date when he means an appointment."

"Sheila. Do you believe in God?"

"I don't know. I never thought about it much."

"Maybe you ought to think about it."

"Okay, I will," Sheila said agreeably. "Now may I go to Peter's?"

"All right," Ellen said.

The girl flew to the door. "Have a good time in church, Mom." Ellen smiled at her daughter; she no longer intended to go, but she didn't say so. "I'll think about that," Sheila said, half out the door already. "I really will."

2.

" 'The air bites shrewdly; it is very cold,' " Sheila read, softly and happily.

" 'It is a nipping, and an eager air,' " Peter read back, in the same tone.

They stopped and smiled at one another.

"Oh, Peter." Sheila said. "I'm so glad it's going to be you."

Peter nodded. "So am I."

"You love this just as much as I do, don't you?"

"Yes," Peter said, and Sheila knew that for once neither of them was being artificial. They were so sure of one another's pleasure in it that they did not have to hurry to read the scene through; they could save, for a moment, between them, the joy of finding someone who shares your purest feeling for a kind of doing.

"Now," Sheila said, and he nodded. They began again to read the scene, tossing the lines lightly back and forth, volleying, not competing, not trying for expression or effect, only and easily finding the rhythm together and the meaning.

When they finished, they smiled at each other again and Sheila knew without question that Peter was where he wanted to be, doing what he wanted to do, no less than she.

"Shall we keep going till we've done all our scenes together?" Peter asked.

"Oh yes," said Sheila.

And when they had been through once:

"Shall we start with the first again?"

"Oh yes."

The foils stood untouched in the corner; another day they could start learning to fence. They were too happy working with the words, the lines, for any interruption; how smart Peter was about the meanings, how lucky Sheila had prepared—there was no argument, no dumbness, only a sharing of discoveries, a dancing back and forth of light. It had never been like this even with Amy; it would not be with any of the other kids. . . .

What a surprise to have Mrs. Held knock on the closed door of Peter's room and ask if they were all right; how peculiar, to realize what Peter's mother meant by saying that she thought they ought to have the door open, for the sake of better circulation of the air. As if. . . .

Peter grimaced, and got up, and opened the door, and told his mother that Sheila had been helping him with geometry, golly, Mom, she's a whiz.

And then another surprise: Mrs. Held said, when Sheila asked, that it was after one o'clock.

Reluctantly, Sheila got up and said she must get home for lunch. Peter glanced at the books they had been reading from, meaningfully, and asked if Sheila couldn't come back and do more theorems. Sheila wanted terrifically to say yes, but she couldn't; she said she had stuff to do for her mother.

382

She didn't want to tell Peter that she was only going to have a sandwich, and eat it on the street, trotting over to the Cuzenus' house to work with Theodore and Amy; and then, a little after five, stop, as she had arranged that morning, at Rosemary Bernstein's to get Rosemary started.

3.

"Do you think Killer Hubert should try to kiss her or something here?" Tom asked.

It was Monday. He had spent the weekend painfully writing a skeleton first draft of the *Carole* script. It was one of the hardest things he'd ever tried to do, and the result was awful—hardly half the length that it was meant to be, full of long unnatural speeches in which people explained what they were thinking and what they were going to do next; he was not even writer enough to write a bad script, Tom conceded. And just as he was ready to destroy it and give up, Ned had called and offered to come and help.

Now they were breaking down the speeches, filling in action, and Tom's mind had started to work a little better on it.

"No," Ned said. "An attempted kiss would be wrong. He can't do anything that might make him sympathetic."

"Would that?"

"If the actor played it that way. Attempts to kiss are either sympathetic or funny. No, he's got to do something mean. I think he probably slaps her and says that's just to show her he's not kidding about keeping quiet."

"Okay," Tom said. He typed:

HUBERT
(SLAPS HER)
That's just to show you I'm not
kidding about you keeping quiet
CAROLE

"What does Carole say? 'Yes sir?' I think she ought to say something defiant."

"What?"

"Oh, I don't know. How about, 'If you didn't have that gun. . . .' "

"You've got the idea," Ned said and Tom typed in the speech.

"Ned," he said. "You must have done this before, haven't you?"

383

"No, but I've been subjected to an awful lot of it. You know, I begin to think now, after working with you, that I probably could do it. I'd never thought much about it before."

"You going to try?"

"No," Ned said. "Not unless somebody does with me what Steve did with you. Gives me an assignment; and there'd be no reason for anyone to. There are so many people around who can string the clichés even easier than I can."

"When I go through again, I think I can get the clichés out," Tom said. "Some of them anyway."

"Poor Paul Wuss."

"Why?"

"He's the editor on it, isn't he?"

"Yes," Tom said.

"You take the clichés out, he'll just have to put them patiently back in again."

"It can't be that bad," Tom said.

"Maybe it isn't . . . oh, sure it is, Tom. I've done it myself."

"What?"

"Put a cliché back where the writer has been careful to avoid one. Sometimes even thrown out a pretty good line to do it."

"Why?"

"Well," said Ned. "The actors are kind of stupid. I get stupid myself. The producer gets stupid. We're stupid and in a hurry. With a cliché, you don't need time. The actor knows how to act it; I know how to direct it, the producer knows how to . . . produce it . . . I don't mean that we're conscious of this, at the time. Just that we come to something that looks like it might need practice and elucidation, and we say to one another: what's a different line that will make the meaning clear? The cliché pops up, we tell each other it's great and hurry on. It's not so true on some of the hour shows, Tom. . . ."

There was a knock on the door.

"Oh, hell," said Tom. "Is it three o'clock already?" He looked at his watch; a quarter of. "My friend Eddie's early."

"Tom," Ned said, getting up too, as Tom went to the door. "Find out when they have the run-through of the next *Carole* show and let's go to it together. Before you do the next rewrite on your script. Would you like to?"

"Very much," Tom said, and opened the door for Eddie.

384

4.

Imagine walking in and finding your friend, Tom Beniger, old J. Christ Beniger himself, sitting in his goddamn walk-up furnished apartment, entertaining a fruit. There happened still, even after all these years of watching him, to be one crud in all the world, one, on whom the crud had not settled quite so thickly; one, out of all the two-legged tuning forks who twang around the walk-up, furnished world, who did not vibrate exclusively, as Eddie saw it, to the dull thud of crud. One. J. Crud Beniger. La de da.

This being the situation, life and humanity being what they are, the misshapen testicle of a world turning as crookedly on its axis as any astronomer would have to confess it did (look, if you kicked it, it wouldn't even roll straight, la de da), all this being so: then out of your whole miserable acquaintance it is quite certain that if you're going to catch some person entertaining a fruit, the person will be Tom Beniger. Yes or no?

"Ned Kildeer, Eddie Bissle. Ned's helping me write a script."

"How do you do? Excuse me for running, I was just about to go."

What else would they say? If it were a female floosie, just slipping off as you came early for an appointment, they would say: this is Betsy, we were just rehearsing a television script.

"How are you, Mr. Kildeer?" Eddie said. "Don't hurry off on my account. I'm early."

"We're through for the day," Tom said.

Through with what, friend Tom? Isn't it a pretty little pink and white thing, putting on its overcoat. . . .

"You in television, Mister Kildeer?" Eddie asked.

"Yes. Oh, yes. Tom and I are colleagues."

Colleague? You're no colleague, Wingy, you're the greatest little flying machine since the helicopter.

While they were waiting for Guy to come and take them to the painter's studio, Tom told Eddie that Lala was going to have a baby. Eddie was sure voice, when it replied, sounded congratulatory enough, and that face showed nothing. You can't spend your life feeling the way Eddie did about things and not be able to count on face and voice not to show. Nevertheless. Nevertheless.

385

Nevertheless, when he thought about Lala, with whom he did not get along very well, and the baby, though he disliked babies, generally speaking, off in England, and saw Tom being so bland, so at ease, so unguilty, Eddie had to excuse himself a minute; he went and sat in the bathroom.

Didn't a man ever learn not to care? Didn't he ever learn not to be upset, just to take things as they cruddy well came? Why should he let it matter to him if Tom Beniger liked a dish of fruit, now and then?

All right, it was the surprise. No more suprises.

La de da on you, Bissle. Oh yes.

5.

Ernest Goswith was unquestionably the dirtiest human being Guy had ever had anything to do with. Take his pipe. It appeared, when you first glanced at it, to be mended, midway along the stem, with tire tape. You looked again, and it was not tire tape; it was adhesive, which had once been white. The teeth in which he held this pipe were dirty, stained with food and tobacco and even, today, a certain amount of red paint wedged between two of the lower front teeth near the gum, apparently from using his jaws as a vise to assist in twisting off the cap from a paint tube.

There was paint all over him, in fact; in his unbrushed grey hair, under his fingernails, around his neck like an extra collar and especially in the back of the neck, at which Goswith frequently rubbed. No point looking at his tee shirt and jeans, at the dirty toes sticking out of the holes in his canvas shoes; it was best, with Goswith, to keep looking at his eyes which were sly and blue and a little yellowish around the edges, but free, at least, of paint and grime.

Goswith was a great belcher, and as Guy presented Tom and Eddie, he belched. Then he laughed as if he'd made a joke. Then he said to Eddie:

"You're the one with dough, huh? Where do you live Mr. Bissle? You the one on Long Island?"

"Yes," Eddie said.

"Whereabouts?"

"Ringlet Harbor. Near there."

386

"What kind of a house you got?"

"An old frame farmhouse," Eddie said. "Unimproved."

"Oh?" Goswith looked suspicious. "You rich guys," he said. Eddie turned away. "Hey, Eddie," Goswith said, putting his crusted hand on Eddie's shoulder. "When you going back out to the Island, Eddie?"

"Wednesday night," Eddie said, without looking around or moving.

"You going to ask me to go out with you, Eddie?"

Guy should have warned Eddie more fully what Goswith was like, he thought; he had called him a moron, an idiot, but neither word conveyed the peculiar quality of the painter's obtuseness, an insensitivity, really, which enabled him to laugh now, as if convinced that he had tricked Eddie into extending an invitation.

"You wouldn't be comfortable," Eddie said. "Can we see the pictures?"

"Go ahead," Goswith said, sulking now. "I'll be back in half an hour. Hey. . . ." He was addressing Tom. "You got a spare buck? When people look at my stuff, I've got to go out and get a drink; I can't stand the things they say."

Tom looked startled, but reached for his pocket. Guy managed to hand Goswith the dollar first; he'd known it was coming. "Here, Ernie," he said. "Go along."

When Goswith was gone, Guy said: "Not the things in this room, Tom. These aren't the paintings Eddie came to see."

They hadn't told Tom anything, really, except that Goswith was a painter, that Eddie might buy some of his work.

"That's a relief," Tom said, sweeping his eyes once more around the front room of the studio. "I mean, this stuff seems well-painted but—it doesn't have much, does it?"

"No," Guy laughed. "Or so I'm told." These were Goswith's serious paintings, here in the front, piled around the walls, hanging, standing a garish half-acre of canvases imitating everybody indiscriminately: Matisse, de Chirico, Feininger, Picasso, Pollock. . . .

"Come on," Guy said, and led the way to the second room. "Now I'll explain, Tom," Guy said, "that what we're going to see are what Goswith does to make a living." Then he opened the door. He stood aside. He wasn't going to look at the pictures again, because he couldn't without thinking of that wretched little girl, Karen Lord.

387

Tom saw: six paintings, each about four feet by six, in heavy, eighteenth century style frames, well spaced out, hanging against clean blue walls and lighted from a skylight. They were representational paintings, rather romantic, beautifully drawn, rendered, composed—deriving not from the Italian or the Spanish schools, but from the French; their style was personal, yet it appeared that the man who had developed the style had done so working in the atmosphere of Poussin, Fragonard, Watteau, Ingres. As if the painter were no one modern, but a Frenchman working in his native tradition between the time of the romantics and the first appearance of the impressionists.

That was the first, the general thing he saw: figures, human and animal, in large canvases with spacious backgrounds of ruins or woodlands or pastured hills.

Then he saw that in four of the paintings, the figures were human couples copulating, another was a gathering of numerous figures, another a study of a girl and some goats.

1. Pretty, dappled woods. A feeling of stillness and sunlight. A stream in the foreground, disappearing back, a narrow, tumbling one. Patches of soft light, where the sun gets through, making the trees magically round, patches of warmth in the cool woods. In one patch, a stand of giant, mysterious mushrooms, meticulously drawn; in another the flank of a great worn rock; in another, a young man and woman, rather pale, young, solemn, quite appealing, just ready to initiate the act of sex. The organs carefully defined, but tiny, of course, because of the scale. The excitement of the couple is muffled by the forest, as is the noise of the stream, the brightness of the foliage. If these were woods creatures—foxes, birds, insects—so engaged, they would not be any more, any less, remarkable.

2. A European city, London perhaps, Berlin. The time of sunset. A glow in the sky, making pink the ruins left by bombing. The streets are empty, lengthy, silent. A man lies dead down one of them. A small fire burns down another, but whether left by the bombers or built from the rubble for cooking cannot be told. A feeling of great space, emptiness. Away to the left, inside what used to be a house, her feet braced on rubble, her back

against a portion of standing wall, leans a girl, accepting an American soldier between her legs. Organs cannot be seen in this one, only one of her breasts. He hunches awkwardly; his face cannot be seen. The girl's face is turned away from him; she stares out and away, sadly, her loneliness unrelieved by the stranger's urgent act.

3. The girl and the goats. Most of the flock is down the hill a way, grazing. Near at hand, the billy goat has mounted a nanny, who appears to be bleating in protest; from behind a rock, their shepherdess is watching them. She is young, tender looking. The rock she has chosen, in her delicacy, conceals her from the goats but not from the viewer; she is touching herself and the organ is very specifically rendered. The eyes with which she gazes at the goats are, at the same time, wistful and greedy. In the long roll of hills, falling off to the left, there is nothing to suggest habitation by any other life.

"Good heavens," Tom said.

"What do you think?" Guy asked.

"I don't know. That one's . . . nothing but pornographic." He indicated the painting in which a number of figures were involved together. "It's kind of humorous, though. Where does the subtlety come from, Guy? The irony? The . . . well, the perception of character. Even the smallest figures have such . . . individualization about them."

Guy nodded.

"Are there . . . have you seen any of these qualities in his other work?"

"No," Guy said.

"Except for the gang job, these move me the way fine paintings do."

"I won't name him," Guy said, "but an enormously influential critic is ready to publish an article on Goswith, which uses, about these paintings and some others, the word 'great.' "

"I'm not that sure of myself," Tom said. "I can only say that if I owned one, I'd want to hang it in the living room."

"And take it down when children came to visit?"

"I don't know," Tom said. "No. Take it down when someone vulgar came to visit. Or go away and let him enjoy it by himself. That one," he pointed to the soldier and girl in the ruins. "That's especially meaningful, I guess. To me. It's a sight I almost feel as if I'd seen. God it's a sad picture. . . ."

389

Eddie came back from the far end. "You think it's art, Tom?" He asked.

Tom nodded. "I think it must be," he said. "If subject matter isn't what makes art, how can subject matter be what mars it?"

"Slower," Eddie said.

"Never mind," said Tom. "I only wish the man seemed a little more human."

"He's a monster, isn't he?" said Guy.

"What do you mean?" said Eddie. "If the guy's a real artist. . . ." They heard Goswith walk into the other room. "I'll talk to you about it later, Guy."

"Flatter him a little on the way out, if you can stand to," Guy said. "Even the stuff in the other room, if he asks about it."

"Why, what's he do? Spit in your face if you don't like it?" Eddie asked.

"No," said Guy. "If you say you don't like it, he fawns on you, agrees with you . . . but according to a woman I know who lived with him once, he cries like a child after you leave."

7.

"We're starting with the last act," Sheila said, and as she had planned, it surprised them all into silence; only Fats had anything to say:

"*Last* act?"

"*Last* act." She mimicked Fats, and the others giggled.

It was Tuesday. The reading the day before had been maddening, a jumble, with different ones trying to read lines that weren't theirs, and others forgetting to pay attention to the book so they'd know where their own speeches came, and it had taken an hour longer than she'd planned. Some of the kids had been very restless before it was over, but she had gotten them through it somehow and gone home to brood over *Worldwide Manual for Direction of the Play* (Boston, 1903).

There, in the chapter on "First Rehearsals," was the advice she needed:

Although it is a practice widely and indeed customarily followed among thespians, and more particularly in the stock

390

companies, with their limited rehearsal time, it need not be considered obligatory to rehearse the play selected in the actual order of its composition, and indeed some advantage may accrue, in certain circumstances, from beginning elsewhere than with Act One, Scene One. Thus it has been the habit of the famed Elston Traynor, as confided to the author of this volume, in preparing the several and successful touring companies of "Lady Jane of Rangoon", which have so delighted our land of late, to imbue a new cast with inspiration and seriousness by commencing, at the very inception of rehearsal period, with the climactic scene in which Lady Jane is held captive by bandits and makes to them the famous speech, so familiar now to all, which begins: "An English woman is not at home to fear." Thus, in returning to rehearsal of the less emotionally high pitched expository passages in the opening scenes, Mr. Traynor has kindly pointed out, the cast knows full well the heights towards which they are working. . . .

This Sheila determined to accept. Following yet another suggestion from the *Worldwide Manual,* she had begun on Monday evening a *Production Diary.* Her first entry read:

"March 3. The reading was a big mess, but Peter was wonderful, and Fats understands all the words in his part, even better than Amy (!) You couldn't hear Rosemary until the part where she goes nuts, and then her voice got higher and you could hear perfectly. Ben Chaffin is the awfullest boy who ever lived; after the reading he wanted me to stay and I had to let him kiss me only then Roy and Fats came downstairs from the third floor where the boys are using the j. (even though the water is *off*), and I pretended I was all flustered and said, "See you tomorrow, Ben," and ran off when I heard them. Anyway, I don't think Ben knows how to kiss very well. I wish he wanted Amy to stay after with him instead of me (no I don't). Anyway, I am going to start with Act V tomorrow, because it's got jokes and riddles and d. words in the first scene, and then the fight so Peter can bring his foils. Note: must think about whether or not believe in God. Famous speech: "An English woman is not at home to fear." (Look up). Note: Change Lafferty's.

The last words referred to the first of several adjustments which must be made in the cast before they could really start walking through Act V. The Lafferty twins had been scheduled to be gravediggers since, as Rosencrantz and Guildenstern they have been sent off to England and killed before the Act begins. But they were not really equal to it; it was the profanity that bothered them, and Basil stammered so you couldn't tell what he was trying to say when he came to the part where the gravedigger tells Hamlet that a tanner's corpse lasts longer than others: "Why, sir, his hide is so tanned with his trade that he will keep out water a great while, and your water is a great decayer of your whoreson dead body." The religious argument in the scene seemed to bother them, too. So Sheila said to the cast on Tuesday, sitting crosslegged and attentive on the floor, looking up at her:

"The Laffertys are going to have all they can do with their important parts. So I want Theodore to be the first clown, because Polonius is dead" (and nothing about a whoreson would bother Theodore) "and Roy will be the other clown, as if the first gravedigger had a little boy helping him. Because the ghost doesn't come back after Act Three, either." The Laffertys nodded, ever polite. Amy had implied when she enlisted them that it was a sort of regular, if secret, school activity they were expected to participate in. Theodore and Roy took the stage.

"Let's put the boxes around like this, outlining the grave," Sheila said. "And you two can be on your knees with shovels, and it will look as if you're down in the hole."

"Where are you going to get the shovels?" Fats asked.

"We'll get some."

"How about a skull?" That Fats had really been studying the play.

"We can worry about it later," Sheila said. "Margaret Jones is going to make a prop list."

"My father's got a skull." They couldn't believe that the voice had come from where it seemed to come, Rosemary Bernstein. "He's a psychiatrist," she said. Or whispered. "He has a skull at home, from medical school. . . ."

"Is it real?" Fats asked.

The question seemed to confuse Rosemary; she stared at Fats, and shook her head. "I don't know," she said.

"I'll bet it's not real," said big Ben Chaffin.

392

Sheila spun towards him: "What difference does it make, as long as it's not yours?" she said, quick and crushing. To shut Ben up might shut them all up, since Ben was biggest. She turned to Roy and Theodore. "You're digging a grave for Ophelia, who killed herself, and that's a crime. . . ."

"A sin," said one of the Lafferty boys.

"A sin," Sheila repeated.

"Hey, Sheila. . . ." Fats interrupted.

"Yes, Fats?" she said furiously.

But Fats had something reasonable to say for once. "The Laffertys, and Freddie and Margaret Jones and Lucy aren't in the last act. Why don't you let them go?"

"I was just coming to that," Sheila shouted. "That's right. Only they can stay if they want to watch, if they'll be quiet."

"Freddie Jones has to stay, because he's Osric," Amy put in.

Sheila slammed her book down on the floor, too furious to speak. There was a shocked silence. She hauled hard at herself, pulling away from the edge of a yell. Then she said, in the smallest possible voice, leaning towards them and spacing the words: "Does - anybody - else - have - any - thing - else - to - say - ?" Then, more normally: "Do any of those kids not in Act V want to leave?" The Lafferty boys looked at one another, then at Sheila and shook their heads. No one else moved. Sheila turned slowly and pointed at Roy and Theodore, kneeling in the grave, books in their hands.

"First Clown," she commanded, and Theodore began.

Rehearsal was underway. They had a little less than four weeks.

8.

That particular Tuesday afternoon in early March was a bad one for Ellen. She had tried to take a nap and couldn't go to sleep; anxiety about nothing, about everything, made the pillow hot and the bed lumpy. It was one of those days. Mostly, she waited for Tessie to call.

She and Tessie had been calling back and forth quite regularly in the afternoon; nice. Ellen didn't always have a drink while they talked, either. What was nice was to know the call was coming, or could be made, so that a drink was possible or not, either way she liked. She put the bottle and glass by the phone, even the ice bucket. Tessie didn't call.

It was because of a little fuss they'd had the day before—is Peter with Sheila, is Sheila with Peter, I don't know, I don't know, don't you know where your child is, don't you know where your child is, oh, goodbye, oh, goodbye. . . .

Why didn't Tessie call and make it up? Ellen was prepared to be gracious; Ellen was damned if *she'd* do the calling. . . .

When it was after three, Ellen tried to call Tessie and got no answer. Then she tried to call Tom, several times, and the line was busy. He must be working on his script, with the phone off the hook. She thought of calling Eddie, at his hotel, but she'd been waiting for him to call her, to suggest another meeting, before he went back, and she practically had the speech of refusal memorized, she had gone over it so often; so she couldn't very well call him and make the speech before he asked her. . . .

Fretfully, Ellen dialed Harrison's office and learned that her husband was in conference. . . .

All right, everybody. Ellen is going to punish you. She is going to take the ice bucket, glass and bottle back to the kitchen and put them all away in their places. Ellen Small Beniger Walle, no drink. Maybe just . . . NO DRINK!

Where was Sheila?

Why didn't Sheila come home?

Didn't that school ever let out early any more?

Of course it did. What was the girl doing, then? Something that involved Tessie Held's famous little angel, Peter? Thursday night Sheila called Peter up and behaved so oddly afterwards. Friday afternoon she was late. All day Saturday, out somewhere; with Amy she said. She said. Sunday, went to see Peter. Sunday afternoon, other kids. A lot of other kids, all of a sudden. Phoning all the time. Stopping whatever she was saying when someone came near. Who were these other kids? Who, for that matter, was Peter? What did she know of him, except through Tessie's star-struck eyes? With that kind of mother, what could Peter be?

Ellen had never seen the boy. Ellen had never seen the other kids. Ellen had seen Amy, and what comfort was that? Amy with the come here, hither, eyes. Was that who taught Sheila to call up boys on the telephone?

And what kind of mother was she, Ellen, letting her only child in for, for . . . For God knew what? Sheila was still a baby, not fifteen yet. What kind of boys did she know? Why should she know any boys? And call them on the telephone? And other kids; and drop her voice when an adult came near? Call them . . . what kind of name was Cuzenus, anyway, Amy Cuzenus? Greek? Turkish? Armenian?

Ellen paced nervously around the kitchen. Ellen stopped and looked at the door of Sheila's room. Closed. Always closed. Was it normal for a girl to want a room way back here, a maid's room, when she could have. . . .

Ellen walked slowly up to the closed door, hesitated. Ellen then opened it. She peered in.

There was no mess.

No mess? But Sheila, Sheila's room was always in a mess.

There was no mess.

There was the desk. Nothing on it. Not one paper. Not one book. And at the right, the drawer. Was locked.

Secrets, orderly room, a locked drawer, full of secrets. There were three sheets of paper, crumpled up in the waste basket. To get them out and straighten them and read them . . . Would be spying. Ellen turned and went out of the room.

Homework, homework, that was all those papers could be, trial sheets of homework discarded in the wastebasket. She was pacing around the kitchen again. No. NO DRINK!

Was Sheila neglected? Was it only homework? Were the secrets in the locked drawer anything . . . sinister? Why shouldn't Ellen, if she wanted, if she were interested in her daughter, if she were not a neglecter, why shouldn't she? Get those sheets of paper from the wastebasket. And see what the girl's, just see what the girl's, homework was about? All right? All right? She went back into Sheila's room decisively, hesitated again by the wastebasket, reached into it finally, and took out the three sheets of crumpled paper. She put them on the desk.

She smoothed out one of them. Nothing on it but initials, various attempts at fancy lettering, as if the girl had been trying to design a monogram, a signet or something:

H, P of D
H., P. of D.
H.R.H. H, P. of D.
(Signed)
H., P. of D.
H.

395

Ellen recrumpled that sheet and tossed it back into the waste-basket, smiling.

Bemused, she opened the next sheet. It had phone numbers on it, and names.

P. — SL 4-9101

That was the Held's number. P. for Peter. Then it said:

Fats — TR 4-8776

Roy the Ghost — TR 4-6152

Freddie (Osric) — SL 4-5833

Luciano ?

Were these children? Fats, Ray the Ghost, Freddie Osric—what sort of name was Osric? And Luciano, and . . . were these the strange children Sheila was always phoning, always dropping her voice? Was living in Brooklyn so wise? Two of them, Fats and Roy the Ghost, lived in another district, another phone exchange. Where? What kind of district? But Peter was from . . . a middle class home. . . .

Neglected children from middle class homes.

Silly. Crumple it, crumple the paper. There. Back in the waste-basket. Why look at the third, if the others are nothing, if the others are silly?

She opened the other, and was struck with horror.

BEN

K. of D.

(King of Dopes)

Dope? It couldn't be. Not Sheila. Dope. She dived for the first sheet, covered with H's. H. Wasn't that what they called, oh God, Heroin? Trembling, holding the sheets of paper all balled up together, Ellen sank onto her daughter's bed. Who was Ben, the King of Dope? She opened the sheet. No. No. It didn't say Dope. It said Dopes. All girls wrote boys' names, *but why should Sheila write a boy's name if she thought he was a Dope?*

The plural form was driving her crazy. She sat up, sorted through the papers for the first she had read. She opened it with trembling hands:

H., P. of D.

Heroin, Prince of Dopes.

Ben was short, was short for, Bennies they called them. Yes. Benzedrine. Ben, King of Dope. Dopes. Heroin, Prince of Dopes. Dope. Silly. Not silly. Not silly.

Ellen sprang up. What should she do with the papers? Were

396

they evidence? Must she save them? Suppose Sheila walked in, right now? They must be put back, exactly as they were, so Sheila couldn't tell. Ellen must get help. Phone Tom. Harrison. Somebody. She began re-crumpling each sheet, trying to achieve the same crumple she had seen them in originally. Could Sheila tell? Oh God.

She hurled the papers into the wastebasket, started to run out, checked herself and stared at the locked drawer. What horrible things could be in it? What packets of white powder, reefer cigarettes, pills. . . .

The girls carry the boys' guns.

She grasped the drawer handle and jerked back; the lock didn't yield. Instead, the handle pulled out.

There she was with it in her hand, tears streaming down her face, when the phone rang.

She jammed the screw, with which the drawer handle had been attached, back into the stripped hole, and ran towards the phone, panting with relief at being called away from that room.

"Hello, Ellie." It was Harrison.

"Oh, thank God."

"What's the matter?"

"What? Oh. . . ."

"You sound out of breath."

Panic vanished, leaving her exhausted.

"I was, I was taking a nap," she said. "The, the phone frightened me I guess."

"I had a message that you called," Harrison said.

"Oh. Oh, yes. I did."

"Well, here I am."

"Oh. Well, it wasn't anything important. I was . . . going to ask you to bring some of that candy Sheila likes. From the store near the subway?"

Harrison chuckled. "Feel we've been neglecting her?" he asked.

"Oh, you know how I get," Ellen said. She was still shaky, but she had her confidence back. How silly. How silly, silly. . . . Of course Sheila wasn't doing anything wrong. She, Ellen, was just . . . "It's silly I know. But children do like surprises, and I kind of forget she's a child sometimes."

"She's pretty mature," Harrison said.

"Oh no. She's . . . she's really a child. She's only fourteen."

"Almost fifteen."

While they were chatting, the doorbell rang.

"That the doorbell?" Harrison asked.

"Yes."

"I'll hang on while you see who it is," he said.

She placed the phone down on the table, puzzled as to who could be ringing but feeling infinitely better, and went to the door. If it had happened five minutes ago, she thought, I would have been certain it was the police. Police! She opened the door and smiled; a man delivering a parcel.

"Be careful," he said, handing her a square, rather heavy package. "These are records."

She gasped. The records Eddie ordered!

"Oh, no . . ." she whispered. She looked back quickly at the phone, as if it were an eye as well as an ear. "Not. . . ." She looked back at the man, and he was holding out something for her to sign. She put the package on the floor, and signed the pad, shaking her head at him. He turned and trotted away and she let the door swing shut. Then she ran back to the telephone.

"Free samples," she cried into the phone. "A man giving out free samples. They're always coming around."

"What's this one?" Harrison asked, good humoredly.

Ellen looked back at the parcel on the floor, by the door. "Its . . . a cleanser, Magic green. It has magic green in it. It cleans anything."

"Just what we need," Harrison laughed. "I'll bring the candy."

"I'm glad you called, Heroin," she said.

"What?"

"I said 'I'm glad you called, Harrison.' " And finally she got the phone hung up.

She had sweat through her dress. There was something worse than dope, more dangerous than zip guns now.

The parcel of records was not really too heavy to lift; nevertheless, Ellen had to drag it down the hall. What could she do with it? She had thought of giving the records to Sheila one at a time, over the coming months, but she couldn't begin tonight because . . . because Harrison had already agreed to bring the special candy for a surprise, and there couldn't be two surprises. . . .

What could she do with these records? Where could so large a package be hidden, where neither Sheila nor Harrison would see it? What could she say if one of them did see it? What?

Mindlessly, Ellen was dragging the parcel down the corridor, past the guest room, her bedroom, Harrison's room. She stopped to rest. She looked around.

In the corridor wall, just by the kitchen door, was a shaft-opening, covered by a flat, spring-hinged metal door. When you opened this door, you could hear, sometimes, faintly, the roar of the building's big incinerator, burning the refuse which people slid down the shaft. Ellen pushed the package over until it was against the wall, just under the opening. Her eye told her it was too wide to go in, but she lifted it and tried to push it in anyway. Wouldn't go.

Working fast, her terror of discovery—Sheila might come banging in any minute—less irrational than the panic from which Harrison's call had rescued her, but a terror, nevertheless, she ran to the kitchen for a knife. She return, squatted, and cut the package open, slitting down the brown tape, breaking up the top flaps. There was an inner package, tied with string. She ripped at it, tore the covering off, lifted out a piece of cardboard. Then she turned the whole thing over, and sixteen LP records in their bright folders were there on the floor, in a slippery stack, sliding about.

She seized one: *Schnabel Plays Beethoven Sonatas*. She got to her feet and opened the metal door. By bending the edges of the folder, so that the record inside it bowed, she could get the thing through the opening; once inside the shaft it fell free.

Second Symphony, Beethoven, Conducted by Arturo Toscanini. Down the shaft. *Fidelio I. Fidelio II.* Mozart, Beethoven, Brahms, Beethoven, Beethoven, Beethoven . . . she could, eventually, hear the roar of the flames picking up.

9.

Eddie hated to change plans. He had said he would stay in town until Wednesday, and he didn't propose to go back a day early just because he had run out of things to do and people to see. Guy was working on a new quiff case; Tom was working, or so he said, on a television script with his little pink-winged friend; Eddie had made all his purchases, seen his broker, got drunk with Jerry Stein just last night—Jerry had had an infantry company in

Eddie's battalion, was now in electronics, and they saw each other about once a year.

Eddie'd even been back to Goswith's studio in the morning—it was now Tuesday afternoon—to sew up that deal, arranging to take four of the paintings, depositing thirty-two hundred dollars to Guy's account in payment, arranging to have the paintings stored where Guy's were, in the stock room of one of the galleries. Eddie could, of course, have had them shipped to Ringlet Harbor, but they didn't belong in his grandfather's house; no painting did. There wasn't a single thing hanging on a single wall in that entire house, not even a mirror; the only mirror was the one Eddie shaved by, on the door of the bathroom cabinet he'd built in. . . .

Eddie was alone in his hotel room, the room he always had, and it was too full of associations with Ellen; being there with nothing to do made him horny.

What the hell? Why shouldn't he see her again, if he wanted and she wanted? Because of a lot of reasons Eddie'd been going over and over in his mind.

But the fusion of remembered and anticipated passion, when a man is by himself, is often more powerful than passion itself. Tomorrow morning?

If he could think something up for tomorrow morning, he'd be okay, because he could get through the afternoon and he was invited to see Jerry Stein again tonight, to have dinner with Jerry and his wife and go to a movie; he'd declined, but he could always call and change his mind.

So, at about three thirty on Tuesday, Eddie picked up the room phone and gave the operator Ellen's number. He got a busy signal. The operator said she'd keep trying and calling, and Eddie gave her the Stein's number to call meanwhile. He got Susie Stein, and she was pleased that Eddie'd changed his mind.

Then they tried Ellen again and that number was still busy. Okay. Eddie hung up. Eddie walked around the room with his hands in his pockets, stopped at the glass-topped dresser, and on it was the slip of paper he'd carried away from Guy's last week with Dorothy Conn's phone number on it.

He had sort of meant to call her just out of curiosity, just to see what sort of thing a dame like that would say, turning him down. . . .

And what kind of pukey jerk was he, burning his heart over

400

whether he could bully poor old Ellen Walle back into bed for another bout, without even trying to connect with a babe that every other guy in New York was panting to get at? What kind of pukey jerk? That was too easy: yellow as an omelet.

The phone rang as he held the slip, and he crossed the room to talk to Ellen.

"Hello. . . ."

"Your party is still busy, Mr. Bissle," the operator said. "Shall I keep trying and call you?"

"No," said Mr. Bissle. "Let's cancel that one. I want you to try this for me," and he read the number of Dorothy Conn from his slip of paper. The operator dialed.

"Hello?" a woman's voice said.

"Look, my name's Eddie Bissle," Eddie said. "I'm calling Miss Conn. You can remind her that she met me. . . ."

"This is Dorothy, Eddie."

She had answered her own phone.

"Oh. Oh, well. Hm, hello. . . ."

"I had a note from Guy last week. He said I might hear from you."

"Oh, yeah," Eddie said. "Well I guess I should have called sooner."

"Guy said he was going out of town. Has he left?"

"Yeah, I guess so," Eddie said. "Well, how . . . how've you been?"

"You know what I keep thinking of, Eddie?" she said.

"No. What?"

"That story you told. About not shooting the German. I still think you were right, Eddie, not to shoot him."

"You do?" Had he really told her that one? Yeah, sure he had. "I'll bet you think so too, really. . . ."

"You're wrong," Eddie said. Being agreeable again, eh Bissle? Oh you sunshine Bissle, that sure is charming. "You're dead wrong. Hey, Dorothy, you wouldn't want to go out with me?"

"When Eddie?"

Well Jee-zuss. "I don't know. Let's see—lunch tomorrow?"

"I'm rehearsing tomorrow,'" she said. "When are you going back to Long Island?"

"Ten o'clock train tomorrow night," Eddie said.

"Would you like us to . . . get together tonight?"

401

Oh, hell. "I can't," Eddie said. "I'm seeing this guy."

"You're seeing Guy?"

"No. No, a . . . a man I knew in the army. Hey, I know. Why don't you let me buy you dinner tomorrow, early, before I take the train?"

"Thank you, Eddie," she said, promptly. "I'd love it."

10.

Wednesday evening, after spending the afternoon telling himself that he would on no account, go to Lordie Lord's party in the character of Ossie Parker, Guy found that he had nevertheless left himself nothing else to do.

So there he was, in blue jeans and a turtle necked sweater, with a bottle of claret in his hand, ringing the doorbell, going upstairs, finding the door with the mutter of voices behind it. He told himself to turn around and go away, and as he did so he knocked. No one answered the knock so he pushed the door open and looked in; and Lordie came flying across the room, took a jump, and there she was in his arms.

"Ossie! Ossie Parker. Oh, honey, look at you."

"Lordie," he said.

"Ossie! Have you seen the Weevil? Is Sandy coming East?"

"The Weevil's going into independent production," Guy guessed; he wondered if anyone there, overhearing, would know if the guess was wrong. "Sandy's too busy to come East."

"Sandy? Busy? What's he doing?"

"He's . . . he's bought a half interest in a Turkish bath," Guy said; the dimness, dampness, clouds of smoke that could be steam, people sitting and reclining on the floor of Lordie's living room, brought the idea of Turkish bath to mind.

"Isn't that just *like* him?" Lordie squealed, and then put her mouth close to Guy's ear. "This is such fun. You were such a sport to do it."

Guy smiled, and Lordie cried for everybody to look, it was Ossie Parker.

A heavy boy with a big nose and a dour face slouched over to them.

"You're Ossie Parker?" he asked Guy.

402

"Yes," Guy said.

"I'd like to hit you one in the mouth, Ossie," the boy said, morosely.

"Reuben!"

Reuben gave Lordie a push, not a very friendly one, and squeaked in a falsetto which was not a bad imitation of her voice: "Reuben." Then he slouched away.

"You shut up, Reuben," Lordie said, after him. "Or I'll ask Ossie to take me right out of here."

Reuben turned back and stared at her for a moment. "Just watch yourself, Ice Cream Cone," he said, after a moment, and resumed walking away.

"Shall I really take you right out of here?" Guy asked.

"Oh no," she whispered. "I couldn't now. Honestly, he's been so awful."

"Reuben has?"

"Yes. You see I used to live with Ossie Parker. . . ."

"I know," Guy said. "You told me."

"And Reuben's jealous. He thinks I want to start *seeing* you— that is, Ossie Parker again."

"Oh."

"And that isn't all . . ." Lordie trailed off, and appeared to contemplate for a moment. Then she smiled and beckoned for his ear. "Listen," she whispered. "Could you be a little bit faggot?"

"What?"

"Come here."

She led him into the kitchen which was empty, and had chartreuse walls. Guy put down his bottle of claret, thinking the only reasonable thing to do was to leave it there and go.

"Look, a friend of Reuben's said he'd heard that Ossie was a big faggot in Hollywood." Lordie said. "He isn't really, just this one producer who took him out West I guess Ossie has to. . . ."

"I see," Guy said.

"But if you could just be a little bit faggot, maybe Reuben would believe it and he'd forget the other stuff."

"What other stuff?"

"Oh . . . oh, I'll tell you sometime," Lordie said. "Will you do it?"

"No." Guy shook his head. "I'm sorry. I'll take my chances with Reuben. . . ."

403

"Please?"

He looked at her, here, in the brighter light of the kitchen; she was wearing a striped, man's style shirt, open halfway down the front. She had pretty shoulders, and had added to her bust for the party. She wore tight, calf-length pants, yellow ones, that pulled her small hips tight, rounded them into a kind of femininity. There was a stain of red wine around the suppliant little mouth, as she looked up at him, and he knew that he could kiss it if he could bring himself to agree to the preposterous request.

"All right," he said, pulled her to him, and tasted the wine she'd been drinking.

After a moment she pushed him away, "That wouldn't look very faggot, would it?" she said, and smiled. "Honestly, it'll be such fun. You don't have to put on much."

"And will you leave the party with me, later?"

She picked up a tumbler of wine, smiled at him, and drank half of it down.

"Maybe. If Reuben gets drunk enough," she promised.

No, Guy thought, she's leading me on, or thinks she is. She has no intention of leaving with me later. But he stayed.

He stayed for half an hour and talked with several people. It had occurred to him to hunt around for another girl like Lordie, and there were several of the same model. He tried to get himself interested in one called 'Gator, who came from Florida—she was quite flirtatious, had a prettier face than Lordie's, and a natural bosom, too; a better girl in every way, but by now his imagination seemed to have fixed itself on that one ridiculous little object. He just didn't want 'Gator; he supposed that leaving her after a promising conversation was acting a little bit faggot. He was aware that Reuben was watching him, so he went up to a pair of young men. They were talking intently about somebody who called himself a method actor; their voices and clothing were just about like those of any of the other young men in the room, and Guy wasn't sure how you were supposed to tell which were the homosexuals. The girls were equally ambiguous. He looked around carefully, and decided that the only reliable indication of sexual orientation was contact. If the person you were inspecting had a hand or arm or hip touching someone else, then you could note whether the second party was of the same or the opposite sex, and your ques-

404

tion might be answered. Or might not. There were forty or fifty people crowded into the room, so contact might be accidental.

In any case, he didn't think he would search for a boy to hold hands with.

They were younger than Guy by eight or ten years, and they were not very exotic to Guy's eyes, whatever their orientation. Some, he thought, were very likely intelligent, and others dull; some, undoubtedly, were genuinely creative, and the others gave them comfort. Guy felt no particular scorn for a group like this; he only felt that he was intruding. And this was not because they were flamboyantly leagued against a society which misunderstood them but because they were so much a part of it—and Guy was Mexican. These were only young Americans, very little different to look at and listen to than a college group, or a gathering of young professional people in any field. Even the most settled homosexual couples, it seemed to Guy, would be less concerned with battling society than with whether or not they could buy a new car, a new refrigerator, a washing machine, for their place.

It didn't interest Guy much.

If I leave now, he thought, rather than hanging around to be turned down later, I'll be a little ahead of her for once. And I'll have a reason to call up, tomorrow or the next day. And perhaps I can start giving this thing the shape of conquest, instead of continuing the pointless improvising I've been doing. He moved towards the door; nobody was paying much attention to him, so he slipped out, seeing only the eyes of Reuben looking after him.

11.

Hey!

Dorothy Conn liked Eddie Bissle.

Imagine this: he had got to her place at seven-thirty, and she sent the maid away and made him a drink herself.

So they'd come to this restaurant Guy'd told Eddie to take her to, very large and French, everyone yelling Hello to Dorothy, and she grabbed his arm in both hands as they went in, and smiled at people, as if she wanted them to see who she was with!

And all Eddie'd done was let her talk.

She had started in as he went in the door of her apartment, and

405

she practically hadn't stopped since. All Eddie'd done was scowl, and smile and grunt like a pig, and drink the drink she made, while she told him about being an actress, and about studying with a famous director Eddie'd never heard of.

Then she got going on some plays she'd been reading, and told him the whole story of each one; and then, when she'd get to the end of the story, she'd ask whether Eddie thought she should do the part she described, and Eddie'd say he didn't know anything about it, but it sounded lousy. Then the third one sounded okay to to him, and he said so, and she acted like she was going to jump on him and kiss him. Only they were in the restaurant by then, so instead she threw her head back and shot this roman candle smile at him that lighted the room.

"But that's the one I'm dying to do, Eddie," she said. "Do you really think I can?"

He shrugged. "Why not?" he asked. He was pretty happy. And it wasn't costing him a hundred bucks for the date, either, no more than thirty or forty for drinks and dinner.

"It's a beautiful play, Eddie, you understand? But not oh, the sort of thing I'm expected to do. . . ."

"No," Eddie said, and scowled. "They want you to get up and show off your body, not act. I don't know how good or bad you are, Dorothy; all I know is you're supposed to be a performer in theatres, not sideshows."

It was his longest speech of the evening, and completely successful. But on the whole, he was just as glad the evening was working out in such a way that there'd be no opportunity for him to try making a serious pass at her; he assumed it would fail if he did, but that he'd have to make himself do it, somehow, if the chance came. It wasn't going to come; as he kept reminding her, he was getting on a train at ten o'clock.

And finally she said he wasn't to hurry dinner and try to get her home, she would go to the station with him instead; Guy was right about her, of course. Guy was always right about dames. Dorothy was a regular enough girl, a little vain, a little insecure, over-friendly because she couldn't bear not to have everyone's approval, and god damn ambivalent about her body—deeply pleased and frantically embarrassed by the response it got. Identifying Eddie, or his point of view towards her at least, with Guy, Dorothy couldn't stand—this is what Guy had suggested—the idea that

406

Eddie might not like her. "Eddie, it's just as well you didn't call her right away; by the time you did, she was wondering why you hadn't." Only Eddie couldn't calculate things that way, and if he kept on doing the smart thing, scowling, being surly, it wasn't out of smartness, but only because he was uneasy in the presence of all that dame; and the more he scowled, smart or not smart, the harder she talked at him, the more often she tossed her head and shot off one of those amazing, roman candle smiles.

It was kind of wonderful; she was kind of wonderful.

Not-Smart Bissle tried to tell her so: "Jesus, you got to ease up on me, Dorothy, I mean . . . well, the thing is. . . ." He knew he was scowling again, and she caught his hand, reaching across the table and said something about not being shy.

When they left the restaurant and jumped into a cab and Eddie said Long Island railroad, she said:

"Eddie, I wish you didn't have to go back tonight. I can really talk to you. . . ."

And Not-Smart said: "Yeah, well, I got a shed needs a new floor on it, uh, 'f I don't get started I won't get done this winter."

He supposed he would have had to try putting an arm around her or something in the cab, and would have gotten his slap for that—Christ, she sat in the middle of the seat, made it hard to know what else to do with stupid arm—but he was lucky: the cab driver recognized Dorothy and kept yacking about it and watching the rear vision mirror, so that excused Eddie from making the try.

She even got out and went into the station with him, over to the locker where he'd checked his bag, and right up to the gate the train left from. And that was damn near another big test for Yellow Belly, because it seemed for a moment he would have to have a try at kissing her goodbye; but he was lucky again. Some jerk stopped to gape, and then another, and in the space of about four seconds there was quite a little crowd gathered around watching; so Eddie just stuck his jaw out at the crowd and his hand out at Dorothy—hand, having an evening paper in it, was unfit for shaking, only intended for waving duty, but Dorothy took it, paper and all in both of hers for a moment, and then Eddie backed away, nodding stupidly to her, other hand full of suitcase. And she cried out,

"Will you call me, Eddie, when you're coming in again?"

And he kept nodding and backing until the whole performance

seemed so asinine that he turned and ran as if the train might be about to leave.

And he was about ten minutes early, though there were already a good many people on the train who hadn't wanted to risk not finding seats. Not finding seats was funny, because this train was never full in the winter. And this one would be a date to remember.

He found a seat. One to remember.

He wished he had Guy's skill; then it might be a date to follow up as well.

As it was, he thought, opening the paper but not reading it, settling into the seat, it really had gone wonderfully; he let his eyes close. He would find a good picture of her, in a magazine or something, and look at it now and then when he needed to be reminded that he had once gone out with a girl like that, and damn successfully, too. . . .

The train began to move. Eddie scrunched down contentedly in his seat, eyes closed, holding the paper in front of him.

A hand caught his shoulder.

He hit the hand off his shoulder first, before he opened his eyes. Then he opened them reluctantly and looked up.

"Well, for Christ's cruddy sake."

There was Ernest Goswith, smiling his cloying, unclean smile, and sort of breathing: "Heh, huh, heh, huh. . . ."

"What are you doing?" Eddie asked.

Goswith sat down beside him. "You said Wednesday night to Ringlet Harbor," Goswith said. "This is the only train."

Eddie told himself this guy was maybe a great painter, and swallowed a number of obscenities. "Ernie," he said. "I got no place to put you up."

"That's all right, Eddie," Goswith said. "I can sleep on the floor, on a rug in the living room if you want. I had to get out of the city. I couldn't stand it and I got no money."

"Got a ticket?" Eddie said.

Goswith shook his head.

"We can buy one from the conductor, I guess," Eddie said.

CHAPTER SIX

1.

"EVERYBODY TALKS DIRTY to Ophelia," Sheila said.

Today she had Rosemary, who was infinitely tractable; Fats, who was inexhaustible and not nearly so fractious when Margaret Jones wasn't around; Theodore, who was Amy's slave; Roy who wasn't in the scene they were going to do, but refused to be absent —and, of course, Amy and herself.

With this group, she could try to get into things that weren't just matters of what a word meant, or where to stand.

"Everybody talks dirty to Ophelia," Sheila repeated, frowning at Rosemary, wondering just what it was she was trying to tell the girl. In the movie, Peter said, Ophelia was just goody-goody; it seemed to Sheila there was more to it. "Well, the first time you ever see Ophelia, her brother is saying goodbye to her. So he says—look at Act One, Scene Three." She waited for them to find the place. Whatever it was she was trying to discover might appear if she kept talking. "Laertes. Her brother. He's saying goodbye to her, because he's going back to college. So he tells her to write to him, and Ophelia says she will. And then he goes into these two long speeches, and all he's saying is, well, 'Don't let Hamlet do it.' On and on about it. . . ."

"Yeah," Fats said, earnestly. "That's what he says all right. Want us to practice it?"

"In a minute," Sheila said. "First I want to show you what I mean. See, it isn't just her brother. The next one who talks to her is Polonius. Her own father! So the old man tells Laertes all that advice, and Laertes goes away; but the last thing her brother does is call Ophelia aside and whisper to her to remember about not letting Hamlet do it. That's what he means, anyway."

The others nodded.

"And right away, after the brother's gone, the father starts in talking dirty to her. I mean, to his son he was all full of beautiful words and poetry about how to behave, but when he talks to his daughter, he starts right in on 'Don't let Hamlet do it.' See what I mean?"

"You mean about tendering a fool?" Fats asked.

"Yes. 'You'll tender me a fool' means have a baby. I asked Miss Flexe."

"Maybe Polonius thinks Ophelia and Hamlet already have," Fats said. "Only Laertes didn't know it."

"Well, he certainly thinks they've been doing something," Sheila said. "Or that they were going to. Because he tells her not to see Hamlet any more, or talk to him. Then the next thing, Ophelia comes and tells how Hamlet was half undressed when he came to see her . . . and in Act Two, Polonius thinks Hamlet's gone crazy because he can't get to Ophelia any more. But then, look at this." She found the place she wanted in Act Three. "First the girl's brother, then her father, and now the man who's supposed to be so much in love with her. Hamlet. Hamlet who's supposed to be such a gentleman and everything. Even he talks dirty to her, the very first time they're alone together."

The others were reading it. "She must be crazy even before she goes crazy," Amy said. "She's not such a little saint."

"That's what I was going to say," said Sheila, but Amy went on:

"If the only things anybody ever says to her are to warn her about doing it, I guess they don't think she has any self-control at all."

All the others nodded except Rosemary, who never made an unnecessary gesture.

"What do you think Rosemary?" Sheila asked.

Rosemary lifted her eyes from the floor and smiled a rare, tentative little smile. "Oh, I think you're right," she said, her voice as still and soft as her face.

410

Sheila said, "No."

Theodore began to snuffle. "If she doesn't give them back, I won't be in your old play," he said.

"If he isn't in the play, he'll never got them back," said Amy.

"Please make her give them back," Theodore begged.

"No," Sheila said coldly. "I told her to hide them."

"But why?"

It was Theodore's collection of train pictures they were talking about, standing in Amy and Lucy's room at the Cuzenus' apartment after rehearsal. Sheila had been working with little Lucy, who was to be the Player Queen, when Theodore discovered his loss and came wailing in.

"Because you were playing with them yesterday when you were supposed to be rehearsing."

"I didn't know, Sheila. Honest. I got mixed up."

"That's no excuse."

"I can't . . . I can't rehearse every day. I have to paste my pictures in."

"You have to rehearse every day," said Sheila. "Except the fourth act. You can paste them in when we're doing the fourth act."

"Please, Sheila. Make her give them back."

"Will you not miss any more rehearsals?"

Theodore nodded, tearfully.

"Will you get those grave digger speeches memorized?"

He nodded.

"And go faster, faster in Act Two?"

He nodded.

"All right," Sheila said. "You miss one more rehearsal or one more speech, or let Ben slow you down again in the second act, and we're going to get those pictures and burn them up. Every one. Understand?"

Six children were grouped, in the oblique sunlight coming in through the rear windows of the deserted living room, ready to begin rehearsing. Sheila, as Hamlet, was not onstage in the scene they were about to do. She was out front. So was Peter Held, standing beside her. Sheila glanced at Peter, sure that he too saw

411

what she saw: a lovely fuzz of sunlight around their heads and shoulders from the backlighting—something they could never hope to achieve, of course, but interesting to look at for a moment.

"Come on, Sheila," Big Ben Chaffin said in his deep, dumb voice. "It's cold."

"I'm waiting for you to spit out the chewing gum," Sheila said.

"Fooled you," Ben grinned. He had been chewing empty jaws, to tease her. "I don't have gum."

"Then why do you always talk as if you did?" Sheila snapped, but it was too late. Fats began to howl with laughter.

"Shut up," Sheila said. "Come on. Places, everybody."

"Places everybody," Fats mimicked.

"We've been in our places for five minutes," Ben began, and Sheila leapt at him.

She thrust her face up at his, and said: "You always have plenty to say, don't you. Talk talk talk till it's your turn on stage, and then what do you do? Open your mouth and nothing comes out. Let's hear you talk, Ben. Act Three, Scene One. You start this scene. What do you say to start it? Come on."

" 'How . . . how fares our cousin, Hamlet,' " Ben said. "There."

"Oh, marvelous," Sheila said. "Very good. You just left out the whole scene, that's all." She turned away, projecting utter disgust. Railing at Ben was her chief means of controlling the others; sometimes he deserved it, sometimes not. This time he deserved it. But she was too wise to leave the hard words between them. "Remember," she said, turning back to him. "It's what I've been saying all along, in this scene and all the others. You're the King. The biggest thing on the stage. All the others wait for you to speak. They look at you. They bow and fall down and do anything they think will make you like them . . . if you just clear your throat, they'll run for a doctor."

"Yeah," said Ben, putting his hands up on his hips. "Yeah."

"Rosencrantz and Guildenstern, remember, don't you get too close to him," Sheila said. "And Queen . . . even you don't forget he's the King. Not in public anyway. Maybe it's different when you get him alone." The kids laughed appreciatively at this. "All right," said Sheila to Roy, who had been made prompter, since he wouldn't stay away from rehearsals, and since he virtually had the play memorized. "Give him the line."

412

Little Roy, crouched in the corner with the prompt book which he didn't need to look at, said in his strange, gravelly voice: " 'And can you, by no drift of consequence. . . .' "

"Oh, yeah," said Ben, the King, and the scene began.

"Margaret, Margie." Sheila ran up to Margaret Jones in the hall at school and hugged her. "That's for being so marvelous yesterday."

"I didn't think I was any good," Margaret said. "I couldn't remember the words. . . ."

"But your voice is getting so beautiful," Sheila said, "that it honestly doesn't matter." She put her hand through Margaret's arm, and walked her along. "Honestly, it's just thrilling to hear your voice."

"I guess it's because I took singing lessons last year," Margaret said doubtfully.

"Did you really? Oh, I'll bet everybody will be talking about your voice after they see the play. Listen, what are you going to do after rehearsal today?"

"I don't know. Go home I guess."

"Let me walk you home?"

"Why . . . you really want to?"

"Yes. You and Freddie and I. Will your mother mind?"

"She won't be there. She works."

"Oh, fine," Sheila said. "Won't it be fun? We can do some lines together in the first scene, all three of us. And you know what? Peter Held has a tape recorder at home and I'm going to ask him to let you sing on it. . . !"

They were on Act III, Scene One, again, and Sheila found herself watching Rosemary. Ophelia had nothing to say in the scene, one line only, and yet Sheila knew the audience would watch Rosemary unless something were done. It was the eyes. Startling. So dark in the pale, still face, you couldn't tell the irises from the pupils. And the way Rosemary stood onstage, more quietly than any of the others, never shuffling a foot or shifting a hand, glancing, as Sheila had directed her to, from the face of one speaker to the next. She was too attentive; she gave herself too

413

completely to the make-believe, as if—as if, Sheila thought, Rosemary didn't want to be herself, wanted to be anything else, even this mad, pathetic Danish girl. Something had to be done about the way this child's presence stole your eyes from the others.

"Ophelia," Sheila said, interrupting. "Would you turn your shoulders away a little more? And about two steps backwards? You're too much in the conversation now. Remember, the queen doesn't have to be shy, but you do." She fussed with the grouping onstage until it was so worked that the distraction of Rosemary Bernstein's eyes would be practically hidden from the audience. It was for Amy chiefly—not Amy, the friend; Sheila would have sacrificed her without a thought. But the Queen had to be attractive, and being close to Rosemary robbed Amy; they had very much the same coloring, except that Amy was swarthier; and Amy's features, boldly handsome normally, looked coarse beside the delicacy of Rosemary's. Sheila must keep them apart.

"Take it from, 'drive his purpose on' " she commanded, and the scene resumed. Rosencrantz and Guildenstern made their Irish bows and went off. The King spoke to the Queen; the Queen spoke to Ophelia. . . .

"No, say it across the stage, Amy," Sheila said. "Don't go over to her. Say it on the way out." It was an unnatural thing, of course, for the Queen not to go over to Ophelia, put an affectionate hand on the fragile shoulder, saying " '. . . and for your part Ophelia . . .' " Unnatural, and so she would have to give Amy a reason; with Amy, there always had to be a reason: "See, the Queen's in a hurry. She knows they're trying to trick Hamlet, and she doesn't want him to catch her being a part of it."

"Oh, I see." Amy swallowed it; it didn't necessarily have to be a good reason. Amy said the line and made the exit as Sheila wanted.

Fats said: "You can get somebody else, Sheila. Honest, I like doing it, but I have a chance to do this work for my old man and he'll pay me."

"How much?" Sheila asked.

"Fifty cents an hour. That's a dollar every afternoon."

Sheila considered a moment, and then got out her wallet. "Here's your dollar for today," she said, holding out a bill. "You

414

tell any of the other kids and I'll ruin you with Margaret Jones. Don't think I can't."

He held the bill hesitantly. "You mean. . . ?"

"I'll give you a dollar every time you have to rehearse," Sheila said.

"Oh. Okay," Fats said happily. "Hey, that'll be swell."

"All right, now listen," Sheila said. "No more yapping in rehearsals. And get Ben here on time. And know Act Four tomorrow, and Act Five day after. I mean know them."

"Well okay," Fats said, putting the dollar in his pocket. "Sure I will."

From Sheila's Production Diary:
March 16. Today we are on Act Four, and Peter is just heaven, even if he's hardly in it. It just makes me feel so sure to have him around. Ben still doesn't know what half the words mean, and I had to stay after with him again. I made him work until it was too dark to see very well, and then he wanted to neck a little and tried to feel my b's. So I let him but it isn't very exciting. I had on my white orlon shirt, and when I got home it was all dirty where his hands were, so if he wants to do it again I'm going to make him feel inside. I had to pretend to be all excited and then push him away and say it's all I can stand (ha, ha). Act IV is okay now and Act V, except Amy yells too loud when she says she's poisoned, and I have to go over her whole part with her and get her to be quieter. Only not tomorrow because Deedie says she can work tomorrow (at last!) Act II and III are still wrong, and must get a little kid for III but next week. Next week will do whole play every day, because dress rehearsal week after.

Once more they were doing Act Three, Scene One. It was the worst of all because she couldn't get Ben and Theodore going fast enough. And it was all between those two, King Claudius and Polonius.

"Faster," she kept saying. "Faster." Maybe the audience would be interested enough in the way they were trying to catch Hamlet. She had to get on to other things. Run throughs. Polishing. So much to do.

Let them go on, now; they've been a little better.

Let Polonius give Ophelia her instructions, and the prayer book. Let King Claudius say the aside about the lash of conscience that Ben would never understand. Sheila moved into position for her own entrance. King and Polonius tramped off to hide, to watch Hamlet's reaction to Ophelia.

With them off, Sheila stood just offstage, counting to herself. Rosemary was to wait two beats, show the audience her eyes, and then drift down to the right. The audience would watch as she closed the eyes, opened them, started to read the prayer book, bait for the Hamlet trap. Then, at the count of five, they would hear Hamlet begin to speak without having noticed him enter, all the way over at the left, his back to Ophelia; they had to believe that Hamlet couldn't see her.

Sheila reached five, slipped onstage, and spoke:

" 'To be or not to be,' and so forth," she said. "All right, let's go down to where he sees Ophelia."

"Say it all, Sheila," Roy Nevins begged. "Please."

"Yes," said Peter Held. "Do it for us, Sheila."

She was tempted: it was something she could relax into for a moment, that speech, a break in the pace at which she had been driving the others. She sighed, shook herself, and said: "Not today. We've got to get through this and back to Act Two again today."

2.

"Boom boom."

"Hello, Karen?"

"Boom boom."

"Lordie?"

"Boom boom."

"This is Guy. I wanted to thank you for the party."

"Boom boom."

"Lordie. Are you saying boom boom because it's me, or because you're saying boom boom today?"

She hesitated, and cleared her throat. He heard Reuben say, "Careful, Ice Cream Cone."

"Boom boom," she said, weakly.

"If it's me you're saying it to, say it quickly. If it's what you're saying today, say it slowly."

416

"Boom; boom." She said it very slowly.

"I'm going to drive my car down Fifth Avenue to Washington Square," Guy said. "It's a whitish convertible. I'll be where the busses stop in exactly half an hour. Please be there."

"Boom. . . ."

He succeeded in getting the phone away from his ear before he heard the second boom.

He'd taken quite a peremptory tone; he wondered whether it might work. He was not surprised to see her standing at the bus stop as he drove up but he would not have been surprised if she weren't; he stopped and opened the door on the street side.

"Get in," he said.

She caught the door and held onto it. "I don't think I'd better," she said.

"Lordie, get in before a bus comes."

"I can't. I just . . . I just came to say sorry for boom boom. You see, we agreed. . . ."

"I understand. Now get in before a bus comes."

She shook her head.

"Lordie, I haven't come to abduct you. I want to talk to you about the other night."

"You mean about being Ossie Parker?"

"Yes."

"Oh." A troubled look had settled over her girlish face. "Oh. Well, all right. I guess I'd better." She got in. He reached behind her and closed the door. "You won't drive out of the Village will you Guy?" She asked.

"All right."

"Reuben's so furious. Are you, too?"

"Should I be?"

"Well, isn't that what you wanted to talk about?"

"I'm very seldom furious at anyone," Guy said. "When I am, I don't ordinarily want to talk to the person about it or anything else."

"You don't?"

"No."

"Why not?"

"This isn't very interesting," Guy said, and smiled at her. "Is it?"

She smiled back uncertainly. They were driving slowly up Sixth avenue; he turned west.

"Why is Reuben furious?"

"He thinks Ossie Parker's in town, and I'm seeing him."

Guy smiled again. "I suppose you are in a way."

"Reuben . . . oh, if he saw you, I don't know what he'd do."

"He mentioned punching me in the mouth," Guy said. "But I don't think I'll let that keep me out of the neighborhood."

"He might call the police," Lordie said.

"What?"

She nodded. "Oh, I wish I'd thought of someone else for you to be. I don't know why I said Ossie Parker."

"Why? What was wrong with Parker?" Guy asked.

"He used to give parties with dirty movies," Lordie said. "And cookies."

"Cookies?"

"Marijuana."

"That's the only word in English I've never before heard used for marijuana."

"We always say it. Reuben thinks Ossie corrupted me, because I said I wanted to have cookies at that party you came to, and Reuben was shocked; I mean, he doesn't mind for anybody else, but he doesn't think I should, and he thinks I wanted the cookies because you were coming, that is, Ossie was coming."

"Oh," Guy said.

"And he thinks I want to start in with Ossie, you, that is. And you know something?"

"What?" They were in the west side dock area now, bumping along cobblestones under the expressway.

"I do," Lordie said, in a small voice. "With you, I mean. Only don't get excited, Señor, because I'm not going to."

"You're not?"

"No, I thought it all out and decided I wouldn't."

In the center of the street a good many large trucks were parked. Guy pulled in between two of them and stopped. They were rather well hidden.

"Oh, don't stop the car," she said, rather pathetically. "Oh, please."

"Lordie, it isn't safe to have the car in motion while you're raving that way," Guy said, lightly. "Now tell me about this."

418

"I'm just not going to," she said. "I mean, look, Guy." It was the first time she had used his name. "I want to like you like anything, but if I do, I'm just one of all those girls—and if I don't, I can always tell myself that Guy Cinturon asked me and I said no."

"Lordie," Guy said. "This is the most childish thing I ever heard. First of all, I haven't asked you to sleep with me yet; I've only asked you to dinner."

"Hey." She looked at him. "Hey, that's right, isn't it?"

"So let's make a date for dinner, and talk about other matters when they come up."

"You don't want to sleep with me?"

"I want to take you to dinner," Guy said firmly.

She leaned towards him. "But why do you want to take me to dinner, if. . . ."

He dropped the arm that had been lying along the top of the seat, behind her, around her shoulders, and pulled her towards him. She went limp. He moved to kiss her, and she neither resisted nor moved to meet his lips. Guy bit off a groan; this was the dead treatment, recommended by high school girls to one another as infallibly discouraging. Years back, the second time he met with it from a girl, Guy had grinned and simply taken advantage of the passivity to get most of the girl's clothes off, before she decided being dead might not work—and by then, it was a little late for her. Now, however, he pushed Lordie away, quite gently, giving the whole thing up.

He started the car.

"Now you're mad," she said.

"No," said Guy, honestly. "Or if I am, it's at myself, not you."

Her voice became sympathetic. "I know what you mean," she said. "I guess I'm mad at myself, too. Hey, Guy?"

"Yes?"

"Instead of you calling me, let me call you next time?"

"All right," Guy said. "That will be fine." He drove back to the bus stop where he'd picked her up, making some remarks about the party, and as she got off, he had an easy enough smile to say goodbye with.

Not only did he feel that his interest had passed in Karen Lord but he experienced, driving back uptown, a deep ennui for sex, for people even. All affairs, business, family, friends were stale,

419

and he kept driving the car around the city, unwilling to go back to where his remarkable telephone would have recorded the voices of connectedness.

If it were summer, he would charter a boat, something he could sail by himself, and go out for a week or two; perhaps he should fly to Florida, or Nassau or Bermuda and do it anyway—or fly to Quebec, and ski—home to Chihuahua to shoot, not birds or small game but, taking a jeep and dogs into the hills, a mountain lion. Once, as a little boy, he'd gotten a lion. He remembered it vividly; unfortunately this reminded him, too, of Angelica, the nurse, who had bestowed—bestowed?—his sexual initiation. He did not like to be reminded of her.

What could he do now, less elaborately? He was driving the car through the Holland tunnel now; go to a small airport, rent a light plane and fly. He hadn't flown in several years. But day was giving out. He could drive, then. He kept going.

More elaborately then. What could he do? What had Tom said? That he'd either achieve his preposterous goal or renounce it. Wasn't it the preposterousness that made it worth achieving? He might not have thought so when he conceived it but now, in his thirties, it seemed to Guy that the unworthiness of a man's devoting his talents to the documented seduction of 350 women was precisely what made it worthy; it was a comment, all the better for being private, a long, smiling, undetectable spit in the face of human life and the other things it offered. For sex was a comic act taken seriously, the male organ a piece of physiological buffoonery, the female organ, hiding behind its funny muff of hair, equally absurd, a slot in the body, hence the placing of one in the other, and rubbing to produce gratification was all travesty, a humorless burlesque of what human bodies can do that has grace and strength; a man and woman making love were as funny as monkeys solemnly scratching one another's backs . . . but if he renounced the goal, what else would he do with himself? Learn to drive racing cars? Make a pilgrimage? Learn to manipulate his family's fortune in dramatic ways? Marry a princess?

Over the sprawl of Jersey flats he went, going towards Princeton. He had a young cousin in college there; the boy would welcome him. Guy could take his cousin out, to dinner, drinking, driving, go down to Philadelphia, get the kid a girl. Philadelphia was full of possibilities, girls who lived there, girls in shows trying

420

out there . . . a road sign read Princeton, pointing to the right. Guy went speeding past it.

In Virginia the following morning, at about three thirty, Guy's car ran out of gas. He had been going over ninety, on a narrow road, skidding the curves, using the whole road to drive on, ignoring any possibility of other traffic. The engine's stopping so abruptly frightened him a little, but he kept control. He got out of the car with weak legs, realizing as he did that there had been no other stops—for eating, drinking, even relieving himself—since he'd left New York the evening before.

3.

Ned Kildeer had to smile at Tom's enthusiasm.

It was camera day for the current episode of *Carole of the Comet,* and they stood on the studio floor among wires and the insignificant-looking shells and furnishings which would photograph as a living room, a bakery shop, Carole's desk in the newspaper office, and the lawn and flower effect to be used in the commercial. Men rode their big cameras like horses, other men pushed them, sound booms swayed, and the ceiling seemed solidly composed of spotlights banked in various directions.

"Isn't it marvelous," Tom kept saying, wanting to look at everything, have everything explained, for though he participated every week in the telecast of *Golden Words,* Tom had never seen the techniques used in sending out a dramatic show before. He was smiling now, at the way the camera could fake, staying on a man to whom Carole had been talking in his living room as he presumably watched Carole going out the door; instead of actually being in the actor's line of vision, the girl who played Carole was being hurried across the floor to the newspaper set so that the next scene could open with a shot of her at her typewriter.

"Not like the movies," Ned said, "where you can have the same character close one scene and open the next. The shooting here is continuous—no recuperation between shots."

"I can see that now," Tom agreed, nodding, moving over to look into a monitor. Ned envied him, briefly, the power of seeing marvels where Ned saw only toil and waste. "It's an extraordinary technique," Tom said.

421

One of the cameras was closing up now on Carole's hands as she typed away at great speed, and the image of the hands on the monitor screen was growing larger and larger. The camera stayed on Carole, but the image on the screen was cut; a second camera, in another part of the studio supplied the next image, showing the juvenile delinquent whom Carole was trying to help in this episode, entering the bakery shop, swaggering up to the counter, asking for some hard rolls and then pulling the gun the older gangster had given him. . . .

"Hold it," said a voice on the loud speaker.

Tom grinned, looking up to try to locate the control room.

"Over there," Ned pointed. The control room window was blocked off by tall flats. "Want to go up?"

They went upstairs to where the director on the *Carole* show and the technical director were working out their shots, sitting in the booth with the blocked and unnecessary window, watching what was going on on the floor by means of three screens, one for each camera.

Ned watched with Tom for a few minutes; going out, they saw Steven Even, as producer, and Paul Wuss as Editor, working on the script. They waved.

"Making cuts, I imagine," Ned said. "When the director gets his shots all blocked, they'll have the first run-through with cameras. Then they'll cut the script, and give the actors notes, and have dress rehearsal. Then they'll give the actors more notes, and a half hour rest and then the air show."

"Only two rehearsals here, both on the same day?"

"Oh yes. Heavens, the full script's probably only been in ten days. Since then they've done all the designing and production, cast it, revised it; I imagine they had the first reading for the cast oh, five days ago. So they started rehearsing four days ago, in a hall. Today they're working with sets and cameras for the first time."

Tom asked. "How can they do it?"

"They learn quickly. They have a lot of experience. It takes a lot more experience than it does talent to do this kind of thing. . . ."

They were back on the studio floor again. Tom said: "It must be a kind of talent, though, or a use of talent anyway. I mean, the whole thing is sort of brilliant: the speed, the coordination of all this intense, effort—it's a brilliant conception, Ned. Putting all these techniques together so infallibly, so that at precisely four P.M., on the tenth day after they started, a show begins, plays for exactly half an hour and ends to make room for the next producer's ten day effort."

"Sure," Ned said. "Meanwhile, three days ago, the same people started being simultaneously concerned with the production of next week's show."

"It's rather like a newspaper," Tom said.

"A newspaper?"

"I worked on one. A roomful of men dashing in and out collecting information, writing words. Others making sketches, taking photographs, others judging the material, others rewriting it, others opening mail, selling advertising, getting news in on tape— all these separate techniques being put together and fed into the composing room, and the whole mechanical process being put into simultaneous operation so that, at exactly four-thirty every afternoon, there was a new collection of reading matter for sale, with as many words in it as the average book . . . and already the staff had started directing their individual energies to the separate parts of the next day's publication."

"It does sound like the same kind of thing," Ned agreed, gloomily. "A great pooling of skills at high speed."

"But it depresses you, doesn't it?"

"Conventionally enough, yes. Doesn't it you?"

"No. I have to agree that all this intelligence and technique achieves a pretty silly result—but it isn't a vicious result."

"No," Ned said. "It isn't. Sometimes I almost wish it were. Have you seen enough?"

"Sure," Tom said. "I think I'll be able to put the script in shape to submit now." They went out and started down the corridor. "I don't think I understand what you mean," Tom said.

"About the result? Tom, the thing that bothers me is that it isn't vicious, but it isn't even silly, really. It isn't anything. It's no result at all. Nobody watches the show, or if they do, they don't remember it. Tomorrow the actors won't even remember their lines. All the people will take home paychecks—that's a result for them. The sponsor—I don't know; I suppose he'll sell his product, if not with this show then another one. The viewer will have half an hour of his life killed painlessly, if this is his kind of thing. But as far as the show goes, there is no show. Nothing's happened, just blah. Indistinguishable, inoffensive blah, to be followed by another half hour of another kind of blah, also reflecting this quality of work, also unnoticeable. It's true hour after hour, day after day; we make our brilliant contributions to nothing, adding zeros . . ."

"That is a nightmare, isn't it?" Tom said.

In the corridor they met Paul Wuss, carrying coffee back upstairs.

"When am I going to see that script, Tom?" He asked.

"Monday," Tom said. "I'll bring it in Monday."

4.

Goswith was pretty pathetic sober; drunk, he was a little more tolerable.

Eddie didn't have him at the house; there was a small cottage Eddie's father had built as a rental property, over near the beach. Eddie put the painter there. It had a little coal stove in it that heated up pretty well; you could walk to town from there in about twenty minutes, to Eddie's house in ten. Goswith had some dough now, Eddie's dough, thirty-two hundred bucks. The painter didn't like spending it much. He started right in charging stuff to Eddie's name at the stores, until the guy at the delicatessen that delivered beer called up one day to check, and Eddie put a stop to it.

Eddie was in a fine mood. He was, in a remote way, and not at all certain whether he meant to do anything about it, in love. He had written a note to Dorothy, the day after getting back, because he was missing his penknife. He thought he might have left in at her place, remembered getting it out to open a bottle for her, wrote and asked. Her reply came by return mail: "Eddie, honey, I couldn't find your knife," and then on and on about other things, and then the next day, by parcel post from Cartier's, came the most beautiful and useless silver cased penknife with a corkscrew, and pretty, sharp little blades that would break off if you tried to cut anything tougher than string with them; Eddie just about cried when he opened the package. A card in it: "I just don't want you to feel you could lose anything at my house. D."

Goswith saw the knife, lying in its packing in the box, and said:

"Present?"

"Yeah," Eddie said. "Pretty little gadget, isn't it?"

"Won't be able to use it, Eddie. Kind of small for around the place, ain't it?" Ernie fancied being ungrammatical.

"No, you can't have it, Ernie," Eddie said.

"Is that the kind of friend you think I am, Eddie? Aw, come on," Goswith said. "I didn't ask you for it, did I?"

Eddie looked at him, picked up the knife, and started up the plain wooden stairs to his bedroom to put it away, package and all, in the drawer where he kept stuff.

"I know, you're right, I'm a terrible sponger," Goswith was calling after him. Eddie didn't bother to answer.

Goswith came to the house a lot; other times, he pottered around the beach, surf-casting with some equipment Eddie'd loaned him, never caught a fish; he sketched some, with a pencil or with charcoal: seagulls, mostly. But his sketching seemed no more than another kind of man's small talk—an aimless reflex, reflecting his mood rather than creating it. The painter had two moods, sober: in one he was abject, seeking things to apologize for, anxious to speak of all the compromises he'd made, all the people he'd betrayed for his art, how low he was. By his art he generally meant the work he had done with serious intention but sometimes, these days, he seemed almost willing to accept the estimate of those who were, with Guy, buying up the pornographic paintings, and he was capable of saying:

"They don't think I knew what I was doing. Heh, huh, heh, huh . . ." This could lead readily to the second sober mood, in which he was transparently sly, in a curiously senile kind of way, seeking advantage with such thin attempts at subterfuge that Eddie would sometimes give in to the man because it was so painful to have him switch from slyness to apology.

When he drank, Goswith became considerably more manly, even arrogant at times, even nasty; Eddie much preferred it. There might be flashes, too, of the sort of young man Goswith had been, and they were rather fascinating; there had been a youth in this hulk who was confident, dedicated, not bright, ever, but able to know much through the power of intuition and sympathy. You could see the man who painted sex so movingly in Goswith, drunk, in these flashes, if you were patient enough to wait for them. There had, apparently, been a woman or two from time to time with

425

enough reason for patience; Eddie supposed it had been years since Goswith had encountered another man who could stand him for more than a few minutes—what difference if Eddie's capacity arose not from patience but simply from the fact that the painter seemed very little worse to Eddie than anyone else?

And Eddie was genuinely interested to learn what Goswith's personal qualities might have been before the man allowed the world to beat them out of him; for there had to be something more than speed and skill of hand and eye, some concealed well of true feeling on which the hand and eye could draw to inform their performances.

Eddie wanted to divine this well. Eddie wanted to know what came out of it, not as pumped into paintings, but in its first form, brought up directly into the man. Eddie set out one evening, in the second week of Goswith's visit, to get the painter really drunk, really talking, give whatever he, Eddie, had to give to the session for priming. He was willing to discuss the pocket knife, where he got it, how he felt about the giver. He was willing to discuss Guy, college, football, his parents. And as he got drunker and drunker, and Goswith did too, damned if it wasn't the painter who was plumbing Eddie.

You started talking to Goswith and found that he could listen like no one else ever had, as if, dirt and all, there was a sympathy, pure, clean and sensitive, in Goswith, like you'd never hoped to see—like, like you might imagine a weary, lecherous, old scab of a priest who can still, at times, project the grave concern and willing forgiveness, in response to a confession, that were available to his personality at the time of his youth, earnestness, and innocence.

Something like that. Goswith brought it all out of Eddie, during the night of hard drinking, at the time Eddie thought he might be in love, everything he'd never spoken before. Even—no names, of course—the whole story of Ellen and the baby. Even that.

All Eddie could feel, waking up the next morning, was that whatever the thing was he'd been looking for in Goswith, he must have found and must have talked to it; all Eddie could hope, waking up the next morning, was that the painter had been drunk enough not to recall very well the things that Eddie had revealed.

And perhaps it was so, for Goswith didn't say a word about the night before, except to whine that he was hung over, and beg some aspirin, and a drink, and stuff like that.

426

5.

Harrison Walle was tired. He wished Ellen would handle these things herself. He said:

"Sheila, you must have lost five or six pounds this spring."

"Oh, no I haven't," Sheila said. "Honest, I'm always weighing over at Amy's, on the bathroom scales, and I think I've gained a little."

"On our scales here, you've lost," Ellen said.

"I don't think ours are any good, Mom."

"We can easily enough check it by making an appointment for you with Doctor Harcome," Harrison said. "And I think that might be a good idea."

"Doctor Harcome's away," Ellen said. "I've already tried to reach him."

"Mother!" Sheila said. "Calling up a doctor, behind my back. . . ."

"Sheila!" Harrison raised his voice to interrupt. "Have you looked in a mirror recently? The circles under your eyes make you look thirty years old."

"Oh, that," Sheila said. "They aren't real. We were just, just trying on some stage make-up, and I guess I didn't get it all off."

Ellen said: "I suggest you go in to my dressing table and take the cold cream and see if you can get the circles off, right now."

"Oh, Mother, I've got my own cold cream," Sheila said.

"Sheila, your mother says you haven't been home one afternoon or at any time during the weekend for three weeks, except to eat and sleep," Harrison said. He wanted to get this over with and settle down; *The Wall Street Journal* lay, tantalizing and unread, right by his hand.

"She doesn't know," Sheila said. "Half the time she's asleep when I come in in the afternoon."

"Sheila, that isn't true," Ellen said.

"How about the time I let Eddie Bissle in? And you were sleeping so hard you didn't even know he was here?"

"Sheila," Harrison said. "That is no tone of voice in which to speak to your mother."

"Well, I'm sorry," Sheila said. "But she. . . ."

"We want to know what's going on," Harrison said, interrupting, and waited.

"Nothing."

"What?"

"Nothing's going on."

"What children are you seeing? Who are Fats, and Roy the Ghost and Freddy Osric?"

"Just kids from school." She said it too fast.

"Where do you go?"

"Oh . . . well, just to each other's houses. And we have to stay at school a lot."

"Why?"

"Well, we're working on a lot of things, like speech lab, and rhythmics and . . . I'm trying out for the paper," Sheila said.

"You're what?"

"Well, there's this girl Rosemary Bernstein, you see, and she's very important on the school paper. And she asked if Amy and I would like to be on it and work, and so we've been getting news, and writing it and things like that. I mean, I was going to surprise you. . . ."

"Oh," Harrison said.

But Ellen would never be satisfied with a reasonable explanation. "Are you going to let the child defy you, Harrison?" She asked.

"Oh, Mom, I'm not defying anybody."

"Sheila, Ellen," Harrison reached for *The Wall Street Journal.* "I think what we want from Sheila is a promise that she'll . . . cut down on her activities somewhat. You're not looking at all well, Sheila, whatever you say. You're tired and fretful and it's quite clear that you've been overdoing. Now let's wait a week or so, it'll give you a chance to cut down gradually without disappointing your friends, and then I'm going to ask your mother whether you seem to be able to comply with a reasonable suggestion, or whether we have to take stronger measures."

"A week or so?" Sheila asked, getting up.

"Yes."

"Oh, I promise. In . . . in two weeks, I'll be coming home every afternoon, right after school. And really, Mom. . . ."

"Yes?" Ellen said, wearily.

"Honest, the . . . the stuff I'm doing now. You'll be proud when you see. I mean, it's really very constructive."

428

6.

Roy Nevins drew his gun and held it close to his side. He made his way, step by step, along the wall of the room from which the fourth floor bathroom that the boys used opened. The gang that had locked him in this deserted house, leaving only Carbuncle and Torpedo on guard, did not know that G-man Roy had hidden a gun upstairs in their hideout. He pressed against the wall, testing each floorboard for squeak before putting his weight on it. He reached the top of the staircase, still pressed against the wall, and listened for Carbuncle and Torpedo's voices. He smiled. They must be asleep; not a sound from downstairs.

He slipped on down the stairs and reached the living room. Ha. Carbuncle and Torpedo were sleeping in that blue plush chair, turned away from him now. Roy crept towards it, gun held forward, ready to surprise them.

Roy levelled his gun at the top, and was about to command them to give up or be drilled, when he heard Sheila's voice say: "Let's breathe a little Ben," and saw Sheila's head, shining in the late afternoon sun, rise past the top of the chair.

She was looking down, and smiling.

Cheeks throbbing, Roy went sneaking backwards towards the stairs, a quick sneak, and Sheila saw him and called out cheerfully: "Roykins." She jumped out of what could only have been Ben's lap, buttoning her shirt, and came running over. "Did you get left behind?"

Roy couldn't speak his reproach. He looked down at his scuffed tennis shoes, swallowing, trying to hold back tears.

Just then Ben went past them, hatefully pausing to give Roy's head a brief Dutch rub.

"Don't work too hard, Roy," he said. "See you, Sheil," and went plunging down the stairs.

Sheila's hand came under Roy's chin and straightened up his face. She was making him look at her.

"What's the matter with you, Roysie?"

"Do you like him?" Roy asked, sobbing a little.

"Who, large and stupid?"

Roy got his face away from her and focussed on the shoes again. "Ben."

"I'll tell you a secret," Sheila said. "I can't stand him."

"But you were letting him . . . you were letting him marry you," Roy said.

"What?"

"You were . . . you were going to marry him."

Sheila said, "Roysie Nevins!" Then she laughed, and pulled his ear. "I wasn't letting him do anything important," she said. "I wouldn't Roy."

"You promise?"

She put an arm around him and said, "Promise, promise, promise."

"Why did you let him do anything at all if you hate him?" Roy tried to push away from her.

"Shhh," Sheila whispered, putting the other arm around him, and gathering him in. "It's just to keep him in the play, Roysie. That's all. I'll never speak to Ben Chaffin again when it's over."

7.

"Hello," Tom said. It was Thursday morning and he was phoning Paul Wuss. "Paul, I really am going to finish over the weekend. Will you be there on Monday?"

"Sure," Paul said. "Bring it in."

"The thing is, Steve said I'd get some money when it was done, even if you couldn't use it. . . ."

"Sure," Paul said. "That's the way it's done."

Tom knew he was being a bore about it, but he added: "You see, I wouldn't bother you Paul but I wanted to know whether it was safe to cash my paycheck and cable some money to my wife, I mean, if I'll be getting a check next week for the script. . . ."

"Sure," Paul said. "Bring it in, Tom. I'll be here."

8.

On Thursday, at 1:50, as Sheila was leaving Biology class, dawdling on her way to Study Hall, she was stopped by Mary Flexe, the school's speech and drama teacher.

"Sheila," said Miss Flexe. "You might have told me."

430

"What Miss Flexe?" Sheila asked, knowing perfectly well that some rumor of their play must have got out.

"Oh, Sheila." Twenty-nine years had passed since Mary Flexe's last professional appearance, but she still managed to look like an actress. It was more than merely wearing bold make-up and costume jewelry—a matter of carriage, gesture, voice and, most of all, the way she worked her face. She made it work so hard for her that the words it emitted were almost like footnotes to her chief meanings. It was a round face, and the bangs and earrings that framed it were a kind of proscenium for the continuous dumb show of wrinkling nose, rolling eyes, and infinite variety of mouth movements. At eleven, Sheila had imitated this, causing her family considerable agony; now, at fourteen, nearly fifteen, Sheila tried not to watch. The only things she admired about Miss Flexe any longer were her enunciation, and the wide separation the drama coach achieved with a small bust; it was a trick of some kind, Sheila thought, and she wished she could get to know Mary—Miss Flexe liked to be called Mary—well enough to ask how to do it.

"Here," Sheila reached into her book bag. "Here's your invitation. I was going to mail them all this afternoon—you weren't supposed to get it until tomorrow."

"But darling," said Miss Flexe, mouth going from moue to smile. "Of course I knew I'd get an *invitation*." Back to moue again. "Come on. I'll get you excused from study hall."

"I have to write a composition," said Sheila. She wanted to mark her script; today was the last run-through, tomorrow and Saturday polishing, Sunday afternoon dress rehearsal; Monday, Monday night, the performance. She really didn't have time to talk to Miss Mary Flexe. "I have to write this composition. . . ."

"No, no. You can talk to Mary. Yes you can." Miss Flexe had her by the arm now and was shoving her along.

"All right," Sheila gave in; there wasn't much choice. Mary Flexe, who had directed Sheila in a dozen roles, who had, three years before, been the first to encourage, even to suggest Sheila's ambition—Mary Flexe had apparently been waiting for Sheila. A treaty would have to be made.

They walked along the corridor, Miss Flexe pressing brightly forward, Sheila a step or two behind. Amy came scooting out of the biology room—she had been told to stay after class for talking—intending to catch up with Sheila, saw the situation, put on

431

the brakes. Sheila beckoned hard and low for Amy to join them; Amy grinned, straightened her face and shook her head.

"I'll just tell the Study Hall teacher, and then we can go to my room," said Miss Flexe.

In the classroom where she taught speech to every class of children in the school, even the kindergarten group, Mary Flexe waved Sheila to a seat, sat down herself, in the next seat, a student's desk-chair, not the teacher's. She sat and looked at Sheila, eyes on the same level, elbows on the writing-arm of the seat, round little chin cupped in her well shaped-hands. It was anything but a relaxed position, and the angle of light was such that Sheila couldn't get her eyes off a thin, pale bluish strip of skin, where the makeup stopped on the right temple, just before the hairline.

"Now darling, Everything. Tell me everything."

"Well, we just thought we'd give this play. *Hamlet.*" Sheila said, cautiously. "Amy and I and some other kids."

"Why dear?"

"Well, just for fun."

"But *Hamlet,* Sheila." Eyes rolled up. "Such a difficult play. I could have given you, oh," she waved her hand at a bookcase full of acting editions. "All kinds of wonderful plays. Why *Hamlet?*"

"No special reason," Sheila said. "Just, Amy and I were doing this scene from it—you know, Hamlet and his mother. Because you told us it was a great acting scene, so we learned it."

"Oh. Oh, *yes.*" Vigorous, approving nod. "And darling, where are you going to give it? In your home?"

Sheila realized happily that Miss Flexe's information was incomplete. "It's sort of a secret," she said.

"From *me?*" Hurt mouth, corners down.

"Well, I thought it would be better if I didn't have any help," Sheila said. Then, aware that it was the wrong thing. "I mean, I thought you'd be prouder of us. Everything we're doing is just the way you've taught us."

"But I gave you and Amy . . . Juliet and her nurse, didn't I? Or. Well, Sheila darling, if I'd known you wanted to direct, *direct a play. . . .*" Miss Flexe finished the sentence with a cascade of facial declarations. Eyes rolled up to say: *directing is impossibly hard.* Chin tilted sideways to say: *I would have helped, you know.* Unexpected smile to say: *but of course you can do it. Wonderfully. There. Now who's your friend?*

432

"Well, I really wanted to act in it," Sheila said, evasively. "But somebody had to direct. . . ." This was more or less true. The passion for acting had been there to start with; a passion for directing had grown, as they went along. "Anyway, you're coming aren't you? It's Monday night."

"Well, dear," said Mary Flexe. "I'm dying to, of course, but I'm not absolutely sure I'll be able to."

Sheila felt real dismay. No matter how much she deprecated The Flexible Flyer to Amy, it was part of her dream of triumph that this woman be proud and astonished. "Oh, please Miss Flexe," she said.

"Oh, it isn't that I don't want to come, Sheila. Oh, you *know* I do. More than anything. But you see, faculty meeting . . . well, you can imagine what faculty meetings are like." The chin went down, eyes swivelling up towards brows to look out at Sheila.

"Faculty meeting?"

"You know, Sheila. You children come here. Go home. On your own except for the very littlest ones. But we're responsible for you when you're coming and going. Oh, yes. If children get home late and parents complain, we *are* responsible." Some nods. Finger on tip of nose. Straight face. Tragic mask. "Sheila darling, if the school administration were against your play, I couldn't *go,* dear. None of the faculty could." She reached across for Sheila's hand. "I—I mean, and all the parents would be told of the school's attitude. . . ."

"They talked about this at faculty meeting?" Sheila cried.

"Don't worry," Miss Flexe said. "I couldn't tell a student what's said at faculty meetings. Not even you. But nothing will happen. Not if I say it's all right."

"Will you," Sheila asked, yearning to get her hand away, but not daring to try.

"I'm your friend, Sheila. And I think there's nothing nobler for young people than . . . the stage." She squeezed on the hand, and stared at Sheila, as if she were trying to press something out of her.

"Would you . . . could you just tell them it's all right?" Sheila asked. "I mean, without coming to rehearsal or anything?"

"Dearest," said Mary Flexe triumphantly, letting go of the hand. "Would you like me to come to a rehearsal? How sweet. But I'd love to. Are you sure?"

"Oh yes," said Sheila, knowing now that she'd been trapped. "Please Miss Flexe. Only . . . ."

433

"What?" Mary Flexe seized the hand again, held it to her chest in the wide space between the breasts, and thrust her chin towards Sheila's eyes; it didn't quite quiver.

Rather forcefully, Sheila removed her hand and stood up. She doubted now that there had been any mention of their play at any faculty meeting, and of course Miss Flexe hadn't really said there had. "Please come. We're going to do the whole play today. But I've had a hard time making the kids listen to me. If you notice anything wrong, will you wait and tell me about it afterwards, where they can't hear?"

Smile. Stricken look. Smile. "Why of course, Sheila." Miss Flexe rose. "Darling, there's only one director. You. Afterwards, we'll go away by ourselves, and have Cokes, and talk and talk."

This was an exchange of notes between Sheila and Amy in study hall:

What did Flexie Flyer want? A.

Ugg. Groan. She made me ask her to rehearsal. S.

1) Who do you think talked? 2) P. H. thinks he's so good-looking. 3) Flexie will try to change everything. A.

1) One of the little ones. Not Roy, I'll bet. 2) Yes, and you agree with him. 3) F. promised not to say anything. S. (Illustration: small heart with initials AC and PH in it; PH was Peter. The message was libelous.)

Did she promise not to make faces? A.

I'm going to make her wear a veil. S. (Illustration, a veiled woman with the caption, *MF as a deaf mute) Over.* On the other side: *1) Will you walk F. to the house? 2) Slowly. 3) So I can can talk to the kids about it first? H.P. of D.*

1), 2), 3) Okay, but take it back about PH. (Mrs G., Q. of D. Okay.

"Listen," Sheila said, when she had the cast sitting and quiet. Since she had begun paying Fats, he acted as a sort of sergeant for her, keeping them quiet, getting them there on time. They love me, Sheila thought, looking at the tense faces; or they're scared of me. I don't care which. Just in four weeks. "Someone talked. I don't know who. I don't care. I don't think it's gotten any farther than Miss Flexe. Tomorrow they'll get their invitations. After that, you can talk and talk. Talktalk, talktalk, talktalk." She imitated a duck for them, and they laughed.

"Talktalk," said Fats to Margaret Jones, but when he mimicked Sheila now, it was to reinforce her points, not mock them.

434

"But we've got to satisfy Miss Flexe. They'll ask her about it. She isn't coming to make trouble. She's just coming to see. I couldn't stop her. So let's make it good. Just like it's going to be on Monday. And no talking, not even between scenes." She looked at Fats, who nodded. "When you aren't on stage, watch the ones who are. Like you were an audience. And listen to them. This is going to be just like the performance, except I'll be out front instead of on the side, and Roy will prompt you. I want it to go fast. Okay?"

They all nodded. Sheila remembered to smile at Peter; it was important to make him feel special. Sheila heard Miss Flexe and Amy on the stairs.

"Places for Act One, Scene One," she said. "Deedie," she spoke quickly to Deedie Freed who, as Bernardo, had the first line. "Watch me. As soon as they come in the room, I'm going to give you a signal to start, before she even has a chance to sit down. Then fast, fast, fast."

Deedie and Frederick Jones, the thirteen year old who played Francisco, took their places behind the battlement, and watched Sheila's raised hand. The other children, sitting along the walls, obediently watched the players. Sheila swung, frowning, towards the door. She could hear Amy assuring Miss Flexe that of course they had permission to use the house for their play. Amy came around the angle at the head of the stairs first, and into the room; Sheila's frown and raised hand stopped Amy in midsentence. As Miss Flexe appeared, perhaps a shade out of breath from the climb, Sheila swung back, pointed a finger at Deedie, and the play began.

Not once did Sheila look behind at Mary Flexe. She was too busy, keeping them moving, speak, cross, pause, step—fast, fast, fast—pouring energy into it as she gestured them on and off stage, conducting them like an orchestra; would point dramatically to Roy whenever she sensed a line about to be missed, so that Roy's prompting, always too fast, was very nearly instantaneous.

They took no intermission. Faster, faster, as if no one were really there but Sheila, the others nothing more than motions in a dream she was having; fast. Fast. On and off stage she went as Hamlet in the wild run-through, leading, prompting, pulling them onstage with beckons, sending them off with flicks. She was hardly aware of her personal performance, except to know that it was good; only now and then, playing a passage with Peter or Amy, she

435

would be aware, for a moment, of another actor doing something out of an initiative not Sheila's own. Otherwise, it was as if, for that afternoon, she were playing all the parts herself.

She was showing Mary Flexe she could.

It wasn't until she and Fats began their final duel that Sheila realized the play was nearly over, that she had been in a kind of ecstasy and given her cast no break. Then her knee was in Ben's stomach as he sat on his orange-crate throne, and she was killing the King and crying,

" 'Here, thou incestuous, murdering, damned Dane,' " before she realized how triumphantly tired she was. The air was turning blue; she hardly knew what had been cut or skipped. She was lying on the floor and Peter was standing over her, saying, " 'Now cracks a noble heart.' "

Deedie came in as Fortinbras and, as arranged, the whole cast except for the dead, followed, marching, as if in his train, quite regardless, of whom they had represented.

" 'Let four captains bear Hamlet like a soldier,' " Deedie commanded. Four boys—Peter, the Laffertys, Freddie Jones—were kneeling by her. They raised her. Offstage, Roy rattled the thunder sheet to represent a peal of ordinance.

The rehearsal was over.

The boys carefully put Sheila on her feet, and Amy caught her before she fell, throwing a coat around her shoulders. Instantly, Sheila straightened up and began to laugh.

"It was wonderful everybody," she cried. "Oh, listen all of you, wonderful." She danced away from Amy's support. "Tomorrow, we'll polish and polish, and work on making stuff and costumes over the weekend, and if you're all as good Monday night . . . it's all anybody could ask." She caught Roy Nevins, running by, and hugged him till he gasped.

Laughing their own relief, the others were going out, struggling into their jackets, calling goodbye to Sheila, looking only covertly at Miss Flexe who continued to sit on a box that had a picture of some pears on one end, her face strangely quiet for once.

Then only Amy, Peter, Ben and Fats were left, and Sheila whispered, "It's all right. I'm sure of it. I'll talk to her and see you at the candy store if anyone wants to wait."

The four went out, calling goodbye and thanks for coming to Miss Flexe as they went.

436

Something was wrong. They all knew it. Sheila knew it. As they left, Miss Flexe stood up but made no move to follow them, or come to Sheila.

"What's the matter, Miss Flexe?" Sheila asked. She had been prepared for extravagant praise, and prepared to discount it; now, suspecting it would not be granted, she was perversely disappointed. "What's the matter, Miss . . . Mary?"

The combination of Sheila's voice and her own name seemed to be too much. Tears rolled out of Mary Flexe's round brown eyes.

"Oh, Mary, what's the matter?" Sheila said anxiously. "Isn't it good? I thought it went . . . it went so . . . all right."

"All right? All right? Sheila Walle, what have you done to that play?" The tears continued to run. "What have you done to that play?"

"Do you mean it isn't any good? Isn't it?" Miss Flexe's tears had stopped; Sheila felt as if her own were about to come.

"I didn't say that."

"It'll be better Monday."

"And I won't be here," Mary Flexe said bitterly. "Never." She backed a step away from Sheila, who was pressing in. "Did you ever read Shakespeare with me, Sheila Walle? Did you? Or do a play with me? Or a Shakespeare scene? Did you? Why did you make it so different?" She put out a hand towards Sheila as if to shake her. The tears began again, and she said, not even trying to wipe them: "There isn't one thing in that performance that you learned from me. Not one."

9.

"Hey, Eddie," Goswith said, coming into the shed where Eddie was nailing in floor boards. "Here's the mail."

"Thanks. Just put it down." Mail; big pleasure. Bang.

"You got an invitation."

"Yeah?" Invitation; big pleasure. Bang.

"On a postcard. To see . . . Miss Sheila Walle perform *Hamlet*. Who's Miss Walle?"

"Oh, just a kid," Eddie said, putting down the hammer and taking the card. "Monday night, huh?"

"Just a kid," Goswith scoffed. "Another one of your actresses, huh? How about cutting a friend in on some of that, Eddie? Come on."

"Shut up Ernie, for Christ's sake. This is a fifteen year old."

"You going to go?"

"I don't know. Yeah, I guess I will." It was Saturday; he'd call Dorothy when he went over to the house for lunch, and ask her. Sheila would like to have theatre people see her. Maybe Dorothy could get someone else, like a producer.

"Fifteen years old, huh?"

"Maybe she's still fourteen. I don't know." Eddie put the card in his rear pocket and knelt again to his hammering.

"Heh, huh, heh . . . I might go with you," Goswith said.

"No, Ernie, this is . . . oh, you know. Just kids in a neighborhood, putting on a play. Nothing you'd be interested in."

"Still, I'd like to go," Goswith said. "You know, maybe Guy will be there, or that other friend of yours. . . ."

Eddie stopped hammering and looked up. "Rather not take you, Ernie," he said. "Do you mind?"

Usually Goswith avoided eyes; this time however he looked back at Eddie, sucking on the filthy pipe, and said: "This the kid you were telling me about, Eddie? About her and her mother, in the war?"

"No."

"Yes it is." The bastard was about to chuckle.

"What makes you think that, Ernie?" Eddie kept his voice calm.

"I saw that picture you keep upstairs, the baby picture. Sheila Walle—that's the name on. . . ." He broke for the door of the shed, but he didn't really need to. Eddie checked his arm before the hammer left his hand, so that it snapped his wrist over and cracked him on the thigh; you don't really sink hammers into the heads of crazy old pukes who happen to be great painters.

Goswith came cautiously back in. "Can I go, Eddie? I'd kind of like an evening in town. . . ."

"All right, you son of a bitch," Eddie said. "You can go. On three conditions. You get drunk and stay drunk. You keep your face shut. And you're staying in town when it's over."

"Aw, Eddie. . . ."

"You got it straight now, Ernie?"

"Aw, come on. . . ."

438

"And if you talk about it," Eddie said, "there isn't anything in this world that will keep me from killing you." He couldn't call Dorothy now. Too bad. He laid in another board, and began to sink nails.

Tom went into the offices of Steven Even Productions Monday morning, the finished script in an envelope under his arm. Ned was coming out through the waiting room, and Tom put out a hand to stop him.

"What luck," he said. "I've been trying to call you all weekend."

"We went out of town," Ned said. He seemed subdued. "I'm sorry."

"Got it finished," Tom patted the envelope. "I owe you a case of absinthe, I guess. But it wasn't the script I was trying to call about."

"No?"

"No. Look." Tom took the postcard out of his pocket, grinning. "I won't ask you if you're busy tonight first, because I don't want to cut off your retreat. Read this. Sheila Walle is my fourteen year old niece." The card was an announcement of *Hamlet*, with time, place, names of the performers, an admission charge of fifty-five cents announced, and a scrawled note at the bottom in Sheila's writing: *If you could get any television stars to come, it would thrill the kids, especially the little ones.*

"The little ones," Ned smiled. "Good heavens, Tom, what can it be like?"

"You're the closest thing I know to a television star," Tom said. "Would it interest you at all? I'll even pay the fifty-five cents."

"Look, go in and see Steve," Ned said. "I'll wait for you."

"Steve? I didn't come to see anyone, just to leave the script for Paul."

"I think you'll find that Steve wants to see you."

"Has something happened, Ned?"

"It was in the *Times* this morning," Ned said. "Didn't you see? The sponsor's dropping *Golden Words*. We're fired."

"What?" Tom was shocked. He hurried over to the receptionist, handed her the script addressed to Paul Wuss, and the girl, who also ran the switchboard, said that Mr. Even had been trying to reach him.

A moment later, Tom was in Steve's office, standing by the big table, and Steve was confirming the news.

"Right out the window, without a parachute," Steve rumbled. "Like a man sliced through below the pockets, and he doesn't know it until his legs walk away and the body falls off. Of course you're unnerved, Tom, you won't find a steady hand in this whole office this morning. We owe you anything?"

"Why. . . ."

"Looked you up, Tom. You got paid for last week? We have you on the books as a consultant, fee basis, so that's it, right? Not an employee with forty-eight days accumulated Christmas shopping leave and life-time men's room rights."

"No," Tom said. "I . . . Steve, I finished the first draft of . . . that scrip. For *Carole*. . . ."

"*Carole?*"

"Yes. You asked me to try a script on that."

"How long ago was that, Tom? Oh yeah, I remember. That's been some time, hasn't it?"

"Four or five weeks," Tom said. "I've been working on it every free minute I had. I just left it for Paul, with the receptionist."

"Oh, yes," Steve said. "Interesting situation on the *Carole* series, Tom. I don't mind taking you into my confidence on this because you're one of the very few people I deal with I'd trust to guard a confidence. The people who were sponsoring *Golden Words* are stuck with a time contract, Tom. They've got a half hour bought, every week for the next seven, and they've got to pay for it. I'm attempting to persuade them that they'd do better to use the *Carole* series, move it back from afternoon to evening, than to send out some combination of organ music and performing dogs. You ever see performing dogs on television, Tom?"

"Steve," Tom made himself say. "I do have three hundred dollars coming from *Carole,* don't I? Now that the script is in?"

"Well, you'd know that better than I would, Tom," Steve said. "I empty the ashtrays around here, and sharpen the pencils, and carry the mail out to the postoffice, but they don't trust me to keep the books."

Tom said: "Steve, about this consultant situation . . . the fee basis. . . ."

"Yes, Tom, I was coming to that," Steve said. "In my ponderous way I was coming to the consultant situation for a number of reasons. Tom, the season's coming to an end and you, you haven't even come to bat yet. I'm like a baseball manager playing an old hack in a key position, when the boy he's been keeping on the bench might be rookie of the year. I've thought about that, Tom, and I think I may have a challenge for a man who's willing to work with me on a consultant basis. A challenge to a big creative imagination, a resourceful, rangy mind. I can't keep you on the payroll, Tom, because at the moment there is no payroll. You understand that, don't you? But. . . ." Steve paused. Then: "Will you keep yourself available, Tom? I mean it."

There was no particular point in Tom's replying that he hadn't come in as a man with a big creative imagination, only one in urgent need of money; he nodded, said goodbye, and walked out. Suddenly all he had were the three hundred dollars due on the *Carole* script, whenever the check might come. Otherwise? Otherwise, he had left, after last week's cable to Lala, the change from a five dollar bill which he'd broken to buy cigarettes in the morning. He was feeling the bottom of his pocket, counting with his fingertips four singles, and wondering where he might start looking for a job, when he almost bumped Ned, who was still standing in the reception room.

"Tom, I'm sorry," Ned said. "I know what this must do to your plans for going to England."

"Yes," Tom said.

"Wretched little industry," Ned said.

Tom nodded.

"I'd like to see your niece's performance tonight."

"You would?" Tom had forgotten that; now he saw that Ned still held the postcard.

"Yes," Ned said, smiling. "You were serious about asking me, weren't you?"

"Oh. Oh, yes," said Tom vaguely, his mind still only fractionally fixed on what Ned was talking about; for mostly he was thinking of Lala.

Sheila had not come home for dinner, but now, at least, they understood.

"I'm rather impressed with her, doing a thing like this," Harrison said, buttoning on a clean shirt.

Ellen swung her eyes to him and held them on his face.

"It takes initiative and ambition," Harrison said. "It's often occurred to me that the qualities that bring success in the arts are the same ones we honor in business. . . ."

Ellen neither nodded nor shook her head. After a moment, she dropped her eyes to the hand that held a drink, and lifted it to her mouth.

"I'd go easy on that, Ellen," Harrison said, lifting his own drink and finishing it off. "That's going to be my last, anyway. Don't want to miss the finer points, if there happen to be any." He chuckled.

Even with the glass in her hand, Ellen looked good to him. She was wearing girdle and stockings, wouldn't know which bra and slip to use until she'd decided on a dress. There were three on the bed, and she didn't seem to be making much progress towards a choice.

Five years ago, Harrison was thinking, I'd have gone over and kissed her, walking around like that in a girdle and stockings. Not any more for some reason. Not that we're cold to one another, exactly, we still, well, still sleep together. Of course we do. Often as most people our age, I guess. But if I walk across the room and kiss her now, she'll . . . be what? Not offended. Just surprised. Not pleasantly or unpleasantly surprised; just surprised. From the amount she's had to drink, maybe . . . maybe stupidly surprised. . . .

He crossed to where she was standing, by the bed, staring at the three dresses. He reached past her and picked up the blue one.

"This one I think, honey," he said. "From what Sheila told us, the place may be dusty."

Guy, too, was dressing. His card had said, in addition to the typed information, "Oh, please, please come and bring Miss Conn if you still see her and tell her I'm sorry for being fresh, I'd love her to see me. Sheila."

Guy had replied by phone, saying that he would certainly come, that he was sorry he couldn't bring Miss Conn; and Sheila had said he was wonderful. Guy felt rather pleased. Attending her play would be a pleasant way to atone to the girl for a wrong she'd never know had been done her, perhaps even an expression of gratitude for a service she'd never know she'd done him. For the whole chain of impulse which had started with responding to

442

Sheila and ended in the crazy drive to Virginia, two weeks ago, had left Guy calmer, more genuinely uninvolved, than he could remember having been for years. In the past two weeks he had had no dates, seen no girls alone; played squash every day, worked hard at some business matters, fulfilled with pleasure several social obligations of a kind he had been accustomed to ducking.

He could not be said to have been torturing himself with abstinence, for no torture was involved. Quite the opposite. A pleasure, mesdames.

He was dressed now, and he picked up the card again to check the address. It was near the Walles, he concluded; plenty of time for the drive over. He read through the names in the cast, squeezed single spaced onto the bottom of the card, and found himself smiling at one: *Roy Nevins.*

"Well, Roy," he thought, not especially surprised. "Imagine you turning up. I know your mother, and I've seen you before, Roy. But I don't suppose you saw me." He smiled again, putting the card down. It could be a different Roy Nevins, of course, but Sarah, whom he had known four years earlier, had had a toddler named Roy. And now the toddler was big enough to be in a play? Guy frowned. It was the same general part of Brooklyn. He decided there was time to clear up the point. He went to his bedroom and got out Volume Two of his notebooks. Sarah was . . . number 157. Three years back, not four.

"Your mother going to be there, Roy Nevins?" Guy found his page. He was merely curious, not alarmed. It no longer bothered him to meet a woman he was finished sleeping with, and Sarah Nevins was one he'd known more casually than most. He looked at a photograph she had said he might have—a handsome woman, in the picture, though he recalled, now, looking at it, that she had been both blousy and boney except for early in the evening. He read in his notes an account of their meeting: ". . . opening of Jacques Snider's show. New group of paintings quite bad. Met subject who is distantly related to Jacques. Uninformed about and not genuinely interested in painting. Looked well when carefully made up and dressed, but a sloppy woman basically. . . ." She had been recently divorced; it was clearer now. Much too wide-open, really. Guy had been taken with her at the art show, regretted being with her later, even before they got to her apartment. Nor had the woman made much sense; not dumb, exactly, but . . . well. He closed the book. Why should he have remembered her? He had barely known her—that was it. He had done something he regretted really, very much. A breach of manners he was quite ashamed of. She had phoned him the next day; he, not wanting to see her again intimately, nevertheless felt obligated to buy her a drink, tell her some gentle lie or other which would help make the experience as casual for her as it had been for him. Made the date and then, because of train connection trouble—he had had to go to Trenton in the morning—stood her up. It was the sort of thing he never did; he must, by all means, look for her at the play tonight and make belated apologies.

He put the book away, and thought of having once seen Roy. During the night in her apartment, the boy had waked and Sarah Nevins left the bed where she and Guy were sleeping to go to her child—and carried the kid back and forth, in the living room, a four year old, walking him up and down, soothing him: "It's all right, Roy; mother's here. It's all right"—and Guy, lying half awake in the bed, had watched them come into sight and out, into sight and out again, through the open bedroom door. . . .

The phone rang.

So now Roy was in a play, Guy thought, no longer smiling over the matter. In Sheila's play. Guy would see him; would seek out and be pleasant to his mother.

The phone rang again and stopped; let the machine answer. Let the mechanism take the message, just as if its master were away. It might be Tom or Eddie, someone to give a ride to Brooklyn. If so, the machine would tell him and Guy would call back immediately. If it were anything else, there wasn't time. He tied his tie. Then he put the machine on playback and listened critically to his own voice, then to the caller's: "Oh, Señor. This is Lordie Lord. If you do come in at all this evening, up to midnight, would you call me? Please? Don't worry about Reuben. He's gone out."

Guy felt an instant and powerful excitement. Of course; of course he would call. Reuben not home? Lordie alone? This was just right: he could take her out to the kid's *Hamlet,* in Brooklyn. An actress, much more the kind of actress who might say something useful to Sheila about her performance than Dorothy Conn. It was all coming together, how nice: Lordie and Sheila, their mutual intensity about acting. Their remote physical resemblance —of course. He might have to slip away to make the apology to Mrs. Nevins. Why not? He dialed.

444

"Hello?"

"Lordie this is Guy."

"Oh, you called back so soon. How could you?"

"Secret," he said. "Lordie, is tonight for us? Are you free at last? Because through sheer luck, there's something marvelous for us to do. . . ."

"Oh no," She said. "No, not free . . . not the way you mean, Guy. Oh, I'm sorry if you thought that. But it's a terrible emergency, and I've got to have a friend to turn to; everyone I know is busy or going out. . . ."

"What's wrong, Lordie?" Guy asked.

"This is going to be an awful imposition, so please say no if you want."

"All right."

"But you said you were going some place?"

"No place I can't take you."

"Oh, no, no." She said. "No, Guy, this is work. I've got a television show, I just got it, and I have to learn it tonight! So . . . so I have to have somebody to do lines with. Just to read me the cues, you know."

"Oh," Guy said.

"Could you take me to this place you thought of some other time? Because if you could, then I could come up there and you could read the cues for me if you wanted to."

"Come up here?"

"Oh yes. I wouldn't dare do it here, because Reuben might come back and find, you know, Ossie Parker."

"Why, I'd be very glad to have you come here," Guy said, his excitement, which had disappeared for a time, returning painfully. "Yes, please do."

"It doesn't mean I've . . . changed my mind, Señor," Lordie said, in a rather forlorn voice.

"You come along," Guy said, thinking, grimly: I haven't changed my mind either, Karen dear. Not in the slightest. "Jump in a cab."

"Not a cab."

"I'll meet you in front of the building and pay it."

"No, the bus will be all right," Lordie said. "There're lights on the busses so I can be studying lines on the way."

CHAPTER SEVEN

1.

IT SEEMED UNLIKELY to Harrison Walle, arriving with Ellen on his arm, that this could be the right house. There seemed to be no lights on in it, nor in any of the surrounding houses. The whole block, in fact, was peculiarly unlit, except for a single street light, and for the lights in the candy store on the corner. But at number 148, the gate stood open, and as Harrison peered down the alleyway beyond the gate, a flashlight beam caught him in the eye.

Ellen started and said, "Oh God."

"Here," Harrison cried, towards the flashlight. "Look out with that." The flashlight turned aside, and an unknown little boy appeared and led them down the alley to a side door. A couple, coming up behind, asked Harrison if this were the place where the children were having their play, and Harrison said, "Apparently." Ellen held very tightly to his arm.

The boy with the flashlight had backed away with it, and was now holding it on the doorstep. A man alone came in behind the Walles and the other couple and, as they moved through the door, Harrison thought for a moment that it was Eddie Bissle.

"Hey, Ed . . ." He started, and then realized he was mistaken.

"David Cuzenus," the man muttered, introducing himself. As

446

far as one could tell now, in the shifting beam of light, Mr. Cuzenus looked nothing at all like Eddie.

"Is it Eddie?" Ellen whispered, very close, and very faintly.

"No, Amy's father I believe," said Harrison firmly, aloud.

Now they were moving, single file, but with Ellen still clutching Harrison's arm from behind, after a second child with flashlight, to the end of a hall, up a flight of stairs.

"I guess they've got permission for this place?" asked a man's voice, possibly Mr. Cuzenus'.

"I suppose so," Harrison said, over his shoulder. "Are you Amy's father? I'm Sheila's."

But Mr. Cuzenus, if it was he who had spoken, seemed not to hear, and Harrison had an uncomfortable image of the man drifting back and away from them, as they moved, Harrison first, Ellen holding on to him, up the stairs in the dark. They reached a point in the flight where a pale, pudgy hand stopped them. Into it Harrison put the two tickets Sheila had sold him; the hand moved out of their way and they continued to climb, emerging, finally, into a limitless and gloomy space.

There were three dim lanterns, points isolated and irregular in what seemed to be a room of indeterminable length, each lantern held by a still child. The three faces were solemn in the slow-flickering upthrusts of light. At one end—the back of the building probably, Harrison thought, though he was not perfectly oriented—might be the stage. It seemed probable if only because people were being seated to face that way.

"There are boxes to sit on," said a new flashlight carrier, the other having turned to go back downstairs. "Or you can stand along the wall if you want."

"Let's find a box, Harrison," said Ellen faintly. "Maybe when our eyes get used to it, we can recognize Tom . . . or Eddie . . . or someone . . ." Her voice trembled away on the final word.

Harrison cleared his throat loudly and deliberately, and patted her arm.

The child led them forward until Harrison said, "Thank you. This will be fine." He had to overcome an impulse to whisper.

"You can light a match to read the program if you want," the child said, thrusting sheets of paper into Harrison's hand, and went away.

447

Matches were flaring now at various points around the room. It was reassuring, in a way, to have this evidence of others, but Harrison said: "Damn fools. Fire hazard."

They sat, crowded against one another on the box. Harrison strained to see the face of his watch. Exactly eight; he sighed. He had gotten Ellen here on time, after all, in spite of her reluctance. He shifted. He thought: how often punctuality is a waste of time, and precisely as he did, he heard Sheila's voice, shrilling from the darkness in front of them:

"House lights, please. House lights. The play is beginning." The lanterns were blown out. " 'Hamlet, Prince of Denmark'."

In the darkness, Ned Kildeer checked his hand as it reached to touch Tom Beniger's arm for company. The gesture might so easily be misinterpreted. He fixed his attention on the front, guessing there would be no curtain, wondering how they would manage to get started.

Again, less shrill as the room grew silent, the voice of Beniger's niece came through total darkness.

" 'The Castle of Elsinore. A platform, on the battlements.' " It was a strange, abstract voice—high, pure and without sweetness, like a boy soprano's.

There was a pause. Then a different girl's voice said: " 'Who's there?' "

That would be Bernardo, Ned thought, opening the play, a soldier coming to relieve the guard. Ned wondered if the cast were all girls. But it was a boy's voice which replied, in the dark, as the other Danish soldier, Francisco, " 'Nay, answer me. Stand and unfold yourself.' "

The girl who played Bernardo lit a candle, held it in front of her face, and gave the password. Francisco lit a candle and was seen, too. As they talked about the evening's watch, both moved forward, knelt, and began lighting other candles set in tin can reflectors, nailed to a board across the front of the stage; they did it just as if it were the business of the hour. It was preposterous, but it worked. By the time the next two, Horatio and Marcellus, joined them, the stage was lit.

Impulsively, Ned began applauding—a childish trick, romantic, illogical, but it had caught him by surprise, caught attention. Not many people joined him in the clapping, but Ned grinned; to the

448

kids backstage, unable to gauge applause yet since they had only begun to hear it, these few claps would sound fine.

Almost at once, however, interest fell off. Marcellus, a thin boy, seemed to be suffering terribly from stage fright. He could hardly speak. For the first moment there had been a partial illusion of soldiers changing guard, beginning to talk about a ghost; now, as Marcellus stammered on about the ghost, trying to persuade Horatio that they had actually seen such a thing here, they were merely four children, in home-made costumes, and helmet liners from a surplus store, having difficulties with recitation. Then something happened: an apparition.

It was neither child nor ghost. It was a gilded helmet liner, charging over an energized swirl of cheesecloth. It had been pushed on stage early, Ned recognized, half a dozen lines before its cue, sent in to rescue those on stage from their confusion; it threw the others into immobility and silence.

It danced ominously a moment, then rushed Marcellus who fell to his knees; it wove in front of him as the others retreated into a corner of the stage and Bernardo said, trembling:

" 'In the same figure, like the King that's dead.' "

Marcellus, groveling in front of the thing, quavered a plea over his shoulder to Horatio to speak to it; there was tension, now, as if Marcellus were in the ghost's power, and only brave words from Horatio could release him.

Finally, stepping forward, Horatio spoke—and Ned knew, as it happened, what had been wrong with this scene as he had watched it played by adult actors twenty, thirty, forty times: you couldn't play the scene and disbelieve in ghosts. Not that these kids needed to believe absolutely; they wouldn't. But they were not too many years away yet, from the age when the embodiment of a dead man in his ghost seems a likely solution to the terrible question: what happens to you when you die?

The ghost drew away, unwilling to reply to Horatio, fled; and the scene was boldly cut, then, by sixty lines, to the question about what such an apparition might portend which cues Horatio's speculative description of the condition of Rome, just before the catastrophe of Caesar's death:

" ' . . . the graves stood tenantless, and the sheeted dead
Did squeak and gibber in the Roman streets.' "

He did it quite well, a little too much charm, perhaps, a handsome boy; Peter Held. Ned suddenly remembered the name from the program. Peter Held was producing, now, just a little too much charm. Nice for the parents, of course; Ned sighed. The boy was poised, he moved well, the voice was obviously trained. But the moment in which he had been an actor, in which he had found the courage to challenge a ghost, had passed, and now the ghost's re-entry and re-exit to frighten the soldiers further did not restore Ned's sense of involvement.

Visually, though, the thing pleased him: the dim lights, the vagueness of the costuming, the constant motion of the players, grouping and breaking, a kind of movement accelerated by the frequent cuts which had been made—these gave the stage a flickering quality, almost dancelike, which was quite exciting. No one ever stood still. The audience was being held through the first scene, Ned decided, removing his attention from the stage to the people sitting on boxes in the shadowy room, not by the story the play was starting to tell, yet, so much as by the strangeness of its appearance, and by the conviction with which the children had begun to do their parts, now that Marcellus was over his difficulties.

They were reaching a decision, Horatio and the soldiers: they were deciding that Prince Hamlet, Horatio's friend, the late King's son, must be told about his father's ghostly reappearance. As they so agreed, and the scene concluded, Ned realized something almost unbelievable: these children were not playing to the audience. Nor were they playing to one another. They were playing to a point in the wings.

Some figure of terror and authority must stand there, someone far more in control of their imaginations, for the evening, than the parents and teachers who watched, a figure exercising what amounted to hypnosis; it would, of course, be Sheila Walle. Throughout the evening, Ned thought, I will always know, whenever she is off stage, at just what point Sheila stands, unseen by us, manipulating her cast.

Ellen felt terribly shaky. She ought to have had one drink more, or one drink less. She had neglected to go to the bathroom before leaving, and now she would be unable to until she was home again. She wished . . . but the kids were starting their second scene, so she finished the wish quickly: she wished she hadn't come. They had lighted more candles.

450

Someone called out that they were now in a room of state in the castle.

There were boxes for furniture, painted in bright colors, red and blue and gold. In the first scene the boxes had been lined out separately, standing on end, to represent ramparts. Now they were stacked in two stacks, and a large boy whom Ellen didn't know was sitting on one stack, bumbling through a long and tiresome speech; at least he bumbled fast. Ellen did not try to follow, but she remembered the play, vaguely, and knew that this was Hamlet's wicked uncle and new stepfather, the present King.

On the other stack of boxes sat Amy as Queen, wanton with coronet, in black blouse with bare shoulders and low bosom; years too old for her; cleavage! So of course the two stacks were meant to be thrones and the kids standing around were the court and . . . but Ellen had almost missed Sheila. Sheila was there, too, sitting on the floor, out of the light, Prince Hamlet at the foot of Amy's throne. Sheila's first appearance and you could hardly see her. She was staring at the floorboards, paying no attention at all to what the King and Queen were saying.

The kids droned on. Some child—was it the boy they called Fats? he had been to the house—in purple sweat pants and a white shirt, was bowing and backing around on the stage. His name was Laertes, and he was supposed to be somebody's son. Amy's little brother's son; Theodore, playing the old man with the silly white beard hanging from his twelve year old chin—Ellen could not remember what this old man's name was, but that's whose son Fats, if it was Fats, was supposed to be. Laertes. And oh, Polones, Polonus . . . Polonius. What was it Laertes wanted? The King's permission to go back to France, to resume his studies, studies interrupted by this trip to Denmark to attend the ceremonies: the old King's burial, the new King's wedding. For the new King has married Hamlet's mother, his sister-in-law, the dead King's wife.

Laertes got permission.

Ellen hitched around on the box, and thought about splinters.

Now, with Laertes gone, the big boy on the throne started speaking to Sheila; still Sheila paid no attention. A flashlight beam darted out from one side and hit her face. She muttered something, and wouldn't look up at the king.

The big boy spoke again, asking Hamlet: " '. . . why the clouds still hang on you?' "

This time the reply was audible. " 'Not so, my lord,' " without

451

looking up. " 'I am too much in the sun.' " Sheila said it sullenly, to the audience—or to the dark beside the audience—refused to give her attention to the King. And it wasn't as if Hamlet had heard about the ghost or anything yet; he was just sulking because his mother had remarried, after his father's death. Sulking. It was just like Sheila.

Now the Queen was speaking to Hamlet, asking what was wrong. Stop that sulking, Sheila; Ellen almost said it aloud. Amy is supposed to be your mother, and she's speaking to you—you won't look at her, she can't even hear what you're mumbling (" '. . . Ay, Madam. It is common.' ")

What's common? Death is common, Amy was reasoning. Then, less patient, with a hand on Sheila's shoulder: if death is common, why should your father's death seem so particular?

Shake her, Amy! Ellen commanded silently. Don't let her sulk.

Sheila leapt to her feet, threw off Amy's hand and started being fresh:

" 'Seems, Madam? Nay, I know not seems. . . .' "

Ellen could have slapped her.

"Are you all right?" Harrison whispered, and it was only a play again. The King was giving Sheila many good reasons why she should stay at home, cheer up, and not go back to school at Wittenberg. Sheila held coldly away. Amy, the mother, added a request of her own that Hamlet should stay home, at court, and Sheila said insolently that she would obey *her*.

And damned—Ellen smiled—damned if the boy, the King in the play, Hamlet's father—no, stepfather—damned if the man didn't do just what Harrison would have done: ignored the insolence, pretended it was *he* who was being obeyed, said a little too much to that effect, and left the room. Ellen laughed.

But Scene Two had lagged, and the audience in general was uninvolved. To those who bothered to judge, it was going a little better than expected. Most, as the King, Queen and courtiers left Hamlet by himself, were simply aware of an evening to be got through.

Now Sheila was alone onstage. It was time for the first soliloquy, " 'Oh, that this too, too solid flesh would melt;' " she didn't say it. She stared out at them and, for the first time, considered the possibility of failure. There had been shifting around and throat clearing while Ben got through his speeches in the scene just past;

452

disturbed, dangerously uninvolved herself, Sheila turned her back to the audience. She would not turn again until she was Hamlet, attracted passionately to suicide as a reply to a world of selfish and corrupt adults. Standing thus, she raised a hand towards her face, with no knowledge of why she was making the gesture, and saw, looped around a finger, the back of her ring, a small topaz in an old-fashioned setting which had belonged to her grandmother as a girl. The hand, in front of Sheila's eyes, was closing into a fist, bringing the sharp little stone into view. With the fist, knowing now what she was doing, Sheila hit herself, a short, cruel blow in the face, and raked the ring across her cheek. She turned back slowly and showed it to them. She tossed her head. She heard them gasp. She touched a finger to the blood, held it away, looked at it, tasted it and wiped it violently across her breast as she began the soliloquy.

Harrison was indignant. The damn little fool. She could infect herself like that. For damn little, he would speak up and stop this whole obscene . . . obscene what? Burlesque. Burlesque against parents. This was not *Hamlet;* he would assert a real authority, stop this before . . . before what? He looked at his wife. What was happening to Ellen? Alarmed, distracted, he watched her: Ellen's chest and shoulders heaved. Her breath was loud. The arm and leg beside him, pressing his side, were rigid. He wondered if she were getting sick.

But in general, the audience was caught by it. That's the way, David Cuzenus thought. Never mind the cheek. You show them, honey. He loved the theatre, had loved it since he was a little boy. He did not know this play, but had seen it once in a movie with Sir Laurence Olivier. And that was good, very nice acting, but not the theatre. Not live people, making mistakes, overcoming them, doing things to win the night's particular audience that they had never done before and would never do again. In a movie, where was the difficulty? Make a scene ten times, take the best, put it onto the best of another scene, string them all together, and you might have nice acting, but dead, dead. This had breath. This was people, kids, all right, but people. Flesh, blood, hair and hide, pitting itself against the sullen will to disbelieve, the disinclination of an audience to come and play. David Cuzenus slipped happily into total belief. He had no need to comprehend all the language,

453

the sum of activity. The parts were what mattered, the individual eloquence, the gestures, the voices, the moving—in Japan, in his exiled-white-Russian boyhood, David Cuzenus had not understood the language in the theatre, but he had learned to give himself, sensually, to the tones, the poses, the swirl. . . .

Others were not caught so willingly, but they were caught; gradually Sheila became for them a strange boy, with a wound self-inflicted on his cheek, with good reason to loathe his uncle and his mother:

"'. . . O, most wicked speed, to post
With such dexterity to incestuous sheets.'"

That was laying it on the line, naked and shocking.

In came the other boy, Horatio, and after him, the soldiers.

Now, for the first time, Ned could get himself to yield a little. Of Sheila's trick with the ring, he had had to disapprove, but now: now there was something in the greeting of Hamlet and Horatio, friends who have not seen each other since the intervention of grave sorrow, something sound: a boyish courtesy, sobriety, joking, between friends so close they might be said to be in love. But not in Ned's sense of love between boys—he made the correction wistfully. These boys were best friends in a way he had envied and never achieved—at school, for instance. There was an ease between them which was the polar opposite of sex—he forgot, in his envy, that they were a boy and a girl acting it.

This thing they had found, between Horatio and Hamlet, was a marvel, Ned thought, something he had never seen in the script though he knew more possibilities in this play than he did in his own life. These were boys who, from the habit of loving one another, spoke lightly, the vernacular of playfulness, though one's heart was broken . . . no! *Because* one's heart was broken. To maintain playfulness, lightness, was the most tender kind of respect on the part of Horatio for Hamlet's sorrow at his father's recent death.

The actual display of this mutual feeling lasted no more than a line or two, but so precisely did the two establish the pattern that it would last out the play, would be there for them to resume whenever they had need of it. And on they went, from the quips, easily into Hamlet's seriousness, weariness, hopelessness—then, from Horatio, an account of the awesome marvel of the ghost. Now, for the first time, hearing this, Hamlet had reason to suspect that the death of his beloved father was not natural; he became excited. He must see this spirit, speak to it, learn its purpose—Peter and Sheila, Horatio and Hamlet, played it together, ignoring Bernardo and Marcellus. Marcellus' speeches even, Ned noticed, had been given to Horatio, so that he and Hamlet could speak the whole discussion apart, off in a forward corner, boys with too heavy a secret, speaking of it in troubled quietness, between themselves.

Hamlet's friends left. Fearful, yet eager to meet his father once again, in whatever form, Hamlet wished for night to come. " 'Till then, sit still my soul.' "

What was this girl? Ned asked himself, as she held the stage alone once more, then turned and went impatiently away. Her voice, a little harsh to his ears at first, lacking in sweetness, now seemed to him to have the joys and sorrows of a woodwind, nothing lush, no overtone, all pure flute and oboe; her form—but he kept forgetting to look at her. Was this Puck as Hamlet? Peter Pan as Hamlet? No, this was a Hamlet, valid somehow. If they could sustain the play, Ned thought, waiting for Scene Three to start, the girl would have created something, no matter how marred and fleeting, something true.

Applause followed Shelia's exit. She stood behind the dyed sheets they had hung to form wings, breathing hard and sweating lightly; she could feel dampness against the gauze Amy had wrapped to flatten her breasts.

"Sheila, is your cheek all right?" Roy whispered.

"Quiet," she said, and, turning on the flashlight she carried, illuminated her left hand and beckoned Fats and Rosemary onstage from the other side.

This was a break in the narrative of Ghost, King, Queen and Prince, a family scene in which brother Laertes, ready to leave for France, warns his sister Ophelia against letting Hamlet love her; they do not realize that Hamlet's present feelings leave no room for love. But narrative break or not, Sheila was sure that Rosemary's stricken beauty, seen now for the first time, would carry the audience into the scene. And then: the way Fats could smirk over the lines, like " '. . . lose your heart, or your chaste treasures open;' " that would do the rest. For the smirk emphasized the pathetic, undefended quality of Rosemary's appearance. It was an effective combination, smirk and beauty, and Sheila had worked hard for it—harder than she should? One day, overhearing Fats teasing Rosemary with these speeches, holding the girl cornered in the schoolyard, with Ben's help, and giving the words far more licentiousness than in rehearsals, Sheila had been a little shocked. Would the audience be? Wouldn't it be like Fats to respond to this public situation by overplaying, by giving them the schoolyard version? Suddenly Sheila had a frightened vision of an indignant Mrs. Bernstein, crying to her daughter to come away from that dirty boy, get off the stage, come home. The Jews; weren't they, weren't they very moral?

Sheila's nerve began to fail. Fats was swaggering into the speech now, ogling, suggestive, worse even than in the schoolyard. His words crawled over Rosemary; he touched her, fondling her; how long could Rosemary's remoteness protect her? What must Sheila do? Only turn the pencil flashlight onto her face and frown at Fats, and he would understand that he must tone it down. Sheila raised the light—but this was effective. This was, in an awful way, real, necessary—a brother-sister encounter of a type unnatural, which would help explain Ophelia's madness later, which would give an extra bluster and guilt to Laertes' violence of feeling against Hamlet, late in the play, when he blamed the Prince for Ophelia's suicide. Who had said, "Everybody talks dirty to Ophelia?" Not Fats. Sheila. This was a horror she had found herself, though it took Fats' bravado to make it whole.

Should she withdraw it? Turn the flash onto her face? The vision of Mrs. Bernstein nearly drove Sheila to it. And yet she didn't; what Fats was doing was good. Hate him, pity Rosemary—still, it was good. Let Mrs. Bernstein yell if she must; Sheila was committed. She moved her thumb from the switch and lowered the light.

It was the evening's only crisis, for Sheila, of judgment or of conscience. Beginning then, she ceased to think of the children or the audience as people; she thought only of her play.

Mrs. Bernstein, a far younger woman than Sheila imagined, sat on a box and watched her daughter's first scene carefully. Her husband, a psychiatrist, working as he did every night at a clinic, would expect a report, and it would be Natalie's pleasure to make him a detailed one; they would sit up, long after their exhausted child had gone to sleep, Philip and Natalie, dissecting the girl's responses, analyzing the experience, trying to find hope in it. For their pale, absent little daughter worried Philip and Natalie to the point of grief. They had been delighted to hear that she had been asked to appear in a play; it meant acceptance by the other children, of some sort. They had been in on the secret long before the other parents, for just as she never revealed, neither could Rosemary conceal. When her mother asked where she was spending her afternoons, Rosemary answered truthfully. And from that point on, Natalie had done all she could to help—practiced lines, bought a book on voice projection to study with her child, saved from household money for the costume, the loveliest on stage, a long white gown, white as Rosemary's skin.

It was a Mrs. Bernstein of another generation Sheila had envisaged; Rosemary's grandmother, perhaps, would have dragged the child indignantly from the stage, a Mrs. Bernstein of wrath and vengeance. Mrs. Philip Bernstein, wife of an idealistic psychiatrist, who worked in one clinic by day and another by night, and had no time for private and well-paying patients, this Mrs. Bernstein felt no discomfort. She watched the scene with relief. It was reassuring to her, and would be to Philip, to learn that Rosemary interested boys; far from resenting Fats, Mrs. Bernstein felt very grateful to him.

The scene continued. Polonius, twelve years old and looking it, came onstage to his two grown children, Laertes and Ophelia.

Tom Beniger saw him, and could not place him in the play. Tom, who could have recited most of *Hamlet,* did not know what Act it was. He was simply standing still, letting time and words move past him, seeing the actors, hearing their sounds, with no attempt at comprehension. He had spent the afternoon phoning people he knew, asking for appointments to talk about a job. He had, so far, not one appointment. He had remembered to dress, to go downstairs, to meet Ned, to come here, only because it was a place he was supposed to be. He had even remembered offering to pay Ned's way in and spent, of his four dollars and seventy-two cents, a dollar ten for two admissions. There had been a heartbreakingly cheery letter from Lala, too, in the afternoon mail, full of planning for his trip to England. It was something of a triumph for Tom, that night, to have arrived at, and to be standing in, a place where he was supposed to be.

As Polonius began to give Laertes, impatient to be off for France, his parting advice—Ophelia standing quietly by—the audience stirred with pleasure at the familiarity of the lines, suddenly feeling a fine roomful of Shakespearian scholars. Ned, for whom, " '. . . to thine own self be true'," had acquired the meaninglessness of a bad popular song, infinitely repeated, thought about the structure of the play, thought of Sheila's problem, any director's problem with the way the scene that they were playing interrupts the building of Act One, from Ghost, to Hamlet, to meeting of Ghost and Hamlet; it was not a really tough problem. Sheila had solved it, he thought, simply by making this interpolated scene itself interesting; but try keeping such indirection, such dramatic illogic, in a television script . . . impatient with such a comparison, Ned turned his attention to Tom. He knew, of course, what the matter with Tom was, but he could not guess how seriously out of money his friend might be. He wanted to help, but he didn't know quite how to offer. Once again, for a different cause, he wanted to touch Tom with his hand, and again he withheld it.

And by now Ned could not keep his attention off the stage for long. It did not quite involve him, but its details kept exciting notice, speculation. What a wonderful cheat Sheila had been in her casting. There, as Polonius, quite unequipped by experience, of course, to deal with the subtleties of rendering a sententious old man, Sheila had found a sententious little boy. There, as Ophelia, a girl who carried in herself, apart from the context of the play, the appearance of her own doom. As a painter may choose colors for what they are, not what he can change them into, so Sheila had chosen actors; she had not been infallible, of course, nor had she completely avoided kids who could act. The boy who did Laertes was acting; the one who played Horatio had facility and, when he was on with Sheila, more; the girl—much the best after Sheila—who was cast as Queen, had seemed full of instinct for the stage in her first scene. Others, on the other hand—the soldiers, minor players, and, most of all, the big fool who played the king—had been wooden and unfortunate so far. Even this Polonius, now hovering over his son's departure, for all the resemblance of the twelve year old bore to an old man, was tiresome, even when convincing. What a puzzle, Ned thought, that this boy should be the Queen girl's brother—yet he mustn't forget, Ned mustn't, that these were children. Adolescents. Charm and talent might descend and drench the boy at thirteen, just as the hot climate of sixteen might dry them out of the sister.

Well, there went Laertes, finally, off for France; Polonius added repetitious advice on sexual conduct to his pale daughter Ophelia, and the scene was over.

Now the crates were stood on end and spaced out to represent ramparts again, and Ned tried to set himself for watching, for giving in, to the first act climax, the meeting of Prince Hamlet with his father's ghost. Night again. On came Hamlet and Horatio, with Marcellus trailing behind, all of them speaking quietly; would the thing appear tonight? Was it time? Then, Horatio:

" 'Look, my lord, it comes.' "

Awfully abrupt, Ned thought; dozens of lines had been left out, between the arrival of Hamlet's party and the coming of the ghost. Such cutting was, well, amateur; yes, but practical; bald, but why not? The ghost, having come on and seen the three, fled; Marcellus and Horatio were wrestling with Hamlet, now, trying to keep him from following. It was a real tussle; the play might have been baldly cut verbally, but no chance for expanding physical action had been missed. Good. Ned watched this in a retrospective fantasy of himself, Ned, helping the children cut their text more smoothly—and rejected the fantasy with irritation. They—she—had needed no help.

For an instant, now, the stage was empty. Then the ghost came flickering back on, the insubstantial thing under the gold helmet, and hid. It was another part of the battlements. Hamlet came following, searching, calling to the ghost.

It rose up; it ascended a gold box, and then another. Then, for the first time in the play, it spoke. Ned's knees went weak at the sound of the voice.

No electronic combination of echo chamber, distorter, amplifier, could have produced that ageless, sexless, disembodied croak.

" 'Mark me,' "

the ghost commanded, and the shiver that had started in Ned's knees went through the room. For this was how ghosts sound—

459

hoarse, lonely, bodiless, longing towards the living with a horrifying weakness and a terrible despair.

" 'I could a tale unfold whose lightest word
    Would harrow up thy soul, freeze thy young blood. . . .' "
But such a tale was not for mortal ears, the ghost cried, and yet the audience could know it from that voice—that the real dreadfulness of ghosts is that they crave so deeply the breath we have, the size, the substance, and know so finally that these things can never again be theirs.

Even Harrison, worried and irritated on the whole by the events, worried in particular about Ellen, was swept by a momentary sense of conviction for this play about a ghost. An adult, tolerantly listening to children telling scary stories, may sometimes feel, if cravenly, a genuine instant of fear if he has happened to relax his guard at the moment when teller meets climax. Harrison jerked himself impatiently out of such a state, and felt justified for he found that Ellen was trembling slightly, regularly, beside him. He murmured something soothing towards her ear, and put an arm around her.

Ellen moved away from the arm, not taking her eyes off the stage, rose from the box and slid over towards the wall, where she stood watching, with her lips apart.

She had forgotten it was Sheila there, that boy on stage, hearing the dreadful revelation of his father, the dead man telling tales: My brother killed me, your uncle. And your mother helped him, an adulteress before my death. Seek my revenge. Kill the murderer; leave the woman to heaven.

Then the ghost was gone and there was Hamlet, alone and horrified in the night, touchingly writing down, schoolboy fashion, a note to remind himself of the unforgettable.

There had come, now, a time when the play was succeeding consistently. The ghost had left; Hamlet, released from fear, knowing the worst, heard his friends' voices again, was relieved, became exhilarated, and he and Horatio called out, locating one another with falconer's cries:

"Horatio: 'Hillo, ho, ho, my lord!'
    Hamlet: 'Hillo, ho, ho, boy! Come bird, come!' "

460

They found one another and fell to extravagant jesting—it was at this moment that Ned forgot himself and touched Tom's arm. Never had he known how to direct the falconer's exchange, the strange, wild joking. Now, seeing it as a product of release, he understood; better than understood, learned.

This was the moment when Tessie Held, Peter's mother, forgot that they had brought her husband's boss and the boss's wife—a slightly older couple—to see her charming boy be charming, and simply watched the play.

It was the moment when Francesca Cavendish, headmistress of the day school all but one of these children attended, gratefully paused in her consideration of the disciplinary problems posed by the event, and watched the Danish Prince and his schoolboy friend skylarking exuberantly over the matter of taking an oath of silence, like kids at recess—so exuberantly that when the Ghost, now unseen, muttered: " 'Swear'," Hamlet could call out to the apparition, so lately terrifying:
" 'Aha, boy? Say'st thou so? Art thou there, truepenny?' "
What a delightfully cocky way to speak to a ghost, your father's, who has just filled your mind with things most awful, demanded a revenge portentous: regicide. This was a true response from Hamlet: to ride the waves of fear on a slim surfboard of cockiness—the true release, the real exhilaration, which springs from knowing, finally, how bad things are.
The friends swore silence. Hamlet, daring now, warned that his strategem might be to pretend madness until he knew the whole truth—a dangerous, a desperate course, recklessly improvised out of exhilaration.
And this was all capped perfectly, for all of them (except, perhaps, for Held's boss, who was asleep; and Harrison, who could not stop fretting; and Sarah Nevins, who thought with staunch vagueness throughout that the children were being uniformly sweet; and Ernest Goswith, who was preparing a remark to make to Eddie Bissle; and one or two others who had come determined to be bored, whatever happened; but there were thirty more, beside these)—capped perfectly for almost all of them, then, by Hamlet's abrupt return to caring. There was a beautiful, weary

461

courtesy that was all that was left in him as exhilaration drained away, and he said to his schoolmate and the soldier, standing aside for him, as Prince, to precede them:

" 'Nay come. Let's go together.' "

It was here that Sheila made a genuinely childish error. Because the book said this was the end of an act, it had not occurred to her that there was any choice but to have an intermission.

The three lanterns were lit. People stood and stretched. Matches flared.

"I don't think we ought to smoke in here," Harrison said, loudly, and was ignored. He crossed to his wife. "Are you okay, Ellen?"

"Oh, yes."

"Maybe we should leave?"

She shook her head.

"Oh, there's Tom," said Harrison. He went over to his brother-in-law, assuming that Ellen would follow. "Hi, Tom. I wonder if we ought to smoke in here?"

Tom looked at him, nodded seriously; then, for it seemed that the meaning had been slow in reaching him, dropped his cigarette on the floor, ground it out with his foot, and turned away.

"Isn't it wonderful, Mr. Walle?"

David Cuzenus hit Harrison on the back.

"Oh, yes," said Harrison. "They're doing quite nicely, aren't they?"

"I could eat them up," Cuzenus said. "What a daughter you have, to do all this, eh? Sons, you expect they'll do things—but daughters! What a country, Mr. Walle. Daughters!"

"Yes, yes," Harrison said, afraid the man would pummel him again. "Excuse me, I must get back to my wife." For Ellen was still standing in the same spot; she hadn't followed him.

"Ellen," he said. "Are you sure you're all right?"

She seemed to come out of it a little. "Aren't they . . . wicked, Harry?" she said.

"What do you mean? That's a strange thing to say." He peered closely at her. She obviously didn't mean wicked. She never called him Harry. Either it was the effect of the lantern light, or there were fever spots in her cheeks.

"Ellen, did Sheila actually tell you that they had gotten permission to use this building?"

462

"She didn't tell me anything," Ellen said. It seemed to Harrison that her voice was trembling.

"I'm going to ask her," Harrison said. "There could be trouble about this."

"Oh, there's going to be trouble," Ellen agreed, but Harrison felt she was speaking of something else—could it be the play?

"I'm going to check with Sheila."

Ellen's hand caught him at the wrist as he moved forward, and her nails dug in.

"Don't you dare," said Harrison Walle's wife. "Don't you dare go check with Sheila."

Sarah Nevins was the only parent trying to find her child. Roy, changing to his costume as First Player, saw her coming and hid until she wandered off again.

Held's boss said he really must go. The smoke was too damn much for him. Should he find the nearest bar and wait for them, or what? It was arranged that Ezra would go with him, that Tessie Held and the boss's wife would stay.

Ernest Goswith took a swill of liquor from the pint that Eddie Bissle held out to him and said: "Look, they're leaving out half the play. Anybody can do all right if he just chooses a few fragments of something and strings them together. It's doing the tough parts—look, like Voltimand and Cornelius; all that stuff about Norway. Where is it? Left out."

"Ernie, they're kids, for Christ's sake," Bissle said.

"That don't excuse them," Goswith said, being deliberately ungrammatical; that sometimes got a rise out of little Eddie. "They're asking to be judged ain't they? Absolutely, good or bad. You think they want to be excused for being kids? No. They want to be told, good or bad. Well, it's bad, ain't it? All that tricky, romantic junk with candles. . . ."

"All right, Ernie."

"What do you mean, 'all right Ernie'? You trying to placate me? Don't you think someone ought to . . . hey, is that her?"

"Is what who?"

"Standing by the wall. Holding the guy's wrist. Is that Hamlet's mother?"

463

"Cut the goddamn clairvoyance, will you?" Eddie said.

"I'll be damned," Goswith said. He was feeling wonderful. He took another pull at the pint and got up. "Hey, I'm going over and have a look."

"You are like hell," Eddie said, calmly, rising too, and putting a hand on Goswith's shoulder.

"Why not?" Goswith pushed away Eddie's hand. "I'll go squeeze her teat if I want to. I'll look at anyone I damn please."

Eddie's blow traveled three or four inches, caught him square in the center of the chest, and practically collapsed his lungs. He found himself sitting back on the box, wheezing, as the call of "house lights" came through the room, and the lanterns went out.

Eddie was laughing at him. "Stop squeaking," Eddie said. "Watch the play."

Mercifully, the second act was short, for it went badly. Cutting a short, unnecessary episode, Sheila had decided to begin it with Ophelia much affrighted, describing to her father how Hamlet had burst into the room where she was sewing, his clothes disarrayed, and behaved like a madman. Unfortunately, Rosemary was not effective in the long, narrative speech; her voice, none too strong at the opening of it, had faded to a whisper, hardly even audible in the wings, by the time she finished.

The audience, straining to hear what had happened, learned only generally that Hamlet was now beginning to carry out his plan of shamming madness; they lost the details of his behavior— the description of his blank stares and tortured sighs—and were annoyed.

There was information enough in the next scene: they understood that the King was suborning two of Hamlet's former intimates, Rosencrantz and Guildenstern, to use their friendship to discover whether the insanity was real or not, what, if anything, Hamlet might know. But information was not enough: the boy who played the King kept missing lines, going back and repeating. It was painful. There were some who found a partly-compensating amusement in the fact that Rosencrantz and Guildenstern were being played by identical twins, identically dressed, but these were limited to the few who could appreciate such casting as commentary—not very subtle, perhaps, but no less broad than Shakespeare's own joke in naming the two with similar tri-syllables, so

464

that one is never certain which is which. To most of the audience, prey to the democratic rule that every player must have a number, each container of individuality a handle, it was irritating not to be able to tell the actors apart.

This was true, even, of the boy's uncle, James Lafferty, a wholesale grocer, with whom the twins lived. It was hard enough to tell George from Basil at home; he felt a sense of insult about the situation, without being quite certain why. Lafferty was an earnest man, and he had brought with him two fellow Knights of Columbus and a priest to watch the young sprigs perform; their indignation was mild, at first, and unspoken, but eventually the priest whispered something about mockery to the more literate of the two accompanying Knights. A moment later, the second Knight said, quite audibly, to Lafferty, hearing the Shakespearian names for the third time:

"The boys aren't supposed to be Jews, are they Jimmy?"

Natalie Bernstein heard this, for one, and looked angrily at the priest, assuming that it was he who had said it.

The muttering of Lafferty's party quieted when the twins left the stage to try to carry out the King's instructions—that they learn what was on Hamlet's mind; then there was a fair degree of attention to Polonius' busy entrance and erroneous announcement that he had diagnosed the cause of Hamlet's madness as unrequited love for Ophelia. Ophelia had been made an interesting, if somewhat mysterious character to this audience, and they were alert to know about her; they listened carefully to discover whether the King would be deceived by the false diagnosis; Ben butchered the lines, of course, but they gathered that the King was not completely satisfied.

Neither was the audience; they were having to work too hard.

They did get further entertainment from the next episode, however, a cruel little scene in which mad Hamlet baited senile Polonius about his age and about his daughter, confirming the old man's error.

The twins came in to join in the baiting—then, when Polonius left, to take over the prying. Hamlet evaded them, too. The Knights and their Chaplain listened carefully for anything to take offense at, but Shakespeare had kept Hamlet reasonably courteous to Rosencrantz and Guildenstern, for the first half-dozen lines. Only when the Prince's questioning of his supposed friends' motives in coming to him turned sharp, could Lafferty's party start to mutter

465

again; there was shushing from others in the audience, and an announcement that a troop of traveling players had arrived at the Castle of Elsinore was nearly lost in it.

Ned was among the shushers. He had been waiting, detached again, for these traveling players to arrive; he had been curious to see what Sheila might do, as director, with a speech of Rosencrantz' describing child actors on the Elizabethan stage. He smiled, understandingly, when the time came for this speech and Sheila had cut it.

What else could go wrong? Several things. The first was the unexpected delivery of the solution to the mystery with which this production had become pregnant in Act One—the mystery of where the children could have found a ghost with such a ghastly voice. A very small boy entered as First Player, and when he began his lines in this character, the thing was solved: it was the ghost's voice again. A slightly incredulous laugh went up. The production lost a good deal of ground.

And why, Ned wondered, only one Player? Why didn't the rest come in? They could at least have made the stage more colorful. Now, instead of more players, crowding around, being colorful, another error, more ground lost. Far, far too much of the action-stopping speech from *Dido and Aeneas* had been left in.

We know, Ned thought, that Hamlet is forming some plan involving these Players, so we can be patient for a little time with their greetings, their discussion of the theatre; but when Hamlet and the First Player go rambling off about a play concerning Dido, and start taking turns quoting speeches from it, Shakepeare's own play dies. The quoting has a function, Ned admitted; it provides material for the second soliloquy, which is about to come, wherein Hamlet will contrast the First Player's facile emotion, in dramatic pretense, with the Prince's own slowness to become stirred to effectiveness by a much graver, unpretended situation. But how much Dido-Aeneas quoting do we need to give us this material?— none, really, from Hamlet; only a few lines from the Player. Why had Sheila, so ruthless with her other cutting, failed to cut her own, Hamlet's share, of this dull stuff?

Why? The only explanation Ned could think of was simple, rather dumb vanity on Sheila's part. Whatever the reason, attention fell perceptibly, as she spoke her part of the long quotation;

466

fortunately, vanity had not required that she leave the Player's continuation equally full; there was little enough of it left in. Hurriedly, now, Hamlet conspired with the Player to stage a play called "The Murder of Gonzago," which would parallel the actual murder and adultery, described by the Ghost as having taken place in the court of Denmark. Seeing this play, perhaps the King would show his guilt—but all of this was merely information, for the audience. It did little to pick up the pace dropped so disastrously by the recitation from Dido.

And now? Ned shook his head slightly, biting his lower lip. Now, there was Sheila onstage again alone, with all the lost audience to win back, and fifty-eight lines of rather cerebral soliloquy left to do it with. Ned thought: she can't start bleeding herself again, she can't trick them, she's got to act now.

Sheila knew this. Whatever she did now must be the real thing, and she must find it, somewhere, in herself. No pause to think (" 'Now I am alone'," she said): just start, and work, and make herself be honest; show them Hamlet.

" 'Oh, what a rogue and peasant slave am I!' "

She said it carefully, bringing it out of a feeling of her own, immediate, personal inadequacies: the awkwardness in her direction as she had seen it fail just now, contempt for her silliness in having tried to save for herself the Dido speech, scorn for her timidity in not having improvised a cut in the middle of it.

She was aware that, with these things to work from, she was starting a little too quietly; no matter. She must test the bladder of emotion to know what it contained; the first pricks of self-dislike must be tentative until she found the tool sharp enough and the bladder full. The liquor began to trickle out through pin-holes:

" 'Am I a coward?' "

Restrain; don't jab until you must:

" 'Who calls me villain?' "

It began to spurt now, with unsuspected pressure from a dozen holes, and the force of the fluid itself was now enlarging the holes, destroying the walls that had contained it, so that emotion came washing, surging:

" 'That I . . .
Prompted to my revenge by heaven and hell
Must, like a whore, unpack my heart with words. . . .' "

467

Something had happened to Sheila and she was triumphantly lost in it. Starting, as she had the first soliloquy, with an audience to win, she had been forced to reject them as a consideration, having neither lure nor plea left to offer, had been forced to leave them, to go into herself for what was truly there. Now it was coming out, and she knew it was right in a way nothing had ever been right before, and she ceased to care whether the audience agreed; she forgot the audience, losing herself in an ecstasy of honest acting, and thereby she won the audience.

To some extent.

For it didn't work with everyone, not even with everyone who was disposed to have it work.

With David Cuzenus, for example, rooting for her to pull her show out of its slump through histrionics, as she had before, and to whom the words were unfamiliar, the content here was disappointing. Here he expected bloody oaths of vengeance and resolution. No background of language study or academic orientation had prepared him for this coupling of self-loathing with a passionate examination of the relation of illusion to reality:

" 'Is it not monstrous that this player here
But in a fiction, in a dream of passion
Could force. . . .
Tears in his eyes, a broken voice. . . .
. . . Yet I
A dull and muddy-mettled rascal. . . .' "

It didn't suit Cuzenus' expectations, nor had Sheila the strength, yet, to force him to be suited by it.

Ned, unhappily discriminating mind, too theoretical for simple responses, too good an audience for Sheila yet, understood her situation as dilemma and approved the solution. But that was as far as he could go for her. Yet, at the same time, it gave him confidence. He felt that she could handle it now, both herself and the production, and he began to look forward to the balance with a keenness he had not felt before.

Tom was, for the first time, caught. Surprised out of himself. He stared at the girl in front of him with a certain amazement. He did not think of her as his niece, and perhaps not as Hamlet, either, but her performance of it made the speech the first meaningful thing he had observed outside of himself for many hours; he began to take interest, even to look forward a little.

To Ellen, entirely rapt with the whole production, the whole strange exposition of evil and innocence, by whom the errors of the second act had gone unnoticed in the totality of her involvement, the soliloquy was only a variation; she was like a woman giving herself to a long passage of love-making, and the soliloquy was like a lover's change of tempo, which gratifies without surprising. At the same time, Ellen's response was not quite as simple as a sustained moan of pleasure, for pleasure was only one of its constituents. There was, in addition, a tremendous sense of identification with Sheila, so that Ellen herself was Hamlet, suffering and eloquent; and identification with the evil, too—the King, Queen, spies, the old man; and finally there was anticipation of climax, a climax neither like orgasm nor purgation but like being cauterized, an agony to be endured and made well by, for the play was pointing towards a scene which she remembered now, between Hamlet and his mother, in which Ellen anticipated a marvel of pain, of burning out, of miraculous cure. . . .

The act was over. There was another intermission.

If Harrison Walle had been concerned for his wife in the first intermission, he was now genuinely alarmed for her. As incapable as any husband and father of real sympathy for the complex and ambivalent relations between a wife and a daugher, he had begun to see the whole production as a morbid attack by Sheila upon Ellen. Whether it was deliberate or not, he could no longer doubt—as Ellen, in something like a trance, pushed away from him—that this was having some effect, temporary, he prayed, upon her sanity.

Nor could he find comfort in the audience at large; it was as if no one would talk to him, or listen, rather: they talked but they refused to make sense. Cuzenus, for example, patting him on the shoulder and saying, compassionately, "There, there"—what did that mean? The smoke, the body heat, the dimness. Some people were angry: "Jimmy, you must take the boys away." "Jimmy, ask the Father." "Is Walle a Jewish name, Father?"—what did this mean? Whose father was here? What was the anger about? If he

469

had before been uneasy, he was now beginning to panic. There was Eddie with some man; why hadn't Eddie brought the man and introduced him? Why did the man look like a beggar off the street? Where was Guy? Where were Ezra Held and his boss? What was wrong with Tom?

He said, "Exuse me," loudly, to Ellen, who paid no heed. He found the deserted stairs. He stumbled down them. In the alleyway between the buildings he breathed cool air for a moment, uncertain what he had come down for in his relief at being away. Then he remembered his intention.

He went out to the street, looked around, and saw the lights of a candy store on the corner. He walked rapidly over to it, entered the store and bought cigarettes, though he already had two packs, to get change. He looked for a phone booth, and saw that there was none, only a naked pay phone hanging on the wall. He waited for the proprietor to lose interest in him, look away, and then went to the phone. He put in a dime and dialed "O."

"I want the fire department."

"Do you wish to report a fire sir?" said the operator.

"No. A violation. May I have the fire department?"

There was a pause; then he was connected with a polite, disinterested man, who listened calmly to Harrison's report of crowding, lanterns, candles, smoking, wooden floors. . . .

"Thank you, sir," the fireman said, having got his name and address. "Thank you for calling." It seemed to Harrison that he was being brushed off, and he started to repeat his description; the man interrupted him with another thank you and hung up.

Harrison hurried back. If they were brushing him off, then he had better get Ellen and take her away—perhaps for a long soothing walk, in the warm spring night.

But when he got back to the huge room, it was dark and the play was starting again. He made his way to what he believed was the box they had been sitting on. It was empty. He remembered where Tom and his friend were standing, and inched over to them, ignoring the proceedings onstage, to ask if they had seen Ellen. There was shushing from all around him. Harrison slumped, defeated, against the wall. They liked this thing; liked it.

A trap was being set for Hamlet, baited with Ophelia. They were hauling the pale, lovely child around, showing her where to stand, how to hold the prayer book she was to pretend to read. They would settle now, by hiding to watch the encounter between Hamlet and the girl, whether unreturned love was the true cause of madness in the Prince, as Polonius insisted, or whether something graver was involved.

Sheila breathed deeply, standing in the wings, and nodded to nobody.

Amy, in particular, had found herself, as if released by Sheila's release in the last soliloquy, and was dominating the stage, even though the King did much of the talking. The audience, instructed, finally, in how to watch and listen, was attentive. On Amy's exit they applauded, and there was more clapping when Polonius and the King withdrew to hide and overhear.

On went Sheila as Hamlet, unable, for a time, to see Ophelia, whose post was on the other side of the stage, and said: " 'To be, or not to be,' " and they applauded. Applause was a help. There had been no way to say those worn out words, except as the announcement of a title. She went on lightly, almost sarcastically, for the first four lines, treating the alternatives of life and death, until she came to the verb, " 'To die.' " She let it stop her. Then she plunged into the great, classic expression of self-pity without trying for anything original, simply saying what the lines said, in a way that moved the audience into something like unanimity.

Further applause. Before it could end, she discovered Ophelia; with this, she and Rosemary were able to sweep on, without loss of momentum, lifting each other through the mockery, tenderness and desperation of their scene together. It was like flight:

"Hamlet: 'I loved you once.' "

"Ophelia: '. . . You made me believe so.' "

" 'I loved you not.' "

" 'I was the more deceived.' "

" 'What should such fellows as I do, crawling between earth and heaven? We are errant knaves, all; believe none of us. . . .' "

" 'O, help him, you sweet heavens.' "

It led to a real opening for Rosemary and, possessed like all the rest now, she made something of her chance: Hamlet left. Ophelia, reviled and abandoned, must now, in ten heartbroken lines, accept as true her lover's madness. " 'Oh, what a noble mind is here o'erthrown. . . .' " Rosemary did it simply, very simply, almost quietly; even Sheila, who had taught Rosemary, she would have said, the inflection for every syllable, was pulled into belief in the girl's shattering and personal sense of loss.

Poor lady.

Out in front, Sarah Nevins cried.

The King and Polonius came out of hiding, no chance, the way their speeches had been cut, of either of them being tedious this time; the King remarked that Hamlet hadn't looked to him like a stricken lover. Polonius admitted that the evidence was inconclusive and suggested that they bait a second trap with Hamlet's mother, and the King agreed. Off they bustled; for once they had held the pace.

Good, Ned thought, very good. For even as the two turned and went off, something curious and intriguing began at center stage. Hamlet's own plot, using the visiting Players, was being set to work. Rosencrantz and Guildenstern, his unwitting accomplices, had entered, and were busily rearranging the painted crates which served for every sort of furnishing. This time the two courtiers were building these crates up, into two walls and an arched opening, a little proscenium, a stage within the stage. It was about four feet high; across the front they hung a length of cloth to serve as curtain.

Rosencrantz and Guildenstern now placed themselves as a screen, from one edge of this interior stage to the left wing, and there was an unseen scurrying, then, as the visiting Players went covertly from the wing to their own little stage, and settled, hidden, within it. The courtiers left.

Hamlet came on to interview the Players, and give final instructions; the First Player answered from behind the curtain of the little inner stage. A surprise was waiting. The whole audience knew it, and enjoyed anticipation.

In came Polonius, doddering; in came the two courtiers, once more, to observe the preparations; still the appearance of the Players was a secret. There was much movement. Off again, Polonius and courtiers; in now to join Hamlet, Horatio, for last words of strategy. The two friends spoke in low voices, and kept glancing at the interior stage; it would be Horatio's job to keep close watch on the King for any sign of guilt during the Player's performance.

Yes. Something extraordinary was going to happen. They were building it up so well; Ned noticed that even Tom, jolted out of

472

himself at the end of the second act, was now excited. Sheila was focussing them all, actors and audience alike. Ned himself began to lose some of his cursed judiciousness, to feel suspense, anxiety; what had they contrived? In came the King and his court at last, to dispose themselves for watching, an audience within an audience.

A last, secret conference behind the reduced proscenium, and Rosencrantz announces that the players are ready whenever Hamlet is. Only Hamlet shows no impatience. He summons Ophelia for dalliance. He speaks naughtily to her. He stretches on the floor to watch, the picture of an indolent young gallant waiting for a show. He tells Ophelia, forced, poor thing, into the role of orange woman, the hobby horse's epitaph:

"'For, O, for, O, the hobby horse is forgot.'"

It is the cue for Rosencrantz to draw the tiny curtain of the inner stage aside.

Collectively, the audience gasped.

There, uncramped by the reduction of space, still and grotesque, like strange dolls posed in a tableau, were four tiny children, as much smaller than the main cast as was the main cast smaller than its audience.

The little ones were lighted not with candles but with flashlights, sconced along the edges of the forward boxes; and they were made up, in this harsher light, big-mouthed and heavy eyed, with preposterous hats, and swords on the two boys who were Player King and Poisoner, elaborately-sashed dresses on the girls who were Prologue and the Player Queen. The tableau they held was of Prologue in a shallow curtsey, front and left; Player Queen kneeling, arms clasped around the Player King who stood at attention, front and center; Poisoner crouching, rear right.

Taste? The audience did not consider taste, not even Ned. They watched intently as the Prologue completed her curtsey, indicated Player King and Player Queen, and backed away. They watched intently as the children solemnly pantomimed a dumb show of wooing and poisoning. Ned was transported. The sheer evil of the little boy's face who mimed the poisoner! The tortured cherub of a King, the sobriety and conviction of their movements—and the perfection of timing with which, just before it all became unbearable, Ophelia's voice said:

"'What means this my lord!'"

And Hamlet cried, leaping up, exultant, and facing King Claudius:

" 'Marry this is miching mallecho; that means mischief.' "

The King leapt up, too, and overturned the little stage; the tiny players scattered, shrieking, and Hamlet and the King opposed each other, giants now, on the scale to which the audience had, for an instant, become accustomed.

Letting the dumb show stand for the whole interior play, Sheila cut through to the cry:

" 'He poisons him i' the garden, for's estate.' "

The shaken King was routed, and Hamlet called after him:
" 'What, frighted with false fire?' "

" 'Give me some lights,' " cried the King, running. " 'Away.' "
And left Hamlet and Horatio alone, as courtiers and Queen followed, in temporary command.

And now, from one focus to the next, the Act swept on. It was known, already, that Hamlet would be summoned to his mother, so Polonius might hide himself to overhear what would be said. Along came courtiers to command Hamlet's presence, in his mother's chamber. For Ned, the moment was over; there would never be another like it. But beside him, Tom had begun to twitch with excitement.

And for Ellen the moment was just now coming: the mother had sent for the child.

" 'She desires,' " said Rosencrantz, " 'to speak with you in her closet.' "

" 'We would obey,' " cried Hamlet, intoxicated, to the ceilings, " 'Though she were ten times our mother . . .' ", and screamed, a high, girl's scream, as an incredibly bright light from behind the audience hit him, directly in the eyes.

"All right, kids," said a heavy voice behind the light. "Let's break it up."

Another beam joined the first. A fireman, directing the second beam steadily in front of him, strode slowly down the room, through the frightened adults towards the terrified children, his footsteps cracking, to their ears, like tank tracks on a wooden bridge.

"Let's break it up, everybody. Let's go home," said the commanding voice from the rear.

No one moved.

474

"Get those candles out, you kids. Come on."

Now the children moved, but back, away from the candles, away from Sheila who still stood center stage.

The fireman was halfway to her, his light steady and bright on her face. Sheila stared back at it. In the audience the adults winced, squinted, looked away, as if their eyes were hers, and saw, at the rear of the room, more uniformed figures, police, joining the firemen.

"Don't let anyone out yet," a policeman said to the commanding fireman, and although he said it quietly it carried down the room. "We'll have to have these names."

No children were left onstage now except for Sheila, still caught in the advancing light, eyes swimming, face pained and crazy under its powder. There was a grunt, a scuffle.

From among the adults, crowded together out of the fireman's way against the wall, a tall form came, flailing, shoving, hurtled into the passage, checked itself, and then leapt at the leading fireman's hands; it was Tom, shouting.

"Bastard, bastard, get that light out of her face," and the heavy flashlight crashed to the floor where it continued to burn. "What are you doing here? They're not hurting anything," and Tom grappled the man, throwing him down. Other men in uniform ran forward.

There was a purposeful shriek. A woman followed Tom and could be seen in the crazy light, punishing a policeman as she might have punished a naughty dog by hitting him with a rolled magazine.

It was Sarah Nevins, Roy's mother, repeating Tom's words: "They aren't. They aren't hurting anything."

There was a chaos now of screaming, shouting and bobbing lights. In it could be heard the voice of Eddie Bissle, cursing at Goswith for holding him back, and the sound of many feet running.

The feet were the children's. Tom's attack was the break they needed, and Ben led them like a king, out of the wings, along the wall, heading for the stairs to get away in the confusion.

A voice, a policeman's, shouted, "Don't let them out. We've got to book these kids."

Near the head of the stairs stood a fireman, blocking the way.

Ben reached this fireman at full run, checked for a second to give Fats time to swing by; Fats took the fireman low, from behind, at the knees, and Ben took him high, butting a head into the solid chest and seeing his man fly back. All the fireman could do was collar Fats as he went down; the rest poured down the stairs after Ben, Sheila last, and out onto the street, past empty police and fire cars, running.

In the room, the calmest place was at the center. There Tom waited for the man he'd bumped to get up; Tom's concern had been for Sheila, and he would have rushed to her, unaware that she was gone, but he supposed his victim would need to hit him. Instead the fireman cursed as he got up, pushed Tom away and moved to retrieve his light.

Beside him, the odd young woman was still trying to whack the policeman with her rolled magazine, but the policeman had caught her hands.

"Oh no, lady," the man was saying. "Lady, lady. No." He took the weapon from her, tossed it away, and caught her by the elbow. Then he hooked Tom's arm with his other hand, and began to move the two away, saying,

"Are you people crazy?" And he marched them quickly to the stairs, out of the building, and into one of the squad cars. Here he told them to sit in back and scolded them, but regretfully; then he wrote down their names and addresses in a book, and settled himself in the front seat to wait for his partner.

Inside, powerful lights were now established from each corner of the room, flooding the center. The firemen were blowing candles out, scraping hot wax off the floor, inspecting the walls. Physical confusion had been replaced by verbal, as a dozen people tried to explain or argue with officials, moving from fireman to policeman to a man in a black raincoat, searching for authority.

"A disgraceful performance," the priest was saying. "I was led to believe it was a school activity. . . ."

"What do you mean, book the kids?" It was Harrison Walle. "You mean as juvenile delinquents? See here, I'm the man who made the complaint and the girl's father as well. . . ."

"These children are in my school, and I will not say that I am ashamed of them or that I consider them criminals. . . ."

Finally it was arranged, with the senior policeman and the man

476

in the raincoat, who turned out to be an assistant fire chief, that the children would not be held. This was concession of principal only, since all but one, a boy who gave his name as Fabian Gunderson and who had been Laertes, seemed to have got away. The parents must undertake to produce them all for the magistrate at Children's Court when directed; the headmistress would be responsible for giving the police a full list of names and addresses. The priest offered to make a deposition. The headmistress snorted at him and insisted that she would make one too.

Several people noticed that Tom Beniger and Sarah Nevins, assaulters of officers, were not there, and supposed that they, like the children, had fled.

Sheila, tears streaming from her eyes, ran along the street. Going fast, teeth chattering, she turned the corner by the candy store and headed for a small park, two blocks away. Halfway down the block she began to pass some of the smaller children. She had nothing to say to them. She kept her eyes on her feet and went by.

When she reached the park, she was running by herself. She was winded to the point of illness. She fell into a small clump of ornamental evergreens, pushing down through the branches until she found bare space, near a trunk, where she could lie, panting, and begin to absorb the dimensions of her defeat. She heard the scuffles, after a moment, of others finding similar shelters, and was very still. They all were. They did not know whether or not they had been followed.

And Sheila did not want to be discovered, not even by her companions. There was no voice in the world she would willingly have heard.

After a moment or two, however, she had caught her breath; she became aware then that someone was in the space on the other side of the same small trunk; she turned on her stomach and wriggled over. It was Ben.

The spring air was mild, but she had sweat so much that she was shivering by now, and she rolled against him for warmth. "Oh my God, Ben," she whispered. The boy was lying on one arm; he dropped the free one around her. Sheila was grateful.

"Did you see my Uncle Tom hit that man?" she asked. "Will they beat him up?"

"Probably will," Ben said.

477

"Oh God."

Then, to her astonishment, Ben started to feel her in the way she had permitted sometimes, following rehearsals. It frightened her. She pressed an elbow into the ground, raising herself, and swung the other hand, smashing him in the face with all the strength she had.

Ben yelled.

Sheila's next impulse was to hit him again; this was followed instantly by a sense of deep confusion. Trembling, she began to get to her hands and knees.

"I'm sorry," she whispered, and as she did she heard someone begin to cry, somewhere near at hand. She crawled under the branches towards the sound, and recognized the sobs as coming from little Roy Nevins. He saw her, stopped crying, and said, desolately,

"Sheila, Sheila," holding out small arms to be taken and comforted.

She stared at him, dim on the ground, wanted to help and, at the same time, felt herself rising from hands and knees to her feet.

"I'm sorry," she said again, and then, her head coming up now, through the branches, called it into the night, out loud. "I'm sorry. Oh, I'm sorry."

Then she ran again, away from the park, a slim, sweat-suited flicker in the night, taking confusion with her; ran through the empty streets of Brooklyn uncertain to whom and for what she had apologized.

478

PART THREE

CHAPTER ONE

1.

LORDIE LORD SAID, *"Señor,* thank you a whole lot."

It was eleven-thirty on the evening of the play, and Guy had been wishing since ten that he had gone.

"Very glad to help," he told Lordie, in an even voice. He was rather tired. The damn girl had kept her overcoat on all the time she had been in his apartment, walking up and down, saying the foolish lines in response as he would read cues from the script she had handed him on entering. She had refused to sit, refused champagne, refused food, refused to talk about anything; now it was not even midnight and she was at the door. Guy firmly wished her on the other side of it; he had not urged her, by a word, to stay.

"Please don't look so sour," she said. "You did tell me you weren't planning anything."

"Yes, of course," Guy said.

"Well, then, it isn't my fault is it? If you'd said you had plans, I wouldn't have come." She made fists of her hands, bounced them off her thighs, and started back across the room towards him. "What was it you missed, Guy?"

"Lordie, you seem to have your lines quite perfectly," Guy said, wondering how he'd ever got started with such a girl. "I think I'd like to get some sleep."

"Ooooh." She made a little mock howl, stood on tiptoes, and

481

kissed at him inaccurately, missing his mouth and slightly wetting his chin.

He patted the padded shoulder of her overcoat, and turned away.

"Ooooh," she howled again, and took the coat off. "Now I've got to stay until you smile and say it's all right. Would it be too late for you to go now, to the party or whatever it was?"

"It was a fourteen year old girl playing *Hamlet*," Guy said. "I imagine it's about over now."

"It was a what doing what?"

"A two year old boy singing *Boris Goudonov*."

"*Señor,* put some music on."

"I like being called *Señor* about as well as you like being called Karen," Guy said. "What would you like to hear?"

"Progressive jazz?"

"All right."

"And a drink with gin in it?"

"Surely," said Guy, starting the phonograph and then turning to go to the pantry. She followed him.

"Do you have a regular bar?"

"All but the neon sign."

She giggled. "I know the price of drinks."

He smiled. "They're on the house tonight," he said. She came up behind him as he mixed, and put her face against his shoulder.

"Now you're being nice. *Señor?*"

"Yes, Karen?"

"Guy, I mean. It's . . . I'll bet you have a way to turn the lights down." She pressed the cheek closer against his upper arm.

"There's a set of switches on the right as you go into the living room," he said, and handed her the drink, holding his own.

She preceded him through the doorway, and found the switches. The first one she tried darkened the room completely. She laughed and tried another. It mingled low-watt, blue and white bulbs in the troughs, making the room dim and romantic.

"Nice," she said, pleased. "Oh my, what an effect."

"Very good for looking at the view."

"Or dancing." She sipped, put her glass down and moved against him; they began to dance. She was wearing tight pants once more, red this time, and a yellow jersey top. Her short hair had been cut recently, and her face, as it passed his at close range, looked elfin.

482

"Tata, tata, ta," she sang breathily, along with an alto saxophone on the record, and they danced slowly around, half-timing music that was already rather slow. She was a wanton dancer, pressing in against him frankly; Guy held back. "Oh, I like this group," she said, of the music. "You can move to this."

"Yes," Guy said. When the number had finished, they stopped and sipped at their drinks; a second tune started and as it ended she took his face in her hands and kissed him. Then she breathed: "There."

Guy smiled, relaxed, and moved his arms around her. At this, however, she slipped away and moved back a step.

"Not tonight," she said. "Please, Guy? Remember, I have to start rehearsing at nine."

He supposed his jaw must have fallen, for he was conscious of having to work the hinges to get his teeth back into occlusion. Meanwhile, she had walked to the light switch and turned on the bright lights again. Guy reached behind him and stopped the phonograph.

"What on earth was the point of that, Lordie?" He asked.

"What?" She turned back to look at him, frowning.

"Did you think you were making things better?"

Now it was her mouth that worked its hinges. "Well . . . well . . ." It appeared that improving the situation was precisely what she'd had in mind.

Guy couldn't help laughing. "Let me help you with your coat, Lordie," he said. "Next time I'll call you."

What sin of pride ever made him think he could have the last word with this girl? "It's a good thing you aren't really Ossie Parker," she said, at the door. "Like you pretended at the party."

"Why? What would Parker have done?" Guy asked.

"He'd probably have caught me and tied me up," she said, with a wicked, sensual roll of her puppy eyes. "He did a couple of times." Then she closed the door fast and was gone.

2.

The sergeant at the precinct house was weary with them, but not impolite. "Thomas Beniger," he said, writing the name on a pad. He looked at it and read it back to himself. "Thomas Beniger."

He looked at Tom. "Tell me, Thomas, did you ever spend any time in a mental hospital?"

"No."

"You sure about that Thomas?"

And later: "What sort of trouble have you been in before, Mrs. Nevins?"

"None."

"Who got the divorce, you or your husband?"

"I did."

"You weren't charged in the case?"

"No."

When he had finished the booking, he told them that the minimum bail in which he could hold them was a hundred dollars each. "Either of you got that much cash?"

Neither of them had.

"All right. Now I'm going to let you use the telephone to find bail," the sergeant sighed. "You can make all the calls you like." Mrs. Nevins was shaking her head, and he went on patiently. "I'm only supposed to let people try three calls, but I'm going to let you two make all you want. Now, Thomas, shall we let the lady go first?"

Tom nodded. Mrs. Nevins shook her head again.

"Thank you," she said, in a soft, vague voice. She was a young woman with a disarrayed look, a face that seemed not quite collected. "Thank you, I don't mind staying until morning."

"Look," the sergeant said. "I don't want to keep you here, and I'm short of transportation to send you over to detention tonight."

Mrs. Nevins said she could only call her parents, with whom she and her little boy lived; she said her parents would be in bed, and that she mustn't disturb them.

"Mrs. Nevins," the sergeant said, still patiently. "Please. I don't want to put you in back. I got a couple of girls back there tonight who aren't very nice. Now please."

"Oh no," she said. "Oh no. I'll wait till morning. I don't mind."

The sergeant sighed. "What about you, Thomas? You want to wait till morning, too? You'll be lonely back there. No company yet on the men's side."

Tom smiled. "I'm sorry, sergeant," he said. "There's no one I could call this late at night who'd have a hundred dollars in cash." He had thought of Harrison, but there would be trouble enough

484

in the Walle house; he had thought of Guy, but it would be inconsiderate to call Guy at home, late in the evening, unless the emergency were really pressing. Tom had never been in a jail before; he found himself more curious than alarmed.

But the cell to which they led him offered little with which to occupy the mind. Its floor and back wall were tiled. It had floor to ceiling bars, spaced four or five inches apart, separating it from the cells on either side, and there were bunks chained to the bars. Tom unhooked a bunk, sat on the edge of it, and thought about Cicero. A man in jail thinks of lawyers.

Wasn't Cicero very much like an American trial lawyer? Tom was remembering Plutarch's comparison of Cicero and Demosthenes, remembering that Plutarch had described Cicero not as stern and censorious but as a man of humor, even unbecoming levity—good-natured, a mixer, changing to the solemn advocate only when the occasion in court called for it. In the weeks of the Cataline conspiracy, finding himself in charge, the lawyer had had a long run in his stern personality, necessarily so, and this had become his legend, whereas. . . .

Tom got up, walked across the cell, and thought about England. He was very far from there, and farther than ever from being able to travel there; suppose he were fined, several hundred dollars? Suppose he couldn't pay it, would he be kept in jail? Suppose they kept him sixty days in jail, he would have no living costs, he would let the apartment go, pay what bills he had to—wouldn't the money due him from the *Carole* script be almost enough to make the journey on then? He smiled. He walked. I am thinking like a bum, he thought; that's a bum's calculation.

Tom walked to the door of the cell and looked out. There was a short corridor with a concrete floor, recently washed and smelling of strong soap. At the end, painted green, was the metal door through which he had been brought from the front part of the police station. He looked at it, and wondered if it would open, if someone else, some man legitimately desperate or hopeless would be brought in. The door did not move.

Tom turned away and went back to the bunk, thinking about bums. Hoboes? No. There weren't any hoboes any more, men, that is, who wandered because they couldn't find work. The bums now were neurotics: winos, misfits.

No criminal would join him here—a real criminal would go

485

straight on to detention; what might he meet? A juvenile, in a purple satin jacket? Some drunks? As for bums, if one came in, it would not be one of the strong and bitter vagabonds of his youth, the hoppers of freight cars, drinkers of canned heat, organizers of trackside jungles. Bums today bought bus tickets and muscatel, slept in city shelters and were bums by psychological necessity, not economic.

The hoboes were a lost tribe. Their songs; he had heard one recently, as a children's record. Their songs, like cowboy songs and railroad songs, like all folk music in a nation whose folk were vanishing, were of interest to anthropologists and to children. The one he had heard? "The Big Rock Candy Mountain"—lemonade trees, baked bean bushes, bulldogs with rubber teeth, jails made of tin so you could break out whenever you liked. It must have been a young hobo's song, a boy wanderer's, for there were cigarettes in the paradise it described but no women, no liquor; a soda water fountain . . . perhaps tribes are lost when their dreams are achieved. Certainly the bulldogs had seized Tom with rubber teeth . . . He heard a latch turn. At the end of the corridor the policeman who had brought him to the cell was coming in, through the green door. Tom stood up, smiling. Company, he thought.

But the policeman was alone. He came to the door of Tom's cell and opened it.

"Come on, Mr. Beniger," he said.

"Mister?"

The policeman grinned. "Haven't we been calling you mister?" he asked.

Tom returned the grin. "The sergeant called me Thomas. Seems nicer."

"He'll probably call you captain now," the policeman said. "He got a call from a Deputy Commissioner about you, and one of the biggest guys in Borough Hall got out of bed to come here with your brother-in-law."

"Oh no," Tom said.

The policeman, who had stood aside to let Tom enter the corridor, closed the cell door behind them. "What's the matter? You like our hotel so well?"

"I know it sounds silly," Tom said, apologetically.

They went out through the green door and into the squad

room. A heavy stranger was talking to the sergeant; Harrison, who had been listening, crossed to Tom and patted him on the shoulder.

"It's going to take a few minutes," he said. "I hope you don't mind waiting."

"You must have been busy," Tom said.

"No one knew you'd been arrested till we started piecing things together, and decided you must have been," Harrison said. "Then I had to mobilize things a little. My lawyer, Held's lawyer—you don't know Held, do you?"

Tom shook his head.

"Useful," Harrison said. "Seems like a silly man but he knows how to operate."

"It . . . it wasn't necessary," Tom said, not meaning to sound ungrateful.

"No?" Harrison frowned at him.

"Is this costing money?"

"Please shut up, Tom," Harrison said. "Come on." He pointed towards a side room. "They're going to let us sit in here, while things are getting fixed up."

3.

Harrison took Tom's arm. He knew he must be tired, but he didn't feel tired. He felt, in an odd, low-keyed way, elated; at the same time, he felt the elation threatened by Tom, by something curious Tom might say in the hearing of the police or the man from Borough Hall. He pushed his brother-in-law into the little side room in which, at a large, plain table, the Nevins woman was already sitting.

"There," Harrison said, relieved, closing the door. Then, pointing to Mrs. Nevins, he said: "I thought we ought to spring her first." He felt like chuckling, and he did. Tom sat down at the table. "They use this room for questioning," Harrison said, and sat down across from them and looked at the prisoners. "They said we could wait here."

"May I talk now, Harrison?" Tom asked. The tone could have been satirical but wasn't.

"Sure."

"What's happening?"

487

Harrison leaned back. "It's a matter of seeing that there aren't any complaints," he said. "If there's no complaint, there's no violation. Held's people are working on the firemen; we have to give the guy you clobbered something; and their fund." He wondered if Tom could really comprehend this kind of thing, but he went on, trying to simplify as much as he could. "The important factor is the firm that owns the house the kids broke into. It's a firm Held's bank does business with, fortunately, and they've been talking."

"But is it really necessary?" Tom asked.

"You questioned that before," Harrison said. "You have strange ideas of necessity, Tom." He thought a moment. "No. I suppose we could have let you and Mrs. Nevins spend a night in jail. But you two are only a . . . well, a complication. The necessity is concerned with the kids."

"The kids?"

"We want the whole thing off the record, Tom. Mrs. Nevins. No complaints, no charges, no . . . no record at all. We don't want our kids in court." That should be something they could understand.

Tom looked at him, about, perhaps, to nod, when, unexpectedly, the woman spoke.

"They were in court," Mrs. Nevins said; her voice was distant. Harrison stared at her. He hadn't really looked before. She seemed to be in her late twenties, with pale, untidy hair, quite a lot of it, tied back. She was rather large, bony, sweet-faced, a trifle pop-eyed, a trifle loose around the mouth. Her dress looked good, but carelessly put on, and she seemed to have made no effort to tidy herself on leaving the cell. Harrison decided she must be a little crazy.

"I mean . . . I mean. . . ." She stopped, and then said, too softly: "They were in the Danish court. . . ." And with that her voice trailed off and her eyes lost contact with his; it was quite clear that she hadn't been trying to make a joke. It was a little spooky.

"Yes." said Harrison. "Well." How very strange, he thought, to be sitting here in a police station, long after midnight on a spring evening, father of an hysterical child, husband to an alcoholic wife, conversing with a crazy woman and a jailed brother-in-law. Harrison Walle, Yale, '40. It was still in the room; then Tom spoke.

"How is Sheila taking it?" He asked.

Harrison heard the question and replied to it, but he was looking at the light, a single large bulb with a green shade, hanging from a black cord, centered over the table. "She wasn't home when I left." It was like the light in a movie police station. "I guess the kids will be straggling in all night."

"You haven't heard about Mrs. Nevins' little boy?"

"No."

Now the woman wrenched herself back into the conversation. "Oh, he'll be all right," she said. "He'll run home to his granny. He'll never miss me."

"Won't anybody miss you?" It was Tom asking; Harrison had let his mind go back to the light. Hadn't small-time criminals, deceitful prostitutes, cracked under this light, confessed?

The woman was saying something, asking a question: "Won't they let me stay here tonight? Just tonight?"

The question seemed to be for Harrison, since Tom didn't answer.

"What?"

"Wouldn't they let me stay? It isn't bad back there." Harrison shook his head, finding her incomprehensible. "I just hate to go home now. So late. When they're all asleep." She paused, then added: "I mean, they're used to having me stay out overnight."

"Oh?"

"I'm divorced you see. . . ." Then she caught herself and blushed, very faintly. "I don't mean that the way it sounds." Her voice ran out, but instead of lowering her eyes, as Harrison expected, she gazed at him intensely.

Harrison shook his head again. The bulging eyes stayed on him a moment, and then got lost. How could he explain to her that people don't voluntarily stay in jail? He felt, suddenly, as if he were about to start shivering, and once more Tom spoke.

"Is Ellen all right?"

"Oh yes."

"She take it hard?"

"Who can say?" Tom would know as well as Harrison how Ellen must have reacted to the play's being interrupted; Ellen had simply gone on home and resumed getting drunk. Tom might know another thing, even, that Harrison had learned over and over, and learned again tonight: that Harrison's fears for Ellen's sanity were never real. That, unless it happens late in life, as a matter of general wear, women like Ellen do not lose their minds per-

489

manently, for they have learned to lose their minds temporarily as often as they need to.

Now Tom was staring at him; for a moment Harrison wondered why. Then he realized it was the tone of his own voice, that there had been no jauntiness in it, no prepared tone at all, when it said, "Who can say?" It was then that the monstrous cat of personality, which had had Harrison's tongue from the time he'd met Tom as a schoolboy, let go. "I can't say about your sister, Tom. Who can say how she takes anything? Can you? I suppose she'd stop speaking to me over a thing like this, except . . . in a way she stopped speaking to me fifteen years ago." I am not myself, Harrison thought, talking this way; but went on. "Fifteen years. Before we were married. And hasn't really spoken to me since. And probably never will. Do you know what I mean?"

"Yes," Tom said, leaning back from the light and becoming a shadow across the table that offered more sympathy than Harrison wanted. "I'm afraid I know what you mean. But why . . . why do you say 'over a thing like this'?"

"You don't know about it? I was the guy at the play who hollered cop."

"You did, Harrison?"

"I got alarmed . . . about Ellen. The kids. The place. I panicked. Was I the only one who felt alarmed?"

In Tom's face he could watch the search for an answer, a mannerism of his brother-in-law's which Harrison had always before considered charming but somewhat forbidding. Now this search and the hesitation in answering it produced, as if Tom, who had nothing to give but answers, was determined that all answers should have full and honest weight, soothed Harrison; the trait had always before seemed to put him at a disadvantage. Now it was quite the opposite; the advantage was Harrison's.

"Yes, I suppose I was alarmed partly," Tom said, at last; "but excited, too. I guess I was more excited. But, well, as Hamlet recently said to King Claudius, about their play, 'We that have free souls, it touches us not.'"

Harrison took out his penknife, opened the large blade, and said, in an offhand way, "Souls free of guilt, it means, doesn't it?" Then he looked up from the knife at Tom, and smiled a deliberate smile. "Not many of those around, are there?"

"I suppose not," said Tom. "Isn't it strange?"

490

"What about your soul, Tom? Why do you suppose you felt so much acceptance of the idea of staying in jail tonight? Why were you even partly alarmed at the play?"

"I suppose it's the idea of children getting at truth," Tom said. "And I don't mind admitting that my soul harbors a certain amount of guilt, but I'm not sure I know what it's for."

"You couldn't know," Harrison said. "But I could tell you."

"You could?" Tom frowned at him, surprised perhaps.

Again Harrison smiled. He must take his time now. He must build this thing. He had never had a chance to attack Tom before, never really known he wanted to. Now, with time stopped all around them, at the interrogation table, under the lamp, he could try. He closed the blades of the penknife and put it away.

"Pretty much of a radical aren't you, Tom?" He began.

"No."

"Weren't you, in college?"

"No." Tom said. "I was a couple of years too young for that."

His subject was wary, Harrison thought; he must be careful. "How do you feel politically then?"

"Just a New Dealer," Tom said. "I grew up loving Roosevelt."

"What are your other ideas?" Harrison asked.

"What about my soul not being free?" Tom countered, smiling.

"We'll get to that," Harrison returned the smile. "Tell me your ideas first, Tom. If you can."

The search began again on Tom's face; finally, finished, he said slowly: "Well. I guess, I guess, in the way you mean, I hate ideas. Political ideas. Religious ideas. All the notions that people can be led to harm one another for. They seem very ugly to me. Democracy's an ugly idea, the way we've worked it out, with all the emphasis on personal property and majority coercion: mine the property, ours the power. Communism's an ugly idea; ours the property, mine the power. Power and property; possession. Control. I dislike those things, Harrison. And religious ideas, insisting that the power and the property belong to some superstitious image. His. His. I don't see anything but indecency anywhere in the whole complex."

Now he had him going, Harrison thought; he would give another push. "Aren't there any decent ideas at all, then?"

"Perhaps," Tom said. "Perhaps the idea that people might aban-

491

don a little power, a little property, for peace. That may be a fine idea."

"One you've served?" Harrison folded his hands across his stomach, and kept his eyes on Tom's face.

"Not as wholeheartedly as I might," Tom said. "Not in the last few years, anyway. Perhaps it's only an excuse but . . . it just hasn't seemed to be one of those ideas whose time has come. I guess we have to smash each other up some more before it does." Harrison waited to see whether he would go on, but all Tom did was add, with uncharacteristic pessimism, "If it does."

"All right," Harrison said. "You think of yourself as a kind of resigned man, disengaged from a self-destroying world. Is that it? Going along as harmlessly as possible, except when the urge to protest overcomes good judgment."

Tom nodded, smiling again. "I'll agree to that. I'd like to say I love the idea of peace, both personal and political—of noncompetitiveness, if you like—as a sort of first philosophic principle but—maybe that's only a way of trying to dignify a mild, resigned kind of character."

Now Harrison laughed. "No, Tom," he said. "No. You're a fighter. You're a big fighter like all the rest of us."

"A fighter?"

"That's where the guilt comes from," Harrison said. He kept his tone light, for he was very sure of what he was saying. "That's the truth today's children will know about you, when they're old enough to write history. We've got a cause, Tom. A big, collective fight we've been engaged in, consciously or unconsciously, all our adult lives."

"I always thought we lacked one," Tom said, mildly.

"Of course you did. You couldn't acknowledge the one we had. Any more than the radicals could, or the aesthetes, or any other kind of intellectual. But being unaware of it doesn't keep you from fighting for this cause, right along with the business men and the housewives and the union labor boys and everybody else. The great, mass, reactionary struggle . . ." He leaned back, grinning, teasing.

"Oh Harrison." Tom grinned, too. "What for God's sake?"

"To recreate the comfort and conservatism of our parents' homes before the depression," Harrison said emphatically. "Probably for you that comfort is a pre-memory affair, one of those infant

492

images." He leaned forward and began to speak even more emphatically, losing, he would remember when he thought about it, that consciousness of time, place and circumstance which had allowed him to start this way in the first place. "It's been a real sacred cause, Tom, conscious or unconscious. How else would you account for where we are politically? Even if you voted against it, you're not deeply uncomfortable living with it, are you? How many radicals do you think there are who give more time to their politics these days than they do to their earning power—I don't mean making livings, I mean getting luxuries; building homes, buying appliances, creating financial estates? How many aesthetes spend more time with art than they do at shop windows? What do they buy when they get their hands on money? Paintings, or automobiles? You want to find the fuel that's driven us? It wasn't losing ourselves in the second war, or fighting fascism; hell, the war was just a sidetrack. We weren't out to make something new out of society; we were out to remake something old, the thing our parents were born to, the thing we were born to and saw snatched away: Comfort. Conservatism. We've been fighting to get our national skin back on, whether we knew it or not, and anything else was just an interruption."

He stopped. That was it.

"Well," Tom said, after a time, grimacing.

"Am I wrong?" Harrison asked, elated now to have said it all, for the ideas had been in his mind, half-formed, for a long time.

"I'll have to think about it," Tom said.

"You don't agree."

"I don't know," Tom said. "I wouldn't like to."

"I don't agree." It was Mrs. Nevins. Harrison had virtually forgotten that she was sitting with them.

"Oh, don't you?" He turned his eyes to her with a certain irritation. "Why not, Mrs. Nevins?"

"Oh. . . ." The invitation to continue the conversation seemed to alarm her. She shook her head instead of completing the answer and was silent again.

"The play, Harrison," Tom was saying. "It isn't really related to what you've been saying, is it?"

"No." In spite of Mrs. Nevins' interruption, Harrison still felt very cheerful. "Only that it was the kind of experience that shakes things loose in the mind, I suppose."

493

"And a place to start after me from?"

"Sure. A resigned man isn't often vulnerable, Tom. I had to get you while you were open."

"You got me," Tom said and sighed. "I don't know just how badly yet. You've been meaning to for a long time?"

"For a long time," Harrison said. "I don't know just why . . . yes, I do." He said it in spite of himself, his voice coming out flat and quiet under the police lamp. "A man's a fool to marry a girl with a brother, Tom."

4.

Eddie and Goswith roamed empty streets, howling at one another. Eddie was furious, furious with guilt towards the painter because of having hit him, with frustration caused by Goswith's having kept him out of the fight with the police and firemen, and now furious because Goswith insisted on criticizing the children's performance bitterly, as if they were serious rivals for the world's admiration.

"Look at the freak show, there in the middle," Goswith shouted; they were walking parallel, on different sides of the street. "That little dwarf girl. Cheap, cheap, cheap."

"You couldn't paint a scene like that in a thousand tries," Eddie shouted back. "You couldn't even imagine a scene like that. . . ."

"Look at the costumes," Goswith yelled. "Sweat suits. Underwear. Where's *their* imagination? They didn't even feel like working enough to make decent costumes. . . ."

"Shut up." Eddie turned and charged across the street. "You shut up." He grabbed Goswith by the lapels of his dirty corduroy jacket.

"Be careful Eddie. You'll tear it. Hey. Hey, I thought you wanted to talk about the play. . . ."

"I don't want to talk to you about anything," Eddie roared, jerking back and forth at the lapels. "See there?" He turned the painter halfway around. "See that hole in the ground?" It was a subway entrance. He pushed Goswith away, violently, in that direction. "Go down it. Go on. Get off the earth."

"I don't know where it goes, Eddie," the painter started whining, but when Eddie charged at him, Goswith ran. Eddie pursued

494

him to the top of the steps. Then he stopped and watched Goswith stumbling down, routed. Eddie waited until the painter was out of sight, around the turn of the stairs, then wheeled and started to trot away. He hadn't gone fifty steps when he heard his name called.

"Hey Eddie. Eddie."

Eddie stopped. It was Goswith again, back up almost to street level, whining after him.

"Eddie, I ain't got the nickel. I got a dime for a token but no nickel to go home." He teetered, grimy, with his hand out.

Eddie turned again, and resumed running.

"Eddie, I don't know where I am. . . ."

Eddie ran faster.

"Eddie, Eddie. . . ."

Eddie went around a corner at a full run, desperate to have seen the last of that red-eyed wheedling image.

After a time he came to a bar. He and Goswith had drunk a pint of whiskey at the play, but he didn't feel drunk. He went in and ordered vodka straight, drank it, got change for a bill, and went to the telephone. I'm not cruddy drunk, he told himself, but he stubbed his toe, getting into the booth. He dialed the Walles' number. The phone rang eight times before Ellen's voice answered.

"Hello?"

"I'm calling to inquire about Miss Sheila Walle. . . ."

"Eddie?"

"This is a friend," Eddie said. "I just want to know about Miss Walle, if Miss Walle's all right?"

"Eddie, I know it's you," Ellen said. "Sheila just got home. She's getting ready for bed."

"Miss Walle has come home?"

"Eddie, stop it. Do you want to come up? Harrison's gone to get Tom out of jail. . . ."

"I only wished to know about Miss Walle, Madam," Eddie said, and hung up the phone. He went back to the bar and asked urgently for a double vodka. Then he paid, left the bar and began to run again, back towards Brooklyn Heights.

He spent the next hour on the street, in front of the Walles' building, watching their lights up on the seventh floor. It was not Ellen he yearned towards; it was Sheila. From the time he had told Goswith about the affair with Ellen, three weeks before, it had been over in his mind; but he was more than ever enrapt with Sheila, and he watched with crazy reverence, believing it possible that the girl might feel his eyes, might hear his thought, might dress and come stealing down, away from that lush apartment, to find her true father waiting in the dark.

5.

When they were outside the police station at last, Tom overheard the man from Borough Hall say to Harrison:

"They won't get any ideas now, will they?"

"Ideas?"

"False arrest suits."

"Oh no," Harrison said. "No, there was no arrest, was there? How could it have been false?"

"Okay." The man from Borough Hall had a car. He offered to drive all of them to their homes but Tom, who was feeling extremely restless, declined. There were two reasons for his restlessness: the first was having learned that his brother-in-law disliked him, a surprise, uncomfortable and unexpected. The second was less easy to formulate; perhaps it was that he'd been cheated twice of climaxes during the strange evening, first of the climax of the play, then of the anticipated night in jail.

He thanked the man with the car; seeing a subway entrance, he said it looked like the quickest way to Manhattan.

Mrs. Nevins declined too; she said she wanted to walk. Harrison and the man argued with her, but she wouldn't get in the car. The two men shrugged, finally, said goodnight, and drove away, leaving the released prisoners standing together on the street.

Not at all sleepy, Tom said: "Shall I walk with you, Mrs. Nevins?"

"Oh, thank you. But I . . . I haven't really decided where to go."

"Would you like the couch at my place? We can have a drink— I ought to explain that my wife is away, but I'm quite faithful to her."

Mrs. Nevins smiled at him. She had a pretty smile. "That's sweet," she said. "Yes, I would like a drink."

They took the subway, rode to Manhattan and walked to Tom's apartment. He made drinks—she protested, in a silly, girlish way,

496

about the strength of hers, though it contained a normal amount of whiskey. She untied her long, pale hair and loosened her untidy clothes, getting comfortable; Tom barely even asked himself whether he found her attractive. She was not a very interesting woman; the things she had to say about the play were uniformly imperceptive; she had not really been moved by it, had merely thought it charming of the children to have done it all by themselves; it did not seem to have occurred to her that her own child might have cause to be unusually upset, and there was something quite synthetic about the alarm she developed when Tom suggested such an outcome to her.

She had not really known, she admitted, what Harrison was talking about, in the jail room, and had only said she disagreed because she wanted to be on Tom's side; she had thought Harrison quite a hateful man, and was piqued that he'd disturbed her just as she was getting comfortable in her cell. Tom wanted to hear about the girls the sergeant had spoken of, but Mrs. Nevins could neither describe nor quote them; she could only say, in a voice too placid to be really compassionate, that she'd felt sorry for the poor things.

Tom continued restless. Mrs. Nevins didn't seem especially sleepy either, so they had another drink and he kept trying to talk to her.

"What an odd night," he said. He was sitting on the sofa, she in the large chair facing him. "So many things, starting and stopping. Sharp turns. Well, I really mustn't keep you up."

She nodded, got up, stepped past where he was sitting, turned around and fell on him. And therewith Tom Beniger, as a consequence of attending a play and knocking down a fireman, found his woman.

6.

Eddie might have stayed all night in front of the Walles', for the lights never went out. But at one point a Cadillac drove up to the building, and Harrison Walle got out and went inside. Eddie, concealed in a doorway across the street, noticed that Tom wasn't with him. Must have gone home. The car drove away. Eddie imagined Harrison arriving up there, Ellen's gratitude. Sheila's admiration. Eddie snarled, and started to run again. He ran till he came to a cab, parked along a street with its driver sleeping in front. Eddie slammed into the back, waking the man, and shouted that he wanted Pennsylvania Station, the Long Island side. On the way through Greenwich Village, however, they passed a particularly bright bar, and Eddie yelled "Stop." He got out, went into the bar, and resumed drinking as fast as he could pour the liquor down him. He tried to strike up a conversation with a black-banged girl, who walked away; Eddie called her a Lesbian loudly and was thrown out of the bar. At around four in the morning he reeled into Pennsylvania station on foot, shut himself in a phone booth and called Dorothy Conn. She was angry at first, a little sweeter when she had made out who it was, but refused to let Eddie come up; she begged him to have a late breakfast with her instead. Eddie concluded that she didn't like him; he was so uncoordinated by this time that he couldn't get the phone back on its cradle in the booth; he tried a number of times, and then left it dangling. He passed out on a bench in the Long Island waiting room, where the porter who stole his wallet was thoughtful enough to look for, and place in Eddie's pocket, his driver's license, car registration and his return ticket to Ringlet Harbor.

7.

Ned Kildeer saw Eddie Bissle thus, slumped on a waiting room bench, recognized him as a friend of Tom's, and went unobtrusively to another part of the waiting room. It was not quite six-thirty, the morning after the play, and Ned still wanted to avoid conversation.

This had been the wish he carried away from Brooklyn with him the night before; the sum of his reaction to Sheila's *Hamlet* was so strong, so awed finally, that he did not want to discuss it. In particular, he had not wished to discuss it with Hubert, who would turn the vision into caricature with a word or two. Ned had spent the night in a hotel and checked out early. He needed money for what he planned now, but could get it from the Long Island bank which he used summers. He wrote a card to Hubert saying he was going away for a while.

There was a train to Lecklie, Long Island, at 6:54, and Ned was on it. In Lecklie, he cashed the check, bought groceries, clothes, and a large bottle of water; he had these things carried down to the wharf. There he had to hire a boat, because the ferry service to Fire Island was not running yet.

Fire Island is that strip of sand three hundred yards wide, which runs through the ocean a mile or so off the shore of Long Island, for about seventy miles. Spread along this roadless, well-less, and quite beautiful sand bar, are several dozen small summer communities, each isolated from the next by two or three miles of waste sand and beach growth. Each community has a separate and rather homogenous character, and one, opposite the mainland town of Lecklie, is a fashionable summer ghetto for homosexuals; in this, Ned was co-owner of a beach house in which he spent most summer weekends.

Now, on the last day of March, the Island was still bleak and the houses boarded up. Ned unloaded his groceries on the dock, and paid his boatman. The man wanted to know when he would be coming off the island, and Ned said he wasn't sure, he had some work to do. They arranged that he would fly a red shirt from the signal staff on top of the dockhouse, when he wanted to come off. The man said he would keep an eye out for it, and the boat chugged away.

The sun was out. Ned carried his overcoat, leaving the groceries, and went off along the deserted boardwalks towards his cottage. There were something like two hundred of the little places, crowded together, fronting on a boardwalk system, gayly painted and grimly boarded. The boardwalks were five or six feet off the sand, and the houses, on stilts, even a little higher, for sometimes hurricane tides washed completely over Fire Island and under its houses.

Ned had expected to see evidence of a few other early visitors —a painter or two of winter seascapes, some hearty early swimmers, but there was no one there and no sign of anyone. He approached his cottage, a small, bright blue one, with yellow trim. He laid his overcoat down, climbed onto the wooden bench beside the door, and reached into the eaves for the nail on which the key hung.

The nail was there. The key was not.

Dismayed, Ned remembered that the other owner had closed the house. As he tried the door he had a second, even more dismaying recollection of a phone conversation, not a very sober one, with

499

this co-owner, and of the term "police lock." He tried to shake the door; something within held it so firmly that it wouldn't even rattle. Ned stopped trying after a moment, and went to a window. The boards on it were fastened with heavy nails. The hammer he had planned to use to pry them off was inside; even the child's express wagon he had planned to get, to haul his load of groceries over the boardwalk, was inside.

The house next door was white; the people who owned it were friends. It was similarly boarded, but perhaps he could get in and get their hammer. He went over and tried the white door. It was as firmly closed as his own.

He must go from house to house, trying doors, and when he found one he could enter, go in, find a hammer or a bar. First though, from an urge for consolidation, he made three trips back and forth to the dock, lugging the groceries to the front door of his cottage, sweating lightly in the cold air. He remembered having discarded a broken beach umbrella under the house. He changed clothes, to a heavy sweater, blue jeans and sneakers, and jumped off the boardwalk onto the sand. The wrecked umbrella was still there, several of the spokes broken, most of the stem gone.

He climbed onto his front porch with it, and spread the canvas over his food. Fortunately, there was nothing perishable except butter; most of what he had was in cans. . . .

Can opener!

The can opener was inside, too.

If Ned had not just finished making three laborious trips to haul his groceries over, he might have gone back and run the red shirt up the signal staff at that moment. As it was, after the first awful gasp, he told himself to be calm. If he could not spend a week, he could still spend an afternoon, and get the signal up around supper time, still in time to be taken off before he got cold or hungry. He could fix some sort of shelter for the groceries, and most of them would still be usable when he returned later in the season.

He decided to do what he had come to do, and walked out towards the ocean. He sat down at the top of a flight of wooden steps, staring at the winter sea, and it soothed him. After a time he was able to think of what he had come to ponder, which was Sheila, her play, the faces of the children acting, the reading they had given *Hamlet*.

. . . . Juliet, we keep reminding one another, is a child, Ned began; what of Shakespeare's other people? Romeo is a child. He got no farther with the formula. Lady Macbeth was not a child. He smiled, thinking of Sheila as Lady Macbeth. She would make something of it at that, Ned thought; the girl was an actress now. Couldn't he, Ned, be a director now, refusing the television assignments that bought cottages on Fire Island, find actors to work with, plays? Couldn't he free himself from the sordid life with Hubert, live sexlessly for art if necessary? He yearned suddenly to be old and grey and free of sex. Could he be an artist then? No, it seemed to him, not unless he were before then. Were art and sex antithetical? Or was it only the weak who found them so, because they could not force their lives to yield all possibilities, and had to make an artificial choice? If the choice were artificial, did that invalidate the art, or the sex for that matter?

It seemed to Ned, looking at the sea, that there were no perfect answers, only innumerable individuals, and a slightly different answer for each. An intelligent dolphin might be able to observe humanity, and formulate the laws of its behavior; to a dolphin, all men would look pretty much the same with a few nonessential differences in size and color; but the wise dolphin would find his own kind mysterious and intractable, for creatures cannot observe themselves.

Having so concluded, Ned continued trying to observe himself. He thought with scorn: I was going to leave this place, retreat, or break into houses to save myself with contrivances. Why? Am I really unable to live here, for a day or two, in the open?

Girl scouts, little campfire girls, lived here in the open, on summer weekends . . . suddenly Ned shuddered, and peered up the beach, towards the place where these twelve year olds did their camping. It was at a place where the sand humped up in the center of the island, making a mild hillside, covered with scrub; on the sides of this, their little tents were hidden from Ned's community. Ned's shudder had been for the recollection of a summer storm, two years before; the clouds had piled up quickly, and the little girls, their tents blown down, had been caught in a drenching rain. Ned and another boy, remembering that the campers were out there, ran out to offer the use of a community building for shelter, meeting, on the way, a determined looking woman, one of those in charge. She thanked them heartily, and Ned and his friend led the band, thirty or forty little girls and three husky women, shivering along the boardwalk; one or two other boys joined them. They got the large community building open; they got towels. The girls were herded inside, just a moment before the lights failed.

And then, as they tried to go inside to continue helping, the first husky woman had barred the way.

"Thank you," she said. "You've been very kind." She said it coldly, indicating that she would, on no account, let Ned and his friends come in to help with the mothering. Ned had thought, at the time, retreating, that the woman was right; she hadn't known what kind of men they were, that their tenderness and anxiety for the wet children could be nothing more than the emotion mules feel for colts. It wasn't until he had got back to his own cottage, and was watching the storm out the window, that Ned saw the Lesbians, little files of them, trotting along the boardwalks, converging on the community building, hearty-looking girls in whom the scout-mistresses would find a general resemblance to themselves, carrying big rough towels and dry sweaters, on their way to strip and dry the little girl campers in the dark.

"How does anyone have a chance?" Ned asked the sea.

I will be analyzed, he told himself next. And I will quit television and direct only plays. And I will not go back to Hubert. If I cannot direct plays, I will do anything else until I can—be a waiter, a clerk—and when I have been analyzed I will marry and have children. But of course there were parts of the program that cancelled one another out: if he were to quit television, he could not afford analysis. If he were not beginning analysis, he would not have the courage to quit television. And if he couldn't do both how would he ever be able to leave Hubert?

He stood up, still looking at the ocean, remembering other things, trying to prove to himself that human problems are no larger than human beings—that they can all be solved. That you must learn to undertake them one at a time, at least until you are deft enough to handle several continuous solutions at once; and his own first problem was simple enough. Men had been solving it for centuries—simply how to sustain life here on an island, with whatever might be at hand, until such time as he felt ready to return. And when he returned, cost what it might, he would leave Hubert.

He went back among the locked houses. A marooned man searches first for salvage.

He began to move from house to boarded house.

502

He had tried forty doors when he came to one that opened, but the house it opened into was stripped. Even the stove was gone. Ned searched it, anyway, looking for anything he might use, and found a piece of pipe, eighteen inches long. He trotted back to his own house, and tried to find a window board loose enough to get an inner edge of the pipe behind. There was none. He considered for a moment, and then hit his door a tremendous whack with the pipe. It scarred the door, stung his hands, but otherwise had no effect. Carrying the pipe, he started off on another boardwalk, trying other doors, checking windows, but found no open house other than the empty one.

So, thought Ned, he would sleep on soft sand, then. He was a little tired, and very hungry. He inspected his piece of pipe. Perhaps he could beat cans open with it. If not, there was bread and peanut butter, and a bag of oranges. The coffee would do him no good, for he had no pan, but he could drink canned milk. He went back to his hoard of food by the blue and yellow cottage.

He spread peanut butter with his fingers on some slices of bread, and chewed hungrily. Marvelous. Sticky. Then he set a can of milk down on the boardwalk, measured the distance, and hit it a sharp blow with his pipe. Immediate success. The end of the pipe tore into the soft metal of the top, leaving a gash. The gash was too close to the center of the can to allow him to drink comfortably from it; he poured the thick sweet stuff into his hand and lapped it out.

He was chilly. He pulled his overcoat around himself. He peered at the sky. It seemed clear. The empty house he had found offered only floor boards; he could sleep under his own, locked house, but the sand would not be as warm there as it would in the open, where the sun had reached it.

He planned: I will move off from the houses. I will come back among them to eat. He took the broken umbrella top, and his overcoat and started up the beach; with the sweater and overcoat and the red wool shirt, he should be warm enough.

It was getting dark, and Ned, who had thought of writing something—a story, perhaps, or a poem—or simply an account of what the children had done with Hamlet, so that he could keep it all—realized that he would have no light for such a purpose; he must either go to sleep at sundown or sit in the dark. He smiled.

Walking in the sand tired him, and he stopped as soon as there was dune enough to hide the cottages from sight. Then, on the slope with scrub bushes, he dropped to his knees beside one, scooped out a hollow trench with his hands, lined the bottom with the overcoat, and set the beach umbrella—what remained of it—over his head for shelter. He lay down in his trench, and watched, under the raised edge of the umbrella, the stars coming out over the ocean. He thought: I will be a long time getting to sleep, because the sand is bumpy, under the overcoat. I ought to heap up a little sand under my head for a pillow. Before he could put this intention into effect, he had gone to sleep.

Dawn woke him, and the noisy birds. He sat up and saw many gulls, all going in the same direction, up the beach towards the empty town. In the summer they were like pigeons in a salt water park, arriving for scraps at mealtimes—on the edge of going back to sleep, Ned jumped up, and started to run. It was slow running through the sand, but he pounded on bitterly, envying the birds their ease of wing. When he reached the end of the boardwalk and vaulted onto it, he had to rest in spite of his pressing fear. But after a minute he resumed motion, no less exhausted, and ran on, his feet at last able to move freely, until the boardwalk delivered him to the sight he had expected; there were gulls uncountable wheeling near his cottage, diving, fighting. By the time he reached them, they had consumed and scattered his three loaves of bread completely. They had tumbled the oranges around, though a few were whole. The can of milk he'd opened was in the sand, and so was his butter.

He yelled at them, ran at them, and they retired. Ned dropped to his knees, found a gull-pecked orange, and began to suck it greedily. He was fiercely thirsty, but, though he had five gallons of water, there was nothing into which to pour it. It was several minutes before he could stop trembling, and eat, systematically, the salvaged food.

When he had fed himself, and transferred the remaining oranges into the suitcase, where the gulls couldn't get at them, however, Ned began to feel like a seasoned castaway. He spent the morning making himself a cup. He did it by bashing in the top of a second can of milk with his pipe, and then hammering the jagged edges down flat against the inner sides. He drank the whole can off, too, though it gagged him, for he had a fierce feeling now about his stocks of food and his dependence on them. He was not, ordinarily, fond of bread, but by the time he was ready for a noon meal, he missed it furiously.

When, with the sun up, nearly in mid-sky, his cup was ready, Ned was extremely proud of it. It seemed to him, squatting off at a short distance and looking at it, that it even had a certain handsomeness; he had stripped off all of the label, and scoured the sides with sand. He poured some water into it, inevitably spilling some, and drank it with a feeling of solemnity. Now he could stay, not abjectly but in triumph.

Now he would begin to learn his strength.

It occurred to Ned that he could make coffee, using the cup for a pan, and he spent a long time gathering dry bits of wood to build more of a fire than he needed; he put raw coffee into his cup, covered it with water and set it into the sand among the flames. It never quite boiled, but after a time the water was black. Careless in this second triumph, Ned tried to lift the cup out barehanded, and burned the tips of his thumb and forefinger quite painfully; nevertheless it was a third triumph, for he spilled no coffee; it tasted watery and wonderful.

He found the place where the seagulls had knocked his butter into the sand, and there was still a little of it stuck, unmelted, to the paper, to dress his fingers with. The sun had gone past, overhead, but it was still bright; Ned decided to go swimming. He swam nude, in icy water; there was little surf. He dressed again and completed his survey of the houses. He found a second empty house, again quite stripped, but in it were some unreturned beer bottles. Ned took them back to the area his food was in. He had no idea of a use for them, but he was feeling ruthlessly acquisitive. When the sun had been overhead, he had thought that he could write, if he liked, during the afternoon, but he now felt nothing at all like doing so. He had more or less stopped thinking about anything but his situation, and he was rather enjoying the extent to which he was now committed to surviving in it. Even Hubert was out of his mind, mostly, if still not out of his guts; no. He still felt, when he thought of Hubert, the sick physical shudder in the stomach which is love's most dependable symptom, but he felt this less strongly, he thought, than he had in many months.

He took a nap in the sun. He woke, and went to squat and look at the ocean for nearly an hour. Toward evening he returned to his cache of food, and determined to open a can of beans; but when he set it up and hit its top, the metal proved not so soft as that of the milk cans. He banged at the bean container with his pipe, but the burned fingers made it painful to use full force. Finally he turned the can on its side and began to batter at it that way, wielding the pipe left-handed. The can bent in many strange ways. It rolled and stopped. Ned pursued it, hitting at it clumsily.

"Yahn," he said with each whack, moving after the can on hands and knees. "Yahn. Yahn."

Finally the metal gave, and the beans dripped out onto the boardwalk. Ned crouched, and ate them off the wood with his fingers. When he was done, he fetched a cup of sea water to the spot, and washed it off as well as he could. It was not an impulse of cleanliness. It was rather to enforce a silent ultimatum: the seagulls were not to eat any more of Ned's food.

8.

They all insisted on worrying about Sheila; why? She wasn't being resentful or sulky. She just didn't happen to feel like saying much to anybody. So they called each other up about it, from Brooklyn to Manhattan and back again, all the next day. By noon she insisted on going to school, just to get away from having to be aware of the telephone. Even her father had stayed home from the office to take shifts on the telephone. Honestly, you'd think the poor instrument would melt, the way they wrapped their sweaty hands around it and breathed.

At school it was a little better. In the library Amy had to be stopped from whispering stuff like, "Honestly, everybody's so proud of you." After Amy stopped that, they walked around together, to afternoon classes and study hall, and Amy acted as if they'd done something funny and wild, made something out of it to interest boys with. That was better; was more like Amy. Sheila wasn't expected to get in on those conversations, and she didn't. The only other thing she had to think about was keeping away from Rosemary Ophelia Bernstein, who kept mooning after her.

In the evening, at home, surprise, surprise. Her parents had made the Helds come over at cocktail time, as if they were just dropping in, and just happened to bring Peter. Sheila was sorry, be-

506

cause she didn't *like* hurting Peter's feelings, she just simply didn't feel she had anything very interesting to say to him, so she excused herself and went to her room. By the time her mother came in with supper on a tray, and the Helds were gone, Sheila had already fixed stuff to eat and eaten it, so she couldn't really be expected to eat the things her mother brought in, though it was perfectly nice of her mother to think of it, of course.

Next day at school was a little better; kids would leave you alone if you wanted, except for creeps like Rosemary and Ben, who you had to keep ducking. Most teachers ignored the whole thing, though she did have an interview in the headmistress's office, but it wasn't bad; she didn't listen to what Miss Cavendish was saying, just said yes contritely in the pauses. The only bad one, really, was Mary Flexe, the drama coach, who caught Sheila in the corridor, and coaxed and coaxed, trying to get her to say what she'd like them to do for a spring play at school—"*As You Like It,* darling? Oh, why don't we?"—until she forced Sheila to say that she didn't think she'd try out for the spring play this year, thank you.

9.

Ernest Goswith.

He had awakened the morning after the play with no words in his head—only a pervasive orange-yellow smoke of sorrow, fury and self-pity—and a twitch in his hand that could only be stopped by the heft of a paintbrush.

Three things drove him that morning, as the smoke made words: bitter hate of Eddie, bitter envy of Sheila, bitter love of God.

He conceived the third, as he painted, in terms of the first two:

Eddie. He must damage Eddie of whom he had thought, just yesterday, as his last friend, damage him by repudiating the pornographic paintings in which Eddie had invested. To repudiate them, he must denounce them morally; to denounce them, he must have a passionate moral position. (But this alone was not enough; Goswith was not that careless of his own finances. There must be a further motive. There was.)

Sheila. Seeing the child had reawakened Goswith's greed for greatness; he was a great painter, after all, and they would all know it, (though he starved to death; and especially the gross ones would know it, to their own loss, the ones who believed that all Goswith could portray was evil; great painters went through that, all great men did).

God. After wallowing in evil, the great found a passionate morality, the great found God.

ALL GREAT PAINTING WAS RELIGIOUS PAINTING.

Goswith did not ask himself what sort of religious man he was; some sort of Christian. Let them haggle over his doctrine when he was dead; Goswith had time now only for work. His mind was layered with ideas, conscious and unconscious, drawn from the subject matter of Christian painting—saints, martyrdoms, madonnas, agonies. He had seen them all, thought them all, dreamed them all. He knew, at first, only one thing clearly enough to paint it: Christ, carrying the cross, mocked at by the people. But as he finished first one and then another hasty version of this scene, something was released, and by evening he had a buoyant foreknowledge of the worlds of images waiting for his brush, gift of his conversion. He worked all night. He slept an hour, two, ate something—he couldn't have said what, drank cold coffee, spilled it down his shirt, looked there and saw in the stain the face of Saint Theresa. Stripped off the miraculous shirt, flung it at the wall where it caught on a frame and hung, and began to paint again, Saint Theresa's martyrdom.

And as for that girl, Sheila, that actress, that bastard daughter of Eddie Pissall—he sneered at a color study of the saint, delicately brushing agony into her mouth—as for that girl she'd make some lucky house a fine wife, yeah. By the third morning he was doing his first full canvas of Saint Theresa, and had already forgotten Sheila and even Eddie in his new absorption. And under the absorption, and the paranoia, and the wretchedness, and the identification with the ten greatest men that ever lived, was an artist's cool, infallible knowledge that what he was doing was very very good.

CHAPTER TWO

1.

Tom beniger's affair with Sarah Nevins lasted one day less than a full week, yet she was, in the sense described by popular songs, the love of his life. Against the strangulation of such love, Tom fought for a breath of humor, calling himself a soap opera villain, a man mistakenly included in the cast of an interminable sentimental movie; but humor seemed as impossible to achieve in his situation as it is in the strips called comic, which serialize the shadow of our problems in the daily papers.

At the moment she fell, untidily, upon him, in the dark of the morning which followed *Hamlet* and the jail, Tom had been thinking of her, gently enough and without distaste, as a sloven, apparently goodnatured but somewhat disoriented; in the next moment, struggling to find a way past the cascade of blue dress material and white underwear that were falling around him, he was conscious of nothing about her but an urgent and amazing need of his flesh to meet hers. His body told him, as it found its way, that in this woman, with him, sensuality would be endless, hunger for it constant; as they plunged together on the sofa, in too violent a hurry to have finished undressing, Tom was a man shaking off an anaesthesia administered to him at, persisting since, birth. Once in middle adolescence, once in late, he had broken out of the cool

509

fog to be, by a young girl named Ruby, an older one named Harriet, pushed back for such behavior; from Sarah, there was no need to return to chill and fogginess. That energy which had dismayed and frightened girls was received by Sarah as a tribute, and hardly had they finished the first blind scramble than they were at one another again; and, in the dawn, waking from a gluttonous sleep, yet again.

She had nothing to say concerning it. Simply got up, when they were finally done with sleep, put on her slip, started picking up, inefficiently, around the apartment, as if the passage of such frenzied nights between them were too familiar to be worth discussing. Wanted to talk, it seemed, about culturally improving matters; put the tritest of classical music on the phonograph, asked to borrow the shallowest of the books on the shelf and waited, in each case, for Tom to approve her taste. Failed either to listen to the records, or to look through the books; spoke of dishes she would like to cook for him, and they were recognizably the culinary pretensions passed on by homemaking magazines. Said she was sorry his wife had left him.

"I didn't say that," Tom said. "As a matter of fact, she's in England, six months pregnant, and I'm very fond of her."

Sarah made no reply, just then; later she referred once more to the sad fact of Tom's having been deserted. Tom noticed this without interpreting it; his mind was occupied too much with wonder at his own physical vitality; he expected, almost, in the boyish concept of sex as generally depleting, as in honeymoon jokes, to feel weak, to stumble, to want to spend the day recovering. On the contrary, towards noon, as he walked towards the kitchen to return a plate and fill his coffee cup, going past where she was standing, still in nothing but a slip, he found that merely to pass close to her brought desire, brought potency, brought her arms and legs around him, sent cup, plate, saucer and themselves all to the floor in a pile of crockery, coffee grounds and rapt bodies.

Words she supplied, of passion and endearment, vulgar and tender, while they were so engaged. Once they were up she had, again, no afterwords. It was as though nothing had happened. And perhaps, thought Tom suddenly, nothing has, nothing that is that need be spoken of, need be discussed, explained, dissected, apologized for, gloried in, rationalized; why must anything be said? Having so concluded, it was late afternoon before his tongue leapt,

510

and, in a moment when she was, for a reason that may have had nothing to do with Tom, looking wistful, he said of all things the most wrong. The tongue leapt, and Tom looked after it, knowing what it said was an enormous error, enormously wrong, enormously unnecessary, and enormously true:

"Sarah, I love you."

She said gratefully, a little surprised, that that was nice, she loved him too. Then she added that she had looked in the refrigerator, but didn't know what to fix for supper.

"There isn't anything, is there?" Tom said, uncomfortably, uncertain whether his statement had been dismissed or absorbed.

"No. I thought you might have a steak or something. I know a wonderful way to fix steak."

"I'm sorry," Tom said. "Let's eat out."

"All right. If you'd had a steak, I do know this wonderful way to fix it," she said, moonily. Then: "Oh. Will you take me to a Bohemian place?"

Tom smiled. He had put a hand into his pocket and counted, without taking them out, three bills which he knew could only be singles. He had thought there was change, too, but his fingers found none.

"I'm afraid it will be inexpensive," he said.

She nodded. "That's what I mean. Bohemian." Then, when they were in the restaurant, an Italian one, she was so attracted emotionally to the name of something on the dinner which cost two dollars that Tom couldn't bring himself to tell her that it was more than they could afford if he were to eat too.

"Lobster fra Diavolo," she said. "That means the devil's father. Doesn't it sound exciting?"

"You must have it," Tom said. He ordered a twenty-five cent glass of wine for each of them, said he wasn't hungry, and smoked while she played with her food. For though Sarah said that *Lobster fra Diavolo* was the best thing she'd ever tasted, she ate only a bite or two, filling herself from the bread basket which supplied what food Tom had as well. Stingy tipping left Tom with a quarter; he suggested going back to the apartment for coffee.

"That would be cosiest," she said.

When they were back there, drinking the coffee, Tom asked: "Are you going back to Brooklyn tonight?"

"What?"

511

"Will you have to be home tonight?"

"Do you want me to stay?"

"Yes. I only thought . . . a change of clothes or something . . ."

Sarah looked down at the same blue dress she had gone to jail in; she turned up the hem and sadly smoothed the slip over her knees.

"I'm sorry," Tom said. "I didn't mean I thought you ought to. I only wondered if you wanted to?"

"I guess so."

Were her feelings hurt? "Even if you go, come back," Tom said weakly, for he had just then begun wishing for a night alone, to sort his feelings over. "Come back tonight."

She shook her head. "No. If I get there, I'll have to stay with them."

"Then don't go at all." Now the idea of her leaving panicked him.

"You're just saying that. I know you really want me to go."

The thought that she might wander away and not come back occurred and was intolerable; he argued with her, but she kept saying, not firmly, only repetitiously, "No, I have to change my clothes. You said so."

And finally Tom gave in: "I'll give you a key," he said. "Come tomorrow, whenever you're ready. I have to be out, in the morning, to collect some money but in the afternoon. . . ."

"All right," she said, and took the key. She had a nickel; it was lucky. That gave her subway fare, and left Tom fifteen cents to go uptown with in the morning.

2.

On the morning of Ned's third day on Fire Island, just before dawn, it rained. Ned was still asleep in his trench out among the dunes, when the storm began; by the time it had rained long enough to wake him he was soaked. He told himself he must run back, up the beach, to look for shelter among the houses, and even tensed his legs to push himself up; then the legs relaxed. The image of adding to his present misery the misery of a jerky and interminable run, through wet sand to cold cover, bled his will. He shivered himself into a tight sitting position, knees up against his chest, pulled the weary canvas of the beach umbrella around his

512

wet shoulders and dripping head, and let the wind rush by. He comforted himself with the thought that, as soon as it was light, he would hurry to the dock and fly the red shirt, the signal that he wished to leave the island.

It dawned stormy; the rain, if anything, came more heavily. The trench which Ned had dug out, and in which he sat, took water in more quickly than the sand could drain it, so that he was sitting in a pool. The sky and sea and land were all so nearly the same grey that one could hardly tell, looking out, where one element left off and another began. Ned got up, finally, too discouraged to want to eat, and, still wrapped in the beach umbrella, trailed through the storm along the beach, across the boardwalks and onto the dock. Once there, he had to remove the red shirt in which he had slept. It was a chilly struggle, getting the thing off, but when he had managed Ned felt better for the exertion. He put his soaked overcoat back on, picked up the shirt and wrung it out. Then he sighed at himself for having wrung out something which would, within seconds, be wet again. He looked, for the first time, out across the bay and stopped smiling. He could not see even a shadow of the mainland. Fog.

He must get the shirt up right away. A fog here might last for days, but there would be minutes in a day when it blew clear, and in one of those minutes, his signal might be seen. Or the boatman, realizing that the fog had cut his recent passenger off, might come part way over to look. Or Hubert might miss him and—Ned ground his teeth. Hubert did not know where he was. Hubert would not know. He would never tell Hubert or anybody else where he had been. And if he should see Hubert again—but as for seeing Hubert again, Ned would sooner die, here on the Island. There was warmth in this thought, and the energy derived from hating Hubert enabled Ned to do something quite athletic: he climbed up on the slippery dock rail, hoisted himself onto the roof of the low building to which the signal staff was attached, and stood there in the wind, sorting ropes. Ned selected a rope led through a pulley on the crossarm, tied the shirt to it, and then let it flutter out, over towards the water. He caught the rope back, and tied on a second corner of the shirt. Now it was flying like a flag. He got back down onto the dock and watched his shirt, brave in the gusts. He smiled at it. He felt, suddenly, quite gay and saluted it.

Ned spent the morning in the empty cabin, wringing clothes,

513

moving to keep warm; he drank a can of milk, and waited trembling, for the sun. He did not know whether he would have to wait a day, or a week and, after a time he lost his capacity for expectation and no longer wondered. Moving about seemed, by now, to use more in energy than it produced in warmth, so he simply huddled, knowing, without thought, that the sun was life. When, at noon, it appeared, Ned went out of the cabin with tears on his face. He threw off the overcoat, stripped off his clothes, and lay down on the boardwalk rolling a little and moaning until all was dry, even the tears.

With clearing weather came higher winds, wonderful for drying. He spread everything out and weighted it, not quite chortling. He looked with pleasure at the high surf and thought, irrelevantly, that there would be waves, in a wind like this, even on the Sound side. Then he walked naked, towards the dock, to spy out whether, in this sparkling weather, the boat might be coming in response to his signal. If it was not, he thought suddenly, he would take the signal down. He was strong now, and wise, good for another day at least, would sleep inside or underneath a cabin; if he did not leave before tomorrow, he would not feel that he had been driven away.

He began to trot along the walks, turned a corner smartly, and was on the dock. The signal staff was empty; his shirt had blown away.

He ran up and down the beach, looking for the shirt, but the wind was carrying towards the Sound. He ran into the choppy water, up to his waist, along the dock, looking to see if the shirt might be caught against a piling, and tore the skin of his thigh quite painfully on barnacles.

He retreated to the boardwalk, and let himself dry off again, sucking as well as he could at the deep barnacle scratches. Well. He must fly another piece of cloth; he told himself, now that the panic was over, that its color shouldn't matter; the boatman must respond. Nevertheless, thinking carefully, he decided he would wait until the wind let up to fly the new signal, for his knowledge of knots was too uncertain to be sure of tying it on securely. He went back to the empty cottage, which had now become his base, to wait out the wind.

That night he tried at first to sleep in the house, but the hard floor, even through the overcoat which was now dry, was torture.

514

He moved underneath the little building, onto protected sand, but the wind kept blowing and his lacerated leg hurt. With the overcoat under him, he was cold; with it over him, he could not keep the sand out of his cuts. He moved back and forth, from underneath the house to within it, several times, without ever managing more than ten or fifteen minutes of sleep at a time.

But sunrise, from under the house, was beautiful. The surf was heavy, but the wind was still. Ned lay for a long time, looking at the sea.

"Good morning," he said, aloud, after awhile; he was speaking to the dolphin he had imagined, out there, making notes on Ned's—on all mankind's—behavior. "Good morning. I'm still here, you see. My leg hurts, but it doesn't seem to be infected. I think, by the way, that I'm making some progress with that matter we were discussing. . . ." With the dolphin, it didn't make any difference that they had not, in fact, had previous discussions; Ned was far from having reached a state of even temporary credence in such a creature. But it was pleasant to use his voice, and to pretend a listener. "The, um, Hubert matter, you know? I find myself much less resentful this morning. Don't you think that's better? I think, after a while, I could even learn to pity Hubert. Wouldn't that be marvelous? And wouldn't he hate it?"

Ned got up, came out from under the house and stretched. He put his hand up to his face and felt the beard there, four days old now. "I must look a sight," he said to the dolphin. "Do you know, I think I'll get an early signal up and leave today? I've a lot to do back in the world."

First, though, to make up for the fact that he had eaten very little the day before, Ned beat open a number of cans. He gorged himself on cold corned beef hash, niblet corn, lima beans, and chewed up sugar and unsweetened chocolate together afterwards. He was so grateful for the change in weather that he even left the bashed cans and the remains of food on the boardwalk for the gulls. There was too much surf to swim in the ocean, but he let salt water wash over and sting his leg and it felt better. Then he went to sleep in the smooth sand, and slept for several hours. Only when he woke did he go about tying his new flags onto the signal staff—a pair of yellow underwear shorts to the right arm, a pair of blue ones to the left, wrapping and knotting the ropes indiscriminately until it appeared impossible for the knots to fail. The shorts fluttered there crisply, all afternoon, but no boat appeared.

He had planned to make a signal fire when night came, raising and lowering his overcoat between it and the mainland perhaps, but his matches, he now discovered, were still useless though he had laid them carefully out to dry.

As dusk came, he was still on the dock, looking wistfully across at the lights coming on in Long Island towns along the shore. Suddenly, though, it occurred to him that it might rain again; and that if it did, he ought to rig his canvas to catch water to add to his supply. Ned turned back, away from the dock, and trotted off quite happily to arrange the contrivance.

3.

Tom stood, waiting for a reply from the receptionist at Steven Even Productions, his mind less than half on what he was doing. The receptionist, finishing her phone conversation with Steve's secretary, said:

"He's very eager to see you, Mr. Beniger, but may not be able to this morning."

Tom nodded and turned away. Love is learning, he was thinking; while we learn from one another, we must love one another. He sat down.

"I don't think he'll be able to see you, Mr. Beniger," the receptionist said.

Tom smiled at her. It isn't that we learn about one another—it's that we learn, from one another, new things about ourselves.

"Shall I tell him you're going to wait?"

"What?" Tom asked apologetically. "Oh. Yes." All he seemed to be willing to hold in mind about his call here, at Steven Even Productions, was that he musn't leave without some money; no, musn't. The money for the *Carole* script. But if love is learning, is acquiring self-knowledge, is it then so very elevated a thing? Is it not still a repetition of that awful clamor in the world of mine, mine?

The receptionist was frowning at him; Tom noticed this without really wondering why. Love is sickness; love is one of those diseases of which we all carry the germs; let any man or woman of us get into a state of low resistance, and. . . .

"I've just checked with Mr. Even's secretary again, Mr. Beniger. She thinks you'd better try another time."

Tom smiled at the girl's frown, nodded at her again, and continued to sit. If Sarah had not returned, let herself into the apartment, was not waiting there when he got back with the money, he would . . . what? Not cry, probably. Feel like it. He saw himself, in masochistic fantasy, bursting into the empty place. . . . "I am acting like a lovesick boy" . . . he formed the words with just enough sound to send murmurs through the roof of his mouth to his inner ears. . . . "Not a lovesick boy, a lovesick man . . . in a man the illness is not becoming . . . one can't be funny and tender about a lovesick man . . . no humorous and nostalgic comparison with adolescence, please. . . ."

He was altogether unprepared for the receptionist saying, in a slightly alarmed voice: "You may go in, Mr. Beniger. Go ahead, Mr. Beniger. Mr. Even will be able to see you."

Steve's secretary looked at him warily as he went by her and Steve said, as Tom went into the office:

"What's this about you muttering in the reception room?"

"What? Oh. Oh, I was . . . is that why I got to see you, Steve?"

"You're damn right it is," Steve said. "The girl was terrified." It was an attempt at joviality, at rough kidding, but with insufficient energy, and it came out querulous. It made Tom look at Steve, give his whole mind to it; Steve was sitting at his big table, in shirt sleeves. There was no work in front of him, no feel of hum in the room. Steve looked dejected. Steve looked a whole size smaller man. And when Tom asked about the *Carole* series, Steve's answer was low-keyed and direct: the sponsor who had dropped *Golden Words* was accepting *Carole* as a replacement, to finish out the season. But they wanted to use re-runs, episodes several years old with new commercials spliced in, to cut costs. This would reduce the income of Steven Even Productions to a point where the present payroll could not be met; employees were either being laid off or taking cuts. As for Tom's script, it would never be used.

"It wasn't too bad," Steve said. "I won't try to tell you it was any good."

"But Steve. . . ."

Steve looked at him, winced, bowed his head; Tom couldn't continue.

"I'll tell you how bad I am, Tom," Steve said, after the pause.

517

"Since you can't seem to get your mouth around the words, I will." But it was a subdued voice; there was none of the old resonance, of a man marshalling force. "I'm lousy enough so that I can sit here gloating that we didn't have a contract. And that you're not in the Guild. If you were, they'd make me pay you for the draft."

"You said you would. I didn't even think about a contract."

Steve rubbed his face. "Good faith. Yeah. You know, I love those stories about the bank presidents who pay off all their depositors with personal dough when the bank fails." He stared off; then he looked back and said, abruptly. "You've got something, haven't you? I mean, the secretaries out there. They got nothing but their paychecks. What's left of them. You know . . . I had to decide who was going to get the good faith, and who was going to get the bad. How would you like that for something to decide? Oh balls, Tom. Oh crap. Why didn't I say I was out when they told me you were here?"

"Steve," Tom said, after a moment. "You're wrong. I don't have anything."

"Shut up," Steve said. "I don't want to hear it."

"My rent's past due. I can't pay it." It was the first time Tom had ever been able to talk to Steve along lines of his own choosing; he was not enjoying it much. "I don't suppose they'll let me stay more than a few days longer. . . ."

Steve sighed. "What do you pay for rent?"

"Ninety-one forty a month."

"Ninety-one forty." Steve grimaced. Then he took a small, personal checkbook from his hip pocket, reached for a pen from the desk set on a side table behind him, and asked: "You got the buck forty?"

"No."

"All right. Eating and riding the subway back downtown's your problem, buddy. Here's the rent." He wrote out the check, folded it, held it out. "You're a lousy con man. Why didn't you say ninety-six forty and make yourself a fin?"

"Thanks Steve." Tom took the check and rose. "It was going to be four hundred for the script; this makes almost two I've collected. As far as I'm concerned, you don't owe me any more."

Steve turned red. "Get out," he shouted. "Take your god damn good faith and your god damn sympathy for my position and get out." It wasn't until Tom unfolded the check and read it, walking

518

towards the elevators, that he understood why Steve had gotten angry. *Payment in full,* it read, at the lower left *for first draft, uncontracted, Carole-Comet episode.* Tom could even sympathize with the anger; it's pretty frustrating to ride roughshod over a man who lies down for it.

Tom stopped at his landlord's office, endorsed the check and handed it over. Then he walked downtown; he was thinking of fifty or sixty cents that might have dropped out of his pants among the sofa cushions where he and Sarah had tumbled the other night. Sarah! He actually started running. In the mailbox, when he reached home, were a letter from Lala and a notice from the phone company; he opened the notice. It advised him that his phone service would be cut off if payment were not received within five days. The amount was forty-one dollars and eleven cents.

He hesitated over Lala's letter, feeling, for the first time, an immense and unhappy contrition. Finally, he put it back in the mailbox, unopened, and started slowly up the stairs, rocked, from step to step so that as his foot touched one, he feared that Sarah would be there, and as it touched the next he feared she wouldn't.

She was not. He was desperate. He did not know how to phone her. The only way that Tom could think of to find out would be to call Sheila, and ask for the phone number of Mrs. Nevins' little boy, an expedient so nasty, under the circumstances, that even desperation could not overcome distaste at first. But by two in the afternoon, a distraught Tom was actually at the telephone, with his finger on the dial, when he heard footsteps sluffing in the hall, and looked up, and it was Sarah, back.

In terms of physical sensation, hearts do not rise or fall; they make some sort of erratic jump, in their cage of ribs, and it would have taken a clearer head than Tom's to decide whether to call the direction of his heart's motion up, or down. As for Sarah, it did not seem to occur to her that she was late. He forgot his annoyance, then, in the excitement of seizing and being seized; to see Sarah was to want her; to want Sarah was to have her. There wasn't a coy breath in her body.

When they were disentangled, she asked about the money collecting, and Tom told her that the rent was paid.

"How wonderful." Later in the afternoon, she found the phone company notice, which had dropped to the floor in the corridor. She was on her way out of the bathroom, where she had been

519

washing her hair, wearing the slip which seemed to be her regular indoor costume—sweet-faced, raw-boned and clucking.

"Poor Tom," she said, holding the thing out. "No telephone?"

"Well," He took it and smiled. "It might be a relief."

"Oh no. Tom, you have to learn to pay your bills." She said it seriously. She reconceived him, from minute to minute, as something less and less like what he was. Now added to his other traits in the account she gave him of himself—general philandery; irresistible charm; a genius for writing because of the television script; carelessness about women's sensitive hearts; callousness towards children, which was all she perceived in his reaction to the play; and a casualness about going to jail—added to these rakish traits now was financial irresponsibility.

It amazed him; reality for Sarah was common enough, observable enough; what she saw simply bore no consistent relationship to the reality observed by anyone else. She had, for example, spoken several times of the nice man who let the children use his house in Brooklyn for their play; she believed she had met him, in one of the intermissions, but couldn't be sure; she had also spoken of the dangerous fire which had started, and of how wonderfully prompt the firemen were in putting it out, and of the policeman who had saved her and Tom from it. Sarah remade the world constantly in her own mind, sweetly stubborn about it—didn't remake it more colorfully, or more conveniently for herself exactly; just, a little nicer. Changed it, as it passed before her eyes, so that its elements were the same but in kindlier combinations.

She was not very sane, this woman of Tom's, not very bright, instinct with small delusions—but she was his woman. He stroked her hair, trying to protect himself by touching her from the things he was thinking, but his mind went remorselessly on: we hear constantly of the sad plight of couples who are carefully matched, adjusted, in every way except the physical. But what of the couple of Sarah Nevins and Tom Beniger, who have physical adjustment to such an extraordinary degree and, most likely, nothing else? He tightened an arm around her thinking, unhappily: love is learning, and I am greedy to go on, but there will come a time, the time of the bell-shaped curve which represents the rate of learning falling off, its plateau, its cumulative descent. He settled her against himself, both arms around her now, and thought: on the arc of the bell-shaped curve a time will come when her silliness is not forgivable, when I will cease to love, then cease to be affectionate, then cease, even, to be polite. As the time must have come for poor Mr. Nevins, whoever he was. And perhaps Mr. Nevins never had even this much with Sarah, this extraordinary physical response or . . . or does she share it with all men? He tightened his arms, and his jaw as well; for the first time in several years, there was a sharp twinge under his shoulder blade where things were slightly out of line.

But that was not the twinge that he minded. The one he minded, the twinge that hurt and twisted and would not stop hurting, illogical or not, began that evening as they played the lovers' obligatory scene of sexual autobiography, of female confession.

". . . it didn't really count," she was saying. "I mean, I only saw him once and, and . . . he's a very romantic, Spanish-type man, and I guess nobody can resist him, Tom. Maybe you've heard of him, Tom?"

"Maybe I have," Tom said, miserably certain. "Guy Cinturon."

4.

"Mother," Sheila said crossly, on her way to the phone. "Please stop telling people to call me up."

"I didn't tell this one to call up," her mother said. "Anyway, they've all been people who wanted to talk to you about your play. I didn't have to make them do it."

"Well, I wish you'd stop," Sheila said. "I wish you'd just forget it. And Daddy too."

"Answer the telephone. The man's waiting."

"I suppose you don't know who it is?"

"As a matter of fact, I don't," Ellen said. "He says his name is Dr. Bernstein, but I don't know him."

"Doctor who?"

"Bernstein."

Oh sure, Sheila thought, picking up the phone, saying hello. Mother doesn't know who he is. Just Rosemary, Ophelia's father, the psychiatrist.

Psychiatrist! Sheila looked around for her mother, shocked. This was getting really stupid, calling in psychiatrists; her mother was out of sight and the man was speaking.

". . . I wasn't fortunate enough to see the play, Sheila, but my wife thought it extraordinary."

"Thank you," said Sheila. *Didn't see the play.*

"She was very moved by what you did. And I think Rosemary's feeling about you now amounts to hero worship."

"Thank you." *Rosemary's feeling; the only feeling that girl has is in her fingers.*

"Sheila, I want to tell you how important this experience has been for Rosemary. It . . . it brought her to life in a way nothing else ever has." This was pretty clever, trying to pretend the problem he was getting at wasn't Sheila's at all. "I don't . . . I don't suppose you knew my daughter very well before your play, but she was a terribly withdrawn little girl. To have been involved in this community of effort was wonderful for her. Just wonderful. We're very grateful to you for having included Rosemary."

"You're welcome," Sheila said. *And would you please keep her out from under my feet doctor? I don't want to step on her.*

"It's . . . I'm tempted to think the therapy might have been almost complete if it hadn't been for the interruption. I mean it. My wife says that a real projection of personality was building up in Rosemary. That if you'd gotten to the mad scene, for instance, she might really have let loose in an important way."

What should Sheila say now? Thank you, or you're welcome? The man was waiting for a reply, so Sheila said: "She was talking louder, anyway."

Dr. Bernstein laughed. "You seem to understand what I'm saying, Sheila. If you do, you know that we have a great deal to thank you for."

"You're welcome."

"I'm afraid I can't say that Rosemary's in terribly good shape today, though. Or was yesterday. You probably noticed that she wasn't in school."

Oh, wasn't she? "Sure," Sheila said.

"But . . . well, it will pass I'm sure."

"Sure."

He cleared his throat. "Sheila, I called to make you an offer."

Now it would come. Now he had all the guff out of the way, and whatever her parents had put the psychiatrist up to would come. "Thank you, but. . . ."

"You see, we live in a house out here. It has a big finished

522

basement, and here's what I'd like to do." He paused, but Sheila saw no need to say anything. "I'd like to have the partitioning completed. I could get plasterers in, and have it ready in two or three days. Then I'd like to build you a real stage, at one end; it would be quite large, with room at either side—not much room behind, I'm afraid. But I'll put in lights, a curtain, everything needed. And folding chairs for an audience. We could seat thirty, maybe one or two more, if we use small chairs. Does this interest you Sheila?" She made a mumbling sound, and stopped listening, while he went on enthusiastically. "You'd have complete freedom to stage anything you wanted. I mean, I thought you'd probably want to complete your *Hamlet* first, but after that, if your group wanted to go on working together, you could do anything you liked. I don't . . . I don't mean to imply that Rosemary would have to be in every play, but we . . . well, Mrs. Bernstein and I would help all we could. With scenery and costumes, that is. If you wanted us to, that is. If you didn't, if you wanted to do it by yourselves. . . ." He was faltering; Sheila started to listen again, out of politeness. "You could be left completely to yourselves. Whatever you want, Sheila. I'm not a wealthy man, but I'd be willing to undertake the expenses I've described . . . no, that's not an important thing to say . . . just, you'd have absolute freedom, Sheila. To do your *Hamlet,* or anything else, without interruption." He stopped. She didn't answer. It confused her to think that her parents should go so far. "Shall I call in the plasterers, Sheila?"

The direct question startled her. "Well, no thank you, Dr. Bernstein," she said. "I mean, it's very nice of them . . . of you."

"But don't you want to finish your *Hamlet?* Rosemary . . . we've had Rosemary working on her lines. . . ."

"Well, it's very nice of you, Dr. Bernstein, but I don't guess we'd want to do anything more with *Hamlet* right now."

"Sheila . . . !" the doctor went on, talking and talking. She supposed he was trying to earn his fee. Or maybe, to do him justice, he was really worried about her. But he didn't have to be; Sheila considered telling him this, and decided not to. He was a psychiatrist; he could probably tell by now that Sheila didn't really need him, she wasn't crying, or laughing hysterically or anything.

Maybe if she explained, but she didn't, how well she understood her situation. . . . but he could tell. A psychiatrist could tell. The thing was, Sheila hadn't done something wonderful, and the other

523

thing was, she wasn't crying or laughing hysterically. It was just that there was a part of it she would have to get used to, a shame to which she couldn't, at the moment apply her former, cheerful, childish doublemindedness. And that was being caught naked.

The interruption had had to come just as the play reached its highest, most exalted time of flow, with Sheila Walle completely stripped, an unclothed self, for action. To be dropped, suddenly, from such stark exaltation to pure terror in an instant was a shock you could not talk about to anyone; how could you? Instinct told her that its effect could neither be described by talking nor healed by sympathy. A wound may be disinfected, stitched and bandaged, but its healing is a function of one's own body, not another's. As for the scar, it may be minimized, but it still shows, still throbs with a change in weather. Sheila knew, already, what her scar was going to be when the healing was done, knew that from the shock would develop, inexorably, a permanent trait of personality, knew pretty well what the trait would be.

It would be a certain tentativeness, a caution, to temper her former ability to commit herself wholeheartedly, and a doubt: a doubt that she had ever reached or, if she had, could ever reach again, the elevation of the instant just before the fireman's light blasted her eyes. She hung up the phone, saying goodbye, no thanks, to Dr. Bernstein, rejecting his perfectly kind interest in her, hoping quietly that this would close the subject.

5.

On Friday morning, his fourth day on the island, after a good sleep, walking the beach at low tide, Ned found a fresh human footprint in the sand. He looked up, alarmed, and saw no one; then he remembered that the blue and yellow underpants were still flying from the signal staff, and thought that the footprint might be that of the boatman. But would the boatman be barefoot? Ned looked to his right, inland, and there, coming around a dune, his pants rolled up and delicately carrying his shoes, came Hubert.

"Hello, dear," Hubert said, and two other boys appeared, following, also carrying shoes. "There were a couple of phone calls for you while you were out."

524

Ned's only impulse was to run.

"My," said Hubert, coming closer and stopping. "You do look like a piece of garbage." Then, turning his eyes to the others when Ned didn't answer. "Perhaps he's forgotten how to talk, poor dear."

"No savvy white man palaver, Johnny?" asked one of the others, and they all laughed.

"Got big fella white fishing boat allasame dockside," said the other one, less successfully. Ned shifted his feet and looked down.

"Oh, no," said Hubert to his friends. "No. I think we'll leave it for the gulls. It's the sort of thing they love to pluck up off the beach and then drop from fifty feet onto a big rock, so that it bursts open, exposing all its little edible parts."

There was a great laugh at this, and then Hubert said, quite severely: "Come along, Ned." He pointed to the boy on his left. "This is Reed. He might have a show for you to direct."

"What?" Ned asked. It was the first word he had managed to say.

"I could hardly blame him if he's changed his mind after all this," Hubert said. "We found your little food messes on the board-walk—really, Ned. And then trailing you up the beach . . . and dear, what were you trying to advertise with those pantie signals? Hmmmm?" Hubert was advancing, wrinkling his nose, pretending to gag as he got closer.

And Ned couldn't run, though he longed to, sending a glance, wistful and furtive, down the limitless slow curve of the sand over his shoulder, imagining himself huffing through it with Hubert and his friends not even bothering to pursue, simply sitting and watching until, somewhere between here and the horizon, an exhausted Ned would fall frail to the beach. Then they would beckon and Ned, frightened of being left after all, would crawl painfully back.

Now Hubert was behind him, making shooing motions. "Go along, go along," he was saying, amusing the others by making his hands behave as if they were unwilling to touch Ned. Ned started moving, slowly, in front of him. "Perhaps when you get home, and scrubbed and purged and dressed in something nice, Reed will be able to face talking to you about his play."

Play? Ned stopped and looked at the one called Reed.

"Oh yes," Reed said, quietly, and, with a covertly sympathetic look and just a touch of emphasis: "Yes."

525

Ned looked at Reed's feet and ankles, pale and bare in the sunlight. Then he began to trudge along again. Hubert had overplayed his hand, now, for whatever joy there was in knowing it. It had been said without words, by the boy with pale ankles, that Ned might leave Hubert, after all, and direct plays—if Ned would leave Hubert for Reed. Ned sighed and looked from Reed's feet, just before they turned up onto the boardwalk, out to sea; there was no sign, today, of the wise dolphin, enumerating the behavior traits of the human species; but Ned supposed that the dolphin already knew that, in problems of human division, answers never come out even, there is always something left over.

6.

On Friday night, Tom and Sarah went to bed at ten fifteen, Tom wearied with guilt, jealousy and the impossibility of communication, Sarah, as always, unwilling to be aware that things were anything but tender and romantic.

By ten-thirty, with Sarah sleeping sweet beside him, Tom was still feeling entirely wakeful and entirely craven, the insomniac oaf of the world. To prove that he was this, he had only to let his imagination touch on scenes of Sarah and Guy, meeting at an art gallery, sharing laughter, sharing mouths. These were images of bilious magic; the merest outline of one, in the hollow cavern of his head, could turn his other limbs, his trunk, to caverns, too, caverns enclosed by cold skin, in which winds blew.

At midnight, not yet having slept, Tom got up and smoked a cigarette, and tried to fix his mind on nothing. Tomorrow, somehow, he was going to have to get money; in three more days the phone would be off. He had to forestall that; he hated the telephone but it might ring, at any time, with some news about the work he'd been seeking, even—he thought sadly—a message from overseas. Thinking about the telephone reminded him that Ellen had called early that evening to say something (what? that the girl was strange) about Sheila. To ask (how? drunkenly) Tom's advice. (To be given what? Stupidity, inattention). If there had been any hope of finding Ellen still rational, Tom would now have called her back. Since he couldn't, the midnight cigarette ritual added to his guilt instead of calming him. He got back into bed.

At three A.M. Tom had still not slept. He got up again. Moon-light lit the room. Sarah, hearing or sensing his movement in her sleep, threw the cover off and twisted towards where he had been lying, naked, nearly awake for love. The instant and infallible excitement which she generated in Tom caused him to take the first of the two steps between him and the bed; there is a special fear of things which are knowable, but have not yet been thought through. This fear, and the feeling that disengagement from Sarah was still possible without catastrophe, caused him to stop. Yet he knew he could not stay in the room with that nakedness and not cover it. He turned abruptly and went into the hall.

Naked himself, Tom put on his overcoat; he could not risk re-turning to the bedroom for his other clothes. There were galoshes in the closet and he put his feet into them, closing up the snaps. Then he went out of the apartment, leaving the door ajar, and down the steps, almost to the first floor. He sat on the third step from bottom, staring out of the glass rectangle of the door that led to the sreet, not quite able to see the streetlight in front of the building, a little cold.

He said: "Balls," out loud, and then, more quietly: "Balls."

He tried to think.

He felt no conviction of guilt for infidelity, intellectually, but as a physical sensation, guilt suffused him. It seemed to him that this consideration was not a part of the real morality involved, only of a kind of fake morality which had scarred him in child-hood, which ought to have as little to do with his behavior now as the rules of a card game one doesn't play; but if the body is sick, with love and guilt, can the mind tell it it is wrong?

Discarding this, as far as he was able, he began to see his set of choices. Whichever he should make he could, for better or worse, impose on Sarah all too easily, so that he must choose for her, too. And, since they could have no voice in the decision, un-der the circumstances, he must choose for Lala and for the unborn child.

Break now with Sarah? Continue, planning to break later? Con-tinue, planning to make the relationship permanent? Continue without plan; see what happened?

The last he discarded as being no choice at all; if there is any such thing as immorality, Tom thought, it is in neglecting to make use of the minds we have. One choice crossed off.

527

Break now? Continue, planning to break later? Continue, planning to make permanent?

He plucked the next discard out of the middle. If he continued, meaning to break, even though he might persuade Sarah to share the intention, nothing would be served but gratification. They would risk destruction of the intention to break, either through growth of the relationship or through outside occurrence. Hence, this choice would be no different from continuing and seeing what happened, and was no choice either. Two crossed off.

Break? Continue, planning to make permanent?

He considered the latter first. He must think of it, he told himself, from four points of view: *Lala's*—she would be hurt, but not deeply; her nature was too sensible, her temperament too philosophical; if Tom were to suggest that they end their marriage, Lala, as he understood her, would take it calmly, sorry to lose the companionship and affection which they both enjoyed, curious to see what other, heretofore unexpected things life might have for her; she was attractive, and would marry; perhaps she, too, would learn a more vivid kind of love; she might, in addition, improve her life in general; and then, of course, she might not; but above all, she would think it highly interesting to find out. Thus only in an immediate way could it matter to Lala. *The child's point of view*—its future, Tom winced to think, might be improved by Tom and Lala's separating, or might not; this would depend on how its mother fared in a second marriage; since its mother was Lala, she would probably fare well; since the child would never, from its first moment of breath, see Tom, it could hardly be affected traumatically by losing Tom. No moral imperative, then, could be drawn by thinking of the child's point of view. *Sarah's*—how would a permanent relationship with Tom affect her? Badly, he thought. Destructively. Just now his ardor was useful to her, as Tom understood Sarah, giving her the illusion that she was all right, that her imprecise orientation, her misuses of mind, were of no importance. Tom did not know whether his ardor would continue; it felt to him as if it would; the experience of mankind in general indicated it would not. If it cooled, he foresaw himself lancing Sarah like a boil. Even if the ardor remained constant, Tom thought that he could not forever refrain from irritation with Sarah's ways of thinking and expression, knew he would start, eventually, to snipe at them, mock them, quarrel with them, be-

528

have, in short, if he were to become her husband, like a husband. What would this do to Sarah? Either expose her fantasies, or drive her into more extreme ones; destruction, either way. *Tom's, Tom's point of view*—what was there for him in continuing, making permanent accommodation for, this love of Sarah? Gratification. The torrent of self-knowledge. The mysterious gift of physical virility. But no dignity, no honor, only the destruction of the object loved. He would not let himself prophesy his own destruction as well; that was romantic. That was assuming, even, that if it should become intolerable, he would, for some reason, accept a second bargain with a woman as more binding than the first. No, he thought; there are many good reasons for discontinuing one marriage, undertaking another, but none apply here. No reason, only an excuse, and of all excuses the paltriest: love.

Was there another choice, before he was left with the simple one of breaking off? Only that he might break off from Sarah and from Lala, too. But this he noted only to complete the roster of possibilities, for Tom knew himself to be uxorious; and he knew that, since he was to spend his life in marriage or in marriages, there was little chance of his finding another woman as fine as Lala, or one as arousing as Sarah. He sighed, briefly, for the sort of male temperament which is not uxorious, which lives most equably without a mate, but there was little of this in Tom.

That left no choice but breaking off with Sarah now. Permanently. Saying goodbye, explaining in any way he had to.

Very well. He would send her home in the morning.

He was chilled enough, uncomfortable enough, sitting on the third step, in his overcoat and galoshes, so that the solution seemed as easy to accept as it was logical. He stood up, with a grateful sense of difficult decision made, and stretched. Then he opened the mailbox, and took out the three letters from Lala which had accumulated there. He opened and read them, one by one, in the order of their postmarks, with a wonderfully fond feeling for her dearness, levelness, courage and candor.

He put the letters in his overcoat pocket and turned upstairs, thinking first, happily, of the warmth of being back in bed. Then he remembered what there was in bed, turned towards him, waiting; he stopped, clenched his fists, turned around and scurried into the street. It was three in the morning.

Cold wind splashed against the openings in the overcoat, spilled

529

over the loose tops of the galoshes, eddied around his ankles, even trickled down to where his feet slapped and paddled at their rubber confinement. Nevertheless, he walked so until dawn, his head full of many things, and finally—his shoulder aching, his frame tiring—knew he could not abandon his passion for Sarah, no matter what the logic. Realizing this, he grasped it as the antidote to exhaustion, and began hurrying back towards his building, block after block, seeing sharply, now and then, in the face of an early wayfarer, astonishment at Tom's bare neck and legs. He rushed, gasping, up the stairs, trembling to abandon himself to his succubus, craven, perhaps, but needing the particular warmth of sexual connection as an addict needs his drug. He thrust into the apartment with his teeth chattering, letting the overcoat fall to the floor behind him as he rushed towards the bedroom, a tall, quavering man, trying ridiculously, laughing, to kick buckled galoshes off cold feet. Without stopping to resolve this comic struggle, he opened the bedroom door. The bed was empty.

Forgetting the problem of galoshes, Tom ran to the kitchen, the living room, opened the bathroom door. He rushed back to look again in the bedroom. Sarah was gone.

On the table by the telephone, he found a note which read, in grammar school handwriting: "You want me to go away. I know it. I knew it all along, so don't be sorry. You can call me up if you want to. Please buy yourself something to eat. Love, Sarah." With this note she had left fifteen dollars; three five dollar bills.

7.

In the middle of the morning, ten days after the play, Guy had a phone call from Ellen Walle. She was, Ellen said, trying to find someone who would talk to Sheila, someone Sheila respected who could cheer the girl up, straighten her out. Sheila wouldn't listen to her father; she had never, Ellen said, listened to her mother. Tom would be the obvious man to come to Sheila, but he was unapproachable since he'd lost his job. This was the first Guy had heard of Tom's losing it.

Sheila's friends and teachers, Ellen went on, didn't seem to get through to the girl.

"What could I say?" Guy asked.

"Tell her she was wonderful in the play," Ellen said. "Build

530

her up a little. Tell her the world's still a nice place, and she's not being persecuted . . . I don't know. A man she likes could talk to her . . . you'd be perfect for it, Guy."

"Ellen," Guy said. "I would. I'd do anything for Sheila, but I didn't see the play."

"You didn't?"

"Wasn't it noticed? No. I didn't make it. Eddie called to tell me about the firemen and so on, but I wasn't there. I'm very sorry."

Ellen hesitated. Then she said: "Sheila . . . *thinks* you saw it."

"I'll never tell her otherwise," Guy said. "But I couldn't fool her for long if we tried to talk about it, do you think? Sheila's too smart for that. Look . . . why don't we confess that I didn't make the show, and I'll take her to lunch and a matinee? Would that help?"

Ellen thought not, not yet anyway; later it might be just the thing. They said goodbye and hung up. Perhaps, thought Guy, if he couldn't do anything for Sheila, he could for Tom. If he had lost his job, Tom must be in need of money; Guy dialed Tom's phone number. On the other end, there were two rings; then an operator's voice cut in and said:

"What number are you calling please?"

Guy told her.

"That number has been temporarily disconnected," the operator said, and hung up. Guy thought for a moment. Then he dressed to go out, phoned for his car, and drove himself over to Tom's neighborhood. On the way, he couldn't help driving past Lordie Lord's building. He had neither seen nor heard from her since the night of the play. He slowed a little as he went by, long enough to glance up at her window. There was no particular point in doing so, it was a window curtained like any other; he speeded up and went on.

There was no buzz in answer to Tom's bell when Guy rang. He pressed other buttons on the panel; the front door buzzer responded, and he went in and upstairs. He knocked on the door of Tom's apartment, very loudly. After a moment he heard shuffling inside, and then Tom opened the door and peered out. He was wearing pale blue underwear shorts, a red sweater with holes in the sleeves, and a pair of galoshes over bare ankles. Nothing more. He did not appear to have shaved for several days.

Tom stared at Guy for what seemed a long time, and then hiccupped; it was not a drunken sound, and there was no smell of liquor.

"Hi, Tom," Guy said. "Let me in."

Tom backed away, leaving the door open, and Guy followed him in.

Tom was muttering something.

"What?" Guy asked.

Tom shook his head and went into the living room. Again Guy followed. The mess was extraordinary. It was a mess, chiefly, of books, dozens of them lying around on floor and furniture, some open.

"What on earth have you been doing?" Guy asked, falsely cheery. "Cramming for midterms?" He forced a grin; he felt that he could conceal his dismay over his friend's condition if he could get past the first shock.

Tom looked unresponsively down at the open book that was nearest him and shook his head.

"You're a mess, *compadre*," Guy said, in Spanish. "Come on. Let me help you put some of these books back." He picked up a couple of volumes and took them over to one of the shelves; it was nearly empty; parallel lines of dust showed on the bared wood. "Put them in anywhere?"

"Yes," Tom replied in Spanish. "Anywhere."

It was helping Guy to be active; he began picking up books briskly, loading his arms, moved to the shelf, put his armload down and asked cheerfully, over his shoulder:

"Any of these you want to keep out?"

There was no answer. Guy looked around; Tom had left the room.

Guy found his friend in the bathroom, sitting on the edge of the tub in his absurd costume, sobbing dryly.

"*Tomasito,*" Guy said, compassionately, putting an arm around Tom's shoulders. "What is the matter? What?"

"Nothing," Tom said in English. "Nothing."

"Have you got a drink around this place? Some coffee?"

"No. No, Guy. No coffee."

"There must be tea, then. Lala must have left some tea."

Tom nodded.

"Wait," Guy said. He went into the kitchen; all the pans were dirty; he rinsed one out, filled it with water and set it on the stove.

532

He went back to the bathroom. "Come on," he said. "I know what I'm going to do. I'm going to shave you." He closed the toilet seat lid and sat Tom on it. "You'll feel much better. Come on." He found a wash cloth, filled the sink with hot water, and sponged Tom's face; Tom made no move to help and none to hinder. Guy cleaned the safety razor that was on the sink rim, put in a new blade. Put a bath towel around Tom's neck, wet the face again, soaped it from a can of aerosol lather, and began to shave Tom, using small, careful strokes. The beard came off quite easily.

"You see," he said. "Your personal barber, *Tomasito*. Now."

When he had shaved him, Guy washed the face and massaged it for a moment with his fingers. He seized a hair brush and started, roughly, to brush Tom's hair. Tom grabbed at the brush.

"I'll do it," he said, getting to his feet. "I'll do it, Guy."

"Okay," Guy began to grin. "Okay, that's better. And get those god damn galoshes off your feet and some clothes on. Come on. I'll make the tea."

Back in the kitchen, Guy checked the refrigerator and the food shelves. There wasn't much around to eat. A cheese sandwich with one bite out of it probably represented the level of Tom's current diet and the extent of his appetite as well. Guy shook his head. His friend was starving himself; this had to be more than just losing a job. On the counter, by the sink, was a phone company notice demanding payment of $41.11. Guy put it in his pocket. He heard Tom moving around in the bedroom; by the time Guy got to the living room with the tea pot and two cups, Tom was there, sitting stiffly in a straight chair by the phone table, clean and dressed.

Guy poured a cup of tea and put it down on the table, near Tom's elbow.

"Now," he said. "What is all this?"

Tom picked up the cup and sipped from it before answering. Then he said, in a low voice. "I've been . . . I've been kicking a habit."

"What do you mean?"

"I've been . . . having an affair. I've been . . . in love. I'm kicking it." Tom shivered visibly. "You know what they call that?" He asked. "Cold turkey."

"What sort of affair, Tom?" Guy asked, gently. "Who with?" Then, when Tom didn't answer, "You lost your job, didn't you?"

"Yes."

"Out of money?"

"No. No, Guy, I'm not."

"How much do you need, Tom? I've got my checkbook."

"No," said Tom. "No. I've got money. Look." He touched three five dollar bills which were lying on the phone table.

"That's not much, Tom."

"Yes. It is."

"How about the phone?"

"What about it?"

"It's been cut off."

"I know."

"Don't you want it back on?"

Tom shook his head.

"Why not?"

"I don't want it to work. I might call up . . . my habit."

"What's to stop you from going out and using a pay phone?"

Tom sipped again at the tea. "That's why I didn't get dressed," he muttered.

"Tom," Guy said. "I know something about affairs. I mean, if I know about anything. You don't want to tell me?"

"No." Tom's voice was unaccountably fierce. "No I don't. You don't know anything about this one."

A little astonished at such vehemence, Guy said, placatingly: "Okay, Tom. Okay."

"Not anything," Tom insisted. "You wouldn't know anything."

It irritated Guy a little; maybe he did, maybe he didn't. But you don't refuse to tell an experienced mechanic what's wrong with your car, or a television repair man about the trouble with your set. You don't tell an expert he knows nothing.

"What can I do, then?" Guy asked, finally.

"Nothing, Guy, nothing." Tom was still jerking his words out. "I'm all right. I'm all right, Guy."

"Sure."

"I was just reading a few books." It could have been a joke, had it been meant that way.

"Do you want me to stay a while, Tom? Help you clean up? Then we can go to dinner."

Tom looked at him fully; his mouth opened once and then closed again. He put his tea cup down, and seemed to shake him-

534

self. When he spoke again, his voice was quietly dull. "No," he said.

"Okay." Guy rose, thinking he had better leave while his irritation was still concealable. He took a hundred dollars in tens and twenties from his pocket and put it on the phone table. "You listen, Tom," he said. "When you come out of this, you'll need more money. All you have to do is call up and tell me how much."

Tom neither looked at nor spoke to him.

"You call up," Guy said. "You hear? Use the pay phone. Or come to my place. Look, this is a post-hypnotic suggestion: When you wake up, call on Guy."

As he went out, Tom was still sitting in the straight chair, the tea cup half-empty, its contents growing cold beside him.

Guy stopped first at a fancy grocer's. He bought and paid for fifty dollars' worth of food, and ordered it delivered to Tom's apartment. Then, thinking things over, he stopped by a phone company branch office and paid Tom's phone bill; it seemed to Guy that any of a number of things might come up which would make it important to Tom that he be reached. The girl who took the check said the instrument should be reconnected some time the next day. Guy got his car and drove back, going, for no good reason, past Lordie's window once again.

8.

The morning after Guy's visit Tom had another caller. When this caller knocked, Tom was unwilling to open the door, thinking it might be Guy come back. Tom had fought anger and despair all the time Guy was with him the day before, and the arrival of the groceries in the late afternoon had put him into a state of silent hysterics. He had had no feeling that such reactions were reasonable or proper; nevertheless, he had been profoundly distressed at seeing Guy, and particularly so when Guy asked about the affair. Tom was having trouble enough with his feelings without trying to discuss his crazy love; to have discussed her with Guy would have been past bearing. Guy. Guy who might, coolly and with truth, have spoken of Sarah intimately, who might have said, Tom could hear him, "No *compadre*. Not with Mrs. Nevins. No man could be in love with such a woman. Even for me, Tom, she was

535

too weird." Tom could hear Guy say that. Had he said it? Or something like it? After twelve hours, Tom was no longer sure, one way or the other; all he could be sure of was that it was a good idea to see no one; and, if someone talked to you, not to listen very closely.

So, when the knock came, thinking it was Guy back, Tom didn't go to the door. Then, because he hadn't altogether closed it after the groceries, the door opened and Ned Kildeer looked in.

Ned, too, had tried to call and found the phone cut off. Ned, too, had thought Tom might need money; and talking to. Ned added two more ten dollar bills to the pile of money on the phone table. Ned was full of talk: news, plans—and an adventure he assured Tom was quite fantastic. Tom sat and let Ned tell it, glad that he was dressed less idiotically than he had been yesterday, hoping the idiocy didn't show on his face. He had the sensation of knowing what Ned was talking about without being able, exactly, to hear what Ned was saying. It was a familiar sensation, known before somewhere, and Tom found himself, instead of trying to attend to Ned, trying to place the sensation. It took a while. When he got it, he realized it was the sensation of being in a bathtub, with one's ears underwater, soaking soap out of the hair or something, and having someone—a wife, mother, friend—try to talk. You see the lips move, the face smile, hear a kind of sound . . . What was Ned saying now? Occasionally dutiful, Tom would resume trying to listen. Ned had made a trip of some kind? Eventually Tom caught the name Sheila, and thought, gratefully, that here was something he could comment on.

"Ellen, my sister that is. . . ." But already he had lost the thread of what he was trying to say.

"What about your sister, Tom?"

"I'm sorry." Tom shook his head. He didn't mind Ned's being there; he wouldn't mind when Ned left.

"I was asking about Sheila?"

"Oh yes. Ellen's worried."

"Sheila's mother is worried?"

"Yes. Very anxious about the girl. Asking, asking everybody to go talk to Sheila. . . ."

"Shall I?" Ned asked.

Should Ned what? Tom tried to puzzle it out. He had forgotten again.

536

"Shall I go to see Sheila? I'd like to."

Tom got up and went towards the kitchen. Halfway there, he began to wonder whether what he assumed—that he had offered Ned coffee which Ned had accepted—had actually taken place.

He turned to ask Ned, whether they had discussed coffee, and a thoroughly normal thing happened. The phone rang. Tom started back to the living room, to answer it, and had come even with where Ned was sitting before he remembered.

"That phone can't ring," Tom said, stopping. "It's cut off."

"That's what I thought," Ned said.

It rang.

"Would the company turn it back on, so they could call up and scold me or something?" Tom said.

"No. They'd send a man."

"Yes."

The thing rang again.

"You sure you didn't pay your bill, and then forget you'd done it? So it's back on now?" Ned asked.

Tom shook his head. "I couldn't have paid it. I wonder. Maybe this woman. . . ." It rang.

"I'll answer it," Ned offered, and stood up. Tom nodded yes. Ned went over to the phone, picked it up and said, "Hello."

Then: "Oh, yes. But this is Ned Kildeer."

Then: "No, I just dropped in at Tom's. His phone's been off, and this is the first call since he paid the bill. He seems to have paid it and forgotten."

Then: "Just a moment." Ned covered the receiver with his hand and spoke to Tom. "It's your friend Eddie Bissle."

"Oh," Tom said.

"Want to talk to him?"

Oh, of course; if Eddie was calling, he wanted to talk to Tom, not Ned. "Yes, sure," Tom said. He took the phone and talked to Eddie. Or more, listened to Eddie. Or more, tried to listen to Eddie, for he found himself having the same trouble he had had with Ned. He couldn't seem to keep his mind, from one word to the next, on what his friend was saying. There was some reason why he welcomed this numbness that was setting in towards people who meant something to him, and sometimes, happily, he could go as long as ten or fifteen minutes without remembering what the reason was.

9.

Eddie called Guy after he finished talking to Tom. It was positively pee-culiar, the way Tom talked. It was comparatively piss-culiar that Ned should have answered the phone. It was superlatively puke-culiar when he remembered that Ned and Tom and gone to *Hamlet* together.

But it was what Guy said that put the cherry on the fruitcake.

"Tom's been having some strange sort of affair, Eddie. He wouldn't tell me anything about it."

"Yeah." . . . that put the fig in the newton,

"He was absolutely mysterious about it. I got the feeling he didn't want me there. Do you suppose he's been entertaining a giraffe or something?"

"Yeah, a giraffe." . . . that put the cream in the oreo sandwich,

"Anyway, the place was the strangest sort of mess. Books all over everywhere. I gathered Tom hadn't seen his love for a while, and had been trying to take his mind off it. I wanted to tell him—best way to get over a thing like this is wallow in it. Give yourself a chance to get tired of it. Then it doesn't hurt to give it up. If he'd let me, I'd have told him to get her back right away. . . ."

"Yeah," Eddie said. "Yeah. Well, that's probably what he did."

. . . . the crunchies in the nestles, the tuttis in the fruttis, and the nutsies in the Hershey bar.

"You heard about Goswith?" Guy asked.

"No, and I don't believe I want to," Eddie said.

"You'd better anyway. And brace yourself."

"Never mind," Eddie said. "If it's about the paintings, you can have mine. I don't even want to think about Goswith. You can have them for half-price."

"It's just as well you feel that way," Guy said. "Half-price is about what they're worth."

"What do you mean?"

"Our friend's got something new," Guy said. "He's got religion."

"Goswith?"

"Yes. I called him up the other day. The boys in Mexico wanted to get moving, so I called Goswith. We were going to have the first show down there; I was going to take Goswith down."

538

"What'd he say?"

"He said God might forgive me for my intentions, as nearly as I could make out," Guy said. "He said he was painting over every canvas in the studio, the only great painting was religious painting, and if we tried to show any of the sinful work he'd done in his deluded effort to make money, he'd repudiate it."

"Well, well," Eddie said.

"You want to sell yours back, you can probably sell them to Goswith for a prayer."

"What'd you plan to do?" Eddie asked.

"What can we do? Hold the stuff till he dies."

"Yeah," Eddie said. "Well, if the son of a bitch crosses my path again, it may not be too long."

"What's got you so sour?" Guy asked. "I thought you were the rare man who could stand him."

"Not any more," Eddie said. "Hey, what do you hear about Sheila? I keep wondering if she's okay."

"Oh, Ellen's looking for someone to talk to Sheila. Look, maybe you could, Eddie."

And that led to the thing that put the pink white mountain frosting in the pastry tube and squeezed "Happy Birthday, Dear World" on the old fashioned, brown-sugar spice cake. Because when Eddie called Ellen to ask about talking to Sheila, you see maybe, maybe he'd just happen to be the guy who could, Ellen said there was someone with Sheila right now, talking to her, they were just now going back to Sheila's room, that was a good sign, Sheila hadn't let anyone, not even Amy, into that room in two weeks, wasn't it wonderful? Someone had turned up, and Eddie asked who, and Ellen said that nice little friend of Tom's, maybe you don't know 'um, Ned Kildeer.

Not a giraffe. Not Henry Wadsworth Longfellow. Not William Makepeace Thackeray. No. Maybeyoudont Knowumned Kildeer.

10.

Sheila told Mr. Kildeer to sit on the bed. Then she sat down in her desk chair and looked at him.

"I thought," he said, "I'd like to try to tell you what you did."

"What did I do?" She was suspicious. Maybe he was a television and play director, a friend of Uncle Tom's, as he said; and maybe another psychiatrist or something, sneaking in. But if it wasn't just a story about his being a director, maybe he *could* tell her something. Sheila was just beginning to want to hear something. That was why she'd asked him to her room.

"What did I do?"

"You made something," Mr. Kildeer said. "You put something into the world that hadn't been there before."

Sheila kept her face sombre, and her eyes on him.

"You took a text by Shakespeare and a dozen children and yourself, and turned them into something nobody'd ever seen before."

"Well," said Sheila. "It's gone."

"Is that what troubles you—or that you weren't allowed to finish?"

"Who said anything troubled me?" But he didn't look like a psychiatrist; in a funny way, he looked like a kid. So she said: "Both."

"You've got to understand," Mr. Kildeer said. "You had to be stopped. They'll always stop you if they can. Making something is a crime. Sedition. Rebellion."

"I don't get it," Sheila said.

"To want to make something is to say the world lacks something."

"Oh," Sheila said. "That's what you meant."

He nodded. They were both silent for a moment.

Then she said: "It wasn't me that made anything. It was Shakespeare."

"No." He got excited. "A writer uses words. A painter uses colors. A sculptor uses stone. But the feeling's already there in a word, the impact in the color, the solidness in the stone. No artist gives his material its basic worth; he only exploits it. A performer makes, too. His material has already been partly exploited; that's the only difference."

Sheila considered that, and shrugged. "Anyway, it's gone," she said.

"That's another thing; about permanence. . . ."

She waited, perfectly quiet, to see what he would think of to say. She liked the way he talked.

"Permanence is the idea that breaks performers' hearts. It's

540

the idea that makes a great dancer or singer feel humble before a tenth rate poet. But it's a hoax, Sheila. A writer's hoax. Even permanence is relative, after all. Homer's the oldest thing we have that's meaningful, and he's less than three thousand years old. Three thousand years before him there were Homers—Hittite Homers. Egyptian Homers. Who knows? An archaeologist finds their work and reconstructs it from the clay tablets; translates it, publishes it—does that make it alive? Has it endured? Does it speak to anyone? Its permanence is gone in half a dozen centuries. Will Homer speak to the South American or the African civilization that succeeds ours? Maybe Shakespeare will, but will he to the nations, in the languages that prevail three thousand years from now? Will Christ? Words and music die. Painting fades. Sculpture and buildings wear away. Performance dies more quickly, yes, but can any of the others be so brilliant? Isn't the instant death of a great performance what makes it so overwhelming, so much more immediately moving than anything else can be? We waste breath, trying to cheat mortality, Sheila. After all . . ."

"All right," she said.

"After all, Sheila . . ."

"All right." That was enough. Anyway, having him there had given her an idea, the first idea she'd had in days: "Listen, Mr. Kildeer," Sheila said. "Do you think I could get a part on television sometime?"

CHAPTER THREE

1.

To ELLEN IT seemed that, in the period that followed, there was movement apart among the three men with whom her emotions had always, if secretly, been most closely engaged. For Ellen was aware that she had given little more than time to her marriage, as a man, perhaps, gives nothing of himself but his time to a job that does not interest him. It was herself in relationship to Tom, Eddie and Guy that seemed to affect Ellen most deeply. This had been so even in periods like that of the war, like others since, when physical separation or involvement in individual affairs put the three out of immediate touch with one or another—so long as their mutual feeling was close and Ellen had just one to see or hear from now and then, the waters on which her fantasies sailed were high and calm.

Now, in the middle spring of the year, she felt the three men grow distant to one another and indifferent, therefore, to herself.

Tom, she thought, was not aware of distance, not aware of much of anything these days. He was living like a zombie, from the way it sounded, if a zombie lives.

Eddie was in one of his epochs of disgust, nothing unusual for Eddie except that he had, in the past, been able generally to exempt his friends and his mistress. Now, it seemed, they were all included, Tom most of all, herself next, Guy least. For herself, she insisted to her mirror, she didn't care.

542

It was not in Guy to be either zombie or disgusted; in fact he even arranged the lunch and matinee for Sheila, just as promised, only not, it turned out, with himself—with a young cousin from Princeton who Sheila said was the most beautiful man she'd ever met. But when Ellen called Guy, a few days later, to thank him and tell him how successful the afternoon seemed to have been, the machine on Guy's telephone reported Mr. Cinturon out of town; indefinitely; no forwarding address.

So, for a time, all three were gone. Well. At least Sheila was fine now. She had even resumed speaking to her father.

2.

Tom wanted and received no more visits after the one from Ned; it had been too difficult, trying to listen, trying to care. Now and then the phone would ring; sometimes he answered it, sometimes he didn't. Only once did he break, and try to call Sarah; the phone was answered by a little boy with a memorably harsh voice. Tom knew who it was; Roy, the Ghost. Tom said it was the wrong number and hung up.

After that he took to walking a great deal around the city. Occasionally—through Ned, ordinarily—he would have an appointment with someone about a job, but he forgot the appointments as often as he kept them. It probably made no difference; when he did keep one, he was inattentive and dull, sat there for the most part thinking about his eyes and how to keep them open, yearning for the interview to be over so that he could leave.

His memory, which retained whole pages of books he'd read in his middle teens, failed now to hold more than a tentative outline of anything that had happened since he'd walked with Sarah away from Harrison and the jail.

Often his walks ended in a little park on the lower East side of the city, a park where no children came, for bums sat there on pleasant days, taking the spring sun. Tom had thought about bums in jail, and was vaguely attracted now to watching them, the winos and the psychos, much as he had imagined they might be.

He never tried to approach or talk to the bums; he was not really that interested in them, nor they in him. Yet on one particularly bright day, when the April sun was like July, a bum came to sit on the same bench with Tom. It was quite unusual;

543

these men treated the benches with the same respect for routine that married people have for one another's customary chairs.

This was a rather portly bum with a newspaper he had fished from a garbage can. Tom had noticed him in the park before, a man with touches about his clothing if not of elegance, then at least of some impulse towards the picturesque. If, for example, he wore his shirt open at the neck, this bum would have its collar spread over the outside of his jacket collar. His pantlegs were always carefully rolled, so that, if the cuffs were frayed, it didn't show. The man was avoided by the others to some extent—not that they socialized a great deal, but they often stood or sat in wordless groups of two or three. To what extent they were acquainted Tom couldn't tell; there must have been certain friendships among them, but not for the careful dresser who now sat down, put his hat on the bench beside him, and ran his fingers through his light, thin hair. Tom looked at him; he seemed to be Tom's age. Most of the men were older; perhaps that was why they avoided this one.

The man noticed Tom's glance and smiled ambiguously; it wanted to be a smile of friendship, but reserved the right to call itself a smile of disdain if not returned. Tom nodded. The man hitched over until there was only about two feet between them.

"You're looking . . . you're looking at someone. I was real famous once," he said in a Southern voice, and paused, holding his breath, the light blue eyes searching Tom's face for interest or approval.

Tom smiled back. "Were you?" He asked.

The man was relieved. "Yes. I was real famous one time." Now, satisfied with the impression apparently, he settled back, and for a minute Tom thought he would not go on.

Finally the man said: "You might have read about me in the papers. I was in the papers a lot."

"Maybe I did," said Tom, and there was another long pause.

"You wouldn't remember," the man said sadly.

"I might," Tom said. "What's your name?"

"Haynes," said the man. "They called me . . . see, they . . . aw, you wouldn't remember." He paused again for a minute then said, softly, "Lover Man Haynes."

"But I do remember," Tom said amazed out of his stupor. "I certainly do."

"You're kidding, aren't you?"

544

"No," Tom said. "I always wondered whether you ever learned to drive that car."

"Car?"

"One of . . . your wives bought you a second hand Chevvie coupe." Tom said. "For a hundred and forty dollars. According to the papers, you couldn't drive it, but you liked to sit in it and play the radio—I always wondered if you ever learned to drive it?"

"I can't drive no car," Haynes said, vaguely.

"But the Chevy coupe, what happened to it?"

"I guess she must have took it back," Haynes muttered. It was clear that he didn't recall it himself, and thought Tom had him confused with someone else.

"You married two women in California," Tom said. "And then a third wife turned up."

"Hey, that's right. That's me," Lover Man Haynes said, delighted. He sat back and the smile of pleasure turned to one of dreaminess. "There was always something about me they liked."

"I remember," Tom said. "I certainly remember."

"You wouldn't have," Haynes lowered his voice. "You wouldn't have a quarter?"

Tom hesitated a moment and then nodded. He had in his pocket, he was fairly certain, two quarters. He took one out and passed it along. "Can you get a bottle for that?" He asked, careful not to smile.

"Not for no bottle," Lover Man Haynes said. He snorted. "I ain't like them." His voice was loud enough to be heard by the other bums, but no face turned; whatever impulse towards defiance had impelled it now left Haynes, and he nodded his head in a tiny, almost frightened gesture, towards the others. Tom looked at Haynes again; it was true. He was not like the others. He was shaved, for one thing, and his pudgy hands were more than half clean. His clothes were filthy enough, but with that odd effect of foppishness. "Tell you a secret, mister."

Tom leaned closer to hear. Lover Man smelled a little, but it was not the sour, wine smell of the others.

"See, I know this girl," Haynes said. "She, she gits fifty cents for it, but to me—a quarter." He stood up in triumph, leering, grinning, nodding his head. He shook out his clothes. He stepped jauntily away.

Tom watched him leave and, after a time, got up to go himself.

It occurred to him, as it had during their conversation, that he must call Ellen right away, she would most wonderfully enjoy knowing of this, it would even be worth going to Brooklyn to see her react when he told her. But the intention went in and out of his mind in a baffling way in the ensuing days—he would either recall that there was something interesting he meant to do, without knowing what it was, or he would suddenly remember what it was without being able to think why it was interesting.

3.

Guy had intended taking Sheila to lunch himself, of course, and had set the date for a Saturday. On Thursday preceding, late in the afternoon, he drove in from a business visit to Westport; this visit had taken the pleasant form of going up to have lunch with a man who held some Cinturon Cie. securities, and helping this man launch his sailboat. It was a small boat, a Snipe, and its spring paint and varnish were just dried. Guy had helped load the boat onto a trailer; they had driven it to the water, launched and rigged it, and had their first sail of the year. Guy was feeling excellently vigorous from the afternoon in the sun as he swung the convertible into the garage where he kept it, on Second avenue. He jumped out, tossed the keys to an attendant, ordered the car washed and polished, and went out of the cool, greasy building. It was just five o'clock.

Beside the garage was an alley, and in its opening sat a man on an Italian motor scooter. Guy smiled at the vehicle; its rider seemed familiar, so Guy smiled at him, too. He supposed it was one of the boys from the garage; he walked on past.

The next moment a surly voice said, "Parker," very loudly. Guy did not connect it with himself, and continued to walk.

"Hey, Parker." Now the voice was in his ear, and a hand caught Guy's arm at the elbow. Almost before the touch, Guy had pivoted away. He found himself facing the young man from the motor scooter, a dour, heavy-nosed boy, somewhere in his early twenties.

"Goddamn you, Parker," the man said. "Where is she?"

Guy didn't want to be angry; he felt too well. He smiled and said in a relaxed way: "You've made a mistake, haven't you?"

546

"Don't give me any of your Hollywood crap, Parker," the man said.

Guy shook his head, still smiling. "My name's not Parker, friend," he began, levelly enough. Then, all at once, he recognized who he was talking to. "Oh," he said. "You're Reuben Shteuben . . . that is, Reuben Andros."

"Yeah," Andros said. "And you're Ossie Parker, you pimping son of a bitch. Where's Lordie?"

"Look, Andros," Guy said. "First, I'm not Ossie Parker. That was a gag. When I went to the party. . . ."

Reuben's big fist punched him softly in the chest; if it were meant for a blow, it wasn't much of one. Guy sidestepped lightly towards the alley, as Andros yelled: "Cut it out, Parker. Don't give me that crap, Parker." He tried another of his silly punches, missing completely. "That's the same stupid story all over again." He was panting already, but he found breath to mimic Lordie's voice: " 'No, he's not Ossie Parker. He's Guy Cinturon.' Ha, ha, ha. And I'm the Aga Khan. You listen, Parker. . . ." Andros kept stepping towards him, trying to grab or hit him; Guy, trying to stay no more than amused with this, kept sidestepping while the boy spouted. "I checked the Cinturon bit. I found guys who know you, Parker. They've seen you in town." He succeeded in pushing Guy. "They've seen Lordie with you. And I know your car. You shouldn't drive down our street so much, Parker. You're pretty goddamn easy to follow. . . ."

Guy's smile, he knew, must look the same, but the feelings behind it were changing to anger—anger, partly, at himself, because he *had* come down Lordie's street just now, anger chiefly, though, at the real Parker, who must actually be in town, who must actually have Lordie with him. He was still reluctant to fight Andros, who was a fellow sufferer, not an enemy, no matter what he thought; and who couldn't hit very well.

"You tell me where she is, or I'll beat it out of you," Andros was yelling. "I don't care how much older than me you are."

The last surprised Guy, coming from this heavy, undermuscled clown. They were within the alley now; they could very likely have a fight, here, uninterrupted. Didn't Andros realize that his sour face would be ripped up, his heavy body punished unendurably— no, probably not; for Reuben thought that Guy was Parker, and Parker was no athlete, from all accounts, a user of dope, rather,

547

a celebrated degenerate. Guy was growing angrier; he was, however, still reluctant to use his anger in a fight with slow Reuben. He saw the big, soft fist wallow towards him again, towards his face this time; he slapped it away.

"Don't be a fool, Andros," he said. "You don't want to fight me."

Again Andros tried to hit him, bringing the punch up from somewhere around his hip pocket; Guy bobbed his head out of the way, still smiling; almost sorrowfully he countered, three jabs, fast and sharp, into Andros' face to sting him, one catching the nose where it would hurt; then, as the boy's hands came up, a hard hook into the body to make him grunt. Guy stepped back, dropping his fists.

"I said, you don't want to fight me," he smiled. At the same time, some of his reluctance for the event was leaving him; he hadn't had a fist fight in years, a serious one, only punched bags now and then, and done some sparring; part of keeping in shape. He confessed to himself that it didn't feel bad at all, using the old weapons in something like earnest; but he could not relish the worthlessness of his opponent. Calming, he hoped that Andros' lesson might be learned and said, in a friendly way: "Hell, let's drop it, Reuben."

Andros, who had stood there panting, holding the hurt nose, now bellowed, raised his arms and charged.

Guy said, crisply, setting his feet: "I said, 'Drop it.'" Then, as Reuben came on, he stepped in and hooked, left and right to the head. He did not aim at the nose this time; he didn't really want to hurt Andros. But neither his timing nor his aim was quite precise, and he caught the nose from the side on the second shot, taking a push on the chest against which he hadn't bothered to guard. As he recovered, thinking out the next combination, Reuben caught him with knuckle points on the cheek, a wild swipe; it pushed Guy's anger over the line. He jabbed the face four times, hard, and then smashed at the body until Reuben backed off. This time Guy followed, no longer wanting to spare the kid, hitting hard, cutting the face methodically, working solid hooks into the body whenever his man straightened up. Andros kept flailing back, off-balance blows mostly, hitting Guy's arms now and then, or whacking a hand on the top of Guy's head.

After about a minute of this, Andros began to sag and stagger. Guy was aiming straight shots, now, at the chin; his arms were tiring and he wanted to put Andros down. His hands were hurting, too. He switched to uppercuts, to take the impacts on a different knuckle surface; Andros wouldn't go down. The slob must have an iron jaw.

Through all this the big, soft boy continued to stumble around and clobber back and suddenly he had hit Guy's own nose, quite painfully. Out of breath, Guy danced back, wanting an instant to recover. Andros poured, hulking and uncoordinated, after him. It took Guy several seconds to wrestle the youngster off, and get him far enough away to start hitting again. Guy began to wonder why he'd ever thought the day was cool; he wished he'd taken off his jacket before they started this thing. He began to regret the energy spent in launching the sailboat. He had taken a little sun on his face, and Reuben's soft, grazing punches were starting to make it sting uncomfortably. He continued, however, driving fists at the fat and wavering chin; there was blood on Andros' face and it made the chin slippery as well. Guy wondered, from the way his hands felt, if some of the blood could be his own; as he did, Andros grappled for him again and, as Guy moved to evade it, butted Guy hard in the chest. It brought Guy's hands down for the first time, and suddenly Andros had landed a funny, clumsy, two handed punch in Guy's face.

Guy jumped away. He had been working to finish Andros quickly and couldn't; now, if the boy was going to get lucky, Guy must start to think in terms of saving himself; he moved back. Andros followed and, changing tactics, kicked Guy hard in the left shin. Guy was so surprised and pained that he yelled. Instead of remembering to save himself, he sprang in and hit Andros as hard as he could, first in the nose, then on the ear; then, as the head twisted sidewise, Guy opened his hand and hit the exposed neck with all his waning strength, sidehanded. Andros went down to his knees and Guy jumped back, too tired to close further and assuming, in any case, that the fight was now over. Andros crawled heaving towards him and tackled him. Guy had no spring left in his legs to jump away with; he felt himself go down.

Andros was on top of him; Guy was almost too exhausted to shift him off. With great effort, however, he managed it, crawled away, and got painfully to his feet. Andros, also on his feet again, seemed tireless. He was charging Guy again, hitting again, more of the soft, stupid blows; but now they hurt. Guy's arms were too weary to hit back; he could only try to defend himself. He was

549

taking a beating and he couldn't think why. Andros, punching at his body now, caught him one over the kidney which almost crumpled Guy. All Guy could do was slap at the big boy's nose, which would stop him for an instant, but an instant only. He would howl and come in again. Guy's strength was gone; how could Andros have any left?

And suddenly, bitterly, as he tried to cover himself, tried to back out of the alley with Reuben lumbering after him, Guy knew what Andros was hitting him with: youth. Andros might be a slob, inexperienced, soft, but he was twenty-two or three; and Guy Cinturon, trained, in condition, even skilled, was thirty-six, couldn't make it back to the street. Thirty-six years old, and about to fall, under a storm of cream puffs. Gratefully, as he tried to push away at that bloody, rubbery nose for what had to be the last time, he heard an astonished voice from the opening of the alley say: "Hey, it's Mr. Cinturon. Hey."

Two attendants from the garage, fresh, twenty-odd themselves, came running down. One rushed between them, pushing Reuben away. The other caught Guy as he fell.

"You all right, Mr. Cinturon?" this second was asking. Guy took a step away from his support, and nodded, exhausted.

"Who?" Reuben was asking stupidly, as the other held his arms. "Who'd you say his name was?"

"Mr. Cinturon, that's who," one of the attendants said roughly.

"Yeah," said the other. Guy was dragging out of the alley, disinterested in waiting for the explanation.

"Hey," one of the attendants yelled. "What do we do with him? Call the cops?"

Guy stopped, turned and tried to shake his head. They were holding Reuben between them now, and the second attendant was saying, "Let's finish the punk. You want us to finish him?"

"No," Guy gasped; it was a mighty effort. "Let him go. Just let him go." Then he moved on out of the alley and, and a moment or two later, heard the sound of Andros' motor scooter starting away.

When Saturday came, Guy's face was nothing for a fourteen year old girl to have to look at across a lunch table, so Guy drafted the cousin from Princeton to keep his date with Sheila. The cousin was nineteen, nice-looking, a runner; he had a varsity letter in track.

4.

Eddie spent the spring doing the same things that his neighbors did, up and down the road—plowing and harrowing, planting and spreading fertilizer. There was only one regular activity he had that was especially different from those of other bachelor farmers of the neighborhood: every evening after supper, in the final half-hour of daylight, Eddie would go out behind the house and shoot trap. He would cock the trap and load it with clay pigeons until it had thrown twenty-five; the trap shells came in boxes of twenty-five, and he always shot through a box. They were twelve gauge shells, and a box cost two dollars and eighty cents. Adding that to the cost of the pigeons, it ran him about $22.50 a week, a sum he thought about from time to time but did not care about.

Almost always he hit them all. He was strict with himself about it; he did not count it a hit unless the clay disc actually disintegrated into black powder in the air. If he merely caught the thing with a pellet or two on the outside of his shot pattern, breaking but not powdering it, he called it a miss; a cripple.

Even counting this way, he generally scored twenty-five. When he failed to, he was hard on himself, deprived himself of some small evening pleasure—the sports page of the morning *Times,* most often, which he customarily saved to read in the bathtub. If he had missed two or three clay birds, he'd deprive himself of the bath as well.

He thought about nothing except what he was doing during this half hour of shooting; he did not pretend that the clay pigeons were really birds, or, indeed, endow them with any properties except those they actually had—clay targets, with black edges and yellow domes; they were, it said on the box, as fragile as eggs; they must not, it warned, be thrown where hogs fed; pitch necessary in their manufacture was toxic to hogs.

5.

Although the meeting with Lover Man Haynes had made a disproportionately small impression on Tom at the time it occurred, in view of its curious nature and connections, it was nevertheless a delayed turning point for him, the beginning of his convalescence from love. For his mind kept returning to the episode from time to time, of its own volition, less, perhaps, because of the intrinsic interest of the matter than because minds do seek proportion; Tom's would not be satisfied until its client's emotional response became adequate.

And from this foolish beginning, balance gradually returned until the day came when Tom was once more doing necessary things and caring how they turned out. One of these, the most necessary, was reinstating with some vigor his search for work; he began phoning, again, for appointments and suggestions, and, in the course of this, he one day called his friend Paul Wuss, the editor and writer at the Steven Even office.

"Yes," Paul said. "I'm glad you called Tom. I do know of something, and I'd even thought of you for it but I didn't know where you were or what you were doing."

"Been right here," Tom said.

"You haven't been answering the phone, then," Paul said. "Never mind. You know Latin and Greek, don't you?"

"Yes," Tom said. "I've taught both."

"All right. Listen then. This wouldn't be big dough . . ." he went on to explain. There was a foundation, with money to spend. They'd hired a man Paul knew, a producer, to work out ideas for a television series based on classic literature in translation. It would probably use a combination of narration and dramatization, along with historical background. The writing, however, would not be Tom's problem; the work for which someone was needed now was preliminary. It involved surveying the literature from a television standpoint, modernizing texts, writing summaries of them, retranslating, perhaps in some cases, and compiling background material—thus providing material from which writers could later work . . .

"I'd be a square peg in a square hole," Tom said. "Really, Paul, this couldn't fit me better."

Two days later, Tom spent a morning with the producer, and came away from it employed. The show was to be called "The Classic Anthology;" Tom's assignment was to deliver a body of writing for it, arranged as a book bearing the same title; he was endowed with a charge account with which to buy the books he would need; he had a check for a thousand dollars, in advance, and a contract which provided for a second thousand on delivery of the manuscript sometime during the summer.

It would not be early in the summer, Tom had warned the producer; before he started work, he told the man, there was a trip he'd been planning which he was now enabled to make, a trip to England.

6.

Guy's eyes were still puffed, his hands still sore, from the fight with Reuben, when the waiter knocked at his door one morning and brought in breakfast and Lordie Lord.

"This all right, Mr. Cinturon?" The waiter asked, hooking a thumb back towards Lordie.

Guy couldn't quite get his damaged mouth around the word *no,* and the man left.

"Poor Guy," said Lordie. Guy moved away from her. "Oh, poor Guy."

"What do you want?"

She gave him her abominable cute look, cocking the head sideways. "Cup of coffee?" she chirped.

"Help yourself."

"I heard Guy. Oh, I heard." She poured herself coffee; she poured a cup for him too, and handed it to him. He took it and set it down. "And what you did to Reuben . . . he can't breathe through his poor nose. He goes around with his mouth open."

"You're back with Reuben? Last I heard you were with Ossie Parker."

"Ossie left. He was only here a few days."

"And Reuben—understands and forgives?"

"Poor Guy," she said.

He turned away.

"Reuben walked out night before last, when I came back. He just—he just breathed through his mouth and walked out. I heard he's . . . well."

"He's what?"

"Gone back to a girl in Philadelphia that he used to be engaged to," Lordie said forlornly. "She has a theatre group he's going to work with."

"Breathing through his mouth?" Guy asked.

"Reuben walked out on me," Lordie said. "I thought you might walk in."

"In that messy little apartment?" Guy asked. "No thanks. Do you want to try staying here?"

"Oh no, I couldn't," said Lordie. "I'm still in love with Reuben."

"Then what would I be doing down in your place if I accepted?" Guy asked. "Just keeping you company?"

Amazingly enough, she nodded. "Please, Guy?" She said eagerly, ignoring the sarcasm of his tone. "I'm so lonely for someone to stay with me. Somebody nice. If I'm there alone, I go out of my mind. I really do."

"Stay here a day or two. Then we'll see."

"I told you, Guy. I still love Reuben."

"What about Ossie Parker?"

"Oh, that was such a mistake," Lordie wailed. "But I just can't say no to Ossie. I never could. I just do whatever he tells me, it's so awful."

"You'd better find another girl to stay with you," Guy said, turning away from her again.

"I couldn't stand another girl."

"I suppose I could *stand* being down there on the terms you suggest," Guy said. "But I'd dislike it. So I shan't."

"Guy, I'd . . . I'd do other things for you. Anything you like, except not really . . . you know."

Her circumlocutions were clear enough; Guy even felt a certain appeal in the decadence of the suggestion. But he said:

"It's impossible, Lordie."

"After a little while, I know I'd start to love you, and then . . . well."

She came over and put a hand on his chest, and repeated: "Well. Won't you, Guy?"

Where had he conceived such a feeling of being obliged to her? This was what Guy couldn't understand. It was as if he owed whatever she requested of him.

"Guy." She dropped the hand. "Guy if you won't, I'm afraid I'll just . . . oh, start going to parties and bringing men home, just so as not to be alone. And oh, I hate doing that, Guy, you get in such messes . . ."

554

"All right," Guy said. "Damn it, all right."

"Honestly," she said, later, following Guy and his suitcases into her apartment and closing the door. "Honestly, we'll both like it this way."

Decadent or no, she looked as girlish, as sweet, as silly as ever; sweeter, in a way, now that she had him there. She was, he finally realized, and supposed it must have been her adolescent manner and appearance that had concealed it from him for so long, a girl who wanted to take charge. And so, since it was basic to his approach to women to let them be whatever they liked, he determined to let Lordie lead on in the way she had suggested though, in the more obscure part of his mind, there was resistance to the arrangement; rationally, at least, he felt neither protest nor shame. Chiefly he felt relief that, after four tortuous months, he was here; now, unless he pressed too hard, in another week, another month, success would have to come, and the figure 205 in his record book would be changed to 206.

He was prepared to give the matter all the time it needed. He had left a message on his machine that he was out of town indefinitely; he had left Lordie's phone number with the hotel clerk, but to be given out only for a real emergency.

7.

In early May, with his plane reservation made, his passport issued, his bills paid and his affairs in order, Tom received a cablegram from England:

FINE DAUGHTER PREMATURE LALA FINE. HERALD.

So, because it meant that Lala and the child could start back earlier than expected, Tom didn't go to England after all.

8.

A jackpot is made up of bellfruit. There is a ringing sound and your machine is full of bellfruit. Eddie hit the jackpot. There was a ringing noise one evening and his machine was full of Bellfruit. William Makepeace Bellfruit Beniger.

The baby, said Makepeace, was born premature.

A girl. Margaret, after Lala's mother.

So there'd be no trip to England.

And this was where the jackpot came in: "Eddie, how about the cottage? Could we still have it? I'd like to let the apartment here go at the end of the month, and have the cottage ready to bring Lala and the baby there, straight from the plane."

"Whenever you want," Eddie said. "As long as you like." For years you beg Tom Beniger to take your cottage, live in it free, be near you. But he waits, all crafty-cruddy, until the spring you learn that you can never again stand the sight of his face, the sound of his voice, and then accepts.

"I'll come the first of June," Bellfruit said. "Lala and, hmmm, Margaret should be along a week or so later."

"Sure, Tom," said Eddie. "I'll get the place in shape."

"Don't do anything; please don't. I can get it ready. Look, Eddie, Ellen's going to ship out a crib and some blankets and stuff. I'll be out to unpack them; don't you. I know you've got spring work."

Sure. Eddie had spring work. But he figured he could put away the trap, and hang up the shotgun, and have time evenings to build another little room on the cottage, so this damn baby'd have a place to say goo in.

9.

The cottage, into which Tom moved at the end of May, was cramped and charming. It had a bedroom, full of double bed; it had a slightly larger living room with a big South window which provided a glimpse, if not a view exactly, of sea and shore. It had a tiny kitchen fitted like a ship's galley, a bathroom with a stall shower, and the nursery which Eddie had built on. Eddie had painted the place, too; Eddie had forgotten to remove a shipping tag from inside the oven of the steel stove in the kitchen. But when Tom tried to thank him, Eddie muttered something about the place having been full of unsanitary crud from a time when Ernest Goswith stayed in it.

Lala was due on June 14. Meanwhile Tom began his work, finding a joy in it he hadn't known since college. It was early for swimming, but Tom rented a bicycle on which he rode for exercise, even using it to go to the station once, leaving it in the baggage room, when he had a trip to make to New York. He did this in spite of Eddie's having urged him to make free use of Eddie's car; it was hard to accept, for some reason, such further favors from Eddie, something about the solicitous formality with which the offer was made, as if Tom were a stranger welcomed to a land where hospitality was an important ritual, practised for its own sake, not the summer guest of a friend he'd had for eighteen years. Yet Tom was too pleased with the turn his life had taken to be much upset; he ascribed Eddie's behavior to the fact that this was Eddie's busiest time of year, and tried to avoid occasions which might lead to further generosity.

Tom had planned to hire a car to use in meeting Lala and Margaret, but Eddie not only insisted that his own be used, he even insisted on doing the driving himself.

"You'll have to help with the kid, Tom," Eddie said. "What time's the plane?"

So they drove down to Idlewild one day in middle June, with Eddie making courteous conversation on the way, and Tom too excited at the idea of seeing Lala and his child to pay particular attention.

At the airport Ellen and Sheila met them, having come out from the city by airport bus. Everybody was quite nervous.

Nervous Tom heard nervous Eddie—why should Eddie be?—trying, clumsily, to compliment Sheila on her play. Eddie hadn't seen the girl since.

"Oh, I wish people'd be quiet about that," Sheila said.

Then nervous Ellen made Sheila apologize to Mr. Bissle, and that embarrassed poor Eddie further. Ellen had always been a little bit mean to Eddie, Tom thought, and wondered why. Male and female pattern, probably, whether or not they realized it themselves.

"You really should call Mr. Bissle Eddie, Sheila," Ellen was saying. "He's such an old family friend, even if he never comes to see us any more."

Sheila picked up her mother's tone of inscrutable feminine sarcasm, and said: "Should I do that, Mr. Bissle? Did you used to dandle me on your knee?"

"No," Eddie said gruffly. "No, I was in the war when you were little, Sheila."

Tom tried to signal Ellen to lay off; people were sometimes unaware that Eddie was sensitive, though Ellen ought not to have been, after all this time.

Then the plane was announced, twenty minutes early, and they all got excited, and, in a few minutes, there was Lala in a line of people waiting for an Immigration officer, and in her arms was an unmistakable bundle.

A uniformed girl, apparently the stewardess from the plane, took the bundle from Lala as they waved to her and she waved back, separated by glass panels and thirty yards. The stewardess brought Margaret out with her; Tom stepped forward and took the the baby. They all laughed quite a lot because Tom had difficulty finding his daughter's face among the wrappings.

And finally, there she was, a daughter, squinting up at him with weak blue eyes. Tom tried to think what he felt, but couldn't. He looked gratefully after Lala, trim and marvelous in a new suit, going now to the customs section.

Then Ellen took the baby. Then Sheila wanted to hold her. Then Ellen even made Eddie hold Margaret, and laughed a little harder than the joke was funny, really; Eddie blushed and passed the bundle back to Tom and, at last, Lala came out. Tom had never been so glad to see anybody in his life.

There was a good deal of embracing. Tom said he'd like to buy everybody a drink. Ellen took Margaret again, Tom hooked his wife's arm and they went to the bar. Everybody had a champagne cocktail, even Sheila; not Margaret, someone said, and they laughed.

Ellen and Sheila went off, after the drinks, to catch a limousine home. Tom, Lala and the baby got in the back of Eddie's car, and Eddie drove them slowly out of the parking lot.

As they rode out the Island, Eddie hugging the right and going more slowly than was safe, Tom kept looking at Margaret's squinty face and shaking his head. Once she began to make some sort of sound; it was barely audible over the noise of the cars. Lala said it was crying.

"She can't cry very loudly yet, poor lamb," Lala said, and Tom was alarmed.

"How could she wake us up at night, if . . . if she had to?" He asked it fiercely. This child's right to breathe the world's air without suffocating, to yell effectively for help if she needed it, seemed, suddenly transcendently important. Lala hugged him and whispered that he mustn't fret, the softer a child cries, the lighter a mother sleeps, everything would be all right.

558

CHAPTER FOUR

1.

ONE SATURDAY MORNING in late July, Tom was kneeling in the beach grass which grew around the cottage, vigorously washing diapers. He used a washboard and a galvanized tub, but without much soap, for he had emptied the soapbox this morning. He had been washing diapers daily, for about three weeks now, since letting the diaper service go. And he had let the diaper service go because a quiet look through the checkbook on the first of July had shown a balance of a little under a hundred dollars.

Lala came out of the house and said, "Tom. Thomas Beniger. Let me finish doing those; I feel too marvelous to keep on sitting still."

Tom stood up grinning. "Don't come any closer," he said, threatening her with a wet diaper.

"Tom. Stop. You should be out catching us a fish or something, now that your work is done." For Tom had mailed off the manuscript on Tuesday, and they were waiting for the check.

Tom pointed a finger at her. "Food, medication, light exercise and rest," he said, quoting doctor's instructions.

"Let me do the wringing out, then. That's light exercise."

"No," Tom said. "You're neglecting your child."

"Nonsense. My child's asleep with a silly smile on her face. She looks quite like her father." But Lala went back in, and Tom knelt and resumed his washing. He would do two dozen today, he decided, since it was the last of the soap. Then if the check didn't come in the mail, it wouldn't matter that he was unable to buy more soap for the weekend. He wondered, as he scrubbed, how much chance there'd be of success were he to take Lala's suggestion and try to catch them a fish. He supposed Eddie must have surf-casting gear, and they could certainly make use of some food from the sea. There were two difficulties: one was that Tom had never done any surf fishing, and had no faith in it—he had never seen a surf-fisherman with anything but an empty creel. The other difficulty was Eddie: Tom wasn't eager to ask Eddie for anything, not even the loan of a fishing rod. Eddie's attitude towards them seemed to grow no less distant, as time passed.

Nevertheless, without a fish it was going to be a slim weekend for food; there was a box of macaroni and some cheese he could cook for his and Lala's lunch, when he finished the laundry. He must count the jars of baby food, check the milk. He had, he thought, about thirty cents left; and a check for a thousand dollars due.

He finished wringing the diapers and sat back on his heels; his shoulder hurt, as it had, constantly, all spring and now all summer. It bothered him only as something to be concealed from Lala—he smiled down suddenly at the thin soapsuds floating in the tub. There were a number of things he had kept from Lala: their exact financial state. His ailing shoulder. And the fact that he'd been having, now and then, recurrences of his boyhood asthma attacks in what amounted, he supposed, to a general physical decline. The decline, however, was more then offset by the remarkable enthusiasm he'd developed for his whole existence, a steady and effective enthusiasm which had enabled him to finish his manuscript two weeks earlier than planned, and to have undertaken, simultaneously, the household work.

Tom put his hand into the water, and searched the bottom of the tub to see if there might be an overlooked diaper in the bottom; there was not. He could take care of his family, Tom thought; he could provide for and protect them. The conditions under which it was done might change, from age to age, but it was still and eternally a man's first function; it should be undertaken, Tom thought, as a matter of course, without discussion, without involving the family in its details. Thus he said nothing about the way

560

he felt; indeed it was only when waking in the mornings, when he was too sleepy to prevent it, that Tom allowed even himself to feel the real effects of his physical condition; they appeared as quite a terrible lassitude on awakening. He overcame the lassitude by a willful gathering of energy, a reviewing of tasks and objectives, which enabled him, after a minute or two, to hurtle out of bed, as full of cheerfully directed energy as a schoolboy on a Saturday.

He carried the washing he'd done over to the clothesline. As he hung the things, he thought: that there was another item of concealment, of which Lala must be somewhat aware. She must know that his physical response to her was more spontaneous, more genuine, than it had been before. His sexual constraint was permanently lost, though there was never anything for Lala like the fierce, even continual, excitement he had felt with Sarah, and there were keen and melancholy moments when he missed Sarah, very secretly and very much. Such moments came less frequently, of course, as the weeks passed. Lala, Tom thought, knew this, or something of it, probably had learned it when they slept together on her first night back; but if she did, she never indicated it.

"Tom." It was Lala, in the doorway, with a pan in her hand, speaking in tones of dismay. "Oh, Tom, look. It's what I deserve for disobedience."

"What's the matter?"

"I was going to cook the macaroni for lunch, behind your back, and now I've burned it."

Tom went to her, took the pan out of her hands and set it down. Then he hugged her. "It's all right," he said. He wondered whether it was time, now to stop treating her like an invalid; perhaps it was. But he said: "Macaroni's terrible stuff anyway. We'll have the hamburger."

"You were saving it for dinner."

"Doesn't matter. I'll get on the bike and ride after some groceries later on."

He didn't mention to this wife he was hugging, though he suddenly began to feel that such protectiveness on his part was probably silly and even demeaning to so robust and sensible a woman, that thirty-two cents was all he had on hand for weekend groceries.

A few minutes later, when she was not watching, he counted to be sure, and found that it was not thirty-two cents at all; he had spent the quarter he remembered, yesterday, on cigarettes,

561

and all the cents he had were seven. Tom shrugged cheerfully. He was quite confident, for some reason, that the mailman would bring a thousand dollar check for them when he came; and when the mailman came, he did.

The same mailman, continuing his Saturday round, had something for Eddie, too. It was a note, from Dorothy Conn, originally addressed to Guy and sent on by Guy to Eddie. It read:

"Baylor's Pond, Long Island, July 24th.
Dear Guy:
    Here I am in summer stock and loving it. We're doing *Amphytrion* this week, and I'm good for once; I really am. Would love to have you see me or, if you can't, would love to have you pass the invitation on to your friend Eddie. Doesn't he live out this way? I can't find his address anywhere. Some people named Ring are giving a cocktail party for the cast Saturday afternoon; I thought maybe Eddie would like to come (you, too, if you can) and then see the show afterwards. Would you send this on to him? Always, Dorothy."

That was the note which Guy'd sent on, adding a note of his own: "Hey, Eddie. Go to this thing." It sounded to Eddie like the girl was just trying to reach around an Eddie-shaped corner to get a hand on Guy again, and he started to throw the invitation away. Hell, he knew Dorothy Conn was nearby; saw her picture on the posters every day. Then he stopped himself. Old Bellfruit Beniger and his English muffin might want to go dip their snouts in the martini trough. What the hell; Eddie hadn't been around to check on them in a while; maybe he'd just stop by and turn this over to them. If he was lucky, he could hand the thing to Lala and not even see Bellfruit who'd probably be working. But suppose it was the other way around, and Eddie had to see Tom alone; maybe he wouldn't take the thing . . . undecided, Eddie walked to the door and scowled out at the dusty driveway. The phone rang.

Eddie turned back and answered it. He thought he knew what it was; he was expecting word on delivery of some tractor parts, and thought it would be the express office. It wasn't. It was, for Christ's sake, Goswith. Goswith.

Goswith was not entirely coherent. ". . . I've got some paintings
562

you've got to see, Eddie. Then you'll see, Eddie. Listen, these . . . when you see these, it'll explain everything. Eddie, I'm not crapping you . . . Eddie, I gotta come back to the cottage. It's too hot to work here, see. It's important, Eddie, I can work in the cottage, what do you say Eddie?"

"You're drunk," Eddie said. "Anyway, I don't want to talk to you and I don't want to see your cruddy paintings and there's someone in the cottage."

"I don't believe you, Eddie," Goswith said. "There can't be someone in the cottage, Eddie, that's the place I gotta work . . . wait, listen Eddie. I'm going to bring a painting. Just one, it's a saint, see? Saint Sebastian. Listen, I'm going to get on the train, Eddie, I'm going to bring it out, you've gotta look, just look . . ."

"You bring a canvas out here, I'll shoot holes in it, Goswith," Eddie said. "You show one hair of your ass and I'll shoot it off. I'm not kidding." And hung up. He did not suppose the painter would come; too much of a coward. But he might as well warn Tom and Lala, and so he might as well pass on the invitation, too.

On his way to do it, he was driving by the tractor shed at the west end of Dio's, the adjoining farm, and saw a sight he could just barely believe. Hanging outside the shed was a long clothesline, full of shirts and overalls. The shed was just past the place where Dio's property touched Eddie's, with no fence between, and there were somewhere around a dozen brownish kids playing a ballgame along the rows where Eddie's potatoes were coming up. He stopped the car, leapt out and yelled at them. They all went flying into the tractor shed, and Eddie drove on singing, of course.

He stopped off at the summer chalet of Mr. and Mrs. T. Puke Beniger and gave the lovely Mrs. Beniger, née Lala Herald, now charmingly attired in Bermuda shorts, print blouse and trusting soul, the invitation from Miss Dorothy Conn to attend a cocktail party given by a Mr. and Mrs. Ring, originally directed to Señor Guy Cinturon and forwarded to Edward M. Bissle, Jr., a local farmer. Mrs. Beniger said she did not anticipate their being able to attend the function, but thanks. Farmer Bissle did not, after all, advise the Benigers of the possibility of a visit from Maestro Ernest Goswith of Manhattan.

If Goswith showed, he'd come to Eddie's house first.

Thankful that Tom hadn't been there, Eddie started home; on the way, he saw the kids working over towards the potato field again. This time there were brownish mothers and sisters, too,

563

sitting out in front of the shed; the minute they saw Eddie's car, the kids dashed for the shed. Eddie stopped the car and got out, quite deliberately. The mothers and sisters all got up and went into the shed, too, shooing small children and dragging babies. By the time Eddie reached the yard, there was no one in it. He went up to the door of the tractor shed and looked in; an unbelievable number of large brown eyes looked back at him.

The shed was dirt-floored and unpartitioned, not much bigger than his living room. In it, with nothing to sleep on but worn blankets on the ground, were twenty or thirty of these brownish people.

"Hey," Eddie said, to them all. "Would you keep the kids off my potato field please?"

None of them answered.

"Anybody in there speak English?" Eddie asked. Then he noticed that some of the women seemed to be getting a rather wrinkled man off the floor and into his pants, so Eddie stepped back and waited. Pretty soon the wrinkled one came to the door and stepped outside. He was a little paler than the rest; he wore a creepy little mustache, blue jeans and an underwear shirt; he was barefoot and looked about fifty.

"*Si, Señor?*" he said.

"You speak English?"

"No, *Señor.*"

"All right. I'll go see Mr. Dio," Eddie said; as he turned and left he was aware that children were slipping out around the door to watch him. Some of the little boys didn't have any pants on.

Eddie found Hector Dio drinking iced tea on the porch of his house.

"Hiya, Eddie," Dio said. He was a short, fussy man, not much taller than Eddie, who'd inherited a good farm and ran it pretty well; he was an officer of the co-operative; he was a slob. His grandfather and Eddie's had been pretty good friends.

"Dio," Eddie said. "What the hell's the idea of turning my potato field into a gypsy camp?"

"My Puerto Ricans going onto your place?" Dio asked. "I told them not to."

"Sure. Only how could you? They don't speak English."

"I told them in Italian. They understand."

"I hope you know the Italian word for shotgun," Eddie said. "I'm not kidding, Dio."

564

"Naw, I know you're not, Eddie," Dio said. "They gotta stay off the plants. Hell, they know better. They're farmers, too, where they come from."

"How many you got in that shed anyway?" Eddie asked. "It's going to be a cesspool down there in about a week."

"Oh, they're gonna dig a privy and fix it up," Dio said. "They just got here yesterday. Three families."

"I thought we had an agreement, we were supposed to provide decent housing. And I also thought we weren't getting them till harvest."

"Well, Eddie you know," Dio's voice grew more and more conciliatory. "A couple of us figured we get ours in early. Listen, you could use a hand or two right now, couldn't you? I'll lend you a couple . . ."

"No, goddamn it," Eddie said. "I couldn't use a hand right now, but I sure as hell could use a couple of words with the Welfare Department if that pigpen doesn't get cleaned up fast."

"Come on, Eddie," Dio said. "That's more of a house than they had at home. Listen, they're satisfied. Listen, they're tickled with it."

"Sure, so am I tickled with it," Eddie said. "You hear me laughing, don't you? I start laughing when the Welfare department hauls your fat ass off to court, Dio. Maybe I ought to take you down there now to have a look at that shed." He put a foot on the first step. Hector got out of his chair, looking alarmed. "I'd like to hear you make them a little sanitation speech in Italian . . ." But Dio wasn't a man who was going to fight. Dio was going to say, please. Dio was going to say, sure, Eddie, glad to come, if you want. Dio was going to squirm and wiggle and fart and smile and crap all over the porch if Eddie didn't take his foot off that first step; Eddie sighed, and took his foot off.

"I'm not kidding about Welfare," he said. "Or about the shotgun, either." And started, disgruntled, out of the yard.

"Listen, Eddie," Dio was saying, after him. "Listen, there's more than I thought. See, they brought cousins. . . ."

"Ah, clean it up," Eddie said, and trudged off.

Guy couldn't decide. He was very much inclined to jump in the car, drive on out to Ringlet Harbor, check into a hotel, see Lala and Tom and the baby—he hadn't even seen the baby yet; see Eddie, sweep them all off to the cocktail party, take them to dinner and the play. Very much inclined. He could leave what clothes he had at Lordie's place and send a messenger to pick them up and never see the damn girl again. The trouble was, he wasn't sick of her yet, only appalled.

He was sitting in his own rooms, where he came daily to pick up mail and check phone messages, thinking, as always, of Lordie. He had, he realized with a shudder, never known a woman so well, for he had been living with her eight weeks now, the longest time he had ever spent with anyone. Their relationship was still technically chaste; at the same time, the circumventions she employed were the wanton and absolute antithesis of chastity, both in flesh and in spirit. He had learned, by now, that the worst thing he could do with her was to press; the only chance left was to outwait her, and that, if he could do it, was not a chance but a certainty. The waiting couldn't go on forever. Or was he throwing good time after bad? It was pride, rather than physical ardor, which was now involved. Suddenly he found himself considering rape. Suppose he should—she could hardly be so silly as to make a complaint; would she, under the circumstances, even technically have a case against him? He grinned. The idea, for now, had far more the aspect of a last recourse than of a firm intention, but he was glad he had thought of it; he wasn't altogether weaponless in the struggle after all. Encouraged, he gave up the notion of driving out to Long Island. He put on a clean shirt, and headed downtown, still grinning.

That Saturday noon in late July, Ellen found herself troubled with an awful feeling that something had happened to Tom and Lala. She could not phone them, for they had no telephone, and the phone at Eddie's, which she tried repeatedly, didn't answer. Harrison was away on his annual visit to the home office of his firm. Sheila was away, spending two weeks with the Cuzenus family at their summer place in New Jersey.

Ellen then tried to call everyone she knew in New York who also knew Tom and might have heard from him. She got nobody. In New York on summer Saturdays, phones don't answer. Ellen started to drink, and, in the middle of the afternoon, decided she would go to Ringlet Harbor to see Tom and Lala; she had forgotten by then that it was originally a premonition about their

566

being in trouble which had turned her mind to them. Now she merely recalled that they had asked her several times to come for a weekend. Ellen told herself that, well, then, she was accepting. She also knew that this was not true, that she was going to see Eddie. She knew that he had been in New York several times since Sheila's play without seeing her. She had thought that seeing her at the airport would bring him to her, but it hadn't. All right then; all right. Tom and Lala *had* asked her to come out, hadn't they?

At about three-thirty Saturday afternoon, Lala having gone for a walk on the beach, Tom was again counting his money. It still came out to one thousand dollars and seven cents, and only the cents were in cash. He had not stopped to think, in the joy of receiving a thousand dollar check, that it was of no use to them until Monday, when the banks would be open again. And meanwhile he could not cash a small personal check at the only store where he was known, the grocery, because he had given them, through an error in his check stub figuring, a bad check on Tuesday. He considered borrowing for the weekend from Eddie; he decided he would, if he had to, but not, considering Eddie's odd behavior, if he could think of something else. He thought: the seven cents will buy one jar of baby food. We have enough milk for tonight and for morning. If only there were something left for himself and Lala to eat tonight, they, too, could last through breakfast time tomorrow—neither of them ate much breakfast. Now: suppose he could get them through till then; could he call Guy, perhaps, or Ellen, ask either of them to come out on the morning train—or Guy could drive—to bring cash? It wasn't preposterous; Ellen kept saying she'd come, and Guy, if Tom could reach him, ought to want to. Guy hadn't seen the baby yet.

Tom checked the refrigerator. A jar of strained peaches. An open can of milk. Some left-over peas, and a jar of mayonnaise. Salad. Ummm. Seven cents. One more jar of baby food—suddenly he thought: I'm three cents short of the dime I'd need to attract the operator's attention from a pay phone, even though I mean to call collect. He frowned over this. Go ask to use Eddie's phone? He kept coming back to his reluctance to ask anything of Eddie.

He went next into the little room where Margaret was sleeping, not because he thought she might be awake or need him, only be-

567

cause he liked to look at her. She was still undersized; not unexpected, the pediatrician said, in a premature child. She'd grow out of it. She didn't move, the man said, quite as much or as vigorously yet as other babies her age, did very little rolling, clutching, looking. But Tom's interest in his child demanded no variety; it astonished him to look at her, even when she slept.

Love is learning, Tom thought, looking at Margaret. Eventually the capacity of two adults to contribute to one another's self-knowledge is exhausted, as it would have been for me and Sarah. With a child, it's different. The contribution a child makes to a parent's self-knowledge is inexhaustible. At least until the child is grown; what happens then?

"Why don't you go?" Lala whispered.

Tom jumped.

"I'm sorry. That was mean." There she was, back from her walk, smiling at him, and he backed out of the baby's room so that they could talk in normal voices.

"Go where?" Even as he asked, he knew what she meant: the cocktail party. And he thought: of course. I can ask to use the phone.

"That party for Dorothy Conn. It's close enough so you could ride your bike over, isn't it?"

"Three or four miles," Tom said, smiling. And dinner! He could take a paper bag, fill it with hors d'oeuvres. Maybe there'd be a cold roast or something. Meat! And cigarettes. By God, he could steal some cigarettes. He said, to conceal the excitement he felt about envisioning such a raid: "I hadn't really considered going. It's Eddie she wants, not me."

"Curious girl," Lala said. "Nevertheless, you could have a drink to celebrate the check coming. You deserve a drink. You've got to go as far as the village anyway."

"Do I?"

"Don't you? To get milk and baby food and something for us?"

"Oh. Oh yes," Tom said, putting his hand in his pocket, as if it would prevent her spying out the seven unaccompanied cents. "Yes, I do have to get some things."

When Ellen's train reached Ringlet Harbor, it was evening but not dark. Ellen got off and found a cab driver who knew where

Eddie's place was. She had had a drink or two in the café car, and had managed to reassure herself about her innocence of purpose: why had she come? To see Tom and Lala and Margaret. But, she assured herself, she must have directions from Eddie in order to find the cottage where Tom and Lala were.

She had never seen the house where Eddie lived; she was mischievously pleased with the idea of coming upon him there, unaware.

But when she saw, as the cab stopped in an unpaved drive, that it was a plain frame house, grey, without paint, her sense of mischief failed. She got out; she paid the driver quickly so that he would go and take escape with him. Pensive now, she stood alone in the hard, hot evening sun, staring up at Eddie's house. A moment passed. Then she saw him in the window, wearing a workshirt open down to the waist, staring back at her.

She stood in the dust and waited for him to leave the window and come to the door, but it seemed a long while before he moved, and during that while she became a little frightened because he didn't smile, or wave or even nod. Nor, now that he was out of sight, did he immediately reappear. She began to wonder, finally, whether of her own accord, she might step up, onto the porch, out of the sun, when the door did open; there was Eddie again. Now his shirt was buttoned.

"Hello, Ellen," he said. Still he didn't smile.

Uncertain and unasked, she walked up the grey porch steps. She felt a kind of bewilderment that this should really be a farm, and Eddie a farmer. "I . . . I was going to see Tom, but the cab driver didn't know where the cottage was," she said.

"Oh? Tom expecting you?"

"No. A surprise. Eddie, may I come in?"

He stood aside. "Sure. You want me to run you over to Tom's?"

"Could I have a drink?"

"Sure."

He stood aside, followed her in, seated her at the kitchen table where, she could tell, he must have been eating supper when he heard her cab drive up. He had removed the plate and tableware —she saw them on the drainboard, by the sink—but not his coffee cup. Now he brought her some whiskey in a jelly glass, with an ice cube floating in it. He sat down opposite, his face noncommittal, and picked up the coffee.

"Aren't you going to have a drink?" she asked.

"No. I don't drink much in the summertime."

"Why?"

"Doesn't mix with work," Eddie said. "And heat."

She drank off what he had fixed for her quickly, and it gave her courage. "Eddie, I didn't really come to see Tom. I was alone in the city and . . . well." She tried to smile at him, and knew that whatever it was on her face, it wasn't much of a smile; it might be a look, even, of pleading.

"You shouldn't have come," Eddie said. "Tom might be over."

"Does he drop in a lot?"

"No."

"Oh."

"You want another drink?"

"Not unless you'll have one with me."

He considered this a moment. Then, his face unchanged, he nodded and said: "All right."

In a bedroom, overlooking the garden where the people named Ring were giving the cocktail party for Dorothy Conn, Tom was using the telephone. He called person to person collect for Guy, first, and heard Guy's voice on the machine tell the operator that Mr. Cinturon was out of town; then he tried Ellen's phone and got no answer. He returned to the garden, where the guests were, and got a second drink. It was a very large party. Tom, who had meant to introduce himself and say something about Guy and Eddie's apologies to Miss Conn, hadn't actually seen her yet, and had more or less decided not to try; he did not know which of the people were the ones whose house he was in, and made no effort to find out.

He concentrated, instead, on the buffet which exceeded his hopes and frustrated them at the same time; the food was elaborate and plentiful, and no one was eating it. But behind the table were posted half a dozen uniformed caterer's men, willing to serve the food but limiting Tom's chance of accumulating a significant quantity. He had been past them once, for ham, turkey and cold roast beef, taken his plate to a secluded spot, scraped off the helpings of salad into a flower bed, and put the meats in his paper bag. But the caterer's men had not been generous with meat; Tom had eaten a couple of slices, and there were only three more in the bag which he now had in his outer jacket pocket.

He was waiting for some other guests to pick up plates and start down the line. None did. He sipped the drink. Finally he put the glass down beside an ornamental evergreen and made his second trip to the buffet. This time he picked up two plates, as if he were filling one for some other guest, walked past the first salad man, and stopped at the turkey.

"Yes, sir?" said the man, somewhat coldly.

Remembers me, Tom thought. To hell with him. "The lady'd like white meat," he said sternly. "She's allergic to dark," and shoved one of the plates across the table. He kept holding it out while the man reluctantly piled meat on it. Then Tom held the other out. "White and dark both on this," he said. At the beef, he repeated the same general tactics for rare and well-done, staring down the man who carved it. He could not avoid potato salad, and didn't think he'd better press his luck on ham. It was quite a good haul, this time, though some mayonnaise from the salmon he'd acquired involuntarily was getting on the meat. Again he went to his flower bed and dumped the salad; he ate the salmon himself, and stowed away the beef and turkey. Then he cached the plates, recovered his drink, and began to ponder the problem of milk.

He considered whether he might get a glass of milk by pleading ulcers; possible, but he didn't suppose he could balance a glass of milk for four miles by bicycle. He scouted around a bit in the area behind the kitchen, looking for a bottle of some sort he could take to a bathroom and rinse out. No luck.

He went back into the crowd of people, bright in their summer clothes, no longer even curious as to whether there might be anyone there he knew. He finished the drink, and decided against having another; taking one to Lala presented the same problem as milk. No loose cigarettes around either. He went inside to try phoning Ellen again. The bedroom to which he now returned was the one through which male guests were directed to go to use the bathroom.

Once more he placed the call to Brooklyn; once more there was no answer. It began to look again as if he might have to go, this evening, to Eddie's house, and he tried to decide whether, this being so, he would ask to borrow a few dollars or merely to use the telephone; and should he continue to pretend unawareness of

571

Eddie's coolness, or should he try to find out what the trouble was? Tom walked to the window.

The window overlooked the garden. Only one man was at the buffet being served. Tom pulled the paper bag out of the side pocket of his jacket and weighed it in his hand. There still wasn't much meat; if he could get some more beef, he could make hash. There were a couple of potatoes left at home. Beef, and some ham; with the turkey, that would take care of three meals. Tom decided to wait; when there was a crush around the table, he could take a couple more plates through the line. He thought he might do the waiting here, in the bedroom, and began looking for something to read. There was a stack of magazines on top of a small, antique desk. He crossed the room to look through them, and noticed a jar, pushed around behind the stack, which held paper clips, rubber bands and a collection of change—a tarnished fifty cent piece, several quarters, some nickels, dimes and pennies. Idly, by eye, he counted the accumulation; something over two dollars—well over, almost three. Without hesitation, he moved back to the window to make sure no one was on the way into the house. Then he walked quickly back to the desk, emptied the jar into his hand, picked out the money, poured the clips and rubber bands back into the jar, put the money in his pocket and left. It occurred to, but did not concern, him that the money might be missed.

He went out of the big house by its front door, into the parking area, found his bike, mounted it and rode away. Let them blame who they liked—guest, servant, trade rat; let them even have seen Tom. He didn't care. Suddenly, pedaling along, he smiled; it was a trade rat, he thought. For he had left the bag of beef and turkey slices on the desk when he picked the money up.

Ellen was trying to think what move to make. Eddie, it seemed to her was practicing a new kind of meanness, holding himself away from her, offering her a new kind of humiliation by leaving her with the initiative. It was a humiliation she was willing enough, eager in an awful way, to undertake; but she didn't quite know how.

Would it be enough just to lie down, somewhere? Or would she have to go and push against him? Crawl to him on her knees, for heaven's sake? She couldn't do any of those things; she really couldn't. She never had. Or perhaps, if she had another drink, she

572

could, and so she looked at Eddie without speaking, and held out her empty glass, and he filled it.

Guy told Lordie that he damn well did want to go to a movie when they finished dinner, their evenings at home were getting to be a real bore; he said it deliberately to provoke her, because he began to feel like having a real quarrel with her, just to see what would happen.

Lordie said all right, only not a movie, some kids she knew were in a show that was about to close at the Cherry Lane, could they go to that, tickets would be easy enough to get closing night.

Singing under his breath, Tom pedaled smartly into the gravel turn-around in front of the combination filling-station-grocery at the crossroads where their road turned off. In the store he bought two cans of milk, six jars of baby food, a can of beans, a loaf of bread, a can of corned beef for hash, one of soup, two onions and four eggs and a pack of cigarettes for Lala. It left eighty four cents. He went to the meat counter, inquired what sort of meat eighty four cents would buy, and decided on a small, rather pallid roast of pork which came to seventy-six. That left eight cents, and by returning his first choice of bread for a brand which cost two cents less, he was able to buy two candy bars. Dessert.

He got all these things except the meat, which was in a separate bag, into the bike basket, and rode away one-handed, carrying the meat bag in his left. About half-way between the store and home, just as he had begun to notice that his front tire was a little soft and was slowing him down, a dog came running out at him. He knew and disliked this dog; it was a medium-sized one, part collie, which habitually chased the bike, barking and snapping, coming out from the only yard along the road to the cottage. Generally Tom could speed up and outdistance the beast, but this time the soft front tire reduced his advantage. As the dog caught up, on the right, Tom turned a little in the saddle and kicked at it; the kick, by intention, missed. Tom did not really wish to hurt the animal; the kick made the dog pause, circle away. Tom gave his energy to pedaling. The dog now crossed behind the bike and came up from the left. Tom began to lose poise. He hitched around to meet the new angle of attack, slipping his left foot off the pedal; the dog

573

stopped. Tom re-engaged the pedal and pumped; as he did, the bottom dropped out of the swinging paper bag in his left hand and the roast of pork fell after it onto the road. Before Tom could stop the bike, the dog had dashed in, grabbed the meat and was going away, towards home.

Tom wheeled the bike and rode after it, yelling. The dog, unable to move quickly with the roast in its mouth, left the road for a field at the side. Tom stopped, got off, remembered everything, even the eggs; lifted the foods out of the basket, laid them quickly on the ground, laid the bike over them so that its rear wheel covered the food. Then he started off across the field, after his adversary, who had stopped, thirty yards away, and was crouching over the meat, eyeing Tom.

Tom stopped. The dog growled. Tom ran at him, and the dog jumped up, meat in its mouth, and started to run, trying to get back to the road. Tom dashed to his right, and headed the dog off, making it turn and run the other way. Tom ran in a parallel, between dog and road, but a little behind. The field they were in was open; across the road were hedges and gullies, into which the dog could disappear if Tom let it cross.

The dog ran heavily; it was not a young dog, a little fat in fact, and the meat encumbered it. Nevertheless, it had speed on Tom. Tom widened the angle between them to give himself more chance if the dog should make a dash towards the cover. He must keep it headed off; he must also keep it running, so that it couldn't stop and eat.

Now the dog wheeled and started running back, past him. Tom paused, saw a stone, picked it up and threw it. He had never been good at throwing things but this stone, which he aimed at the dog's jaws, hit the creature in the flank. The dog turned again, and started going even faster, heading now for its house. Tom ran after it, stopping only to arm himself with more stones on the way. He wanted the dog to go to his house; if the people who owned it were there, they would shout, whether at Tom or the dog didn't matter, and it might make the animal drop the meat. Wily, he dropped his stones.

Now they reached the gravel driveway; it led to the house, a small white wooden one, and past a small white garage. One garage door was open. There was no car there. Tom shouted. No reply. He shouted again. The house seemed empty, too. He looked back to the driveway and the dog was gone.

574

The garage. The dog must have gone in it or around it. Tom ran down one side and looked behind. No dog. He ran around to the front again; he slowed himself and moved up to the open door. The dog was inside, against the back wall, crouched under a wooden shelf. The meat was again between its front paws and the animal emitted a continuous low-pitched growling.

Tom felt joy; stupid opponent, to have given up its chief advantage. He stepped into the garage and closed the door behind him. The pitch of the growling rose, to a snarl, to a hard, bitter barking. Tom moved in, leaning forward, his arms swinging in front of him like a wrestler's. He saw now, but without fear, the yellowness of the bared teeth; it was the dog, Tom thought, which was afraid; he regretted having dropped his stones, and sneaked a look, without discontinuing the advance, for something to hit with. There was a piece of two by four, two feet long, in the corner to the right. But getting it might be an error; his hand twitched for the weapon, his arm ached for the smashing it could do; but a change of direction would risk loss of advantage.

While he was still moving forward, still trying to calculate, even beginning to be afraid of being bitten, Tom's eyes dropped for a moment to the meat. He saw that the dog had let it fall in a grease spot, and he lost his temper. He sprang forward, kicked at the meat; the dog lunged for the foot. Tom jerked his leg back, and, as the dog followed it, caught the beast by the loose skin of its back and neck, threw the animal hard against the left hand wall, and grabbed his meat.

There was a yowl. Tom backed away, clutching the meat. The dog was on its feet, limping. It held one paw up, and looked at Tom, whining and sidling toward him. Tom backed away, out of the garage, closing the dog inside. It took a moment for him to stop trembling; then, his shoulder aching from the wrench he'd given it, his head entirely clear of thought, he trotted back up the road to where he had left the bike, and reassembled the food for his family.

Eddie's plan was working. It wasn't a very complicated plan. It was to get Ellen as drunk as possible and put her on the ten o'clock train back to New York. The ten o'clock had a chair car, and its porter could be paid to take care of her.

He was now merely irritated with Ellen for coming out, but on first looking out the window, two hours ago, seeing her standing in the cruel sunlight, he had taken her at first for Goswith and been shaken with hate; then, recognizing Ellen, the hate had grown even crueler. Imagine Eddie, sitting at supper, thinking of Dorothy Conn; he feels perfectly alone and perfectly suited by loneliness; he is thinking about Dorothy not because he wants to see her, but because he likes to think about her; she has joined Eddie's collection of timeless memories, now, a beautiful woman with whom he was once permitted to fall in love, with whom, boorish and obtuse as he is, he never had a chance. He hears the cab drive up and stop, and when, finally, looking out, he recognizes Ellen, he is looking at what the obtuse and boorish deserve. As he stares, the sun, the heat shimmer, the falling dust trick him; the hair shines, the face softens, her girl's prettiness is hers again, but he knows it is a trick and he knows who stole the shine and the softness, and, like any thief who does not know how to evaluate or use his booty, who sees it tarnishing and in the way, he wants now to destroy it. He thinks of rushing out and strangling Ellen to prevent her coming into his house; then he reminds himself that Ellen is his child's mother, and gets himself in hand. . . .

And, in fact, they had spent the two hours talking, quite amiably, about college and the old days. Except that she twitched a little, from time to time, Ellen seemed content enough to sit across the kitchen table from him, chatting and getting stewed. After a time, the talk even began to please Eddie, and he wondered why he hadn't let himself enjoy talking this way with Ellen before. But he didn't forget to keep pouring liquor into her, as fast as she would drink it.

By eight, the conversation was losing aim; Ellen was on her feet, poking around the way she did, and Eddie figured she was past or getting past whatever feeling of amorousness might have been driving her earlier. He had deliberately withheld offering her food, nor had she asked for any. He got up and carried her drink over to her.

"Here," he said, putting an arm around her, and raising the glass to her mouth. "You didn't finish."

He wondered how many other guys had ever set out to get a woman drunk in order to keep her from going to bed with them.

"You look tired," Lala said.

Tom found a smile somewhere and brought it up for her. "I
576

feel fine," he said. They had finished supper; his corned beef hash had turned out quite well.

"Did you have an accident of some kind with the bike?"

"Accident?"

"I noticed the front wheel was wobbly, as you were coming down the road. And that piece of meat you've got hidden in the refrigerator . . ."

"What about it?"

"It looks as if you'd fallen onto it, and then had to pull little bits of gravel out or something."

"Is this what you've been working out so quietly?" Tom asked, smiling again. She nodded. "You're amazing," Tom said. "Yes, I did take a fall. Not an accident exactly, but that front tire's low. The bike and I went spilling over."

"Where?"

Tom tried to remember where some gravel was. "Right in front of the store," he said. "The cracker-barrel philosophers had a great country cackle at me for it." He chuckled; it was a chuckle, though, that wanted to be a sigh, wanted him to let go and tell Lala everything—about the dog, about the money, about the way he'd been feeling and how close he was, now, to having got them through. But he said: "I guess I'd had a few too many drinks at that party."

Lala was quiet for a moment; then she said, in the even voice that meant that she was emphasizing: "Tom, I'm going to do the dishes."

He looked for protest in himself and found none. He nodded.

"Tonight, and tomorrow and always."

"I'll take a shower then," he said. "I got kind of sweaty cooking."

"You've cooked your last meal, too, Old Father," Lala said.

He took the shower, staying under it until the hot water was gone. Then he sat in his bathrobe, with Lala light on his knees, and they looked out the window together, around the dune and towards the water until the late twilight was spent. "Monday, when I cash the check, I'll buy a bottle of whiskey," he said.

"Poor Tom," said Lala. "That will be nice."

All at once he began to feel that the energy on which he had been able to call all summer was leaving him, and he slid Lala off onto her feet and stood up. He did not want the energy to go, not yet, not ever. "I think I'll make a foray," he said.

"The bank, or a train robbery?" His fault, for using a word like foray.

"Just a cabbage. Eddie has some early ones. I rode past today but didn't have a knife to cut one with."

"Nothing a wife could say could halt his desperate career," Lala mocked fondly. "Once he had embarked upon it. Going now?"

"When it gets a little darker," Tom said.

Once during the drunken evening, Ellen told Eddie something of such importance that he forgave her completely for having come out to him, and would, had it been anyone but Ellen, have embraced her for the news.

"Sly Tom," she was saying. "Sly, sly Tom."

"Yeah. Sly."

"You know about it? The little Ghost's mother?"

"No. What?"

"You know Tom went off to jail with the mother of the little boy who was the ghost?"

"Oh yeah. I heard there was some dame they locked up. Who was she?"

"Ghost's mother," Ellen said. "Sly Tom. See, Harrison was with these men, at the police, they were going to give Tom and the . . . the lady . . . a ride. Home. So she said no. And Tom said no, and they walked off together."

"What are you trying to tell me?" Eddie asked.

"Not trying to tell you anything," Ellen said. And then: "Sheila came home from school one day, been talking to the little boy. Little Roy. And she said, she said: 'Roy's says his mother's always yakking about Uncle Tom'." Ellen laughed and choked. "Sheila said: 'I didn't know Uncle Tom knew her.' " Ellen laughed again, quite hard. "Then Guy called me up. 'Tom's having a big affair, won't tell me about it, got him in a mess. You know anything?' So I said, 'Little Ghost's mother, sure.' So . . ."

"Ellen," Eddie interrupted. "Are you sure?"

"Course I'm sure," Ellen said. "But here's the part; soon as I told Guy her name, Guy started laughing and said, 'That's why, that's why'. Eddie, listen . . ." Eddie, unable to sit down with this

578

news, had sprung up. "Listen, the reason Tom wouldn't tell Guy was because this Ghost's mother was one of Guy's . . ."

She went on but Eddie stopped listening. If it had been anyone, anyone at all, but Ellen, he'd have hugged her, embraced her, kissed her feet. If he'd been free he'd have run across two miles of field and hugged Tom. As it was, as it was, he poured Ellen another drink. And another.

At about nine-thirty, a hitch developed in Tom's plan for getting them a cabbage. In the laundry he had done that morning he'd neglected to wash himself any underwear.

"That should teach you," Lala said. "Washing is woman's work."

"Nonsense," Tom said. Because it offered him an excuse for not doing something for which he was feeling less and less enthusiasm, he was determined to solve the underwear problem. He picked up one of the clean diapers, and tossed off his bathrobe. He exhibited the diaper. "Practical for every member of the family," he said. "A needed simplification of our overspecialized lives." And he tucked the thing between his legs without doubling it, brought the corners up along each side, and knotted them over his hip bones.

"I don't know why anyone thought we needed whiskey in this house," Lala said, and laughed as Tom pulled pants on over his diaper. And then: "Look, silly. It's started raining."

"Mist," Tom said scornfully, for that was really all it was. "Drizzle. Fog. I thought you were supposed to be British?"

"So aggressive," Lala said, and gave him a push and then a hug.

It was still a warm evening, in spite of the faint wetness that came sifting out of the sky, and Tom decided to go without a shirt.

There was one drink left in the bottle; Ellen had had two thirds and Eddie the rest, but it didn't seem to him that he felt his; now she said that she didn't want any more, thanks anyway, she was rather tired.

"You can rest on the train," Eddie told her.

"Train?"

"Yeah. Your train goes in about twenty minutes."

"Oh." She nodded, and the nod pulled her after it into a

579

stumble; he caught her. There was a kind of a bad moment, right there, of wanting to carry her off, up the stairs, not in spite of her repulsive state but because of it. He resisted. He took the bottle in one hand, and Ellen's arm with the other, and led her out to the car. He pushed her into the seat, closed the door, went around and got in. He settled her so that she'd ride upright, and drove off. That was all there was to it, after all.

Except one more bad moment, as they drove along; for there came Big Brother Bellfruit—no, Tom, Tom—pedaling along towards them on his stupid bike with his shirt off, and Eddie pulled Ellen down onto the seat not absolutely certain that Tom wouldn't be able to see in. That would have been something; this Eddie-Ellen thing really did have to be over now, after this, after fifteen years of keeping it from everybody, keeping it especially from Tom. That would have been something, having Tom catch them now, on the last possible night. It would have been something.

Eddie felt a great stirring of emotion as, finally and successfully, they got by Tom, so long and pale in the freshening rain; hell, that's my friend, Eddie thought. That's my friend.

The chair car porter on the ten o'clock knew Eddie. He was very solicitous about the lady and promised to see that she got into a reliable cab when they arrived in New York. Eddie gave him a ten, checked Ellen's purse to be sure she had cabfare, and jumped off just as the train began to roll. And as it did, the drunkenness which he'd been holding off hit Eddie a staggering blow in the back of the head and he fell forward with a grunt, almost into the moving train.

He managed to pull himself away and stared at the lighted windows going past him, faster and faster. Then, as the last car cleared and his breath began to come normally again, he was attacked by a truly terrible lust for Ellen, now that she was gone; it was so violent that he actually ran a writhing step or two after the train, and fell to one knee when he realized that he couldn't catch it and get it back.

Sobriety and drunkenness were alternating now, hot and cold, and in the chill which suddenly followed fever he thought: My God, what would I have done to her if I'd kept her here? Chopped her up with an axe? In this sober instant, he felt a sense of extraordinary escape, for both of them.

The last lights, the last noise of the train were gone now, leaving him alone in the quiet station.

580

As he returned to his car, he was writhing again, and he reached into the car for the whiskey bottle, to have the last drink, only when he got it raised off the floor it wasn't the bottle, it was the shotgun he'd tossed in that morning, after his run in with Dio about the Puerto Ricans. He threw it back on the floor and then chill came for a moment as he remembered that the goddamn thing was loaded with number four magnums, a goose load, and could easily have gone off. Fever came again; he found the bottle and had the other drink, and threw the empty way, way up in the air, so high that he was in the car and moving out of the station yard before he heard the crash of its coming down.

The air was still lower in the low front tire of the bike as Tom pushed along. It made the thing hard to pump, and the rain was cooler on his bare chest than he'd expected. What height of spirit he had now was artificial and he would, in fact, have turned back except that there was a certain figure he was cutting for Lala.

One or two minutes in the rain had been enough to tell him that to go out stealing cabbages was really rather silly, and the sort of thing that might quite reasonably irritate Eddie. He had decided, instead, to go by Eddie's house and visit him, perhaps ask if he might cut a cabbage; and clear some air, get some air cleared.

But, as he rode towards Eddie's house, he saw the car start and pull away, and he thought: it's Saturday night, and maybe Eddie has one of his cleaning women out from Ringlet Harbor and is taking her home, and he would not much like having me a witness to this part of his life, so, when the car passed, Tom looked steadily down at his front wheel until he realized that this was silly, too, he couldn't see into the car, past the headlights, anyway.

Though Eddie had gone out, Tom must still take Lala a cabbage, and he could tell Eddie in the morning; he turned the bike and headed for the cabbage field, grim at first; then he had to smile. It was a pretty ludicrous thing to feel grim about—a man his size, riding along shirtless on a bicycle with a low front tire, wearing, under his trousers, a diaper, and on his way to steal a cabbage.

The car stalled at the stop sign, going out of town, and skidded slightly, starting up again. Eddie cursed it both times. Because it was a car made to go fast, he punished it by driving slowly. He tried to remember where the bottle was, so that he could stop and

581

have a drink. But the car might stall again. Stupid car. He would, he would go to his friend Tom's house, visit Tom at last, and Tom would give a friend a drink.

When Tom reached the field where he had seen the cabbages that afternoon, he turned off the main road, onto a smaller asphalt road that ran between the cabbage field and another like it. He stopped, twenty or thirty yards along, laid the bike down, got the paring knife he'd brought from home out of the basket, and went in among the young heads.

He went three steps into the field before he realized that it was muddy; instead of going further in, he knelt there in the drizzle. He found a head with his left hand, moved the hand down until he had located the stem, held it with the fingers, moved the knife until the blade was just under them, and began to slice into the tough fibre. He had it cut in a moment, going through the inner stem quite easily once the skin was cut, and settled back on his heels, holding the cabbage, trying to see its size, when car lights caught him, went by him, and there was a harrowing noise of brakes on the wet road.

Tom rose, panicked, too stupid to drop the cabbage, and jumped back a step, away from the car.

Then he heard Eddie's voice shout, "All right, goddamn it, come out of there," and Tom felt warm with relief that it was only Eddie who had caught him.

He laughed. He waved the hand that held the paring knife. He held the cabbage joyfully high with the other hand. He stepped forward. He thought, "There's nobody here but us chickens," and shouted it aloud to Eddie, in Spanish:

Aqui no hay nadie sin nosotros los pollos.

On the train, Ellen was sleeping, hunched into her seat; the solicitous chair-car porter turned off the reading light, and delicately pulled her skirt down to cover her knees.

Eddie knew it was Tom when he heard it, the old joke of Tom's and Guy's, speaking Spanish to stupid Eddie, and loved the old joke, and forgave Tom everything at last, and forgave himself, and knew it was one of Dio's Puerto Ricans, speaking Spanish, coming at him with a knife, and meant the man no harm, and could see that it was Guy with a football, Goswith waving Sheila's head,

582

and recognized his grandfather's voice. Knew he held a shotgun, too, but this time he was very careful to get the carbine's safety off before he let the big, blond German prisoner have it, bang spang and splatter. Right in the cruddy chest.

It was intermission time at the Cherry Lane Theatre. Guy stood beside Lordie; they were talking with a village married couple, whom she knew, about the play. Lordie was saying something asinine, and Guy prepared to contradict her as insultingly as possible.

And Tom could feel, in the particular instant, the shot rushing towards him, knew it was an error, knew it was no mistake, knew it for a gesture of forgiveness, knew what for, was grateful, knew he was being killed. Was happy that his aching shoulder would not trouble him any more. Knew he could not die, for he had not endorsed the check to Lala, he had never talked to Sheila about *Hamlet,* not told Ellen yet about his meeting Lover Man Haynes.

2.

Ellen was the first one Lala called in the morning. Ellen was a long time answering the phone, and screamed when she heard it. Americans, Lala thought, go to pieces just when they most need steady hands. Look at Eddie, the tough one, completely shattered, the glimpse Lala'd caught of him sitting in the State Police car which he'd apparently called himself, crying. You could understand that, of course. It was going to be hardest of all for poor Eddie. Awful for him; already Lala blamed herself more than she did Eddie. She understood perfectly how he felt about his fields. About the Puerto Ricans; it had even crossed her mind—this was why she blamed herself—to mention it, when Tom was proposing to go out last night. Crossed her mind, but she hadn't said a word; hadn't wanted to spoil Tom's lark. Poor old darling. Poor old diapered darling.

Now then. She mustn't get to weeping herself. She decided to call Guy next; he was Mexican. Perhaps he wouldn't scream.

Guy lay in bed at Lordie's Sunday morning, listening to the phone ring. He heard Lordie answering, and he lay still. Last night's attempt to provoke a quarrel hadn't worked; she wouldn't fight, only acted hurt. He was thinking out a new plan for angering her, one that might work since it would begin by teasing her about Reuben, when she came in and said the call was for him, some woman.

Guy pushed the blankets off.

"And what are you grinning about?" she asked crossly.

He didn't answer, merely widened the grin, and stood up, stretching, in his pajamas.

"Some woman," she repeated. Guy was not surprised. Though this number was one he had left with the hotel clerk to be given out only in emergencies, many people knew by now that he was staying at Lordie's. Too many. As he picked up the phone, he stole a look at Lordie's puckered little face, sulky without its pixie make-up, and thought that this morning, before either of them was dressed for the day, he might have all matters out with her.

"Hello," he said cheerfully. "This is Guy."

And found that he was speaking with Lala Beniger, hearing her apologize for disturbing him, hearing her say that Tom had been killed.

"May I ask your help, Guy? I know it's a horrid thing for you, but Harrison Walle seems to be out of town. Ellen's trying to reach him, but of course, she's very upset herself."

"Lala, of course I'll come," Guy said. "I'll be there as soon as possible."

"Yes, please," Lala said. "And . . . and Guy, bring some money? Tom left me with a rather large check but he hadn't, well, endorsed it, and I suppose it will take some time to have a new one drawn."

"Of course," Guy said. "Oh, God, how awful." Then he wondered, having heard what terms Tom and Eddie were on, whether Lala was availing herself of Eddie. "I'll drive right out," he said. "And Lala, don't be reluctant about calling on Eddie for help, too."

When she didn't answer, he repeated: "Get hold of Eddie, Lala. I know he'll want to do all he can."

584

That broke her control, poor Lala, though he didn't understand why it should at first, not until, recovering, she managed to make it clear that it was Eddie who, making a terrible error in the fog, had shot Tom down.

Guy was sobbing when he hung up, sitting on the daybed by Lordie Lord's telephone and crying.

"Guy, what is it?" Lordie asked.

He didn't want to tell her. He wanted her to go away. She wouldn't. He thought then that if he did tell her, she would have to go away, so he pushed the words out and she came over and knelt by him.

"Oh, Guy honey," she said. "Poor Guy."

"Not poor me," he shouted at her. "Poor Tom, poor Lala, poor little Eddie."

"Come on Guy," she sank down and opened her arms to him. "Baby, come to Lordie Lord."

What was this? As he began to understand her intention, Guy was too horrified even to exclaim. He opened his mouth to shout at her to get out, and something happened that hadn't happened to Guy in years; his English left him, he couldn't think except in little boy Spanish.

"*Andale*," he said. Go away. Get out. "*Andale pues.*"

"What honey?" Her face was over his. She was pushing him back against the wall. He shuddered. "Poor baby," she said. "He's trembling. Lie down, Lordie'll call the garage and tell the man to send your car. Lie down, honey. Trust Lordie."

"*No quiero,*" he said, twisting helplessly under the lightest of hands. I don't want to. "*No quiero . . .*"

4.

Sheila said that she must go to Long Island, her uncle had been killed.

Amy said, "Oh, Sheila, I understand."

Actually, her mother had told Sheila to stay right where she was; Guy was already out on Long Island, making funeral arrangements, helping Lala and the baby. Sheila's father was flying in, and would be met by her mother at the airport to go on out to Uncle Tom's funeral tomorrow; nothing had been said about Sheila's going, too.

Sheila did not intend to be left out. Her parents couldn't say anything much if they arrived and found that Sheila was already there. She would go straight to where Lala was staying, and could help mind the baby, and they would all be grateful to her, and maybe tell her what had really happened. What she knew so far was confusing; her mother said that Mr. Bissle had thought Uncle Tom was a thief, stealing something. What would Uncle Tom steal? It was a tragic thing for Mr. Bissle, anyway, even if Sheila had never liked him, she could see that. She reproached herself for not having liked him, and she thought perhaps she could help everyone by being nice to Mr. Bissle, along with watching the baby, etc.

Mr. Cuzenus said that he would be glad to drive her to the train, and gave her a ten dollar bill, though she didn't really need any more money than she had. Amy and she cried together in the back seat, going to the station, which was soothing. And then Sheila was very lucky, when she got to Pennsylvania Station, in New York, and went down to the Long Island part; she had only fifteen minutes wait, just time enough to eat two yummy hamburgers, before the next train left for Ringlet Harbor.

The next thing that turned out well was that the cab driver Sheila found to take her to the cottage knew about it, and was very sorry for Sheila, being the niece of the man who was killed and everything, and wouldn't even let her pay a fare. And it was a good thing she'd come. Lala and Guy were in the cottage when she arrived, and they'd been trying to find a nurse for the baby, but there was no phone at the cottage and they had to keep going out some place to make their calls, and they had a million other things to do. So they hugged her. Lala said Sheila was an absolute angel. Guy said it was marvelous of her to come. They both said she could start sitting with little Margaret right away. Uncle Tom was at the undertaker's, and would be buried tomorrow, and Sheila could sit then, too.

Mr. Bissle was in jail, they told her, and that was a surprise; but he would probably be released soon, and that was rather disturbing. And still no one told her exactly what had happened. They left, and Sheila settled down to her job—which was important but not very interesting—and her thoughts.

586

5.

The halo of crud which had circled Eddie Bissle's skull at birth, and formed the brim through whose radiance he had seen the world, had sagged, and slipped, and settled. There was crud in his eyes, now, and up his nose and in his mouth, and it wound down from there, a tight binding of crud, pinning arms and chest, round and round, stomach, pelvis, thighs, knee, ankles. He was mummified in crud.

He had been released, on his own recognizance, and was sitting in his car, under the steering wheel, with his lawyer sitting in the seat beside him. The lawyer was saying, very sympathetically, that no jury in the world would feel anything but sorrow for him, there was quite a lot of feeling already about the Puerto Ricans, they were known, unfortunate folk, to have criminal tendencies, there was no question but what poor Beniger had had a knife in his hand, yes. And the world was full of people willing to testify that Beniger had been Mr. Bissle's closest friend, even Beniger's wife on whom the lawyer had paid a call, wasn't she splendid? a splendid woman, wanted to give such testimony. . . .

Eddie's own recollection, as he waited for the lawyer to stop talking and get out of the car, was unconfused. There is no confusion in a blank.

He remembered a voice shouting in Spanish, and he remembered, next, calling the cops and then going back to the cabbage field and sitting there with Tom's body, blubbering, till the troopers came. He could not remember exactly what had made him stop the car, whether he had seen anything in the lights or just had a feeling that he ought to stop. He didn't deny having had some drinks, but since he knew he had kept himself sober in order to get Ellen onto the train, he said, as it seemed to him honestly, that he hadn't been drunk. He said nothing, of course, about Ellen's having been there. No reason to hurt Ellen. No connection. It was only Ellen he was concerned with protecting, for nothing could hurt Eddie any more, he was well and truly mummified.

He didn't have a feeling left in his body, nor an open orifice; an answer to a necessary question would work its way out of that mouth somehow, but nothing more, only answers in the way of speech.

He knew, why deny it? that there was a big clot of grief for what he'd done, somewhere inside him, but the clot was never going to move. None of the things that were clotted up inside Eddie were ever going to move again. Eddie could, as the lawyer finally said goodbye and left the car, see the rest of his life very clearly. He would have nothing more, after the funeral, the hearing, the jail term if he served one—he didn't care—nothing more to do with anyone or anything. He would live alone in the farmhouse, work alone, have the telephone ripped out, chop down the mailbox and burn it; and burn up, while he was at it, the contents of his bureau drawers: the shirts, ties, city underwear and city socks, and especially of the top drawer, the medal, photographs, mementoes. All the clothes Eddie was going to need could hang in the closet; memories he would not need. He started the car, put it in gear, and switched the lights on. It was just barely dark enough to need lights.

It would not matter whether anyone spoke to Eddie in the life he was going to live, because there was no voice left in the world that was going to get through to Eddie. Beginning now, no voices could. Not even Guy's. Certainly not Ellen's. So for now, he thought, he must go and say something to Lala whose voice, though it might yet hurt to look at her, could not reach him either. He drove to the cottage.

Knocked, when he got there, and didn't listen to the voice that said, "Come in," for it was words he registered, not sounds. Walked in, well and truly wrapped.

But it wasn't Lala.

It wasn't Lala. It was Sheila, looking up at him, in the twilit room, with an expression which changed slowly from inquiry to fright. "No," Eddie said. "Oh no."

He felt his hand moving, in some kind of feeble little gesture; it took a long time for him to say: "Sheila," and at the same time she said:

"Oh God," and put a hand to her heart.

He shook his head; she shouldn't swear, a young girl.

He took a slow step toward her. Just as slowly, she got up. He stopped, but she kept moving, until she had put herself between him and the door to the little extra room he'd built.

"I'm . . . I'm guarding the baby," she said, and the soft young

588

voice cut through Eddie's wrappings with the hiss and purr of newly sharpened scissors, made for the job.

"What?"

"They'll be back in a minute," she said, warningly. "Guy's coming back."

"Sheila." He shook his head. "Sheila, are you scared of me?"

"No. Of course I'm not."

"I guess I startled you?"

"Yes. That's all."

"I'll go if no one's here."

"They're in town," Sheila said. "There's no one here." Then, "but they're coming. They'll be back soon."

"Don't be frightened," Eddie said. "I'll go." He backed away a step, and then said: "Sheila, forgive me, honey. I loved your Uncle Tom. We all did." Then he turned and went towards the door; her whisper caught him on the threshold.

"No. You didn't love him," it said. "You killed him."

Eddie stopped. He clenched his fists.

Now it wasn't a whisper but a quavering voice that said, defying its own fear: "How could you have killed him if you loved him?"

Eddie turned around, slowly; she moved back, away from him.

"Didn't they tell you?" Eddie asked. "Sheila, it was a mistake. An awful mistake."

"Oh sure," Sheila said, getting a straight chair between them, behind which she seemed to grow bolder. "Sure, they told me. They all believe it, don't they?"

He had seen her this way before, overexcited. "Sheila, calm down, honey. Please calm down."

"You hated him," she said. "Yes, you did."

"No honey," he said. "Don't say things like that."

"Don't you call me honey, either," she said. "Because . . . because you hate my mother, too. You hate my whole family, and I hate you."

"Don't," Eddie said. "Don't."

"What makes mother so scared of you, then? Did you do something to her? Why'd you want to kill him if you didn't hate him?"

"Sheila, I didn't want to. Sheila!"

"You did. You wanted to kill him. Why? Why? Were you drunk?"

Eddie could only shake his head.

"People don't make mistakes like that unless they're drunk, so it wasn't a mistake."

"I was," Eddie shouted. "I was drunk."

"You weren't. You weren't, you said it yourself. You're a liar."

"Please," Eddie begged. "Sheila. Sweetheart. . . ."

"Then you explain it. Go ahead, explain it." Her voice lowered, without becoming any softer. She hissed at him now. "You'd better explain it. I never have known what you were doing with my family. They hate you and you hate them." Eddie was shaking his head; it wasn't true, she knew it wasn't true. He kept telling himself that she was acting, only acting, she would stop in a minute, she must. "You hated my uncle. You hate my mother. You hate my father . . ."

"Your father." It stunned him, coming as it did.

"I can tell. The way you talk to him."

He took a step towards her. She fled to behind the table.

"Yes, yes, yes," she shouted. "And he hates you."

"But Sheila. . . ."

"Yes he does. He does." Her voice, starting in that horrible hiss, rose to a scream of rapid words. ". . . you murdered my uncle. You stay away. Stay away from the baby. You do awful things to my mother, don't you? Don't you? Stay away from me, I hate you, I always hated you."

"Sheila, Sheila . . ."

"You don't believe my father hates you, well he does, worst of anybody, except me. I hate you more."

"No," Eddie shouted, starting towards her again.

She screamed. "Help, someone, help help help," and again the scream came from her, a long, high, sustained note that was still sounding as he stumbled backwards, away from it, and out the door.

Legs, stiff and jointless, moved Eddie from cottage to car. Left hand opened car door, right hand turned ignition, hands and feet worked wheel and pedals, steered him home; eyes showed him kitchen light on, legs took him into house, right hand turned on stove, lighting flame under big blue enamel farm style coffee pot.

But then he decided not to have a cup of coffee.

The cops had his new shotgun, the twelve-gauge automatic, stupid cops. As if anybody would care about an automatic when he still had the English double barrel twenty gauge that had folded

590

more quail than there were cops on Long Island, powdered more clay pigeons than cops could count.

Eddie got the twenty off the rack in the closet, and warmed the cold barrel with his hands; he was briefly shaken with remembered anger at the gunsmith who had done its latest blueing job. Could you call an ape like that a gunsmith? Were there any gunsmiths left in the decline of the world?

He started to load it with number fives, and then shook his head quite seriously, and put in trap loads instead. The bird he was after was strictly clay, yellow-domed, black-edged, toxic to hogs—a true flyer, fragile as an egg.

He remembered that he had decided against coffee, and turned out the flame under the pot so as not to waste gas. He wondered if he would be criticized for not showing up at the funeral. He wondered if Sheila had stopped screaming yet. Then he sat down at the kitchen table, and promised the world that she would never scream again.

He snapped the gun closed, pushed the safety forward and set the butt on the floor between his feet. He slid his mouth over the muzzle of the gun, closed his teeth on the barrel, just below the sight, tasting oil with his tongue. He was careful in locating the forward trigger, improved cylinder for close range, around three pounds of pull. He wanted to know exactly when he did it, just when it happened, and he pushed and pushed against the trigger with the nail of his index finger but three pounds, an easy pull, was a hard push; then the trigger started to move; and the last thing Eddie knew was the sorest throat a man ever had.

The head exploded, splattering walls and windows, fragments of hair and scalp hitting and even adhering to the ceiling. The short, muscular arms flew away from the gun, and then relaxed, dropped slowly back to the sides again, all tension gone.

6.

Lala did not want to ride in the lugubrious limousine provided for immediate family by the undertakers, so she borrowed Guy's convertible; she wanted to drive to the funeral alone. Guy went in the limousine with Ellen and Harrison; Sheila was sweetly staying with the baby.

591

At first Lala's driving was jerky, for it had been months since she was last behind a wheel; when she had the car going more smoothly, she looked at her watch, calculated that she had twenty minutes before the ceremony, and turned off the road onto a narrower strip of asphalt whose thin shoulders merged with unfenced cabbage fields on both sides. About thirty yards up, she stopped the car, opposite the point where the heavy pellets had shattered Tom's ribby chest, night before last.

She thought if she were going to do any crying she'd get it done here, not in public at the cemetery.

She got out and found herself thinking, absurdly, that if only she'd made Tom wear a shirt, instead of letting him go out into the rain with his bare chest unprotected . . . and banished the thought for the furious nonsense it was. The next image in her mind, as she stood at the edge of the field, was of the crippled bicycle, as she had seen it, arriving at this place a few minutes after the body had been removed, and as Eddie was being driven off.

The bike had been lying on its side in the drizzle, and just as Lala came up a police photographer shot off a flashbulb, taking its picture. The flash burned into Lala's mind precisely what would appear on the photograph itself—black glare from the road, the forlorn mechanism lying with its limp tire, a State Trooper's hand pointing the direction in which the cabbage had rolled.

Now, as Lala stood by the car, there were no signs of violence left along the asphalt. She walked among the cabbages, not quite through growing, their leaves a pretty, light blue-green as they filled towards the harvest.

She didn't cry, after all. Instead she thought of her two brothers, Bert and Chrissie, dead in the war. Then her mind went back to Tom, and she thought what might have been one of his thoughts: that the world had not changed enough yet to make her very different from Homer's women. Homer's women, too, lost men, their brothers, sons and husbands, and watched the cabbage grow.

7.

Walking away from the grave, Guy found himself beside Ned Kildeer, whom he had never met before and who seemed to Guy an odd friend for Tom to have had.

It was one of those moments when it is necessary to discuss almost anything but what is on the general mind, and so Guy asked:

"You saw the kid's *Hamlet?* I understand it was quite good."

"Oh, no," Kildeer said, and then, hesitantly: "It wasn't . . . good. Or bad . . . it was extraordinary. Beautiful, brilliant, stupid, boring . . . full of apparitions. But there wasn't any bad in it, or any good. . . ."

"No, extraordinary," said Guy heartily, recalling the word from the opening of Kildeer's statement and using it to stop the man from starting round again.

Then Guy excused himself to go over to Lala. He thought he had better get his car back from her. Eddie had not shown up for the funeral, understandably enough. In fact, no one had seen Eddie at all since some time yesterday, and Guy thought he would drop in at the farmhouse and see what he could do about cheering the poor little monkey up.

CHAPTER FIVE

1.

Past, present and future are items of indifference in this un-remembering world. Does it matter if we use, just now, past tense in speaking of the future? It is a convention devised by prophets in their business, and one perhaps that we may borrow from them for our own task of tracing out the generations:

Sheila Walle Winengrad's children—she married Winengrad, her sociology instructor, while in college—show no promise of producing *Hamlet,* though one of them is something of a prodigy on the cello. He stands to play the instrument, for he is not yet tall enough to bow it from a sitting position. Most of the others who were in the cast of the Brooklyn production—Ben Chaffin, for example, he who played the king—are, like Sheila, married and raising families. Ben's cousin, Fats Gunderson, who played Laertes, who never got to wrestle with Sheila in the Act V grave, has a grave of his own now, down in Georgia, for he joined the para-troops and was killed in one of those training accidents.

It was Amy Cuzenus, not Sheila, who went on to dramatic school; Peter Held did, too, of course, but that was more expected. Amy, to the disappointment of several people, did not apply her-self much—she and Sheila finally quarrelled over this and Amy left her training and went on to become, in Sheila's words, "kind of a

594

mess." Amy married a first husband with money, and a second with charm, and a third, people say, with nothing at all. She is divorced again, now, and she drinks a little which is not good for her figure, and which has made her face look heavy and old in the morning. But it is when she is drinking that there are traces, in her voice and eye, of the imperious dignity which once commanded the Danish court.

So it is Peter Held who is a professional actor now, though not on the stage. Those who appeared with him take some pleasure in pointing it out, when one of his movies is shown in the various towns and cities where they live. Not that Peter is a star; he was tried, once or twice, in leads, but the movies were inconspicuous ones, and his particular magnetism, strong enough face to face, was too diluted by reduction to two dimensions. Still, Peter's craftsmanship and presence are excellent, and he works steadily in offbeat, secondary roles—effete gunmen, neurotic brothers, things like that. He has half-abandoned, now, the goal of stardom which once seemed virtually in hand, and will settle smoothly into character work in which he should age well. None of the others, except for Roy Nevins, to whom we shall come presently, scorns Peter's achievement, though not many have seen him personally. Amy met him at a party once, in Las Vegas, and they laughed together for a few minutes. Sheila is another who has seen him personally; oddly enough, she went to bed with him. It's been six years.

She had been married to Winengrad a little over a year and was restless. Sexually impulsive up to the time of her marriage—a factor which had something to do with bringing the marriage about—she found the encounter with Peter, who was making personal appearances in New England at the time, mechanical and unexciting. It was the end of sexual impulsiveness for Sheila. Since then her fidelity to Winengrad, though subject to the mild tests of faculty life from time to time, has been total and unstrained—and has exceeded, be it said, the Associate Professor's fidelity to Sheila. She doesn't mind very much; she takes enormous pleasure in her children, and especially in the little boy with the cello. Her mother and father, whom she thinks of as getting old now, and who were visited last spring in Brooklyn Heights, have offered to pay for conservatory training for the child when he is ready, should he merit it. Tom and Ellen's mother, old Mrs. Coombs, lives on, in her nineties now, at the rest home in Arizona. Sheila saw her there; Mrs. Coombs does not acknowledge that Tom is dead.

When Sheila thinks, as she rarely does, of the silly episode with Peter Held, it is not as something belonging to the period of adulthood and marriage, but rather as a hastily conceived and innaccurately directed attempt to maintain or reinstate something that belonged to the time of her youth.

Still, she has not completely given up the hope that love will come to her sometime.

Ellen getting old? Age began to show in her almost from the time of the funeral on Long Island. She and Harrison are a good deal closer now than they were before that sad event; they quarrel more, which is a sign of closeness, and are, at last, quite dependent on one another emotionally. Ellen took a cure for alcoholism, quite successfully, in the fall which followed Tom's and Eddie's deaths, and does not drink at all; Harrison is home early from the office every night of the week. He has recently been promoted from Chief of Section to a general supervisory position which promises vice-presidential rank in his company before long. Harrison was always able.

Speaking of abilities, Ernest Goswith's religious paintings, when inspected after his death, caused some excitement. It was clear that he had been reaching for something extraordinary, when the heart attack intervened.

There was, perhaps, with the publicity that came with the discovery of these late paintings, financial opportunity for those who controlled his early and opposite works. But Guy, the chief among them, had put such matters out of his life upon marrying.

He married at the age of forty-three, and thereby made his final appearance in the newspapers, a dignified one for once. It is true that U.S. columnists tried to make something of the fact that he took to wife a girl of eighteen, a Brazilian girl just graduated from convent school in France, but to Latin American journalists the match seemed entirely conventional. Guy and his wife live in Mexico City. There are four children, with a fifth expected in the spring.

Another marriage: Lala Herald (Beniger) to Colin Hastings, an Australian importer whom she met in New York through Guy, about a year after her first husband's death. Thus Margaret Beniger is an Australian schoolgirl now, a pretty girl and a fine swimmer, with two half-brothers, six and seven.

But to return to the Brooklyn cast: Roy Nevins. He is just entering college, and he is a poet. It may have been misleading to say that Roy scorned Peter Held's achievement, for Roy's scorn is general, according no man the honor of being singled out as target. Roy has published a poem or two, but he is so young a poet that only other poets, equally young or very old, will speak yet of Roy's poems in terms of judgment. Even among these there is no present consensus as to his worth.

There is only one, from Sheila's *Hamlet,* who is still close to the living stage, and here is a surprise: it is Theodore. Who's Theodore? Theodore Cuzenus, Amy's younger brother, the one who did Polonius. He is not an actor. In fact, he took a degree in electrical engineering, and then a job, a very good one, in the same field. But the candles, the costumes, the intensity, the transfixed audience and transfigured players—these were too much magic for the recollection of the stolid Theodore to hold in comfort. Acknowledging a lack of vividness in himself, he had been too close to vividness to give it up. Theodore's career was a circling back; he was pulled from his excellent job, from his industrial laboratory, from his engagement to a girl the company would have liked, from his down-payment on a house the girl would have liked—pulled from all these quiet, substantial circumstances of half life to the theatre where, if you can ignore the man in the box-office, circumstances are flimsy and noisy and life is doubled. Well. Theodore's tremendous command of the intricate possibilities of circuits and lights is of use to the theatre, box-office man and all. There is a point at which sheer competence is delivered in so great a measure, supplied with so much love, that the difference between competence and creativity disappears, and it is this kind of competence which Theodore brings to the shows he lights. Ned Kildeer, of whom it is said: "He's a sweet, dignified old girl, and an artist to his finger-tips," always asks that Theodore light his shows, and Ned directs a new play every season.

Ned had a good deal to do, back four or five years, with the discovery and brief career of Rosalie Burton, who had been Rosemary Bernstein. There was, after all, one of those children who grew up to act professionally on the stage for a time. But Rosemary's feeling for it went beyond Theodore's: she did not ask of

597

the theatre only a more vivid kind of life, she asked of it an alternative to life . . . critics who saw her in her first role, in a toga, in a modern drama of Greek derivation, were astonished by her physical beauty and said so. But there were infrequent parts thereafter for an ingenue, no matter how beautiful, whose single and overwhelming projection was the quality of tragedy. And when, finally, a part was written especially for Rosemary by the smitten young playwright who also married her, Rosemary could not do it. Her voice was the trouble, trained and exercised into audibility and, as ever, a haunting thing to hear, it simply would not last three acts. It was an organic frailty that could not be overcome. And so the theatre was no alternative to life—indeed, it contained precisely the expectation and orderly realization of severe disappointment of which Rosemary had always found life to consist.

It was this expectation and realization brought to a pitch so high that Rosemary could not tolerate it. She kept the inability within her, where she had always kept the intolerable, kept it through childbirth even, screaming no louder in the delivery room than any other patient. And then, in the depression which attacks many women after childbirth, Rosemary gave up. There is, after all, an alternative to life and Rosemary accepted it. Her suicide was not one of the sensational ones.

And the child—well, the child. It is a little boy, four now, slender, with the dark, desperate eyes, the shining pallor of his mother. But it seems, too, that he will have something of his playwright father's midwestern height and physical strength, and it is likely that there will be produced in him some refinement of his father's virile midwest intelligence as well.

They are taking no chance with this boy; they are taking no chance that he will fail to become an actor, and a serious one, for he is to be his mother's memorial. This is his father's intention, and his grandparents' reason for living. Already, at four, the boy goes weekly to a speech teacher, and daily to a ballet-master.

See him cross the street, holding his grandmother's hand; they are coming home from a puppet show. We do not notice the woman for the boy absorbs our eyes too completely. His gravity, beauty, litheness, grooming, and more than these, his air of being marked for something—madness, doom, greatness, or a great imitation of all three—can this really be true of a child four years old? Is he really marked so, or is it a trick of light in the late afternoon? Will we, if we see him again, see this again? Oh yes—for did we not, do we not, shall we not—sit in an audience and see him like this?

Past, present and future are items of indifference in this unre-membering world. Our present eyes, as we pass him, are compelled. If we had not been brought up so politely, we would stare. He is aware of this, too, but unresponsive, the little goon, creep, dope. Prince. Prince of Dopes.